SHATTERED NATION

An Alternate History Novel of the American Civil War

By Jeffrey Evan Brooks

This is a work of fiction.

Published by CreateSpace Independent Publishing Platform

Map by Steven Stanley
Cover art by Meredith Scott

Dedicated to my parents, Lonnie and Barbara Brooks,
Who taught me to be a good man and to love learning.
All that I have done or will do with my life
Is built on the foundation they gave me.

All great things hang by a hair. The man of ability takes advantage of everything and neglects nothing that can give him a chance of success; whilst the less able man sometimes loses everything by neglecting a single one of those chances.
- Napoleon Bonaparte

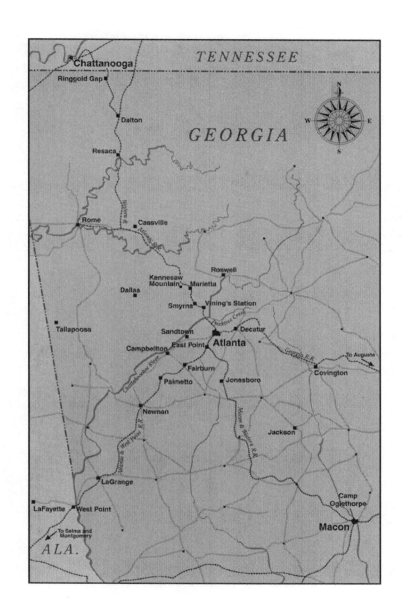

Chapter One

June 27, Morning

In a long trench carved into the slope of Kennesaw Mountain, surrounded by the endless pine forests and red clay hills of northern Georgia, the men of the 7th Texas Infantry Regiment waited in silence.

Birds drifted in the light breeze above them, oblivious to the turmoil that had engulfed the land. Although the sun had peeked over the horizon only an hour or so before, the air was already becoming stifled with the humid heat that had plagued the regiment since the campaign had begun. If the past few days were any indication, it would be over a hundred degrees by mid-afternoon.

The soldiers themselves remained still, clutching their Enfield rifles as they stared intently down at the enemy lines at the base of the mountain. When the regiment had marched out from Texas nearly three years before, it had numbered over a thousand men. Now, barely one hundred hungry survivors remained.

Among the hardened veterans was Sergeant James McFadden. Slightly smaller than his fellow soldiers, his face was covered with a thin mustache and goatee very different from the bushy beards sported by most of his comrades. His skin was deeply tanned, giving him a vaguely Latin appearance that belied his Scottish blood. His cool gray eyes reflected a sharp intelligence, but where there should have been emotion there was only emptiness.

"The Yankees are coming up the mountain," Private Billy Pearson said. He quickly glanced about to see if anyone would respond.

McFadden said nothing in reply, hoping that his silence would deter Pearson from speaking further. Sometimes the trick worked, but on this morning it did not.

"Do you think the Yankees are coming up the mountain, Sergeant?"

"No," McFadden said simply.

"I think they are," Pearson replied. "It's just too damn quiet. Usually we can hear the Yankees talking, chopping wood, all that kind of thing. Can't hear a damn thing this morning, though. They're getting ready to come up this mountain, sure as hell."

"Doubt it," McFadden replied resignedly. "Attacking us straight on isn't Sherman's style. He'll try to get around our flank again, just like he's done, over and over."

"Two dollars says they attack before the morning's over."

"Go to hell." McFadden knew that Pearson didn't have a dollar to his name anyway, having lost all his money to Private Balch in a series of disastrous card games.

"You think I'd win, don't you?" Pearson said with a grin. "I think that's why you never take my bets. You think I'll win. Ha! I expect I'll have taken a hundred dollars off the rest of you fellows by the time we get back to Texas."

McFadden wanted to remind Pearson that the odds of any of them making it back to Texas were not particularly good, but decided that it was best to try silence again. The soldiers on either side of them followed McFadden's lead. Pearson continued his chattering until the authoritative voice of Captain James Collett, commander of the regiment, came down on him like a thunderbolt.

"Billy, shut your damn mouth and keep your eyes peeled!"

"Yes, sir," Pearson meekly replied.

"Sergeant McFadden, please keep the men of your company quiet."

"I will, sir. Sorry, sir.

Collett nodded and moved on to the next company. McFadden glared menacingly down the line of the twenty or so men who made up Company F, nicknamed the Lone Star Rifles, which was under his command. Ordinarily the command of a company should have been held by a lieutenant. But with so many officers having been killed, each company in the 7th Texas had become the responsibility of a sergeant.

Silence again descended upon the line and McFadden gripped his rifle more tightly. As the long minutes passed, he found his mind drifting, which was not unusual. He wondered if the seemingly endless trench warfare was beginning to wear on the minds of the men. Since the great Yankee offensive against Atlanta had commenced two months earlier, the regiment had been involved in one vicious fight after another, interspersed with endless marches or the labor of constructing fortifications. There had scarcely been a single day of rest. Such a constant strain was bound to erode even the toughest of men. His own spirit was undeterred, however, and would remain so as long as he had the opportunity to kill Yankees.

From somewhere off to the north, there was a noticeable increase in the soft booming of artillery. The thunder of distant cannon had been a constant companion since the onset of the campaign, but changes in its tempo were always worthy of attention. The men lifted their heads and strained to hear. The artillery fire continued for several minutes, then reached a crescendo. A sudden silence was followed, a few minutes later, by a far-off crackling sound that the men recognized as sustained musket fire.

"The Yankees are attacking up north," Private Tom Harrison said. "We may get a battle today after all."

McFadden nodded. Harrison was one of the few men in the regiment that he genuinely liked. "Sounds like the fighting is where Polk's corps is," McFadden observed.

"Not Polk's any more. Poor fellow got himself killed by Yankee artillery a couple weeks ago. Not sure who's in command of it now."

"Who cares? Think they can hold?"

"If they're dug in as good as we are, should be no problem."

"Isn't that what we said at Missionary Ridge?"

The mention of that horrible day brought a slight but noticeable shudder among the Texans. For just a moment, McFadden bitterly recalled how their division had held its portion of the line at Missionary Ridge, only to have the rest of the army give way in the face of the Yankee attack. The result had been a shameful rout of the entire army, which the 7th Texas had barely been able to escape.

The crackling sound to the north went on. Veterans like the men of the 7th Texas had long since learned to read the sounds of distant battle. Had the sounds of musket fire suddenly ceased, it would probably have meant that the Yankees had breached the line and that hand-to-hand fighting was taking place. If the sound gradually faded, it would have meant that the attack had been repulsed. The fact that it continued unabated indicated that the Yankees were still pressing on with their attack, the outcome yet uncertain.

"Stay alert, men!" Captain Collett shouted. "The attack to the north could be a diversion. They could be planning to mount their main attack along our lines."

McFadden couldn't fault the captain's logic, but the idea that the Yankees would launch a frontal assault on such a strong position seemed ludicrous. The men of the 7th Texas had had days in which to transform the slopes of the little mountain into a veritable fortress. The very hour they had arrived, they had begun digging a regular trench and thrown up a parapet in front of it with the excess dirt. A head-log had been mounted on top of the parapet, the foot-high gap between the log and the parapet allowing them to shoot down at their foes with little risk of being hit by return fire.

Their fixed defenses were not the only obstacle to any attacker. They had cleared the slope in front of them of any trees that might provide cover to Union soldiers, while laying out barriers of chopped branches to make the ascent as difficult as possible. Closer to the line, barriers known as chevaux-de-frise had been erected, consisting of thick logs with sharpened stakes sticking out of them from four angles.

After nearly three years of war, the men of the 7th Texas had mastered the art of preparing defensive positions. McFadden was sure that they could hold their line against anything short of an attack by the Devil himself.

Still, he hoped that the Yankees would attack. It would give him the opportunity to kill more of the enemy, exacting slivers of vengeance with each shot at the people whom he held responsible for the death of his family out on the plains of central Texas. More importantly, somewhere out there was the Yankee captain with the scar across his left cheek, from whom he had sworn to extract a more direct form of revenge. Would today be the day he finally had the man in the sights of his Enfield? He prayed that it would be so, even if he was no longer certain of the existence of God.

After about an hour, the sound of musketry from up north began to fade. The Union attack had clearly been beaten off. But relief was quickly transformed to alarm when a series of loud, dull thudding sounds suddenly emanated from the Union lines directly across from them.

"Get down!" Captain Collett shouted.

"Down!" McFadden repeated to the men of his company.

The men needed no encouragement, instantly diving to the bottom of the trench. A second later, explosions rocked their position as artillery shells slammed into the mountainside. The shells that exploded as they hit the parapet or the ground in front of it threw up great chunks of earth, tossing dirt every which way. More dangerous were the projectiles that exploded in the air, showering the men of the 7th Texas with shrapnel.

McFadden hugged the earth as tightly as he could. The noise of the explosions pounded his eardrums and the impact vibrations shook his body. He knew a shrapnel fragment might take his head off at any instant, but he felt no fear. In his first battle, fought more than two years before at Val Verde in distant New Mexico, he had been absolutely terror-stricken, shaking so much that he had nearly dropped his musket. But the many battles he had gone through since then had cured him of that ailment. If it was his destiny to die on this particular day, there wasn't much he could do about it. Besides, he was one of the lucky ones who did not particularly care whether he lived or died.

"Told you!" he could hear Pearson shouting over the sound of the bombardment. "I told you they were going to attack! You owe me two dollars!" He had never taken the bet and considered shouting this fact back to Pearson, but decided that to do so would be a waste of breath.

McFadden hoped the bombardment wouldn't last long, as the noise was extremely annoying. It was common for the Yankees to try to soften them up with artillery fire before launching an infantry attack. It usually did little good, as the fortifications were strong enough to survive the shelling virtually intact. In fact, by giving away the intentions of the enemy, the artillery fire probably helped the Confederates more than it hurt them. But that didn't make the noise any less annoying.

Over the sound of the shell explosions, McFadden heard a man scream somewhere off to his right. Glancing over, he saw Lieutenant Martin Featherston grasping at his leg, which was suddenly half the length it should have been. What had been his foot a moment before was now nothing but a bloody stump. The stretcher bearer team immediately dashed forward to rescue him. Such wounds all too often became infected and led to an agonizing death.

Some of the men were shouting. "Cleburne! General Cleburne's here!"

McFadden looked back to where they were pointing, and there he was. General Patrick Cleburne, mounted on a reddish-brown mare, was riding behind the lines as if on a regular inspection tour, seemingly unconcerned about the explosions shattering the earth all around him. Two staff officers followed him at a respectful distance, along with a color-bearer who was carrying the distinctive flag of the division, a blue field with a white ellipse in the center. Cleburne's division was the only one in the Confederate Army permitted to carry a non-regulation battle flag, a fact that filled the men with pride.

McFadden thought that Cleburne's uniform looked more like that of a private than a general. Their division commander, perhaps just shy of forty, was not a physically imposing man. He was slightly taller and rather more thin than most men, with a well-formed if undistinguished face covered with a thin red beard. Though his appearance might not have attracted attention, the look on his face was fierce. His eyes seemed to blow out fire.

The men cheered as Cleburne rode past and he responded by taking his hat off and waving it. "Stand firm, 7th Texas!" he shouted. "Treat them the same way you treated them at Pickett's Mill!"

McFadden remembered that fight, exactly a month before. His mind involuntarily recalled the horrific sight, after the battle was over, of hundreds of Union soldiers lying dead or mangled in front of the Confederate lines. They had been mowed down like so many blades of grass. McFadden had been convinced he could have walked forward several hundred yards without his feet ever touching the ground. The sight had pleased him enormously.

Cleburne rode on, and the bombardment continued. It went on for what seemed like an hour, but was probably only five or six minutes. Then, quite abruptly, the firing ceased. From long experience, every soldier in the regiment knew what that meant.

"Stand up!" Captain Collett yelled.

"Up!" McFadden repeated.

As one, the men of the 7th Texas rose from the ground and took their places on the fire-step. Looking through the gap between the top of the parapet and the head-log, McFadden could see clusters of blue-coated Union soldiers emerging from the trees at the base of the hill, forming their lines for an attack.

"Don't bother with bayonets, men!" Collett shouted. "They'll just get in the way of reloading. This here's going to be a rifle battle from start to finish!"

McFadden took a large swig of water from his canteen, thinking it might be the last he would taste for awhile. He went through the automatic task of loading his rifle: bite off the top of a cartridge, pour the gunpowder down the barrel, insert the musket ball, use the ramrod to shove the ball and powder down the barrel, lift the weapon to firing position, pull back the cock, and place the firing cap on the cock. It had been somewhat complicated the first time he had done it. He now did it automatically, without thinking.

Many of the Enfield rifles which with the men of the 7th Texas were armed had only recently been acquired. At the beginning of the campaign, the regiment had been equipped with an jumbled assortment of weapons, not only Enfields but also Springfield rifles captured from the Yankees and Lorenz rifles imported from the Austrian Empire and run through the blockade. The Texans considered the latter two models inferior to the Enfield. Fortunately, after their victory at Pickett's Mill, however, the men had taken a sufficient number of Enfield rifles off the corpses of dead Yankees to reequip the entire regiment. They now went into battle as one of the best-armed regiments in the Confederate Army.

Turning his eyes back to the base of the mountain, McFadden was astonished to see that the numbers of Union soldiers had massively increased in the minute or so since his previous glance. Packed into dense columns, they were moving steadily up the hill like some giant snake, their obvious intention being to overwhelm the Confederates by sheer force of numbers. To the men of the 7th Texas, however, such a tightly-packed formation simply made for an easy target. The barrels of a hundred rifles poked out from beneath the head-log, aimed directly at the oncoming mass of men.

"Hold your fire until the command!" Captain Collett shouted. McFadden could hear other officers shout commands to the men of neighboring regiments on either side of them. He gripped his Enfield tightly. He felt no fear, but rather a sense of anticipation not unlike that he had often experienced just before a visit to one of the camp prostitutes. The few remaining minutes seemed to last forever.

When the Northern soldiers were about a hundred yards away, the Yankee officers gave the order to charge. The Union men rushed forward, letting forth a tremendous deep-throated battle cry, their bayonets glinting in the morning sun. They could be on top of the parapet within less than a minute.

"Fire!" Captain Collett yelled. Instantly, the Confederate line erupted in a tremendous crash as every soldier pulled his trigger at the same moment. The troops of the regiments on either side of the 7th Texas opened fire at almost the same moment. To the attacking Federals, it must have seemed as though a volcano had exploded in their faces. Blue-coated men immediately began to fall in droves and the sound of bullets whistled through the air.

It was not just musket fire that sliced down the Yankees. Positioned on the left of the 7th Texas was a concealed artillery battery of four cannon that opened up with canister shot. These deadly munitions spewed out containers packed with small lead balls, effectively transforming the cannon into gigantic sawed-off shotguns. McFadden could see great gaps being torn in the Union ranks, but the Northern men stoically continued up the slope.

"Send them to hell, boys!" Collett was shouting, walking up and down the line behind the men with his sword in one hand and pistol in the other.

McFadden quickly fell into the relentless pattern of load-and-shoot, load-and-shoot. The noise of the fighting was deafening, with the roar of musket fire mixing with the pounding sound of artillery blasts, the screams of wounded men, and the maniacal laughter of those pushed to the edge of sanity by the pressure of battle.

McFadden fired as quickly as he could load. He had to kill as many of the enemy as possible. He squeezed off another round and was pleased to see the stout-looking Yankee at whom he had been aiming fall to the ground, clutching at his chest.

"The Yankees must be crazy!" Harrison shouted as he reloaded. "We're butchering them!"

McFadden had no time to reply, but didn't disagree. As he aimed and fired, he could already see that scores of Yankees had fallen, some writhing in pain, others simply dropping like sacks of flour, never to move again. The formation was melting away, like a piece of ice tossed into hot water. He noticed that some Union soldiers were instinctively raising their left arms to shield their faces, as if they were walking into a heavy rainstorm.

Remembering his duty as a noncommissioned officer, McFadden began shouting out encouragement to his company. "Keep up your fire, boys! Slaughter the sons of bitches!"

Not many Yankees got close to the Confederate line. Many, unable to force themselves forward but unwilling to retreat, stopped where they were and began firing back. Little spits of dirt popped off the parapet as bullets hit it and he heard other shots whistle past, but McFadden felt adequately protected. Besides, most of the enemy soldiers who stopped to fire were killed within a few seconds.

A few Yankees, braver or luckier than the others, actually reached the parapet. As he withdrew his rifle to reload yet again, McFadden glanced through the opening under the head-log and was astonished to see a Union officer charging forward from less than ten feet away. Within seconds, the man was over the head-log, waving his sword.

"Surrender, you traitors!" the Union officer yelled.

"Go to hell!" Harrison shouted, shooting him in the head at point blank range. The body fell unceremoniously into the Confederate trench, where it was quickly kicked out of the way.

The unequal contest went on for an astonishingly long time, the two sides simply blazing away at each other. But the Southerners were well-protected behind their fortifications, whereas the Federal infantry was completely exposed. It was less a battle than a mass slaughter. The ground in front of the regiment's position was soon red with blood, slowly trickling downhill through the grass.

McFadden's ears began to ring. He wanted desperately to take a swig of water from his canteen, as his lips were parched and cracked from biting into his gunpowder cartridges and the heat of the musket fire all around him was intense. But he couldn't bring himself to waste even a few seconds, as he continued to load and shoot.

Finally, the Yankee officers realized the futility of pressing the attack further. McFadden could hear the sound of Yankee buglers blowing the notes for a retreat. It was a slow movement at first, with many frustrated Northern soldiers continually pausing and firing potshots back at the Southerners. But eventually, with the fire continuing to pour forth from the Confederate line, the retreat became rushed. The men hurried back downhill, amazed at having remained alive and desperately hoping to avoid death now that the attack had failed.

McFadden didn't reload. He hated the Yankees, but he saw no point in shooting men who were already running away. Besides, he was tired. While the rest of the regiment removed their hats and waved them in the air, cheering wildly, McFadden simply stared out onto the ground over which the Yankees had attacked. For hundreds of yards, it was littered with unmoving Yankee corpses and the pathetic forms of badly wounded men trying to drag themselves down the hill to safety.

It had been Pickett's Mill all over again.

*　　　　*　　　　*　　　　*　　　　*

General Patrick Cleburne was in a good mood. Truth be told, repulsing the Union attack had not been particularly difficult. But his men had behaved admirably, fighting a long engagement with little respite on one of the hottest days of the year.

Mounted on his favorite horse, Red Pepper, he rode behind the lines, trailed by Lieutenant Stephen Hanley and Lieutenant Learned Magnum, his two personal aides-de-camp. Also following was the color-bearer carrying the unique flag of Cleburne's division. When Joseph Johnston had taken command of the Army of Tennessee in January, he had ordered a standardization of all divisional battle flags, but Cleburne had successfully persuaded him to allow his men to retain their distinctive standard. From what Yankee prisoners had told him, the enemy had learned to dread seeing the white moon on a blue background facing them across the battle lines. This gave him more pride and satisfaction than anything else in his life, aside from the love of his fiancée, Susan.

The men of his division turned and cheered when they saw him and he raised his hat in salute as he passed his regiments, one by one. Other generals might have reined in and personally congratulated the men with some grandiloquent oration, but Cleburne was a shy man and not much given to making speeches. His men didn't take any offense. For them, the raised hat was enough.

Major Calhoun Benham, his divisional chief-of-staff, galloped up, an urgent look on his face. "General!" he shouted out excitedly.

"Yes, Major! What is it?" Cleburne was suddenly worried, as Benham was not easily alarmed.

"A brush fire has started directly in front of the 1st Arkansas! Dozens of wounded Yankees are lying out there, screaming for help! Our men are still taking some fire from the enemy lines. Colonel Martin requests authorization to raise a flag of truce and allow the Yankees to come get their wounded."

"Yes! Immediately!" Cleburne said without hesitation. Nobody should suffer so horrible a fate as being burned alive, even if they were Yankees. All brave warriors were worthy of respect. Whatever else they were, the Yankees were undoubtedly brave.

Benham kicked his horse and dashed off. He didn't waste time saluting, but Cleburne didn't care. He did not demand strict military protocol from his staff officers, and every second was precious if it meant saving the lives of wounded men.

He heard the light thundering sound of a party of horsemen, and turned to see Lieutenant General William Hardee, his corps commander and immediate superior, followed by a party of staff officers considerably larger than Cleburne's own. He wasn't surprised to see a smile on his face.

"We whipped them, Pat! We whipped them good!" Hardee reigned in alongside him, and Cleburne clasped his outstretched hand. "You and your men performed most admirably, my friend. Congratulations!"

"Thank you, General. What's the word from the rest of the line?" Cleburne's thick brogue easily betrayed his Irish origins.

"The Yankees attacked everywhere, all up and down the line. Cheatham's division had a particularly heavy attack, but it wasn't anything he couldn't handle. We repulsed the enemy at all points. A great victory, Pat!"

"Excellent. This day will greatly improve the morale of the men, I imagine."

"Have you any word on your division's casualties?

"No exact numbers yet, but very light. Less than a hundred in the whole division, I think."

"If there's a better example of the stupidity of attacking veteran troops protected by fortifications, I can't think of it. Having achieved such a great victory at such a small cost in blood is certainly something to celebrate."

For a moment, Cleburne found himself thinking about the bloodbath at Chickamauga, where the Southern triumph had been purchased at the cost of thousands of Southern lives. Even then, the victory had been squandered by Braxton Bragg. Today, by contrast, was a much better day.

The sudden sound of artillery rumbling far off to the north caused them to instinctively look over in that direction, although of course they could see nothing. Hardee's tone shifted from lightheartedness to seriousness. "Another attack?"

"I doubt it, sir. The Yankees are probably just shelling us out of frustration. I don't hear any musketry." He quickly glanced at his pocket watch. "It's still early in the day, but the drubbing they have received will surely have taken all the fight out of them. It's over for today, I think."

Another general appeared out of the dust, trailed by a single color-bearer. Cleburne tensed when he recognized the man as General William Walker, the commander of one of the other divisions in Hardee's corps. Walker saluted as he approached the group, eyeing Cleburne warily. He saw a flash of hatred in Walker's eyes. He was not surprised.

"General Walker," Hardee said simply. "You may report."

"The Yankees attacked my line with a heavy force, but we repulsed them handsomely. Our losses are light, but the losses inflicted upon the enemy are heavy."

"Good," Hardee replied. "Very good. Please convey my congratulations to your brigade commanders."

"Oh, I will. I certainly will," Walker said with a snide smile. Cleburne had the distinct impression that Walker's pleasure had less to do with earning Hardee's approval than it did with the sheer joy he derived from killing people.

Hardee went on. "You'll be happy to know, General Walker, that the enemy attacks have been equally unsuccessful at other points along the line. General Cleburne here repulsed a very heavy attack, as a matter of fact."

"Did he now?" Walker said.

"Indeed," Hardee replied.

Cleburne could see what Hardee was trying to do. He wanted Walker to offer congratulations to a brother officer in view of the assembled staff officers. Cleburne did not expect Walker to offer any such sign of respect and was unsurprised when the man merely grunted.

"Well, I thank you for your report," Hardee said to Walker. "Best get back to your division in case the Yankees try again."

"Yes, sir." Walker raised his hand in a salute to Hardee and, without casting another glance at Cleburne, turned his horse and rode off.

Hardee chuckled softly as soon as Walker was out of hearing. "As agreeable as ever," he said to Cleburne with a wry grin. Cleburne nodded to acknowledge Hardee's joke, but he did not consider Walker any laughing matter.

The smile on Hardee's face dimmed and he became serious once again. "If you think it advisable, Pat, send out pickets in the more heavily-wooded sectors. It might be worth picking up some of the wounded Federals as prisoners, especially if we can get any officers."

Without speaking, Cleburne turned and nodded to Lieutenant Hanley, who galloped off to make Hardee's order happen. In the meantime, Hardee turned to one of his own staffers and told him to report to General Johnston's headquarters. He then turned back to Cleburne.

"Keep your men on the alert, just in case the Yankees try again. I don't think they will, but we must be prudent."

"Of course, sir."

They quickly exchanged respectful salutes, and Hardee and his staff rode off. Cleburne watched him go. Serving in an army as torn by bitter personal and professional rivalries as the Army of Tennessee, Cleburne always counted himself lucky to serve under a man as decent as Hardee. Over the years, their excellent professional relationship had developed into a strong friendship.

Major Benham returned with the good news that the Yankees facing the 1st Arkansas had agreed to a temporary truce and had come forward to rescue their wounded comrades. Cleburne continued moving down the line of the division, occasionally stopping to chat briefly with regimental officers. The initial reports of low casualties proved even better than expected, with the division having suffered only two killed and nine seriously wounded. At no point had the enemy come close to breaking the line.

He allowed himself the luxury of a small smile.

*   *   *   *   *

The Confederate battle flag fluttered slightly in the breeze above the cluster of tents that contained the headquarters of the Army of Tennessee. Controlled chaos swirled about everywhere, as staff officers talked and argued, couriers came and went, and secretaries hurriedly scribbled orders and reports. The shade offered by the tents and trees provided only a slight respite from the heat. The sun had reached its zenith and begun its long descent toward the western horizon.

General Joseph E. Johnston, commander of the Army of Tennessee, sat at one table, intently reading a message just brought in from a dispatch rider. Of medium height, his body language did not convey strength so much as a leathery toughness and a wound-up energy that belied his fifty-seven years. His mustache, goatee and sideburns were carefully trimmed and his uniform appeared impeccably clean and well-pressed. His hat, rarely off his head as he preferred to conceal his baldness, was decorated with an ostrich feather, his only obvious concession to vanity.

The sounds of battle had been clearly audible throughout the day, though they now was now gradually tapering off. While he had naturally felt some apprehension, Johnston had been quite confident in the outcome of the battle. He had chosen the position well and the men had constructed excellent fortifications. Moreover, he knew the men under his command were among the toughest soldiers in the world.

He had been rather surprised at Sherman for abandoning his flanking strategy in favor of a frontal attack. From the commencement of the campaign nearly two months before, the Union commander had continually used his superior numbers to maneuver Johnston out of one defensive position after another. But if Johnston had been surprised by the frontal assault, he wasn't about to complain. After all, successfully tempting Sherman into launching such an ill-considered attack was precisely what Johnston had been trying to do since the campaign had begun.

In the distance, a courier appeared, galloping toward the tent at top speed. Johnston heard someone say that it looked like a staff member from Hardee's corps, whereupon he hurriedly rose from his chair and walked to the edge of the tent. The man reined in about ten paces out.

"Report!" Johnston called out.

The man shouted so that everyone in the vicinity could hear. "General Hardee presents his compliments, sir! He wishes to inform you that the attacks have been repulsed all along the line! The Yankees never got close!"

The headquarters staff cheered, but Johnston called out again, asking about casualties.

"Hardly a man in the whole corps hit, sir! But we sure killed a god-awful lot of Yankees!"

The men cheered all the louder and Johnston smiled. He was not a man given to bloodlust and, in quiet moments, felt very keenly the horror and sorrow of the war in which he fought. But he told himself that every Union soldier killed was one less enemy trying to kill his own men. As the army commander, it was his responsibility to put human emotions aside and deal with the cold logic of warfare.

"Thank you, lieutenant!" Johnston called. "My compliments to General Hardee! Tell him it was a job well done!"

"Yes, sir!" The man saluted and galloped off.

Johnston indulged in the victory ritual of shaking hands and receiving congratulations from most of the staff. For a moment he felt a feeling of exultation, as the victory at what eventually would come to be called the Battle of Kennesaw Mountain was his most significant achievement in the campaign to date.

Brigadier General William Mackall, chief-of-staff of the Army of Tennessee and Johnston's principal staff officer, extended his hand as the commander reached his seat.

"Congratulations, General!"

"Thank you, my friend. I recall that when we received news of Lee's victory at Cold Harbor earlier this month I complained that no person would ever attack me in such a perfect defensive position. I must now stand happily corrected."

"Indeed, sir. I dare say that even President Davis will be pleased, assuming that it is possible to please that man."

Johnston smiled. Any words critical of Jefferson Davis were music to his ears. He gestured back toward his table, where he retook his seat as Mackall sat down across from him. "I don't know what Sherman was thinking today. If this war has taught anyone anything, it is never to launch a direct infantry assault on a prepared position."

Mackall nodded. "You'd think the Yankees would have learned that, having had their noses bloodied at Chickasaw Bluffs, Fredericksburg, and a half dozen other places."

"And as I have well learned by studying carefully what has happened to our own troops at Malvern Hill and Cemetery Ridge."

"Point taken, sir. Much better to receive and repulse an attack by the enemy than to have our own men slaughtered in front of impregnable defenses."

"Quite so. Still, as happy as I am that we defeated Sherman today, this victory does little to change our strategic situation. Now that Sherman has discovered the futility of launching a direct assault against us, he will certainly return to his previous strategy of using his superior numbers to maneuver around our flanks."

Mackall nodded. "No doubt. I just hope the beating we have given him today will give us at least a few days of breathing space. The army is tired."

"Sherman will move to outflank us, and soon," Johnston said with conviction. "He is far from foolish. My guess is that he will attempt to get around our left flank, where Hood's corps is currently posted. Sherman always goes after our left." His fingers traced the route on the map that covered the table.

The map showed something else troubling. Only a few miles south of Kennesaw Mountain was the Chattahoochee River, the last major natural barrier between Sherman and Atlanta. If Johnston could not prevent Sherman from crossing the river, he doubted he would be able to hold the city.

Mackall stared down at map. "I do not believe we have sufficient men to extend our left flank, sir. Our right flank is already stretched dangerously thin. In some places we have had to dismount units of Wheeler's cavalry and deploy them as infantrymen in the trenches."

Johnston thought a moment. "Draft a letter to Governor Brown. Remind him that he has repeatedly promised me that he will send forward all the militiamen he can muster. We have yet to receive so much as a single regiment. Tell him that we need those men, and we need them now."

"You intend to field Georgia militia against Sherman's men?" Mackall asked. "Old men and young boys with no training won't last long against seasoned veterans." Mackall certainly had no love for the Yankees, but he respected them very highly as fighting men.

"We can put the militia in quiet sections of the line, freeing up our reliable troops for more active sectors. Even old men and young boys are better than no men at all. In circumstances such as ours, we have to make do as best we can."

"True enough."

Johnston tapped the table impatiently. "Too many Yankees," he said absent-mindedly. For a moment, he found himself wondering if the people of the Confederacy would blame him if they lost the war.

A courier handed Mackall a note, which he quickly opened and read.

"What is it?" Johnston asked.

"It's from Senator Wigfall, sir. He wishes to inquire if it would be best for him to postpone his visit to headquarters, what with the battle and all."

"No, tell him to come straight away. The battle is over, and the sooner Senator Wigfall and I have a chance to discuss matters, the better. I am sure he is anxious to continue on his way to Texas."

"I will notify him, sir."

"In the meantime, please find out the estimated losses we have sustained in this morning's engagement."

"At once, sir." Mackall stood, saluted and walked off.

Johnston let out a deep breath and stared back at the map. He was quiet and still for some time, as the staff of his headquarters continued to swirl around him.

*   *   *   *   *

General William Tecumseh Sherman, commander of the combined Union armies in the Western Theater of Operations, shook his head in intense frustration, chewing his cigar until it nearly disintegrated. Couriers kept arriving with message after message, all of them saying the same thing. Every single one of his attacks had been repulsed with heavy losses. At no point did his men even come close to breaking through the Confederate lines. The attack had been a complete fiasco.

"Take a telegram for General Thomas," he said to a nearby staff officer, who immediately prepared to accept the dictation.

Do you think you can break any part of the enemy's line today?

"Have that dispatched at once, and let me know as soon as he replies. Right away, as soon as he replies. No delays, you understand?"

"Yes, sir." The officer scurried away to carry out his task.

For a moment, Sherman reflected on the telegraph lines which connected him with the command posts of his chief subordinates. The very thought of the instant communication they provided filled him with amazement and fleetingly distracted him from the day's disappointments. He wondered what use Napoleon, Marlborough or the other great generals of the past would have made of such an invention. He shook the thought from his mind and tried to focus on the task at hand.

He was angry at himself. Nearly two months of marching and fighting throughout northern Georgia had gained a lot of ground, but had failed to inflict a decisive defeat on the Army of Tennessee. So long as the Army of Tennessee continued to exist as a formidable fighting force, the capture of Atlanta and the defeat of the Confederacy would remain an elusive dream. After countless failed attempts to run his opponent to ground, he had finally given into frustration and launched a full-scale frontal assault.

He had played right into the hands of Joe Johnston. Three thousand Union soldiers had paid the price.

A few minutes passed. "Sir, we have just received the response from General Thomas."

"Read it to me, please."

From what the officers tell me, I do not think we can carry the works by assault at this point today, but they can be approached by saps and the enemy driven out.

Sherman frowned and shook his head. To have the men approach the Confederate trenches by means of digging zigzag trenches, all while under fire, would effectively mean resorting to siege warfare. It would take weeks, perhaps more than a month, for such tactics to work.

Sherman knew the Union had unlimited resources of men and material. He also knew that one thing it did not have was time.

"Take the return message, Lieutenant."

"Go ahead, sir," the officer said, readying his pencil.

Is there anything in the enemy's present position that if we should approach by regular saps, he could not make a dozen new parapets before one sap is completed? Does the nature of the ground warrant the time necessary for regular approaches?

Again, the officer hurried off to the telegraph tent. Sherman didn't like the idea of remaining stuck before the Kennesaw line. After all, using siege tactics would simply give Johnston time to build a new defensive position slightly farther back. It would also provide a respite for the Confederates, allowing them to recover their strength, and Sherman felt it critical to keep them as hard pressed as possible.

To make matters worse, every day that Sherman remained stymied at the Kennesaw line was another day in which the Confederates might unleash a cavalry raid on his supply lines. Such an operation was the thing Sherman feared more than anything else, the terror which kept him awake at night. The three armies under his command constituted one of the most powerful military forces ever assembled in the history of warfare. However, for their supplies they were dependent on a ramshackle network of railroads that stretched hundreds of miles to the north.

For a man as worry-prone as Sherman, his shaky supply lines made him decidedly uncomfortable. The fact that the commander of any such raid would likely be the dreaded Nathan Bedford Forrest made him worry all the more.

Thomas's response was quickly received.

Enemy works exceedingly strong, so strong that they cannot be carried by assault except by immense sacrifice, if they can be carried at all. Best chance is to approach them by regular saps. We have already lost heavily today without gaining any advantage. One or two more such assaults would use up this army.

The staff officer reading the message to Sherman glanced up nervously as he recited the last sentence. The language Thomas used could easily be interpreted as a criticism of Sherman's decision to attack, and for a subordinate to criticize his superior so openly was simply not done.

If Sherman thought the words were critical, he didn't show it. He knew that Thomas didn't want to resort to siege tactics any more than he did. It was clear that his subordinate was trying hard to dissuade him from launching another frontal attack and he was doubtless correct.

Sherman took a deep puff on his cigar as he contemplated his options. The Confederate defenses could not be taken by assault, and he didn't have the time to break them down by siege methods. The only alternative, therefore, was to revert to his previous strategy of outflanking Johnston. To do that would require moving the bulk of the army away, at least temporarily, from the railroad that brought them their supplies. For a few days, most of his troops would have to carry with them all the food and ammunition they would need to both survive and fight. If the movement somehow went awry, the consequences could be grave.

It would be a risk, but there was no other choice.

Sherman called for his maps and spread them on the table, ideas whirling through his mind as he began dictating his orders.

*   *   *   *   *

June 27, Afternoon

Those who saw General John Bell Hood often came away thinking that he looked like something out of Beowulf, for the commander of the second infantry corps of the Army of Tennessee did indeed resemble a bearded, angry Anglo-Saxon tribal chief. On the face of it, he was a powerfully built man in his early thirties, whose eyes and facial expression positively exuded strength and ferocity. But all that was belied by the physical torments which the war had inflicted upon his body.

His left arm dangled uselessly in a permanent sling, shattered beyond recovery by an exploding Union shell at the Battle of Gettysburg. His right leg was missing, having been amputated after being smashed by Yankee musket fire at the Battle of Chickamauga. Because of his grievous injuries, Hood had to be strapped into the saddle of his horse if he wanted to ride anywhere. He was, quite literally, a broken man. His eyes remained strong, but perceptive observers could see a dark element in their gaze that had not been there before he had suffered his wounds.

Hood was sitting quietly in his tent, listening to the steady rumble of cannonading off to the north. Clearly, something had happened on the right, on the opposite end of the line from the position held by his own corps, but he had no idea what. Staff officers he had sent to investigate had not yet returned. If anything particularly important had taken place, Hood assumed that General Johnston would have notified him immediately. In the absence of any such message, Hood assumed that the Yankees had attacked the Confederate lines, probably around Hardee's corps, and had been successfully repulsed.

Until he knew for certain what was happening, he would withhold judgment. He had ordered his division commanders to be ready to repel any attack, but there seemed to be little activity on his own lines. As the sun began its slow descent toward the western horizon, it became increasingly clear that June 27 was going to be an uneventful day for John Bell Hood.

As he shifted uncomfortably in his chair, his peg leg accidently thumped onto the ground. In an instant, shocking pain screamed through the stump that was all that remained of his natural leg. He tightly gripped the table with his one good hand, grinding his teeth against the agony and resisting the almost irresistible urge to cry out. His peg leg was of the highest quality, custom-made in England from the finest cork available and run through the Union blockade. It had been paid for by a subscription raised by the men of his old brigade in General Lee's army. However, even at the best of times it caused severe discomfort. Often, the torture it caused him was unbearable.

Glancing outside to make sure that no one was in a position to see him, he quietly reached into his pocket and pulled out a small bottle of laudanum. Removing the cork with his teeth, he took a quick swig of the concoction of alcohol and opium. Very quickly, he replaced the cork and put the bottle back in his pocket.

"General Hood, sir?" a staff officer outside called.

"What?" There was irritation in his voice.

"General Wheeler is approaching."

Hood hobbled up, holding the table for support. Ordinarily, he would receive another general in his tent, since his comrades were more than happy to accommodate the limitations imposed by his physical condition. But Joseph Wheeler, commander of the army's cavalry, was one of the few genuine friends Hood had in the army and Hood figured he deserved the courtesy of a proper greeting.

Hood threw back the flap of his tent and stepped outside, just as General Joseph Wheeler reined in a few yards away, trailed by two staff officers.

"Hello, Sam!" Wheeler said, using the nickname by which friends customarily addressed Hood.

"What is happening up north, Joe?"

"The Yankees attacked all along the line, but we beat them back, by God! Killed us a whole mess of Yankees!"

"Very good!" Hood said, trying to sound enthusiastic. Intense pain still shot through his leg, but he tried to ignore it. "I only wish my boys could have joined in the fun!"

"Oh, you'll get your chance soon enough, my friend."

"Join me for a glass of whiskey?"

"I believe that I shall take you up on that, sir," Wheeler responded with mock formality. He sharply dismounted, the reins being taken by one of Hood's staff officers. Hood gestured into the tent, and a moment later they were sitting down at the table while Hood poured two glasses of whiskey.

"General Johnston will be in high spirits this evening, I should think," Wheeler observed.

"I suppose so," Hood replied. "Of course I am very glad at the day's success. But is Old Joe going to follow up with a counter attack? I frankly doubt it."

"No argument here," Wheeler said, his face becoming more serious. "You know that I've been saying all along that we need to be taking the fight to the enemy. Hell, every time my boys have come up against Yankee cavalry since the campaign started, we have sent them running. I can't see why the infantry can't do the same."

Hood frowned and shook his head. "The main result of today's engagement may well be to encourage the men in the belief that they should never fight unless they are protected by strong fortifications. When I served under Lee in Virginia, all my successes- at Gaine's Mill, at Second Manassas, at Sharpsburg- were achieved the old-fashioned way, by charging the enemy with the bayonet!"

"I know it, Sam," Wheeler said. "It was your record of success in the East which made me so pleased when you took command of one of our infantry corps. And I must say, your record in the present campaign has fully vindicated my hopes."

Hood, smiling modestly, responded with a slight nod. Though he was more than happy to accept Wheeler's flattery, he knew quite well that his fighting record over the past two months had been mixed at best. Try as he might, Hood had been unable to replicate as a corps commander in the West the brilliant success he had achieved as a brigade and division commander in the East. Memories of the missed opportunity at Cassville and the botched attack at Kolb's Farm flickered through his mind. The latter had cost the lives of hundreds of Southern soldiers.

Wheeler raised his whiskey glass. "To offensive action, and soon!"

"To offensive action," Hood replied as they clinked their glasses together.

A few minutes of trivial conversation passed quickly, focused mostly on horses, but both men soon realized that their minds were turning elsewhere. Excusing himself politely, Wheeler soon mounted his horse and rode on.

Seeing no reason not to, Hood poured himself another glass of whiskey. He then pulled out writing material and began the laborious process of writing a letter with his right hand without being able to hold the paper down with his left. Since it was apparent that there would be no action along his front that day, it seemed like a propitious time to address a letter to Sally Preston, the sophisticated and beautiful Richmond socialite he hoped to soon call his wife. He had a letter of substantially greater political and military significance to write afterwards.

*   *   *   *   *

June 27, Evening

General George Thomas, commander of the Union Army of the Cumberland, shook his head sadly as a staff officer handed him the most up-to-date report on casualties from the day's attack. Hundreds of his men had been killed in front of the Confederate defenses, while nearly fifteen hundred were wounded. Many of the latter would undoubtedly perish in agony in the rudimentary field hospitals over the next few days. Farther north, the Army of the Tennessee had also suffered heavy losses. All of the fallen men had had friends and loved ones back home, but Thomas tried not to dwell on that.

His men had fought bravely; that much was clear. Two of his best brigade commanders, Colonel Daniel McCook and Brigadier General Charles Harker, had been killed while leading their men from the front. If eyewitness accounts were to be believed, the color-bearer of the 52nd Ohio Infantry had reached the Confederate line and planted his flag on the parapet before being shot down. But as the war had proven so many times, even the greatest gallantry was no match for the brutal firepower of entrenched infantry.

The few prisoners Thomas's men had captured, all from the Confederate picket line well in front of the fortified position, had said that the division holding the line where the strongest attack had been made was that of General Patrick Cleburne. If that were true, it was no wonder that the attack had failed.

Thomas was a big man, not tall but possessing such bulk that he reminded many people of an oversize Scottish terrier. His whole form seemed to combine manly strength with a certain grace and dignity. His eyes sparkled with an intense and clear intelligence and his thick beard was speckled with shades of gray. Though his face could on occasion express a comforting warmth that cheered those around him, it was just as likely to solidify into an indecipherable mask.

Since their earlier telegram exchange, in which Thomas had forthrightly expressed his view that they could not hope to break the Confederate lines through frontal attack, Sherman had been pestering him with telegrams asking his advice about their next course of action.

To Thomas's mind, there were two possible courses of action. They could adopt siege tactics and attempt to blast their way through the Confederate defenses by approaching them with saps. It would probably work, but it would take several weeks even under the best circumstances. Thomas knew Sherman would be unwilling to wait that long. Accepting such a long stalemate might give the rebels time to mount the cavalry raid against their supply line that the Union generals so dreaded. More importantly, President Lincoln would be far from pleased.

The second possible course of action would be to attempt a wide-sweeping flanking movement to the south to get around the Confederate left flank. This had been done several times since the commencement of the campaign, always with success. But in this particular instance, the nature of the terrain and the respective positions of the armies would make it necessary for the bulk of the Union forces to abandon the railroad on which they depended for supplies. It was hard to say how long such a movement would take, but it might turn out to be several days. If they failed to force a Confederate withdrawal, the flanking forces would have to make an inglorious retreat as soon as their supplies ran out. Meanwhile, the portion of the Union forces left holding the railroad might be vulnerable to a surprise Confederate attack.

The first course of action was unthinkable and the second was very risky. Between unthinkable and risky, however, one had to go with risky.

"Take a telegram for General Sherman, Lieutenant," he said to a staff officer.

"Go ahead, sir."

I believe the movement of a large portion of our forces against the enemy left flank to be risky but feasible. I think it decidedly better than butting against breastworks twelve feet thick and strongly abatised.

Sherman might interpret the last sentence as a subtle criticism of his decision to attack at Kennesaw, but Thomas didn't care. A subtle criticism was exactly what he intended.

About twenty minutes later, Thomas received Sherman's response.

We shall move to the south against the enemy left flank with the whole army. Go where we may, we will find breastworks and abatis, unless we move more rapidly than we have heretofore.

Thomas grinned and chuckled lightly. The last sentence was clearly a rebuke to the perceived slowness of the Army of the Cumberland, but Thomas let it go. He and Sherman might not have been the best of friends, despite having been roommates at West Point in the old days, but there was no reason they couldn't work together effectively. It was true that any unbiased observer could see that Thomas' military record was considerably superior to that of Sherman. If the world had been fair, Thomas reflected, he would have been given supreme command of the Union armies in the Western Theater rather than Sherman. But Sherman's close friendship with General Grant had been the decisive factor.

It had not been the only factor, as Thomas well knew. While few of his brother officers had ever said anything to his face about the fact that he had been born in Virginia, he knew that it was often on their minds and that it certainly colored their opinions.

For a brief moment, he remembered the dark days of 1861, when secession had swept across the South. He and his fellow Southern officers had been faced with the most difficult choice of their lives. Should they follow their states out of the Union or should they remain loyal to the oaths they had taken to protect the United States Constitution? Most had followed their states. Thomas had remained loyal to his nation, donning a blue uniform rather than a gray one. And for that, he had been vilified by his own people.

He had been told that his family had turned his portrait to the wall. He felt a sharp pang of pain when he remembered reading the only letter he had received from his two sisters since the start of the war, in which they had sternly suggested that he change his last name. According to rumor, whenever General Thomas was mentioned in the presence of his sisters, they drew themselves up stiffly and replied that they had no brother.

The pain was the price he paid for doing his duty. In his mind, he had had no choice. An oath wasn't something a honorable man could cast aside.

He shook his head. Dwelling on the past was useless. It was better to focus on the task at hand. He called for his maps, and began dictating the marching orders that would take the Northern armies around the Confederate left flank.

*   *   *   *   *

As the curtain of night drew over the Georgia sky, the mood at the headquarters of the Army of Tennessee was still celebratory. There was a great deal of laughter around the campfires, the sound of banjo playing and singing mixing with the crackling of burning logs. The smell of fire, whiskey and roasting pork hung tantalizingly in the air.

Isolated from the celebration inside his tent, illuminated by the light of a few oil lamps, Johnston pondered his army's next move. He had no doubt that, on the other side of the lines, Sherman was even then sitting in his own tent, trying to devise a new plan after having seen his frontal attack repulsed. Johnston knew he had precious little time before his Yankee adversary acted again.

In view of current realities, Johnston did not see any option but to try to anticipate what Sherman would do and then take appropriate action. Looking at the map, he couldn't see any means by which he could take the offensive. The Yankee troops always began to entrench the moment they came to a halt, constructing formidable fortifications in a matter of hours. Launching frontal assaults on such positions was little short of suicide, as the Yankees had themselves discovered earlier in the day.

The location of Sherman's flanks, as reported to him by his scouts, did not present him with much of an opening, either. They were strong and secure, with their approaches carefully screened by Yankee cavalry. Any attempt to attack his opponent's flanks would quickly be detected. When Johnston had last attempted such a maneuver, in the closing days of the fighting around New Hope Church a month earlier, the result had been a bloody repulse, costing Johnston several hundred men that he could not afford to lose.

Johnston had previously considered detaching a large force of infantry and sending it on a long march around Sherman's line to attack the railroad which brought the enemy his supplies. But the Confederate lines were stretched terribly thin as it was, and if such an attacking force were discovered and attacked by superior numbers, it would be unlikely that any of his men would make it back to their own lines. It would be impossible to supply such a striking force in any event. While it would have been a daring move, Johnston had determined that it was far too great a risk. It was imperative above all that he keep the army intact.

He continued staring down at the map, as though wishing it would change on its own, until his thoughts were interrupted by the voice of an aide-de-camp.

"General Johnston?"

"Yes?"

"Senator Wigfall is here to see you."

"Ah, excellent!" Johnston said, rising from the table. "Send him in."

Wigfall threw back the flap of the tent and strolled inside. Wearing the dark civilian suit of a politician rather than the uniform of a general, Wigfall presented a large and formidable appearance, enhanced by his reputation as a rough man of the Texas frontier and an accomplished duelist. His age and increasing plumpness were only just beginning to wear away at his intimidating visage.

Wigfall extended his hand and Johnston gripped it firmly.

"Good to see you, my dear friend," Wigfall said.

"And you, Senator. Please, take a seat. I hope your trip is proceeding well?"

"Well enough, I suppose. Our rail network still functions in the Carolinas and in that part of Georgia which has not yet fallen to the enemy. More or less, anyway."

"How do you intend to proceed from here?"

"I can take the train from Atlanta to Meridian, rickety as the ride will surely be, but then I must find a way to cross the Mississippi River, which is infested with Yankee gunboats. If I can get to Shreveport, it will be easy for me to complete my trip to Texas."

"You hazard a great deal merely to touch base with your constituents, Senator," Johnston said with a grin. "And how are things in Richmond? How is your lovely family?"

"All very well, thank you. My wife and our two daughters miss you and Mrs. Johnston very much, of course. If you'll forgive me a moment of sentimentality, I must say that the days in which our two families lived under the same roof were some of the most pleasant of my life."

"Mine as well. I happily forgive your sentimentality."

Johnston poured two glasses of wine, deciding that Wigfall's visit fully justified the expense. The Yankee blockade had made wine expensive but not unobtainable. As they sipped on the wine, the two men recollected happy memories for a few brief minutes. After Johnston had been severely wounded at the Battle of Seven Pines in 1862, Wigfall had been kind enough to offer his home to Johnston for his recuperation. Despite their vastly different personalities, Johnston and Wigfall had become fast friends, drawn together particularly by their shared loathing of Jefferson Davis.

"I hope the closeness of the war to Richmond does not unduly trouble your wife and daughters," Johnston said.

Wigfall let out an exasperated sigh. "The sound of Yankee artillery is always present. Lee will continue to hold the Yankees off for some time yet, but having the enemy so close to the capital is not pleasant, to say the least."

"I would imagine so. And how are things in Congress?"

"Deadlocked, of course. Jefferson Davis and his cronies continue their efforts to consolidate the power of the central government at the expense of the states, asserting that such measures are necessary to win the war. I am sad to say that many members of Congress have been seduced by such arguments. They seem to forget that it was exactly such illegal and unconstitutional usurpations of power which caused us to secede from the Union in the first place."

Johnston nodded. "It seems we have rejected a king in Washington, only to be faced with a king in Richmond."

"Exactly. And a rather incompetent king, if you ask me."

"I am well aware of that, I can assure you! The President's incompetence may yet be the ruin of my campaign to defend Atlanta. All my recommendations for officer promotions or transfers are ignored. All my letters requesting improvements in the logistical system are ignored. And I am denied the authority to communicate with other theater commanders in order to properly coordinate operations against the Yankees. I feel like I am fighting with my hands tied behind my back."

Wigfall slowly shook his head. "It is even worse than you realize, my friend," he said soberly.

Johnston's eyes narrowed. "What do you mean?"

The senator leaned forward. "Rumors are swirling around Richmond these days. I know you are well aware that Davis did not want to appoint you to command the Army of Tennessee last December. Had he been able to avoid it, he would have."

"I am aware of that," Johnston said.

"But from what I am hearing now, he is actually planning to remove you from command of this army. In order to justify it to the public and the press, he is withholding reinforcements and other forms of support from you in the hopes that you will suffer some sort of setback at the hands of Sherman."

Johnston's eyes widened. "From whom did you obtain this information?"

"Trusted friends who are in a position to know. Beyond that, I should say nothing. They spoke to me in confidence."

Johnston nodded, even as his mind raced. He thought he had known the depths of the hatred Davis felt for him, but this was devilishness of the worst form. To think that the President of the Confederacy would jeopardize the outcome of the most critical military campaign of the year- jeopardize the survival of the Confederacy itself!- merely to settle a personal score was utterly beyond the pale.

"I must admit, my dear friend, that I find this rather difficult to believe. Could even Jefferson Davis be so duplicitous?"

"Answer the following question. Am I right in assuming you have requested that the President order Nathan Bedford Forrest's cavalry to move out of northern Mississippi and attack Sherman's supply lines in Tennessee?"

"I have asked him to do so many times, yes."

"Why has the order not been given, then? Forrest virtually destroyed the Yankee forces stationed in western Tennessee weeks ago at the Battle of Brice's Cross Roads. Davis could unleash him against the Yankee railroads with the stroke of a pen, yet there he sits in northern Mississippi, twiddling his thumbs. Meanwhile, supplies and reinforcements flow freely to Sherman."

Johnston's faced scowled into a mask of anger and resentment.

Wigfall went on. "I see you are upset, Joseph. Another glass of wine, perhaps? I have more to tell you."

Johnston poured each of them a new glass, no longer even thinking about the expense. "What else can there be to say? What you have already said has left me thoroughly distressed."

"It is about General Hood."

"General Hood? What of him?"

"It has been made known to me from these same trusted friends that General Hood is secretly communicating with President Davis, writing him regular letters that are highly critical of your conduct in the present campaign."

Johnston instinctively rose to his feet, nearly spilling his wine glass all over the map. "What?!" he said, his voice quivering with anger. "That is a violation of military protocol! Hood is my subordinate. He can only be permitted to communicate with the higher levels of command through me!"

"Military protocol is observed by gentlemen. Whatever else he is, Hood is no gentleman."

"How could he do such a thing?"

Wigfall sighed. "He's a different man than he was before he suffered his wounds. Early in the war, he and I were friends. Hell, my daughter Louise herself made the battle flag for the 4th Texas Infantry when Hood was in command of the regiment. But he's changed. Something left him when he lost those limbs. What's left of him is rotten to the core."

Johnston calmed himself, as he certainly did not want anyone outside the tent to hear any of the conversation. He sat back down, but his blood was boiling with rage. He shook his head. "He was one of the finest brigade and division commanders of the Confederacy when he served under Lee. I was so hopeful when he was assigned to command one of my corps."

"It is a shame."

"And, pray tell, what exactly is Hood telling the President in these letters of his?"

"I have not seen the said letters myself, but from what I have been told, Hood is telling President Davis that he has constantly urged you to take the offensive against Sherman and that you have always refused to do so. He also says that the numerous withdrawals the army has been compelled to make were done against his advice."

Johnston took a deep breath and his lips curled into a bitter smile. "The true facts are precisely the opposite. Hood has not urged the offensive at any point in this campaign. Indeed, on those occasions when I have attempted to strike a blow at Sherman- at Resaca, at Cassville, at New Hope Church, and at Pine Mountain- I entrusted the critical role in the attack plan to Hood's corps, because of his reputation for aggressiveness. However, on each of those occasions, the attacks either sputtered out quickly or failed to materialize at all."

"I have heard about the incident at Cassville. What happened, exactly?"

Johnston leaned back in his chair, remembering. "We had been able, through rapid marching, to take up positions where we would could concentrate our full force against only a portion of Sherman's army. It was a situation few generals in history can ever hope for and I felt we were about to inflict upon Sherman a defeat so devastating that it would bring his entire campaign to a halt. Hood's corps was positioned on the right flank, ordered to sweep down on the unsuspecting enemy forces, who were walking right into our trap. When the time came for the advance to begin, I was waiting impatiently to hear the sounds of cannon and musketry, but no sounds of battle came."

"Why not?"

Johnston took a sip of wine before continuing. "I sent General Mackall to investigate. When he arrived at Hood's headquarters, he was stunned to find Hood's entire corps in retreat. Hood claimed that he was being attacked in the rear by a force of enemy cavalry, though Mackall had seen no such force. In any event, by the time we might have been able to sort the mess out and move forward, the enemy had discovered our intentions and prepared for defense. With the element of surprise lost, we had no choice but to call off the attack."

Wigfall sighed. "It appears that General Hood is blaming you for debacles which are his own fault. And in secret letters to the President, no less."

Johnston chuckled bitterly. "If I recall correctly, Hood finished dead last in his ethics class at West Point. Now I can see why." He paused for a moment. "I could call him to answer charges of insubordination before a court martial," Johnston said menacingly.

"You could," Wigfall replied. "But unfortunately we cannot provide proof of these facts without revealing the identities of the men who gave me this information. This I cannot do, as they did so in confidence."

"I cannot abide this," Johnston said emphatically.

"My advice is to be patient. Keep a close watch on General Hood. Eventually, he will become careless and his insubordination will come out into the open in such a way that he cannot deny it. At that point, we can both remove Hood and strike a blow against President Davis."

Johnston nodded, frowning. "Perhaps you're right."

"Only time will tell, my friend."

Johnston slowly shook his head. "I have always thought of Sherman as being my chief enemy. Now I find myself wondering if Davis and Hood might in truth be more dangerous foes."

As a demonstration of gratitude for their successful repulse of the Yankees, General Hiram Granbury, the commander of the brigade of which the 7th Texas was a part, had pulled the regiment back from the front line and replaced them with another regiment. Now the sound of drunken singing emanated from their encampment as they celebrated far into the night.

> *"Cheer, boys, cheer We'll march away to battle!*
> *"Cheer, boys, cheer! For our sweethearts and our wives!*
> *"Cheer, boys, cheer! We'll nobly do our duty!*
> *"And give to the South, our hearts, our arms, our lives!"*

Private Ben Montgomery, universally considered the best fiddle-player in the 7th Texas, plucked away on his instrument, filling the air with his delightful sounds. Amid raucous laughter, the men were excitedly recounting stories of how many Yankees they had killed that day. Many of them danced like wild Indians around campfires that had been stoked so much that they now resembled miniature bonfires. There was no need for heat, for the Georgia summer was such that even the dead of night was rather warm. But the light provided by the fires lifted the spirits of the men.

Not that they needed much lifting, for most of the Texans were drunk and getting drunker. Cleburne had allowed the regimental officers to issue an additional ration of whiskey in recognition of their victory. The men had needed little encouragement to take full advantage of it.

> *But as we march, with heads all lowly bending,*
> *Let us implore a blessing from on high.*
> *Our cause is just, the right we're defending*
> *And the god of battles will listen to our cry!*

Sergeant McFadden had consumed as much whiskey as any of his comrades, if not more. He had become only slightly inebriated, for three years of heavy alcohol consumption had allowed him to build up an exceptional level of tolerance. Despite occasional entreaties from his comrades, he did not join in the dancing. He would not have enjoyed it and he didn't want to dampen the fun the others were having. He was content to watch the singing and dancing in silence.

He considered the men of his regiment. For the most part, they were good men. He certainly knew they were brave fighters, fiercely protective of one another and dedicated to the Confederate cause. Though often suspicious of the high command, they admired and respected their own regimental and brigade officers and were intensely loyal to General Cleburne. Since Union control of the

Mississippi River had cut them off from Texas, the men of the regiment relied on one another perhaps more deeply than did the men of other units. In a very real sense, the hundred men of the 7th Texas were a family.

There were some men McFadden liked and some he disliked, but he couldn't honestly call any of them a friend. Though he had been with the 7th Texas for more than a year, he remained something of an outsider. He had not known any of the other men before the war, whereas many of them had grown up with each other in the same counties and towns.

The 7th Texas Infantry Regiment had originally assembled in the fall of 1861 in the town of Marshall in northeast Texas. It had journeyed from there to Hopkinsville, Kentucky, where it had endured a nightmarish winter during which scores of men had died of disease. The following February, the regiment had fought courageously at Fort Donelson, only to pass into captivity with the disgraceful surrender of the garrison by its incompetent commanders. For more than six months, the men languished in a vile Yankee prison known as Camp Douglas, where many had perished from illness, lack of food, and exposure to the elements.

In the fall of 1862, the men of the 7th Texas were released after being exchanged for an equal number of Union prisoners. They were sent to reinforce the Confederate defenders of Vicksburg and Port Hudson in the lower Mississippi Valley. The regiment was still there when McFadden had joined it in early 1863.

Since then, McFadden had marched and fought in the ranks of the 7th Texas through battle after battle. Raymond, Chickamauga, Missionary Ridge, Ringgold Gap, Dug Gap, Pickett's Mill, not to mention countless smaller skirmishes. But he had not grown up with these men, nor had he gone through the nightmare winter in Hopkinsville or the miseries of Camp Douglas with them. His natural aloofness kept them at bay. Although the others greatly respected McFadden for his bravery and his soldierly qualities, they had never quite warmed to him.

Captain Collett appeared inside the glow cast by the campfire. There was a momentary quiet, but Collett smiled and waved for Montgomery to continue playing. He then sat down near McFadden.

"Evening, Captain," McFadden said simply.

"How are you, Jim?"

"Well as can be expected. How's Featherston?"

"He lost that leg of his. Poor boy. We'll see whether fever takes him or not."

"Hope not."

"Me, too. He's got a wife and son back in Texas."

McFadden grunted. The captain paused. Without a word, McFadden passed his flask and Collett took a quick swig before giving it back.

"We're going to have to promote one of the sergeants to lieutenant, you know. I was just talking to General Granbury about it."

"Thought you'd ask. The answer is no."

"Just like that, eh? I asked you after Chickamauga, then again after Ringgold Gap. You always say no."

"It's my answer."

"But why, Jim? I know you. Hell, I recruited you myself last year. I don't mind telling you that you're the most intelligent man in this regiment. You can read, write, and do figures better than some of the officers who have college educations. What with so many of the officers getting killed, you could easily have been a captain by now, if you had wanted it."

"That's just it, Captain. I don't want it. I don't want any responsibility. I don't even like heading up a company. All I want to do is fight."

Collett shook his head. "Pity. You'd make a fine officer, Jim, if only you'd be willing to start moving up the ranks. But you've been like this ever since I met you. Whatever the hell happened to you out in New Mexico turned you into one damned stubborn ass."

McFadden tensed, as though he sensed danger. He said nothing to Collett in response, but his mind was flooded with terrifying memories. He remembered the confusing and horrifying battles at Val Verde and Glorieta Pass, the long and hard retreat without food or water, the freezing nights spent without blankets, and the bitter realization that all his suffering had been for nothing.

But those experiences, brutal though they were, had been no different from those of any other Confederate soldier who had gone into New Mexico with General Sibley. His mind was haunted by a memory from the campaign of an altogether more sinister nature. He tried to force it out of his consciousness. But against his will, the ominous name he had heard on that nightmarish day forced its way into his mind, as if a little devil was whispering into his ear.

Cheeky Joe.

He clenched his teeth, then took a long swig of whiskey. Collett didn't see his discomfort, having had his attention drawn elsewhere as Private Montgomery began yet another song. It was *The Bonnie Blue Flag* this time and all the men of the 7th Texas began clapping as a renewed round of dancing around the campfire began. McFadden took another swig of whiskey from his flask, even less inclined to join in the dancing than he had before.

Chapter Two

June 28, Morning

Jefferson Davis, President of the Confederate States of America, stepped out of the front door of the Executive Mansion. In Richmond, it was popularly known as the White House of the Confederacy despite the fact that it was gray. Taking in a deep breath of summer air, he began his regular walk to work down 12th Street. He stood straight as a ramrod, making his height of five feet and ten inches seem rather taller than it was. His face, worn by the stress of the previous three years and a life that had known more than its fair share of grief, seemed chiseled out of granite. His lips seemed frozen in a line of perpetual humorlessness.

As he walked down the street, Davis was occasionally greeted by respectful strangers, with whom he exchanged polite tips of the hat. Some citizens, however, made a point of crossing to the other side of the street when they saw him coming so as to avoid such courtesies. His popularity was not what it had been when he had reluctantly assumed office back in 1861.

After a few minutes, Davis passed by Capitol Square. He circumvented the neoclassical building which presently housed both the Confederate Congress and the Virginia state legislature. He had always admired it, especially as it had been designed by Thomas Jefferson. The author of the Declaration of Independence was said to have based the Virginia State Capitol on an ancient Roman temple he had seen in the south of France. Davis sighed with regret at the fact that he had never been able to visit Europe.

Dismissing that thought, Davis crossed the street and reached the handsome if not quite elegant building that housed the executive offices of the Confederate government. Before the war, it had been the U.S. Customs House. He entered and was greeted with familiarity by the secretaries on the first floor, which housed the Treasury Department. He walked up a flight of stairs to the second floor, most of which was taken up by the State Department, but which also housed the executive office of the President. Outside his door, the President politely greeted Burton Harrison, his young personal secretary, and was handed a packet of correspondence.

A moment later, with considerable relief, Davis stepped into his office, shut the door, and dropped the letters on his desk. Settling into his chair with a tired exhalation, he immediately looked over at the military map that was mounted on the wall. Colored pins showed the current locations of major Union and Confederate military forces. A dark string, tautly drawn across the map, indicated the area of the country that remained under Confederate control. Every morning before he arrived, staff officers would update the map based on the latest reports. Davis was happy to see that there were no noticeable changes from the previous day.

It required a certain concentration to realize that those colored pins actually represented hundreds of thousands of men fighting to the death across a considerable chunk of North America, but Davis did it better than most. Everywhere he looked on the map, his armies were under enormous pressure. In Virginia, General Robert E. Lee and his redoubtable Army of Northern Virginia were battling valiantly against the Army of the Potomac under Ulysses S. Grant. Although they had inflicted terrible casualties on their foes since the opening of the campaign in May, the Southern troops had been steadily pushed back toward the capital at Richmond and the critical rail junction of Petersburg. Both sides had now dug in for a siege and the booming of the artillery was clearly audible in Richmond.

Despite the regrettable loss of territory, Davis felt little fear regarding the Virginia theater. According to the reports he was daily receiving from Lee, the massive losses the Yankees had sustained during their drive south had so demoralized Grant's army as to render it virtually unfit for offensive operations. Indeed, Lee had even been able to dispatch an entire corps, one-third of his army, on a raid northward against Washington City itself. Though he doubted the actual capture of Washington City was at all likely, the thought of Confederate troops operating on the outskirts of the enemy capital brought a smile to Davis's face.

On most other fronts, Confederate troops also appeared to be holding their own. The coastal forts protecting the great port cities of Charleston, Wilmington and Mobile continued to stoutly resist Union attacks. A recent Yankee attempt to invade Florida had been bloodily repulsed. Southeast of Memphis, the ruthless and brilliant cavalry leader, Nathan Bedford Forrest, had defeated every Yankee effort to penetrate into Mississippi or Alabama. And in the distant, near-forgotten theater of the Trans-Mississippi, scattered units of Texas cavalry continued to duel sporadically with Union detachments, with neither side able to gain much of an advantage.

No, he wasn't worried about Virginia. Nor was he worried about Mississippi, or the Carolina coast, or the Trans-Mississippi. What was keeping Davis up at night was Georgia. He stared intensely at the colored pins representing the respective armies of Johnston and Sherman, facing one another just north of Atlanta.

A frown formed across his face. Jefferson Davis and Joseph Johnston had known one another for years. Four decades before, they had been cadets together at West Point. While there, they had come to blows over the affections of a local damsel. When they had served together during the Mexican War, their relationship had been marked by professional rivalry and personal distaste. In 1861, when Davis had been struggling to organize the officer corps of the Confederate Army, he had found Johnston's attitude about his rank to be vain and petulant.

But the distrust Davis held for Johnston was not rooted, at least so far as he was concerned, in their admittedly poor personal relationship. In mid-1862, when Richmond seemed certain to fall to the Army of the Potomac, Johnston had been the commander of the army charged with the capital's defense. But instead of fighting the Yankees, Johnston had continually refused to give battle. Repeatedly stressing his numerical inferiority, he had insisted on a strictly defensive policy.

Davis recalled those dark days very well. Johnston had not launched a counter attack until the Yankees had literally been within sight of Richmond. Even then, he had so botched the attack that the result had been a tactical victory for the Yankees. Johnston had avoided complete disgrace only because of a severe wound he had received during the fighting. Unable to continue commanding the army, Johnston had been replaced by Robert E. Lee, who had promptly launched the great counter offensive that had driven the Yankee host away.

The more he thought about it, the more Davis became convinced that Johnston would have abandoned Richmond in 1862 had fate not intervened. He couldn't help wondering if history was about to repeat itself down in Georgia.

A soft knocking on the door stirred Davis from his musings. A moment later, Harrison appeared.

"Mr. President? Secretary Seddon and General Bragg are here to see you."

Harrison stepped aside and the two men entered. James Seddon, the Confederate Secretary of War, looked like he had just risen from a hospital bed, but that came as no surprise to Davis. The man was forever being afflicted with some ailment or other. Despite his unimpressive appearance, Davis considered Seddon an intelligent and conscientious man. Most importantly, he considered Seddon a man who did what he was told without thinking too much about it.

Braxton Bragg could not have looked more different from Seddon. He wore the gray uniform of a Confederate general. It was likely the most impeccably cleaned and tailored uniform of any general in the entire Confederacy, but Bragg was a general who no longer commanded any troops. Bragg had been Johnston's immediate predecessor as head of the Army of Tennessee, but his tenure as a field commander had come to an inglorious end with the disastrous defeat at Missionary Ridge. President Davis, unwilling to completely abandon a personal friend, had defied public opinion by summoning Bragg to Richmond to be his chief military advisor.

"Good morning, gentlemen," Davis said as they took their seats across from him. "What news this morning?"

"A telegram from General Johnston arrived late last night," Seddon said. He passed a telegram across the desk to Davis, who pulled out his glasses to read.

Secretary Seddon,
At eight o'clock this morning, the enemy launched heavy assaults all along the line. They were handily repulsed at all points. The loss of the enemy known to be great. Our loss known to be small. Our troops fought with great gallantry.
General Johnston

"Interesting," Davis said matter-of-factly, reading through the telegram once more. "It would seem that General Johnston has finally achieved something significant in the fight against Sherman."

"Only a defensive victory, Mr. President," Bragg said quickly. "Nothing more. Unless Johnston follows up this success with a major counter attack, the strategic situation in Georgia remains unchanged."

"Remains very bad, you mean."

"Precisely, Mr. President. While I will withhold judgment until we get a more detailed report from General Johnston, my initial impression is that this was nothing more than a minor tactical victory. Sherman, having been repulsed in a frontal attack, will no doubt return to his previous tactics, forcing Johnston to retreat by using his superior numbers to outflank him."

"Tactics which Johnston has been decidedly unable to counter," Davis spat.

"Indeed not, Mr. President."

Davis grunted for a moment, then glanced at the Secretary of War.

"Mr. Seddon? What do you think of this news from Johnston?"

Seddon shrugged. "I do not entirely know, Mr. President. Any victory is cause for celebration, I suppose. But I fear General Bragg may be correct. Unless this success is accompanied by a dramatic change in policy, I fear it will come to nothing."

"I admit that I am somewhat surprised to hear you say that, Mr. Seddon," Bragg interjected. "As I recall, you supported appointing Johnston to command of the Army of Tennessee last year."

"I did at the time, yes," Seddon said, with ever so slight a hint of defensiveness. "I did not consider him ideal, but only better than the other possible choices. Aside from you yourself, Johnston was one of only four men who held the rank of full general. Lee obviously was needed in Virginia. Kirby Smith was needed in the Trans-Mississippi. To appoint that pompous blowhard Beauregard was clearly unthinkable. Johnston was the best available choice at the time."

"I am afraid that it might have been the wrong choice," Davis said. "In view of what has happened since the opening of the campaign in Georgia, I might have preferred having Beauregard in command, pompous blowhard or not."

Seddon and Bragg laughed, though a more perceptive man than Davis could have sensed that neither found the comment particularly funny.

The President went on. "Why is it that every time Grant attempts to outflank Lee in Virginia, Lee intercepts him and fights him to a stalemate, while every time Sherman outflanks Johnston in Georgia, Johnston simply retreats?"

Bragg shrugged. "I wish I could answer the question, Mr. President. Lee is made of sterner stuff than Johnston, by God."

"According to the letters I have been receiving from General Hood, Johnston has passed up several opportunities to launch a counter attack against Sherman. I am beginning to suspect that the man will refuse to attack no matter how favorable the circumstances might be."

"Unwillingness to be aggressive is a sure way to ensure defeat, Mr. President," Bragg said.

"Precisely." Davis pursed his lips and shook his head. He turned to the map on the wall. "Mr. Seddon, how far is the front line in Georgia from the city of Atlanta?"

"Less than twenty-five miles, if I recall correctly."

"I will confess, gentlemen, that if we lose Atlanta, the game may well be up."

The eyebrows of both Bragg and Seddon shot up at these words. It was highly uncharacteristic of Davis to express doubt about the ultimate success of the Confederate cause. Davis gestured at the map.

"Look at it. All the railroads that connect the eastern and western halves of our remaining territory on this side of the Mississippi pass through Atlanta. The city has become the linchpin of our republic. I believe losing it would be a more severe blow to us than the loss of Vicksburg."

Both men nodded. They recalled, as did everyone in the Confederacy who read the newspapers, how the loss of Vicksburg had brought the entire Mississippi River under Union control, cutting the Confederacy off from the states of Texas, Arkansas, and Louisiana and therefore from critical sources of manpower, food, and other necessities of war.

"It is not just Atlanta's role as a transportation hub, Mr. President," Seddon said dryly. "Aside from Richmond itself, it is the most important industrial center that remains under our control. If we lose Atlanta, we lose the city's factories, grist mills, iron foundries, armories and other critical facilities. We would be deprived of much of our remaining ability to produce rifles, cannon, rail iron, armor for our ironclads, and everything else needed to keep our war effort going."

Davis practically shook his fist at the map. "Lee has stopped the Yankees in Virginia. Forrest is keeping them out of Mississippi and Alabama. The Union Navy can't break down our coastal fortresses. We continue to hold our ground in the Trans-Mississippi. We can win this war, gentlemen. We need only hold out until November, after all. But if Johnston fails to hold Atlanta, the entire country could collapse."

Bragg's eyes narrowed for a moment. "November?"

"November 8, to be exact."

"Oh, of course," Seddon said. "You speak of the presidential election in the North."

"Indeed. Everything now hinges on the election in the North. Lincoln's popularity among his own people has never been high and it is now lower than it has ever been since the beginning of the war. His management of the war is regarded by many as incompetent, with the Yankee armies suffering heavy losses without any meaningful military gains. Outside of New England, with all its abolitionist agitators, there is little support for the Emancipation Proclamation. And opposition to the draft is increasing every day."

"That's what the Yankee papers say," Bragg said. Enemy newspapers were frequently acquired from the front lines around Petersburg due to illicit trading between the pickets of the rival armies.

Davis nodded. "If we can continue to hold out until the fall, especially if we continue to inflict heavy losses on our enemies, then we can expect Lincoln and the Republicans to be defeated in the election. A Democratic administration will be inaugurated that will certainly be more open to negotiations with us. But if we suffer a serious military reverse, such as the loss of Atlanta, Lincoln can go to the Northern people and present it as evidence that they are, in fact, winning the war."

Seddon cocked his head skeptically. "I must confess, Mr. President, that I find it unlikely that the Democrats would be willing to simply let us go, especially after the deaths of hundreds of thousands of Northern soldiers."

"There are powerful factions within the Democratic Party who openly declare their desire for a cease-fire," Davis said emphatically. "If these elements succeed in winning power in the November elections, anything is possible." The President turned back toward the map again. "Assuming, of course, that we can hold Atlanta. With General Johnston at the head of the Army of Tennessee, I'm not sure that we can."

*   *   *   *   *

Major Thomas Eckert, chief of the United States War Department Telegraph Office, was having a relatively quiet day. During and after a major military event, the cramped room on the second floor of the War Department would be swamped by incoming messages, many of them requiring careful decryption. To make matters worse, various government officials would usually hang around the office at such times, demanding that the time-consuming process be sped up and ignoring protests that this was simply not possible.

But aside from Sherman's repulse at Kennesaw Mountain the day before, which had been a fairly straightforward piece of news, not much of any military importance had happened that day. Consequently, he had made use of his free time by borrowing some volumes on military history from the War Department library, even if he technically didn't have permission to do so. A few telegraph operators, all of them surprisingly young, lounged about lazily, patiently waiting for the next time their machines started clicking.

Eckert was deeply engrossed in an account of Napoleon's victory at the Battle of Austerlitz when a familiar visitor to his office, an exceptionally tall man, poked his head in the door.

"Am I bothering you, Major Eckert?" President Abraham Lincoln asked.

Eckert dropped the book onto his desk and stood up instantly. "No, Mr. President. Of course not."

"How is this day treating you?"

"Very well, sir. A quiet day, thus far."

"I see. You don't mind if I take a peek at the latest telegrams, do you?"

"Not at all, sir."

Lincoln smiled and nodded, in that electric way which Eckert had seen so many times and yet which he found difficult to explain. The President exchanged a few quick greetings with the machine operators, who were used to seeing him there. As Eckert pretended to go back to reading his book, Lincoln opened a drawer in the main office desk, where the telegrams were filed in the order in which they had been received. Lincoln plucked a handful of sheets, strolled over to a couch, and sat down to read.

He went on for some time, as Eckert knew he would. Since Eckert had arrived in the Telegraph Office more than two years before, Lincoln's visits had been an almost daily occurrence. They had evolved into a familiar routine, and Eckert had come to believe that, strange as it sounded, the President came to read the telegrams at the Telegraph Office partially as a means to relax.

After about twenty minutes, interspersed with sighs, grumbles, and an occasional chuckle, Lincoln said the words that Eckert knew he would say.

"Well, Major Eckert, I'm down to the raisins." He rose from the couch, put the telegrams back in the drawer, and with a smile and nod, turned to leave.

"Mr. President?" Eckert asked, finally getting up the nerve.

"Yes, Major Eckert?"

"I beg your pardon, sir. For a year or so now, you have always announced that you have finished reading the telegrams by saying that you are 'down to the raisins.' I confess, sir, that I have no idea what you are talking about. Can you please explain it for me?"

Lincoln's head rolled back and he let out a hearty laugh. Eckert smiled, happy with himself for finally asking the question he had wondered about for so long.

"Well, Major Eckert, I had a friend once back in Springfield, who threw a big party for his little girl on her birthday. Fifth birthday, I think. She gorged herself on a massive dinner, and polished off a whole mess of raisins for dessert. That night she got real sick and my worried friend sent for the doctor. When the doctor showed up, the dinner the little girl had eaten was in the process of, shall I say, liberating itself from her stomach. The doctor examined the refuse of the said liberation. He finally came across some small dark objects and told the girl's parents that she was now out of danger. When asked how he knew this, the doctor merely smiled and said that she was now down to the raisins."

Eckert laughed lightly, somehow feeling that the joke contained some hidden piece of wisdom which an unenlightened fellow like himself could never fully understand. Abraham Lincoln seemed to glow from the inside.

"Come to bother my telegraph operators again, Mr. President?"

Eckert and Lincoln turned to see Secretary of War Edwin Stanton walk into the room, staring at them sternly from behind his spectacles. A newspaper was stuffed under his arm. The portly man's beard spilled across his chest like an enormous child's bib. Eckert found the appearance of the Secretary of War mildly ridiculous, but stood to respectful attention. Not only could Stanton be wrathful toward subordinates who failed to meet his high expectations, but Eckert also knew that a powerful mind lurked within the man's head.

Lincoln laughed and responded. "You should know by now, Mr. Stanton, that I always make it a point to acquaint myself with the latest war news. Don't rightly think there's a better way to do that than to read the telegrams that come into this office."

"You can acquaint yourself with the military situation quite well enough by reading the reports I send you," Stanton replied. "Besides, you will have seen that there has been little military news of note since your visit yesterday, aside from the knocking Sherman received at Kennesaw Mountain."

"It says a great deal for how hardened we have become that we now refer to a battle in which hundreds of men were killed as a `knocking.'"

Stanton's expression showed that he had not thought about it. "My apologies, Mr. President."

Lincoln waved his hand. "No matter. You are right that the war situation does not appear to have changed much in recent days. Kennesaw Mountain is just the most recent event telling us that we are well and truly stymied. In Virginia, in Georgia, and everywhere else. If we are unable to pick the locks of the rebels before November, the voters shall not be pleased with me, to say the least."

"I wish I could argue with you, Mr. President."

Lincoln nodded toward the newspaper under Stanton's arm. "What have you got there?"

"This? Oh, yesterday's copy of the *New York World*."

"Ah," Lincoln said. The periodical was staunchly pro-Democratic and hostile to the President. "And what are our Democratic friends saying today?"

Stanton put his reading glasses on, unfolded the newspaper, and began reading.

The reelection of the brute to whom we are compelled to give the title of President of the United States would be the most measureless disaster this country has ever seen! A worse tyrant and butcher has not been seen since the days of Caligula and Nero! Do you want endless and mismanaged war? Do you want your sons rounded up by draft officers and sent to be impaled on Southern bayonets? Do you want no markets for your produce? Do you want Negroes marrying your daughters? If so, cast your vote for Lincoln, and be counted with the traitors and fools. Debt, defeat, taxation and tyranny shall be your trophies.

"Sounds like Vallandigham," Lincoln commented, sounding amused and not in the least offended.

"It is, indeed. He goes on at length. Shall I read the rest?"

"No, thank you. I have become quite well-acquainted with Congressman Vallandigham's literary style and feel no need to brush up on it further. The man inflicts such pain upon adjectives that I am surprised they have not yet murdered him in his sleep."

"I have two men watching him at the hotel he is staying at in Canada. I believe it very likely that he may soon attempt to return to Ohio."

Lincoln waved his hand dismissively. "Leave him be. After he was arrested for sedition last year, my greatest concern was to avoid making him a martyr. That's why I had him kicked out of the country rather than keep him in jail. Taking a firm line with him may just make him stronger. If we don't take him seriously, maybe the people won't, either."

"Vallandigham is but the most public and visible member of these so-called Copperheads, Mr. President. There are uncounted thousands who share his views. Public support for the war is steadily eroding, with the lack of military success at the front being compounded by the agitation spread by these infidels."

Lincoln shook his head. "The Peace Democrats agitate so much that it makes it harder for the country to fight, then they blame us when we don't give them an immediate victory"

"If the Democrats win the election in November, and go ahead with their stated intention of opening negotiations with the rebels..." Stanton didn't need to go on.

Lincoln strolled over to the war map on the wall. Large red pins were in place at Richmond and Atlanta.

"It seems to me, Mr. Stanton, that we are trying to unravel the equivalent of the Gordian Knot. And until we remove one of these pins, I fear the knot will remain too tight for us to untangle."

*   *   *   *   *

June 30, Morning

"What do you think, General?"

Cleburne carefully examined the weapon he was holding. "A Kerr rifle, you say?"

"That's right," the ordinance officer replied. "Beautiful, isn't she? And brand new. It wasn't off the blockade runner in Mobile more than two days before they loaded it up on the train to deliver to us. Hell, it wouldn't surprise me if this beauty came out of the factory in England less than three months ago."

Cleburne examined the muzzle. "Point four five caliber, yes? Just like the Whitworth?"

The man nodded. "Yes."

"It will be hard for you to provide me with a continual supply of ammunition." Both the Kerr and the Whitworth required a special cartridge, longer and heavier than that used in normal weapons. So much powder was required for the sharpshooting weapons that,

- 46 -

according to the men, they felt like a mule had kicked them in the shoulder after using it.

"We received a shipment of Kerr cartridges with the weapons. Not as much as I'd like, of course, but enough to keep your men employed for at least a little while."

Cleburne held the weapon up to his shoulder in a firing position, sensing its weight, feeling how easily the wooden butt of the weapon fit into his shoulder. He tried to imagine wielding the weapon in a trench that was under artillery fire. Accurate fire at a target several hundred yards away required great stability, which was incredibly difficult in the midst of combat. Steady hands were necessary.

"Range?"

"A thousand yards, give or take."

"Not quite as good as the Whitworth," observed Major Benham, who was standing behind Cleburne.

"No, but good enough," Cleburne said. He had formed a special unit of sharpshooters within his division, taking the best shots from each of his brigades. These men were able to kill at an astonishing distance, regularly striking targets that were nearly a mile away. Cleburne mostly employed them against enemy artillery batteries, which helped to neutralize the Union superiority in cannon. They also had been instructed to identify and kill enemy officers whenever possible, although Cleburne's conscience was somewhat troubled by such an unsportsmanlike tactic.

Cleburne turned to Benham. "How many sharpshooters do we have presently?"

"Nineteen, sir. All armed with Whitworths."

"Well, these newly-arrived Kerr rifles should significantly increase their firepower."

"How many have we been allocated?" Benham asked the ordinance officer.

"We got twenty off the train. Orders say that your division gets five."

"I'd prefer more," Cleburne said.

The man shrugged. "What can I say, General? Orders are orders. No one else got as many as you did. All the other divisions got three. I'm not mentioning that to them, of course. Don't want them to get jealous."

"Very well," Cleburne said, satisified. "You'll arrange for them to be delivered to the division?"

"They'll arrive this afternoon, sir."

There was a quick exchange of salutes. A minute later, Cleburne and Benham were back in the saddle and slowly riding north. They had taken advantage of the lull in the fighting to take care of some business with the corps and army administrative officers behind the lines.

As they rode, Cleburne quizzed Benham on a variety of subjects. Had he checked to make sure the divisional hospital was fully stocked with supplies? In the event that no rations would be forthcoming for the division, how long would their present supplies of food last? How many men had turned out for religious services the previous Sunday?

Benham answered each question quickly and easily, which gave Cleburne great satisfaction. He was quite confident that his division was not only the best in the Army of Tennessee in terms of its fighting record, but also the best in terms of its organization and cohesion.

"Oh, I forgot to tell you," Benham said, turning slightly in the saddle. "The officers of the Yankee brigade that attacked General Govan's position the other day, the ones who requested a truce because of the fire that threatened to burn their men alive?"

"Yes? What about them?"

"They sent over a gift to General Govan under a flag of truce the next day. Two new Colt Revolvers."

"Oh, that was thoughtful of them," Cleburne said without much emotion. The fact that Govan would use the weapons to kill Union soldiers had apparently not troubled those who had given the gift. Still, such gestures of chivalry between enemies were appreciated.

As they rode north back toward the front line, they passed through an area in which hundreds of slaves were hard at work. Without speaking, Cleburne pulled his horse to a stop, compelling Benham to do the same. For a long while, the two officers observed the work being done.

Johnston had given orders for a new defensive line to be prepared in the likely event that the Army of Tennessee was eventually forced to withdraw from its current position on Kennesaw Mountain. The slaves, stripped to the waist, were hewing great trenches out of the red clay earth, chopping down trees in front of them to create clear fields of fire and using the logs to strengthen the defenses themselves. Although the fortifications lacked the natural strength of the high ground the Confederates currently enjoyed on Kennesaw Mountain, Cleburne was confident that his men could hold the positions against any enemy. And the work of the slaves was making them more formidable by the hour.

One of the slaves, stopping to wipe the sweat off his forehead, looked up at Cleburne and momentarily met the general's eyes. He looked away and went back to work before a single second had passed.

All around the laboring slaves, whip-wielding overseers walked about slowly, carefully observing the proceedings. Cleburne could see the slaves casting glances toward the overseers as they moved about. He wondered how hard they would have worked had they not been slaves, but instead been paid for the amount of work they accomplished. Cleburne was no abolitionist, but he had never owned a slave and, being a Irishman, had never quite understood the attachment Southern men had toward the institution.

A sound rose above the axes chopping wood and the shovels slicing through the soil. After a moment, Cleburne realized that it was the sound of the slaves singing as they worked. One man would sing a single line, after which the rest of the slaves would sing out in response. It was a strange sort of music that Cleburne found incomprehensible and alien.

> Won't you ring old hammer?
> Hammer Ring!
> Won't you ring old hammer?
> Hammer Ring!

Those who could stamped their feet or beat their tools against wood in rhythm to the singing. It was as though a barrier had been erected around the workers through which no harshness or hatred could penetrate.

> Got to hammering in the Bible!
> Hammer Ring!
> Got to hammering in the Bible!
> Hammer Ring!
> Got to talk about Noah!
> Hammer Ring!
> Got to talk about Noah!
> Hammer Ring!

"They seem happy enough," Benham said.

"Well, we can't read their minds, can we?" Cleburne said in response. He figured that he, too, would do his best to appear happy if the alternative was being whipped. But having encountered the irrational anger that the issue of slavery could raise among Southern men, he decided not to broach the subject. Cleburne clicked Red Pepper back into a walk and resumed the journey back to their division.

"Good that we have the slaves to do such labor for us," Benham said as he got his own horse back into a walk. "It frees up more white men for duty on the front line."

"It would be better by far if we raised combat regiments of blacks," Cleburne responded.

Benham turned and looked at his commander. "Shall we go over this again, General?" he asked. His tone had changed, from that of a dutiful subordinate to a man trying to talk sense into his friend.

"Why not?" Cleburne responded. "It is absurd for the Confederacy to deny itself such a vast pool of available manpower. I believe my proposal to enlist slaves into the army is as valid now as when I first put it forward in January. More so, in fact, because of the heavy losses our armies have suffered both here in Georgia and in Virginia."

Cleburne remembered that strange cold night the previous winter, only a few days after Johnston had arrived to take command of the Army of Tennessee. At Cleburne's request, Hardee had convened a meeting of the high command at the army headquarters. There, warmed by roaring fires and well-cooked food, the division and corps commanders had listened as Cleburne had read aloud his memorandum. It had called for the Confederacy to enlist vast numbers of slaves into the army, giving them their freedom in exchange for their military service.

The reaction from his comrades had not been what Cleburne had expected. General William Bate, who led one of Hardee's other divisions, had been furious and called Cleburne an abolitionist, which was as serious an insult as it was possible for a Southern man to make. General Walker, however, had gone even further, saying to Cleburne's face that he thought he was a traitor. Only the presence of Hardee and Johnston had prevented a challenge to a duel, with all present at the meeting agreeing before departure that the matter was not to be discussed further.

It had been one of the greatest disappointments of Cleburne's life.

"I know your motives were pure, my friend," Benham said. "But you should have never written that memorandum. Certainly you never should have presented it to the high command of the army. When Walker notified the War Department about it, I believe he killed any chance of your promotion to corps command."

"We will see," Cleburne said. "I know Johnston is considering me for command of Polk's old corps. In any case, I do not see how I could have acted other than I did. I believe firmly that the case I presented was correct. My heart and soul are for the Confederacy, so how could I have kept silent about a plan which I honestly believe could save our nation."

Benham shook his head. This irritated Cleburne, who did not like seeing his idea dismissed so glibly, but he respected Benham as both an officer and a friend and tried not to take offense.

"It's difficult for a man not born and raised in the South to understand," Benham said.

"So I've been told," Cleburne responded in a clipped tone. Hardee had told him. His close friend General Thomas Hindman had told him. Just about everyone to whom he had broached the subject had told him, for that matter.

"You must understand that slavery, right or wrong, is central to the Southern way of life. If every other aspect of our society were planets, slavery would be the star around which they orbit. The whole point of secession, the whole point of the Confederacy, is to protect our way of life. Without slavery, we have no way of life, just a bunch of empty fields."

"But surely every Southern man can see that slavery is a millstone around our neck," Cleburne protested. "Slavery is the only reason the Confederacy has not received diplomatic recognition from Britain and France. It allows the Yankees to fill their soldiers with false notions of a crusade to destroy slavery, when in truth their only goal is to reduce us to absolute subjugation for their own profit. It means that every time any of our territory falls into enemy hands, their numbers are increased by freed blacks who flock to join the Yankee army."

"I know," Benham said.

"On every front, the Yankees confront us with armies that are greatly superior to ours in number. Why do we deny ourselves such an immense pool of fresh manpower? Were we to enlist the slaves into our own forces, we could meet the enemy with armies equal in strength to their own, giving us every possibility of success and perhaps even allowing us to invade the North's own territory."

"What makes you think the slaves would fight for the Confederacy?" Benham asked. "If the Union wins, slavery will be abolished, whereas if the Confederacy wins, it shall go on. The slave would gain nothing by fighting for us."

"That is why I say that we must promise the slaves their freedom if they are willing to take up arms on our behalf."

"But if you hand a slave a gun, how do you know which way he will point it?"

"If we offer the Negro his freedom, why should he not fight for us?" Cleburne said heatedly. "I believe that blacks can be properly trained and disciplined as well as white men."

"But in undermining slavery, do you not see that you are striking at the very foundations of Southern society? When we begin to question slavery, when we begin to even consider the possibility that the black man might be equal to the white man, our very identity as a people is thrown into question."

"Surely every patriotic Confederate soldier, if forced to choose between independence without slavery or absolute subjugation to Yankee control, would unhesitatingly choose the former. Surely you would rather give up slavery than be a slave yourself."

Benham considered this. "When you put it like that, I suppose you are right. In that one sense, at least. But so long as the possibility of victory remains without recourse to the proposal you put forward, the vast majority of Southern men will continue to resist proposals such as yours with every fiber of their strength. In truth, I believe that if we ever attempted to recruit black soldiers, half the men in the Army of Tennessee would throw down their weapons and refuse to fight."

Cleburne sighed. "I cannot understand such attitudes."

"That's all right, General. You weren't born with them."

As they continued north, the sounds of the singing slaves eventually faded away.

*　　　*　　　*　　　*　　　*

July 1, Morning

Beneath the shade of his large headquarters tent, General Johnston stood over a table which was covered with a topographical map of the surrounding mountains and countryside. He was surrounded by half a dozen of his principal commanders. It was the first meeting of the high command of the Army of Tennessee since the Battle of Kennesaw Mountain.

"First, allow me to offer my congratulations to you all for our great victory four days ago. Sherman threw everything he had at us, but thanks to the courage of our men and the favor of Almighty God, he was unable to break us. Our success brings us one step closer to victory."

The officers collectively muttered their thanks to the commander.

Johnston held up a finger. "But let us not delude ourselves, gentlemen. While we repulsed the enemy's attack, he will not be idle. We must assume that Sherman will revert to his previous strategy of moving around our flanks and force us back by threatening our line of retreat."

General Hood cleared his throat and began speaking. "My pickets are already reporting Yankee infantry moving southward across their front, toward our left flank."

Johnston eyed Hood closely for a moment before responding. He had trusted Hood and held him in high regard only a few days before. However, he trusted Senator Wigfall nearly as much as he would have trusted a member of his own family. Having heard what Wigfall had had to say about Hood, any trust he might have had in his corps commander had vanished like cigar smoke on a windy day.

"And what size units are we talking about, General Hood? Are we talking about brigades or divisions?"

Hood shook his head. "Not sure. Certainly big formations of infantry."

"I see. Keep your pickets out and inform me immediately of any new information. I would very much like to see more solid information, if it's possible. General Wheeler?"

"Yes, sir?"

"Keep your troopers deployed out in front of our left flank. They must keep a watch for any sign of a Yankee movement toward our left."

"Of course, sir."

"We must be vigilant, gentlemen. If we can accurately ascertain the movements of the enemy, we can maintain our position here on the Kennesaw for at least several more weeks."

Mackall walked up, nodding respectfully to the assembled commanders. "Excuse me, General Johnston, gentlemen. Senator Hill has arrived."

"Ah, yes! Bring him here, please." Mackall nodded and moved to obey his orders. Johnston composed himself for a moment, knowing the potential importance of this meeting. While Senator Wigfall was an avowed foe of the Davis administration, whose views would automatically be suspect, Senator Hill was both a political ally and personal friend of Davis. As such, Johnston hoped he might be able to gain some leverage with the Davis administration if he could persuade Hill that his views on the military situation were correct.

He turned to his officers. "Senator Hill has been visiting his constituents here in Georgia and is soon to return to Richmond. He has asked to be updated on the current military situation, so as to better inform officials in the capital."

"He will be meeting with President Davis?" asked Hood, a bit too quickly.

"I would assume so, yes." Johnston was tempted to ask why Hood would want to know such information, but held back.

Senator Benjamin Hill was led into the tent by Mackall and quickly introduced himself to the assembled officers.

"I do thank you for taking the time to meet with me, General Johnston," Hill said. "I am sure that time is very precious to you in the midst of a military campaign, particularly one as important as this."

"Think nothing of it, Senator," Johnston replied. "It is vital that the Congress in Richmond has a clear picture of the true situation here in Georgia and I believe you are in a unique position to help us achieve this."

"That is my hope."

Johnston gestured for everyone to sit down. "My chief-of-staff, General Mackall, has prepared a brief summary of the campaign up to this point, if you would care to hear it."

"Of course."

The men all turned their attention to Mackall, as two staff officers placed a large map of northern Georgia on a stand. The chief-of-staff began his presentation and spoke for about ten minutes. Senator Hill listened politely, asked intelligent questions, and seemed genuinely eager to learn what had taken place in Georgia. The more he observed Senator Hill, the more confident Johnston became. Most politicians Johnston had met over the years had been utter nonentities, but Senator Hill seemed to be made of more substance.

The story Mackall told was, of course, well-known to the officers themselves. Since the campaign had opened in early May, the Army of Tennessee had repeatedly blocked the route of Sherman toward Atlanta. Each time, however, Sherman had eventually forced the Confederates to retreat by using his superior numbers to outflank them. At Dalton, at Resaca, at Cassville, at Allatoona, at New Hope Church, and at Lost Mountain, the story had always been the same. Every step of the way, the Confederates had inflicted significant losses on their opponents, but had inevitably been compelled to give ground to avoid being surrounded.

In the midst of the presentation, Johnston frowned as Mackall described the incident at Cassville, which had taken place on May 19.

"So, thanks to fast marching and skillful maneuvering, we had obtained an advantageous position, concentrating the full strength of the Army of Tennessee against only a part of Sherman's force. Had the attack been carried out successfully, we could have achieved a decisive victory."

"What went wrong?" Hill asked.

"General Hood, upon moving his corps forward against the exposed Yankee forces, discovered what appeared to be an enemy cavalry force astride his right flank, thus forcing the cancellation of the attack."

Hood sat upright, an angry look on his face. "It was a misfortune of war! If that force of Yankee cavalry had not shown up in the wrong place at the wrong time, my attack would have gone forward and would have put the Yankees to flight."

"How can a small force of cavalry stop an entire infantry corps?" Hill asked, confused.

Johnston didn't say anything. Hood's face betrayed what Johnston perceived to be fear, or, at the very least, agitation. "It doesn't matter," Hood said. "It concerns military technicalities which a civilian like yourself would not understand."

Hill looked at Hood for a moment, examining him with the eye of a politician. "I see, General Hood," he said without much expression.

Johnston considered speaking, wanting more than anything to state his conviction that the attack had failed because of Hood's incompetence. Hood could have easily salvaged the situation by detaching a brigade to cover his right flank and going forward with the attack. But as he looked around at the faces of the other men, including General Hardee and General Wheeler, Johnston felt compelled to hold his tongue. After all, he was a Southern gentleman, even if Hood was not.

Mackall now took back control of the conversation. "From late May until the present, Senator, we have been engaged with Sherman's army in a series of engagements between Allatoona and our present position here on the Kennesaw line. The incessant rain has made maneuvering exceedingly difficult, but we have inflicted heavy losses upon the enemy while being driven back only a few miles."

"Thank you, General Mackall. Your presentation was most informative."

"Do you have any questions, Senator Hill?" Johnston asked.

"Several, General Johnston, if you'll forgive me. First, am I right in assuming that the Chattahoochee River is the last major obstacle between Sherman and Atlanta?"

"Yes."

"And obviously you will want to maintain a position on the north side of the Chattahoochee River for as long as possible, yes?"

"Of course."

"And how long do you believe you can do this?"

"It has taken Sherman more than a month to drive us from New Hope Church to our present position, a distance of only a few miles. You may make your calculation from that."

"Senator Hill," Hood said. "Respectfully, I must disagree with General Johnston. When we abandon the present line of Kennesaw, in my opinion we will retreat across the Chattahoochee River very rapidly."

Johnston jerked his head toward Hood. "How do you figure that?" he asked, anger in his voice. Openly disagreeing with the commanding officer in the presence of others was a serious breach of military etiquette. Openly disagreeing with the commanding officer in the presence of a senator was incalculably worse.

"Because this line on Kennesaw Mountain is the strongest we can expect to have this side of the Chattahoochee. Once we leave this line, any operations we engage in will be mere delaying actions until we cross the river."

"Nonsense," Johnston said sharply. "We have already surveyed multiple defensive positions between here and the river. We can hold out on the north bank of the river for a long time." His tone made it clear that Johnston expected Hood to keep his mouth shut for the remainder of the meeting.

Hill nodded, processing everything he was hearing. "I hope you'll forgive me for asking questions that may sound simple. As I am not a military man, the details often elude me."

"That's quite all right, Senator."

"Please tell me, concisely and specifically, what it is you need to bring this campaign to a successful conclusion."

Johnston took a deep breath. This was the moment he had been waiting for. He stood and stepped toward the map. He ran his finger along a black line that ran along the route of Sherman's advance from Chattanooga.

"This is the Western and Atlantic Railroad. As it has fallen into enemy hands, it is now the key supply route for Sherman's forces.

Virtually all the enemy's food, ammunition, and other supplies come to them along this single railroad."

"A jugular vein, so to speak."

"Exactly."

Hill nodded. "I understand."

Johnston's fingers moved north on the map, above Chattanooga. "The Union supply base at Chattanooga is linked to Nashville, Louisville, and the great cities of the North by only a few railroads. These railroads constitute the weak link in Sherman's plans."

Hill nodded again, and Johnston now spoke what he knew were the most important words of the meeting.

"I believe the key to winning the campaign is to launch a large-scale cavalry raid on the railroads and destroy them, in order to deprive Sherman of his supplies. In effect, this will cut Sherman off at the knees. If we can cut the railroad, Sherman will have no choice but to retreat. Atlanta will thereby be saved."

Johnston was silent for a moment, allowing the words to sink in. The collected officers sat quietly, but looked intently at Hill's face to see his reaction to Johnston's words. After a moment, the Senator spoke up, pointing to the cavalry commander.

"So, you intend to send some of Wheeler's horsemen to attack the railroad?"

The commanding general shook his head. "Not possible," he said emphatically. "What cavalry we have with this army is needed to screen our flanks and monitor the movements of the enemy. Sending even a small force from the Army of Tennessee would greatly hinder our ability to defend Atlanta. If an attack is to be made on Sherman's supply lines, it must be done by another cavalry force."

"Who?"

Johnston motioned to a staff officer, who removed the map of Georgia from the stand, revealing a new map that covered the entire Confederacy east of the Mississippi River. Johnston tapped northeastern Mississippi.

"General Nathan Bedford Forrest commands a force of several thousand cavalrymen, currently positioned here. As you know, he recently won a decisive victory at Brice's Cross Roads, leaving Yankee forces in the region in total disarray. I see no reason why he can not be unleashed into Tennessee or northern Georgia, to wreck havoc on Sherman's supply lines."

The mention of Forrest's name caused a ripple of disquiet through the gathered generals. The man might be an effective soldier, perhaps the most brilliant the South had produced. However, he was a ruffian, as prone to violence off the battlefield as he was on it. Wheeler noticeably shifted in his chair, his discomfort apparent; the two men had a long-running feud, during which Forrest had threatened to kill him. Coming from Forrest, such a threat was very serious, indeed.

"Nathan Bedford Forrest," Hill repeated. "For such an important mission, I can think of no one better. But can you be sure that an expedition against Sherman's supply lines would be successful?"

"With Forrest at its head, absolutely," Johnston said. "Recall that two years ago, during Grant's first campaign against Vicksburg, the Yankee effort was thwarted by means of a cavalry raid on his supply depots, not by defeating him in outright battle. Confronted as we always are by superior numbers, such indirect methods of obtaining victory are the most effective."

Hill nodded, thinking carefully. He was silent for nearly a full minute before he spoke again. "So, let me make sure I understand you, General Johnston. Because of your inferior numbers, you have little hope of defeating Sherman outright, as he will always be able to outflank your defensive positions. All that can be achieved is to delay him for a time. The only hope for victory in the present campaign is a large-scale cavalry raid against Sherman's supply lines, preferably undertaken by General Forrest. Is this correct?"

"That is an excellent summary of the situation, yes."

"Very well. That is the message I shall take to President Davis when I return to Richmond." He rose from his chair and stepped forward to shake Johnston's hand. "I thank you for giving me this briefing, which has been very illuminating."

"I thank you for coming and wish you a pleasant journey back to Richmond."

Senator Hill shook the hands of the other officers, briefly exchanging courteous words with them. Within a few minutes, the generals had left to return to their commands.

Johnston walked with Hill toward the buggy that would take him back to Atlanta. From there, he was planning to catch the evening train that would eventually carry him back to Richmond.

As he opened the door to the buggy, Johnston grasped Hill's arm. "Senator, I cannot stress enough the vital importance of the cavalry raid."

Hill nodded emphatically. "I fully understand, General. Rest assured that I shall do my utmost to persuade the President of the necessity of the expedition."

"You have my sincere thanks."

With a final smile and nod, Hill climbed into the buggy and, moments later, was on his way to Atlanta. As Johnston watched him go, Mackall came up beside him.

"Well, how do you think it went?" Johnston asked.

"About as good as can be expected, I suppose."

"I hope it was good enough. We need Hill's support with Davis. Unless Forrest is unleashed against the enemy supply lines, the fall of Atlanta may be merely a matter of time."

*　　　　*　　　　*　　　　*　　　　*

July 1, Evening

The steam engine of the ferryboat carrying passengers from the Canadian town of Windsor across to Detroit chugged along steadily. Most of the passengers stood quietly against the railings, impatiently waiting for the brief trip to end. Though the geographic distance was short, the journey was carrying the travelers from the British Empire into the United States.

Among the passengers leaning against the railings was former Congressman Clement Vallandigham, though he looked nothing like his widely-known public persona. During the months he had spent in exile in Windsor, he had been made aware that he was under surveillance by United States agents. Consequently, he had decided to take no chances now that he was finally returning to his country.

He had tied a pillow around his waist to increase his girth. He had applied a fake beard to conceal his face. When he had looked in the mirror before leaving his hotel, he had seen a completely different man looking back at him. Indeed, his appearance had made him think of Falstaff. With a little luck, it would be enough to fool the customs agents on the Detroit docks, who had no doubt been given orders to keep an eye out for him.

Somewhere behind him, Vallandigham could hear four men quietly conversing with one another, occasionally glancing in his direction. They deliberately stood several yards away, acting as if they did not know him. In fact, the four men were members of the Ohio Democratic Party, sent into Canada to clandestinely escort him home. All were carrying revolvers, a measure that the former congressman considered likely to do more harm than good, but he doubted they would be needed in any event. Besides, he had to admit that he appreciated the added dramatic element.

He looked across the bow and could see the houses and buildings of Detroit in the twilight. It wouldn't be too long before the ferry reached the dock. Then, assuming he could slip past the customs officials, he would be back on American soil for the first time in more than a year.

Vallandigham was confident that his disguise would work. He had been told that his mother was dying and he wanted to be by her side before the end. But his reasons for returning to America were more than merely personal. He knew he couldn't continue his effort to thwart the reelection of Abraham Lincoln from Canada. To be politically effective, he had to be present at the scene of the action.

Even if the customs officials saw through his disguise and arrested him, his political purposes might still be served. After all, barring a major military event, his arrest would be the big news story throughout the Union for at least a few days. The Lincoln administration would again face questions about its abuse of power, as Vallandigham was doing nothing illegal. Indeed, had never done anything that could be considered wrong except criticize the war effort. Vicious newspaper editorials from New York to Wisconsin would follow, and Lincoln's chances for reelection would suffer yet another blow.

One of his four escorts, a man he knew only as Charles, strode up and stood beside him on the railing.

"Lovely evening, is it not?"

"Indeed." A brief moment passed. "You can dispense with the subterfuge. No other passenger is within earshot."

Charles nodded. "We have purchased you a train ticket that will take you from Detroit to Lima, so that you can see your mother."

"Good. I appreciate your kindness."

"We can also arrange for you to head from there to Dayton, to see your family."

"Thank you, but no. There is no time to lose, and the state Democratic convention will begin in Hamilton in just a few days. I shall spend one day in Lima, then head directly to Hamilton."

"Very well, sir."

"The Democratic National Convention is less than two months away, you know. We have to make sure that the party is united behind a peace platform and, more importantly, that the presidential candidate we put forward will be one who can defeat Lincoln."

"And who will be the nominee?" Charles asked.

Vallandigham turned to look directly at the man and smiled impishly. "That is the question of the day, my friend."

The man's eyes narrowed in confusion, but he choose not to inquire further. "You've been in exile a long time, sir," he said simply.

"Yes," Vallandigham replied. "Nearly a year, in fact." He gazed up at the darkening sky for a moment. The obvious approach of his mother's death had made him rather more attuned to the length of time a person might expect to live. Assuming that he lived an ordinary lifespan, Abraham Lincoln had robbed him of a considerable chunk of his time on Earth. It was for more than Lincoln's tyrannical and unconstitutional actions that Vallandigham wanted revenge.

Two hours later, having successfully bluffed his way past the customs officials, Vallandigham was on his way back to Ohio.

July 2, Morning

"No question about it, sir," Mackall said. "The Yankees are trying to get around our left flank again." He sighed with resignation, as though he was speaking of an annoying yet inevitable infestation of summer flies.

Johnston intently read through the report that had just arrived from Wheeler. The earlier indications that Union forces were moving southward across Hood's front had been proven correct. And rather than being a probing movement by a single division, it was now clear that several infantry corps were on the move. In all likelihood, it was Sherman's entire army, excepting only a small force to guard the railroad.

The news didn't come as any surprise to Johnston, for it was the obvious move for Sherman to make following his repulse at Kennesaw Mountain. "Were I in Sherman's place, I should do precisely the same thing," he said under his breath.

He looked over the map, tracing the course of the Chattahoochee River with his finger. If he attempted to hold a defensive position with a river to his back, Johnston knew he would be running a terrible risk. He and his army might find it impossible to retreat over the river fast enough if the Yankees were to pry them out of their fortified lines. Still, his engineers had worked hard preparing an elaborate defensive position on the north bank, and Johnston felt that there was little danger. After all, it was always best not to retreat until one was forced to do so.

"Well, General?" Mackall asked. "Shall we put into effect the plan we previously discussed?"

"Yes," Johnston said without hesitation. "Issue marching orders that will move the army into the defensive line we have drawn here." His tapped the map near the point where the Western and Atlantic Railroad crossed the river. "General Shoup tells me that he has brought in nearly a thousand slaves from the plantations south of Atlanta and that they have been working on the fortifications for nearly a week."

"If that's so, we can expect our new defensive line to be very strong, indeed. General Shoup knows what he's about when it comes to engineering."

"Yes," Johnston said absent-mindedly, his fingers now tracing the south bank of the river. After a moment's thought, he spoke up again. "William, I wonder if it might be advisable to bring one of our three corps to the south side of the river. With his superior numbers, Sherman certainly could invest our new defensive line and still have sufficient strength to detach a large striking force. If such an enemy force is able to cross to the south side of the river while our entire army remains on the north side. . ."

"We could be surrounded," Mackall said, finishing his commander's thought. "It makes strategic sense, General. However, I would worry that such a move would be poorly received in certain quarters."

"In Richmond, you mean."

"Quite so, sir. President Davis would certainly be aghast to learn that a significant portion of our army has been withdrawn to the south side of the river."

"Do you really think I give a damn what Jefferson Davis thinks of my operations? If the man weren't such a small-minded buffoon, I might value his opinion. But since he is, I don't."

"You are aware, General, that I fully share your opinion of the President's mental acuity," Mackall replied. "His personal animosity toward us all but guarantees that he will always assume the worst concerning our course of action. I fear it is also causing him to deny us the means to defeat Sherman."

Johnston looked up, reading Mackall's mind. "You believe he will withhold the order for the cavalry raid against Sherman's supply lines purely out of spite?"

Mackall thought for just a moment before replying. "I do, sir. To be frank, I often find myself wondering if Jefferson Davis would rather lose Atlanta than have you win a victory which would do you credit."

"I know. You're not the first person to suggest it to me, either. It is the same as during the Peninsular Campaign of 1862 or during the campaign around Vicksburg last year."

"The enemies in front of us are bad enough. I truly wish we didn't have to deal with enemies behind us as well."

Johnston snorted with contempt. He could not afford to ignore the President's actions, since they directly impacted his ability to defend Atlanta. But neither could he call Davis out on them, since it would only result in the President immediately removing him from command. Johnston admitted to himself that he didn't quite know what to do about Davis. For that matter, he didn't quite know what to do about Hood. That being the case, it was best to focus on strictly military questions.

"William, after you issue the marching orders to our new defense line, draw up a set of orders for a contingency plan to bring one of our infantry corps to the south side of the river. If we do decide to implement such a plan, I want to be ready to do so immediately."

"Yes, sir."

"Get to it. We may not have much time."

As Mackall began dictating the marching orders to a nearby secretary, Johnston continued to stare intently at the map. He knew that he had a knack for concealing his emotions and he was heartily glad of it on this day. For Johnston was consumed by an increasing sense of uncertainty and gloom. He admitted to himself that he had absolutely no idea what to do. No course of action his mind conjured up had a chance of preventing the fall of Atlanta. If Davis refused to order the cavalry raid, as seemed likely, all would be lost.

Briefly, he wondered what his old friend Robert E. Lee would do in his situation. But was that useful? While Johnston didn't question his fellow Virginian's military skill, Lee took chances that Johnston was unwilling to take. The great victories at Second Manassas and Chancellorsville should, by all rational calculation, have been catastrophic Southern defeats. As far as Johnston was concerned, Lee won his triumphs more through sheer luck than by skill.

Jealousy tugged at Johnston. Until he had suffered his wound at Seven Pines, the Army of Northern Virginia had been under his command. For just a moment, he wondered whether he might have been able to achieve what Lee had. Lee was now the great hero of the Confederacy. He was being lionized around the world as a military genius on the level of Napoleon or Caesar. Would Johnston have been able to win such glory had he not been wounded that awful day?

He shook his head. Rather than winning immortality on the battlefields of Virginia, Johnston was increasingly certain he would soon be forced out of Atlanta. He knew that he might eventually have no choice but to abandon the second-most important city in the Confederacy in order to save his army. He also knew that the people of the South would never forgive him. When the history of the war was written, Johnston's name would be remembered with scorn.

He continued to absent-mindedly scrutinize the map, not looking for anything in particular. Purely by chance, he then noticed a small rivulet south of the Chattahoochee River that meandered eastward, drawing a neat line directly north of Atlanta. It was called Peachtree Creek.

Johnston's eyes narrowed. The wheels in his mind began to turn.

*   *   *   *   *

July 2, Afternoon

The men of the 7th Texas lounged about behind their defenses. Not much had happened since their successful repulse of Sherman's attack five days before, and the men had taken the opportunity to rest and recover a bit. Although food was, as ever, in short supply, there was plenty of fresh water thanks to the close proximity of the Chattahoochee River. Consequently, the men were cleaner than they had been in some time and several of them had indulged in a much-needed shave.

A few men manned the parapet line, ready to give the warning if the Yankees launched a sudden surprise attack. A few, more cautious or more clever than the others, had rigged small shaving mirrors in such a way that they could look over the parapet without exposing their heads, as they had no desire to be picked off by some nameless Yankee sharpshooter.

Sergeant McFadden sat quietly, leaning backwards against the parapet and simply waiting for time to pass. Private Montgomery was playing his fiddle by plucking at the strings as though it were a banjo, filling the air with soft and unobtrusive music. Next to McFadden, Private Harrison was taking the opportunity to write a letter to his wife. Glancing about, McFadden saw some of his other comrades engaged in the same activity. Most of the men, however, simply laid back with their eyes closed, happy to get a chance to catch up on their sleep.

McFadden had no one to whom it would be worth the effort to pen a letter, as he had buried every member of his immediate family two years before. He supposedly had some cousins who lived in Scotland, but he had never met them and knew them only through stories his parents had told him when he had been a boy. McFadden was, as far as he was concerned, utterly alone in the world.

Private John Balch, who had been reading a newspaper, waved it in McFadden's general direction.

"Done with this. You want it, Jim?"

McFadden nodded and took it. It was a copy of *Atlanta Intelligencer*. He considered it a good newspaper, despite its tendency to balloon minor successes into great victories and to dismiss serious reverses as trivial setbacks. McFadden's mind insisted on keeping abreast of the latest war news, though he was not such a fool as to think that whatever he himself did had any great impact on events. Nor did he particularly care which side won the war. He served as a soldier for his own sake, not for the Confederacy's.

"Anything interesting going on back east?" Harrison asked, not looking up from his letter.

"Not really. Lee and Grant are still fighting around Petersburg."

"Grant won't get into Richmond anytime soon, then."

"Doesn't look like it."

"Rumor says that Lee may soon send us some reinforcements."

"I'll believe that when I see it," McFadden replied. He never trusted rumors, and did not understand why so many of his comrades did. But then, few of them had enjoyed the education his father had given him.

After twenty minutes of reading, McFadden set the newspaper down and leaned his back against the parapet. He found himself thinking about Captain Collett's offer a few days before to have him promoted to lieutenant. He wondered if he had made the right choice in turning the captain down. If he had been the man he had been two years before, McFadden was certain he would have jumped at the chance. But he was not that man, and although part of his mind tugged at him to reconsider, he decided that he had made the correct choice.

Tilting his felt hat forward a bit so as to block the sun from his eyes, he tried to drift off into sleep. Just when he felt blessed unconsciousness beginning to creep up on him, his quest for sleep was thwarted.

"Everybody up! Attention!" the authoritative voice of Captain Collett bellowed.

The men of the 7th Texas were on their feet and moving into a single-file line, ready to hear whatever their commander had to say. Collett waited about twenty seconds for everyone to form up.

"Boys, we're moving out! It looks like the Yankees are moving to get around our left flank again."

The men groaned their collective disappointment. A few muttered curses were heard, damning Sherman and all Yankees to hell. After having occupied the same position for so many days, the idea of marching to a new one struck many as a serious inconvenience.

"The whole division is moving south to block the Yankee movement. Our marching orders have us moving out in less than an hour and we'll probably be marching all night, so get something to eat and be prepared to march in thirty minutes."

"Yes, sir," the men of the regiment said as a group. The line immediately broke up as the men scrambled to get ready. McFadden saw to it that the Lone Star Rifles did their work as quickly and efficiently as possible, sparing only a few moments of thought to wonder where the 7th Texas would next find itself.

*　　　　*　　　　*　　　　*　　　　*

July 3, Evening

Wearing his finest dress uniform, with a ceremonial sword dangling at his side, Bragg strode into the main dining room of the palatial Richmond house. He had no idea why he had been invited to the party, for he knew that he was distinctly unpopular. Being far from a personable man, his first inclination upon receiving the invitation had been to decline. Bragg did not like parties, with all their silly women and meaningless small talk. More enjoyable by far would have been an evening at home with his wife, who had not been able to attend due to illness.

But President Davis had hinted strongly that he wanted Bragg to go and so he had come. He did not plan to stay for long, but he had decided to make the best of it while he was there. After all, an evening at the home of George Trenholm, the wealthiest man in the Confederacy, promised the opportunity to enjoy foods that had become virtually unobtainable due to the Yankee blockade.

Fortunately, it was not an affair that required the guests to sit down together at a table, which would have placed Bragg in the uncomfortable position of having to talk to the same two people for an hour or more. Instead, the guests were milling about the various large rooms, sampling food at their own pleasure from a buffet set up on an immense dinner table. There were slices of roast mutton, oysters, roast chicken in a maple syrup glaze, a sort of gelatin he didn't recognize, iced fruits of various kinds, and many other foods that looked as lovely as they tasted. He sampled some of the fare, finding it more delicious than any he had tasted in quite some time. The mutton, in particular, was cooked to perfection.

Slaves dressed in livery silently circulated among the party-goers, carrying plates of champagne flutes. Bragg did not touch any of them, for he had been a teetotaler since his early days in the army, when he had seen alcohol destroy many a promising young officer. He was not about to break his habit now, even if the drink in question was fine French champagne run through the blockade on one of Trenholm's ships.

In a corner of the room, a string quartet filled the air with soft music. Around Bragg swirled the cream of Richmond society. There was the Reverend Charles Minnigerode, minister of St. Paul's Church, to which most of the social elite of the city belonged. There was Congressman William Miles, the most dapper man in the city, successfully charming a younger woman while his wife looked on with mild disapproval. There was Colonel James Chesnut, one of the President's military aides, along with his annoying wife Mary.

Bragg carefully looked about at those guests wearing military uniforms, wondering who among them might be his enemies. Most of the officers in and around Richmond were Lee's men and had not served in the Western Theater, so he did not recognize many of them. He did not think it worth his time to introduce himself to anyone.

"Ah, General Bragg!" a voice said.

He turned and saw a man in a fine civilian suit and bearing a warm smile approaching him, a glass of champagne in his hand. It took him a moment to realize that the man was George Trenholm, the host of the party.

"Good evening, Mr. Trenholm," Bragg said, shaking his proffered hand.

"Thank you for coming," Trenholm said. "I apologize for sending the invitation on such short notice, but I only decided to organize this gathering last week."

"I appreciate your thoughtfulness. You have a fine house, sir."

"Thank you, General. I am rather proud of it myself. Can I interest you in a glass of champagne?"

"No, thank you."

Trenholm nodded slightly, studying Bragg. He reminded Bragg of a trial lawyer analyzing a witness. No doubt he was even then realizing that Braxton Bragg was an uninteresting fellow and determining not to invite him to the next party.

"I hear tell that there may be a shakeup in the high command of our army in Georgia," Trenholm said matter-of-factly.

"Oh? What sort of shakeup?"

"Rumor has it that you and President Davis are planning on removing General Johnston and placing either General Hardee or General Hood in his place. Any truth to it?"

The mention of William Hardee's name instantly made Bragg grimace. During Bragg's tenure as commander of the Army of Tennessee, Hardee had constantly undermined him. Bragg knew for a fact that that Hardee had counseled President Davis to relieve him of command after the failure of the campaign in Kentucky and the stalemated battle at Murfreesboro. Bragg only wished that the Union shell which had recently killed General Leonidas Polk, another enemy, had killed Hardee at the same time. Of all the generals in the Army of Tennessee, only the cavalry commander Joseph Wheeler held Bragg's trust.

"It's not my place to speak about rumors," Bragg said. "Nevertheless, it should be obvious that we are not pleased with Johnston's performance in the field."

"Oh?"

"He has retreated nearly a hundred miles in the last two months, abandoning territory of great importance to the war effort. The ironworks of Rome, one of our principal producers of artillery, have been lost to us. The ground of northern Georgia is well-suited to the tactical defense, yet Johnston has repeatedly surrendered a number of extremely strong positions and made no effort to defeat the enemy's flanking movements. A change in strategy in the Western theater must be made. If Johnston himself will not make it, we may have to find someone who will."

He realized that he was saying too much, having let his anger at the mention of Hardee get the better of him. He resolved to speak no more on the matter.

Trenholm nodded, sipping his champagne. "Well, I am sure that you and President Davis will make the right decision when the time comes."

"Of course."

"There is another rumor making rounds about the city. Some wags are saying that Secretary of the Treasury Memminger is to leave office soon."

"What's that?"

"Memminger is about to resign, or be forced out, depending on who's telling the story."

Bragg shrugged. The identity of the man who held the portfolio of Treasury Secretary was no concern of his. He had met Memminger on a few occasions, but had never spoken more than half a dozen words to him at any time.

"If you do not feel it to be inappropriate, you may inform the President that I myself am more than willing to do my patriotic duty at any time he may see fit to call upon me."

"Of course. Your fleet of blockade runners has been extremely useful in helping keep our armies supplied with weapons and equipment."

"Thank you, General Bragg. But if there is any further service I can render my country, I want you to know that I stand ready."

At once, Bragg understood why he had been invited to the party. Trenholm knew that Bragg held the ear of the President. If rumors really were swirling that Memminger was on his way out, Trenholm wanted the job and hoped that Bragg would intercede with the President on his behalf. It was perfectly obvious to Bragg that Trenholm would use the position to line his own pocket whenever possible, but if he could bring some order to the troubled public finances of the Confederacy while doing so, he was probably as good a man as any.

"I will let him know, Mr. Trenholm."

Trenholm smiled. "Very good. Before you depart, I should like you to have a basket of French soaps and perfume to take home to your wife, who I understand could not join us on account of illness. Just ask the doorman on your way out."

"Thank you. She will be very happy to receive such a gift."

Bragg forced his mouth into a smile. Trenholm nodded and moved on to the next guest. Bragg went back to the table, taking for himself a slice of the roast chicken and some of the iced fruits. He intended to leave within the next few minutes but wanted to have just a little bit more of the delectable food before going.

He was aware that people were casting side glances in his direction and he thought he heard disparaging comments about him in the whispered conversations of some of the women. Two men he didn't recognize, neither in uniform, were engaged in an animated conversation. The gist of it seemed to be that Joseph Johnston was a great commander, second in the Confederacy only to Robert E. Lee himself. Bragg was tempted to break into the conversation and tell the two men that they had no idea what they were talking about, but decided against it. He wanted to avoid doing anything that might find its way into the Richmond papers.

It was time to leave. Finishing the last of his food and placing the plate on the tray carried by the nearest house slave, Bragg turned and began walking toward the door.

"Well, there goes the biggest buffoon of all!" a loud voice exclaimed.

Bragg stopped in his tracks and turned to face whoever had said such words. He was shocked by the sight of Richard Hawes, a frail-looking man in his late sixties, whom he had not seen in nearly two years. He was, as far as the Confederacy was concerned, the Governor of Kentucky. But he had been living in exile in Virginia ever since the Army of Tennessee had been driven out of Kentucky after the Battle of Perryville in the fall of 1862.

Bragg instantly recalled the farce that had accompanied the inauguration of Governor Hawes that October. Under Bragg's command, the Army of Tennessee had occupied Frankfort, the capital of Kentucky, and had taken over a vast swath of the state. Bragg had been determined to put a genuine state administration in place, so that taxation and conscription could be undertaken on behalf of the Confederacy. He had expected large numbers of Kentuckians to join his army as soon as it had entered the state, but up to that point he had received a surprisingly small number of recruits. Getting a solid Confederate administration up and running had been imperative.

He himself had introduced Governor Hawes inside the Kentucky State Capitol as a pro-Confederate crowd had wildly applauded. Outside, the booming of cannon fire was heard, causing the audience to cheer even more loudly, for they had assumed the artillery was part of the inaugural celebration. In fact, the guns had belonged to the Yankees, who had outmaneuvered Bragg's forces and were commencing their counter offensive. The newly-installed Confederate state government had been forced to rapidly withdraw from Frankfort, making both Governor Hawes and General Bragg look ridiculous.

"There's the man, ladies and gentlemen!" Hawes said, pointing. It was immediately obvious that he had had far too much to drink. "There's the man! There's the man who lost us Kentucky!"

All over the room, people stopped talking to watch the unfolding confrontation. The string quartet abruptly stopped playing and the room was silent except for the words of the exiled Kentucky governor.

"Hope you're proud of yourself, Bragg. You lost Kentucky when you didn't listen to your generals after Perryville. You lost Tennessee when you didn't listen to your generals after Murfreesboro. You lost your chance to destroy the Yankee army when you didn't listen to your generals after Chickamauga. I hope you're proud of yourself! I know I would be!" Hawes then downed the contents of his champagne flute in one gulp.

Colonel Chesnut walked up and took Hawes' elbow. "Governor, perhaps you'd like to try some of the lemon pound cake? It has a lovely custard sauce."

Hawes clumsily freed his arm from Chesnut and pointed accusingly at Bragg. "Sherman is at the gates of Atlanta and Grant is at the gates of Richmond, but if it hadn't been for this miserable incompetent we would have won the war two years ago!"

"You're drunk, Governor," Bragg said calmly.

"Of course I'm drunk!" Hawes said. "I'm damn drunk! I have nothing to do but drink! I was run out of my own state because you were unwilling to fight for it!"

Bragg remembered the criticism that had poured down upon him following his withdrawal from Kentucky. Despite the fact that the Battle of Perryville had been a tactical victory for the Army of Tennessee and with his army still roughly equal in strength to the opposing Yankees, Bragg had elected to retreat back to Tennessee. Inwardly, he burned with regret at having made the wrong decision, but he would sooner die than acknowledge his failure publicly.

"The fault did not lie with me," Bragg said, trying to sound calm but raising his voice for others to hear. "If General Polk had obeyed my orders to attack the enemy when the army was deployed near Bardstown-"

Hawes cut him off. "Oh, always someone else's fault, isn't it, Bragg?" he mocked. "Always someone else's fault!"

"You do not understand what you are talking about, Governor," Bragg said. "You lack an understanding of military matters."

"I know what I see with my own eyes! I know what I read in the papers! You led the Army of Tennessee to one disaster after another. Thank God that General Johnston was able to pick up the pieces after Missionary Ridge. That's all I have to say about it. He's ten times the commander you were, by God!"

Bragg turned on his heels and walked toward the front door without another word. He did his best to maintain a straight face even as anger swirled within him with the force of a hurricane. He ignored the slave who offered him the basket of French soaps and perfumes Trenholm had earlier told him about. He stormed through the door and out onto the street, determined to go home as quickly as possible. As he exited, he heard the violin music begin again and heard many of the party-goers start to laugh. He had no doubt that the laughter was at his expense.

*   *   *   *   *

July 4, Morning

General Thomas sat on his horse by the side of the road, watching as his divisions marched past. It was oppressively hot, but Thomas thought the men appeared to be in good spirits. All the regimental bands were playing patriotic tunes in observance of Independence Day, with the men happily singing along.

The entire Army of the Cumberland was on the move, its columns slowly grinding forward like enormous snakes along the roads and trails that ran between Kennesaw Mountain and the Chattahoochee River. Sherman's two subsidiary armies, the Army of the Tennessee and the Army of the Ohio, hovered on the flanks of Thomas's force, also pushing forward toward the river. Over one hundred thousand Union soldiers were moving southeast, trying to learn whether their rebel foes were dug in on the north side of the Chattahoochee or had scurried off to the south bank.

He heard the thunder of hooves approaching from behind and turned to see General Sherman, along with some staff officers and an escort of cavalry. As usual, Sherman had a cigar in his mouth. He slowed his horse to a walk and reined in alongside Thomas.

"Morning, George," Sherman said pleasantly.

"Cump," Thomas replied, using Sherman's nickname.

"Looks like Uncle Joe is heading to the south side of the Chattahoochee."

"Wouldn't count on that just yet. He held us up for two weeks on Kennesaw Mountain. Would have given him plenty of time to build another line of defense north of the river. Maybe more than one."

Sherman shook his head. "No, no, no. I've got the measure of the man by now. Been chasing him all over north Georgia for damn near two months. He and I were exchanging fire with each other outside Vicksburg last year, too. No, Johnston will be focused on getting his army over the river as quick as he can. He doesn't like fighting with his back to a river. Look at the way he scurried out of Cassville, just north of the Etowah River. That was the strongest defensive position I've ever seen in my life, but Uncle Joe abandoned it, just like that."

Thomas nodded, acknowledging Sherman's point. He had also been perplexed by Johnston's abandonment of the Cassville position, back in the early days of the campaign. But the wily Southern general rarely did what was expected.

They heard the sound of cannon fire from somewhere up ahead of them. Straining their ears, they listened for the telltale sound of musketry, which might have indicated that the advance elements of the army had encountered a new Confederate line. Try as they might, though, they didn't hear anything, and shortly afterward the sound of cannon fire ceased. Thomas sent one of his staff officers forward to investigate.

Sherman spoke quickly. "George, I'm willing to bet just about any amount of money that Uncle Joe is pulling to the south side of the river. I want you to push your men on forward as quick as you can, to try and catch them while they're crossing. If you move fast, we might be able to get ourselves a large batch of prisoners."

"I will push on quickly, Cump. But we shouldn't be reckless. If we advance too rapidly, our lead units could receive a bloody nose if, in fact, Johnston intends to fight on this side of the river."

"Yes, yes, yes, of course," Sherman said quickly. "Very well, very well. You, of course, know best what should be done. But I tell you, George, that Johnston is not going to fight us on this side of the river. I tell you that the whole damn Army of Tennessee is, at this very moment, while we sit here talking, crossing over to the south side in a great hurry."

The sound of cannon fire was suddenly heard again, much more rapidly this time. The sounds of the detonations had a different pitch, a sort of metallic ringing as opposed to the low bass booming sound caused by Union cannon fire. The seasoned ears of Sherman and Thomas recognized it as coming from Southern artillery, whose inferior powder caused it to make a distinctively different noise when fired.

"If the rebels are deploying artillery, it may indicate that they intend to fight on the north side of the river," Thomas suggested.

Sherman shook his head. "No, no, George. We will find no substantial body of rebels this side of the Chattahoochee. Not on this side of the Chattahoochee, we won't."

As if in response to Sherman's words, there was a sudden increase in the volume of fire. They heard the sound of sustained musketry and the level was such that it had to be coming from a large engagement. They listened quietly for a few minutes.

"A rear guard action, perhaps?" Sherman asked.

"Or our men coming up on a new enemy position."

"Let's go forward and see," Sherman said, kicking his horse into a trot. Thomas followed, and the cloud of staff officers and cavalry escorts trailed behind them like a swarm of bees.

As they moved down the road toward the front line, the typical refuse of battle was moving in the other direction. Wounded men who still possessed the ability to walk were heading back in search of the nearest field hospitals, clutching bloodstained bandages to their heads or arms. The more seriously wounded were being carried back on stretchers by medical orderlies. To Thomas's irritation, many of the men passing them seemed unhurt. Their explanations that they had become separated from their unit or been sent back to fetch ammunition seemed less than convincing.

Amidst the confused and often hurt white men scurrying to the rear, an out-of-place black man emerged. He glanced about in confusion and it was immediately clear that he had no idea where he was or what was happening.

"You there!" Sherman said, pointing. "What brings you to this area?" There were no black regiments in Sherman's army and very few black laborers, so it seemed likely that the negro had come from the local area or from the Confederate lines.

The black man looked up. "I'd rather be just about anywhere else, sure enough. Southern cavalry came through the neighborhood of my master's plantation two weeks ago and ordered all us negroes into the wagon. Spent the last week on the banks of this here river, shoveling dirt and moving logs. Hard enough work without bullets flying all over the place."

Sherman looked at Thomas. "What the hell did he say?"

Thomas smiled, realizing that Sherman had not understood a word the slave had spoken because he couldn't decipher the man's accent. Thomas, a Virginian and longtime slave owner himself, had understood him perfectly and quickly translated for Sherman.

"For what purpose were you doing this construction work?" Sherman asked.

"They didn't tell us, sir. Building lots of little forts, seems like." Again, Thomas relied to Sherman what the man had said.

"On the north or south side of the river?" Sherman asked.

The man's eyes narrowed in confusion and he did not immediately answer.

"On this side of the river or the other side, boy?" Thomas demanded.

"This side, sure enough."

"Can you describe them, boy?" Sherman asked. "What kind of forts?"

"Dozens of them. Each big enough for a hundred men, I reckon. Stretched out all along the bank of the river, like a big half moon."

"It appears that Johnston is, indeed, making his stand on the north bank, General Sherman," Thomas said.

"General Sherman?" the slave asked, his eyes sparkling. "Being you General Sherman?"

"I am, indeed."

A wide and delighted smile crossed the black man's face. "Been hearing lots about you down at the plantation, sir. Mighty glad to meet you, sir, I am. Though I doubt if my old master would like it." He laughed at his own joke.

"You head on up the road that way," Sherman said, pointing north. "You're a free man now. Old Abe's Emancipation Proclamation says so. Maybe try to find a job as a cook for one of my regiments or something."

"Will do it, General Sherman. Will do it and be glad! My old master is with some Georgia regiment or other. If you find him, do me the favor of shooting him in the belly."

Sherman laughed. "I will do so."

With a spring in his step, the liberated slave walked away to the north, while the Union party kicked their horses and continued south.

"You might have suggested he head north to enlist in one of the new black infantry regiments," Thomas suggested.

Sherman frowned. "I don't much like the idea of enlisting blacks in the army. I doubt they will make good soldiers, nor do I think our regular troops like serving alongside them."

Thomas already knew Sherman's opinion on the subject, but out of boredom he decided to press the point. "President Lincoln and General Grant are enthusiastic. Our black troops fought well at Fort Wagner, by all accounts. Other places, too."

Sherman grunted.

Thomas pressed. "A black man can stop a bullet just as good as a white man."

"Yes, and a sandbag stops a bullet better than either. But can a black man improvise roads, do skirmishing and picket duty, or organize flank movements like a white man? I say no."

Thomas shrugged. "Blacks defeated Napoleon's finest soldiers during the insurrection in Haiti back in the day, did they not? And their basic human desire to be free certainly gives them a motivation to fight that our white soldiers do not possess."

For just a moment, Thomas remembered being a frightened teenager in Virginia more than thirty years before, frantically snapping at the reins of the carriage carrying his family away from their farm as it was being ransacked by Nat Turner and his band of rebellious slaves. More than fifty whites had been killed, including women and children, and Thomas himself had barely escaped with his life. His fellow Southerners might entertain ideas about contented slaves dutifully wishing to obey their masters, but Thomas knew that this was a delusion. He felt the familiar tug on his soul, feeling in his heart that the blacks of the South should be free but knowing that holding that belief had wrenched him away from his family and everything he had once held dear.

Sherman waved his hand dismissively. From long experience, Thomas knew that the conversation was over. The sound of artillery and musket fire grew louder as they continued ever farther south. At last they came upon the forward headquarters of General Oliver Howard, who was commanding the lead corps pressing against the Confederates. The headquarters was situated next to what appeared to be an abandoned tavern.

"Howard!" Sherman called out upon seeing him. "What's the situation?" Sherman and Thomas quickly dismounted and jogged up to the table Howard had set up and on which he had placed his maps.

"The enemy are firmly entrenched ahead of us. We cannot continue to push forward unless we wish to mount a major attack."

"Oh, nonsense, Howard! The enemy is laughing at you! I tell you now that there is no sizable enemy force on this side of the Chattahoochee. You ought to push right down the road."

No sooner were the words out of Sherman's mouth than a Confederate artillery shell screamed through the air and slammed into the tavern's chimney, which instantly disintegrated. Sherman, Thomas, and Howard dove for cover as stray bricks and a large cloud of dark dust swept over them.

Thomas, slightly dazed, pulled himself up from the ground. His ears rang. Looking down, he saw quickly that he was unhurt and said a silent prayer of thanks. He had not received so much as a scratch since the war had begun, but he felt that everyone's luck was bound to run out sooner or later.

Sherman and Howard were also unharmed. Howard helped the supreme commander to his feet.

"Yes, well," Sherman said as he dusted himself off. "Perhaps you're right, Howard. It appears our enemies are there after all."

*   *   *   *   *

July 4, Afternoon

Cleburne reined in and dismounted next to the large tent that contained the headquarters of Hardee's corps. A sergeant took his horse's reins and he strolled into the tent, glancing around for his commander. He found Hardee hunched over a table, marking off the locations of known Federal units on a map.

"You wanted to see me, General?" he asked.

Hardee glanced up. "Yes, Pat. Thanks for coming. Just give me a minute here. Trying to trace out what the Yankees are doing."

"I assume you got my recent dispatch. They're only mounting minor probing attacks on my front, trying to establish the strength of our position."

"It's the same story all along the line. They won't attack such a strong position head on. Not after the lesson they learned at Kennesaw Mountain, anyway. So we're secure on the north bank of the river for the time being. Now, why don't we take a walk outside?"

The two men strolled out of the tent and wandered to a point where they could not be overheard by the men in the tent. He noticed that Hardee seemed slightly apprehensive and quickly guessed the reason why.

Hardee let out a sharp breath. "I have spoken twice with General Johnston about which division commander should be promoted to permanent command of Polk's corps. Tomorrow morning he will announce that the command has been given to General Alexander Stewart."

Cleburne took a deep breath. "Well, General Stewart is a fine officer."

"Rest assured, my friend, that I strongly recommended you for the position. But Johnston thought it best to promote Stewart."

Cleburne's voice was not angry, but pained. "Does it not matter that I outrank Stewart? My commission as major general predates his by six months, if I recall correctly."

"You are right, of course. I reminded Johnston of this fact. I can only say that you have my sympathy. I think the decisive factor is that Stewart is a West Point graduate and you are not. I acknowledge that this is unfair. I also want to stress, though it should go without saying, that General Johnston has nothing but the highest respect for your command abilities."

Cleburne let out a deep sigh. "I shall say nothing. I shall make no protest. I hope never to be counted among the hotheads who populate this army."

Hardee laughed. "That's good, by God. We have quite a sufficiency of them as it is."

"But William, may I speak to you simply as a friend for a moment?"

"You were the best man at my wedding, for pity's sake. Of course you may speak to me as a friend."

Cleburne pursed his lips. "I find this a bitter pill to swallow. My combat record should speak for itself. Shiloh, Perryville, Murfreesboro, Chickamauga. My division held its part of the line at Missionary Ridge when the rest of the army fell apart. We covered the retreat by holding off the whole Yankee army at Ringgold Gap. Do not mistake me for bragging, but surely the achievements of my division demonstrate my fitness for corps command."

"Truth, indeed. No division commander in this army can come close to matching your achievements. You have added many laurels during the present campaign, too."

"Then why do I remain a mere division commander when other men are appointed over my head?"

"I can only say honestly that I do not know."

He paused a moment before continuing. "Does the fact that I am an Irishman have anything to do with it?"

Hardee didn't respond for several seconds, mulling it over. "I cannot say for certain, Pat. But I would be lying if I said I was sure it wasn't so. Your foreign origin has never been an issue with me, or any other officer to whom I have spoken about it. But how men in Richmond feel about it, I cannot say."

Cleburne's only response was a grunt.

Hardee went on. "If I may now be the one to speak frankly, my friend, I think the memorandum you wrote in January may be partly responsible for the fact that you have not yet been given corps command."

Cleburne's eyebrows went up. "You think so?"

"Well, when an outstanding division commander of enormous reputation calls for the emancipation of slavery and the enlistment of freed Negroes into the army, it certainly raises a great many questions in Richmond. Disturbing questions, if I may say so."

Cleburne pursed his lips and shook his head. "Damn that bastard Walker," he said under his breath.

"I know," Hardee said. "I was not aware that he sent a copy of your memorandum to President Davis, much less the scathing commentary he saw fit to attach to it."

"And I thought he was going to challenge me to a duel."

Hardee laughed softly. "I am glad he did not. I should not have liked having two of my division commanders shooting at one another rather than the Yankees."

Cleburne ignored the joke. "I was frankly glad he sent the memorandum to Richmond. Best way to get it in the hands of President Davis, after all. I felt it was my duty to state the facts as I see them clearly, irrespective of any result to myself."

"I can understand. Remember that I voiced support for your proposal at that meeting. But the authorities in Richmond considered it extremely dangerous, and maybe this is why you have remained a division commander. It may be that it was only your outstanding combat record that kept you from being transferred to some backwater in the Trans-Mississippi."

Cleburne shook his head again. "Well, I won't take it back. I stand by every word. I meant it then and I still mean it now. I shall keep my mouth shut about it, just as General Johnston ordered me to do, but a man cannot change his opinions when they are honestly held."

Hardee slapped him lightly on the shoulder. "Perhaps that's why you aren't yet a corps commander, Pat. You just have too much damn integrity!"

Despite himself, Cleburne smiled. A few moments later, he was accepting Hardee's offer of some freshly cooked pork and some tobacco for his pipe.

Chapter Three

July 4, Afternoon

The man on the stage came at last to the end of his speech, summoning up the most booming voice he could muster.

"And so, my friends, let me conclude by telling you that, on this Independence Day, we want *the Constitution as it is and the Union as it was!*"

The Great Hall of Cooper Union, in the very heart of New York City, erupted in cheers and applause. General George McClellan couldn't help but smile. He usually tried to maintain a serious expression, but the reaction of the crowd was more than enough to pierce through his veneer and touch his vanity.

Some in the crowd were chanting. "Little Mac! Little Mac!" His nickname might have been a play on his height, just under five feet and four inches, but it had been given to him by his devoted soldiers entirely out of affection.

He waved farewell and moved to leave the stage, just as a brass band began bellowing forth patriotic tunes. As he walked down the steps off of the platform, several dozen people swarmed up to shake his hand. He didn't know any of them, but was beginning to learn the politician's trade of asking a few searching questions that would enable a brief conversation to take place. The next day, hopefully, they would all be telling their friends that George McClellan was a fine man who would make an excellent president.

The crowd in the hall gradually quieted down and began filtering outside. After about ten endless minutes, McClellan was finally able to extract himself from the crush of well-wishers and walk over to the man to whom he actually wanted to speak. Throughout the speech and the subsequent mayhem, Manton Marble, editor of the viciously anti-Lincoln, pro-Democrat newspaper *New York World*, had been patiently waiting.

"Well, how do you think it went?" McClellan asked.

"Very well, General," said Marble. "Very well, indeed. Your last line was one for the history books."

"It does have a certain ring to it, does it not?"

"It does. Rest assured that the entire text of your speech will be reprinted in tomorrow's paper, along with a very complimentary editorial."

"I am glad to hear it."

A few minutes later, the two men were in a carriage, rolling through the streets of New York City. The clip-clopping of the horse's hooves was largely drowned out by the noise of the people on the sidewalks, of which McClellan took little notice. Marble's eyes occasionally glanced quickly out his window, drinking in as much visual information as he could even as he focused on his conversation with McClellan.

"Well, I believe your speech today will remove any doubt about your intention to seek the Presidency," Marble said.

"That was the idea. You, and every other citizen of the United States, may now consider me a candidate for the highest office in the land. I shall not deign to make any sort of official announcement of the fact, but I shall instead let the facts speak for themselves."

"I noted in particular your repeated statements asserting the supremacy of the Constitution. These statements will, of course, be seen as attacks on the Lincoln administration, because of the high visibility that has been given to the arrest of anti-war advocates and the closing down of newspapers."

"Good," McClellan said emphatically. "That is precisely how I intend them. But I wish to be as subtle as possible when it comes to Mr. Lincoln specifically. Obviously, I would consider it beneath my dignity to openly criticize Lincoln by name. That is a task I shall leave to you and others."

"And a task I fully intend to accomplish. With great pleasure, if I may say so."

McClellan smiled, looking out the window as the streets of New York City flowed past him. "That man will pay dearly for his treatment of me, rest assured."

Marble nodded. "Lincoln's removal of you from command of the Army of the Potomac was entirely unwarranted, particularly as it came on the heels of your victory at the Battle of Antietam. A few months from now, he will be looking back on it as the greatest political miscalculation he ever made."

"History will so record it," McClellan answered.

With great effort, Marble was able to hide his amusement at this response. McClellan had a habit of making such pompous statements, all of which struck Marble as faintly ridiculous. Clearly, the frequent comparisons of McClellan to Napoleon earlier in the war had gone to the man's head. As far as Marble was concerned, the two men were similar only in terms of their short statures and massive egos.

"I believe the strategy we have agreed upon will work to perfection," the newspaper man said. "The military campaigns in both Virginia and Georgia have bogged down, which is exactly what you told me would happen months ago. Casualties are higher than they have ever been and it is clear to everyone that the Lincoln administration is completely mismanaging the war. Inflation is wrecking the economy and opposition to the draft is increasing daily. All we have to do is sit back and maintain our criticisms in the press. The Republicans will destroy themselves."

"I have heard it said that one should never interfere with one's enemies when they are making a mistake. I am quite confident about our chances in November."

"I have no doubt that we will easily carry New York, New Jersey and Pennsylvania, which by themselves garner us sixty-six electoral votes. That's more than half of what we need to win the election. Throw in Indiana, Ohio, Kentucky and a few other states, and we will achieve a decisive electoral victory."

"I am glad you are so confident," McClellan said.

Marble smiled. "Oh, I should have mentioned it earlier. Vallandigham is back."

McClellan's eyebrows shot up. "Is he?"

"He crossed the border from Canada a few days ago, according to a wire I received from Detroit."

"And Lincoln hasn't had him arrested again?"

"Apparently not. I doubt he will, considering the public outcry the first time. Lincoln might be a backwards Illinois guttersnipe, but he does have sound political instincts. He will avoid making Vallandigham into a martyr if at all possible."

"I suppose having that Copperhead whipping people up around the country could suit our purposes."

"Agreed. But if I may venture an opinion, General McClellan, you should personally keep your distance from the man. Direct association between the two of you would leave you open to charges that you are unpatriotic and don't support the war effort."

McClellan nodded. "I am fully aware of that. I agree that he and I should not meet. You, however, should do so if you think it worth your while."

"We'll see."

"Vallandigham is an agitator. Let him agitate, I say. The more embarrassment he causes Lincoln, the better it will be for me."

"Very well," Marble said. "Let the wheels begin to turn, then."

*   *   *   *   *

July 5, Morning

President Davis held Hood's most recent letter in one hand and a telegram just received from Johnston in the other. He read through both with growing alarm, periodically glancing up at the military map on the wall.

Johnston's telegram informed Davis that the Army of Tennessee had evacuated the Kennesaw line and withdrawn into a defensive position on the north bank of the Chattahoochee, centered near the Western and Atlantic railroad bridge. Johnston expressed confidence that this line would be held for some time. Hood's letter, however, expressed his opinion that Johnston would not hold this line for very long and would likely withdraw to the south bank of the river without making much of an effort to hold the north bank. Clearly, one of them was not to be believed.

"Mr. Harrison!" Davis bellowed.

An instant later, the dapper young Creole opened the door. "Yes, Mr. President?"

"Would you inform General Bragg that I wish to see him at once."

"Right away, sir." The door quickly closed.

Davis continued to read through Johnston's telegram, which ended with the now familiar demand that Forrest and his cavalry be sent to attack Sherman's supply lines. Davis's face settled into a frustrated scowl.

Twenty minutes passed, which Davis filled with routine administrative work, including the commutations of four death sentences for soldiers who had been arrested for deserting. Davis could not remember the last time he had allowed a scheduled execution to go forward, for he saw no point in shooting his own soldiers.

Finally, General Bragg arrived and was shown into the office by Harrison.

"I assume you want to discuss the news from Georgia, Mr. President?"

"Indeed. I have just read through Johnston's latest telegram. Do you think he will attempt to fight a major battle north of the Chattahoochee River?"

"It's impossible to say with any certainty, sir."

"And if you had to guess?"

Bragg thought for just a moment, then shook his head. "If I had to guess, Mr. President, I would have to say no. I do not think he will fight on the north bank. I think he will do what he has always done. He will hold a strong defensive position until Sherman moves to outflank him, then he will retreat."

"But look at the map, General Bragg. There is no more room in which to retreat! The Chattahoochee River is the last major natural barrier between Sherman and Atlanta. Once Sherman is across the river, he will be at the gates of Atlanta itself!"

"You are correct, Mr. President. If I recall, the telegram ends with another request for a cavalry raid on Sherman's supply lines."

"Yes," Davis said resignedly. "One gets tired of hearing about that. I have turned down his request for Forrest's assistance more times than I can count, yet he continues to pester me about it, over and over again. When will the man learn?"

"And he again repeats that he cannot dispatch the cavalry of his own army, because he needs it to protect his flanks?"

"Yes," Davis said, anticipating that Bragg would soon say something worth hearing.

Bragg smiled. "It may be of interest to you that I recently received a letter from Johnston's cavalry commander, General Wheeler. According to Wheeler, he has repeatedly asked Johnston for permission to take five thousand troops on a raid against Sherman's supply lines, but has been repeatedly denied."

Davis sat back and folded his arms, looking like a schoolmaster hearing of a disobedient student.

Bragg went on. "According to Wheeler, Sherman's cavalry is disorganized and ineffectual. In every skirmish between our cavalry and the enemy's, our men inevitably emerge the victors. Wheeler is of the opinion that taking five thousand cavalry on a raid against Sherman's supply lines would present no difficulty, because the enemy cavalry is not a threat."

"So, Johnston tells us that he lacks sufficient cavalry of his own to undertake a raid on Sherman's supply line, but his very own cavalry commander says the exact opposite. Whom are we to believe?"

"I commanded General Wheeler for some time. Believe me when I tell you that he is a man in which you can have full confidence."

Davis stared at the map for a long time. "But if Johnston genuinely believes that attacking Sherman's supply lines is the only way to achieve victory, and if his own cavalry commander is telling him that he has the means to do it, why doesn't he do it himself?"

"Do you want my honest opinion?" Bragg asked.

Davis nodded and waved for Bragg to go on, impatient at such a needless delay.

"Mr. President, with all due respect to General Johnston's obvious talents, he is a man of immense vanity. I believe that he is unwilling to risk a decisive battle with Sherman because he fears that were he to suffer a defeat it would destroy the reputation as a great general that he has gained among the people, deservedly or otherwise.

In short, he cares more about protecting his popular image than he does about winning the war."

Davis pursed his lips tightly and shook his head. "I must admit that I have had this very thought many times. But could it really be true? Surely losing Atlanta without a fight would do far more to destroy his reputation than a lost battle. Lee lost at Gettysburg, yet the people still revere him."

Bragg raised a finger. "Ah, but if he abandons Atlanta he will be able to say that he could have held the city if only you had been willing to order Forrest into Tennessee."

Davis's face turned red with fury. It was a minute before he spoke again. "So, that's it. Rather than risk a battle for the sake of his country, he cowardly refuses to budge from his defensive positions. He consigns the army to a passive strategy that will mean the fall of Atlanta, which he will then blame on me. And all for the sake of his precious military reputation!"

Bragg waited for Davis to calm down, which he did after a minute or so, though he was still fuming. "I agree with you fully, Mr. President," Bragg said carefully. "With our forces successfully resisting the Yankees on all other fronts, the loss of Atlanta would be a disaster. And to lose it simply because of one man's ego would be more than a disaster. It would be a disgrace."

Davis let out a deep breath and spoke very slowly and carefully. "Then perhaps it is time for us to consider relieving Johnston of command, before it is too late." The thought had long been in his mind, but Davis felt relief at finally being able to say it out loud.

Bragg responded soberly but quickly. "Replacing an army commander in the middle of a major campaign is a very serious matter, Mr. President. Even under the best circumstances, confusion and delay will result for at least a brief time during any transition. With Sherman at the gates of the city, such a move could prove fatal."

"Keeping Johnston at the head of the army could prove fatal as well!"

"Of course, Mr. President. If you do decide to remove Johnston, to whom shall the command go?"

Davis frowned and shook his head. "That is a difficult question. General Lee is needed here, at the head of the Army of Northern Virginia. General Beauregard is of sufficient rank, but has never proven adequate as an army commander. General Longstreet has not yet recovered from the wounds he received at the Battle of the Wilderness."

"What of the corps commanders of the Army of Tennessee itself?"

"General Polk was killed a few weeks ago," Davis said, his voice betraying no hint of the grief he felt at the death of Leonidas

Polk, who had long been one of his closest personal friends. "Hardee and Hood are the two remaining choices."

"Well, what of them?"

Davis shrugged. "I offered command of the Army of Tennessee to Hardee in December, before approaching Johnston. He declined it, despite my earnest entreaties. My sense was that he did not wish to have such a heavy burden placed on his shoulders."

"From my acquaintance with the man, I am not surprised. Hardee is a highly overrated general, if you'll excuse me for saying so. General Hood, however, might be worthy of consideration."

"I have been getting regular letters from Hood since he arrived in Georgia, as you know. He seems to be of the same mind as you and me, believing that we can only win in Georgia by taking the offensive against Sherman. He has objected strongly to Johnston's habit of merely reacting to the maneuvers of the enemy."

"He certainly has a reputation for favoring the attack," Bragg said. "In his service with Lee's army as a brigade and division commander, he achieved many well-known successes through offensive action. When he served under my command at the Battle of Chickamauga, he led the attack that shattered the enemy line. Certainly, his courage and boldness are not to be doubted."

"Indeed not, but do courage and boldness a good general make?" Davis asked. "Machiavelli tells us that a great captain must be both lion and fox. A good general must have boldness, but also good sense and high intelligence. Would you call Hood a sensible and intelligent man?"

"From my rather short acquaintance with him, I cannot honestly tell, Mr. President."

"Perhaps we will gain some insight when Senator Hill arrives and reports on his meeting with General Johnston. We can expect him any day now, according to his last telegram."

"I hope so, Mr. President. Because if Sherman gets across the Chattahoochee, the fall of Atlanta could be only days away. The replacement of Johnston might be the only measure by which you can save the city."

*   *   *   *   *

July 6, Morning

The men of the 7th Texas kept their heads down, as more Union artillery shells hit the walls of their enclosed redoubt, bouncing off like marbles being thrown at a brick wall. A more serious threat was the constant peppering of musket fire from small squads of Yankee skirmishers, but even that posed little danger so long as the men didn't do anything stupid.

Private Balch clambered up onto the fire-step and squeezed off a round from his Enfield before ducking down again, just as a series of shots splattered around the space he had just occupied.

"Cut that out, Balch!" Sergeant McFadden spat. "You're not going to hit anything!"

"I think I got one!"

"You couldn't hit an elephant in the ass if it were standing ten feet away! You're wasting ammunition and putting yourself in danger. Now get down and stay down or I'll shoot you myself!"

Balch sullenly sat back down on the fire-step. Three more enemy artillery shells slammed into the redoubt in quick succession, but they had no noticeable impact aside from the noise they generated.

Little impressed McFadden these days, but he had to admit that the redoubt the regiment occupied was something of a marvel. They had marched into it the day before, and they had also seen that it was only one of several dozen laid out in a large semi-circle centered on the point where the Western and Atlantic Railroad crossed the Chattahoochee River. It was the strongest fortified position the men of the Army of Tennessee had ever seen.

The Yankees were refusing to attack, which didn't surprise McFadden. Having learned his lesson at Kennesaw Mountain, Sherman certainly would not be such a fool as to throw his men against such a strong position. But McFadden was still disappointed, as he would certainly have enjoyed the opportunity to send more Yankees to hell.

McFadden might have been a lowly infantryman, but thanks to the reading his father had forced him to undertake as a child, he felt he knew much more than most about military strategy. Though he could do nothing himself to influence events beyond the sight of his Enfield, he couldn't help but speculate as to what was going on. The Yankees were feeling out the Confederate position, hemming them in but not attacking. If McFadden had to guess, this meant that Sherman would certainly attempt another flanking maneuver in the very near future.

Over the course of a few hours, the enemy skirmishers vanished back into the woods north of their position. At the same time, the federal artillery fire gradually diminished and eventually stopped altogether. For a few minutes, the Texans continued to remain close to the ground, waiting to see whether the cessation of enemy fire was real or just a temporary lull. After about ten minutes, they concluded that the firing had stopped for the time being and began to relax.

Some of the men got campfires going, in order to make coffee and cook some bacon. A few precious hogs had been slaughtered the day before and the men were anxious for some meat. Other men got out their sewing kits and tried to stitch up their uniforms and what remained of their shoes. Two privates began playing chess, with a cluster of a dozen others gathered around them offering advice and placing bets on who would emerge the victor.

Someone from brigade headquarters arrived with mail, and most of the men eagerly crowded around him as he passed around letters. Correspondence from home were few and far between for the men of Granbury's Texas Brigade. The fall of Vicksburg the previous year had secured Union control over the Mississippi River, preventing easy communication from the Trans-Mississippi to the Confederacy on the eastern side of the river. The men and women who braved Yankee gunboats to smuggle packets of letters across the swamps of Louisiana and Mississippi were greatly loved by the Trans-Mississippi men who served in Johnston's army, and McFadden assumed that the same was true of those who fought in the ranks of Lee's army.

Those men who were lucky enough to receive a letter howled with glee, as though they had discovered buried treasure, and hurried off to a quiet place where they could read the precious letter in peace. Those who did not receive a letter, a decided majority of the hundred or so men of the 7th Texas, turned away in disappointment, with a few doing their best to hide tears. McFadden, of course, had known from the moment mail call had been announced that he would not be receiving a letter.

Two hours after the Yankee fire had ended, Collett called McFadden.

"Sergeant McFadden!"

"Sir!" McFadden stood to attention

"Since the fighting seems to have stopped, I'd like to have the men clean up. We'll go one company at a time down to the river. The men will wash their clothes and take a bath. You will go first."

"Certainly, sir. Company F! Prepare to move out!"

The men of McFadden's company gathered the necessary equipment for washer duty and collected them into the regiment's last remaining twenty-five gallon oak bucket. Then, with pairs of men taking turns carrying the rope on either side of the bucket, the twenty-two survivors of Company F began walking south toward the river.

They headed south on a dusty road some pioneering unit had scratched out of the ground. McFadden led the way, not only because he was in charge of the company but because it would minimize the efforts by his comrades to engage him in conversation. The Texans behind him chatted amiably with one another, and occasionally called out to friends they recognized from other units as they passed by.

"What flag is that?" Pearson asked as they walked past the encampment of yet another regiment.

"Are you blind?" McFadden called back. "65th Georgia. Walker's Division."

The Texans groaned. The loathing that existed between General Walker and their beloved General Cleburne was an open secret throughout the army. It didn't much matter, as Texas troops tended to hold Georgia troops in contempt anyway.

"Hey, Georgia boys!" Private Montgomery called out.

"What do you want?" a Georgia soldier shouted back.

"If you end on up on either of our flanks in the next fight, you'd better hold your damn line! Otherwise, we will shoot you ourselves and no mistake!"

"Go to hell, Texas!"

The men laughed and continued marching. McFadden knew that Montgomery had been joking, but he himself would happily shoot down a fellow Confederate who ran away. Such cowardly actions put others in danger and increased the likelihood of defeat. If a few examples were made, it would be to the benefit of everyone.

The Lone Star Rifles kept moving south, passing by numerous other regiments as well as the general detritus that formed in the rear area of an army. There were broken down wagons being repaired, makeshift bakeries turning out loaves of bread, improvised workshops attempting to repair broken firearms, and other such random sites. Occasionally, clusters of officers could be seen talking earnestly with one another. As always, there was the large number of men wandering about in confusion, no doubt searching for excuses to avoid returning to their units on the front lines.

Finally, they reached the bank of the Chattahoochee River. They came upon it suddenly, as the ground on both banks was thickly wooded. It struck McFadden as a lovely sight, quite wide but not very deep. Numerous rocks poked out from the water at various points of the stream.

A pontoon bridge crossed the river directly from the point the road met the water, and two other pontoon bridges were visible several hundred yards downstream. McFadden directed his men over to a patch of ground just off to the left of the bridge, and there they set up their cleaning station.

McFadden directed Private Pearson to get a fire going, for as irritating as he found Pearson, he had to admit that the man was the best in the company when it came to starting a fire. As water was heated over the fire in one of the few cast iron pots the regiment had left, the men stripped naked and soaked their clothes thoroughly in the river, happily splashing about and dunking one another while doing so. As time passed and the water began to boil, the clothes were dumped into the pot and left for a time. Lice and other pests which inhabited their uniforms were boiled away. After they had boiled the clothes, the men began the laborious process of scouring them on rough scrub boards.

They sang songs while they cleaned. They chatted and felt relieved to be away from the pressures of the front line, even if it was only for a short amount of time. When they put their clothes back on, they felt the blessed sensation of clean cloth on their skin for the first time in weeks.

As he helped boil another bunch of white shirts, McFadden heard a sudden excited but hushed conversation among of his men. He looked to see what the matter was and found that several of his men were intently staring at a fashionable two-wheeled buggy passing on the road and onto the bridge. Immediately he saw what had caught their attention. Sitting next to the older gentleman holding the reins was a woman.

During the months of winter encampments, women had constantly been with the army, whether the officer's wives in elegant dresses, old washerwomen, or syphilitic prostitutes whom wise men avoided. But when the campaign for Atlanta had commenced two months before, General Johnston had ordered all females sent away for their own safety. Seeing any woman at all had become an exceedingly rare and pleasant occurrence.

This particular woman was far from ordinary. She had raven black hair and a soft, milky-white complexion. McFadden found her exquisitely beautiful. He quickly checked himself, for most of the women he had known had been either the assorted females of the winter camps or the rough women of the Texas frontier. Surely he was not qualified to make any judgment on feminine beauty. But looking at her face, he was suddenly reminded of the poems by Dante about the lady Beatrice.

McFadden suddenly realized that many of his men were still naked. Horrified, he spun around.

"Cover yourselves, men! Quickly!"

"Why?" Pearson asked with a grin. He raised his voice loud enough for the woman to hear. "I want the lady to see these fine goods! I'll give them to her for free if she wants! Want this, lassy?"

Upon hearing these words, the woman turned and looked at Pearson, horror on her face. The man seated next to the woman shouted out.

"Damn you, sir!" he said. "You're speaking to my daughter!" McFadden noticed that the man had a wooden leg, which likely meant he was a veteran.

"I'll speak to anyone I want, old man!" Pearson rejoined laughingly. "She's a fine morsel, your daughter!"

McFadden turned and punched Pearson in the face as hard as he could. Letting out a pathetic yelp, Pearson was sent rolling over like a log and splattered down onto the ground in a large puddle of mud.

The men laughed, happy to see Pearson get the treatment most of them felt he had deserved for far too long. The father of the girl said nothing, whipping the horse into a slightly greater trot.

Turning back toward the buggy, McFadden had a moment of eye contact with the girl. At this distance, he couldn't tell whether her eyes were blue or green, but they seemed to be some combination of the two and more beautiful than either. She smiled at him and he felt some unfamiliar emotion tug at him.

He turned away, not wanting any more distractions. The buggy soon began to creak over the pontoon bridge, taking the woman away. He was certain he would never see her again and that the whole episode would simply be remembered for the pummeling of Private Pearson. He turned his attention back toward finishing the clothes washing job. The sooner they finished, the sooner they could return to the redoubt. Besides, he was hungry.

McFadden's determination to complete his immediate work lasted less than a minute. From behind him on the river, he suddenly heard the sound of sharply cracking wood, followed by the sound of a woman screaming. Turning, he saw that one of the wheels on the buggy had disintegrated, perhaps fifty yards down the bridge. To his horror, the entire wagon dipped over the right side of the bridge and plunged into the water, throwing both the woman and her father into the river and dragging the horse in as well.

Without thinking, McFadden tore off the white shirt he had just put back on, dashed to the edge of the river and plunged in. He didn't consider himself a good swimmer, but he doubted if any of the men in his company even knew how to swim at all. When would they have ever learned? Frantically, he swam toward the collapsed buggy, which was rapidly sinking. The confused horse jerked about in terror as it was pulled beneath the water.

"Help us!" the man's voice screamed.

McFadden swam for all he was worth. Though it was difficult to see as his arms pulled him through the now churning water, he headed toward the two flailing shapes he thought must be the man and the woman. The fall of the wagon had tossed them a few yards away from the bridge, but by the way they were struggling it instantly became clear to McFadden that neither of them knew how to swim. Fleetingly, the thought dashed through his mind that it would be a shame for them to drown with the bridge so very near to them.

"Help!" the voice of the woman cried out.

"Help my daughter!" the father shouted.

"I'm trying!" McFadden shouted back as he came within reach of the woman. As he approached her, she frantically grabbed his arm, causing him to momentarily panic as he lost the ability to control his swimming. The urgent need to save the woman's life instantly superseded any sense of propriety, so he jerked his arm free from her grip and then wrapped it around her waist.

A dozen or so members of the Lone Star Rifles were running toward the spot on the bridge where the wagon had overturned.

"Over here, Sarge! Swim this way!"

He started kicking toward the sound of the shouting and slowly he and the woman began inching closer to the bridge. She quickly calmed down and stopped struggling, enabling him to swim more easily.

After what seemed like several minutes but was actually only thirty seconds or so, McFadden was able to bring the woman within reach of his comrades waiting on the bridge. They lifted her up out of the water.

"Please help my father!"

McFadden kicked away from the bridge back toward the struggling man. He had to swim around the wreckage of the buggy, making it a considerably greater distance than he had thought. The man was rapidly losing strength, but this actually helped McFadden as it meant that he could approach him without fear of being accidently struck by the man's wild flailings. Even as he felt his own strength diminish, McFadden was able to clasp one of the man's arms and began pulling him toward the bridge. A few moments later, the soldiers pulled him up onto the pontoons as well.

McFadden felt great relief as he was helped up onto the planks of the pontoon bridge by Private Montgomery and Private Harrison. When he stood up, he saw that all of his men were looking intently at the woman. She was drenched, causing her white cotton dress to cling tightly to her body. Ever the gentleman, Harrison threw his own uniform coat over her to protect her modesty. The father was coughing, having swallowed a fair amount of the river water, but staggered to his feet as McFadden was doing the same.

"God bless you, son!" the man said between coughs. "God bless all of you!"

"Are you all right?" McFadden asked.

"Yes, I think so. Dear Lord, we might have drowned!" He turned to his daughter. "Are you all right, Annie?"

"Yes, father. I am fine." She clutched the uniform coat more tightly around herself, using it as a shield against the gazes of the men.

"We should get off the bridge," McFadden said, seeing a battery of artillery coming up from the south bank. It wouldn't do for them to cause a traffic jam.

"What is your name, son?" the man asked as they walked.

"Sergeant James McFadden. 7th Texas Infantry."

"I'm Robert Turnbow. This is my daughter Annie." He took a deep breath, still recovering. "It seems that we are both very much in your debt, Sergeant."

"Not at all, sir."

"Thank you for coming to our assistance. Without your help we would surely have died."

"It was nothing." McFadden did not believe this. Having witnessed their struggling in the water before he had reached them, he was convinced that both of them would surely have drowned. The girl obviously had no idea how to swim, and Mr. Turnbow had been too encumbered by his peg leg to save himself. Without intending to, McFadden caught Annie's eyes. She quickly glanced away.

As they walked back over to the north bank of the river, Mr. Turnbow looked out at what was left of their buggy. The horse had ceased to struggle. "Shame," Turnbow said. "Gypsy was a good horse. Good horses are hard to come by these days, since so many have been taken into the army."

"I apologize," McFadden said without thinking. He immediately thought it had been a stupid thing to say. It wasn't his fault that the horse had drowned.

Turnbow looked at him. "Did you say 7th Texas?"

"Yes, sir. Granbury's brigade, Cleburne's division."

Turnbow nodded quickly. "I served in the 18th Georgia under General Lee. We fought alongside Texas regiments in Hood's brigade. Good soldiers, you Texas boys."

"Thank you, sir. Where were you wounded, if you don't mind my asking?"

"Seven Pines. The Yankees were apparently keen to take me out of the war as early as possible. I guess they were scared of me."

McFadden smiled. He decided he liked Turnbow.

"I told the War Department I could still serve with a peg leg. Plenty of other people do, after all. General Hood. General Ewell. But they wouldn't have it. They wanted me back in Atlanta to run the iron works."

"The iron works?"

"Yes. The Turnbow Iron Foundry. Built it from scratch, I'm proud to say. We turn out cannon for the army."

"Oh. I suppose it's good to manufacture a product for which there is such a high demand."

Turnbow laughed, although McFadden hadn't intended his comment as a joke.

"How will we get back to the city, father?" Annie asked.

"Hmm, good question. Sergeant, I don't suppose I could prevail upon you for further assistance?"

"Come and rest for a few minutes with my men," McFadden said, doing his best to sound reassuring. "I will try to arrange transportation for the two of you back to Atlanta."

"I thank you very kindly, Sergeant."

"It is my pleasure, sir."

They reached the edge of the river bank and McFadden directed them to sit down with his company. He was relieved that his men had had the foresight to clothe themselves once again and he saw that the task of washing the clothes was completed. Private Pearson was on his feet again, though a trickle of blood was coming out of the left side of his mouth. He eyed McFadden with resentment, but said nothing.

McFadden sent Private Montgomery off to find an officer who would be able to help. Robert and Annie Turnbow sat down and dried off, and McFadden had his men do what they could to make the two of them comfortable. Soon, Robert Turnbow was engaged in a heated but cordial discussion with Private Balch about whether Robert E. Lee or Joseph Johnston was the better general.

Annie stood apart from the men. She didn't look physically uncomfortable, but McFadden could see that she was obviously distraught at having nearly been drowned. He also sensed that her father was unaware of how much it had troubled her. McFadden approached her.

"Are you all right, ma'am?"

She shook her head.

"It's just a buggy, ma'am," McFadden said. "You and your father should be thankful to have survived the accident."

"I know," Annie said. "But I could have drowned. I have never been so scared in my life."

McFadden nodded, though inwardly he thought Annie's statement rather childish. He came close to death on a daily basis and the thought of being killed held no terror for him. Then he thought back to his first battle in New Mexico and remembered how frightened he had been. Clearly, this girl had been sheltered from the horrors of war more than most.

"Well, you'll soon be safe at your home in the city."

"As safe as that is, at any rate."

"Why have you not yet fled the city? I can understand why your father remains, as the iron foundry is no doubt important to the war effort. But the enemy is now only a few miles from the city. I thought all women had been sent away for safety."

"My mother says that she shall not allow the Yankees to dictate to her where she shall make her home."

McFadden considered this. "I suppose that's admirable." He didn't add that he thought it was foolish.

"Yes," Annie said, her voice momentarily becoming lighter. "My mother is a strong woman. She says that if you soldiers can't stop Sherman's advance, she'll pick up a gun and do it herself."

"Yes, well, war is not a proper business for women." Rumors abounded of women disguising themselves as men and engaging in combat, but McFadden thought such stories absurd.

"No," Annie said. "I would prefer to keep the war at as great a distance as possible. I cannot fathom the arrogance and pride that drove the politicians to plunge our people into such a nightmare. The war brings such suffering." She paused for a moment. "And it took away my brother."

He nodded. "I'm sorry." He surprised himself by feeling sincere sympathy, an emotion he had not experienced in years. After all, hundreds of thousands of other people across the country had lost loved ones in the war. One woman's grief compared to the grief of uncounted numbers of others was merely a drop of water in the proverbial bucket. Yet McFadden found his heart going out to this woman, whom he had known for less than a half hour.

She nodded. "He was killed at Second Manassas."

"Was he? I'm sorry."

Annie shrugged. "It's been two years. They say time heals all wounds, don't they?"

"Yes, they do." McFadden knew it wasn't true. More than two years had passed since he had been forced to watch his own brother be tortured and killed, and the scarred face of the demented Yankee captain haunted his dreams as much now as it had then. Nor had the passage of time done much to erase the memory of the bodies of his parents and sisters, impaled by Comanche arrows.

The memories were like the still-smoldering embers of a campfire. If you tossed even a little bit of kindling back onto them, the fire would burst forth again.

"You look angry," she said, confused. He glanced at her, feeling defensive. But the softness of her voice and the tender way she was looking at him caused his anger at the old memories to vanish almost as quickly as it had appeared.

"I am sorry. My mind wandered off for a moment."

"If Father and I had drowned, Mother would have been left entirely alone. I cannot thank you enough for saving us."

"As I said to your father, it was nothing. I am glad I was nearby and able to help. Besides, you might have been able to get out of the river on your own." McFadden said the last bit even though he knew it was false.

"We are not imposing on you and your men, are we?"

"No, not at all. Private Montgomery should be back very soon, and I know Captain Collett would be very upset with us if we failed to assist people in need."

As if on cue, McFadden saw Private Montgomery jogging back up to the clothes washing station, which was now almost cleaned up. When he arrived, Mr. Turnbow rose from his conversation and walked over to McFadden just as Montgomery reached him.

"Well?" McFadden asked.

"A commissary wagon train will be crossing the pontoon bridge shortly. Not more than three minutes behind me, in fact. The lieutenant commanding the escort said that they are heading for the Car Shed in the center of the city, and that they would be more than happy to bring along the civilians."

"Thank you, Montgomery. Get your stuff ready and tell the men that we'll move out shortly." Montgomery nodded and moved off.

"Well, Sergeant McFadden," Turnbow said. "Again, please let me express my deepest appreciation for rescuing my daughter and myself. And thank you for looking after us and making sure we reach the city. We are both in your debt."

"It is my pleasure and my duty to assist you, sir. And if I may say so, your daughter is a most gracious young lady."

Turnbow's eyebrows rose and he eyed McFadden warily. "Thank you, Sergeant."

McFadden stole a glance at Annie, who faintly blushed and looked away from him. At that moment, the first wagon emerged from the tree line. The man sitting next to the driver, who wore a lieutenant's uniform, called out for them to jump into the back.

"Please extend my best wishes to your commanding officer. He leads good men."

"Thank you, sir," McFadden said. Turnbow extended his hand and McFadden shook it firmly.

The wagon slowed to a halt just long enough for one of the soldiers to assist Annie and her father inside. The driver then whipped the mules back into a steady walk, and the wagon began to cross the bridge.

McFadden watched them go. Just before he turned away, Annie cast a glance back over her shoulder and saw him looking at her. For an endless moment, her expression remained unchanged. Then, she smiled and faced forward once again.

*   *   *   *   *

Sherman had set up his field headquarters near the small hamlet of Vining's Station, a few miles north of the Confederate defensive position. A nearby hill offered a good vantage point from which to observe the surrounding countryside, so he had asked his senior commanders to ride with him to the summit. They could hear the sounds of their men skirmishing with the rebels and the ever-present booming of distant artillery.

The reports filtering back to headquarters described a line of fortifications more formidable than any yet encountered since the beginning of the campaign. Attempting to carry them by assault would bring about a bloody repulse even worse than that at Kennesaw Mountain. Faced with an impregnable defensive position, Sherman realized that he would once again have to find a way to outmaneuver Johnston.

Just to their right, a putrefying body was hanging from a large tree. It had been there when they had arrived, so presumably the man had been hanged by the Confederates just before they evacuated the area. Sherman had briefly wondered who the man had been. Perhaps a deserter of whom an example had been made or perhaps simply a common criminal. Conceivably the man might have committed suicide. No one particularly cared, as evidenced by the fact that no one had bothered to cut the body down.

Thomas was scanning the area below them with his telescope. "I've never seen a line so well built," he said. Sherman knew that the man nicknamed 'The Rock of Chickamauga' did not make such comments lightly. As he observed the position with his own telescope, he had to agree with Thomas. The Southern line arched for several miles, its flanks firmly anchored on the Chattahoochee. There was no way to outflank the position without crossing the river.

"A rather pretty river, I must say," commented General John Schofield, commander of the Army of the Ohio.

"Yes," replied General James McPherson, commander of the Army of the Tennessee. "But right now I'm more concerned with finding a way across the river than with assessing its aesthetic value."

Sherman had been the commander of the Army of the Tennessee before McPherson and the unit held a special place in his heart. It always annoyed him that the Army of the Tennessee had a name which led many newspapermen to confuse it with the Confederate Army of Tennessee. From the beginning of the war, the Union had named its armies after rivers, while the Confederacy had named its armies after states.

Sherman liked McPherson a great deal. He had been first in his class at West Point and had achieved a solid record as a division and corps commander in earlier campaigns. Tall, handsome, and possessing what Sherman thought was the kindest heart of any man he had ever met, McPherson meant a great deal to his commanding officer.

Schofield, on the other hand, always reminded Sherman of a bird, and a rather fat and ridiculous bird at that. Before the Atlanta Campaign had begun, he had seen little combat, having commanded forces in the military backwater of Missouri. While Sherman respected Schofield's intelligence and thought him a decent enough man, he had never really warmed to him.

Sherman's grand host was made up of three constituent armies. Thomas's Army of the Cumberland was by far the largest, with seventy thousand men. Indeed, it outnumbered Johnston's entire force by itself. McPherson's Army of the Tennessee numbered about twenty-five thousand, while Schofield's Army of the Ohio had only fifteen thousand and was scarcely larger than a single infantry corps. In his maneuvers, it had become Sherman's preference to keep the Army of the Cumberland in the center, with the other two armies, smaller and more mobile, operating on the flanks. In a certain sense, Thomas was the body, while McPherson and Schofield were the arms.

"Look across the river," Schofield said, pointing. "Over there."

The others scanned the area indicated. There were several large Confederate camps, where men were digging entrenchments. Smoke rising from cooking fires was clearly visible.

"A division?" Sherman asked.

"A few divisions, I should say," Thomas replied. "There's another one over there."

"So," Sherman said. "Johnston has pulled at least part of his army to the south bank of the river."

"No surprise," said Thomas. "It's exactly what I'd do in his place. The force on the south bank is there to launch a counter attack against any effort on our part to cross the river."

"What do you think?" Schofield asked. "Maybe two corps holding this fortified line on the north bank and one corps on the south bank?"

"Sounds about right," Thomas said.

Sherman took a deep breath. Crossing a river in the face of the enemy was one of the most daunting maneuvers for a military commander to attempt. His army would necessarily be divided while it was crossing, giving the opponent the chance to fall on only a portion of the army with his full strength. The result could be a disaster.

"What battle was it in which Alexander the Great had to cross a river in the face of the army commanded by that Hindu king?" Sherman asked.

"The Battle of the Hydaspes, I believe," McPherson answered. "In 326 BC, if I remember my West Point history lessons correctly. He used a massive feint, making the enemy think he was crossing at one point, causing him to rush his forces there, whereas the actual crossing point was several miles distant."

"It may be that we shall require a similar movement here."

"Would you like to borrow my copy of Plutarch?" Schofield said in a humorous tone. "You can brush up on the details."

"Yes," Sherman answered, not realizing his subordinate had been joking. "I would be much obliged to you."

The sun was gradually burning away the morning mist, and Sherman saw something on the distant horizon that he had not noticed before. There was a purple smudge of some sort, and he focused his telescope on it. The domes and church steeples of a city were clearly visible.

"Atlanta," Sherman said soberly.

"Only eight miles away," McPherson said.

Seeing the ultimate objective of his campaign for the first time filled Sherman with excitement. He knew better than anyone how heavy a blow the Confederacy would receive if he succeeded in capturing this city. If he could take from the South the transportation links and industrial facilities in Atlanta, he would tear the heart out of the Southern rebellion. It would be a defeat from which the Confederacy would never recover.

Sherman snapped shut his telescope and leaned forward on his horse, deep in thought. If he could get his army across the

Chattahoochee River, the city would be at his mercy. But how to do it in the face of an enemy that yet remained dangerous and diligent? He gazed up and down the river and was silent for several minutes, as the other three continued their visual surveying of the area.

Finally, he spoke again, and did so in a commanding tone.

"George, I want the Army of the Cumberland to encircle this Confederate position. Keep your boys skirmishing with the rebels in those damn forts. Keep them pinned down and do your utmost to make them stay put. I don't want a single additional rebel regiment crossing to the south bank if you can prevent it."

"Yes, sir."

"I'm going to have the cavalry swarm around the river to the southwest of Johnston's current position. They'll be noisy and visible, the idea being to make Johnston think we intend to make our crossing downriver. Since we have always gone after his left flank, he will hopefully fall for it."

The three men nodded, and Sherman went on, speaking now to McPherson and Schofield.

"I want the Army of the Tennessee and the Army of the Ohio to swing northwards, upriver from the Confederates, and try to find suitable crossing points. Load up the wagons, because you will be away from the railroad for a few days. Use your cavalry to scout the way, but try to avoid detection by the rebels for as long as possible. When you find a crossing point, get your men across the river as quick as you can, and be sure to fortify in a bridgehead as soon as you are across. Johnston could well try to counter attack the moment he finds out he's been flanked."

The men muttered their understanding, and Sherman asked if there were any questions. There weren't.

"All right, let's get to it, then. With any luck, we'll be having our dinner in Atlanta within a week or two."

*   *   *   *   *

July 7, Evening

Johnston had set up his headquarters at a large house owned by the Campbell family, on the south side of the Chattahoochee not far from the Western and Atlanta Railroad. Somehow, being on the opposite bank from the front lines gave the assembled Confederate generals a certain psychological distance from the fighting, like being in a room with a door only slightly ajar.

Hardee, Hood and Wheeler were all there, listening as Johnston described the current situation on the maps laid out on the table. Also present was General A.P. Stewart, recently promoted to command the army's third corps following the death of the much-mourned General Polk.

"Our engineers have done a remarkable job," Johnston said with satisfaction. "Our current position on the north bank is all but impregnable, and its flanks are securely anchored on the river. Sherman will not easily outflank us this time, by God."

"I agree it's a strong position," Hood said. "But I am not comfortable being backed up against the river. During my time with General Lee, we made the mistake of doing that at Sharpsburg and nearly lost the whole army."

Hardee sighed a little too loudly. Hood was always talking about his service with Lee.

"What are you suggesting, then?" Johnston asked.

Hood spoke adamantly "I strongly recommend that we pull the entire army to the south side of the river without delay."

"That would be disastrous!" Hardee exclaimed. "So long as we remain on the north side of the river in force, Sherman cannot risk dividing his army."

"And you think the Yankees are simply going to sulk outside our fortified lines, then?" Hood's voice rang with mockery. "Just like they did at Dalton and Resaca, eh? No, they'll just flank us again and turn this mighty fortified line of ours into their biggest prison camp!"

Hardee's eyes angrily flashed at Hood's tone. Had it not been for Hood's crippled state, Johnston would not have been surprised to see Hardee's hand move to his sword.

"So you want to run away?" Hardee asked. "Just like you advised us to do at Cassville?"

"I consider that remark an affront to my honor!"

The conversation descended into a shouting match for the next minute or so, but Hardee's words had suddenly caused Johnston to think of something he had not previously considered. The incident at Cassville still perplexed him. Despite his reputation for aggressiveness, Hood had on those two days displayed a shocking lack of fighting spirit. Not only had Hood thrown away an excellent chance of launching what would have been a devastating surprise attack, but had then insisted that they retreat from what was, in the view of Johnston and Hardee, an outstanding defensive position.

Johnston recalled his meeting with Wigfall little more than a week before. His friend had told him that Hood was writing secret letters to President Davis, accusing Johnston of lacking in offensive spirit and of being overly disposed to retreat. But here was Hood now, advocating retreat yet again.

Everything snapped together in Johnston's mind at that instant and his eyes momentarily widened in shock. The thought was nearly unspeakable, but he couldn't deny its logic. Might Hood's duplicity go beyond unauthorized communication with Richmond? Could Hood be deliberately sabotaging the operations of the Army of Tennessee in order to discredit Johnston's leadership? Was Hood trying to persuade Johnston to retreat again because he thought it would cause the President to remove Johnston from command and appoint Hood in his place?

Anger flared within him, and he suddenly stood up and slammed his fists down on the table. Sudden silence descended upon the collected group of officers, who looked at him in great surprise. It was the first time any of them had seen a physical manifestation of Johnston's anger.

"Gentlemen," he said, controlling his emotions and refusing to let his subordinates see what he was thinking. "Please calm down. It is our duty to fight the Yankee invaders, not each other. Don't we agree?" He paused for a moment, letting himself calm down. "Now, General Hardee, please tell me your recommended course of action."

"We must remain on the north side of the river. That much is certain. The cavalry and infantry we already have in position on the south bank are sufficient in case Sherman attempts a major crossing."

"I understand your position. Go on."

"By maintaining our current position, Sherman cannot maneuver with his full force. The Chattahoochee is a sufficiently wide barrier to allow us to defeat any crossing attempt with minimal forces. If we keep to our present position, the Yankees will be well and truly stymied."

Johnston looked around. "General Stewart? What are your views?"

Stewart cleared his throat, somewhat nervous at his first participation in the deliberations of high command. "I agree with General Hardee. If we can block Sherman's advance by maintaining our position and protecting the river crossings, we can potentially hold the Yankees off long enough for an attack to be made on the enemy supply line."

"Assuming President Davis ever gives orders for such a raid," Johnston said sourly.

"I must protest!" Hood exclaimed sharply. "Suppose that Sherman merely takes up a position directly opposite ours and fortifies with a force equal to ours? That would leave forty thousand or so men with which Sherman could mount a major crossing operation to the south bank. Two divisions and a few cavalry would not be able to stop such an attack."

Johnston turned to his cavalry commander. "General Wheeler, how confident are you at being able to detect a Union crossing attempt before it takes place?"

"Quite confident, sir."

"Can I rely on you, therefore, to be able to inform me of any Union crossing attempt at least four or five hours before it occurs?"

"I obviously can't make such an exact promise, General. Anything can happen in war. But I would certainly expect to be able to do so."

"Make sure your patrols downriver are especially vigilant. Sherman always goes after our left. Never forget that fact."

"Yes, sir."

Johnston turned back to Hood. "With a few hours warning, we will have sufficient time to withdraw a few brigades from our bridgehead and march them to the threatened point. You disagree?"

"Respectfully, sir, I do. I believe standing our ground on the north side of the river risks disaster. We should immediately retreat to the south bank."

Johnston looked around at his assembled commanders, who waited for him to speak. Unknown to any of them, his mind was racing. For reasons he was not yet prepared to tell them, Johnston actually wanted to withdraw to the south bank of the Chattahoochee. He wanted Sherman to get onto the same side of the river as Atlanta, so long as he crossed to the north, rather than the south, of the present Confederate position.

Johnston also knew what game Hood was playing. If the Army of Tennessee was withdrawn to the south bank, Hood would falsely tell President Davis that he had opposed a retreat on which the army commander had insisted, even though the exact opposite was true. Such a communication might be enough for Davis to remove Johnston from command.

Johnston did not know what to do.

Hardee and Stewart glanced at one another, obviously confused as to why Johnston had been silent for so long. The Virginian finally looked up.

"The conference is over, gentlemen. Return to your commands and await my orders."

*   *   *   *   *

July 9, Morning

Davis and Bragg listened quietly as Senator Hill recounted his conversation with General Johnston and the other senior officers of the Army of Tennessee. It had taken him a week-and-a-half to reach Richmond along the Confederacy's dilapidated rail system.

"I concluded the conversation by asking him directly to say what he needed to win the campaign," Hill was saying.

"If Johnston's reports to me are any indication, his answer involved sending General Forrest's cavalry to attack Sherman's supply lines," Bragg said.

Hill nodded. "As a matter of fact, that is precisely what he said. So, Mr. President, on behalf of the citizens of the state of Georgia, I request that this order be put into effect without further delay. Forrest should be sent to attack Sherman's supply lines forthwith."

Davis removed his glasses and rubbed his temples, nursing a pounding headache. He was quiet for some time before responding to Hill. When he did, he gestured to the map on the wall.

"As you can see, Senator Hill, Mississippi is threatened by the Yankees as well. They have twenty thousand troops in Memphis, whereas we have a mere nine thousand men in northern Mississippi to oppose them. If we send Forrest to attack Sherman's supply lines, the Yankees might easily overrun the state, losing us valuable territory that includes, I might point out, the very farmland that keeps Johnston's troops fed. Furthermore, many of our Mississippi troops serving with both Lee in Virginia and Johnston in Georgia might desert the colors and return to their homes if they feel their families are in danger."

Hill nodded. "I see. Johnston did not seem overly concerned with Mississippi, I must admit."

"I would think not. He cares only about his own department."

"Are there any other cavalry units which might serve as a substitute? Morgan's men in southwestern Virginia, perhaps?"

Davis shook his head. "Morgan recently launched a raid into Kentucky which turned out to be a disastrous failure. They are currently in no condition to undertake another major operation. The simple fact is that if Johnston is to defeat Sherman, he must do it with his present force."

"I must state to you, in all frankness, that he did not seem confident in his ability to defeat Sherman with his present force."

"But why not, I ask you? If his reports of inflicting heavy casualties on Sherman since May are true, then the Union army must be significantly weaker in strength that it was at the commencement of the campaign. We have already sent him over ten thousand infantry as reinforcements, stripping essential theaters of war to do so. If he is being truthful when he claims that his army has avoided high losses, his own army should be stronger now than it was at the beginning of May."

Hill thought for a moment and nodded. "I can't argue with that, Mr. President. Mathematical logic, you might say."

Bragg spoke up. "And there is no reason to think that Johnston cannot use his own cavalry for an attack on Sherman's supply lines. Indeed, we have received word from General Wheeler himself that he has repeatedly asked Johnston for permission to raid the enemy supply lines, only to be denied."

Hill's eyes widened. "That certainly was not something I was told when I met with Johnston. Wheeler was present, but told me no such thing."

"He would not have been willing to speak out of turn in front of his commanding officer," Bragg replied. "Military protocol, you see."

"Tell me," Davis said. "How long did Johnston say he could hold out on the north bank of the Chattahoochee?"

"A month. Perhaps longer."

Without a word, Davis slid a piece of paper across the desk to Senator Hill. It was the latest telegram from Johnston's headquarters. Hill put on his reading glasses and quickly scanned through the document.

President Davis,

Last night the enemy crossed the Chattahoochee River several miles north of our position. They immediately entrenched, making an attack inadvisable. In consequence, the Army of Tennessee are withdrawing to the south bank of the river in order to avoid being outflanked.

General J. E. Johnston

"Johnston is withdrawing to the south bank already?"

"That's about the size of it," Davis said tiredly.

"So," Hill said. "Rather than hold the north bank for more than a month, Johnston managed to do so for little over a week."

"That is correct."

Hill pursed his lips tightly. "I can't speak intelligently on military operations, Mr. President. I'm a politician and not a soldier. But I must admit to feeling deceived."

"Tell me, in all frankness, what you think of Johnston's will to fight."

Hill exhaled deeply, thinking before answering. "My impression was that he is a general more concerned with not losing than he is with winning. In certain situations, this might be admirable. But in the present context, I believe that we must value boldness over caution. Times like these call for a Scipio rather than a Fabius."

Davis nodded. "I agree. My greatest concern is that Sherman will now move to cut Atlanta's rail links with the rest of the Confederacy and that, rather than fight, Johnston will simply abandon the city."

"It is not inconceivable, Mr. President," Hill answered. "And losing Atlanta would be a catastrophic blow to our cause, perhaps equaling the evil consequences stemming from the loss of Vicksburg. Or even New Orleans."

Davis stood up and stepped toward the map. "It would be worse than either of those losses, severe though they were. If Atlanta falls, Lincoln will be able to claim that the Yankee war effort is making progress, thus contributing greatly to his chances of reelection in November. We can win the war only by outlasting the Yankees and inflicting such losses upon their armies that Lincoln is turned out by the voters."

"And do you think this is possible?" Hill asked.

"It's not only possible, but likely. The North is war-weary, and on all other fronts we are successfully resisting their armies of conscripts. Lee is continuing to hold the lines around Richmond and Petersburg. By God, he has even been able to detach an entire corps to cross into Maryland and threaten the enemy capital itself!"

"I was entirely unaware of that," Hill said with admiration. "General Lee never ceases to astonish me. If Johnston had but a fraction of Lee's boldness, I would have no fears for the future of Atlanta."

"Nor would I," Davis said, sitting back down. "If things continue to go as they have gone for the past few months, Lincoln will lose in November and an administration more inclined to peace shall be set up in Washington. If that happens, I believe the independence of our Confederacy is assured. But if Johnston abandons Atlanta, all will be lost."

"Mr. President," Hill said, speaking carefully. "Have you considered replacing Johnston?"

Davis nodded, sitting back down. "You are not the first person to suggest this to me. And with the recent news that he has withdrawn to the south side of the Chattahoochee, my inclination in that direction are increasing."

*   *   *   *   *

July 9, Afternoon

It felt good to be alone for a change. Having given the necessary orders to his corps commanders for an orderly withdrawal to the south bank of the river, Johnston had felt comfortable leaving the headquarters in the capable hands of Mackall and venturing off on his own for a few hours.

He had decided against an immediate counter attack. Instead, Johnston had decided to pull the entire Army of Tennessee to the south bank of the river and deploy it in a line running west to east a few miles north of Atlanta. It would take several days for the Yankees to get all of their men across the river, so the chances of any serious fighting for the next week or so were remote.

Johnston was riding slowly through the woods north of the defenses of the city, with only his horse for company. Lee had Traveler, Stonewall Jackson had had Little Sorrel, but Johnston had never taken to any one particular mount. Instead, he simply got into the saddle of whichever horse his staff happened to provide for him on any given day. He did not even know the name of the horse he was riding, but it seemed friendly enough.

He rode north for a considerable distance. The area was densely forested and it became difficult to see more than a few hundred yards in any direction. Insects buzzed about and filled the forest with their eerie sounds. He spotted an occasional deer or wild turkey and wondered how they had escaped the ravenous hunger of his fifty thousand men.

The heat was oppressive, but he enjoyed the fresh air and the feeling of being liberated from the prison of his headquarters. Without having reports shoved across his desk every five minutes, he could reflect on the situation more clearly.

Johnston had known for a long time, perhaps even before the campaign had begun, that he could not hold the Yankees on the north bank of the Chattahoochee River indefinitely. Sooner or later, Sherman had been certain to get a large force onto the southern bank. Johnston might have attempted to maintain a foothold on the north side, but if the plan he had devised was to have any chance of success, he would need to have the entire Army of Tennessee concentrated into a single, solid force on the south bank of the river.

He said a silent prayer of thanks to God once again that the eventuality he had most dreaded had not come to pass. Sherman had crossed the river upstream from Atlanta, rather than downstream; he had gone around the Confederate right flank, rather than its left. That seemingly innocuous fact, combined with the realities of the local geography, could well determine the outcome of the war.

Johnston continued north, feeling more serene than he had since the beginning of the campaign. He knew that he would soon he going into battle against a strong and dangerous foe, led by a crafty commander whose forces considerably outnumbered his own. He knew that President Davis distrusted and despised him and was almost certainly planning on removing him from command. He knew at least some of his own subordinates were actively subverting the operations of his army. Yet despite all this, Johnston felt strangely untroubled.

God was in control. Of that Johnston had no doubt. Though he had always been an Episcopalian, he had admitted to himself a few months before that his faith had not been as strong as it should have been. He had not felt the presence of God in his life in some time. But when the campaign had begun in early May, Johnston had been seized by a strange feeling that his actions were being directed by a higher power.

He had mentioned this to his wife Lydia, who had responded by writing a letter to General Leonidas Polk, one of his corps commanders. Polk had been an Episcopalian bishop before the war and had continued to perform sacramental duties. The night before the attack on Cassville was supposed to have been mounted, he had approached Johnston and shown him the letter from Lydia in which she asked Polk to baptize her husband. He readily agreed.

With Hardee and Hood standing as witnesses, the headquarters illuminated only by the flickering light of a few candles,

Polk had momentarily discarded the uniform of a Confederate general and donned the robes of a bishop. Johnston had knelt and received the sacrament, feeling cleansed of his sins. It had been one of the most deeply solemn and moving moments of Johnston's life.

It had also made it all the harder to bear the death of Polk, killed two weeks before the Battle of Kennesaw Mountain by Union artillery fire. Johnston had not been especially impressed with Polk's military abilities, but he had been a good man and a good friend. He had helped bring Johnston closer to God.

Johnston recalled cradling Polk's body, which had nearly been torn in two by the enemy cannonball. Later, he had discovered a blood-splattered piece of paper in one of Polk's coat pockets, on which the bishop-turned-general had jotted down a poem before he had been killed.

> *There is an unseen battlefield,*
> *In every human breast,*
> *Where two opposing forces meet,*
> *And where they seldom rest.*

Yes, whatever happened was God's will. That thought gave Johnston comfort. He would, of course, do his best, for he was deeply committed to the Southern cause and hoped to live to see an independent Confederacy. If he failed, if would be through no fault of his own. He would have the satisfaction of knowing he had done his best. But he did not expect to fail.

His horse whinnied ever so slightly, alerting its master that there was an obstacle ahead. Johnston wasn't surprised. Indeed, he had been expecting it. A few moments later, he was riding along the edge of a large creek with a rocky and uneven bottom. Green, foamy moss coagulated along its muddy banks. The water itself did not appear deep. Indeed, Johnston was relatively sure that the water wouldn't have reached his waist. But the banks of the creek were quite steep, in some places as much as ten feet.

Johnston rode along the creek for some time, deep in thought. It ran for miles, flowing from east to west until it reached the Chattahoochee River. Along its entire length, it maintained its disjointed character of uncertain depth and steep, uneven banks.

He smiled. The creek would suit his needs perfectly.

Perhaps an hour later, having seen all that he needed to see, he turned his horse south and kicked it into a trot. Before the sun disappeared over the western horizon, Johnston was back at his headquarters.

The creek was Peachtree Creek.

   *   *   *   *   *

"Who are you?" the staff officer called.

"7th Texas!" Captain Collett called back. "Granbury's Brigade! Cleburne's Division!"

The man glanced briefly down at the orders in his hands. "Okay. You can go ahead and cross."

Collett turned to his men, who were arranged in a marching column on the road leading up to the bridge. "7th Texas! Forward! March!"

The men shouldered their Enfields and stepped off. Within moments, the crunching sound of their feet on the grassy clay soil was replaced by the thunking sound of marching on the wooden planks of the pontoon bridge. On either side of them, the vast expanse of the Chattahoochee spread out like a romantic painting. Along with the rest of the army, the men of the 7th Texas were abandoning the north bank of the river.

"What the hell is this about?" Private Pearson said, to no one in particular.

McFadden hoped that no one would respond, but Private Montgomery did.

"What the hell are you talking about, Pearson?"

"Why are we retreating again? No way the Yankees could have ever knocked us out of the line we held. I bet even old Napoleon couldn't have taken those redoubts."

McFadden sighed. He doubted if Pearson knew anything at all about the campaigns of the Emperor of the French.

The regiment continued marching over the bridge. Pearson was still talking. "I'm getting fed up with this, boys! We've retreated damn near every day since we left Dalton back in early May. Every time we fight the Yankees, we whip them. We whipped them at Dug Gap, we whipped them at Resaca, we whipped them at Pickett's Mill and we whipped them at Kennesaw Mountain. But whenever we whip them, the next day, Johnston orders us out of the trenches and marching south again. Why do we keep retreating after we win all the fights? What the hell is Uncle Joe doing?"

"Shut your mouth, Pearson!" McFadden said harshly. He didn't much care for Johnston's strategy of retreating either, but he was not about to allow a mere private in his company to disparage the commanding general in front of other soldiers.

"What, Sarge?" Pearson said, adding to McFadden's irritation. "Am I wrong?"

"It's not for you to criticize our commanding general, Private," McFadden said. He emphasized Pearson's rank as clearly as he could. "You say one more word about it and I'll shove you right off this bridge."

Up at the front of the regiment, Captain Collett heard the exchange and glanced backwards. Seeing that McFadden was dealing with the situation, he looked forward once again and gave the matter no more thought.

"What'd I do to make the sergeant so upset?" Pearson asked Montgomery, doing his best to sound aggrieved. "I'm just talking, is all." He said this just loudly enough for McFadden to be able to hear it.

Montgomery grinned. "The sergeant has got other things on his mind than the war, you know. Like that fine-looking gal he saved from drowning the other day."

The men of Company F laughed, but their good-natured tone convinced McFadden that it was not really laughter at his expense. His first thought was to upbraid Montgomery the same way he had just upbraided Pearson. However, he rather liked Montgomery and therefore kept quiet.

Besides which, what Montgomery had said was far from false. McFadden had scarcely been able to stop thinking about Annie Turnbow since he had rescued her three days earlier. The night before, he thought he had dreamed of her beautiful face, but could not be sure. His dreams had always been rather troubled and he usually tried not to think about them. To dream about Annie was a refreshing change.

He shook his head. It was stupid to think about Annie, for there was virtually no chance that he would ever see her again. She might even have left Atlanta, as most citizens had already fled the city by train to either Macon or Augusta. Now that the Yankees were on the south side of the Chattahoochee and the Army of Tennessee was abandoning its position on the north side, McFadden assumed that those few who remained would also make the decision to leave. It was, after all, basic common sense.

He stopped thinking about Annie as he heard his men continuing to discuss the retreat.

"I don't care whether Uncle Joe wants us to fight on the north side or the south side of this damn river," Private Harrison was saying. "I'm ready to fight just as soon as he gives the word."

"Damn straight," Montgomery said emphatically. "You ask me, Uncle Joe has lured the Yankees all the way from Dalton down to Atlanta itself as a trick. We're about to catch them in a trap, I say."

"A trap?" Pearson said, incredulous. "What the hell gives you that idea?"

"Two years ago, Uncle Joe waited until the Yankees were almost within sight of Richmond before he launched his big attack on them. Only failed because Johnston got himself wounded. That's what I read in the papers, at any rate."

"And you think that's what Johnston is doing to Sherman now?" Harrison asked. "Letting his whole army march all the way to Atlanta before we turn and attack him?"

"Sure," Montgomery said with a smile. "After all, if we can beat them in a fair fight on the south side of this river, they won't be able to run away like they did after Chickamauga."

McFadden's pulse quickened at the thought of that terrible but glorious battle, fought ten months before. The 7th Texas had lost half its strength during the two days of slaughter, but McFadden could not forget the feeling of unbelievable exaltation at the number of enemy soldiers he had killed. He was certain that four of them had died from the fire of his Enfield rifle and he had impaled a fifth on his bayonet. He remembered how enthralled he had been when the regiment had taken part in the great breakthrough on the Union right, tearing a huge gap in the enemy lines and putting the Yankees to flight. His joy had been raised to even greater heights when it became clear that the Battle of Chickamauga had been a tremendous Confederate victory.

The memory of Chickamauga stirred a certain giddiness inside McFadden, as if he had consumed a large amount of good whiskey. He remembered how he had been tempted the night the battle ended to take the scalps of some dead Yankees as victory trophies, in the same way that the Comanches had taken the scalps of his father, mother and sisters. Only concern for what his fellow soldiers would have thought had snapped him out of his vengeful trance.

As he continued walking along the pontoon bridge, something happened that McFadden did not expect. He suddenly felt confused as he found himself wondering what Annie Turnbow would have thought if she had been able to see him that night, taking such delight in killing his enemies. Imagining how his bloodlust would have appeared to her, he felt a foreign emotion rise up within him.

For the first time in as long as he could remember, James McFadden felt shame.

Behind him, the men of the Lone Star Rifles were laughing and chattering away amiably, making jokes about the stupidity of Braxton Bragg and the unreliability of troops from Georgia. None could see the emotional anguish that was sweeping through McFadden's mind. That, he decided, was obviously for the best. The regiment was coming to the end of the pontoon bridge and, a few moments later, McFadden's feet left the wooden planks and were again treading the familiar red clay soil.

*   *   *   *   *

Sherman sat on his horse, cigar in his mouth, watching regiment after regiment file past him as they marched onto the pontoon bridge and across the Chattahoochee River. Every minute that passed put more Union soldiers on the same side of the river as Atlanta, the supreme goal of the campaign.

General McPherson walked his horse up beside Sherman.

"All going well, Cump. The entire Army of the Tennessee should be on the south bank by the end of the day."

"Good," Sherman said. "Schofield's boys are already all across, and once you get over, Thomas can start getting the Army of the Cumberland over as well. It will take a few days, and perhaps a week to build up enough supplies for an advance, but we have time."

"You appear to be a happy man," McPherson said with a smile.

"I am. But I'm also a confused one. Why didn't Johnston make it more difficult for us to cross the river? I'm frankly surprised by how easy it was."

"Maybe the rebels are really whipped. Maybe they have no fight left in them."

"Considering the beating they gave us at Kennesaw Mountain just two weeks ago, I doubt that."

McPherson shrugged. "From the beginning of the campaign, Johnston has demonstrated a reluctance to engage in combat except when his troops are protected by fortifications. By now, Atlanta has to be the best fortified city on the continent, aside from Richmond and Washington. Perhaps he wants to fight us from his fortifications."

Sherman shook his head. "Try to withstand a siege? That would be foolish. Johnston is no fool. Whatever else he is, he is no fool."

"Well, all we can know for sure is that he's pulled his forces back and is allowing us to cross the river unmolested. Cavalry reports no Confederate forces within miles of our position."

Sherman nodded. "I haven't heard any cannon fire for days."

"I know. Odd, isn't it?"

For just a moment, the thought entered Sherman's mind that Johnston actually wanted his entire force on the south side of the river, so that he might lead the Union forces into some sort of trap.

He shook the disturbing thought out of his head, angry at himself. It was paranoid thinking like that which had gotten him removed from command at Louisville at the very beginning of the war, an experience he had no desire to repeat. It had led to a complete mental breakdown and his attempt at suicide. Had it not been for the intervention of Grant, he might have never gotten another command.

"James, when your army is across, I want to move it into position on Schofield's left. Thomas will take position on Schofield's right when he gets across."

"Very well. And then?"

"The Army of the Cumberland will advance directly south toward Atlanta, while you will maneuver to the east side of the city and cut off its railway links with Augusta, then close up toward the city itself. Schofield will serve as a link between you and Thomas."

"If I move my army in such a manner, my left flank will be exposed," McPherson pointed out.

"I know. Nothing to do about it. If Johnston plans to fight for the city, I imagine he will do so by attempting to strike your flank. It's a risk, I know. But a pitched battle in the open against the rebels is something to be desired, not feared. If Johnston means to attack you, we shall meet him. Yes, by God, we shall meet him."

"And after that?"

"Battle or not, once we have cut his rail links to the east, we shall pin him in the defenses of the city and send our cavalry to break his rail links to the west, leaving him with only a single railroad to ensure his supplies. We can then extend our trenches to threaten that final rail link, at which point I believe Johnston will evacuate the city and retreat southwards. We shall march into Atlanta with a minimum loss of life."

"A sound plan," McPherson said.

"Yes. In the meantime, unless the rebels attempt an attack, which I consider very unlikely, there is going to be a lull in operations for several days while we bring the Army of the Cumberland across the river. Make sure your men take the opportunity to rest and refit. When we move south again, I want our boys to be as ready as they can be. And when we march through the streets of Atlanta, I want them looking like proper soldiers."

*   *   *   *   *

July 9, Night

"All aboard for Danville!" the train conductor called. As if to give added emphasis to his words, the train's steam whistle blew sharply a few times.

The people who had been patiently waiting in the Richmond and Danville Railroad depot stirred themselves. A few exchanged hushed whispers and pointed at one man in particular. More than a few gave him angry glares.

General Bragg clasped his carpetbag and rose from his seat on the bench. He was aware of the attention he was getting from the rest of the people in the depot, but he paid no mind. If the fact that he was likely the most despised man in the entire Confederacy bothered him, he gave no indication of it.

The conductor took his ticket without meeting his eyes and Bragg stepped aboard the train. He hoped that the trunk carrying his clothing and other necessities had been loaded properly. A moment later, he found an empty seat and sat down. The two men sitting across from him, one of whom wore an officer's uniform, immediately got up to find other seats. Letting out a deep breath, Bragg resigned himself to the fact that he would spend at least the next forty-eight hours in uncomfortable confinement aboard multiple trains.

The President's request that he travel to Johnston's headquarters to personally examine the situation had come as a greater surprise than it should have. After all, the stream of telegrams and letters from Atlanta could easily be misunderstood and Davis had long since ceased trusting anything that Johnston said. A personal inspection by a person on whom the President could rely was clearly necessary.

He thought over the route in his head. From Danville, he would go to Greensboro; from Greensboro, he would go to Columbia; from Columbia, he would go to Augusta; from Augusta, he would go to Atlanta. It was going to be a long and unpleasant trip. The Southern railroad system had been barely adequate before the war and now it verged on total collapse. Rail iron and replacement parts for locomotives had been imported from the North or from Europe before the war. With the blockade having cut off those supplies, the Confederacy had been hard pressed to manufacture their own. Occasional Yankee raids on the railroads only made the problems worse. It was a near miracle that the trains continued moving at all.

After a delay that nearly sent Bragg forward to complain to the conductor, the engine finally began chugging and the train slowly pulled itself out of the Richmond station. Bragg opened his carpetbag and pulled out a packet of papers, laying them out on his lap. Some were copies of the official reports and telegrams which had been received from General Johnston. Others were letters written by Wheeler to Bragg, and by Hood to Davis. He would spend the journey reading through all the material and trying to filter out fact from fiction.

If, as Johnston claimed, he had suffered light losses while inflicting heavy losses on Sherman since the campaign had opened in May, why could he not take the offensive? After all, if Johnston was telling the truth, the Confederate army had to be much stronger vis-à-vis the Union forces now then it had been at the beginning of the campaign. This question was especially relevant considering Hood's claim that Johnston had missed several opportunities to attack.

He thought of Johnston's constant requests for reinforcements, which both mystified and irritated him. Johnston had to have been aware that every regiment which could possibly be spared from other theaters of war had been sent to the Army of Tennessee. More than fifteen thousand men had been stripped from Mississippi and the lower Atlantic Gulf and dispatched to Johnston, leaving those other fronts dangerously undermanned. Yet Johnston continued to assert he was too weak to take the offensive.

Then there was the matter of the proposed cavalry raid on Sherman's vulnerable supply line. Every piece of information that

Bragg had seemed to confirm that the railroad was, indeed, quite vulnerable. But why did Johnston insist that Forrest be sent from Mississippi to do the job, rather than dispatching a force of his own cavalry? Wheeler himself was telling Bragg that he was personally eager to undertake such a mission and that it could be done without endangering the operations of the Army of Tennessee in the slightest.

As Bragg was mulling these questions over in his mind, his attention was drawn to the conversation of two women sitting directly behind him.

"Did you see General Bragg waiting to board this train?"

"Bragg, you say? What an odious brute!"

"My husband tells me that it was his fault we didn't capture Chattanooga right after the Battle of Chickamauga."

"And I heard Forrest threatened to kill him one time. Perhaps if he had done so, the country wouldn't in such sorry shape now."

"All will be well with Johnston in command. He's ten times the general Bragg ever was."

Bragg scowled severely. He considered standing up, turning around, and berating the poor women in front of the entire car. That obviously would not be the proper behavior of a Confederate general officer and it would certainly get into the newspapers. After what had happened at George Trenholm's party the other night, news of which had rapidly spread throughout Richmond, Bragg was determined to avoid any such publicity. Hopefully, the women would stop talking and go to sleep and he would not have to endure their sneers any longer.

They weren't going to sleep anytime soon, however. Indeed, their ridicule of Bragg continued for nearly twenty minutes, interspersed with praise for Johnston. He tried to focus on his papers to shut out the anonymous mockery emanating from behind him. Eventually, a gentleman who was sitting across the aisle rose and whispered quietly to the two ladies, causing them to fall into an awkward silence.

Johnston. Everyone was always talking about Johnston. He had been one of the heroes of the First Battle of Manassas back when the war was young. His name had been on everyone's lips. But he had never achieved any significant success in the years since that battle. He had failed to halt McClellan's advance on Richmond before being wounded in the Battle of Seven Pines and he had failed to act aggressively enough to break Grant's siege of Vicksburg. Why everyone continued to speak of Johnston as second only to Lee in the Confederacy's pantheon of generals was a mystery to Bragg.

The words of Governor Hawes from a week earlier suddenly came back to him. The political exile from Kentucky had said that the war would have already been won had Johnston been commander of the Army of Tennessee instead of Bragg. Those words had burned, because Bragg had heard them many times before.

The previous November, a disgraced Bragg had resigned as commander of an Army of Tennessee that had been utterly shattered and demoralized following the disaster at Missionary Ridge. The following May, a rejuvenated and restored Army of Tennessee commanded by Johnston had gone forth to battle against Sherman's hordes with a renewed enthusiasm and spirit. The difference had not been lost on the Confederate press or in the idle chatter of Richmond dinner parties.

Bitterly, Bragg shoved his papers back into his bag, tried to get comfortable in the confines of his chair, and closed his eyes. Sleep, however, didn't come easily.

Chapter Four

July 10, Afternoon

It was an unusually hot day in New York City, but Vallandigham was in a good mood. He had expected a crowd of about fifteen hundred people, but at least twice that many packed the ground in front of the speakers' platform. Judging by their clothes and appearance, the vast majority belonged to the working class. Many were waving signs denouncing Lincoln and Grant.

The man currently speaking was Congressman Fernando Wood, one of the stalwarts of the Tammany Hall political machine. He had been serving as Mayor of New York City when the war had broken out. He created enormous controversy when he had called for the city to secede from the Union and set itself up as an independent city-state.

The crowd cheered and applauded as Wood denounced Grant's generalship in Virginia and condemned Lincoln for enlisting blacks into the army. Vallandigham didn't catch his exact words, as he was concentrating on the text of his own speech, which he was going to give as soon Wood had finished. The crowd evidently liked it, as they were cheering wildly.

Vallandigham thought things were going well. As he had expected, no one had arrested him in Ohio, even after his presence back on American soil had become public knowledge. Lincoln no doubt feared the political backlash which would have ensued had the authorities done anything to him. Free to move about the country at will, Vallandigham had embarked upon a speaking campaign, addressing a dozen "peace rallies" throughout Ohio. Now, setting his sights higher, he had traveled to the Democratic stronghold of New York City.

He considered himself in friendly territory. Just a year earlier, New York City had exploded in three days of deadly rioting against the draft, leaving scores of people dead. The large turnout at

- 113 -

the rally confirmed for Vallandigham that the greatest metropolis in the Union was adamantly opposed to the President and his policies.

The cheering of the crowd rose to a crescendo as Wood came to the end of his speech. The former mayor turned and glanced at the row of chairs behind him, filled with local Democratic leaders, and met Vallandigham's eye. He dipped his head, wordlessly asking if Vallandigham was ready. Upon receiving a nod, Wood turned and faced the crowd again.

"And now, it is my pleasure to introduce to you fine people a true patriot. A man who has endured arrest, abuse, and even exile for his country. A man who refuses to be intimidated by the bullying brutes of Lincoln. A man who stands up for the liberties of the people! A man who loves our Constitution! Ladies and gentlemen, Clement Vallandigham!"

He rose and walked forward, shaking Wood's hand before advancing to the podium. The crowd roared its approval, applauding madly and waving their signs.

Vallandigham raised his hands to call for quiet. As the applause died down, he began.

"My friends, I am happy to be here in New York City, among so many true patriots and Democrats! As you know, my journey was a little longer than I expected." He paused for a moment while the crowd laughed at his joke. "You may have heard about what happened to me. I had the gall and temerity to ask questions about how King Lincoln was running his war. I had the gall and temerity to ask why ten thousand good Northern men had to die under the guns of the rebels at Fredericksburg. I had the gall and temerity to ask why rich men reap the profits of the war while working men like you are sent to fight and die in it!

"And what happened to me, you ask? In the middle of the night, armed men broke down my door and hauled me away, even as my wife and children wept and begged them to leave me alone! I was tried before a military court, denied a writ of habeas corpus, found guilty of sedition, and exiled from the country! Was this legal?"

"NO!" the crowd roared.

"Was this Constitutional?"

"NO!"

"Was this right?"

"NO!"

He paused a moment, waiting for the tumult in the audience to die down. "But I have returned to the United States, my beloved country, and I dare King Lincoln to do anything about it. I am not afraid and I know you are not afraid, either. But we must be on our guard, friends. For even as your husbands, brothers, fathers, and sons die by the thousands in Virginia and Georgia in useless battles under incompetent generals, and even as agents of conscription scour the streets for more fresh bodies to send to the slaughter, the seeds of tyranny have been planted in these United States. Newspapers have been shut down, good men have been arrested, and the President is setting himself up to be a dictator!"

He went on, listing the names of bloody and indecisive battles and describing the number of men killed in each.

"What would these men have done with their lives had they not been sent like sheep to the slaughter? What does King Lincoln have to say to their wives and children?"

Vallandigham had found his rhythm, and his speech went on for more than an hour. At every denouncement of Lincoln, the crowd cheered and waved their signs. At every mention of General Grant or General Sherman, the crowd hissed.

He knew he would be giving speech after speech until Election Day. His campaign to bring the Lincoln administration crashing to the ground was off to an excellent start. If all went well, Vallandigham was confident that the Democrats would be victorious in the upcoming elections. If the Democrats won, so would Clement Vallandigham.

*　　　　*　　　　*　　　　*　　　　*

July 11, Afternoon

Johnston and Mackall stood on the large and elegant porch, complete with columns in the Greek revival style, of the very fine house owned by a man named Dexter Niles. They had appropriated it as the headquarters of the Army of Tennessee. Like so many other civilians, Mr. Niles had fled before the advancing Yankees. Johnston hoped the man did not mind having his house commandeered for military use. He had given strict orders that none of the furniture or ornamentation be disturbed and that care be taken not to damage anything unnecessarily. Had he known that Mr. Niles was a Yankee from Boston who had moved south only to pursue a career as a slave-trader, Johnston might not have bothered being so considerate. He considered slave-traders to be at the lowest rung of society.

The house was a few miles north of Atlanta, roughly midway between the city and the Chattahoochee River. From somewhere off to the north, several miles away, an immense pillar of dark smoke was rising into the sky.

"What's that?" Mackall asked.

"Roswell," Johnston answered without emotion. Roswell was a small town on the riverbank near where Sherman's men had first crossed the Chattahoochee.

"The Yankees are burning it?"

"So it would seem. There were a couple of textile mills there, making uniforms for the army. It seems that makes the town fair game as far as the Yankees are concerned."

"Bastards," Mackall growled. "They are destroying the livelihoods of innocent civilians. Honorable men do not make war on helpless women and children."

"Truth, indeed," Johnston replied. "But we shall have our revenge soon enough."

"Oh?" Mackall said, intrigued.

Johnston merely nodded and turned back into the house, leaving Mackall with a perplexed look on his face. There was a sizable central hall with a large dining room off to the left and a parlor room off to the right. In both rooms, staff officers puzzled over tables strewn with maps and reports. Upstairs were three bedrooms. One had been designated for the officers, one had been set aside as Johnston's private office and the third as his own living quarters. He strode up the steps and soon was sitting down at his desk.

He looked down at the pile of reports. The last few days had been relatively uneventful. Sherman was steadily crossing his army to the south side of the Chattahoochee, while fortifying the opposite bank at any point where the Confederates might be tempted to cross back to the north side. Wheeler's cavalry reports indicated that the Yankee infantry was not yet on the move. Johnston felt certain that Sherman wouldn't begin his maneuvers against Atlanta until his whole force was across the river.

Enemy cavalry were on the prowl, though. Wheeler reported large units of Union horsemen probing eastwards toward the railroad linking Atlanta to Augusta. Now that the two armies were beyond the geographical barrier of the Chattahoochee, the Union cavalry could range far and wide. Although Sherman's mounted arm had been relatively ineffective during the campaign thus far, they posed a threat that Johnston couldn't afford to ignore.

The thought occurred to Johnston that a Yankee cavalry raid might be mounted toward the gigantic prison camp at Andersonville, a hundred miles south of Atlanta. If a few regiments of Yankee horsemen set off for Andersonville, they could reach it in a few days, perhaps arriving before Wheeler's men would have a chance to catch up with them. Tens of thousands of Yankee captives were imprisoned there. If liberated, they might conceivably try to head north and link up with Sherman or head south to the Union base at Fort Pickens on the Florida coast. While doing so, they would likely ravage the country in a desperate bid to avoid starvation. Such a situation would bring chaos and devastation across southwestern Georgia, which had thus far avoided the ravages of war.

Johnston considered this very unlikely, but it was not a matter that could be ignored entirely. He wrote a quick telegram to the President, suggesting that the prisoners be moved elsewhere. Handing it to an aide to transit to Richmond, Johnston gave the matter no further thought.

He spent the next half hour dealing with various administrative issues, wrote a note to the governor of Georgia to urge speed in calling up the militia, and after much effort finally looked down at a desk clear of annoying paperwork.

It was time.

"Send for General Mackall!" he shouted to the guard posted outside the door. A few minutes later, the door opened and the chief-of-staff appeared.

"Yes, sir?"

"Come in, if you please." He gestured to the chair and Mackall sat down, closing the door behind him. "Can anyone on the other side of the door hear what is being discussed in this room?"

Mackall's eyes narrowed. "Not if we keep our voices down."

"Good, because I am about to tell you something which must be kept in strict confidence."

"General Johnston, I do hope I have not done anything which would cause you to doubt my circumspection."

"No, not at all. I know I am always able to count on you. But what I am about to tell you is much more sensitive than anything I have ever told you and I must emphasize the need for secrecy. Absolutely no one but you and myself can know about it for at least the next few days."

"Of course, sir." His voice betrayed a boyish excitement.

Johnston pointed to a line on the map. Mackall looked down.

"Peachtree Creek." Johnston said simply.

"Yes. What of it?"

"That is where we shall fight, and win, the decisive battle for Atlanta."

Mackall leaned back. "Well, this promises to be an interesting conversation," Mackall said. "Go on."

The army commander did so, running his fingers across the map as he traced out what he was saying. "Sherman will wait until his whole army is across the Chattahoochee River before he moves on Atlanta. I have gotten a good measure of the man during the course of this campaign. I know what he is going to do. When he begins to move, he will send about a third of his force, probably the Army of the Tennessee and the Army of the Ohio, southeast, to cut off our rail link with Augusta and then move against the city from the east."

"That seems plausible enough," Mackall said. "Cutting us off from Augusta would present a serious problem, as it would sever the most direct line of communication and transportation between us and the Carolinas, not to mention Virginia."

"Perhaps, but we must ignore this threat for the time being."

Mackall's eyes widened. "Ignore it?"

"Bear with me while I explain. While the two smaller Yankee armies are moving east of Atlanta, the Army of the Cumberland will march directly south toward Atlanta. Sherman has always relied on

Thomas to do his dirty work while giving his beloved boy McPherson the cushy assignments. He will be using his largest army in an effort to distract us from the threat to the east. They won't realize until it is too late that we are deliberately ignoring their actions east of the city, focusing instead on the Army of the Cumberland."

"I don't understand. If the advance of the Army of the Cumberland is only a diversion, what will we gain by repulsing it?"

"I don't propose to repulse the Army of the Cumberland, General Mackall. I propose to destroy it."

Mackall's eyes widened and his face drew back in confusion. The idea of destroying the Army of the Cumberland seemed absurd. At no point during the war had any commander, North or South, ever succeeded in completely obliterating an opposing army. And the Army of the Cumberland was one of the most formidable military forces on the planet.

"Destroy it?" Mackall asked, stunned.

"Destroy it. Or at least inflict such casualties on it and reduce it to such a state of disorder as to render it unfit for further action. This will be the ruin of Sherman's campaign against Atlanta."

"General, forgive me for being skeptical. How can such a decisive victory be possible?"

"Look here," Johnston said, pointing at the map. "In order for Thomas to present a credible threat to Atlanta, sufficient in Sherman's mind to distract us from the activities of McPherson and Schofield to the east, he has to cross Peachtree Creek."

"Naturally. It's not particularly large, though. Compared to the Chattahoochee, it is a mere rivulet."

"Indeed, but its banks are quite steep. I rode along it for some time just the other day. It reminded me of nothing so much as the moat of a medieval castle."

"Go on," Mackall said, more intrigued with every passing minute.

"When Thomas crosses Peachtree Creek, he will be separated from the other Union armies by several miles and by a substantial geographic barrier. The moment a significantly large portion of the Army of the Cumberland is across, we shall attack. If we time the attack correctly, we will strike the Yankees before they have had time to entrench and while many divisions of the army still remain north of the creek, unable to intervene. Thomas will be caught by surprise, with his back to Peachtree Creek. It will be very difficult for him to retreat and it will be impossible for him to bring his full force to bear. If we succeed, we can utterly wreck the Army of the Cumberland."

"Yes," Mackall said, slowly beginning to nod. "Yes, I begin to see what you are saying. Perhaps it is possible. We will need to execute the attack perfectly, especially in the matter of timing, and have quite a bit of luck. But yes, it could work."

"There's more, William. If our plan is successful, Sherman will find his largest army destroyed or in disarray, with us closer to the crossings of the Chattahoochee than his intact units east of Atlanta. If we can beat Thomas and then advance just a few miles northward, we can cut Sherman off from his supplies and trap him on the south side of the river."

Mackall was silent for several moments, imagining the immense possibilities. "What you are describing to me, General Johnston, is nothing less than a plan that could win the war."

"I believe it to be so, William. And with God's help, we shall succeed."

*　　　　*　　　　*　　　　*　　　　*

July 12, Morning

President Davis could not believe the telegram he was reading.

> *President Davis,*
> *I strongly recommend the distribution of the enemy prisoners, now at Andersonville, immediately.*
> *General Johnston*

He slammed the paper down onto his desk. The simple and straightforward telegram provided nothing in the way of explanation or details. He glanced up at the map. Andersonville wasn't marked, but Davis recalled that it was about a hundred miles south of Atlanta. How could it possibly be under threat by Sherman's army?

Davis didn't like to think about Andersonville. In the prison camp, roughly twenty thousand Union prisoners were contained in an enclosure designed to hold less than half that many. Scores of men were dying every day from starvation and disease. He would have liked to improve conditions for them, but with the South barely able to feed its own troops, what could he do?

His mouth turned down into a scowl when he recalled that Confederate troops in Union prison camps were living in equally miserable conditions and dying in roughly equal numbers, despite the North having an enormous surplus of food and an outstanding transportation system. That fact did not change anything about Andersonville, of course, but it helped ease his mind somewhat.

He shook his head, trying to focus on the matter at hand. If Johnston thought that the prison camp at Andersonville was under threat, Davis could only conclude that the commander of the Army of Tennessee was planning yet another retreat. If that were true, it could only mean that Davis's worst fear was about to be realized. Johnston was about to give up Atlanta without a fight.

Davis stood up, stretching his legs. He stared at the military map for some time, momentarily relishing the site of a red pin marking Jubal Early's small army of fifteen thousand men outside Washington City, perhaps lobbing artillery shells at the White House itself. He didn't think that Early could actually capture the Federal capital. Most likely, he would soon have to retreat at the approach of Union reinforcements. But the image of a Confederate force harassing Washington City would certainly help discredit Lincoln and hurt his chances of reelection.

Even better, by forcing Grant to send reinforcements northward, the pressure on Lee at Petersburg had been considerably reduced. At the same time, Southern forces in the Trans-Mississippi and on the Atlantic seaboard continued to maintain their positions.

Everywhere but in Georgia, the Confederate armies were either holding their own or bringing the fight to the enemy. Davis saw no reason that they couldn't continue to do so. If events continued along this path, Lincoln would be kicked out of office in the fall and the incoming Democratic administration would call a cease-fire and open negotiations with the South. If a cease-fire went into effect, the war was as good as won. Political reality dictated that the fighting, once stopped, could not possibly be resumed.

However, if Atlanta fell to Sherman, all of this would fade away like a dream in the morning. If Johnston abandoned the city, the Confederacy was doomed.

If he did decide to replace Johnston, Davis would then have to select his successor. It could only be Hardee or Hood. Hardee seemed like the obvious choice, but he had turned down the position before and Davis felt that this indicated a lack of self-confidence. Hood was nothing if not self-confident, but Davis was uncertain as to his other qualifications.

He needed advice. He took out writing materials from the desk drawer and began frantically scribbling.

General Lee,

General Johnston has failed and it seems certain he will abandon Atlanta. He recommends evacuation of the prisoners at Andersonville. It seems necessary to remove him from command at once. Who shall replace him? What think you of Hood for the post?

President Davis

"Mr. Harrison!" he yelled. His aide opened the door a moment later.

"Yes, sir?"

Davis held up the paper. "Have this sent by telegraph to General Lee at Petersburg immediately. Please be discreet about it."

Harrison took the paper and left. Davis went back to the administrative minutia of the executive branch. He wrote a note to

Secretary of the Navy Stephen Mallory complaining that blockade runners were not reserving half of their cargo space for government needs, despite a recent law to that effect. He signed a few new commissions for officers and commuted three death sentences for desertion. Upon reading a request from someone in Texas to lead an expedition against Colorado, he threw it in the trash, deeming such nonsense unworthy of his attention.

An hour after Harrison had left with the telegram for Lee, he returned.

"General Lee responded right away, sir." He handed him a copy of the return telegram.

> *President Davis,*
> *I regret the fact stated. It would be undesirable to remove the commander of the Army of Tennessee in the midst of the campaign. We may lose Atlanta and the army, too. But I know nothing of the necessity, being occupied with events on my own front.*
> *Hood is a bold fighter. I am doubtful as to whether he possesses the other qualities necessary to lead an army.*
> *General Robert E. Lee*

Davis read it over a few times. It was not the ringing endorsement for which he had been hoping. Quietly, he folded it up and put it in the drawer under his desk. He would have to think very hard on the matter, but knew he had little time.

*　　　　*　　　　*　　　　*　　　　*

July 13, Noon

"Mr. President," Stanton said in a scolding voice. "I really must take issue with your behavior at Fort Stevens yesterday. You were very lucky to have emerged unscathed."

"I was unaware that the purview of the Secretary of War includes acting as mother to the President," Lincoln said with a boyish grin.

"This is no laughing matter, Mr. President. To wander around a fort that is under attack, merely to satisfy your own curiosity, is irresponsible in the extreme. Think of the consequences to the country if anything had happened to you!"

Lincoln simply smiled and shook his head, reading the latest telegram. Jubal Early's Confederate raiders, apparently lacking the strength to mount a serious attack, had contented themselves with firing a few artillery shells into the city and skirmishing with the defenders of Fort Stevens. Now they were withdrawing back to Virginia. Lincoln had given orders that the raiding force be ruthlessly pursued and destroyed.

"Well," Stanton said. "It is no matter now that the rebels are gone. But if another such raid occurs, Mr. President, you will remain in the White House, even if I have to post guards to keep you there!"

"Is it true that you ordered a ship on the Potomac kept at readiness to evacuate me in the event that Early had been able to enter the city?"

"I felt it was a worthwhile precaution, Mr. President."

Lincoln waved his hands dismissively. "I never felt the capital was in much danger, Edwin. Early's ragged and hungry band of men could not have penetrated the defenses of Washington once the reinforcements sent by Grant arrived."

"Those reinforcements arrived only in the nick of time, Mr. President. Besides which, those ragged and hungry men you describe once marched with Stonewall Jackson. Underestimating such men, rebels and slaveholders though they may be, is ill-advised."

Lincoln nodded, somewhat sobered. Glancing down at his desk, his eyes narrowed when he saw a letter there he had not previously noticed. He picked it up and quickly scanned it. As he did so, his face furrowed and he let out a deep sigh.

"What is it?" Stanton asked.

"A letter from Raymond," Lincoln replied. Henry Raymond, a prominent New York politician who had founded the *New York Times*, was the Chairman of the Republican National Committee. As such, he was effectively the man in charge of the overall Republican electoral campaign.

"Judging by the look on your face, the news he sends is not good."

"No," Lincoln said simply. "Vallandigham is raising hell in New York City. He spoke to a very large crowd just a few days ago and apparently caused quite a ruckus."

"I'm sorry to say that it is likely to get worse before it gets better, Mr. President."

"Probably," Lincoln agreed. "And I believe the rebel raid on Washington City, though it may have only been a diversion from a military point of view, will lead to more political trouble. To have a sizable Confederate force arrive on the outskirts of Washington is embarrassing, to say the least."

"I'll say," Stanton replied. "Vallandigham will make a lot of hay out of it in his upcoming speeches. Editors like Manton Marble and others will fill their editorial columns to the brink with exaggerations and outright lies about what happened."

"I fear that any advantage our reelection campaign has garnered by the successful crossing of the Chattahoochee River will be more than offset by the embarrassment caused by Early and his raiders."

"Respectfully, Mr. President, I do not believe that any event less momentous than the capture of Richmond or Atlanta will have much impact on the present political situation. The tide is quite frankly running strongly against us."

Lincoln nodded soberly. "I agree. Every day I receive letters from Republican leaders in every Northern state and they are becoming increasingly pessimistic. Our friends in New York seem to have almost given up hope of keeping their state out of the Democratic column in November. Pennsylvania, sadly, seems to be moving in the same direction and even my own state of Illinois is becoming wobbly."

Stanton shook his head. "I cannot imagine that buffoon McClellan occupying the White House. I can still picture him when he commanded the Army of the Potomac, strutting around as if he were Napoleon. If he becomes President, I see nothing but national disaster in our future."

"You're not likely to be wrong there," Lincoln said. "McClellan may claim that if he were elected President he would carry on the war until victory is won. But anyone who believes him ignores, willfully or otherwise, some basic political facts."

"Such as?" Stanton asked.

"Well, McClellan will not have been able to win without the support of Vallandigham and his coterie of Copperheads, the very ones inflaming the people against me in the newspapers. Having earned their chips during the campaign, they will insist on cashing them in once McClellan enters the White House. The price of their support will be a cease-fire and an opening of negotiations with the rebels. There they will humbly ask that the rebels rejoin the Union, dangling a carrot in front of them by promising never to interfere with slavery."

"The rebels would immediately reject such terms," Stanton said with conviction. "Jefferson Davis would happily be drowned in a pool of his own blood before agreeing to return to the Union, slavery or no slavery."

"You know that and I know that, but far too many Democrats have deluded themselves into thinking otherwise. Imagine it for a moment. A cease-fire goes into effect, negotiations are opened, and Davis rejects McClellan's terms. What then? Do you think that the political will would exist for hostilities to be resumed? Having once again tasted peace, do you think the people would accept a return to bloody war?"

"Certainly not, especially because Republicans and abolitionists would be unwilling to fight under McClellan's banner in any event. If the destruction of slavery is no longer to be a condition of peace with the South, the abolitionists would no longer see the war as worth fighting. New England would, for all practical purposes, drop out of the war altogether."

"Precisely, Edwin." The President shook his head. "The more I think about it, the worse it gets. If we do not capture Atlanta by the fall, I don't see how we can win the election. And if we don't win the election, I do not see how the Union can be saved."

*   *   *   *   *

"All out for Atlanta!"

Bragg stepped off the train into the enormous red-brick train depot known simply as the Car Shed, where three different railroads met in the center of Atlanta. Although under the shade of the immense roof, the heat was almost unbearable. He glanced around for a moment, wanting to cup his hands over his ears to shut out all the shouting and confusion. Everywhere there were crowds of people, most clutching carpetbags or other small pieces of luggage. All were frantically trying to board any train which might take them out of the city. Most of them had fearful expressions on their faces, terrified by the approach of Sherman and his Yankee hordes.

After seeing to his baggage, he walked to the telegraph office of the Car Shed, still clutching the carpetbag containing the reports and letters from Johnston, Hood, and Wheeler. As he walked through the door, the telegraph operator rose to attention at the sight of a man in a lieutenant general's uniform. Bragg sensed the immense surprise and discomfort when the man recognized his face.

"General Bragg, sir! Welcome to Atlanta."

"Thank you," Bragg said without warmth. "I require you to send a telegraph to the War Department in Richmond. It must be done immediately."

"Certainly, sir. You can write it, or dictate it to me, as you please."

He took the offered piece of paper and jotted out his message.

> *President Davis,*
> *I have arrived in Atlanta. Indications seem to favor the entire evacuation of the city. I shall proceed at once to General Johnston's headquarters and make myself fully acquainted with the situation.*
> *General Bragg*

A few minutes later, Bragg climbed into a buggy which Johnston had sent for him and was on his way northwards toward Johnston's headquarters. Judging from what he had seen at the Car Shed, he was not surprised to find that the streets were nearly deserted. Every civilian with an ounce of sense had gotten out while the getting had been good. No doubt they were adding to the flood of refugees from cities like Nashville, Memphis, and New Orleans who now crowded into Richmond, Mobile, and other cities that still remained in Confederate hands.

The smell of the Georgia air suddenly and powerfully reminded him of the time he had spent in command of the Army of

Tennessee, from the early summer of 1862 to the fall of 1863. During that time, he had led it in bitter fighting in Kentucky, Tennessee and northern Georgia. He immediately pushed the memories from his mind. Whatever else he was, Braxton Bragg was not a sentimental man.

After an hour's ride, during which he said not a word to the driver, the buggy pulled in front of the Niles House. Having notified Johnston by telegraph that he would be coming, he knew his arrival would not be a surprise. Nevertheless, he didn't expect his welcome to be cordial.

Mackall was waiting for him at the door.

"General Bragg, sir," he said as the former commander of the army approached.

"General Mackall." The two exchanged professional and polite salutes, then shook hands briefly. Neither smiled.

For six months, Mackall had served as Bragg's chief-of-staff during the last phase of Bragg's command of the Army of Tennessee. He considered Mackall competent enough, though the two men had never warmed to one another personally. Mackall had requested a transfer following the Battle of Chickamauga, disillusioned by Bragg's failure to pursue the defeated Union army. But the man had resumed his duties as chief-of-staff of the Army of Tennessee when Johnston had taken command. As far as Bragg was concerned, this reflected a belief that Johnston was a better commander than Bragg. Such a personal insult could not be tolerated.

Bragg decided in that moment that, as soon as he had taken down Johnston, he would move against Mackall. If Bragg had anything to say about it, Mackall would finish his service as the commandant of the smallest prisoner-of-war camp that could be found in some godforsaken backwater of the war.

"General Johnston has been expecting you, sir. If you will follow me, please."

They entered the Niles House. The rooms on each side of the central hall were filled with the humming that a large collection of military staff officers always made as they pursued their various, arcane administrative duties. Bragg remembered the sound well, though he couldn't help but notice that the staff officers seemed happier and more eager in their duties than they had during his tenure as commander. Bragg and Mackall walked up the stairs. A few moments later, Mackall knocked softly on the door to Johnston's private office and opened it.

"General Bragg has arrived, sir."

"Good," Johnston's voice said from within the room. "Please send him in. And please make sure that we are not disturbed except in a case of necessity."

Bragg nodded politely to Mackall and stepped inside. Johnston stood from behind his table, and the routine exchange of salutes and handshakes took place.

"It is good to see you, General Bragg. Please have a seat."

"Thank you."

"Can I get you anything? Coffee, perhaps?"

"No, thank you."

"Very well."

There was an awkward silence for a moment. While he struggled to keep an impassive expression, Bragg seethed inside as he looked across the table at Johnston. Bragg had met Johnston countless times before, but somehow it seemed as if he were now seeing him for the first time. This was the man who had replaced him? This was the man who everyone said was the better general? This was the man who had rebuilt the army that Bragg had allegedly wrecked? He seemed like nothing so much as an vain and overblown peacock.

On nearly half a dozen occasions during Bragg's tenure as commander of the Army of Tennessee, a cartel of corps and division commanders had petitioned President Davis to replace him with Johnston. On each of those occasions, Johnston had defended him. Bragg did not feel the least bit grateful. Quite the opposite, in fact. Braxton Bragg was not the sort of man who needed others to do favors for him.

Johnston nodded toward Bragg, inviting him to begin.

Bragg obliged. "General Johnston, as you know, the President has asked me to come to Atlanta to gain a firsthand account of the situation here. I do hope I am not taking up any of your time unnecessarily."

"Not at all. It is obviously important for the President to be as well-informed as possible."

Bragg nodded. "Of course. Now, can you summarize the general military situation at the moment?"

Johnston gestured to the map on the desk. "You'll have had my telegrams describing the crossing of the Union forces onto the south bank of the river?" Bragg nodded and Johnston continued. "Not much has happened today, or for the past few days, for that matter. Our army is all on the south side of the Chattahoochee. Sherman has been spending the past several days crossing his entire force over the river, miles north of our present position, and building up his supplies."

"I wouldn't expect him to remain idle for long. Is there any indication on when he will begin to move on the city?"

"Nothing specific, but it must happen within the next few days."

"And you plan to oppose his movement, yes?"

"Of course I plan to oppose him." Johnston's tone suggested that this should have gone without saying.

Another awkward silence followed. "And what is the condition of the army?" Bragg asked.

"Good, very good. Morale among the troops remains quite high. There has been very little straggling. We continue to field about fifty-five thousand men, and every unit is in generally good condition. Considering the arduous campaign in which we have been engaged since the beginning of May, the strength of our force is much higher, in numbers, morale, and general well-being, than we had any reasonable right to expect."

"Well, that's good news," Bragg offered. "And what do you anticipate will be Sherman's next move?"

"I believe he will send the Army of the Cumberland, perhaps sixty thousand men, directly south toward the city. At the same time, he will send the Army of the Tennessee and the Army of the Ohio, totaling perhaps forty thousand men, southeast to attempt to cut our rail connections with Augusta."

Bragg's eyebrows went up. "If they cut your rail links to the east, it could jeopardize our lines of transportation and communication between Georgia and the eastern portion of the Confederacy."

"Perhaps. But, of course, we shall have a bloody battle before such a thing is likely to happen."

Bragg's face betrayed nothing. But inwardly he scowled at the words. He didn't want to hear Johnston say such things, for it did not suit his purposes. The commander of the Army of Tennessee sat with an expectant look on his face, awaiting Bragg's next question.

Bragg removed his glasses and rubbed his sinuses. "General Johnston," he said slowly. "I apologize, but I find myself very much exhausted from my long journey from Richmond. Would it be possible for us to resume this conversation tomorrow morning, after I have had a chance to rest?"

Johnston's eyes narrowed slightly in surprise, but he nodded. "Yes, that would be fine. There is much I wish to tell you, but I suppose it can wait until tomorrow."

"And perhaps we might be able to assemble your corps commanders as well?"

"I see no reason why not, assuming that there is no sudden emergency."

Bragg smiled and stood. "Very well. I shall return at eight tomorrow morning."

"I look forward to it."

The two men rose and exchanged salutes. Without another word, Bragg turned and left the room. Johnston watched him go, a worried look on his face.

July 13, Afternoon

"So, you'd give your vote to Private Williams?" Collett asked.

McFadden nodded. "Best shot in my company. I've seen him take down Yankee skirmishers from four or five hundred yards. Can't speak to his being the best shot in the whole regiment, though. You'd have to talk to the other sergeants."

"I will, I will," Collett said tiredly.

"I'd hate to lose Williams, though. Not only is he the best shot in the Lone Star Rifles, but he's often a calming influence on the other men. There is a dynamic at work with such a group, you know. I'd worry about my men getting rowdier."

"I know. But orders are orders. One man from the regiment is joining the sharpshooter company. We have to choose the best man."

McFadden nodded. It wasn't an abstract question in his mind. He went back to the innumerable times the 7th Texas had been subjected to ferocious Union artillery fire, with Southern guns nowhere to be seen. At such times, Cleburne's sharpshooters would come jogging up with their deadly Whitworth rifles and, within minutes, silence the offending battery by picking off the gun crews at an astonishing distance. It really was remarkable what the men could do with those weapons and it had probably saved all of their lives on more than one occasion.

Collett stood up from his tiny desk, threw the tent flap back and strode out into the sunlight. McFadden followed. Around him, the companies of the 7th Texas were cooking their rations. They had actually received some meat that morning, rather than the usual issue of simple cornmeal, and the smell of cooking pork delighted McFadden's senses. He made a mental note to hurry back to the encampment of the Lone Star Rifles as soon as his business with the captain was completed. Otherwise, Private Pearson was likely to sneak off with a chunk of McFadden's lunch.

A traffic jam was unfolding along the crude road that had been hacked through the woods near the camps of Granbury's Texas Brigade. A wagon train had halted on account of protesting mules, who refused to move despite all the pulling and cursing of the teamsters. Behind them, an impatient limbered-up artillery battery was trying to get by, the angry shouts of the gunners adding to the cacophony. The nearby Texas infantry found the proceedings hilarious and were shouting whatever jokes they could think of at the men and animals.

"My men are enjoying their meat, Captain. Any chance we could get some more tomorrow?"

"Probably not," Collett said. "Getting closer to Atlanta has eased the supply situation a bit. So I'm told, anyway. But the commissary people are sitting tight on the meat. Rumor is that Uncle Joe is preparing to withstand a siege of Atlanta and wants to conserve the food as much as he can."

"So it's back to cornmeal tomorrow?" McFadden did not find this a pleasant prospect at all.

"Cornmeal it is, I'm sorry to say. But that's better than the blue beef, don't you think?"

McFadden's stomach nearly revolted at the memory of the spoiled gunk he and the men had been forced to eat during December and early January, when the supply system of the Army of Tennessee had nearly broken down completely. It had been so rancid that many men had been willing to go hungry rather than eat it. When Johnston had assumed command of the army, one of his earliest priorities had been to improve the supply of food for the men. The blue beef had soon vanished, replaced by decent rations, and for that the men of the army had been deeply grateful to Johnston.

"Who's on the picket line today, Captain?" McFadden asked. Their regiment had done picket duty the day before, so hopefully they might have some time behind the line.

"The 10th," Collett replied. "The 6th/15th will be out there tomorrow, though. Still, the Yankees could come at any time. Make sure your men are ready."

"They will be."

Collett sighed and looked away to the north, though nothing could be seen through the dense forest. "Sherman's been quiet lately. I'm betting he'll move soon. We could see action at any time."

McFadden nodded. The brief interlude since crossing the Chattahoochee had been welcome, and had allowed the men some time to rest and refit, but it was obviously going to come to an end soon. Old soldiers like McFadden and Collett could sense it, just as a farmer could sense a gathering storm.

Cleburne's division, along with all the units of Hardee's corps, was deployed in a line running from west to east a few miles north of Atlanta. As far as McFadden and his comrades knew, Stewart's corps was off to the west and Cheatham's corps was off to the east, leaving Hardee's men in the center. When Sherman and his Yankees finally made their big push on the city, they had no doubt that they would be in the thick of the fight.

"Bragg's in town," Collett said. "Or so rumor has it."

"That's too bad, sir," McFadden replied. There was no love lost between Braxton Bragg and the rank-and-file of the 7th Texas Infantry. "What is he doing here?"

"Nobody knows. Nothing good, I reckon."

McFadden sneered. "Bragg's as cold a bastard as they come. Remember the day he was removed from command? The men celebrated deep into the night."

"I remember," Collett replied. "If you treat the men under your command like scum, why should you expect them to fight for you? I lay the blame for the fiasco at Missionary Ridge right at Bragg's door, sure as hell."

McFadden grunted agreement. As far as the men of the 7th Texas were concerned, to say nothing of the rest of the army, Braxton Bragg had driven them like a teamster drove cattle rather than led them like a commander leading soldiers. Joseph Johnston was an infinitely better man.

A rider approached, whom McFadden took to be a messenger. He reined in before them and saluted.

"Captain Collett?" he asked.

"I am," Collett said, returning the salute.

"Message for you, sir." The man handed Collett a folded piece of paper and, without another word, kicked his horse back into a trot and disappeared down the road.

Collett unfolded the letter and began reading. For some reason, he glanced up at McFadden with a mischievous smile on his face.

"From General Granbury," he said. "Well, this is certainly interesting."

"What is it?"

"It's about you, actually."

"Me?" McFadden had no clue why his brigade commander would be sending his regimental commander a message about him. He was just a sergeant, after all. He suddenly worried that he was somehow in trouble and tried to think of anything he might have done which could have earned the displeasure of the brigade commander. Nothing came to mind.

"Remember that fellow you saved from the river the other day? Him and his daughter?"

"Of course." McFadden could not have forgotten Annie Turnbow even if he had tried. Part of him had wanted to forget, for useless thoughts about beautiful women had no place in the midst of a war. Still, another part of him had held on to the memory of the final smile she had cast at him as she had left.

"Well, apparently this Turnbow fellow wishes to thank you for rescuing him and his daughter by inviting you to dinner at his home in Atlanta. He did not know exactly how to reach you, so he contacted General Granbury."

"I'm sorry?" McFadden said, stunned. What on earth could Robert Turnbow want with him? After two months in the trenches, fighting and marching across practically all of northern Georgia, the idea of sitting down to a dinner in a civilian home in Atlanta seemed ludicrous.

"I say, this fellow's name is Robert Turnbow?"

"Yes, I believe so," McFadden said. He was trying to process the import of the message.

"You're aware that he's one of the wealthiest men in Georgia, aren't you? Hell, half the cannons in the Army of Tennessee were probably made in his foundry." Collett smiled and smacked McFadden's shoulder. "Looks like you made friends with the right fellow!"

"I'm not sure what to say about this, sir. Obviously, there is no way I can go."

Collett looked at him quietly for a long moment, studying him carefully. McFadden found this somewhat unsettling. He knew how distant he kept himself from other people, but Collett surely knew him better than anyone else. What was going through the man's mind?

"No, you can go."

McFadden's face betrayed his confusion. "But you just said that the Yankees could move forward at any time. My place is with my company."

"We're close enough to Atlanta that it should be all right. For all we know, Sherman won't make his move for another week or so. You can be in Atlanta inside of two hours. You can borrow one of the horses. Leave in the morning, have dinner, and then come back. Shouldn't be a problem."

Suddenly, the full implication of the message began to weigh on McFadden. The idea of sitting down to an elegant dinner in the home of a wealthy man filled him with an anxiety greater than he had ever felt when faced with a line of Yankee muskets. He was a rough man from the Texas frontier. He was a mere sergeant, not an officer. Anyone else sitting at the table would dismiss him as a country bumpkin, especially the lovely Annie.

"My uniform is a disgrace."

"You can borrow my dress uniform. You and I have about the same build, after all."

"I can't go, sir."

"You can and you will. After all, McFadden, if you decline the invitation, you will be ignoring the wishes of the brigade commander."

"Please, sir, I don't wish to go."

"Sorry, James. You're going." The strong words were belied by the smile on Collett's face.

July 13, Evening

Hood frowned as he pondered the matter before him. As near as he could tell, the message had something to do with which road a wagon train was to take in order to deliver rations to his men. Hood knew little and cared less about such administrative matters. He set the paper aside, confident that some staff officer would deal with it in good time. Meanwhile, he had more important things on his mind.

He returned his attention back to the letter he was writing to Sally Preston. On the whole, his words seemed wholly inadequate. He certainly did not fancy himself a Shakespeare or a Byron, but surely he could do better than the drivel he had thus far accumulated on the page. He took up the paper, crumbled it into a fist-size mass, and contemptuously threw it away. It was the third time he had done so over the past hour.

He thought back to the day he had first set eyes on Sally Preston, back in March of 1863. He had been a full-formed man then, strong and powerful, commanding the division widely considered to be the best in General Lee's army. Hood and his men had been moving through Richmond on their way to rejoin the Army of Northern Virginia after having been on detached duty. The march through the city from one train depot to another had become an impromptu parade, with thousands of Richmond residents lining the streets to cheer the brave men of Hood's division.

Riding at the head of the column, Hood had recognized the familiar face of Mary Chesnut among the crowd and had naturally trotted over to say hello. When he had seen the young, beautiful Southern belle standing next to Mrs. Chesnut, he had become immediately transfixed. Some women manifested female sensuality by their very being; Sally Preston was certainly one of these. Hood had instantly decided that he had to have her and since that day his obsession with her had only increased.

The courtship had not been smooth, to say the least. Sally at first declined Hood's calls at her home. Even after the two of them began to spend time together, Sally insisted on keeping Hood at arm's length, though she never actually rejected him. Sally's parents considered Hood no better than a bumpkin and had made it clear that they had no intention of allowing her to marry an unsophisticated provincial from Texas. At every awkward proposal of marriage, Sally had managed to evade giving a plain answer, employing her infinite reserves of coyness.

Following the Battle of Gettysburg, when his division was hurriedly moving by rail to join the Army of Tennessee prior to the Battle of Chickamauga, Hood had seen Sally again. Upon receiving yet another evasive reply to a proposal of marriage, Hood had decided to be as bold off the field as he was on it. He simply declared to Richmond society that he and Sally were engaged. Horrified, she had insisted that they were not. The gossip mongers of the Richmond evening party circuit had had a field day.

It had not been until the next winter in the capital, while Hood was recovering from the loss of his leg and was being lionized by Richmond society as a wounded knight, that a clear engagement between the two had finally been established. Some wagging tongues said that Sally had only surrendered out of pity for the shattered warrior.

Now, six months later, the marriage still had yet to take place and Hood continued to feel he was on shaky ground. Sally's parents continued to firmly oppose the match and rumors had reached Hood of Sally's continued flirtations with other men.

As these thoughts floated through his mind, Hood's face tightened. He was consumed by a determination to achieve something which would finally silence Sally's parents and convince Sally to give herself completely and utterly to him. Before he could do that, he had to climb above the rank of a mere corps commander. Joseph Johnston was an obstacle that had to be removed.

A courier arrived. It was a man Hood did not recognize, and he was wearing civilian clothes. These unusual circumstances alone were sufficient to make Hood pay special attention to the message he was handed.

> *General Hood,*
> *I have arrived in Atlanta and wish earnestly to meet with you as soon as possible. It goes without saying that absolute discretion must be observed. Please inform me of the best time and place at which you and I may meet.*
> *General Bragg*

Hood's heart suddenly raced. He had to resist the temptation to reach for his laudanum. Below the message was scrawled the name of the hotel in Atlanta where Bragg was staying. Immediately, Hood sent one of his aides with a message to Bragg, telling him that he would be welcome at his corps headquarters at any time.

Johnston was in trouble; that much was clear. It had been obvious for weeks. Jefferson Davis had hated Johnston for years. The long retreat from Dalton to the outskirts of Atlanta had surely only stoked the fire of the President's discontent. Now that the rumors of Bragg's arrival had been proven true, it could only mean that the President was on the verge of removing Johnston from command of the army.

Obviously, the man who would replace Johnston could only be Hardee or Hood himself. Stewart, the third corps commander, had only just been promoted and was therefore not likely to be considered.

Nor were there any prominent generals from outside the Army of Tennessee who could be called upon for the job. Longstreet was still recovering from the severe wound he received in the Battle of the Wilderness, Kirby Smith was far away in the Trans-Mississippi, and Robert E. Lee was obviously needed with his own army.

The decisive battle for Atlanta was likely to be fought within a matter of days. Hardee and Hood had to be the only conceivable choices.

Hood knew that Bragg detested Hardee, who had wasted no effort in maligning him during Bragg's tenure as army commander. If Bragg was to be the decisive voice in making the decision, as seemed likely because of his presence in the city, Hood figured his chances of gaining the command were excellent.

A sudden rush of excitement filled him and this time he did reach for the laudanum. After all, since Bragg could be expected to arrive at his corps headquarters at any moment, Hood would need to appear as calm and collected as possible.

He looked down at the letter he was writing to Sally, and decided to put it away for the time being. It seemed better by far to wait to write her until the next day, when his situation might be much more clear. And much more to Sally's liking.

A few hours passed as the curtain of night descended over the Georgia countryside. Hood's expected visitor finally arrived.

"General Bragg is here to see you, sir."

"Very well. Send him in." Hood took a deep breath as Bragg pulled back the flap of the tent and stepped inside. The interior was illuminated with the soft yellowish glow of a single lantern. Although the sun had set hours before, the air was still humid and hot.

Outside, the only sound was the crackling of the campfire. Hood had orders his staff officers to keep people a reasonable distance away from the tent, so as to prevent anyone from overhearing what transpired.

"General Bragg, it is very good to see you again. How are things in Richmond?" He had considered offering Bragg whiskey, but decided against it as he wanted to present as serious and professional an appearance as possible.

"Well enough, but I fear I don't have time for pleasantries. The President has asked me to inspect the Army of Tennessee and report to him on the military situation here in Georgia. The situation is grave and I believe it necessary for you and I to be as open and frank with one another as possible."

"You will get no argument from me, General."

"Good. Let us begin then. The President is concerned that General Johnston lacks the spirit to take the offensive and that he may, in fact, have no plan at all for defending Atlanta. What is your view? Again, I ask you to speak frankly."

Hood thought for just a moment before replying. "General Bragg, I am sad to say that the President is quite right. General Johnston has no spirit for the attack. Over the past few months, we have had many chances to attack the enemy when they have divided their forces or left their flanks open. However, on each occasion, Johnston failed to take advantage of the situation. Had a more aggressive general been at the head of this army, I believe we would have defeated Sherman long ago."

"And how have the other officers of the army reacted to this?"

"Me and General Wheeler have constantly told General Johnston to take the offensive against the Yankees. General Stewart, too. General Hardee, on the other hand, has always gone along with Johnston's strategy of avoiding a fight."

What remained of Hood's conscience tugged at him. He knew he was telling an out-and-out lie. He also knew that it would not redound to his credit as an honorable Southern gentleman if it ever became known. He thought momentarily of Sally Preston's voluptuous figure, and knew that achieving his objective was well worth the cost.

Bragg nodded. "I see. And how would you view the prospects of success if our army were to take the offensive?"

"The prospects of success? I think they'd be excellent. Sherman is a poor general. He makes many mistakes. Were we to attack, I believe it would be easy to take him by surprise and catch him at a disadvantage. Moreover, returning to the offensive would immediately revive the spirit of the men."

"In what way?" Bragg was looking at him in much the same way as a professor looks at a student under examination.

"If the men fight only when they are protected by strong entrenchments, it saps their natural offensive spirit. Our men are Southerners, and naturally aggressive. They want to come to grips with the invader and beat him fair and square in an open field fight."

Bragg nodded and waved for Hood to continue.

"I feel it worth pointing out that all the tactical successes we have gained in the campaign to date have been entirely defensive in nature. After achieving any success, such as at Kennesaw Mountain, there has been no counter attack. The enemy has been entirely left alone."

Bragg nodded again. "Go on."

"I contrast this to the men I commanded when I served under General Lee in the Army of Northern Virginia. At Gaine's Mill, for example, I ordered my brigade to fix their bayonets and charge the enemy directly with unloaded rifles. We broke through and won a decisive victory. And, as you will recall, when I served under your command last fall, I broke the enemy line at Chickamauga using the same tactic."

"I remember it well," Bragg said, smiling thinly for the first time. "And how has General Johnston responded to your advocacy of taking the offensive?"

"I have so often urged that we attack that I think both Johnston and Hardee have come to regard me as reckless. Whenever Wheeler and I have urged an attack, Johnston and Hardee have decided to retreat. Every time, without a single exception."

Bragg frowned. "I'd like to move on to another subject. Johnston, in messages to the President and myself, has constantly requested that General Forrest be sent to attack Sherman's supply lines, claiming that the cavalry of the Army of Tennessee is needed here. What are your views on that subject?"

"General Bragg, I know for a fact that General Wheeler has urged Johnston to allow him to take five thousand troopers and raid Sherman's railroads. Johnston has always refused permission. As a result, we have thousands of cavalrymen sitting idly around our camps for want of a mission. The Yankee cavalry are ineffective and disorganized. They pose no threat to us. I say quite firmly that there is nothing holding us back from such a raid except General Johnston's lack of will."

"That is a strong statement, General Hood."

"You may ask General Wheeler himself, if you like."

"I believe I shall do that. Now, before I leave, let me ask you a very basic question. What do you think should now be the strategy for the Army of Tennessee?"

Hood took a deep breath. What he said in response to this question could very well determine the future of his career. But he felt he knew exactly what Bragg wanted to hear.

"General Bragg, we must abandon this strategy of passive defense. Only offensive action will suffice to save Atlanta. If we continue as we have done, Sherman will inevitably cut all our rail communications and drive us out of the city. We must strike the enemy a hard and decisive blow, even if we have to cross back to the north side of the Chattahoochee to do so. I regard it as a great misfortune that we failed to give battle to the enemy far north of our present position."

Bragg nodded. "You'll be happy to know, General Hood, that I fully concur in your assessment of the situation."

"Then please say to the President that I shall continue to do my duty cheerfully and faithfully. I will strive to do what I think is best for our country, as my constant prayer is for its success."

Hood and Bragg both stood, shook hands firmly, and saluted.

"Thank you, General Hood. I shall perhaps speak to you again before I depart."

"I am always at your disposal, General Bragg."

Bragg nodded, turned, and left the tent. Hood was left alone, almost unnerved by the unnatural silence. He sat back down and did not move for several minutes, staring blankly at the light cast by the lantern for a long time.

*　　　　*　　　　*　　　　*　　　　*

July 14, Morning

Cleburne sat in his tent, going over administrative paperwork and trying to complete a report on the number of casualties his division had suffered since the Battle of Kennesaw Mountain. Outside the tent, some of his staff officers were frying bacon and boiling water for coffee.

"General Cleburne!" Lieutenant Hanley called out. "General Hardee is approaching!"

Cleburne stood up and walked outside, just in time to see Hardee rein in near the fire and quickly dismount.

"Morning, Patrick!" he said. "Bacon smells mighty good."

"Will you join us for breakfast?"

"Thank you. That would be lovely."

A few minutes later, the two generals were in Cleburne's tent, downing their hot breakfast of bacon and cornmeal biscuits. The coffee, unfortunately, was barely drinkable. The Union blockade had raised the price of coffee so much that most people now resorted to a brew that combined coffee with cornmeal. It tasted awful, but it was better than drinking water.

"So, all of the corps commanders are to meet at General Johnston's headquarters to speak with General Bragg?" Cleburne asked.

"That's what the message said. Rumor also has it that Bragg visited with Hood and Wheeler last night. I can't imagine Johnston would have given them permission to speak with Bragg privately."

"Has Bragg contacted you since his arrival?" Cleburne said as he chewed another piece of bacon.

Hardee let out a scornful laugh. "No, not even so much as a courtesy note. But that's to be expected, Bragg being Bragg."

"Why do you think Bragg is here, William? Simply to discuss strategy with General Johnston? Seems strange that he would travel all the way out here just to do that."

Hardee shrugged. "Your guess is as good as mine. As for myself, I have little idea what is going on. Johnston rarely consults me, and often it seems to me that Hood is the one doing most of the strategy."

"And you told me that Hood is constantly advocating retreat?"

"Almost always, yes. He advised Johnston to retreat from Cassville, right after he botched that attack. He advised Johnston to retreat from the Chattahoochee lines, which I think could have been held. When he came to our army in March, we thought we were getting an aggressive, fighting general. But if you ask me, Hood has little fight in him."

Cleburne shook his head. "It does seem strange, considering how well he served under Lee as a brigade and division commander."

"I wonder if the loss of his leg and the use of his arm also robbed him of his fighting spirit."

Cleburne nodded, having seen such things happen to other men. Losing a limb took something away from a person beyond their physical appendage. Losing two limbs doubtless took much more.

"William, is it possible that Bragg has come to determine whether or not Johnston should be removed from command?

"Why do you ask?" Hardee replied.

"There are rumors."

Hardee waved his hand. "There are always rumors."

"But do you think it is possible?"

"Anything is possible, Pat. It's certainly no secret that there is no love lost between Johnston and the President. And obviously Johnston has retreated nearly a hundred miles without fighting a decisive battle. If we wake up tomorrow morning to the news that Johnston has been sacked, I would not be too surprised."

Cleburne's eyebrows arched up. "If that happens, you are the obvious choice to take command of the army."

Hardee shrugged. "I am the senior corps commander."

"If Davis offers you the command, would you accept?"

"I suppose I would," Hardee said without much enthusiasm. "In December, it was clear to me that Johnston was better suited to the command than I was, because he was more able to restore the army's morale after the disaster at Missionary Ridge. But if Davis does decide to replace Johnston and offer me the command, I shall accept."

"This army could not have a better commander than you, my friend," Cleburne said with a smile.

"Thank you." He paused a moment. "But, truth be told, I do not expect to be offered the command."

Cleburne's eyes narrowed. "Why not?"

"I think that I lost a lot of credibility with Davis when I turned down his offer to take permanent command back in December. Besides, if Bragg has anything to say about it, I have as much chance of being appointed commander of this army as Abraham Lincoln."

"Then who?"

Hardee said nothing, answering only with a knowing look.

Cleburne understood. "Surely not Hood!"

Hardee shrugged. "If not me, who else could it be?"

Cleburne frowned and shook his head. "Setting aside questions of his fighting spirit, Hood can barely manage the administrative details of a single corps. If Bragg and Davis think that he is qualified to command an entire army, they are deluding themselves."

Hardee smiled grimly. "Well, when it comes to deluding oneself, no one can match the skill of Braxton Bragg."

*   *   *   *   *

Sherman stood on the north bank of the Chattahoochee, flanked by two men in colonel's uniforms, watching with interest as his engineers labored to complete yet another pontoon bridge. Behind him, several regiments of infantry waited impatiently to cross.

"You've done a marvelous job, Colonel Wright," he said to the engineering officer in charge of bridge construction. "But we need to be moving faster."

"Sir, I'm sorry, but we can't go any faster. My men are exhausted. We've thrown up half a dozen bridges in just the last few days. There are limits to human endurance, you know."

Sherman let the last comment go. He might not have under normal circumstances, but he could see how tired Wright was and knew the man had probably not slept for the last forty-eight hours.

"You realize, Colonel, that until our entire army is on the south bank, our forces are split in two. If the rebels decide to attack, they might have a significant advantage. Your bridges could be the only thing that could save us from defeat." Sherman was exaggerating and knew it, for he thought an enemy attack to be unlikely and his men on the south bank were already entrenched. Still, it seemed a good way to spur Wright on.

"We shall do our best, General," Wright said resignedly.

"Good," Sherman said, then turned immediately to the other officer. "Colonel Anderson? The supply wagons?"

"I've got several hundred at the railhead we've established at Marietta. They'll be fully loaded up with food and ammunition by this time tomorrow and on their way to the crossing site."

"They'd better be," Sherman insisted. "I may have the best army in the world, but it can't fight if it doesn't have food and ammunition. I know that getting it all across the river gives you even more problems, but I'm sure you'll figure out a way to solve them."

"Of course, sir."

Sherman closed his eyes for a moment and reflected on the massive effort that went into supplying his army. The products of the vast agricultural and industrial machinery of the North, which dwarfed that of the South by several orders of magnitude, were collected at the great government depots of Louisville and Cincinnati on the Ohio River. From there, they went by train to the enormous supply base that had been established at Nashville, which had fallen to Union forces more than two years before. The mountains of food, ammunition, and other supplies at Nashville were sufficient to supply Sherman's army for at least a few months.

From Nashville, two railroads weaved southeastward to the major Union base at Chattanooga, carrying tons of supplies each and every day. Having two railroads from Nashville to Chattanooga provided a certain amount of redundancy.

But it was the line from Chattanooga to the front line that kept Sherman up at night, for it was dependent upon the rickety and vulnerable single-line track of the Western and Atlantic Railroad. Johnston's men had torn it up thoroughly as they had retreated and the main task of Sherman's engineers had been to repair it as they advanced, mile by mile.

For every hour that Sherman spent figuring out how his army was to march and fight, he had to spend at least six hours figuring out how to keep it fed. If Sherman's railroad lines were cut, his army would begin to starve and the campaign against Atlanta would have to be abandoned. Sherman felt very much like a man dangling from the roof of a tall building by a rope. If the rope broke, he would fall to his death.

"Have any of the guard units behind the lines reported anything out of the ordinary?" Sherman asked.

Anderson answered. "No, sir. A few guerrilla attacks only. There are occasional reports of rebel cavalry, but they seem more intent on reconnaissance than raiding the railroad."

Sherman shook his head. "I do not understand why the enemy has not made a significant effort to break our railroad. I am not complaining, mind you, but I cannot understand it."

"If they do attempt to attack our supply lines, sir, we have strong defenses everywhere. Every railroad bridge is protected by blockhouses. We have continuous patrols moving up and down the line. Repair crews are also stationed at every depot, ready to deal with any damage the rebels might inflict on the railroad."

Sherman tried to fathom what Johnston was thinking. While he had fought tenaciously during the campaign up to this point, the wily Confederate had withdrawn across the Chattahoochee without a fight. He also seemed to be making no effort to cut his supply line. Was Johnston truly whipped? Or was it some sort of ruse?

Sherman silently reminded himself not to give way to paranoia. If Johnston had wanted to fight a major battle, he could have done so north of the Chattahoochee with greater odds of success. Every calculation Sherman's mind made told him that the rebels were whipped. They would abandon Atlanta, he and his Northern troops would march in, Lincoln would be reelected, and the war might be over by Christmas.

He smiled. He shouldn't have.

"You're certain?" Johnston asked.

"Without any doubt," Mackall said. "Bragg and Hood spoke privately for some time and afterwards Bragg went to confer with General Wheeler. It is extremely inappropriate, I must say."

Johnston shook his head. "I suppose I am becoming naïve in my old age, trusting in the honor of Southern officers. But then, considering their recent behavior, I should have expected no less."

"What recent behavior?"

"I have not told you up to this point, but it has recently been made known to me that Hood and Wheeler have been engaging in a secret correspondence with both President Davis and General Bragg for some time."

"What?" Mackall's faced flashed with anger. "Insubordination! All communications relating to military matters must be sent through this army headquarters."

"You are quite right, William."

"I shall have court martial papers drawn up at once!" Mackall began to head toward the door before Johnston stopped him.

"Wait, William! Sit back down. We can't be too hasty. Politically, we are on very sensitive ground. President Davis is clearly looking for any justifiable reason to remove me from command. That's obviously why he sent Bragg here. Bringing charges against Hood, who is the President's personal friend, would only make that more likely to happen."

"A letter of reprimand, then."

"No. Not yet, anyway."

Mackall sat back down, pursing his lips and shaking his head. "These rumors of your impending removal make me furious, General. We have done the best we could under very difficult conditions. We have only surrendered territory when we had no other choice. The fact that we have been pushed back to Atlanta is not your fault. Certainly no one else could have done any better."

"President Davis apparently thinks otherwise."

"Would he have been happy if we had committed the army to an open battle, so that it could have been crushed by Sherman's superior numbers?"

"He may be a West Point graduate and a veteran of the war in Mexico, but Davis has always been more a politician than a soldier. He does not understand military realities, especially when they refuse to correspond with his fantasies."

"But what should we do about Hood and Wheeler?"

"I'm not sure," Johnston admitted. "I suppose we could confront them about their actions, but if they are then left in command of their respective units, it would only lead to discord and rancor, jeopardizing our upcoming attack when the enemy crosses Peachtree Creek. But I confess to having great fears about Hood's involvement in the operation."

"Why?"

"It's only a suspicion, but the thought has recently occurred to me that Hood, in previous actions on this campaign, has deliberately sabotaged our army's operations."

Mackall sat back. "Surely you can't be serious."

"Like I said, it is only a suspicion."

"No Confederate officer, even one as unscrupulous as Hood, could sink to such a low. Incompetence is one thing, but sabotage? To jeopardize the success of our cause merely to satisfy his own personal ambitions? I cannot believe it. It would be treason."

"Can you not? Recall that he abandoned the attack at Cassville, which would have crushed one-third of Sherman's army had it gone forward, because he claimed a small force of Union cavalry had appeared behind his lines."

"I grant you that. When it happened, I had just passed through the area where he claimed the cavalry was located and saw nothing at all."

"And even if they had been there, Hood should have detached a force sufficient to deal with them and gone forward with the attack. How could a small force of cavalry threaten an entire infantry corps?"

Mackall nodded. "Yes, I see what you mean."

"And in late May, right after we beat the Yankees at Pickett's Mill, I ordered Hood to move his corps around Sherman's left flank and attack it. I even reinforced him with brigades from the other two corps. But he again shrank back from attacking, even though the tactical situation seemed close to perfect."

"The two golden opportunities of the campaign, and each time Hood botched the attacks."

"Botched? Your choice of words implies an accident. I am beginning to suspect that his failures were deliberate."

"Yes, I see. A coincidence does seem rather too convenient, doesn't it?"

"Needless to say, considering his letters to Davis, his secret meeting with Bragg, and these hard-to-explain actions over the course of the campaign, I am hesitant to trust him with a serious role in the upcoming attack. Indeed, I hesitate to trust him with anything at all."

*   *   *   *   *

July 14, Noon

President Davis was reading Bragg's telegram for the third time.

President Davis,
I have visited General Johnston's headquarters and will do so again today. I cannot see that he has any more plan for the future than he has had in the past. I have also spoken with Hood and Wheeler. Full details of these meetings will be transmitted later today.
General Bragg

Davis fumed at the lack of information, but he knew that Bragg was only making sense in waiting to send a more detailed message until he had a chance to confer with Johnston at greater length. Still, the only two solid pieces of information Bragg had given him were bad enough. It appeared as though Atlanta was being prepared for an evacuation and it did not appear that Johnston had any plan to defend the city.

He made his choice. Davis would, of course, have to wait for Bragg's full report, but there could be no delaying the decision beyond that. If Johnston was left in command, Atlanta would be in Yankee hands before another week had passed. Lincoln would win reelection and the defeat of the Confederacy would be only a matter of time.

Johnston had to go.

Chapter Five

July 14, Afternoon

Johnston and Mackall stood upright, in full dress uniforms, their hands clasped tightly behind their backs. Behind them stood Hood, Hardee, Stewart and Wheeler. In the distance, Bragg's horse and buggy were approaching.

Mackall leaned over and spoke softly. "Are you going to tell him about our plan to attack the enemy at Peachtree Creek?" he asked.

"I'm not sure," Johnston replied. "There is security to consider. To prevent the Yankees from discovering our intentions, it would be best for as few people to know about our plan as possible. Thus far, not a soul knows about it save you and me."

"But Bragg has the ear of the President. If he reports back to Richmond that you have no strategy to defend Atlanta, Davis might order your removal at once. Besides, we shall have to inform the corps commanders in a few days anyway."

"I know, William. I know." Johnston pursed his lips. He was not entirely sure what he was going to do and this very fact filled him with unease.

Bragg's buggy pulled up to the front of the Niles House and Bragg emerged. "Gentlemen," he said simply as he strode up the steps, raising his hands in a salute. The senior commanders of the Army of Tennessee collectively returned the salute, stiffly and professionally.

"Welcome back to my headquarters, General Bragg," Johnston said with a forced smile.

"Thank you, General Johnston." There was an awkward silence. With Bragg there were always awkward silences.

"Let us go inside." As the officers walked through the doorway, Johnston saw Bragg nod knowingly in Hood's direction. He pretended not to notice.

A few minutes later, after coffee had been provided, Mackall began a presentation on the general military situation, going into much greater detail than Johnston had the day before. Mackall explained where the three infantry corps of the army were situated and what was known of the enemy positions. The Union forces had not moved for several days, though scouts reported that the buildup of supplies was almost complete. It seemed that a renewed push to capture Atlanta would likely begin in the next few days.

Bragg did not seem particularly interested in the presentation. At times, he seemed not to be paying attention at all, which Johnston considered very rude. His loathing for Bragg increased. To Johnston, it was apparent that Bragg had only come to the briefing for the sake of appearances. He had clearly already determined what he would say in the report he was going to send to President Davis.

Mackall came to the end of his presentation, and Bragg glanced at the generals assembled around him.

"General Hardee?"

"Yes?"

The tone of these words was ice cold. Johnston felt distinctly uncomfortable as he watched Bragg and Hardee gaze at one another with scarcely disguised hatred. Everyone in the room was well aware of their detestation for one another. No one else spoke, as though fearing that the slightest disruption of their conversation would set off an explosion.

"What is the present strength of your corps?"

"Eighteen thousand men, more or less."

Bragg grunted. "Their morale?" he said after a moment.

"Very good, I would say. They have beaten the Yankees repeatedly since the beginning of the campaign."

"They have not been dispirited by the long retreat?"

Hardee glanced at Johnston for just a moment. "Not in the least."

Bragg nodded, then looked at Stewart.

"And the strength of your corps, General Stewart?"

"Roughly the same as Hardee's, I would say. Between eighteen and twenty thousand men. Their morale remains unshaken, despite the death of their previous commander, who was much loved and respected."

Bragg's face hardened into cold granite at the mention of the late Leonidas Polk. During their service together, Bragg and Polk had grown to loath one another with an intensity that surpassed even the hatred between Bragg and Hardee. Johnston wondered why Stewart would have said something certain to goad Bragg. Had it been a simple moment of awkwardness or had it been calculated impoliteness?

"A pity the regard in which General Polk was held by the men was been matched by his performance on the battlefield," Bragg said.

"One should not speak ill of the dead," Hardee said instantly, anger in his voice.

"Gentlemen," Johnston said quickly, anxious to defuse any argument before it started. He held out his hands, palms down, as though to smooth troubled waters. "We should remain focused on the matter at hand."

"Agreed," Bragg said sharply. He turned to Hood. "And you, General Hood? What is the strength and morale of your corps?"

"Fifteen to eighteen thousand men, give or take. They are anxious for battle, I should say. Months of fighting from trenches has made them more determined to come to grips with the enemy. They're tired of being on the defensive. They are ready to fight."

Johnston scowled ever so slightly. Hood had certainly told Bragg everything he had wanted to know during their secret meeting the night before. He wondered just how foolish Bragg and Hood thought he was.

He couldn't resist a slight jab. "The strength of Hood's corps is slightly lower than that of the other two corps due to losses it sustained at the Battle of Kolb's Farm, where its attack was repulsed by the enemy with heavy casualties."

Hood's head jerked slightly, but he said nothing. Inwardly, Johnston smiled. He then reminded himself not to get carried away. He had to maintain control of himself if he was to have any chance of keeping his command. The tension was thick enough to be cut with a knife and Johnston knew it would be unwise to unnecessarily increase it.

Bragg ignored Johnston's comment. "Well, I believe I fully understand the military situation and have a sound idea of the condition of the army."

"Excellent."

"Now, can you tell me what plans you have to oppose Sherman's advance? Obviously, he must begin his move on Atlanta soon."

"Within days, I should say. As soon as he gets his entire force across the river and builds up sufficient supplies."

"And when he does advance, what will you do?"

This was the moment Johnston had known would come. Obviously, if he told Bragg of his plans, Bragg would immediately notify President Davis. That would mean that every telegraph wire between Atlanta and Richmond would be humming with the details of his strategy and every telegraph operator in Georgia and the Carolinas would become privy to them. Shortly thereafter, every clerk in the War Department would be talking about them as well. Then the Richmond rumor mill would begin inexorably turning.

Richmond, Johnston knew, was infested with Yankee spies. If a single one of them got so much as a hint of the plan to attack Sherman at Peachtree Creek, it would be a simple matter to get the news across the siege lines to General Grant. A simple telegram from Grant to Sherman would then put an end to all of Johnston's hopes.

However, if Bragg was told nothing, he would report back to Davis that Johnston had no plan to halt Sherman's advance on Atlanta. The President, Johnston knew, would conclude that Johnston intended to abandon the city without a fight. This would certainly lead to Johnston's removal from command.

Then there were Hood and Wheeler to consider. With those two schemers obviously doing everything in their power to discredit him, Johnston had to assume that Davis would think the worst of him no matter what Bragg's report said.

Johnston began cautiously. "General Bragg, you are aware that the enemy has more than twice our number. My plans, therefore, depend largely on the movements of the enemy. We hope that the coming days will present us with an opportunity to attack the enemy when the advantage is ours."

"Do you believe the appearance of such an opportunity to be at all likely?"

"I do, yes." He took a deep breath, glanced around at his corps commanders, and decided to tell Bragg his plan. It was a risk, he knew. But it was a risk he would have to take if he wanted to remain in command of the army.

Bragg was now talking. "Well, in war a commander must obviously look for every possible advantage. But suppose such an opportunity does not occur. Are you prepared to resist Sherman if he attempts to capture Atlanta by siege?"

Johnston's eyes narrowed. "The defenses of Atlanta are too strong to be carried by assault and too extensive to invest. A siege of Atlanta is simply not a feasible strategy for the enemy."

"I see."

"But let us return to the matter of catching the enemy at a disadvantage."

"Very well," Bragg said, his voice sounding both tired and disinterested.

Johnston did not respond right away. It suddenly occurred to him that if he were to discuss the plan with Bragg, he would necessarily have to reveal it to his corps commanders as well. He was not prepared to do that just yet. If the corps commanders knew of the plan, they would obviously share it with their division commanders, who would then share it with their brigade commanders, who would then share it with their regimental commanders. It would filter down through the ranks until, at least in the form of rumor, ordinary soldiers in the ranks would begin to hear of it. If any of them were unfortunate enough to be captured by the enemy, or if any of them simply deserted, information about the upcoming attack could be presented to Sherman as though on a silver platter.

His original intention had been to inform the corps commanders two days before the attack was to be launched. That would give a sufficient amount of time for the necessary reconnaissance to be undertaken and for other preparations to be made, while minimizing the chance of an intelligence breach. But as Sherman still had yet to begin his advance from his bridgehead over the Chattahoochee, it might still be a week or more before the decisive battle would be fought. That was too long.

"General Johnston?" Bragg asked. "You were speaking of catching the enemy at a disadvantage?"

"Yes," Johnston said, pausing uncertainly while he pondered how to answer. "The strength of our fortifications will allow us to use the city as a pivot, if you will, while we maneuver against Sherman as he approaches. I am completely confident that we will be able to strike Sherman a decisive blow at a time and place where it would do tremendous damage."

Bragg's eyebrows went up in a clearly feigned effort to appear interested in what Johnston was saying. " I see," he said. "Well, I shall certainly transmit your confidence to President Davis. It goes without saying that the President expects every effort be made to defend Atlanta from the enemy."

"Of course."

"Well, I should be going." Bragg pushed his chair back and rose, a movement quickly repeated by Johnston, Mackall, and the four other commanders. "I bid you gentlemen a good afternoon and wish you luck in the upcoming battle."

"I shall walk you to your buggy, General Bragg," Johnston said.

"Very well."

Bragg exchanged salutes with the assembled generals, then shook the hands of Hood and Wheeler before turning toward the door. Johnston considered it a calculated rudeness that Bragg did not give Hardee, Stewart and Mackall the courtesy of a handshake, but restrained himself from mentioning it.

"And are you heading back to Richmond?" Johnston asked as they walked down the front steps.

"Not immediately. I shall travel to Mobile to confer with General Taylor regarding the coastal defenses of the Gulf. It is feared that the Union Navy may soon attack Mobile Bay."

"I see. When you return to Richmond, present my compliments to President Davis and General Lee."

"I shall do so."

Johnston turned his head to look back up the steps, seeing that no one else was within easy earshot. "Do you have one more moment, General Bragg?"

Bragg's face betrayed confusion. "Of course," he said in a measured tone.

Johnston leaned slightly forward. "General Bragg, I did not wish to speak of this in front of the others, but I will tell you now that the Army of Tennessee shall attack the Army of the Cumberland when it crosses Peachtree Creek. I have drawn up a plan I believe gives every chance of victory. Please inform President Davis of this."

"You plan to attack?"

"I do. Two corps will attack the Army of the Cumberland while the third corps holds off the rest of the Yankees. I believe that we will be able to catch the enemy while his forces are divided and defeat them in detail."

Bragg was silent for several infinite moments, his eyes studying Johnston's face carefully. "You have drawn up the plans?"

"General Mackall will be preparing the orders this very evening."

"So nothing is on paper just yet?"

"Not yet, no. I thought it best to wait until tonight, in order to maintain proper secrecy."

Bragg said nothing in reply, at first looking back at Johnston with a blank expression. There was a pause that seemed to last forever. Then, very slowly, one end of Bragg's flat, thin mouth curled up slightly, forming a sneer of infinite hatred.

Involuntarily, Johnston stepped back. He took a moment to recover. "I wish you a safe and pleasant journey," he said automatically.

"And I wish you success in the coming battle."

Johnston doubted that very much. "Thank you, General Bragg."

*　　　　*　　　　*　　　　*　　　　*

July 15, Morning

As President Davis walked into his office, Mr. Harrison handed him the latest telegram from Bragg. Although he was anxious to open it immediately, Davis managed to remain calm enough to chat for a few moments with Harrison. The conversation was brief, focusing mostly on inane Richmond social gossip.

When Harrison finally closed the door, Davis hurriedly opened the telegram. It was a very long message, but the exertions that the telegraph operator must have been forced to make were justified by the importance of the message.

President Davis,
I have made General Johnston two visits and have been received with courtesy. I have also held discussions with his senior

commanders. *Johnston did not seek my advice and it was not volunteered.*

I find nothing here to be encouraging. Our army has suffered twenty thousand casualties since the commencement of the campaign, without inflicting proportional losses on the enemy.

I do not believe Johnston has prepared any plan to resist the enemy advance on Atlanta. Therefore, I believe that he should be removed from command at once.

Davis nodded as he read, sipping a cup of lukewarm coffee as he did so. It was reassuring that Bragg had also come to the conclusion that it was now necessary to replace Johnston. The only question was whether Hardee or Hood was to be Johnston's successor. As if reading his mind, that was the subject to which Bragg next turned his attention.

I do not believe that General Hardee has the confidence of the army, and it seems more than likely that his appointment would result in the continuation of Johnston's passive strategy, as he has apparently been its strongest supporter among the high command.

If the change be made, Hood would give unlimited satisfaction and would certainly engage in a more aggressive policy than has hitherto been the case. Do not mistake me as proposing him to be a man of genius, but I do believe he would be far better in the present emergency than anyone else we might have.

During the whole campaign, General Hood has been in favor of giving battle and mentions to me numerous instances of opportunities lost.

God grant you wisdom in this difficult decision.

General Bragg

Davis briefly wondered if he could trust that Bragg's rejection of Hardee did not stem from Bragg's well-known personal distaste for the man. After a moment's consideration, he decided that he could. After all, Davis himself felt comfortable that his own decision to replace Johnston was not motivated by his poor personal relationship with Johnston. If he could put patriotic duty ahead of personal matters, surely Bragg could do the same.

Davis now tried to play out the scenario in his mind. If Hood took command of the Army of Tennessee, the long retreat would certainly come to an end. All possibility of abandoning Atlanta without a fight would be gone. Bloody fighting was certain to commence. Perhaps Hood would instill the same spirit and élan in the Confederacy's main western army that had so long inspired the Army of Northern Virginia to such glorious victories as Second Manassas and Chancellorsville.

Davis knew that replacing Johnston with Hood would result in tremendous controversy, perhaps more so than any other decision he had made since the beginning of his presidency. He would certainly be accused of allowing his personal prejudices to dictate his military policy. Johnston, after all, had many powerful friends. Louis Wigfall and many others in Congress would denounce the measure with all their fury. Many of the newspapers would certainly cry foul. But his detractors were already criticizing his leadership and had been for years. Davis was not particularly concerned about them. There was no pleasing such people, after all.

He pulled out some stationary and began drafting a message to Secretary of War Seddon, directing him to remove Johnston from command and appoint Hood in his place. As Davis wrote, his pulse quickened.

*   *   *   *   *

July 15, Afternoon

Sherman was in his headquarters discussing logistical matters with McPherson when the messenger arrived. "Telegram from General Grant, sir."

Sherman took it and nodded a thanks.

General Sherman,
The rebel raider Jubal Early has withdrawn from the Washington area and is returning to Virginia, with between twenty and twenty-five thousand men. Their future operations are uncertain, as General Lee cannot feed such an additional number of men at Petersburg.
It is therefore not improbable that Early shall be dispatched to reinforce the rebel army at Atlanta. Do not be surprised if you find within the next two weeks enemy reinforcements on your front in number mentioned above.
General Grant

"What is it?" McPherson asked.

"Telegram from Grant. He says that Jubal Early and twenty-five thousand men may soon reinforce Johnston."

McPherson pursed his lips in a silent whistle. "That could certainly complicate matters."

"An understatement if there ever was one, James. We have a bit more than a hundred thousand men. Our latest intelligence says that Johnston has a bit more than fifty thousand. If Grant is right and Early is on his way to reinforce Johnston, we may soon find ourselves confronted with an army of seventy thousand rebels."

"Behind some of the strongest fortifications in the world, no less."

Sherman nodded as he did some calculations in his head. "They would need to rest and refit for a few days, I would guess. And obviously moving them by railroad all the way from Virginia to Georgia would take awhile."

McPherson thought a moment. "When Longstreet and his two divisions were transferred from Virginia to Georgia just before the Battle of Chickamauga, it took them two weeks, if I recall correctly."

"If they do as well this time around, we might reasonably expect Early's arrival in early August, then."

"It's possible that we will be in Atlanta by then," McPherson offered hopefully.

"We'll see," Sherman replied. "That depends on many factors. I'd actually welcome this reinforcement of Johnston if it would get him to come out of his trenches and fight us in the open field. But he's too smart to do that, the old fellow. He'll stick behind his trenches, just as he has done every day since the start of this whole thing."

"If Johnston is reinforced, he might use his newfound strength to hold the defenses of Atlanta more securely, while maneuvering outside of the city with a large force that might be used to threaten our flanks."

"Or worse, our supply lines to the north. Were I in Johnston's shoes and received twenty-five thousand reinforcements, my strategy would be to send an infantry corps back across the river to cut the Western and Atlantic Railroad. I shall instruct the commanders of all our units guarding the supply lines to strengthen the blockhouses protecting major bridges and be more diligent in sending out cavalry patrols."

"That should go without saying," McPherson said.

"Yes, yes, of course. But I wish to be as careful as possible."

"You know, Cump, it's entirely possible that no rebel reinforcements are coming from Virginia. Grant might have sent us that message merely to advise us of the possibility."

"I know. But I always tend to assume the worst case scenario. That way, I shall never be surprised."

Sherman sighed and looked down at the map. His army was all on the south side of the river now, aside from a few units guarding the crossings to make sure the rebels did not try to launch a raid to the north bank. After several days of enormous logistical effort, sufficient supplies had been built up to allow for a period of unrestricted maneuver. More bridges were being built all the time, so he had little to worry about on that score.

If twenty thousand rebel reinforcements were on their way to Johnston, it seemed to Sherman that the best course of action would to move forward even more quickly than he had planned. That way, he could defeat Johnston and capture Atlanta before the additional troops had time to arrive.

It was time to move forward again.

*   *   *   *   *

It had been a long time since McFadden had ridden a horse. In order to enable him to attend this foolish dinner with the Turnbows, Captain Collett had loaned him his own mount. McFadden was beginning to silently curse his commander for doing so. The animal reared up with annoying regularity and neighed loudly at the slightest disturbance. It was clear that the horse did not like McFadden one bit, a feeling he heartily reciprocated.

He was riding down Marietta Street, which paralleled the route of the Western and Atlantic Railroad into the center of Atlanta. Everywhere around him, the city was in a tumult. The news that the enemy had crossed the Chattahoochee, the last major natural barrier that had shielded Atlanta from the Yankees, had clearly sent the civilian population into a panic. Everywhere McFadden looked, frantic people were loading up wagons with every conceivable household item, both useful and useless. The noise was loud and irritating.

McFadden frowned when he saw more than a few healthy-looking men in civilian clothes hauling furniture out of their homes. Why, he wondered, were these men not in uniform and serving on the front lines? The horses hitched to the wagons also appeared to be in considerably better shape than those belonging to the army's cavalry and artillery. He shook his head in disgust. If these men were not willing to put their own lives and fortunes on the line in defense of the Confederacy, why should he and his comrades shed their blood to protect them?

He looked with skepticism at the black slaves helping their white masters load up the wagons and the black teamsters sitting on the front benches ready to drive the horses away. In the confusion, and with the Yankees so near at hand, he imagined that several of these slaves would take the opportunity to escape. After all, he would do the same in their place.

Off to the east, pillars of black, inky smoke rose into the sky. Despite the proximity of the Union army, some of the war industries of Atlanta continued to work without letup, their factories churning out ammunition, rifles and cannon. If there were any truth to the rumors McFadden had heard, though, a good portion of the heavy machinery had already been evacuated south to Macon or east to Augusta on the orders of General Johnston. He wondered whether this was just a sensible precaution or evidence that Atlanta would soon be abandoned.

As he continued southeast, he came closer to the immense structure known as the Car Shed, where three railroad lines came together. He could hear steam whistles of locomotives either coming or going and saw immense crowds of people milling about all around the building, no doubt hoping to find a way to board one of the departing trains. The only thing McFadden saw that was even somewhat heartening was a battery of heavy artillery being unloaded from the trains and hitched up to wagons. He figured that the big guns were to be taken north and incorporated into the defenses of Atlanta.

He passed on, entering the business district known as Five Points. Uniformed men stood about, leaning on their rifles and eyeing him warily. McFadden assumed that these were the provost marshal's men, whom Collett had advised him to avoid. Though ostensibly charged with ensuring law and order in Atlanta, they were said to be little more than brigands with a tendency to get drunk and steal from just about everyone. He rode on, avoiding eye contact.

McFadden struggled to concentrate and remember the directions to the Turnbow home that he had been given. Having departed the camp of the 7th Texas at around eleven in the morning, it was almost three in the afternoon when he finally reined in the horse in front of the house.

It was a lovely house, picturesque without being overly ostentatious. The front door was sided by two small pillars in the Greek style and the brick structure of the entire house was completely white-washed. Unlike many of the finer houses in Atlanta, it did not have a second floor balcony. To McFadden, the home seemed designed more for comfort than display. Compared with the noise and confusion everywhere else, the Turnbow house seemed strangely quiet and calm, as if a bubble had descended to protect it from the adjoining chaos.

He dismounted and tied his horse to the fence by the sidewalk. He then paused, looking around. With all that was going on, someone desperate to flee the city was likely to steal the animal. But if Collett lost his horse, the captain would have only himself to blame, since he had pressured McFadden into going to this dinner in the first place.

McFadden opened the small, wrought-iron gate and began walking up to the door. He then stopped. In concentrating on the city and the chaos sweeping through it, he had almost forgotten why he had come into Atlanta in the first place. He had thought the invitation to dinner at the Turnbows was rather ludicrous, coming as it did in the middle of a war and only a few miles from the front lines. Still, McFadden had been serving in the Confederate Army long enough to have learned that the line between the ludicrous and the mundane was often quite blurry.

The last time McFadden had sat down to a proper dinner in a respectable household had been before the war. Not only had that been years before, but he had been an entirely different man then. But he desperately wanted to see Annie again, for reasons he found difficult to articulate. He had only met her once, and then only for a few fleeting minutes, yet the very thought of her made his pulse quicken and his face flush.

It had not just been a physical attraction, he was sure. Granted, she had been stunning, perhaps the most beautiful woman McFadden had ever seen. Even in their brief conversation, he had sensed that something more had been at work, something that had warmed his heart in a way he had not experienced since before his family had been killed.

And then there was Robert Turnbow. The gratitude he had displayed toward McFadden for saving his life and that of his daughter had also sparked something in him. For the past few years, those who had expressed any kind of admiration for McFadden had done so only in regards to his ability to kill. To have a man like Robert Turnbow hold him in esteem for something other than slaughtering other human beings was a new and refreshing experience.

He glanced down at himself one final time. The new uniform that Collett had provided fit reasonably well, but he was suddenly overcome with concern that it had become unacceptably dirty during his ride from the regiment's encampment into the city. However, if that were the case, there was nothing he could do about it now. Steeling himself, McFadden knocked loudly on the door.

A moment later, a black woman in her early fifties opened the door, staring out at him with a cautious gaze.

"Sergeant McFadden?" she asked.

He nodded but said nothing. He never felt very comfortable around slaves.

"Well, come on in," she said, stepping aside. McFadden stepped inside the house, looking around uncomfortably at the elegant furniture with which the parlor was filled. "The Turnbow ladies will be with you shortly. Mr. Turnbow is in the study. If you will follow me, please."

She led him through a short hall to the left of the foyer and he emerged a few moments later in what looked like a library. The walls were covered with tall bookcases filled to capacity with volumes bound in attractive red leather. Mr. Turnbow was standing at one end of the room, a glass of whiskey in his hand.

"Ah, Sergeant McFadden!" he said with a warm smile. He set his glass down and walked over, extending his hand. "I am very glad to see you again."

McFadden shook his hand firmly. "I am glad to see you, too, sir. I greatly appreciate the invitation to dinner."

"Not at all. After all, I owe you my life, as does my daughter. Set against that, dinner is a small matter. A whiskey?"

"Certainly," McFadden said, gazing at the bookshelves as Turnbow poured his glass. "You have a fine library, sir," McFadden said. "The leather binding of these books is quite impressive."

"Thank you. A good many of the volumes belonged to my father-in-law. He spent a fair amount of his fortune on these books, though I doubt if he ever read more than a handful of them. He was one of the first white settlers to arrive in the Atlanta area. Made his money by helping bring the railroad to the city."

"A pioneer," McFadden said with admiration.

"Yes, I suppose you could call him that. But you would know more about pioneers than I do, wouldn't you? What with being a Texan and all."

McFadden nodded.

"When did your family arrive in Texas?"

"In 1837, just after the revolution freed it from Mexican rule. They left a comfortable life in Scotland for the Texas frontier."

Turnbow's eyes narrowed. "Why did they do that?"

"My father was a Presbyterian minister. He wanted to help establish the Presbyterian Church in Texas."

This was only partially true. His father had owned, or at least had thought he owned, a healthy bit of land in the Scottish Highlands. Due to legal trickery, he had lost control of the land during the Highland Clearances, which saw large numbers of small landowners lose their property to wealthier men backed by corrupt government officials.

His father had not told him about that anguish until he had been older. McFadden remembered his father as a strong and happy man, but he had seen both sadness and anger in his eyes when he had told the story of the hired thugs who had arrived at their home and told them that they had to leave.

"You're Presbyterian?" Turnbow asked in some surprise.

"I am," McFadden replied. He found the question slightly alarming and worried that Turnbow might be the type of man who found certain churches objectionable. He also was not sure if his answer was, strictly speaking, true any longer. He had not felt any particular religious impulse since his family had been killed.

Turnbow's mouth curled into a wide smile. "So are we," he said with delight. "Coincidences abound, I say."

"So they do, sir."

"Your parents? They are still in Texas?" Turnbow asked.

McFadden shook his head. "No. They were killed by Comanches in the spring of '62."

"I am sorry," Turnbow said. It was not an empty platitude. His voice was respectful, speaking as one man does to another.

McFadden shrugged. Comanche raiders were a fact of life on the Texas frontier, rather like the thunderstorms that would occasionally come booming out of the northwest with scarcely an hour's warning. That made the loss no less heartbreaking, though.

"I thought the threat of the Comanches had been eliminated," Turnbow said.

"Before the war, to a degree. They had been pushed into the western part of the state. But when the Yankees started the war, the system which had secured the frontier fell apart. They've been raiding the settlements of central Texas with impunity for the last few years."

Turnbow nodded. "The Yankees have much to answer for, certainly."

McFadden decided to move the conversation in a more suitable direction. "My father was an educated man and had a library of his own. I doubt it would have filled a single one of your bookshelves, however."

"You are too kind."

"Not at all."

"Did your father have any particular favorites?"

"Mostly theology," McFadden said, a hint of the dismissive entering his voice. "But he loved Robert Burns. So did my mother. My mother taught me to read with the Bible in one hand and the collected works of Burns in the other."

"I assume that regular schooling was hard to come by on the Texas frontier?"

"Nonexistent, rather. Everything I know I learned from reading on my own and I owe the ability to read to my parents."

"Well, you are surprisingly articulate for a sergeant."

McFadden momentarily thought that perhaps he should have found this comment insulting, but he did not. For one thing, he was only a sergeant because he wanted to be a sergeant, having turned down previous offers of promotion. Furthermore, Turnbow was only being honest.

McFadden's eyes were drawn to a portrait hanging on the western wall of the study. It was of a man possessed of broad shoulders, wavy black hair, and eyes that burned with a passionate intensity. He wore the uniform of the Continental Army from the age of the American Revolution.

"Who is he?" McFadden asked, waving his whiskey glass toward the portrait.

Turnbow smiled. "That is Thaddeus Kościuszko."

"Kościuszko?" McFadden asked, struggling to make sure he pronounced the name correctly. It sounded vaguely familiar.

"One of the greatest men in history!" Turnbow said with enthusiasm. "A Polish noble and a patriot of the highest order. He was so moved by reading the Declaration of Independence that he left Europe and came to America to join our fight against the British. He served as the chief engineer for George Washington. After the war was over, he returned to Poland and fought against the Russians, pursuing the dream of an independent Poland."

"Impressive," McFadden said. "A man can hold his head high if he fights in a single revolution. To fight in two different revolutions represents an even greater service to mankind."

"I should say so."

"I'm embarrassed to admit that I know nothing of this man. I may have heard his name before, but I could have told you nothing about him other than what I have just heard you say."

Turnbow thought for a moment, then limped over to one of the bookshelves and swiftly withdrew a volume. He extended it to McFadden.

"A biography of Kościuszko," he said with a smile. "My gift to you, Sergeant McFadden."

McFadden shook his head. "I thank you, sir, but I could not accept a gift from you."

"Nonsense. You saved my life. The least I can do is give you a book."

He took the book, rubbing his hand with admiration over the elegant red morocco leather. "I thank you very much, sir."

"I am glad for you to have it."

"If I may ask, sir, why do you have his portrait on your wall? Is it simply due to admiration or is there some other connection?"

"The father of my father-in-law was one of the Polish soldiers who came to America with Kościuszko."

"Your wife is Polish?"

"As Polish as Frederick Chopin, I should say."

McFadden had no idea who Chopin was, but decided against asking for fear of looking foolish. "And your own family, sir? From what country do your ancestors come?"

Turnbow's eyebrows arched slightly upwards and he took another sip of whiskey. "I don't know, actually."

"You don't?"

Turnbow waited a moment before continuing. "They found me on the street in front of a Presbyterian church in Baltimore. No one had a clue who my mother was, much less my father. I was raised in the orphanage."

"I'm sorry, sir."

"No reason to be. I have no reason to complain. After all, look what I have made myself into, without any help from parents or family. I built every inch of my fortune, bit by bit. I started out as a poor clerk in a Baltimore merchant house, but now I am one of the richest men in all the South." He sipped his whiskey and laughed slightly. "Of course, all that might be lost if the Yankees prevail."

"And you were raised in the Presbyterian Church, I assume?"

"Yes. This created problems for my wife's family, as Poles are more Catholic than the Pope. We eventually came to a compromise, though. She adopted my religion and I adopted her culture. We are a family of Polish Presbyterians, you see. Perhaps the only such family in the world!" He laughed at his own joke, or perhaps the absurdity of it.

At that moment, a somewhat stout woman about Robert's age appeared in the doorway. Her white hair was pulled up tight and short and she eyed McFadden warily.

"This is the sergeant you told me about?" she asked Robert, with an odd rustling accent that McFadden assumed was Polish.

"Indeed, it is the man who saved the lives of your husband and daughter. May I present Sergeant James McFadden. And Sergeant McFadden, this is my wife, Teresa."

"How do you do, ma'am?" McFadden said, bowing his head respectfully.

She looked him up and down as though she were inspecting a prize horse. The expression on her face was that of a woman who was far from impressed.

She grunted. "I do well, sergeant. I welcome you to my home."

"I am much obliged to you, ma'am."

"It's my husband to whom you are obliged, sergeant. He was the one who invited you. Now, let's move to the dining room."

McFadden and Turnbow set down their glasses and followed her through the door into the dining room. The table was set with elegant dishes, but McFadden noticed that some of the china cups were slightly chipped. He glanced about, looking for Annie but seeing no sign of her.

"Annie is not quite ready," Mr. Turnbow said, sensing McFadden's confusion. "I believe she'll join us in a few minutes."

"Perhaps she'd have been ready sooner if you'd invited a proper officer to dine with us, rather than a sergeant."

"Teresa!" Turnbow snapped. "We agreed that you would be polite this evening."

Teresa's face curled into a girlish scowl, making it abundantly clear that she felt she owed McFadden nothing. Turnbow turned toward McFadden.

"I apologize for my wife's behavior, sergeant. She can be rather spritely."

McFadden nodded. He considered the dismissive attitude of Mrs. Turnbow extremely rude rather than spritely, but was not about to say so.

"And whose fault is it that I can no longer entertain proper guests in my own home?" Mrs. Turnbow asked. "Whose fault is it that we have been able to hear the booming of cannon for the last month?"

"The Yankees, ma'am?" McFadden offered. It seemed the most obvious answer.

She gave a dismissive snort, causing Robert to frown in mild dismay.

"Please calm yourself, dear," he said gently. "Can we not try to have an enjoyable evening?"

"How can we have an enjoyable evening when the Yankees are just a few miles from my own dining room, with our army too frightened to stand and fight?"

McFadden shifted uncomfortably as he took his seat. He and his comrades were no cowards and he deeply resented the implication that they were. He thought of all the men he had known in the 7th Texas who were now lying in graves across northern Georgia.

Turnbow seemed about to respond to his wife when Annie suddenly appeared in the doorway. He had not forgotten how beautiful she had been when he had first seen her on the north bank of the Chattahoochee River, yet he was still taken aback. She was wearing a blue dress that would likely have been laughed at before the war, but was a model of elegance in the third year of the conflict.

Annie's father rose to his feet, and McFadden instinctively followed suit. She took her place at the table, directly across from him, and everyone sat down.

"Good evening, Miss Turnbow," McFadden offered.

"Good evening, Sergeant. It is good to see you again. I am glad you came."

"Well, I expect the dinner I shall have here will be considerably better than I would have had in my regiment's camp."

"I do hope so," Robert said. "The war has been unkind to everyone, but it is still possible to acquire decent food in Atlanta if one has the means and knows where to go. But I hope you will accept a meal that is somewhat less than extravagant. Our fare tonight will be a glazed ham, some sweet potatoes, and I believe some green beans. My woman Mattie is a fine cook, as you shall soon see."

McFadden's mouth watered. Turnbow might disdain such food as shoddy, but McFadden had not eaten such a meal in years. Two slaves, a man and a woman, brought in a salad dish and laid the plates on the table. He assumed the woman was the aforementioned Mattie.

"Sergeant McFadden's father was a minister," Mr. Turnbow said. "Perhaps he would like to say the blessing?"

Annie and her mother both glanced at him. McFadden felt distinctively uneasy. He hadn't spoken to God since the day he returned to the family farm to find it a burned ruin containing the corpses of his parents and sisters. He tried to think of something to say, but neither his mind nor his heart could find any words. An anguished and uncomfortable minute passed.

"I'll say it, father," Annie offered.

Annie's prayer was warm and concise, but McFadden scarcely heard a word of it. He was ashamed at himself for having been unable to say anything and was certain that he had committed an unforgivable social blunder. He tried to imagine how his father might have reacted had a person come to dinner at their home on the Texas frontier and declined to say the blessing.

Conversation was limited during the eating of the salad. When those awkward minutes were over, the two house slaves withdrew the salad plates and placed dishes of ham and sweet potatoes in front of everyone.

"Thank you," McFadden said absent-mindedly to Mattie as she served him.

Her eyes widened in surprise, as the faces of the Turnbows betrayed some confusion.

"It is not customary to thank slaves," Mrs. Turnbow said.

"I am sorry," McFadden replied. "I was trying to be polite."

"There is no need," she said. "Mattie is a slave."

"Perhaps there are different customs on the Texas frontier," Annie observed to her mother.

"Forgive me, ma'am," McFadden said. "My family did not own slaves."

"Ah. Poor, were they?"

"My family was not rich, no. But there are few slaves on the Texas frontier even among the well-to-do. Most of the plantations are in the eastern part of the state." He paused for a moment, weighing whether or not he should say what he wanted to say. "In any event, my mother found the institution of slavery distasteful. I doubt we would have had any slaves even had we been able to afford it."

McFadden could see disapproval in Mrs. Turnbow's face and had to repress a smile.

"What sort of men are in your regiment, Sergeant?" Annie asked, rather too anxiously.

"All sorts," McFadden answered. "The recruits of 1861 came mostly from the northeastern part of Texas. New recruits raised in late 1862 came from all over the state."

"And the rest of the brigade?" Robert Turnbow asked, a professional interest in his voice.

"There is the 10th Texas Infantry, an independent regiment like the 7th. The other regiments were made by consolidating other infantry regiments and cavalry units that have been dismounted. No one could ever agree on what to call these new regiments, so they just jammed all the numbers together. There is the 6th/15th Texas, the 17th/18th Texas, and the 24th/25th Texas. It sounds awkward, but somehow it works. Sometimes they attach other regiments to the brigade for short stints, boys from states other than Texas, but we don't pay too much attention to them. We're a Texas brigade through and through."

"Can any of the men read and write?" Teresa Turnbow asked.

"I know none who cannot, actually," he answered, suppressing the offense he took at her question. "Most of the men could read before they enlisted. A few of our men were schoolteachers before the war, and they gave regular lessons to those who could not read or write until they became proficient."

"Oh? That is surprising."

"Not all Texans are savages, ma'am."

Teresa Turnbow's face became darkly clouded. She was obviously not used to being corrected. McFadden heard Annie laugh softly, which pleased him.

He continued. "The men value their reading and writing skills because letters to and from home are the only contact they have with their families. Since the fall of Vicksburg, it's been virtually impossible for anyone to the regiment to visit Texas."

"How do the letters cross the Mississippi River?" Mr. Turnbow asked, enjoying the conversation and apparently not offended by McFadden's retort to his wife.

"They are smuggled across by brave and dedicated men. It would warm your heart to see the faces of the men of my regiment when a packet of mail arrives."

"And when did you last receive a letter, Sergeant?" Teresa Turnbow asked.

McFadden didn't answer immediately. Out of the corner of his eye, he saw Robert Turnbow shake his head slightly, telling his wife that it was not a good subject to discuss. Annie frowned, uncertain as to what the problem was but sensing that McFadden deserved her sympathy.

"I have not received a letter in some time. I have no living relatives."

"Oh," Teresa said, embarrassed at her mistake. "I am sorry. None at all?"

"Some cousins in Scotland, I believe. But I have never had any contact with them. Truth be told, I would not know how to contact them."

"Perhaps one day?" Annie offered.

McFadden smiled slightly. "Perhaps. I actually would very much like to meet them. I do long to see the mother country."

It had been a long time since McFadden had thought this, though it was true. His mother had often cried softly after recounting to him how beautiful Scotland was and how sad she had been when they had left.

The ham and sweet potatoes were delicious, being far better than anything McFadden had eaten during his time with the 7th Texas. The punch was also good. He listened to Teresa and Annie tell stories about life on the home front, some silly and others sobering. He and Robert discussed the similarities and differences of the Army of Northern Virginia and the Army of Tennessee and gamely debated which force was superior. Over time, McFadden was surprised to feel himself relaxing.

He would have gone back to his regiment a happy man had he eaten nothing but the ham. When the dessert, a freshly-baked chess pie, was placed before him, he thought he had gone to heaven. The smile on his face must have been obvious.

"You seem to be enjoying your pie," Annie observed, a hint of playfulness creeping into her voice.

"Truly, I have not eaten anything so delicious in a very, very long time."

"You seem somewhat surprised," Mr. Turnbow observed.

"I was simply wondering where all the produce has come from. We have next to nothing on the front lines aside from army-issued cornmeal. Any beef or pork we are given is barely this side of rotten. If I knew how you came across all this, I thought I might collect some money from the men of my regiment and perhaps supplement our rations with some proper food."

Teresa's face curled into a disapproving scowl and she dropped her napkin onto the table. But Robert's face lit up with a smile.

"His name is Ponder. He runs what I might call a grocery store here in town. If you have the money, he can get you just about anything you want. You name it. Chickens, hams, flour, sugar, even coffee. How he gets the coffee, I have no idea. But then, I don't ask."

"It's unseemly!" Mrs. Turnbow interjected. "A negro having that much money. A negro having any money at all, by God! How can you do business with a negro, Robert? How can you do business with a negro who should be out in the cotton fields!"

"Ponder is a negro?" McFadden asked, confused.

"He is," Robert responded.

"Free?"

"No, he's technically still a slave. But his owner is a clueless white woman who lives outside of town. She gave him permission to let himself out as a laborer here in the city a few years ago, having little interest in what he was doing. He still pays her a trifling sum each month to keep her out of his hair and the law off his back. In the meantime, he has made himself a fortune as a merchant trader. Like I said, if you have the money, he can get you just about anything you want."

"I should like the address of his store, if you don't mind," McFadden said.

"Easily done."

"Unseemly," Mrs. Turnbow said again. "The proper place for a negro is either in the field or serving at the table."

She was saying these words just as Mattie and her male counterpart came back in to take away the plates of the dessert service. McFadden noticed that it had not occurred to her to tone down what she was saying when the two slaves had reentered the room.

"If this Ponder fellow has a good head for business, I don't see why he shouldn't be allowed to make as much money as anybody else," McFadden said. He knew he was goading Mrs. Turnbow now, but did not mind. He sensed that it pleased both Annie and her father, who were the two whose opinion he genuinely valued.

"How can you say that?" Mrs. Turnbow asked. "God clearly intended the white to rule over the black. Why else would He have created them with such distinctions of color?"

McFadden said nothing, but his mind immediately conjured up a memory of his parents singing beside the fireside during the long winter nights. As if he had heard them yesterday, he remembered the words of "The Slave's Lament" by Robert Burns.

> *It was in sweet Senegal that my foes did me enthrall,*
> *For the lands of Virginia, -ginia, O;*
> *Torn from that lovely shore, and must never see it more*
> *And alas! I am weary, weary O!*
> *Torn from that lovely shore, and must never see it more*
> *And alas! I am weary, weary O!*

McFadden himself did not know what he thought about slavery. His father had considered it nothing but an eccentric aspect of Southern culture which they, being immigrants, should simply accept. His mother, though, had been staunchly opposed to it, finding it utterly incompatible with the principles of Christianity.

When he really thought about it, which was not often, McFadden thought that perhaps slavery was wrong, but that there was nothing to be done about it. The institution was so deeply engrained in Southern society that one might as well have tried to drain the Mississippi River as to eradicate it. While he had listened to his father discuss and debate issues such as the Mexican War, the tariff, the possibility of a trans-continental railroad, he had never heard him discuss slavery outside the family. McFadden had taken this as a sign that talk on the subject was probably inadvisable.

He glanced over at Annie and was somewhat surprised to see her pursing her lips and looking at her mother with disapproval. Was she embarrassed by what her mother was saying? Might she, perhaps, harbor emancipationist sentiments similar to what his own mother had often expressed?

Mr. Turnbow decided to subtly change the subject. "If the men of your regiment are lacking in proper provisions, perhaps I can help organize some relief."

"Relief, sir?"

"Perhaps I might arrange the purchase of some produce and arrange for it to be sent to the 7th Texas? Perhaps some meat as well?"

McFadden considered this for a moment. He worried that the other regiments in Granbury's Brigade might be resentful and jealous, but the thought of fresh beef and perhaps even fresh vegetables was simply too much to pass up.

"We could not accept such generosity, sir."

"Nonsense. It would be little trouble for me."

"Well, I am sure all the men would be deeply grateful."

"Annie can help organize the effort," he said, nodding across the table at his daughter.

"Me?" she asked, incredulous.

"Of course," he replied. "Daughter, my time is constantly taken up with affairs at the iron foundry. We're still producing artillery in some quantity, and I will also be seeing to the evacuation of some of the heavier equipment in the next few days. Obviously, I have no time to devote to a charitable project. And you yourself have been complaining of boredom quite a bit of late."

"Boredom?" McFadden asked, glancing at Annie.

"My school has shut down. My parents forbid me to serve in the hospitals as a nurse. I have been sewing socks for the soldiers with a collection of other ladies, but there are only so many pairs of socks one can sew before going mad."

"Perhaps your father is correct, then," McFadden said. "Helping organize food packages for the men of my regiment would not only be very much appreciated by the men on the front lines, but would help you find something to do with your time." A hint of playfulness was now creeping into his own voice.

"It is decided, then," Mr. Turnbow said with decisiveness. "Annie, I shall place a certain amount of money at your disposal. You can take it to Ponder's shop, or wherever else you think you may be able to acquire produce at a good price. You and Sergeant McFadden can then arrange between yourselves how to transport the supplies to his regiment."

"I shall not have my daughter go into that negro's store!" Teresa exclaimed, an aghast expression covering her face.

"Why not?" Robert countered. "My dear, she is no longer a girl but has become a young woman. She must learn to fend for herself. Surely she is capable of going into a shop on her own."

"We shall discuss it later," Teresa replied firmly.

Annie's eyes flashed and she suddenly began speaking quickly and angrily to her mother. It took McFadden a moment to realize that she was not speaking English. For a moment, he thought it was German, which was the native language of many farmers he had known from the Texas Hill Country. But it sounded rather more flowing and sharp. He immediately concluded that it had to be Polish.

He couldn't understand a word the mother and daughter exchanged with one another, but obviously they were quite heated. He remained awkwardly silent while the dispute went on for a minute or two, when Annie and her mother finally fell silent once again.

Teresa turned to McFadden. "I am very sorry, Sergeant."

"That's quite all right, ma'am."

There was a momentary pause, and McFadden suddenly felt that it was time for him to depart. He did not particularly want to leave, for despite the abrasiveness of Mrs. Turnbow he realized that he had, against his own expectations, enjoyed himself a great deal. Robert Turnbow's warmth and obvious respect for him had been refreshing, while simply being in Annie's presence and exchanging a few pleasant words with her had been more than worth the trip.

He rose from the table. "I must get back to my regiment," he said.

"I shall walk you out," Mr. Turnbow said, clambering up from his chair.

McFadden turned to face Annie and her mother. "I thank you fine ladies for a lovely evening."

"Good evening, Sergeant," Teresa said without enthusiasm.

Annie gave him a beaming smile. "I do hope I see you again soon."

"And I, you, Miss Turnbow."

Mr. Turnbow and McFadden walked toward the front door. He made sure that McFadden remembered to take the biography of Thaddeus Kościuszko with him, then guided him outside.

"Thank you for a fine evening, sir," McFadden said.

"And thank you once again for saving my life. If there is anything else I can do for you, please let me know."

McFadden hesitated for just a moment. "There is one thing, sir."

"Yes?"

"May I have your permission to write to Annie?"

Mr. Turnbow drew himself up, looking suddenly surprised and uncertain. The words of Mrs. Turnbow, dismissing McFadden as a mere sergeant and not a proper officer, came back abruptly. McFadden wondered if he had just made an unforgivable error.

"Write to my daughter?"

"Yes, sir."

"For what purpose?"

McFadden paused uncertainly for a moment. "Well, I suppose because I have no one else to whom to write."

Turnbow nodded, seeing this as an acceptable answer. "I see no reason why you may not write her, McFadden. After all, you will need to discuss the provisions." The words were spoken without a noticeable tone, but they lifted McFadden's heart.

"Thank you very much, sir."

*   *   *   *   *

July 16, Morning

Hood poured Wheeler another glass of whiskey as the cavalry commander continued to happily recount the story of his raid on Harpeth Shoals in early 1863. He had begun the story about ten minutes earlier, right after Hood had finished regaling Wheeler with an account of his own actions during the Battle of Sharpsburg in September of 1862.

With a hearty laugh, Wheeler finished his story by telling Hood how many hundreds of enemy prisoners he had taken on the raid. He then cheerfully took the proffered glass of whiskey and drank a third of it in a single gulp.

"Well," Hood said. "I think it likely that you will soon have more stories of martial heroics to tell our friends."

"Yes," Wheeler replied. "My scouts are telling me that the Yankees are finally moving again."

"Major fighting will resume within the next few days, I reckon. Your boys should have more than their fair share of fights with Sherman's troopers in the coming weeks."

"I certainly hope so," Wheeler said with frustration. "I'm sick and tired of doing nothing but screening Johnston's flanks and sending back reports on where the Yankee divisions are. My boys want action and they want it now. We're sick of being scouts."

"Scouting doesn't get your name in the paper, does it?"

"No."

"My boys want action just as much as yours do. They're damn tired of sitting in trenches."

"Do you think Johnston has any plan to deal with Sherman?"

Hood shook his head. "If he does, he hasn't told me. No, I'll tell you what will happen. He'll fall back into the Atlanta defenses, Sherman will come up and invest the city, a few Yankee corps will move around toward our railroads, and Johnston will retreat. Simple as that. We've seen it all before."

"I agree. I only hope that whatever Bragg has told the President will jar him into doing something about the situation out here. With Johnston at the head of the army, we can't expect anything good."

"You really think Davis will remove him? It's a serious business to replace a commanding general right before a major battle."

"We had Bragg's ear during his entire inspection tour. He barely said a word to Hardee, Stewart, or anybody else. Whatever he told the President in his report, it was based solely on what you and I told him."

"You're certain?"

"About as certain as I can be about anything. Now that the Yankees are moving, I expect to hear word from Richmond that old Uncle Joe is out of a job." Wheeler smiled at what was, for him, a very pleasant thought.

Hood tried to keep his tone neutral. "And you think Hardee will be appointed in his place?"

Wheeler shook his head. "Not if Bragg has anything to say about it. You weren't here when Hardee served under Bragg's command. You can't know the depths of the loathing between those two men. I expected them to fight a duel more than once."

"I have only heard about it secondhand. But I could sure see it in their eyes two days ago."

"Besides, I don't think very highly of Hardee. He can fight a good battle now and then, but mostly he's a stuffed shirt. Been riding his reputation from before the war for too long, if you ask me."

"I see," Hood said. "So, if Johnston is removed from command and Hardee is not going to succeed him, who is?"

Wheeler turned and smiled at him. "Oh, I think you know the answer to that as well as I do."

Hood chuckled. Wheeler was right. If Johnston was going to be removed and Hardee was not going to be put in his place, then Hood was the only person Richmond could possibly appoint as the commander of the Army of Tennessee. No other general of comparable seniority was available and his own friendship with President Davis would surely have shifted the scales in Hood's favor even if there had been.

Hood felt like a Crusading knight who was about to be given a magnificent suit of armor and weaponry with which to go forth and battle the heathen. He had achieved glorious victories at the head of his brigade and division in the Eastern Theater, so what might be possible for him to achieve at the head of an entire army? Could the name of Hood one day be ranked among the great military captains of history?

He remembered the euphoria he had experienced the night of June 27, 1862, when he and his brigade had launched the decisive attack at the Battle of Gaine's Mill. Throughout the day, Confederate brigades had hurled themselves against the Union defenses, only to be bloodily repulsed with horrendous casualties. In some desperation, Lee had turned to Hood and his gallant Texas Brigade, making it clear that they represented his last throw of the dice.

When the order had come, Hood's Texas Brigade had charged into the fires of hell. At every step, men had been cut down by withering artillery and musket fire. But his brigade had kept going, following the figure of Hood as he dashed forward, waving his sword over his head, yelling like a demon, miraculously remaining unharmed. As they had approached the Union line, the blue-coated soldiers had wavered, awestruck by the fury of the attacking Southerners. When his men had finally swarmed over the defenses, the Yankees had turned and fled.

Hood's attack at Gaine's Hill had shattered the Union line, winning the Confederacy a victory as unlikely as it was decisive. He had saved Lee's army, saved Richmond, and probably saved the Confederacy. Accolades had poured in from President Davis, from General Lee, and from every newspaper in the South. The name of John Bell Hood and his gallant Texas Brigade was enshrined in history.

Hood nodded sharply. That kind of spirit was what the Army of Tennessee needed now. Not sitting in trenches. Not hoping for the enemy to make a mistake. What the Army of Tennessee needed to do now was simply to find the enemy and attack him in full force, trusting to Southern courage and cold steel to drive the hated Yankees back. The Confederacy didn't need Joe Johnston; it needed John Bell Hood.

Wheeler was still talking, prattling on about why he stayed loyal to Bragg when so many other generals had turned against him. Hood tried to focus his attention on what Wheeler was saying, but found it difficult to distract himself from the visions of glory which kept welling up inside his mind.

The conversation was interrupted by a courier who galloped up. "Message from General Johnston, sir." He handed the paper over to Hood, saluted, and galloped off. Hood unfolded the message and read it.

"What is it?" Wheeler asked.

"Nothing. Just routine marching orders. He wants my corps on the right flank, Hardee in the center, and Stewart on the left. We're to take battle positions in readiness to oppose Sherman's move south."

"Or to cover a retreat."

Hood crumpled the message and put it in his pocket. "We'll see, won't we? But I wouldn't be surprised if this is the last order I ever receive from that pretentious bastard."

*   *   *   *   *

July 16, Noon

Davis looked down at the message he had written, which he was about to send to General Johnston through the War Department telegraph.

As you have failed to arrest the advance of the enemy to the vicinity of Atlanta, far in the interior of Georgia, and express no confidence that you can defeat or repel him, you are hereby removed from the command of the Army of Tennessee, which you will immediately turn over to General Hood.

He read through it once again, then a third time. Finally, he nodded. It was brief and to the point, and expressed his thoughts and instructions in as polite a manner as the circumstances required. Had it been a message to any general other than Johnston, he might have tried to craft the language in such a way as to assuage the recipient.

He glanced down at his desk. There were the telegrams sent from Atlanta by General Bragg, as well as several of the letters sent by General Hood. Letters that Wheeler had written to Bragg were also there, having been provided to him by Bragg for his perusal. Next to them were reports from the War Department on the progress of the fighting in Georgia, including several telegrams sent by Johnston himself. There were also newspaper articles clipped by his staff detailing the events which were taking place in the Western Theater.

All of this led Davis to the same conclusion. Johnston was afraid to fight and would be unwilling to risk battle to defend Atlanta. If he remained in command any longer, the city would be abandoned to the Yankees.

Johnston had to go. Hood would replace him.

Davis nodded, steeling himself. Removing Johnston would be a controversial move, but he had dealt with controversy since he had accepted the position of President of the Confederate States of America. He folded the copy of the order and began to slide it into an envelope for delivery to the War Department.

A flickering in the corner of the office suddenly caught Davis's eye. Looking closely at it, the Confederate President was surprised to see a tiny butterfly flapping its wings. He tilted his head in confusion, wondering how such an out-of-place creature had found its way into his windowless office. He glanced over to remind himself that the door was closed, but when he looked back the butterfly was gone.

There was a brief knock on the door, which opened instantly thereafter.

"Mr. President? A telegram from General Lee has just arrived."

Davis nodded, immediately forgetting about the mysterious butterfly. "Give it here, if you please." Unlike Johnston, Lee was so communicative that multiple telegrams on a single day were nothing unusual.

President Davis,

I have been contemplating the matter on which you earlier requested my opinion. I now wish to take the opportunity to strongly urge you not to remove General Johnston from command of the Army of Tennessee. On the eve of what may be the decisive battle of the war in the West, replacing the army's commander would necessarily entail confusion within the army's command structure and dishearten the men.

General Johnston is not a perfect commander. However, judging from a distance, I cannot see how any other commander could have done better in the present campaign than he has done. I have no doubt that he understands the importance of holding Atlanta and that he will make every effort to do so.

I must frankly admit that General Hood, while undoubtedly a gallant soldier, is not the proper sort of officer to be entrusted with the command of an army. His successes under my command were achieved through boldness, but an army commander requires a large measure of prudence as well. I regret that I do not believe Hood possesses prudence in the necessary quantity.

The greatest hope for the salvation of Atlanta now is to retain General Johnston as commander of the Army of Tennessee.

General Robert E. Lee

Davis was stunned. As he had just done with the order he had been about to transmit to the War Department, Davis read through Lee's telegram three or four times, making sure he understood every word perfectly. He focused in particular on the final sentence.

His head spun. He felt as though he were in a carriage whose wheels had just flown off while riding at high speed. Davis took advice from only a very few people and even then only with the greatest reluctance. But among those very few, Robert E. Lee was certainly at the top of the list. Disheartened, he lowered the telegram onto the table, then sat back in his chair, his hand on his chin, lost in thought for several minutes.

Lee and Johnston were old friends and fellow Virginians. They had served together in Mexico. Perhaps Lee was simply fulfilling his honorable duty as a Southern gentleman by expressing his support for a fellow officer. Davis shook his head, dismissing that thought out of hand. Lee's tone in the telegram was too rigid to be anything other than a strongly held professional opinion. Besides, Lee was the last person in the world whom Davis would expect to allow personal feelings to come before the good of the nation.

But there was more to it than that. Lee had never communicated to him in such a blunt manner on any other subject before. Although he knew how much Davis valued his advice, Lee had always made a point to be artful and diplomatic with the President, rarely disagreeing with him directly. For Lee to say so forthrightly that Davis was wrong could only mean that Lee believed it so fervently that he was willing to risk unsettling their otherwise harmonious relationship.

Another thought then crossed Davis's mind, which he hadn't considered before. What if he replaced Johnston with Hood and Hood subsequently lost Atlanta to Sherman? If that happened, Davis knew that he would be blamed for the loss of Atlanta, for his enemies would assert that it had been the replacement of Johnston that caused the fall of the city. Even worse, they would further assert that Davis had removed Johnston purely out of personal spite.

He would be the one on whom the blame would fall, not just for a lost battle, but a lost war.

He picked up Lee's telegram and read it through once again. He was struck by Lee's insistence that the best chance for retaining control of Atlanta was to maintain Johnston as commander of the Army of Tennessee. In military matters, Lee was as keen a judge of character as walked the Earth. The question was whether Johnston would fight for Atlanta. Davis had come to believe that he would not. But Lee evidently thought differently and Lee was to be trusted in such things.

Another point Lee made was undeniable, in that replacing the commander of an army would necessarily cause considerable confusion within its command structure. If Hood replaced Johnston, then a division commander would have to be appointed to succeed Hood in command of his corps, and a brigade commander to succeed the new division commander, and so forth. If the decisive battle for Atlanta were only days away, it would obviously be best if the men commanding the units of the Army of Tennessee were not in new and unfamiliar positions.

Despite himself, he realized that he was trying to find ways to agree with what Lee had said in his telegram. Somewhere in his mind, his respect for Lee was vying with his distaste for Johnston.

Lee's point that removing Johnston would dishearten the men was also worthy of consideration. As flawed a general and man as Davis considered Johnston to be, he had to grudgingly admit that the rank-and-file of the Army of Tennessee liked and respected him. Indeed, if certain newspaper stories were to be believed, they adored him to the point of worship. Davis had been a soldier before he became a politician and he was also an astute student of military history. He knew that men going into battle had to have confidence in the man who was leading them.

Davis imagined for a moment that Lee was in the room with him, watching him as he made his decision. He looked up at the military situation map on the wall, carefully studying the locations of the red and blue pins. He thought of the upcoming elections in the North and what their result would mean for the Confederacy.

He looked down at the two pieces of paper on his desk. One was the order removing Johnston from command. The other was the telegram just received from Lee. Very carefully, he picked one of them up and systematically began tearing it into tiny pieces.

*   *   *   *   *

July 17, Evening

The headquarters of the Army of Tennessee was illuminated by scores of candles and oil lanterns, as the officers digested the reports coming in from Wheeler's cavalry. Columns of Union infantry were snaking their way southwards from the Chattahoochee crossings. There was no doubt any longer that the lull in the campaign was over and that the Yankees were once again on the move.

Staff officers tried to translate the reports into reality on the maps. Units which had been identified as belonging to McPherson and Schofield were marching southeast toward Decatur. The immense Army of the Cumberland was lumbering directly south toward Atlanta itself. The situation was developing precisely as Johnston had expected it would.

By themselves in Johnston's private room, the commanding general and his chief-of-staff sat huddled over a map of Peachtree Creek and its environs.

"Two corps will make the attack. Stewart's corps will be on the left and Hardee's corps on the right. This small stream, the Tanyard Branch, will be the dividing point of the two units, where Hardee's left should meet with Stewart's right.."

"Looks good to me," Mackall said. "Where will Hood be?"

"Hood's corps will be assigned to guard the far right flank, east of the city, keeping an eye on McPherson and Schofield. Furthermore, Hood will send Clayton's division to Hardee, where it will be positioned as a reserve for the attacking force."

Mackall smiled. Johnston's orders left Hood out of the attack altogether and deprived him of a third of his troops. The man who cared so much for glory on the battlefield would get no glory from this engagement.

"How many Georgia militiamen have arrived?" Johnston asked.

"About five thousand, General."

Johnston grunted. "Governor Brown promised me three times as many."

"I know. He makes many promises he cannot keep. He is certain to go far in politics."

Johnston chuckled and waved his hand dismissively. "It doesn't matter. Make sure the militiamen are manning the Atlanta defenses themselves and working to improve them as much as possible. I would not risk such units in an open fight with Sherman's men, but they can at least hold a fortified line. That will allow the movements of the army to be freer and wider as we mount our attack. If anything goes wrong, we can withdraw into the Atlanta defenses."

"I agree, sir."

"Send a message to all corps commanders to join me for a council of war here tomorrow morning. It is time for them to be informed of the army's plans."

"Very good, sir."

There was a soft knock on the door, and moments later a staff officer entered. "Telegram from President Davis."

Johnston frowned at the sound of the man's name, but took the telegram and quickly opened it.

General Johnston,
The fate of Atlanta is in your hands. May God grant you victory in the coming battle.
President Davis

"That's odd," Johnston said, passing the telegram over to Mackall. "It's not like our President to engage in such sentimentality." Since the chief executive had not asked for a reply of any sort, he set the telegram aside and promptly forgot all about it.

*　　　　*　　　　*　　　　*　　　　*

July 18, Morning

Thomas rode at the head of one of his divisions, happy to be moving once again. It had required more than a week to construct the bridges across the Chattahoochee, move the armies across, and bring up sufficient supplies for an extended period of operations. The delay had been unavoidable, of course, but that had not made it any less frustrating.

His men had taken the opportunity to rest, refit, and write a few letters home. He was glad that his men had had the chance to write their loved ones one last time before moving out. Several thousand of them would never get the chance to do so again.

Occasional pops of musket fire could be heard up ahead, but the lack of anything substantial told him that they were simply rebel cavalry patrols. This didn't worry him, as the Army of the Cumberland was so enormous that it would have been futile to attempt to conceal its movements.

A courier galloped up beside him. "Message from General Sherman, sir."

General Thomas,
Advance your men forward toward Peachtree Creek, but halt a few miles north of it. McPherson and Schofield require more time to reach their positions east of Atlanta. Lack of opposition makes me question enemy resolve to hold the city. I consider an enemy attack

unlikely, but if it happens it is most likely to be directed against McPherson.

    General Sherman

Thomas nodded and barked out the necessary marching orders. Several hours marching would be sufficient to get the army into the position Sherman desired and they would then have all night to entrench. While Thomas agreed with Sherman that a major attack on the Army of the Cumberland was unlikely, it could not be ruled out altogether and therefore the men would be ordered to entrench. The work would take all night, but he knew none of his boys would object. Better to be tired and alive than be well-rested and dead.

Thomas thought about Sherman's assessment that Johnston might abandon Atlanta without a fight. Certainly the rebels had not made much of an effort to prevent them from crossing the Chattahoochee, nor had they launched an attack when the Union forces were divided. This flew in the face of all military logic. He wondered if perhaps the Army of Tennessee was weaker than they imagined it to be. By all accounts, however, the defenses of Atlanta were immensely strong and even a weak army could fight well from sturdy fortifications.

Thomas shook his head in frustration. Johnston was no fool. He had to know that if he drew his army into the Atlanta defenses to withstand a siege, the Federal armies could simply cut the city's railroads and wait for the Confederates to run out of food. What was Johnston thinking?

Sherman's belief that an enemy attack, if it happened at all, was likely to be made against McPherson seemed logical enough. After all, as he was advancing toward the city from the east, his left flank would be unprotected. The right flank of the Army of the Cumberland, by contrast, was protected by the Chattahoochee River. It also seemed plausible that the Confederate defenses of the city were strongest on the northern side, where an assault on the city might be considered most likely. In that case, the Confederates might consider McPherson and Schofield's operations to the east to represent a greater threat than that posed by Thomas.

Thomas smiled, optimistic about the operations that would take place within the next few days. If Johnston was preparing to evacuate Atlanta, he would hurry the Army of the Cumberland south and attempt to seize the city as quickly as possible. If the rebels sought to attack McPherson, he would do precisely the same in order to relieve the pressure on his comrade. Either way, Thomas expected to be marching at the head of his troops through downtown Atlanta within the next few days.

He wondered what his sisters would have to say when they learned their brother had commanded the first Union troops to enter the South's second-most important city.

*   *   *   *   *

"They're here, General Johnston," Mackall said.

"Very well. Send them in."

The commanding general stood up straight and placed his hands behind his back as the four corps commanders of his army entered the room. He eyed them one by one. There was Hardee, the senior corps commander and gifted soldier who, Johnston knew, had felt left out of the army's councils during the campaign to date. In light of Hood's machinations, Johnston had resolved to rely much more on Hardee in the future. His plan for the attack at Peachtree Creek was a step in the right direction on that score.

Johnston glared at Hood, the betrayal still stinging. Up until the revelations of Senator Wigfall, Johnston had trusted Hood more than any other of his senior commanders. Having had the wool pulled over his eyes and then having it pulled away so abruptly had been a bitter experience. After the battle, there would have to be a reckoning of some sort, but that would have to wait.

Wheeler was as bad as Hood, Johnston had decided. His performance in the campaign to date had been less than satisfactory, especially in the opening days, when his failure to conduct adequate reconnaissance had nearly led to disaster during the Battle of Rocky Face Ridge. He had obviously been Bragg's lackey since Johnston had arrived at the Army of Tennessee.

Then there was General Stewart, the newest corps commander, who had only recently been promoted to take over Polk's corps. He had made a name for himself as an effective brigade and division commander and no one doubted his bravery on the battlefield. But he was still an unknown quantity. Johnston knew he would have to keep a close eye on him until he had become comfortable at a higher level of command.

He began. "Gentlemen, I do not exaggerate when I say that the next few days will be the most important of the campaign. We are about to engage the enemy in what may be the most decisive battle ever seen in America. If we succeed, we shall save Atlanta and the Confederacy. But make no mistake. The retreating stops here."

Johnston glanced at Hood and Wheeler. Both of them shifted uncomfortably, dark expressions of doubt suddenly clouding their faces. Johnston quickly put the pieces together in his mind. The two of them must have told Bragg that Johnston was going to evacuate Atlanta without a fight. Perhaps they had even persuaded themselves of this. How were they going to explain to Bragg what was happening now?

Johnston gestured to a large map on the wall, showing Atlanta and the surrounding territory. "According to our latest information, the Yankees are approaching the city from two different directions. General Thomas and the Army of the Cumberland are marching directly toward Atlanta from the north, while Schofield and McPherson are swinging around to the east with the Army of the Tennessee and the Army of the Ohio."

"What strength?" Hardee asked.

"Our current best estimates are that Thomas has sixty thousand men coming down from the north, and McPherson and Schofield have a combined strength of forty thousand men swinging around to the east."

"And we have but fifty-five thousand men here in Atlanta," Hardee observed. "It appears that Sherman wishes to catch us in a pincer movement, crushing us between two forces each roughly equal in numbers to our own."

"Yes, but the hunter is about to become the hunted."

The faces of Hood and Wheeler had both become stony and expressionless.

Johnston went on. "I believe Sherman expects us to do one of two things. He thinks that we will either evacuate Atlanta without a fight or attempt an attack on McPherson's vulnerable left flank. We shall do neither, gentlemen."

"And, pray tell, what shall we do?" Hood asked, sounding annoyed.

Johnston tapped the map. "Here is Peachtree Creek. I assume you've all seen it. Deep, uneven banks. A difficult natural barrier to any large formation of troops. In order to threaten the city from the north, the Army of the Cumberland will need to cross it."

He paused and looked around for a moment, studying the faces of the men. When he spoke again, it was with fierce determination.

"We shall not contest the crossing, gentlemen. Instead, we shall wait until the Yankees cross to the south side of the creek, then fall on them with the full force of two entire corps. Our goal shall be nothing less than the destruction of the Army of the Cumberland as an effective fighting force."

Johnston stopped there, wanting the impact of his words to sink in. He could see skepticism in their eyes, but the expressions of Hardee and Stewart also exhibited cautious excitement.

After an appropriate period of silence, Johnston continued. "The attack will be made by the corps of Stewart and Hardee, with Stewart on the left and Hardee on the right. General Hood, you will detach Clayton's Division and place it under the command of Hardee. It shall act as a reserve for the attacking force."

"And where shall my corps be positioned?" Hood asked, confused.

"You will take up position on the east, to keep an eye on McPherson and Schofield, should they attempt to come to the aid of Thomas or move directly on Atlanta."

"You want me to face the combined forces of McPherson and Schofield with only two divisions?"

"Wheeler will deploy a few brigades of cavalry to assist you. You will also be reinforced by the Georgia Militia, which numbers five thousand men."

"Those are old men and young boys!" Hood protested.

"There's nothing to worry about, General Hood. If the Yankees to the east mount a major attack at the very moment we are attacking Thomas, you need only to delay them for a few hours and then fall back into the Atlanta defenses. Surely you should be able to do that, yes?"

"Two divisions and a bunch of militiamen against two entire Yankee armies?"

"You'll be fine, General Hood. All you'll need to do is show us some of that fighting spirit of the Army of Northern Virginia that you are always going on about."

Hood's face became flushed with anger as Hardee and Stewart chuckled at what they assumed to be a good-humored jest. Johnston smiled slightly, though not nearly enough to be justified by the elation he felt inside. He reminded himself to maintain his composure.

"When shall this operation take place?" Hardee asked.

"Timing will be the key to success. The Army of the Cumberland is already moving south, though at a slow pace. Thomas is always slow. I believe that they won't start crossing the river until tomorrow evening, and that the bulk of their forces will not move across until the morning of July 20."

"That seems to be the thinking of my scouts, General Johnston," Wheeler said. The cavalry commander's voice sounded more respectful toward Johnston than it had for many weeks, but this made no impact on Johnston. As far as he was concerned, Wheeler had burned his bridges and it was far too late to try to repair them.

"Good," Johnston said, deciding he might as well make some use of Wheeler for the time being. "In the meantime, make sure your men delay the Yankees as much as possible until tomorrow night, then withdraw them all to the south bank of the creek."

"Very well, sir."

He spoke again to all the generals. "We have to hit them at exactly the right moment. If we attack too early, not enough troops will have crossed to make the assault worth the risk. If we attack too late, the enemy will have had a chance to entrench and bring up enough troops to outnumber us. If we are right and the Yankees begin crossing the creek in large numbers on the morning of the 20th, I believe we should attack at one o'clock in the afternoon."

Hardee nodded quickly. "Yes, that would seem like the most likely moment for the conditions you have outlined to be met. It will also allow us plenty of time to position our own divisions for the attack, and the wooded areas south of Peachtree Creek will provide excellent cover for us to do so unobserved."

"Indeed," Johnston said, happy to see Hardee so enthusiastic. "I want both you and General Stewart to carefully reconnoiter the ground tomorrow morning. Memorize every hill, every stream, and every grove of trees. Have every member of your staff do likewise. When we advance against Thomas, I will need you to have a clear picture of the ground onto which you are leading your troops."

"Of course, sir," Stewart said, as Hardee nodded agreement.

"As I said, Sherman likely believes that we are evacuating Atlanta, and it serves our purposes to make him think so. Mackall has already sent selected enlisted men toward the Yankee lines, who will allow themselves to be taken prisoner or feign desertion, and who shall give misleading information to the Yankees about troops being loaded into trains heading south. At the same time, we shall move large numbers of empty trains south along the railroads to the south and southwest, hopefully causing Sherman to give more credit to such reports."

"A fine idea, General Johnston," Hardee said.

"Yes," Hood said. "And considering all the strong positions we have abandoned without a fight since the onset of this campaign, he may well fall for such a trick." His voice was that of a petulant schoolboy.

Johnston ignored Hood's comment. He could have retorted that the majority of those positions were evacuated on Hood's own advice, but he thought it best to let it go. For the moment, all that Johnston cared about was that Hood was sidelined and could do nothing to squander their chances of success in the upcoming battle. After the fate of Atlanta had been decided, Hood could be properly dealt with. Until then, he could be safely ignored.

Johnston looked around at the generals. "Mackall will provide written copies of the orders in about two hours. They shall specify the details of deployment. Does anyone have any questions?"

They shook their heads.

"Very well. We shall meet again tomorrow evening. In the meantime, return to your commands and inform your division commanders. Keep word of the operation from brigade commanders until tomorrow night, and regimental commanders until the morning of the 20th."

"Yes, sir," they said as one, and quietly filtered out of the room.

Johnston saw them go, and a staff officer closed the door, leaving Johnston alone in the room. He was pleased, feeling that he had encouraged Stewart and Hardee, partly marginalized Hood, and moved Wheeler to a place where he could still be useful to Johnston. His objectives for the meeting had all been achieved.

He recalled the famous phrase from the Suetonius he had read when he was a cadet at West Point: *Alea iacta est:* The die is cast. The Roman historian was describing how Caesar had reached the point of no return when he ordered his troops to cross the Rubicon, starting the civil war against Pompey and the Roman Senate. Johnston, too, had now set in motion events which he would do his best to control, but which he had to acknowledge would be largely determined by fate.

And fate was a fickle mistress.

*   *   *   *   *

Hood returned to his corps headquarters, was pulled down from his horse, and then hobbled into his tent without a word to any of his staff officers. Aside from the routine saluting, they made no effort to communicate with him. The look of fury on his face made it abundantly clear that he had no wish to speak with anyone.

He fell heavily into his chair and immediately took up his pen. But he then paused, not sure what to write, or even to whom he was intending to write. With a howl of rage, he tore the paper on the desk in front of him to pieces, then threw the quill and inkpot off the desk and onto the ground.

Hood angrily realized that he had been made to look a fool. He had been sending letter after letter to President Davis for months, all of them asserting that Johnston was weak, that he would not fight for Atlanta, that he had no plan to defeat Sherman. During Bragg's inspection tour, he had told Bragg the same thing. But now Johnston had announced that, contrary to all his assertions, a bold and determined battle would be fought in defense of the city after all.

From this moment on, Hood was sure, President Davis and General Bragg would consider him entirely unreliable. The information he had provided them had been completely wrong. His influence with the President, on which he had staked so much, would vanish as though it had never existed.

Pouring salt into the wound was the fact that Hood would have no part to play in the upcoming engagement, which could well be one of the great battles of the war. With his corps off to the east, assigned an entirely passive role and deprived of one of his three divisions, he felt very like an actor who had been playing the lead role in the production but who had now been relegated to a bit part just when the biggest performance of the season was about to begin.

He couldn't understand why there had been no word from Davis or Bragg. After all the letters, his private meeting with Bragg, and everything that Wheeler had told him, Hood had expected a telegram to come from Richmond at any moment saying that Johnston was being removed from command and that he himself was being appointed in his place. Indeed, when he had received orders to report to Johnston's headquarters, he thought it was to receive news of his appointment.

He had sacrificed his honor as a Southern officer to achieve the goal of army command. Now, it seemed he had nothing to show for it.

A darker thought crept into Hood's mind. In previous attempts to attack Sherman, Johnston had always entrusted the most important role to Hood. Now, in the greatest gamble of the campaign thus far, Hood was to play no role at all. Could it be that Johnston had somehow learned of his insubordinate activities and was marginalizing him as an act of retribution?

Hurriedly, he poured himself a whiskey and downed it in a single toss. If Johnston had learned of what he had been doing, he would be within his rights as army commander to call him before a court martial. That, in turn, would certainly bring into the public gaze details of the events at Cassville and New Hope Church which Hood certainly did not want to be made known. If such a thing happened, the reputation he had earned on a dozen battlefields in Virginia, Maryland and Pennsylvania would be ruined, perhaps forever. His mangled body would have been mangled for nothing. It would be even worse if Johnston actually won the upcoming battle, for such a victory would make Johnston a hero across the Confederacy.

With a sudden horror, he found himself wondering what Sally Preston would think when she learned the news. The thought stunned him with nearly as much force as the Yankee shell fragments that had shattered his arm. The size of the scandal would be so great that her parents, already opposed to the match, would make sure that their daughter never laid eyes on John Bell Hood ever again. Indeed, she probably would be not even be allowed to open his letters. And how the Richmond gossip-mongers would sneer!

Suddenly, the constant aching pain in his arm and what was left of his leg seemed to increase unnaturally. He had to bite his lip to keep from letting out a cry of pain. Instinctively, he reached into his pocket for his laudanum. He felt certain he would need more of it very soon.

*   *   *   *   *

July 18, Evening

Around noon, the forward units of the Army of the Cumberland had arrived with little warning in the tiny hamlet of Old Cross Keys, a dozen or so miles north of Atlanta. While most of the Yankee soldiers had continued marching due south toward the city, some remained behind, setting up rear-area supply depots.

The family of the nicest house in the village had been told to vacate immediately so that a proper headquarters for the Army of the

Cumberland could be established. A few men had proceeded to remove some of the furniture and load it onto carts, while others stuffed the silverware into their pockets. Thomas had considered issuing an order to stop such looting, but decided against it as he knew any it would only have been ignored.

Sherman, McPherson, and Schofield had ridden over from the east to hold a conference. All four men hovered over the dinner table, which was covered with the ever-present maps. The light cast by the oil lanterns projected their enormous shadows onto the walls, making the men appear far larger than they actually were.

"Everything is working in our favor, gentlemen," Sherman said. "Yes, by God, everything! I believe we will be entering the city within the next two days or so. I don't think Uncle Joe down there is going to even defend the place. Not anymore, I don't. Your thoughts?"

"I am of the same opinion," McPherson declared. "My scouts have been reporting all day that they can see and hear trains heading out of Atlanta to the south, on the Macon and Western Railroad track. It seems that Johnston is moving supplies and perhaps his heavy artillery out of the city."

Thomas nodded. "Two rebels surrendered to my pickets earlier today, one from the 37th Tennessee and the other from the 7th Arkansas. Both men report that their units had been ordered to march to the Atlanta train station. According to our latest intelligence, these two rebel regiments belong to two separate divisions, which would indicate that a large-scale troop movement out of Atlanta is under way."

Sherman nodded. "One or two of these pieces of information I might ignore. But all of it put together? No, it is fitting into a clear pattern. Uncle Joe has had it. He's leaving Atlanta in one big hurry."

The Union generals shared a smile around the table, as a staffer quietly refilled their glasses with whiskey. Sherman continued to speak.

"Still, it would not do to be reckless. As we advance on the city, I foresee our greatest danger will be to the east, where the left flank of the Army of the Tennessee will be exposed and open to attack. I therefore have ordered our cavalry to screen this flank carefully and watch for any sign of the enemy."

"A wise precaution," Thomas said.

"If the rebels attack anywhere within the next few days, it will be on the east side of the city."

"I have no fears on my front, " Thomas said. "The Army of the Cumberland by itself outnumbers the entire rebel army. To tell you the truth, if you feel it necessary to reinforce the units advancing from the east, I can certainly spare a few divisions."

Sherman thought for a moment. "Perhaps. But I see no need to take such a course of action as yet. If the rebels do intend to defend the city, the Army of the Cumberland would possibly be doing a greater service by threatening the city from the north, forcing Johnston to keep larger numbers of his troops on your front."

"Very well, sir."

Sherman traced lines on the map with his fingers, vocalizing his thoughts as he had them. "The Army of the Cumberland will advance across Peachtree Creek on the morning of the day after tomorrow, thirty-six hours from now. The Army of the Tennessee will move with all speed to this town here, Decatur, and cut the railroad between Atlanta and Augusta, after which it shall advance directly toward Atlanta from the east. The Army of the Ohio will position itself on the right flank of the Army of the Tennessee. Our plan will be for all our forces to be in position on the morning of the 21st, and to enter Atlanta on the afternoon of that day. Any questions, gentlemen?"

Sherman's three subordinates shook their heads.

"Good. We may not all be together again until after we are in the city, so I will simply conclude by wishing you all good luck in the coming days. If fortune smiles on us, we shall capture the city with little loss. If we do, perhaps Uncle Abe will give us each twenty days leave, to see the young folk."

*   *   *   *   *

July 19, Morning

Cleburne rode alongside Hardee as they wound their horses through the trees about half a mile south of Peachtree Creek. The terrain was slightly rolling, with low hills and ridges scattered about everywhere, and occasional streams that meandered away from the creek in a southerly direction. Aside from a few small open fields, the entire area was covered with trees. It was difficult to see more than a hundred yards in any direction.

"This is a good place for an ambush, William," Cleburne said.

"Yes, it is," Hardee replied. "The trees will conceal the presence of our troops from the Yankees, assuming our picket line keeps their infantry at a distance long enough."

"The forested and slightly uneven nature of their terrain will also make it difficult for the enemy to employ their artillery, negating one of their principal battlefield advantages."

Earlier in the day, they had sent out their staff officers to comb the entire area. If the attack was to succeed, it was critical that they understand the ground as accurately as possible. Since the Yankees would be advancing into unknown terrain, knowing the ground would give the Confederates a decided advantage. During the afternoon and evening, the staff would be updating their maps and correcting whatever mistakes they had previously made.

"Will we have guides assigned to us?" Cleburne asked.

Hardee nodded. "Many of the men from Stovall's Brigade were recruited from around here. They know the area better than anyone. Three or four of these men will be assigned to each brigade."

"Sounds good. Too many battles in the past have been lost by foolish mistakes that could have been avoided by having local men assigned to units as guides."

"If this is going to work, we can't afford to make the same mistakes we have made in the past." Both men could easily remember the disappointments and lost opportunities of so many past battles.

Cleburne decided to sound an optimistic tone. "I think Johnston's plan is a good one, at least so far as you have described it to me. I only hope the attack isn't canceled at the last minute, as it was at Cassville."

"That was Hood's fault," Hardee said sharply. "If you ask me, I think Johnston has finally realized Hood is not the effective, aggressive general his admirers have claimed him to be. That's why he's been assigned the task of guarding the east flank. Better to have him out of the way, giving you and me a chance to actually achieve something meaningful."

Cleburne nodded, but felt it wise not to say anything.

"Let's ride forward to the creek itself," Hardee said.

With a quick kick, they sent their horses into a trot. After fifteen silent minutes of riding, their mounts stood on the banks of the creek. They slowed to a walk and moved a few hundred yards downstream, surveying the rivulet. It flowed unhurriedly westward toward the Chattahoochee and was obviously not very deep. In many places, stones protruded from the surface of the water. Cleburne thought it likely that a man could walk across it with no trouble at most points.

On the other hand, the banks of the river were very steep, eight or nine feet in some places. Cleburne found himself thinking that if he accidentally fell in, it wouldn't be easy to get out without someone's help. From a military point of view, that made a formidable natural barrier.

Cleburne glanced around. "I don't see any peach trees."

"What of it?"

"Why is it called Peachtree Creek?"

"I have not the foggiest idea," Hardee responded.

Cleburne shrugged, dismissing the question. "If we can break the Yankee line tomorrow, they won't be able to run away," he said. "They'll be trapped with their backs to this creek."

"I agree. We can wreck the Army of the Cumberland."

Cleburne nodded. For a long time, they walked their horses along the banks of the stream, staring down into it, lost in thought. Then, just as the sun began its descent toward the western horizon, they turned their horses to the south and headed back to their command posts, to prepare for the struggle that the next day would bring.

*　　　　　*　　　　　*　　　　　*　　　　　*

July 19, Afternoon

"Today's correspondence, Mr. President."

Unceremoniously, Lincoln's secretary John Hay dropped a pile of paper nearly an inch thick on the President's desk, creating a sound not unlike that of a gunshot. Lincoln, who had been reading a report from Grant, took off his glasses, rubbed his sinuses, and looked at the pile of paper.

"Oh, dear Lord."

"I apologize, Mr. President," Hay said sympathetically.

"It looks thick enough to stop a cannonball. You are sure Mr. Stoddart has gone through these letters and removed everything extraneous?"

"Quite sure, Mr. President."

"I do wish you gentlemen would try to be more thorough," Lincoln said. "Yesterday I found myself reading a proposal from a very silly man who requested government assistance for the construction of some sort of balloon airship which he was convinced would provide regular mail service between New York and London. Such nonsense should immediately be thrown in the trash."

Hay nodded. "I'll tell Mr. Stoddart to be more thorough, Mr. President."

Lincoln picked the first letter up from the pile and glanced through the first few lines. "Oh dear," he said, almost absent-mindedly. "It seems that tomorrow I am to entertain a delegation of Shawnee chiefs who are upset about white settlers encroaching on their lands." He set it down and picked up the next piece of correspondence. "And here is Secretary Seward advising me to take a harder line on French actions in Mexico. I must say, Mr. Hay, that I never cease to be surprised at how my office requires me to attend to issues which have little or nothing to do with the war. How can I attend to these matters when I daily face the pressure of ordering thousands of men to their deaths?"

Hay allowed himself the familiarity of a shrug. "You are the President of the United States, sir. The people choose you in 1860. If you were not to do the job, who would?"

Lincoln sighed, then looked longingly out the windows of his office, across the Potomac and into Virginia. "Someone younger than me, perhaps? Better able to stand the strain? I tell you, Mr. Hay, this war is eating me up inside. Whenever I visit one of our military hospitals, I feel an internal scream that I cannot silence."

Hay was slightly taken aback. "Don't speak so, Mr. President. Every day brings us closer to victory."

Lincoln's face suddenly brightened. "You may not be far wrong there, Mr. Hay. The latest dispatches from Georgia are very promising. Sherman seems confident that we shall capture Atlanta in the next few days."

"Is that so?" Hay asked expectantly. "What of Johnston and the Army of Tennessee?"

"Sherman seems to think that the rebel forces are preparing to abandon Atlanta. This Johnston fellow is apparently the cautious type. He doesn't want to risk losing his army in a doomed attempt to withstand a siege."

"So the fighting will go on, even after the fall of Atlanta?"

"Perhaps so. But as you say, every day brings us closer to victory. And after the election, the eventual triumph of our cause will be but a mere matter of time."

"I dearly hope so, Mr. President."

Lincoln looked up and smiled. "If Grant can keep Lee pinned down in Petersburg and Richmond, we can tear the guts out of this so-called 'Confederacy' and end the rebellion, placing America back on track toward its rightful destiny."

Hay was intrigued. "Oh?" he said.

Lincoln smiled. "Hay, since I took office, I have signed the Homestead Act, opening vast tracts of the West to settlement. I have laid the groundwork with the Union Pacific Railroad Company for a trans-continental line to link the Atlantic with the Pacific. I created the National Academy of Sciences. I have been told that our manufacturing output will soon be greater than that of the British Empire. Every day, boatloads of hardworking immigrants arrive in New York, ready to put their talent and industry to work here in the United States. We have it in our power, Mr. Hay, to make America into the greatest nation the world has ever seen."

Hay nodded. He knew Lincoln was a visionary. He and John Nicolay, Lincoln's other personal secretary, had often sat up into the wee hours of the morning with the President, listening to him expound on what he would do once he had brought the war to a successful conclusion. "Where does the defeated South fit into this, Mr. President?"

"As a regular part of the United States, Mr. Hay. I know the Radicals like Thaddeus Stevens and Charles Sumner want the government to place its foot on the throat of the South for a generation or more, but what would that achieve? It would only breed more bitterness and hatred between the North and South. There's been far too much of that, by God. No, far better to welcome them back into the Union as brothers. If they recognize the authority of the federal government and agree to abolish slavery, it shall be as if the war had never happened."

"I hope to be a part of all this, Mr. President."

"You will, John. You will. After the war you will go on to greater things than being the humble private secretary of a highly-flawed President, believe you me. And I can personally assure you that I shall use whatever influence I have left to assist you in finding a position worthy of your talents. Mr. Nicolay and Mr. Stoddart, too. I expect all of you to play critical roles in shaping America into the nation that, God willing, it shall become."

"Thank you, sir."

Without another word, Hay turned and left the office. Lincoln turned and again gazed out across the Potomac, not knowing that his dreams for the future of America would soon lie in ruins.

Chapter Six

July 20, Morning

As the eastern horizon began to glow with the coming of the dawn and the chirping of the birds was only just beginning, a loose row of Yankee skirmishers appeared through the mist on the north bank of Peachtree Creek. Several yards separated each man and they moved in near total silence. Their eyes were alert, their muskets ready to be raised into a firing position at any moment. As they reached the bank of the creek, they paused, straining their eyes for any sign of the enemy on the other side.

They waited there for several minutes, seeing nothing. Then, the officers made silent hand signals. Picked men clambered down the bank into the creek. It wasn't easy. Most handed their rifle to another man and then had him hand it back when he finally reached the bottom. They found the creek itself very shallow. Some crossed while barely getting their boots wet, while a few waded over with the water reaching their waists. Those remaining on the north bank covered the crossing of their comrades, raising their weapons to their shoulders and aiming at every shadow on the other side.

The picked men found it very difficult to climb up the steep southern bank while holding their muskets. It was only by clasping onto exposed tree roots or rocky outcroppings that the first few managed to get up. They then set their weapons down, feeling themselves in no danger as there seemed to be no enemy troops nearby, and turned to assist their comrades.

This scene was reenacted up and down the length of Peachtree Creek that morning. In ever increasing numbers, the men of the Army of the Cumberland began to cross over Peachtree Creek. They were now only a few miles from Atlanta.

As soon as their hold on the south bank was secure, the engineers immediately began working to erect improvised bridges to make the crossing easier for the vast host which remained on the north bank. Within hours, the trickle of Northern troops crossing Peachtree Creek became a flood.

Among them was General Thomas, who crossed over to the south side at about ten o'clock, walking his horse across what the locals had called Collier's Bridge, which the rebels had mysteriously left intact. It connected to Peachtree Road, one of the few good thoroughfares in the area. He smiled at the thought that there was now no natural barrier between him and Atlanta. Had there been no war, he could have kicked his horse into a trot and been in the middle of the city in about an hour.

He drew over to the side of the road, followed by some of his staff and the color bearer of the Army of the Cumberland, and watched as yet another infantry division began to march across. Thousands of his troops were now on the south bank of the creek and every minute that passed brought yet more over. A few minutes later, General Joseph Hooker, the commander of Twentieth Corps, rode up to him.

"Good morning, General Thomas," Hooker said without warmth.

"And to you, General Hooker."

Among near-equals in rank, informality was the norm, but not with Hooker. Easily the most vain man Thomas had ever met, Hooker was the disgraced former commander of the Army of the Potomac, who had been outwitted and defeated by Stonewall Jackson and Robert E. Lee at the Battle of Chancellorsville in Virginia the previous year. That defeat aside, Hooker's combat record was actually fairly good, but the blow Chancellorsville had inflicted on Hooker's immense pride had caused him to be extremely touchy on matters of rank and prestige. Thomas had learned to tread carefully with the man.

"Two of my divisions are across," Hooker said. "One more to go."

"Good, very good. Any sign of the rebels?"

Hooker shook his head. "Some cavalry pickets up front, but nothing to indicate the presence of large units anywhere nearby."

"I see," Thomas said. He thought for a moment. "I'm beginning to suspect that Sherman is correct. Maybe Johnston has given up the city."

Hooker sat up straight in the saddle and spoke hurriedly. "If that is the case, General Thomas, I request that my corps be the one to lead the Army of the Cumberland into the city."

Thomas sighed with quiet exasperation. "It's too early to discuss such things, General Hooker. Let's just get the army over this creek and form them up for the advance."

"With respect, General, I believe that under all the observed rules of civilized warfare my seniority in rank to the other corps commanders in this army entitles my corps to the honor of leading the advance into Atlanta."

"Like I said, General, we shall discuss such things later. Rest assured, only military considerations are on my mind when I determine marching orders." He saw the look of injured pride on Hooker's face, which struck him as mildly ridiculous, so he sighed and went on. "But unless there is a specific reason otherwise, you shall have the honor of leading the advance."

"Thank you, sir." Hooker saluted and rode off. Thomas watched him go, shaking his head. All that damned idiot wanted was to see his name in the papers again.

He turned in the saddle and looked back north, over the bridge. It was crammed with blue-coated troops. The crossing was going well. Hooker's corps was nearly finished crossing and was taking up position in the center of the developing Union line of battle. The other two corps were crossing on either side of Hooker's corps, using the bridges hastily thrown up by the engineers. Within the next few hours, assuming things continued to go smoothly, the entire army would be across.

"Sir!" a staff officer shouted. He pointed to three Union soldiers approaching, leading what appeared to be a Confederate prisoner.

"Bring him over here!" Thomas called out. Perhaps the man would have some useful information. "Who are you, son?"

"Stephen Carpenter, sir," he answered, appearing rather stunned to be addressed by a Union general. "38th Tennessee. Cheatham's Division."

"Prisoner or deserter, Carpenter?"

The man shrugged. "Oh, I just had to give up, General. Got a letter smuggled in from my family back home, in occupied territory. They need me to come home and keep the farm safe from your boys, who've been stealing all the hogs and chickens."

Thomas grunted. War was hard on everyone. "Answer some questions for me and I'll make it easier for you to get home."

"Happily, sir." The man's eyes lit up.

"Where are the closest Confederate troops?"

"Well, the Atlanta defenses are manned by the Georgia militia. I think they're the closest ones. Nothing between them and you, near as I can tell. But I was trying to stay out of sight, you see."

Thomas nodded. "Where was your division when you left it?" Cheatham's division was one of Johnston's best, so its location might say a lot about the Confederate commander's intentions.

"Oh, way out there," Carpenter said, waving his hand. "Out east and south of the city. We marched through Atlanta the day before yesterday."

"Other divisions out there, too?"

"I think so, yes. But I can't say for sure. They don't tell us privates much. Probably the same in your army, I reckon."

"Thank you kindly, Carpenter." He turned in the saddle and spoke to a staff officer. "Get this man some food and make sure he gets processed properly." A moment later, Carpenter was gone.

Thomas pulled his notebook out and hastily scribbled a message for Sherman.

General Sherman,

Crossing proceeding normally. No sign of enemy. Deserter just brought in reports Atlanta defenses held only by militia and Confederate troops southeast of the city. Recommend McPherson watch his flank. I shall prepare to advance if opportunity presents itself.

General Thomas

He tore the paper off and ordered a courier to take it to Sherman. The deserter's claim that the defenses of the city were being held only by the Georgia Militia seemed to confirm the reports of his cavalry that there were no formations of Confederate troops between the Army of the Cumberland and Atlanta. Either Johnston was pulling out or he was massing his troops for an attack on McPherson. In either case, Thomas had little to fear.

Sherman had ordered all forces to be ready to move into Atlanta the following day. Thomas now felt that the prize was within his grasp already. The Georgia militia would not last long in a fight with the hardened veterans of the Army of the Cumberland, even if they were behind stout defenses. Once the entire army was across the creek, they would move south toward the city. There was no time to bother entrenching and Thomas did not want the men to be too tired to make a forced march. Even if Johnston did intend to attack him, Thomas was fully confident in the ability of his army to maintain its position. He had, after all, done it all before.

*   *   *   *   *

Captain Collett looked tense and perhaps even apprehensive as he glanced around the group of two lieutenants and nine sergeants. McFadden felt his patience instantly wear thin. Collett had just returned from a hurried conference with General Granbury, the brigade commander, and everyone was frantic to know what was about to happen.

"Listen carefully, men," Collett began. "It's look like we're about to have one hell of a fight on our hands. The Army of the Cumberland is crossing Peachtree Creek, just a mile or so north of here. In a couple of hours we're going to hit them with everything we've got. The whole corps is going in. Stewart's corps, too, over on our left. Our goal is to drive them into the creek and destroy them."

As Collett spoke, a rustle seemed to breeze through the assembled officers and sergeants. A few men smiled, while others appeared more pensive. McFadden's face betrayed no reaction, for Collett's words didn't particularly surprise him. The strict orders of the previous evening had made it obvious that something big was about to happen. The 7th Texas had made a night march to its present position, instructed not to speak or to make any unnecessary noise. All their gear except their rifles, ammunition and canteens had been left behind in a rear depot, though many of the men had stuffed some biscuits in their pockets, not wanting to go into battle on an empty stomach.

"Two corps against the whole Army of the Cumberland in an open field fight?" one of the lieutenants asked, incredulous.

"If I understand what General Granbury told me, the plan is to strike them while they are still crossing the creek, catching them by surprise while their forces are divided. Sherman's other armies are too far away to come to their support. Something like that, anyway."

The lieutenant shook his head. "Those Cumberland boys don't run."

"They did at Chickamauga," Collett said. "Besides, it's not for us to worry about the big picture. We must place our trust in God and General Johnston." Collett squatted down and used his finger to sketch a diagram in the dirt. "Now, our division will hold the far left of the corps' line. Our brigade has been designated the division reserve. We'll advance behind the main line. The other brigades are going to make contact with the Yankees before we do. When old Pat Cleburne gives the word, we'll be sent in to break the bastards."

The men around the captain nodded stiffly and he stood up and went on. "Every man has been issued sixty rounds of ammunition. Hopefully that will be enough. Make sure that everyone's canteen is filled. We'll all be in hell before the day is over and we're going to need the water."

A few men chuckled at what they assumed had been Collett's attempt at a joke, but the stern face of his captain persuaded McFadden that he had not meant to be funny.

"Now, get back to your men and get them ready. The attack is scheduled for one o'clock."

The group of officers and sergeants quickly broke up and McFadden jogged back to the Lone Star Rifles, who had been placed on the far left of the rough line in which the 7th Texas was deployed.

His mind raced. Kennesaw Mountain had been a bloody fight, but had been brief and had involved only portions of the respective armies. The vicious engagements at Pickett's Mill and Dug Gap had also been brutal, but in the grand scheme of things had been little more than large skirmishes. If what Captain Collett had just told him was true, the Army of Tennessee was about to fight its biggest battle since Missionary Ridge. The fate of the campaign, perhaps even the entire war, might well turn on its outcome.

McFadden knew that there was a very good chance he would not be alive by the end of the day. He had never had much fear of death. Before the nightmare of the campaign in New Mexico, he had been a sincere believer in the doctrine of salvation through faith in Jesus Christ. After coming out of New Mexico, after what had happened to his family, he honestly hadn't much cared whether he lived or died. Death, at least, would have been an end to the agony which gripped his soul. Indeed, he had embraced death as he had plunged into the maelstrom of war on so many battlefields in Arkansas, Mississippi, Tennessee and Georgia. Imminent death had become almost like a companion to him, something comforting that he could caress as warmly as a lover.

McFadden suddenly stopped in his tracks, confusion clouding his face. He was not afraid, but he was abruptly and unexpectedly possessed by the intense realization that he no longer wanted to die. Something had changed. Some new factor had entered the equation of his life.

Since the dinner he had had with the Turnbows, nearly a week before, he and Annie had exchanged three letters, two from him and one from her. They had been innocent enough. Mostly they had discussed her father's plan for providing fresh produce to the men of the regiment. He had asked her about her favorite authors and poets, telling her of his love for Robert Burns and Sir Walter Scott. He also had made what he considered a pathetic effort to describe camp life, trying hard to make an incredibly dull topic sound interesting.

She had replied almost immediately, telling him that she had read and enjoyed Scott and would now try to read Burns. She liked Shakespeare and Milton very much, so McFadden resolved to try and find copies of those writers and brush up on them.

Annie had ended the letter by expressing concern for his well-being and safety, noting the prevalence of tuberculosis in the army and the prospect of renewed fighting. He hadn't thought about it when he read it, assuming that it was nothing more than a general statement of good will. However, with the biggest battle of the campaign at hand, the words suddenly had a much deeper resonance. Even if only slightly, he meant something to someone again.

McFadden took a deep breath. Steeling himself, he resumed his run.

He found the Lone Star Rifles just where he had left them, sitting in a large circle with disgruntled looks on their faces. Just before leaving them a few minutes before, McFadden had forbidden them from starting a fire to make coffee, citing strict orders.

"Can we make our damn coffee now?" Pearson demanded.

"Shut up, Pearson," McFadden said sharply. "We're going into battle, men. A damn big battle, from the looks of it."

The men stiffened and some stood up, looking to him for more explanation.

"Near as I can tell from what the captain said, the Yankee army is crossing that little river north of here right about now. Our plan is to hit them before they are all across, or something like that. Johnston wants to trap them on the south bank and crush them."

The eyes of the Texans lit up and their lips tightened. McFadden scanned their faces carefully, watching for any sign of fear or hesitation.

"What enemy?" Private Balch asked.

"Army of the Cumberland."

"Shit."

"Mind your tongue, Balch."

"We're dead men, sure as hell," Pearson said resignedly.

"That'll do," McFadden said, his tone making it clear that there would be no further discussion. "Rest up. Make sure your Enfields are clean and you have enough ammunition. If you brought any food with you, even though you were told not to, I suggest you eat it now."

"Can I make my coffee?" Pearson asked again, his tone much more polite.

"Sorry. No fires. Orders are orders. We don't want the Yankees to see any smoke, after all."

And after that, there was nothing to do but wait.

*   *   *   *   *

July 20, Noon

East of Atlanta, the twenty-five thousand Union troops of the Army of the Tennessee were marching south. In their midst rode Sherman and McPherson, surrounded by their respective staffs and followed by a large cavalry escort.

A courier galloped up. "Lead brigade reports it has entered Decatur. No rebels there, General!"

A cheer went up from the nearby federal troops. Sherman smiled and turned to McPherson.

"Well, that's good news, James. It means we now have a force on the railroad between Atlanta and Augusta."

McPherson nodded. "It does, indeed, Cump."

"I want you to get your engineers down on that railroad and start tearing it up. I want it so thoroughly wrecked that not a single train will pass between Atlanta and Augusta from now until doomsday. You hear that, James! From now until doomsday!"

"I understand completely, sir."

"Now that Johnston is cut off from his main rail connection to the east, he'll certainly pull out of Atlanta, if he hasn't already. We've cut him off from easy communication with the Carolinas and Virginia. If Lee really was sending him reinforcements, they'll have to come by a different route now." Sherman's face beamed and his voice was giddy.

Another courier arrived and handed Sherman a note.

General Sherman,
Crossing proceeding normally. No sign of enemy. Deserter just brought in reports Atlanta defenses held only by militia and enemy troops southeast of the city. Recommend McPherson watch his flank. I shall prepare to advance if opportunity presents itself.
General Thomas

"Well, James!" Sherman said happily. "Old Tom tells me that there are no rebels in his front and that the defenses of the city are held only by militia."

"Is that so?" McPherson said.

"Yep. He also tells me that, according to a deserter, the rebels are massing southeast of the city. Right against you, James."

McPherson shook his head. "I have received no reports of any serious enemy activity anywhere in that area. And my scouts have been pretty busy."

Sherman nodded. "Well, we know that trains have been pulling out of Atlanta in a big hurry, and prisoners and deserters have been telling us that their units were on their way out. If I wasn't sure before, I am sure now. Johnston has abandoned Atlanta. No doubt about it. Probably trying to regroup somewhere to the south."

"If that's so, then Thomas may be walking into the city even as we speak."

Sherman thought quickly. "How soon for you to get three or four divisions in battle line and march west, toward the city?"

McPherson considered it. "I can probably get General Logan and Fifteenth Corps lined up in an hour or so. They're at the head of the marching column. That's four divisions."

"Uh huh," Sherman replied, still thinking. "I know we discussed entering the city tomorrow, but if the rebels have pulled out already, I see no reason why we can't move things up by a day."

"Better to arrive too early than too late," McPherson said with a grin. "I can leave a brigade or two here to get started on wrecking the railroad, and some cavalry to guard the wagon train, and form up the rest of the army behind Fifteenth Corps."

"That sounds good. Make the necessary arrangements. Get Fifteenth Corps in formation and head directly for Atlanta, with the rest of them following as they get organized. The militia should run away at the first volley. Frankly, I'd rather let the Army of the

- 195 -

Tennessee have the honor of being the first to enter Atlanta than the Army of the Cumberland."

*   *   *   *   *

Moving quietly, Cleburne and Hardee scrambled up to the edge of a clearing. A few yards behind them, Lieutenant Hanley and some of Hardee's staff officers were holding their horses. Both men knew they were taking a terrible risk, moving up so close to the enemy. But they felt it was important that they get a clear estimate for themselves of exactly where the Union line was located. The risk was no greater than hundreds of others the two men had taken during the course of the war.

There was movement on the far side of the field. Hanging back in the trees to stay out of sight, the two men wordlessly surveyed the scene with their binoculars. Blue-clad regiments of Yankee soldiers were milling about the field. They were not setting up camp, but neither were they digging fortifications.

"Must be waiting for other units to come up," Hardee said. "Then they plan on continuing south."

"I see the flag of the 78th New York. It's in Twentieth Corps, I think."

"So it's the Army of the Cumberland for sure."

"They're not digging in," Cleburne said. "Never figured old George Thomas would ever get careless."

"Maybe Johnston's right, then. He's convinced them that we're abandoning the city and the Yankees are focused on getting into it as fast as they can."

"Maybe."

"Don't get cocky, though," Hardee cautioned. "The lead units are deploying into a battle line. They may not expect an attack, but they aren't letting their guard down too much."

There was a moment's pause as the two continued to scan the Union line, relatively sure they weren't being observed. After a few minutes, Hardee slapped Cleburne's shoulder and the two men crawled back toward their horses. Mounting quickly, the two generals and their staff officers walked their horses quietly away from the front line, careful not to kick their mounts into a trot. None of the Yankees saw them go, for none had seen them arrive.

When they had walked back south a considerable distance, Hardee pulled to a stop and Cleburne reined in next to him. Hardee pulled out his pocket watch.

"It is almost twelve. Are you prepared to move forward, General Cleburne?"

His pulse quickened. "Yes, sir."

A pause. "Then let the battle commence in exactly one hour. I will notify General Stewart that we are in position, so that he will be ready to send forward his corps as well. You've sent an officer to liaison with the rightmost division of Stewart's corps?"

"Of course."

"Very well. God go with you, Patrick."

"And with you, William."

Cleburne and Hardee exchanged sharp salutes, then Cleburne tossed his head toward Lieutenant Hanley and the two men rode off into the woods to the southeast, back toward the main body of the division.

*   *   *   *   *

Johnston felt his years as he hoisted himself up into the saddle. His leg muscles protested as they gripped the side of the steed. He wasn't the man he had been in Mexico. Still, if his body was aging, his instincts remained as combative as ever.

"What's the name of this horse?" he asked. It was a large and lovely brown mare with a streak of white along her snout. It was apparently the latest attempt of his staff to find a horse that Johnston liked.

"Fleetfoot, sir," Mackall answered.

"Nice name for a horse."

"Are you sure you want to ride forward, sir? The corps commanders have their orders. Once the battle commences, there will be little we can do to influence the course of events."

Johnston laughed. "I'm surprised at you, William."

"How's that, sir?" the chief-of-staff replied, mounting his own horse with considerably less effort than Johnston had required.

"Today is likely to be the most important day in both of our lives. Damned if I am going to spend it confined to a comfortable house while my men fight and die on the battlefield."

Mackall said nothing in response, but Johnston could still see the skepticism in his face. He didn't mind it. Part of Mackall's job, after all, was to keep Johnston out of harm's way unless absolutely necessary. Johnston did not doubt that Mackall would unhesitatingly put his own life on the line to protect him. Mackall might have been a staff officer rather than a battlefield commander, but Johnston did not doubt his courage for a single moment.

Besides, Mackall was talking good sense. Johnston only needed to recall the grievous wound he had received at the Battle of Seven Pines to remind himself of the dangers an army commander faced when venturing too close to the front lines.

They rode northwards, followed by a coterie of staff officers who had been assigned to serve as messengers and a small escort of cavalry. Off to his left, Johnston could see some of the formed units of Stewart's corps, deployed to form the left flank of the battle line.

Somewhere off to the right, hidden by the thick woods, was Hardee's corps.

He admitted to himself that he was nervous. He was not a gambling man by nature and he knew he was gambling now. He had rolled the dice, and though he had planned as carefully as he could and had taken every precaution he could think of, he could now do nothing but wait and see how the dice fell.

"Where are we going?" Mackall shouted above the thunder of hooves.

"Stewart's headquarters!" Johnston shouted back.

Mackall nodded. Excepting only James Longstreet, Hardee was the most experienced corps commander in the entire Confederate army. Stewart, by contrast, had only recently been elevated from the command of a division to the command of a corps. Hardee could be safely relied upon, but it was quite possible that Stewart would require the presence of the commanding general in order to be as effective as possible.

After riding for a few minutes, Johnston slowed and reined his horse to a stop. Without a word, Mackall and the rest of the assembly halted as well. The air seemed deathly silent, and Johnston strained to listen over the thin movement of the wind and the chatter of cicadas. He turned to Mackall.

"What time is it?"

Mackall checked his pocket watch. "Ten minutes to one o'clock, sir."

The corps commanders had been ordered to attack precisely at one o'clock, so there was no reason for him to hear the sounds of battle yet. Nevertheless, he found the silence unsettling. For a moment, he recalled the frustrating day in May, when he had waited to hear the sound of the guns that would have marked the opening of Hood's flank attack at Cassville. Those sounds had never come. Later that month, he had awaited the sounds of the guns which would have marked the beginning of the attack at New Hope Church. Again, those sounds had never come.

Now, every second that passed without the sound of firing was an endless agony. He didn't move. Behind him, men exchanged nervous glances with one another, wondering what their commanding general was thinking.

The minutes ticked away. He thought he heard something off to the right. He strained his ears to their absolute limits. Yes, there was the popping sound of musket fire off to the right, coming from the direction of Hardee's corps. He continued to wait. The sound of musketry seemed to gradually roll over the land, quiet at first but slowly reaching a higher volume, like the sound of crashing waves over the dunes of an Atlantic seashore.

After a few minutes, he heard a series of low booming sounds, which could only have been artillery fire. Continuing to listen intently, Johnston could now hear the sound of musketry from the left as well as the right, indicating that Stewart's corps was also involved in combat.

Mackall walked his horse up alongside Johnston.

"It's begun," Johnston said simply.

"Yes, sir."

"We've put our cards down on the table, William. Perhaps we have a pair of kings. Let us hope Sherman doesn't have a pair of aces."

"Your plan is good," Mackall said reassuringly. "The men are brave and strong. We shall emerge victorious."

"We shall see."

They sat silently and listened, their horses occasionally stirring uneasily as the sounds of battle grew louder. Eventually, Johnston reached over and placed a friendly hand on Mackall's shoulder. "Remember this moment, my friend. If God is with us, we shall today achieve the greatest victory of the war. But if not, I hope that you and I can both be proud of what we have done and know that we have both acted in an honorable manner."

"Of course, sir."

He paused for a moment, looking again to the northeast.

"Let's get to Stewart's headquarters."

"Yes, sir."

With a wave of the hand and a few kicks into the sides of their horses, the two men were off, the collection of staff officers following dutifully behind them. All around, the sounds of battle were growing ever louder.

*   *   *   *   *

Thomas was talking with a staff officer about getting some supply wagons across Collier's Bridge when he stopped talking and jerked his head about. He distinctly heard a sudden crash of musketry from somewhere off to the southeast. Many nearby officers stopped what they were doing and looked in the direction from which the sound had come. It sounded too intense to be a mere exchange of fire between picket lines.

His first thought was that some of his advance units might have stumbled upon a Confederate brigade, perhaps even a division, that was acting as a rear guard. But a few minutes later, a similar crash of heavy firing rang out from the southwest as well. In the midst of the sounds of musketry could be heard the occasional boom of cannon fire.

Over the din of heavy musketry and artillery fire, Thomas thought he could make out another sound, only partially muffled by the forest. After a few moments, he recognized the distant high-pitched yipping sound. It was the Rebel Yell.

He'd heard it before. At Stone's River, at Chickamauga, and countless other battlefields. Thomas was not a man given to fear, but his ears could tell him instantly that the Rebel Yell he was hearing was coming from the throats of tens of thousands of men. For just a moment, his blood turned cold. Thomas took a deep breath as he realized how completely wrong he and Sherman had been about Johnston's intentions. The Confederates were not abandoning Atlanta. Nor were they planning on attacking McPherson, east of the city. Instead, they had unleashed a full-scale offensive against the Army of the Cumberland, determined to drive it into Peachtree Creek.

His men were unfortified with their backs to the creek, having been caught completely by surprise. Suddenly and unexpectedly, Thomas found himself facing the most serious crisis of his military career.

But Thomas was not called The Rock of Chickamauga for nothing. Despite himself, Thomas found his lips curling into a sly grin. He turned and began yelling orders to his staff officers. Couriers were sent galloping to the various corps headquarters to obtain information on precisely what was happening. Artillery batteries were ordered into positions from which they might best bombard the attacking Southerners. Word was sent to the divisions still remaining on the north bank of the creek to speed up their crossing.

Satisfied, Thomas lit a cigar and waited for events to unfold. The blood which had turned cold for a moment had now become hot once again. "Very well," he said to himself. "If it's a fight Johnston wants, it's a fight he'll get."

*　　　　*　　　　*　　　　*　　　　*

Cleburne rode back and forth behind his advancing line, trying to drive his division forward through sheer force of will. The only people with him were Lieutenant Hanley and a private who had been given the honor of bearing the division colors. Major Benham and the other staff officers were trailing somewhere behind the advancing division, attempting the impossible task of keeping everything in order. Under Cleburne's saddle, Red Pepper breathed hard, frightened by the dreadful tumult into which his master had driven him but still obeying every tug and flip of the reins without hesitation.

It was difficult to see what was happening. Gunpowder smoke already covered the area, as if the Almighty had pulled a curtain of hot and acrid mist over everything. The roar of musketry seemed to be coming from every direction except from behind him, and even his finely tuned ears could not sense whether it was louder in one direction as opposed to any other. From somewhere off to his right, he thought he could hear the louder booming of artillery, which might have been a Union battery pouring its deadly fire into his men. But he couldn't be sure. All was confusion and chaos.

He glanced up at the sun. The rising smoke of the battle was already beginning to obscure what was an otherwise cloudless sky. The light from the sun punched through the canopy of grayish gunpowder smoke, but took on a ghastly blood red appearance. That Cleburne had seen the same effect on many other battlefields made it no less forbidding. Death was happily having a feast.

Half an hour earlier, the men of his division had marched out of the trees and into a large open space near the center of the battlefield. That field had now become a slaughterhouse of epic proportions. Although his men had caught the Yankees by surprise, it did not seem to have gained them much of an advantage. The tough veterans of the Army of the Cumberland, when faced with an unexpected attack, had quickly formed themselves into solid battle formations and begun to slug it out with their Southern foes.

Cleburne's men were still moving forward, exchanging fire with the Yankee troops opposite them, but only at a very slow pace. As he and his two companions advanced, the ground they passed over was littered with the corpses of dead men from both sides, as well as a larger number of wounded soldiers who were pathetically calling for help.

Though he was behind the front line of his division, bullets shot by Cleburne every few seconds, creating a sharp and frightful buzzing sound as they whistled past. Lieutenant Hanley ducked low in his saddle.

Cleburne laughed. "Ducking does no good, Lieutenant!" he shouted over the din. "By the time you hear them, they're already past!"

"I'll keep ducking, if you please, General!"

An artillery shell soared over Cleburne's head and slammed into the ground a few yards behind him. It exploded immediately upon impact, showering him and his two companions with dirt. Cleburne's hearing faltered momentarily, but recovered after about thirty seconds.

"Let's go forward!" Cleburne shouted, waving his hand. Hanley and the color bearer nodded and kicked their horses into trots. Suddenly, Cleburne realized that he did not know the name of the color bearer. He felt slightly guilty about this and considered asking the man, but just as quickly dismissed the matter as irrelevant in the middle of a battle.

Cleburne had deployed two of his brigades in line, holding his third brigade in reserve. On the left was Govan's brigade of Arkansas troops, while Lowrey's brigade of Mississippians and Alabamians was on the right. A few hundred yards behind the center of the line was Granbury's Texas brigade, held in reserve and ready at any moment to charge forward on Cleburne's command.

His division was on the left flank of Hardee's corps. The leftmost regiment of Govan's brigade was touching the right flank of Stewart's corps, near a tiny rivulet called Tanyard Branch that ran directly north into Peachtree Creek. On the other side of the division, the rightmost regiment of Lowrey's brigade was touching the left flank of Cheatham's division, which was made up entirely of Tennessee troops. Having Cheatham on his right was comforting for Cleburne, who greatly respected Cheatham's fighting abilities and the toughness of his troops. He could count on Cheatham is a way that he could never count on Walker.

In his mind, the positions of these various brigades and divisions were organized and tidy, like neat little lines one could draw on a map. The reality, as he well knew, was completely different. Amidst the swirling chaos of battle, most regiments had only the faintest idea where they were and perhaps no idea at all where the rest of their brigade was. If they maintained even the semblance of a line facing the enemy, and had some idea of which regiment was on each of their flanks, they counted themselves lucky.

As Cleburne and his companions drew closer to the front line, the sound of musket and artillery fire grew exponentially. His nostrils protested at the burning smell of gunpowder and Red Pepper made his displeasure known by shaking his head and whinnying vigorously. Cleburne glanced over at Hanley, seeing an expression on the lieutenant's face that was apprehensive, but not fearful.

Walking wounded, many of them holding bloody bandages up to their faces, drifted back away from the front lines. Hanley pointed some of them in the direction of the division's hospital tents, but Cleburne knew that they would find little comfort there. If anything, the horrors the wounded would experience at the hands of the surgeons would be worse than those they had already encountered on the battlefield. But that would be something he would think about later, when the battle was over and if he managed to survive.

They finally reached the battle line itself. Ragged and disorderly, it yet remained intact, with the men standing shoulder to shoulder as they loaded and fired continuously. Through the smoke, Cleburne could just make out the line of blue-coated Union soldiers perhaps a hundred yards father on. Neither side seemed willing to budge, but neither appeared able to mount a bayonet charge. Both sides simply stood their ground, pouring deadly fire into one another. Every few seconds, another one of his men fell, some dropping quickly and silently, others shrieking in agony as they were hit.

Somewhere off to the right, obscured by smoke, was a Union artillery battery. He couldn't see it, but he could hear the booming of its guns and see their deadly effect. As he was watching, a solid shot passed neatly through the body of a young soldier, perhaps only sixteen or seventeen, slicing him in half as trimly as though it had been done by a butcher's knife. He hadn't had a moment in which to scream. The men on either side were drenched with the boy's blood, but they ignored it and kept firing, instinctively scooting slightly closer to one another to close the tiny gap in the line.

"Where is General Lowrey?" Cleburne shouted to the first officer he encountered.

"Over there, sir!" the man shouted, pointed toward the center of the brigade.

Cleburne trotted over, spotting Lowrey a few moments later. The brigade commander was on foot, his sword drawn and a fierce expression on his face. Mark Lowrey was a good friend who had long served with him and who had loyally supported him when he had issued his proposal to free the slaves. He was a devout man of God and, as far as Cleburne was concerned, the bravest man in the Confederate Army. Simply seeing him in command of his troops gave Cleburne a sense of comfort.

"How are things, Mark?" Cleburne shouted.

Lowrey shook his head vigorously. "The Yankees won't break! We're giving it everything we've got, but they won't break!"

Cleburne glanced back at the firing line. Men were falling with grim regularity and it seemed that the tempo of firing from the Union line was becoming more intense. Canister fire and solid shot from enemy cannon swept in every few seconds, taking clusters of men with it.

"There's a Yankee battery over there!" Lowrey said, gesturing frantically to the right. "It's firing at an angle that's enfilading our line."

"I'll summon sharpshooters," Cleburne said. He nodded toward Hanley, who galloped off.

"I need support!" Lowrey said. "Can you bring Granbury up?"

Cleburne thought quickly. He did not want to commit Granbury except at a time and place where it would be decisive. If he sent in his reserve brigade at the wrong place or at the wrong time, it might fail to have any impact and be chewed up for no gain.

"Not yet! Can you hold?"

"I think I can hold, but I can't move forward!"

"Keep the pressure on!" Cleburne shouted as he turned his horse away. He needed to consult with Govan on the other end of the division's line. He kicked Red Pepper into a gallop, wanting to get to the other brigade as quickly as possible. As he shot past the men of Lowrey's brigade, many of them sent up a cheer.

A Union artillery shell slammed into the ground scarcely five yards off to Red Pepper's right and exploded. The force of the blast tossed Cleburne out of his saddle like a ragdoll and he fell heavily onto the ground. The wind was instantly knocked out of him and he struggled to maintain consciousness. He felt faint for what could have been just a few seconds or perhaps longer than a minute. He couldn't tell. As he began to try to pull himself up, the color bearer was at his side helping him.

"Are you all right, sir?" the color bearer asked.

Cleburne looked down and twitched his toes. Everything felt intensely stiff, but he did not think any bones had broken. "I think so, yes."

"A few more feet and that shell would have exploded right under your horse."

Suddenly startled, Cleburne glanced about for Red Pepper. With great relief, he saw the animal standing a few feet away, quietly gazing at him and seemingly impatient for Cleburne to get back in the saddle.

He looked at the color bearer. "What's your name, son?"

The young man looked confused. "John Hatch, sir. 45th Alabama."

Cleburne clapped his shoulder. "Good to know. Now, get mounted up again and follow me."

Moments later, Cleburne and Hatch were again riding westwards toward the right flank of the division. They arrived within a matter of minutes.

"Where is General Govan?" Cleburne asked the nearest officer.

"He's dead, sir! Shot through the chest!"

Cleburne pursed his lips tightly. In an instant, he had lost a trusted subordinate who was also a dear friend. He had known Daniel Govan for years and respected him as he did few others. But grief would have to wait until after the battle was over.

He located Colonel Warfield, the ranking officer, and ordered him to take command of the brigade. Such transitions happened all too often in the midst of battle, but Cleburne trusted his men enough to know that any unnecessary confusion would be avoided. He spent a few minutes riding back and forth behind the brigade, feeling for himself what the situation was.

It looked little different from the situation on Lowrey's front. The Arkansas troops were exchanging heavy fire with the Yankees, but neither side seemed to have the gumption to charge forward. It was a stalemate.

All around, men were collapsing, dead or wounded. He knew that his men could only take this punishment for so long before the number of casualties forced them to break off the action. Something needed to be done, and fast.

Behind the line, he knew, the Texans of Granbury's Brigade were waiting. Cleburne knew he needed to do something with them. If he simply committed them to the fighting by pushing them up to the front line, they might also lack the strength for a decisive attack and simply be cut to pieces like the other two brigades.

He looked across the line at the enemy. They presented a long, continuous battle line, with scarcely any gaps between formations. There were no flanks that could be turned, nor any particular pieces of terrain he could see that might give his men some sort of advantage. He knew his division lacked the strength to overwhelm the enemy by brute force and he could not see any way to outmaneuver them.

It was then that he had his idea.

*   *   *   *   *

The phenomenon known as acoustic shadows had been reported many times since the beginning of the war. Battles could be seen clearly a mile or so away, though they appeared to make no sound. Odder still, people at a considerably greater distance could hear the sounds of fighting quite distinctly. No one understood what caused acoustic shadows and they were the subject of much debate and discussion.

The particular combination of air pressure, temperature, humidity and the topographical realities of the north Georgia terrain happened to come together during the early afternoon of July 20 to form an acoustic shadow over the battlefield just south of Peachtree Creek.

West of Decatur, Sherman and McPherson watched the four divisions of Fifteenth Corps form up for an advance on Atlanta, entirely unaware that the Army of the Cumberland was even then engaged in a desperate battle for its life just a few miles away.

*   *   *   *   *

July 20, Afternoon

Thomas sat silently in the saddle of his favorite horse, Billy, serenely smoking an enormous cigar. Less than twenty yards away, two four-gun artillery batteries thundered every few seconds, sending their deadly shells out into the midst of the attacking rebels. Clearly visible in a clearing a quarter mile to the south, the rival battle lines were continuing to slug it out. The loud and constant crackle of gunfire rose into the skies.

Inevitably, the stream of wounded men was painfully making its way back from the front line in search of the hospitals in the rear. A few confused men also arrived, frantically asking staff officers to direct them to their units. Some of these men, Thomas knew, were shirkers seeking to avoid combat, but he hoped most of them were genuinely lost and trying to get back into the fight.

He raised his field glasses to his eyes and surveyed the scene. Most of the ground over which the fighting was taking place was heavily wooded, but there were also numerous open fields where heavy fighting was easily observed.

According to what he saw, and all the reports coming to him from his commanders, the Confederate attack had been stopped dead in its tracks. While momentarily taken by surprise when the rebels had emerged from the trees to the south, the individual brigades and divisions had rallied quickly and given up only a small amount of ground in the first half hour of the engagement. Everyone now appeared to be holding their positions with relative ease. In a few cases, some individual brigades had even launched counter attacks. Heavy casualties had been sustained, but that was inevitable.

As information from the front line filtered back to the army command post, an increasingly clear picture of the situation formed in his mind. Some of the enemy units carried the distinctive blue battle flags of Cleburne's division, which meant that Hardee's corps had to be involved in the attack. A few prisoners from regiments identified as being from Polk's old corps had been brought in, who provided the useful information that the corps was now under the command of General Alexander Stewart. There was no sign of Hood's corps, which Thomas therefore concluded had to be deployed east of the city to protect it from McPherson and Schofield.

Thomas did some fast mental calculations. He had briefly considered halting the movement of his troops over Peachtree Creek, for in the event of a disaster the bridges would need to be cleared in order for the men on the south bank to retreat to the north bank. He had never doubted the ability of his men to hold their ground, but Thomas was a careful man and always planned for every eventuality. As it now appeared that the enemy attack was faltering, such a precaution seemed unnecessary. He sent orders to speed up the crossing if possible.

In an instant, Thomas saw a breathtaking possibility. The rebel attack was in the process of being repulsed. When that was achieved, the enemy formations would be in great disorder and would have suffered heavy casualties. A few fresh Union divisions, formed up for battle behind the main Union line, would be in a perfect position to launch a devastating counter attack. Two-thirds of the Army of Tennessee could be shattered in a matter of hours. If Hood's corps could be dealt with by McPherson and Schofield, not only would the city of Atlanta be in Union hands before nightfall, but the main Confederate army in the western theater of the war would be completely destroyed.

He breathed in sharply. The possibility before him was nothing less than a chance to bring the war to an end as a decisive Union victory.

He pulled a message pad out from his saddlebag and began furiously scribbling.

General Sherman,

I have come under heavy attack by two enemy corps. The fighting is severe but I am holding my position and am confident I can continue to do so. I intend to counter attack as soon as possible. Recommend McPherson and Schofield advance from the east. I believe we can crush Johnston between us.

General Thomas

He tore the paper off the pad and handed it to a nearby aide.

"Take this to General Sherman as quickly as possible. Ride like the devil, Captain!"

"Yes, sir!" the man said, shoving the paper into his saddlebag before kicking his horse into a full gallop.

*   *   *   *   *

As he rode across the landscape, trailed by his staff, Johnston kept glancing to the north. The sounds of battle continued to increase with every passing minute, becoming a constant low roar and seemingly coming from every direction. It sounded like an endless piece of paper was being torn in half. In a few places, darker smoke was intermingled with the grayish mist caused by the mass expenditure of gunpowder, indicating that underbrush in many areas had caught fire. As in past battles, the flames would certainly consume many of the helpless wounded men.

The earth had broken open and hell had been let loose.

Before him suddenly was General Stewart. They had traveled across the length of the battlefield and were now near the left flank of the line. The corps commander was mounted on his horse, frantically issuing orders to his own officers. For the first few moments, he seemed entirely unaware of Johnston's presence. Nearly a full minute passed before a staffer quietly told Stewart that the army commander had arrived.

Stewart quickly composed himself and saluted. "Good afternoon, General Johnston!" he said. It seemed a ridiculous thing to say.

Johnston returned the salute. "What's the situation, General?"

Stewart didn't respond right away, but his expression told Johnston everything that he needed to know. Stewart looked frazzled, like a man who had just lost a fortune at the gambling table. This worried Johnston, but he was somewhat comforted by another emotion he could see in Stewart's fierce face. The Tennessee warrior was also enraged.

"The Yankees won't drive worth a damn!" Stewart blurted out. "We caught them by surprise at first, and pushed them back a half mile or so. But then they stiffened up and brought up artillery. We haven't gone forward an inch since then!"

Johnston nodded sharply. He quickly recalled the division Stewart had held in reserve. "Have you sent in Walthall's division yet?"

"I did," Stewart said quickly. "I had to! French's division was shattered by Yankee artillery and an enemy counter attack. But Walthall is barely holding his ground as we speak."

"And Loring?"

"He's holding his own, but says he can't move forward without support. Dear God, General, I've already lost more than two thousand men!"

There was a sudden crash of artillery fire from somewhere off to the north. Instinctively, Johnston looked in the direction from which the sound had come, but could see nothing through the smoke and trees. In all likelihood, yet another Union artillery battery had gotten into position, set itself up, and started pouring fire into the ranks of his army.

As he was listening, Johnston realized that the sound of battle had changed. An hour earlier, he could distinctly hear the yip-yipping sound of the Rebel Yell over the din of artillery and musket fire. It had signaled that his army was attacking and pushing back the Yankee enemy. But he no longer heard the Rebel Yell. Instead, as he listened intently, it was apparent to him that the deep hurrah sound made by the Northern soldiers was becoming ever louder. The sounds of battle were coming closer, not getting farther away.

Johnston pursed his lips. The gamble had clearly failed. The attack had not achieved the decisive success he had sought. He was now caught in an open field fight with a foe that outnumbered him. He faced the very real possibility that his two corps would be shattered on this field, that Atlanta would fall, and that the name Joseph Johnston would be written in history as the name of the man who had lost the war.

He had to find Hardee.

Johnston left orders directing Stewart to rally his men and continue the attack with whatever strength he could muster. After assuring himself that he had been properly understood, Johnston saluted and kicked his horse back into a gallop, heading east this time, followed by Mackall and the rest of the staff.

Ten minutes later, as they continued to ride across the battlefield, Johnston saw a horrifying sight. Out of a white cloud of gunpowder smoke, he could make out Confederate soldiers running toward the south, many of them weaponless and all of them frightened. Worse still, none of them appeared to be wounded. As he watched, the number grew from a handful to a few dozen, and then scores of men running together. Something on the front line had obviously gone terribly wrong.

Johnston sent a courier galloping back to Stewart to tell him something was amiss, but he knew that it would take too long for the message to reach the corps commander and for proper action to be taken. Although he hesitated to interfere with the chain of command, he knew he had to intervene personally. He kicked his horse northwards, riding into the midst of the retreating soldiers.

"Stop!" he shouted. "Turn around! Don't run like cowards!" To give his words added emphasis, he drew his sword.

Most of the fleeing troops continued running as though they had not heard him. Only a few of the men stopped, looking up at him in confusion.

"What brigade are you from?" he demanded.

"Quarles' Brigade, sir! Walthall's division!"

Johnston's mind instantly recalled that the brigade was a hodgepodge of regiments from Alabama, Louisiana, and Tennessee. The crowd of retreating Southerners was growing larger.

He spotted a corporal whose eyes seemed intelligent. "What is happening?" he demanded of the man, pointing toward the front with his sword.

"The Yankees wheeled up two batteries of artillery and blasted us, sir! Then a whole new brigade of Yankees showed up and charged at us!"

Johnston pursed his lips in anger. He turned to Mackall.

"William, if I am not mistaken, General Reynolds' brigade of Arkansans was designated as Walthall's reserve. Find him and bring him up at once."

Mackall nodded sharply and was gone in an instant, disappearing off to the south. Johnston began walking his horse back and forth, waving his sword over his head to gain the attention of the fleeing soldiers.

"Halt!" he shouted. "The men of the Army of Tennessee do not run!"

Some of his staff officers, taking their cue from their commander, dashed about on horseback, halting and organizing the retreating soldiers back into a semblance of a line as if they were herding sheep. As the precious minutes passed, a thin line of men was slowly strung across the surrounding area. Johnston could only hope that its flanks would connect with steadier Confederate units on either side of them.

Artillery shells began to fall around them, leading Johnston to conclude that the enemy was moving their guns forward and preparing to mount an even larger attack. Having broken one Confederate brigade, it stood to reason that the Yankees would see this particular position as a weak point and attempt to break through completely.

He glanced around. The thin line of frightened men his staff officers were struggling to put together could no more resist a determined Union attack than a fragile piece of glass could resist the blow of a sledgehammer. If a fresh enemy brigade charged toward them, the Southerners would be lucky to get off a single volley before they broke and bolted for the rear. At best, they might delay the enemy attack for a few precious seconds.

He glanced to the southeast, hoping to see Mackall leading the Arkansas brigade into position. There was only an empty field. Johnston quickly said a silent prayer that Mackall had located reinforcements and was hurrying to the scene. If he didn't arrive in the next few minutes, it might be too late.

He had begun the battle as the attacker, confident of victory. But now his own army stood on the brink of defeat. For if the Yankees broke through his line, they might split his forces in two. In such a case, Johnston thought he would be lucky if he managed to get back into the defenses of Atlanta with even a portion of his force. His heart turned to ice when he contemplated the very real possibility that the Army of Tennessee was about to be destroyed.

There was a tremendous cry of alarm from the haphazard line. Looking northward, Johnston could see the first rank of blue-coated infantrymen coming into view. They were advancing at a walk and were not yet charging. He sensed the wavering of his own men and decided to take a calculated risk.

Looking as serene as he possibly could, and in spite of the fact that his heart was pounding in his chest with the force of a steam engine, he calmly walked his horse out in front of the line formed by Quarles' men. He pointed his sword at the advancing Union troops but turned in the saddle to face his own soldiers.

"Men of the South! You must maintain this position! I am bringing up reinforcements! If you can hold your ground for a few minutes, help will come!"

There was silence from the men. He could still see demoralization in their faces. They had already been through severe fighting and were utterly exhausted, both mentally and physically. Johnston knew from a lifetime of soldiering that there was only so much strain a man could take. He needed to get these tired and frightened men to bear that strain for just a little bit longer. Bullets began zinging by, but Johnston paid them no mind.

"Will you allow the name of the Army of Tennessee to be disgraced?"

"No!" a man from the ranks shouted.

"We will hold, General!" another cried.

Johnston quickly scanned the eyes of the soldiers. Many were glancing left and right at their comrades, seeking strength and reassurance. Others began calling out to the army commander, expressing their determination to hold their ground and follow orders. It was as if a rope was tying them together and holding them in place. It might yet snap under pressure, but it was better than nothing.

Satisfied, he nodded sharply and kicked his horse back into a trot. The men parted momentarily to let him pass through the line. As he continued to ride southwards, he began hearing a sharp increase in firing from the spot he had just left. The Yankees were indeed attacking again, hoping to press their advantage, but Quarles' men were offering a least some measure of resistance. Johnston knew it could not last long.

His heart leapt as he saw the reassuring form of General Mackall riding up to him at a canter. Even more heartening was the formation of Confederate infantry coming up behind him. Row upon row of hundreds of Southern fighters were coming up at the double-quick. A glance at the battle flag of the lead regiment confirmed for Johnston that it was the Arkansas Brigade of General Reynolds.

Coming close to the fighting, the officers shouted commands and the men expertly deployed from a marching column into a battle line. The entire maneuver took scarcely a minute. As they formed up shoulder to shoulder, gripping their rifles tensely, Johnston rode up to the front of their line.

"Men of Arkansas! All before you are giving way! You must advance and drive the enemy back!"

"We will, General Johnston!" several men shouted simultaneously.

"I will lead you!" Johnston cried. He trotted to the center of the Arkansas battle line, stopped just long enough to point his sword in the direction of the fighting and kicked his horse into a walk.

Mackall rode up beside him, a cross between anger and concern in his eyes. With extreme impertinence, he grabbed the bridle of Johnston's horse.

"What the damn hell do you think you're doing, General Johnston!" he demanded. "Get away from here! General Reynolds can lead his own damn brigade in the counter attack!"

Johnston felt a surge of anger, wondering how his chief-of-staff could dare speak to him in such an insolent manner. "Let go of the bridle this instant, Mackall!"

"I will not, sir! You must retire to the rear immediately!"

"Let go!"

"General Johnston, the army has plenty of brigade commanders, but only one man to lead the army!"

Johnston's face flushed. For just a moment, he was white-hot with anger. But his ears heard the cries of his soldiers, calling for him to move behind the brigade. Like raindrops falling onto a campfire, their cries smothered his fury.

General Daniel Reynolds, the commander of the unit, galloped up. "Please retire to the rear, General Johnston," he pleaded. "My brigade will counter attack and restore the line, but you must retire at once. The men are refusing to charge unless you are safe!"

The rational part of his mind quickly realized that Mackall

and Reynolds were entirely correct. Leading an infantry charge was not the duty of the supreme commander of the army. He saw that he had acted with gross irresponsibility and potentially placed the army in danger. Allowing his grip on the reins to slacken, he let his chief-of-staff pull the horse away from the fighting and lead him to the south.

Once their leader was safe, the men of Reynolds' Brigade wasted no time. They dashed past Johnston and Mackall at the double quick, plunging northwards into the confusion of the battle. The Rebel Yell rose from the throats of a thousand Arkansas soldiers and there was a sudden explosive crackling of musket fire as the two sides collided. Johnston glanced over his shoulder just long enough to see General Reynolds falling out of his saddle, dead or wounded.

As the fighting behind him increased in intensity, he saw two Confederate artillery batteries rolling up behind the line. The gunners unlimbered their deadly weapons and loaded them with canister. Though they held their fire out of fear that they might hit their comrades, the presence of the eight artillery pieces gave some measure of reassurance to Johnston that this section of the line was now safe. It had momentarily broken, but disaster had been averted.

Instantly, Johnston's mind returned to the battle as a whole. Stewart's attack on the left side of the battle line had obviously been repulsed and all his reserves had been committed merely to prevent the Yankees from breaking through themselves. Thomas and his Army of the Cumberland were fighting ferociously. Johnston had to get to Hardee and discover what the situation was on the other side of the battlefield.

He thought for a moment that he should immediately order Stewart and Hardee to call off their attacks and retreat at once into the Atlanta defenses. Doing so would save the army and preserve whatever combat power it had left. But doing so would also mean the end of his effort to win a decisive victory. Sherman would place Atlanta under siege and the city's fall would become merely a matter of time.

There remained one ace-in-the-hole for Johnston. Clayton's division, which he had detached from Hood's corps, remained deployed to the south as the final reserve for the attacking force. It was a strong force of about five thousand men. If Johnston could find a way to tear open a gap in the Union line, no matter how small, he could send Clayton's division charging through to the enemy rear, shattering the federal position and driving the Army of the Cumberland into Peachtree Creek as originally planned.

It seemed a forlorn hope. Yet it was the only chance Johnston had. He was not prepared to give up just yet.

Johnston, Mackall, and the swarm of staff officers and escorting cavalrymen thundered eastwards. Off to their left, the battle continued to rage. As they moved, couriers from various points of the battlefield rode up and shouted news. Almost all of it was confused and disjointed. Within minutes, two messages arrived from Stewart, one saying that he was having difficulty holding his ground and the other saying that he was about to resume the attack. Which message was most recent was anyone's guess. The only thing that seemed certain was that the fighting was severe all along the line and that the casualties were already heavy.

Johnston and his party splashed across the small stream running down the center of the battlefield, which had been designated as the dividing point between the corps of Stewart and Hardee. Twenty minutes later, they located General Hardee.

"What is the situation?" Johnston asked quickly after the customary salute.

"We pushed them for a mile or so. We've taken many prisoners and half a dozen battle flags. We also captured a battery of Yankee artillery. But resistance has stiffened since the first hour of the attack. I haven't been able to push forward an inch for some time. Lost of a lot of men."

"Stewart's attack has been repulsed. The enemy broke his line at one point before a counter attack sealed the breach. We need to find a way to get the attack moving again."

"Can I put Clayton in?" Hardee asked.

Johnston thought quickly. He had considered dispatching Clayton to Stewart's front in order to shore up his obviously shaky line, but that was a move designed to prevent defeat rather than to achieve victory. And it was victory that Johnston was after.

His original plan had called for both Stewart and Hardee to drive the Yankees back to Peachtree Creek in a single, sweeping assault. But as usually happened, the chaos of actual battle had created a situation in which the original plan no longer applied. Instantly, Johnston's mind drew up a new plan. Stewart would continue to press his assault if at all possible, but from now on Johnston would consider his attacks to be a diversion, designed only to keep the Yankees occupied on the west side of the battlefield and prevent them from dispatching reinforcements to the east side. In the meantime, Clayton's division would be released to Hardee, who would use it to try a last-ditch effort to break the Union line.

"Yes, put Clayton in," Johnston said decisively. "Where to deploy him is a decision I leave to you."

"Very well, sir." Hardee saluted and, with a kick to his horse, was off.

Johnston watched Hardee go. With him, Johnston thought, went the hopes of the Confederacy.

Unlike the ground to the north of Atlanta, the terrain east of the city was largely barren and empty of trees. Much of the woods in the area had been cleared for lumber to be used in the fortifications which protected the city. Indeed, the most prominent elevation in the area was known simply as "Bald Hill" because of its complete lack of foliage.

Atop Bald Hill, Hood stared out to the east with growing alarm. Enormous formations of Union infantry were visible from his position, formed up for battle and marching directly on Atlanta. It was hard to tell from such a distance, but Hood thought he counted four divisions. Behind them, great clouds of dust rose from the ground, indicating the presence of yet more marching columns. It appeared to Hood that the entire Army of the Tennessee was heading directly for him.

He lowered his telescope and glanced northwards from Bald Hill. Since Johnston had taken Clayton's division away from him, Hood had only two divisions manning the fortifications on the eastern side of Atlanta, those of General Brown and General Stevenson. All told, he had perhaps eight to ten thousand men in line. Even behind stout fortifications, Hood wasn't sure how long they might be able to hold against McPherson's twenty-five thousand men. Moreover, Schofield was also out there somewhere with fifteen thousand more.

He heard the scattered popping of musket fire, and trained his telescope in the direction of the sound. The advance elements of the Union infantry were just now coming into contact with the skirmishers he had deployed out ahead of the fortified line. Ordinarily, this was done to force any advancing enemy to deploy into a battle line, thereby buying time for the troops in the main line to get ready. But the Yankees were already deployed in a battle line, so little was achieved besides a few minutes delay and a couple dozen casualties on each side.

Hood figured that the Union infantry would reach his line within the next half hour. They would then perhaps take a short time to study the defenses before forming up for an attack. At most, Hood had perhaps an hour-and-a-half before his men would be called upon to withstand an enemy more than twice their number.

He turned to an aide. "Captain, you are to ride as fast as you can to General Johnston. Tell him that an enemy force considerably superior to my own is advancing upon my position. I must have Clayton's division returned to my command at once or I will be overwhelmed."

"Yes, sir!" The man saluted, kicked his horse, and was away.

Cleburne rode eastward behind the line of his division, feeling the hot and angry wind of the battle raging just a few hundred yards away. Red Pepper was becoming increasingly tired and upset, neighing his protests more loudly than before. Cleburne gently patted the animal's neck and spoke words of reassurance, but Red Pepper wasn't much comforted.

He had more important matters to worry about than the agitation of his mount. Cleburne knew he had to act quickly if his plan to break the Union line was to have any chance of success. He knew it was a good idea, but it would depend on many different factors falling into place at exactly the right time. Above all, it would depend on his ability to keep his division under control in the midst of a ferocious battle, a difficult if not impossible task.

Just minutes earlier, he had given the necessary orders to Colonel Warfield, temporarily in command of Govan's Brigade following Govan's death. Warfield was a good regimental commander, but Cleburne wasn't sure if he would have the stomach to assume command of the whole brigade. There was no time to worry about it. Cleburne had to trust that Warfield would be able to do what he had asked him to do.

He approached Lowrey, who was continuing to frantically direct his regiments. The brigade commander saluted sharply as Cleburne approached. He wasted no time with small talk.

"General Lowrey, when I give the command, your brigade is to fall back!"

"What?!" Lowrey shouted. "Why? I may not be driving the Yankees, but as God is my witness I'll not let them force me to retreat!"

"We're not retreating, Lowrey!" Cleburne shouted over the din of the musketry and artillery fire. "I don't have time to explain it! We're going to trick the Yankees into thinking that you are retreating! When I give the word, pull your brigade back six hundred yards or so, then halt!"

Lowrey's face did not betray fear, but it did betray anxiety of a sort. Every soldier of any experience knew that a orderly withdrawal in the face of a superior enemy in the middle of a battle was the most difficult and dangerous maneuver imaginable. The slightest hint of confusion could send the men into a panic. If even a single company lost its composure, its fear would instantly spread to the rest of its regiment, and from that regiment to the entire brigade. The entire unit might then disintegrate into a confused and frightened mass of men and tumble into a headlong rout. Cleburne had seen it happen before.

Cleburne was gratified when Lowrey finally nodded, kicked his horse, and went to find his regimental commanders. A lesser officer might have demanded further clarification or angrily disagreed. It spoke volumes about Lowrey's confidence in Cleburne that he did neither of these things. Nor did Cleburne remain to oversee Lowrey's movement, instead simply counting on him to perform the duty that had been entrusted to him.

Cleburne turned and kicked Red Pepper into a gallop, heading south. Moments later, he came upon the steady ranks of Granbury's Texans, not yet committed to battle. Granbury, mounted on a gray mare, sat stoically in front of them, patiently waiting. To Cleburne, he seemed like nothing so much as a steady Roman centurion, commanding a cohort of heroes. Indeed, the very sight of the Texas soldiers, gripping their Enfield rifles, gave Cleburne a feeling of superb confidence.

"How's it going, General?" Granbury asked, as naturally as if he were discussing a horse race.

"Govan's dead. Warfield's taken over command of his brigade."

Granbury nodded. He and Govan had been friends, but he betrayed no hint of sadness. "Well, that's too bad. Leading from the front, no doubt."

"The attack is stalled, but I want to get it moving once again. I want you to move your brigade a few hundred yards to the left, and prepare to attack in a northeasterly direction."

"Northeast?" Granbury asked. "Pray tell, what is it you have in mind?"

"Lowrey's going to pull back a few hundred yards. The Yankees will think they have broken the line and will charge forward to exploit the breach. When Lowrey halts and turns to fight, the right flank of the enemy formation will be exposed to your attack. Your men will then open fire and charge, just as Lowrey's men do the same. The combined attack by both brigades will shatter the enemy formation by catching them in a crossfire."

Granbury nodded as he listened. "A brilliant idea, Patrick. Truly inspired."

"Compliment me after we have succeeded. Any question?"

"No, sir."

"Good. You have ten minutes. Now, get to it!"

Granbury dashed off without taking the time to salute. Cleburne turned and gazed northward, back toward where the brigades of Warfield and Lowrey were fighting. The steady rolling sound of intense musketry combined with the regular booming of artillery continued to pummel his ears. He wondered if he would be able to hear anything when it was all over.

He sent a courier to bring the divisional artillery to the position Granbury's men were expected to take. Their added firepower would pack an enormous punch when the time came. He was attending to their deployment when he saw General Hardee ride up.

"Stewart's attack has failed!" Hardee said without preamble. "Our own corps has been halted all along the line. We have to break through here, Patrick. Put Granbury in right away. Clayton's division will be right behind."

"Give me five minutes!"

"If we don't break them now, the battle is lost!"

A wry grin crossed Cleburne's face. "Watch this, William!"

*   *   *   *   *

The battle had now been raging for hours, but McFadden had not yet fired his Enfield. Nor had any other soldier in Granbury's Texas Brigade. Somewhere in front of them, the men of Govan's and Lowrey's brigades were fighting for their lives. They had seen a steady stream of wounded men drifting back toward the rear since the commencement of the battle. But despite the obvious fierceness of the fighting, the Texans remained uncommitted. Thus far, their only casualties had been a few men wounded by artillery fire.

He had tried to follow the progress of the battle by listening to the sounds of the fighting, but had soon given the task up as impossible. Unlike other engagements, in which heavier firing could clearly be heard in one direction and lighter firing in another, this battle simply seemed to be one constant roar of explosive force somewhere up ahead. McFadden felt like he and his comrades were standing on the edge of a volcano.

"What's going on, Sarge?" Montgomery asked, his voice betraying nervousness.

"Your guess is as good as mine, Private."

"Why haven't they sent us in yet? I can't stand this waiting a minute longer!"

McFadden nodded quickly, trying to appear composed. In truth, his heart was in his throat, his breathing was quickening, and he felt his hands shaking ever so slightly. Aside from his baptism of fire at Valverde, he had never been nervous before going into battle before and he struggled to understand why he should be nervous now. He didn't want to die, not now. Not after Annie Turnbow had come into his life and allowed him to glimpse the possibility of something other than a bleak future.

Out of the smoke suddenly emerged General Cleburne, mounted on Red Pepper, staring down at the massed group of Texans with a cool and determined gaze. Over the din of battle, he raised his voice for all to hear.

"Texans! You are the sons of the defenders of the Alamo! You are about to perform a maneuver that will decide the outcome of the battle! Be brave and hold steady, my Texans! I shall lead you to victory!"

"We will follow you to the gates of hell, General!" a man in the ranks yelled out. His words were followed by several seconds of wild cheering. Cleburne nodded sharply and rode off.

Officers began shouting out orders. The brigade had been deployed in a standard battle formation two lines deep facing directly north, with the 7th Texas being one of the regiments in the front line. But to McFadden's confusion, the orders did not send them forward into the fight as he had expected. Instead, they were directed to shift from a battle line into a marching column. Although perplexed, the men did as they were told quickly and efficiently. Within two minutes, the entire brigade was trotting steadily to the west.

"What's going on, Sergeant?" Pearson said from somewhere behind him.

"I don't know," McFadden replied, dearly wishing that Pearson would stop asking so many questions.

They moved west for a few minutes, closer toward the left flank of Cleburne's division. McFadden was reasonably certain that they were now somewhere behind Govan's Brigade. He trusted the Arkansas troops, who had fought beside them in so many battles. He couldn't see any reason for Cleburne to have ordered the Texas Brigade to this particular position. From all McFadden could see and hear, Govan's men were holding their ground just fine. He began to wonder if they were being sent to another part of the battlefield altogether, perhaps to reinforce Stewart's corps on the other side of the battlefield. But the words Cleburne had spoken led McFadden to believe that something altogether extraordinary was about to happen.

They veered slightly to the right and started moving northwest. They had not gone far, however, when Granbury shouted the order to stop.

"Halt!" Collett repeated.

"Company! Halt!" McFadden shouted to the Lone Star Rifles.

More orders were shouted, which McFadden repeated as loudly as he could so that his own men could hear them. The brigade again metamorphosed, going from a marching column back into a battle line, now facing directly to the northeast, at a forty-five degree angle to the position they had been in a few minutes before. But there was no enemy in front of them.

Scarcely thirty seconds after that had been accomplished, orders were shouted that took McFadden quite by surprise.

"Lie down!" Collett shouted.

"Lie down," McFadden repeated for his own men, trying to keep the confusion out of his voice.

Exchanging befuddled glances with one another, the men of the Lone Star Rifles did as they were told and lay chest down on the ground. They did not much mind this, as stray bullets from the front lines were continually zipping past them. Being prone provided at least a measure of protection.

This illusion was quickly shattered. A shell from a Yankee cannon whistled overhead, then slammed down into the ground and exploded amidst the regiment just to the right of the 7th Texas. A horrific and momentary chorus of screams told McFadden that a number of men had been killed together in the same instant.

"What the hell are we lying down for?" Pearson asked.

"Cleburne knows what he's doing," McFadden snapped back. "Now shut up!"

Then began several tense minutes of motionless waiting. The battle continued to rage all around them, as if they were in the eye of a tremendous hurricane made of fire rather than water. Bullets continued to zip over McFadden's head and shells periodically slammed into the ground around them.

"Something's happening with Lowrey's men!" Montgomery cried in alarm.

McFadden raised his head and glanced over to the right. Sure enough, it appeared as though Lowrey's men were retreating. For just a moment, rage filled McFadden. The Arkansas men of Govan's unit were holding their ground, and the Texans themselves had not yet even fired a shot, but it now seemed that the battle would be lost because Lowrey's men had been unable to stomach the fight. Now that they had given way, the Yankees would come pouring through the breach like a swarm of devils.

"Cowards!" a chorus of voices from among the Texans cried. "Alabama bastards!"

McFadden remembered Missionary Ridge, eight months before. All day, their brigade and the rest of Cleburne's division had fought with all their strength, holding their ground against a vastly superior enemy. But the shameful rout of Confederate units on another part of the battlefield, miles away, had rendered all their sacrifices completely irrelevant. It looked like it was about to happen all over again.

However, something was not quite right. Even as Lowrey's men fell back, they did not have the appearance of a defeated brigade. While it was difficult to tell through the smoke and haze, it looked to McFadden as though every man was still holding his rifle. Indeed, he spotted several men reloading even as they jogged toward the south. Usually, the men of routed units threw away their weapons in a panic. Equally telling, McFadden could not hear any shouts of alarm. If anything, the men of Lowrey's brigade appeared eerily calm.

Suddenly, everything clicked in his mind and he could see Cleburne's plan as clear as crystal. Lowrey's men were not retreating. Instead, they were falling back according to a prearranged plan to lure the Yankees into charging forward. When they did so, the enemy flank would be exposed to the fire of the 7th Texas and the rest of the

Texas brigade. It was as if Cleburne had just made an unexpected and masterful move on a chess board. McFadden smiled, realizing that he was watching an artist at work on the battlefield.

He didn't wait for orders from Captain Collett or anybody else. "Get ready!" he shouted to the Lone Star Rifles. "Load your rifles and fix bayonets!"

On the very edge of McFadden's vision off to the right, the officers of Lowrey's Brigade suddenly stopped and began waving their swords. The gray-clad troops stopped running and quickly gathered into a steady line, turning to face northwards once again. All told, they had probably retreated only six or seven hundred yards.

Looking back to the north, McFadden could now just make out a large formation of Union troops, perhaps an entire division, racing southward, imagining themselves to be in pursuit of a defeated foe. He could hear the distinctive low and steady battle yell of the Northern troops and felt a momentary loss of courage. He had fought the Yankees on enough battlefields and, loathe them though he did, he knew that they were brave and determined fighters. He gripped his Enfield tightly and glanced around at his men. On their faces he could see the same combination of momentary doubt and fierce determination that he himself felt.

"Stand up!" the booming voice of Captain Collett shouted over the din.

The Lone Star Rifles rose to their feet, as did every man in Granbury's Texas Brigade. The Yankee division was continuing to advance at the double quick, its formation now in disorder, probably unable to clearly see either Granbury's Texans or Lowrey's brigade because of the thick smoke. McFadden speculated quickly that the gray and butternut colors of the Confederate uniforms helped conceal them in the midst of the swirling smoke, while the dark blue uniforms of the Yankees made them much easier targets.

As the Northerners continued forward, their right flank seemed to present itself like a gift to the men of Granbury's Brigade. The Texans were in a perfect position to pour fire into the Union formation at its most vulnerable point, being able to concentrate all their fire at the right end of the Yankee line. Bullets fired from Granbury's lines would sweep the Union formation lengthwise, while few of the Northerners would be in a good position to shoot back. As far as tactical advantages went, the situation was close to perfect.

"Ready!" Collett shouted.

The men of the Lone Star Rifles raised their Enfields to their shoulders. McFadden waited for the order of his captain, glancing back and forth. Ahead of him and slightly to the right, he could see the men of Lowrey's Brigade swiftly reforming. Their obvious discipline made him consider the possibility that he might have been wrong in his earlier estimation of Alabama and Mississippi troops. As far as McFadden could see, they were behaving with great steadiness.

"Right flank!" some of the Union troops were shouting in a panic. "Watch out on the right flank!"

"Aim!" Collett shouted. The same order was repeated by every other regimental commander in the Texas Brigade at the same time. They aimed their rifles directly into the right flank of the Union formation.

"Fire!"

Instantly, the line of the 7th Texas exploded in an eruption of musket fire. The sound momentarily deafened McFadden. The blunt shock of the butt of his rifle kicking back against his shoulder was no less uncomfortable for its familiarity.

An instant later, he saw the effect of his regiment's volley. Scores of Union troops were cut down in an instant, as though a scythe had slashed through their lines. Those who remained standing appeared staggered and stunned at receiving such a deadly barrage at close range from an unexpected quarter. At the same moment, the other regiments of Granbury's Texas Brigade were opening fire as well. Seconds after them, the reformed units of Lowrey's Brigade unleashed their own devastating volley into the ranks of the Northern troops.

Faced by Granbury's men to the southwest and Lowrey's men directly to the south, the Northerners were caught in a deadly crossfire, as volley after volley tore through their ranks from two different directions. A few Yankee troops returned fire, but many had not reloaded their weapons during their charge and the officers seemed confused as to the direction in which they should direct the fire of their men.

As he reloaded and fired again and again, McFadden watched as the Union division melted away. Several frightened men in the enemy ranks threw down their weapons and fled back to the north, unwilling to stand against the ferocious fire that seemed to come from all sides. Compared to the rolling volleys being delivered by the Confederates, the return fire of the Yankees was minimal.

"Charge bayonets!" Collett shouted.

The men of the Lone Star Rifles reloaded one final time, then thrust their Enfields forward like spears, their bodies tense as they awaited the order that they knew would follow.

General Granbury rode out in front of them, gripping his saber and glaring fiercely at the enemy. He waved his saber over his head a few times, then pointed it straight at the Yankees and kicked his horse into a canter.

"Charge!" he yelled. The cry was immediately taken up by every officer in the brigade.

"Go, boys!" McFadden shouted. Screaming like banshees, the Lone Star Rifles dashed forward, with all the rest of the brigade charging forward with them. All the tension of the endless waiting vanished in an instant, exploding in a burst of furious energy. It was like a taut rope had just snapped.

It took only a matter of seconds to cross the distance to the Yankee line. Already staggered by the ferocious fire coming from the Southern ranks, the Union resistance broke quickly. Many Yankees dropped their rifles as they turned and fled. A few, braver than the others, held their ground, swinging their weapons like great clubs or stabbing forward with their bayonets the moment the Southerners reached them. It was no use. Stunned, outnumbered, and already having lost most of its strength, what was left of the Union formation swiftly collapsed. Most of the Yankees fled northwards. The few who stood and fought were swiftly killed or captured.

"After them!" Collett and other officers were yelling, gesturing with their swords toward the fleeing Union troops. "On their heels, men! Forward! Charge!"

McFadden tried desperately to keep his company together. Glancing around, he could already see a few faces missing, but he couldn't be sure if they had been killed or wounded or if they had simply become separated from the company in the confusion. In the midst of trying to hold his unit together, McFadden loaded and fired his weapon at the few Union soldiers he could see who were trying to stand their ground. A few Union officers were trying to rally their men into ad hoc formations to deliver fire at the oncoming Confederates, but these small batches of men were quickly and easily dispersed by a handful of volleys.

As the men continued to advance northward, they passed over a field covered with the corpses of Northern soldiers and the assorted detritus of battle. McFadden momentarily halted his company to reorganize the men and give them time to take ammunition from their dead foes. Over the sound of constant firing, McFadden could hear a sudden upsurge in cheering and shouting from off to the left. Looking in that direction, he saw a large formation of gray-clad soldiers which he hadn't seen before, joining the attack. An Arkansas flag told him that it was Govan's Brigade.

As he glanced about, McFadden suddenly realized that Cleburne's division had punched an enormous hole in the center of the Union line and that all three brigades were now charging through it. He and the Lone Star Rifles were right in the thick of it.

*   *   *   *   *

After watching Hardee depart, Johnston had considered riding back to the other side of the battlefield to check on Stewart. But it had become clear to him that the outcome of the battle would be determined on Hardee's front, so he had decided that it would be best to remain where he was.

Couriers and staff officers found it easier to locate him when he was staying in one place. Within a few minutes, a captain he recognized as belonging to Hood's headquarters galloped up, an expression of alarm on his face.

"General Johnston, sir!" he cried, snapping a salute.

"Report!"

"General Hood reports that the enemy is advancing in superior force against his lines to the east. He urgently requests that General Clayton's division be sent to his assistance."

Johnston's heart skipped a beat. He ordered the man to repeat the message once again. After he had done so, Johnston glanced nervously at Mackall.

"It appears our enemies on the east side of the city are moving faster than we anticipated."

"But who is it?" Mackall asked. "McPherson, Schofield, or both?"

Johnston turned back to the courier. "Can you identify the Union formation?"

The man shook his head. "Don't know, sir. All Hood said was that the force was considerably superior to his."

Mackall fumed. "So like Hood to give such little information."

Johnston pursed his lips and considered what to do. He had already told Hardee that Clayton's division was released to be deployed when and how he saw fit. But if the Yankees were really about to attack Hood's lines with greatly superior numbers, Sherman might force his way into Atlanta from the east. This would not only result in the city's fall, but would trap the Army of Tennessee between Thomas in the north and McPherson and Schofield to the south.

Then again, if he acceded to Hood's wishes and sent Clayton's division to the eastern defenses, any chance of achieving a decisive victory over the Army of the Cumberland would be lost. He would have to pull Stewart and Hardee back into the defenses of the city. After that, the Army of Tennessee might hold Atlanta for a few weeks, but inevitably Sherman would cut the railroads and he would be forced to retreat.

Another courier arrived, this one from Hardee's headquarters. Unlike Hood's man, this messenger bore an expression of triumph.

"Cleburne's broken them, sir!"

"What?"

"Cleburne's broken them! Tore a hole in their line half a mile wide, I tell you!"

The assembled staff officers and cavalry escort raised a cheer. Johnston found this irritating, as it made it difficult for him to converse with the courier.

"Did you see this?"

"Yes, sir! Damndest thing I ever saw, sir! Cleburne pulled back Lowrey's men, made it look like they were running away. The

Yankee chased after them, but then Cleburne hit them from the left with Granbury's men. Just then, Lowrey's men stopped running, turned around, and opened fire, too! The Yankees were caught in a crossfire and cut to ribbons! Never seen so many dead bluecoats in one place, I reckon. Not even at Chickamauga!"

"And what is Cleburne doing now?"

"What's he doing now? Why, he's charging his whole division through the gap, sir! What else would he be doing?" If the courier thought his words were impertinent, he didn't show it.

Johnston thought quickly. If Cleburne had broken the Union line, he would need support to properly exploit the breakthrough. That support could only come from Clayton's division, which Hardee was almost certainly ordering into the breach at that moment. Conceivably, there was still time to send word to Hardee that Clayton's division must be sent to aid Hood rather than support the attack on the Army of the Cumberland. Johnston's caution momentarily tugged at his aggressive instincts. But he shook his head. The chance of achieving a truly decisive victory over the Army of the Cumberland could not be forsaken.

"Do you know where General Clayton is?" Johnston asked Hardee's courier.

"I do, sir."

Johnston turned to the messenger from Hood. "Inform General Hood that Clayton's division is already committed and that he must make do with what he has." He turned back to Hardee's man. "Ride as quick as you can to Clayton. Tell him he must drive northwards through the gap and seize the bridges over Peachtree Creek. Tell him that if he succeeds, the entire Army of the Cumberland will be trapped!"

"I will tell him, sir!" The man saluted and was off.

*   *   *   *   *

Having left McPherson to advance directly west toward Atlanta, Sherman had ridden north to confer with Schofield, whose Army of the Ohio was positioned a few miles to the north of McPherson's position. Sherman was there, speaking with Schofield about the possibility of sending his fifteen thousand men eastward toward Augusta after Atlanta had been secured, when the temperature and humidity just south of Peachtree Creek begin to subtly change.

"Do you hear that?" Sherman asked, his head arching up slightly.

Schofield listened carefully. "Yes. Artillery."

"Coming from where?"

"West of here, I think."

"Somewhere near Thomas, then." Sherman felt a tingle of fear move up and down his spine, awakening unpleasant memories.

"Could be siege artillery in the Atlanta defenses. The militia firing off some rounds out of panic."

Sherman shook his head. He could hear it more clearly now. "No, that's field artillery, sure as hell."

"The pitch of the ring is too high. Sounds like rebel guns to me."

"Something's not right."

At that moment, a courier covered in dust appeared, both man and rider out of breath and exhausted. Hurriedly, he handed over a dispatch.

General Sherman,

I have come under heavy attack by two enemy corps. The fighting is severe but I am holding my position and am confident I can continue to do so. I intend to counter attack as soon as possible. Recommend McPherson and Schofield advance from the east. I believe we can crush Johnston between us.

General Thomas

Sherman's eyebrows went up. "Well, it appears that Uncle Joe is again doing the unexpected. He has decided to fight for Atlanta after all." He passed the message over to Schofield, who read through it quickly.

"Interesting," Schofield said. "I can move my men to Thomas's assistance if you so wish, but it would be a few hours before we can reach him."

Sherman shook his head. "If Thomas says he can hold, I think we should take him at his word. Thomas has always been good on the defensive, at least."

"Very well, sir."

"McPherson is already moving on Atlanta south of here. That should force Johnston to reinforce the eastern defenses. Looks like the wily old fox has finally rolled the dice for a change. But I don't think his number will come up."

"Indeed. If I am not to go to Thomas, what shall I do with my men?"

"Remain in position here for the time being," Sherman said. "That way, you can move to the support of either Thomas or McPherson in the event that either gets into any trouble." This seemed like a sensible policy.

"Fair enough, sir. I must say, things seem to be going well. Yesterday, we were expecting to capture Atlanta. It now appears that we will capture Atlanta and crush the Army of Tennessee at the same time."

Sherman nodded, but did not share Schofield's confidence. He couldn't quite put his finger on it, but something seemed amiss. He had been hoping since the beginning of the campaign that Johnston would leave his fortifications and fight him in the open field. Now that he had, however, Sherman felt unease rather than elation. Having convinced himself that the rebels had already given up the city, he was unsettled at having been so completely wrong. And if he was wrong about that, perhaps he was wrong about other things, too.

He shook his head, as if to rid his mind of such thoughts. He had to guard against such paranoia just as surely as he had to guard against enemy cavalry raids.

A courier rode up at full speed.

"Message from General McPherson, sir!"

"Go ahead."

"McPherson begs to report that the defenses of Atlanta are not held by militia but by regular Confederate troops. They are deployed in considerable strength and he is therefore halting his advance to reconnoiter the enemy position properly."

More uncertainty now rose in Sherman's heart like a dark cloud. If McPherson had halted his advance, the threat being presented to Atlanta was lessened, which in turn would allow Johnston to concentrate on his attack against Thomas. McPherson had often been slow and overly cautious, which had led to the missed opportunity at Snake Creek Gap in the early days of the campaign. Was that mistake about to be repeated once again?

"Ride as quick as you can back to McPherson. Tell him that the enemy is engaged heavily with Thomas north of the city and that there cannot be many enemy troops facing him. He is to press the enemy hard, with all possible strength. Ride quick, man!"

"Yes, sir!" The man saluted and dashed off.

*   *   *   *   *

It had turned into a fox hunt.

Trailed only by his color bearer, Cleburne rode forward behind his advancing men, sometimes walking, sometimes trotting, sometimes cantering. He kept glancing in every direction to get as clear an idea as possible of what was going on. All around him was smoke, confusion, gunfire, and shouting, but the din of the Rebel Yell permeated the air and seemed to overcome every other sound.

They had left behind the field where they had shattered the Union line and were now moving into more heavily wooded terrain. They were getting closer to Peachtree Creek with each step. Cleburne passed by innumerable corpses lying where they had fallen. Many wore Confederate gray, but a great many more wore Union blue. He also passed by clusters of unarmed Union men being marched to the rear as prisoners, escorted by a small number of his own troops.

Lieutenant Hanley rode up to him. "I just saw General Cheatham, sir!"

"And?"

Hanley smiled. "He's broken through as well! Once Lowrey's brigade made a right wheel into the flank of the Yankees facing him, they collapsed like a house of cards. Now Cheatham's moving north alongside us, driving the Yankees just fine. Captured two four-gun batteries, he has!"

Cleburne nodded sharply. He had figured as much. Once he and his division had smashed the Union line open, he had sent Granbury's brigade directly through the gap into the Union rear, while ordering his other two brigades to wheel to the right and left and charge into the flanks of the adjacent Union divisions. Being hit from the front and flank would cause the Union line to come unhinged, spreading disorder and widening the gap.

The five thousand men of Clayton's division had followed Granbury's brigade through the gap and were charging northwards at the double quick. He tried to imagine what Thomas was doing at that moment. An excellent fighter and a tough soldier, particularly when on the defensive, he was no doubt trying to organize sufficient forces to plug the gap that had been torn in his line. With Granbury's brigade and Clayton's division pressing the attack with all their strength, that was likely going to be very difficult.

The sound of gunfire picked up to the north and Cleburne heard the distinctive boom of Northern artillery. Now that they were moving through more heavily forested ground again, the impact of superior Yankee artillery was somewhat negated. But enemy shells were still going to be killing a lot of his men until he could capture the guns or eliminate their crews.

A sergeant and private emerged from a cluster of trees, leading a group of eight or nine Yankee prisoners. The private was holding a lowered Springfield rifle at the bluecoats, while the sergeant held a Union battle flag in his arms. Cleburne noted that one of the Yankee prisoners had a major's stripes on his shoulder.

"What regiment are you from?" Cleburne asked.

"19th Louisiana, sir!" the sergeant answered.

"Congratulations on capturing this flag. From what unit is it?"

"154th New York Infantry," the captured Union major said resignedly.

"Your name, sir?"

"Major Lewis Warner, sir."

"My men will treat you properly, Major. For you, the war is over. Keep heading that direction." Cleburne pointed directly to the south. The men vanished into the tree line a few moments later.

"154th?" Hanley said in astonishment. "How can a single state raise one hundred and fifty-four regiments of infantry?"

"The Union possess manpower and material resources that we can never hope to match," Cleburne answered. "Let us remain focused on the battle."

"Of course, sir."

"Ride over to Loring's Division on the left, observe the situation, then come back and find me. I know what's happening on my right, but I need to know what's happening on my left."

Hanley saluted and, without a word, dashed away. Cleburne again found himself with only his color bearer, Private Hatch, as company. He turned Red Pepper northwards and began walking forward.

"Are we winning the battle, sir?" Private Hatch asked.

"I think so, yes. But ask me again at the end of the day."

*   *   *   *   *

Thomas had mounted his horse and ridden forward as soon as he had heard the sound. There had been a tremendous crash of intense musketry followed by a dark and ominous silence. Conceivably this could indicate that the rebels had punched through his line and were now using the bayonet on his men. Unfortunately, the forested nature of the ground meant that he could not see what was happening. Riding forward was a risk, but he felt it was necessary. Besides, he had an escort of cavalry with him in case he got into any trouble.

It did not take Thomas long before he realized that something had gone horribly wrong on the front lines. As he and his escort rode forward, they begin encountering frantic soldiers, individually or in small groups, all of whom had the unmistakable air of defeat hanging over them. Many were unarmed, running in a panic toward the rear. Others simply seemed bewildered, like men who had been hit on the head and had just awoken.

Thomas spotted a captain who was running about frantically with his sword, trying to stop the men from fleeing.

"You there!" Thomas roared. The man stopped and saluted when he saw who was addressing him. "What is happening?"

"Captain David Thompson, sir! 79th Ohio! It's a damn disaster, sir! Cleburne's men routed our division and are pouring through the gap like a bunch of devils! Another bunch of rebel brigades are pushing through, too!"

"My God," Thomas said under his breath. He tried to recall to which division the 79th Ohio belonged. "Where is General Ward?"

"Dead, sir! I saw him hit in the head and fall from his horse. Lots of the officers are killed or captured. Dammit all, sir, the division has fallen apart!"

Thomas glanced around. Seeing the streams of disorganized and dispirited men flowing toward the rear, he couldn't disagree. He sprang into action, firing off orders and dispatching staff officers and messengers in every direction. He sent one man off to find General Hooker, who commanded the corps in this sector. Others were simply sent to locate division commanders in order to get a better picture of the situation. Two men were dispatched to hurry the reserve brigades forward to plug the gap.

As a small army of dispatch riders dispersed from his position, Thomas rode forward once again, with two dozen cavalrymen riding alongside him. He reminded himself that he had been in tight spots before. On the first day of the Battle of Stone's River, his line had been battered by Hardee's assault, yet he had finally held. On the second day at Chickamauga, the entire right wing of the Union army has dissolved into rout, but he had held on long enough to cover the retreat despite being assailed by superior numbers. Thomas was not a man given to panic under any circumstances.

Even as he kept his head, he silently admitted to himself that the situation now facing him was the most critical and dangerous he had yet encountered in the war. His army had its back to a river and the center of its line had been broken. Thomas knew from long experience that panic could spread through an army like a prairie fire through a dry grass prairie. More than at any time in his career, he now faced the possibility of a complete disaster. Still, so long as he remained calm, the situation might yet be salvaged.

He ordered the cavalry escort to spread itself out into a line about two hundred yards long. The retreating infantry found themselves confronted by saber-wielding men on formidable horses, all shouting for them to stop running and get back in line. Thomas remained in the center of this line, watching with increasing apprehension as the majority of his men continued to dash past the line of horsemen without stopping.

*   *   *   *   *

The Lone Star Rifles had gone into battle with twenty-four soldiers. Now, including McFadden himself, the company had only ten men left. Three men had been detached as part of a detail to escort prisoners to the rear, but the other eleven were unaccounted for. McFadden worried about the missing men, knowing that many of them had to have been killed or wounded, but he had no time to think about it now.

The 7th Texas was a shadow of its former self. Not only had it suffered heavy casualties, but it had become completely disorganized over the course of the battle. McFadden was not sure if the Confederate troops on either side of him were even from the 7th Texas. Some of them belonged to the other Texas regiments in Granbury's brigade, but others belonged to the Georgia, Louisiana, or Alabama brigades of Clayton's division. All was confusion and chaos, but the

Southerners instinctively understood that they had to continue to push forward, no matter what the situation.

The Yankees were on the run. Since punching through the Union line two hours earlier, the Confederates had been steadily grinding their way forward, driving the enemy before them and taking large numbers of prisoners. The Lone Star Rifles had captured the battle flag of the 82nd Illinois, which McFadden hoped would redound to their credit when the battle was over. They had also taken over two dozen enemy prisoners, who had been sent to the rear under an armed guard led by Private Montgomery.

Bullets whizzed by McFadden's head, causing him to spin behind the cover of a thick pine tree. Seconds afterward, he heard two dull thuds and saw little spits of splinters fly off the trunk. Obviously, there were Yankees up ahead who were still full of fight.

"Careful, boys!" he shouted to his men. He hoped other nearby Confederate soldiers from other units would also heed his warnings.

Pearson raised his rifle and squeezed off a round, then took cover behind the same tree as McFadden and began reloading his Enfield. "I think I got one, Sarge."

"See how many there were up ahead?"

"Nope," Pearson answered. "Too many damn trees."

Pearson finished reloading, then bolted from the cover of the tree to another one, a few yards away. Two bullets narrowly missed him as he ran. From his new cover, he ventured out for an instant to fire in the direction he thought the Yankees were located, but did not wait to see whether he hit anything.

Harrison and one other of the remaining Lone Star Rifles were prone on the ground a few yards away, laboriously attempting the difficult task of reloading their rifles while lying down. "Bunch of Yankees in that clump of trees just ahead, Sarge!" shouted one of them.

"Stay down!" He wished Harrison had not shouted so loudly, as it would certainly tell the enemy where he was.

McFadden peeked around the tree, catching a momentary glance at the group. There were perhaps ten of them, huddled around a cluster of four or five trees. He could see some of them reloading their rifles, while another leveled his weapon directly at McFadden. He ducked back behind the tree just as the man fired, sending a bullet smacking into the trunk.

The only other Southern troops he could see were perhaps a hundred yards away on either side. He considered calling out to them for help, as they would be able to get around this bothersome group of Yankees with little trouble. But they doubtless had their own problems to deal with. Throughout his field of vision, as individuals or in small groups, frightened Northern troops continued to run past in a bid to escape the fighting.

"Private Harrison!"

"Yes, Sarge?"

"Take Pearson and Balch and see if you can work your way around those boys. We'll keep you covered."

"Why does Tom get to be in charge?" Pearson asked.

"Because I said so, dammit! Now move!"

The three men crawled toward the rear, dragging their rifles with them and staying as low as possible to avoid enemy fire. McFadden ordered his six remaining men to pepper the cluster of trees with shots in order to give their comrades sufficient cover to get a reasonable distance away. He watched them go a few dozen yards, then they stood up and vanished into the trees off to the left.

A few minutes of tense waiting then passed. Even as enemy bullets continued to thud into the trunk of his tree, McFadden felt reasonably safe. He suddenly realized how tired he was, having been marching or fighting for several hours without a break. He took a quick swig of water from his canteen and was surprised at how full it remained. He had not drunk from it much over the course of the day.

Ignoring another splattering of bullets against his tree, McFadden tried to read the battle by listening to the sounds around him. The low booming sound of artillery had considerably lessened over the past hour or so. He hoped that this might be because Union artillery batteries were falling into Confederate hands, but he was not about to indulge in such optimistic speculation just yet. Still, near as he could tell, everything was going well.

"Ready to surrender, Yanks?" he called out.

The reply came immediately. "Damned if we are!"

"Plenty of your friends have surrendered already today! You should see all the prisoners we have in the rear!"

"Go to hell, Reb!"

McFadden leaned out just long enough to aim and fire his Enfield, though he was not sure whether or not he hit anything. A flurry of bullets hit the tree trunk as he swung back around, proving to him that the Northerners were far from ready to give up.

He reloaded his rifle, motioning for the rest of his men to do the same. He figured that Harrison and the others would be in position within the next two or three minutes. After all, it had been nearly ten minutes since they had scurried away. Surely that would have given them long enough to work their way around the Yankee position.

"Leave here or you will all be captured!" a familiar voice shouted. "The rebels are surrounding you!"

The voice was calling to the federal troops, but McFadden recognized at once that it was Private Balch. The other soldiers had often made fun of his accent, saying it made him sound more like a Wisconsinite than a Texan. He was the perfect man to play such a ruse of war.

"Who are you?" a Yankee voice shouted.

"Captain Mitchell! 82nd Illinois!" That was the regiment whose flag had been captured by the 7th Texas.

"Trick!" one of the Yankees said. McFadden could just barely hear him over the sounds of battle. "It's a rebel trick! Don't listen to him!"

"I'm no rebel, you damn fool! You want to end up in Andersonville? Now let's get the hell out of here before we all are taken prisoner!"

Shots were fired near the Yankee position. McFadden couldn't see exactly what was happening, but guessed that someone had gotten nervous or perhaps one of the enemy soldiers had gotten a good look at Harrison, Balch, or Pearson. One way or another, Balch's ruse had failed. But perhaps he had created enough confusion among the Union group to give the Lone Star Rifles an advantage for a brief moment. If so, now was the time to take it.

"Go!" McFadden shouted. He dashed around the tree and darted toward the wooded cluster where the enemy troops had been sheltering. The six other men with him either rose from the ground or dashed around their own trees at the same moment, screaming a primal battle cry. It took only a few seconds to cover the distance to the clump of trees. During that time, McFadden stopped just long enough to discharge his Enfield, then continuing running forward.

The Union troops fired back. Off to his right, McFadden saw the chest of one of his men explode, spewing out an eruption of syrupy red liquid. Seconds later, McFadden ran through the gap between two of the trees and swung the butt of his musket into the head of one of the Yankees, knocking him senseless. A few confusing seconds of hand-to-hand combat followed. Two of the Yankees were killed by bayonets, five were captured or rendered unconscious, and the remaining three ran for their lives.

On the ground, McFadden saw Private Harrison's body, with one enormous bullet hole in his chest and another in his left abdomen. He glanced back over the ground he had just covered, realizing that the man who had fallen during the quick charge had been Private Donald Parker. For a brief moment, he recalled that Parker had a wife and two children who lived in Marshall. He had been some sort of shopkeeper.

McFadden was now down to eight men. There was no way to continue pushing forward with such a small force, for they would likely be destroyed if they encountered so much as a single intact Federal company. They would have to wait until some other Confederate unit appeared.

"Reload your rifles," McFadden barked. "Balch! Pearson! You watch these prisoners here. The rest of you, take position around those trees and keep your eyes peeled to the north. And cover up Harrison and Parker!"

A group of Yankee soldiers was visible a hundred yards or so to their left, retreating northwards in a hurry. It appeared to be about the size of a regiment, though in considerable state of disorganization. McFadden ignored them. With so few men, he did not want to get involved in a fight with a force so much larger than his own. Besides, they were running away and clearly posed no threat.

A few minutes later, a Confederate captain appeared on horseback, trailed by a few dozen men. He looked over the survivors of the Lone Star Rifles quickly.

"Who are you?" the captain asked.

"Company F, 7th Texas," McFadden answered. "I'm Sergeant McFadden."

"Captain Ben Randals, 16th Tennessee. You boys are with Granbury's Brigade, right? Hell, boy, you have wandered over a mile away from your unit!"

"Confusing battle, sir."

The captain smiled. "That it is. You can take those prisoners on back to the rear. My boys will take over here."

"With respect, sir, we'd like to continue with the drive forward."

Randals nodded quickly and ordered two of his men to take the five Yankee prisoners back to the rear. "That's done," he said to McFadden. "Now, organize your boys and follow along with us."

"Any idea what's happening on the rest of the battlefield, sir?"

"No idea whatsoever."

The eight Texans moved on to the right end of the line of the 16th Tennessee, which appeared to have been reduced to roughly fifty or sixty men. They moved forward, holding their loaded Enfields carefully, ready to hoist them to their shoulders at a moment's notice.

There was still cannon fire audible in every direction. The steady popping of musketry continued as well, though without the roar that had previously characterized it.

"What do you think?" Balch asked.

"I think we've broken the enemy line and routed them. They're now running to the north to try and get away."

"Just like Chickamauga!" Pearson said excitedly.

"Or like Missionary Ridge," Balch added. "Except the folks doing most of the running that day was us."

There was a chorus of laughter among both the Texans and the Tennesseans, which struck McFadden as odd. Jokes about Missionary Ridge were usually sarcastic and bitter, since no one remembered that disastrous day with any fondness. It seemed that the experience of victory was giving the men considerable cheer.

As they advanced, they came across several Yankee soldiers who had discarded their weapons and simply sat down to await capture, too exhausted to continue running. They also encountered numerous Confederate soldiers who had become separated from their units during the chaos of the advance, most of whom fell in with the ad hoc Texas-Tennessee unit. As they continued moving north, the group grew larger and stronger, while the enemy troops they encountered appeared increasingly stricken with panic.

*   *   *   *   *

"We should retire to the rear, sir," the cavalry escort officer said sternly.

Thomas glared at him with anger. "We are not going one step backwards, Captain! Nor is the Army of the Cumberland!"

"Respectfully, sir, we are too far forward. Rebel troops are approaching and it is dangerous for us to remain here."

Thomas grunted. The captain was correct, of course. But Thomas could not justify retiring to the rear himself when he was trying to prevent his army from doing just that. The few regiments he and his cavalry escort had managed to rally were forming up in a thin line, but the men were disorganized and still shaken. If he and the cavalry troopers departed, the reformed infantry would probably bolt at the first sign of the enemy.

But Thomas knew he couldn't afford to stay, either. It would be difficult for dispatch riders to locate him so close to the front line and the first responsibility of an army commander was to exercise efficient and effective control over the entire battlefield. He obviously couldn't do that if he was doing the job that should be done by a brigade commander.

Thomas was about to tell the cavalry escort commander to prepare for a departure when a shout of alarm rose from the unsteady infantry line. He glanced up and saw a large formation of rebel troops approaching. He frowned. The enemy unit easily outnumbered his own troops and were doubtless fired up with confidence by the success they had had during the battle. His own men, by contrast, had had their morale shattered.

If he ordered his men to retreat, they would immediately fall apart in a rout. He also knew that he could not ride off himself, for he could never imagine abandoning any of his men in the face of the enemy. Even if logic dictated that doing so would be best for the Union cause, his own heart and soul would never forgive him. There was only one thing to do.

Thomas kicked his horse and trotted to a point just behind the center of the line he had created. He pulled his sword and lowered it toward the rebels.

"Send these traitorous bastards to hell, boys!"

The officers ordered their men to fire. The volley appeared effective enough at first. Thomas saw several of the rebel troops fall dead or wounded. But the remainder raised their rifles and responded with a volley of their own. When the bullets struck his thin and unwieldy line, his greatest fears were realized. Having been pushed to the breaking point, the Union soldiers broke and bolted for the rear.

"Stop!" Thomas shouted. "Stop, men! Turn around and fight!"

They ignored him, continuing their flight. The Southern troops unleashed a fearsome Rebel Yell and charged forward, bayonets lowered.

Thomas gripped his sword, though he knew that the blade was next to useless against men armed with rifles. Not far away, the captain commanding his cavalry escort was shot through the chest and fell off his horse and onto the ground. The few Union infantrymen who were attempting to resist were shot to death or clubbed down with the butts of muskets. Less than a minute after ordering his men to open fire, the fight was ending less with a bang and more with a whimper.

"General!"

Thomas turned and found himself staring down the barrel of an Enfield rifle pointed directly at his head.

"I must ask you to surrender, sir!"

He considered swiping at the rebel with his saber. If he were quick, he might be able to slash the man's face, thus creating an opportunity to escape. But the man would be able to pull his trigger far more quickly than Thomas could swing his sword. At such close range, he wouldn't miss.

Thomas sighed. "I suppose I have no choice, do I?"

"I will kill you if you don't, sir."

"In that case, I surrender." He pulled his saber back and carefully took hold of the blade. He then extended it toward the soldier, whom he noticed wore sergeant's stripes.

The man's eyes narrowed in confusion and he took the sword awkwardly, sticking it into the ground. He then nodded sharply and backed away, careful to keep his weapon pointed at Thomas.

"Please get off your horse, General."

Thomas dismounted. "To whom am I surrendering?"

"Sergeant James McFadden. 7th Texas."

"One of Cleburne's men. Bloody hell."

"Are you who I think you are?"

He drew himself up with as much dignity as he could muster. "I am General George Thomas, commander of the Army of the Cumberland."

"I thought so."

Thomas eyed the man warily. He would have expected a rebel noncommissioned officer to holler for joy upon learning that he had captured the commander of the enemy army. Instead, this man simply kept his rifle pointed at him without wavering, looking at him as though he were some sort of potentially dangerous animal. There was fire in the man's eyes, though.

"Who's this?" a rebel captain said, walking up.

"It's General Thomas, sir!" McFadden replied. "The enemy commander."

"You're serious?"

"He is telling the truth," Thomas said. "I am General Thomas."

The captain reacted the way Thomas would have expected. He took off his hat, waved it in the air, and whooped loudly enough for all nearby to hear. Word quickly spread through the Confederate unit that had shattered his line, all of whom were soon cheering wildly. A large group formed a circle around him, looking at him as though he were one of Darwin's apes at some sort of public exhibition. Thomas felt a vast darkness closing in around his soul.

"No dishonor in it, sir," McFadden said.

"What?"

"No dishonor in being taken prisoner, I mean. Happens to lots of soldiers."

"Oh," Thomas replied, surprised that the sergeant had spoken. "Yes, I suppose it does."

"Better than being dead, sir."

Thomas considered that for a second, thinking of his reputation, his sisters, the humiliation he was certain to endure in the very near future. "I wouldn't be too sure about that, sergeant," he finally replied.

*   *   *   *   *

July 20, Evening

"Pat! Are you all right?"

Cleburne turned in the saddle to see Hardee and three of his staff officers ride up.

"Yes, William, I am fine. And you?"

"No holes in me, though two bullets passed through my jacket." He pointed to the spot on the left side of his uniform coat. Cleburne's eyes widened for a moment when he saw how close his friend had come to being hit. Wounds in that area of the body were almost always fatal and those who suffered them did not die pleasant deaths.

"You should take better care of yourself, my friend," Cleburne observed. "It doesn't do for corps commanders to move so close to the fighting."

"Don't worry. The bullet that will kill William Hardee has not been cast!"

Cleburne frowned when he heard these words. The grin on Hardee's face reflected the exaltation of victory, but Cleburne felt it was unwise to tempt fate.

"What's happening on the rest of the battlefield?" Cleburne asked.

"It's all going splendidly, Pat! Your breakthrough in the center changed everything. When you sent Govan's brigade into the left flank of the Yankees facing Stewart's corps, their entire line started collapsing. Stewart's men are now driving the enemy north up to the creek. On our front, Bate's men have already reached the creek on the east side of the battlefield and taken one of the Yankee bridges. Cheatham and Walker are pushing hard north, driving the enemy before them. We're herding them toward the creek like a bunch of sheep."

"We have to keep the pressure on," Cleburne said anxiously. "They'll crowd the bridges across the creek. Everything will be confused. If we push hard enough, we can wreck their whole damn army!"

"I know, Pat. I know. How is your division doing?"

"We've suffered heavy losses. General Govan has been killed. But we're still pushing forward and we've got the Yankees on the run. Peachtree Creek is only about a mile further on."

"Well, then, let's go forward together!"

The two men kicked their horses into a trot. Half a dozen staffers and two color bearers followed them. As they moved north, the sounds of fighting grew louder. All around, Confederate units were advancing in clusters or ragged lines, maintaining only a minimal amount of organization as they pushed on. Some Union formations were occasionally visible, but most of them seemed focused on pulling back to the north rather than standing and fighting.

As he rode north, Cleburne realized that he heard little or no artillery fire. Many of the Yankee batteries had fallen into Confederate hands and Cleburne figured that most of the rest were being pulled back across Peachtree Creek as quickly as possible. He smiled at the thought. Those big guns would no longer be killing his men and the withdrawal of the enemy cannon served as yet another confirmation of the Southern victory.

As they trotted north, they passed over a landscape covered with dead and wounded soldiers of both sides. Some of the wounded were missing legs and arms, while others were shot through the stomach and crying piteously for water. Most of these men would not last much longer. Cleburne hardened his heart and kept riding.

One of the staff officers pointed at a cluster of a dozen or so Confederate troops, marching some prisoners to the rear. "General Hardee! General Cleburne! Look there!"

Cleburne squinted. The fading light made it difficult to make out the men. One of the Union prisoners was a strong, gruff-looking man with a gray beard.

"My God!" Hardee exclaimed. "That's General Thomas!" He kicked his horse and cantered over to the group. Cleburne, astonished and somewhat disbelieving, followed quickly.

"Is that you, William?" Thomas said as the two men approached.

"It is, George! Are you injured?"

"No," Thomas replied glumly.

"By God, I never expected to have you as a prisoner."

Thomas sighed and tilted his head, but otherwise made no response.

"Being a prisoner isn't so bad, George. You'll recall that I spent some time as a prisoner of the Mexicans in '46. Back in the good old days, eh?"

Thomas's mouth actually curled into a slight smile. Cleburne recalled that Hardee and Thomas were old friends. Their time at West Point had overlapped for a few years, they had served together in Mexico, and they had both been officers in the Second Cavalry Regiment on the Texas frontier. He couldn't imagine how strange and awkward it had to be for the two to be reunited under such circumstances.

Hardee gestured to Cleburne. "May I present my colleague, General Patrick Cleburne."

Thomas nodded. " General Cleburne," he said with little enthusiasm. "I have heard a great deal about you."

Cleburne nodded in return. "I am honored to meet you, General Thomas."

"I understand that it was your division which broke my line."

"My men had that honor, sir."

"A fine performance." His voice betrayed no enthusiasm whatsoever.

Cleburne thought Thomas was being sincere, but was not surprised to hear deep unhappiness in his voice. "Thank you, sir."

"My men are treating you properly?" Hardee asked.

"Yes," Thomas answered. "This man is the soldier who captured me." He gestured to the sergeant standing by his side. "He has been most gracious."

"Your name, young man?" Hardee asked.

"Sergeant James McFadden. 7th Texas." If the man was at all uneasy being in the presence of so many high-ranking generals, he didn't show it.

Cleburne had not known the man's name, but he recognized him. He reviewed each brigade in his division at least once a week and had noted the man's face on a few previous occasions when walking or riding down the line of Granbury's Texas Brigade. He had mentally labeled the man as "The Fierce-Looking Sergeant." Although he had never thought about him for more than a few moments, it was nice to have a name to put to his face, especially as he had just achieved a noteworthy feat.

"You'll be mentioned in the dispatches for this, Sergeant McFadden," Cleburne said. "It falls to few soldiers in history to capture the commander of the opposing army."

"Oh?" McFadden said. "Thank you, sir."

"George, you will be my guest at dinner this evening," Hardee said.

"Thank you, but I am afraid I must decline."

"Don't be like that, George! This is a reunion of old friends! We can swap old stories about our days at West Point and in Mexico!"

"Forgive me, William. I mean no disrespect. But I cannot find it in my heart to celebrate even a reunion with an old friend while my army lies in ruins. I have just suffered one of the worst defeats that an army has suffered in the history of war." He paused a moment before continuing. "Besides, I do not wish to share a table with those who have turned their backs on their country."

Darkness clouded Hardee's face. He didn't answer for several seconds. "Suit yourself, George. For what it's worth, I would prefer not to endure the company of a man who betrayed his state. Sergeant McFadden, would you please escort this man to General Johnston's headquarters?"

McFadden nodded. "Of course, sir." He tilted his head to the south and Thomas walked on without speaking further. Hardee and Cleburne watched as they disappeared into the trees and the gathering darkness.

Hardee shook his head and didn't speak for a few minutes. Cleburne wondered what was going through his head. He was himself a warm friend of Hardee's. Indeed, he had been the best man at his wedding and had already asked Hardee to serve as his best man at his upcoming wedding to his darling Susan. More than anyone, Cleburne knew the value Hardee placed on friendship. Many times over the past few years, he had heard Hardee talk about how much he respected Thomas. To have been spoken to in such a manner would doubtless wound his friend considerably.

Hardee turned to him. "I shall head east to see how the attack is progressing with the other divisions."

Cleburne nodded. "Very well, sir. I shall continue to push north. Peachtree Creek is not far."

"Good luck, Pat. I shall see you when it is all over."

As Hardee rode off, Cleburne headed back north, still being followed by Hanley and two other staff officers, with Private John Hatch still bearing the divisional colors.

*   *   *   *   *

Sherman rode forward, increasingly frustrated. The roar of battle was still audible off to the northwest, where Thomas was hopefully pummeling the two corps Johnston had been foolish enough to send forward in an attack. Surely McPherson, with twenty-five thousand men and Schofield in support, should be able to deal with the small rebel covering force on the eastern side of the city. Yet no sound of battle could be heard just ahead.

It took some time for the staff officers to locate McPherson, so it wasn't until nearly six o'clock that Sherman reined in alongside his subordinate's horse. A hundred yards away, two Union divisions were formed up in a battle line, waiting patiently.

"What the hell are you waiting for, James?" Sherman asked without preamble.

"It's not the Georgia Militia manning those trenches, Cump. It's the Army of Tennessee! Hood's corps, by the look of it."

"I know that!" Sherman snapped. "I got your message! Why haven't you attacked? Your men should have planted their flags on top of those trenches over an hour ago."

McPherson frowned and Sherman's frustration increased. Was McPherson's caution to rob them of a great victory, as it had at Snake Creek Gap two months before?

A series of low booms announced the firing of several heavy cannon from the Confederate lines. Some shells exploded in the Union formations, tossing many dead and wounded men to the ground like broken dolls. A single shell exploded about thirty yards away, close enough to spook Sherman's horse slightly.

"James, listen to me. Thomas is under attack by two corps of rebel infantry, so the force facing you here cannot be that large. If you push forward with all your force, you can break through at any point along the line. There is still enough daylight left to capture these trenches. Then, we can move into the city tomorrow morning."

Sherman was about to continue when a courier rode up. The man looked apprehensive and exhausted. Covered in dust, he had obviously ridden a great distance at top speed.

"Sir! General Sherman!"

"What? What is it?"

"We are beaten, sir! The rebels broke through Thomas's line at the center and everything fell apart! The Army of the Cumberland has been routed!"

"My God!" McPherson gasped.

"Can it be true?" Sherman asked. "Surely not!"

"There's no doubt, sir! Several officers from the Army of the Cumberland arrived at headquarters in a state of panic! They say the rebels attacked at one o'clock. Things were going well at first, but then the division holding the center of the line collapsed. The rebels poured through the breach and the entire line fell apart."

Sherman's mind raced. He'd been in the midst of a routed army before, when he had commanded a brigade at the First Battle of Bull Run. If the Army of the Cumberland had been routed on the south side of Peachtree Creek, the defeated and confused units would have a great deal of trouble retreating to the north bank. The potential for complete disaster was very real.

"Where is General Thomas?"

"No one knows, sir. No word from him for several hours."

Sherman felt like he had been stabbed in the heart. He shook his head, trying to concentrate. If Thomas had suffered a complete defeat, Johnston might conceivably be able to strike north and capture the Union bridges over the Chattahoochee River, trapping not only whatever was left of the Army of the Cumberland on the south side of the river, but the armies of Schofield and McPherson as well.

He remembered Grant's warning that Jubal Early might soon be arriving in Georgia with twenty thousand rebel reinforcements from Virginia. Was it possible that these men had already arrived? Could they even now be under attack by veterans of the Army of Northern Virginia?

Another courier arrived, having come straight from General Hooker.

"What's the situation?" Sherman demanded. He hoped against hope that things had changed for the better.

"General Thomas is missing, sir! Either dead or a prisoner. Hooker says that he is taking command of the Army of the Cumberland and will try to withdraw to the north bank of Peachtree Creek in as much order as possible. Hooker urgently requests reinforcements."

"Thomas dead?" he said, stunned. He felt like a cold fist was closing around his heart. Their relationship might lack personal warmth, but Sherman knew how much he depended on the steady and solid leadership of Thomas. The loyal Virginian was one of the best generals the Union had. If he were indeed dead or a prisoner, the Union cause might have suffered a blow as severe as the battlefield defeat of the Army of the Cumberland.

The idea of Joseph Hooker being in command of the Army of the Cumberland, even if only temporarily, filled Sherman with dread. Although Hooker was the highest-ranking corps commander and therefore entitled to take command, Sherman considered Hooker a vainglorious blowhard and incompetent to boot. He certainly did not consider Hooker the man to extract the Army of the Cumberland from such a dangerous situation.

"Shall I attack, sir?" McPherson said.

Sherman's mind was spinning. "What?"

"Shall I attack, sir? If I attack, I may create a diversion that could enable the Army of the Cumberland to escape."

"No," Sherman said quickly. "No, an attack is now out of the question. We need to get the Army of the Tennessee back to the north side of Atlanta without delay. Schofield, too. If Thomas has been defeated, Johnston may follow up his victory by capturing our crossings over the Chattahoochee."

"Surely things can't be as bad as that, Cump. Perhaps Hooker can rally the men and restore the situation."

Sherman didn't say anything in response, but merely shook his head. He had no confidence in Hooker's abilities. He could feel his own spirit rapidly giving way to panic. Unpleasant memories from years earlier, memories which he would have liked to forget, were quickly boiling to the surface.

"Cump?" McPherson asked, a little too insistently. "What shall we do?"

He turned to one of his couriers. "Message to Schofield. He is to move his army at once to the assistance of the Army of the Cumberland, while marching one division to Buckhead to prevent any rebel move toward our bridges. Wheeler's cavalry may be about, after all."

The man saluted and kicked his horse into a canter, rapidly disappearing.

Sherman faced McPherson. "James, your army must now march back the way it came. I know your men are already tired, but they will have to march all night. We must get them away from the east side of the city and avoid any trap the rebels might attempt to catch us in."

"Very well, sir."

"You disagree?"

"Not at all, sir." He paused for a moment. "To tell the truth, Cump, I honestly don't know what the best course of action is."

"Neither do I," Sherman admitted. "Our main objective now is not to capture Atlanta, but to escape with as much of our force intact as possible."

*   *   *   *   *

"Where is General Lowrey?" Cleburne shouted to a captain. It was hard to make himself heard over the roar of musketry.

"He's wounded, sir! Shot through the leg!"

He pursed his lips and shook his head angrily. Two of his three brigade commanders were gone, one dead and one wounded. His subordinates were simply too brave for their own good. He said a silent prayer, asking God to preserve the life of General Lowrey and to allow Granbury, at least, to survive the battle unscathed. He asked nothing for himself.

- 242 -

"Who is senior?"

"Don't know, sir! Might be me, for all the regimental commanders are dead, too!"

"I will lead you myself."

Taking direct control of the brigade seemed like the sensible thing to do. He wasn't about to burden a mere captain with the command of an entire brigade. Besides, his division was now scattered over several miles of the battlefield. The regiments of Granbury's Texans, after leading the initial breakthrough of the Union line, had become separated from one another in the confusion of their charge north. Less than ten minutes before, he had left Granbury to the task of locating his units and reforming them if it were possible.

After the breakthrough, he had sent Govan's Arkansans wheeling to the left, shattering the left flank of the Union divisions facing Stewart's corps. The few reports he had received from them since then indicated that they were doing well and helping Stewart's men drive the Yankees northwards. He had sent a staff officer to discover their whereabouts, but assumed that they could take care of themselves.

That left Lowrey's Brigade. They had smashed the right flank of the Yankee division facing Cheatham after the initial breakthrough, then pushed north alongside Granbury's Texans and Clayton's division. Now, they were within a hairsbreadth of Peachtree Creek itself.

It took him a few minutes to get the brigade under control. The Alabama and Mississippi men were stunned at the ferocity of the combat they had gone through and shocked at the heavy losses they had sustained, but they were also seized with the fire that victory lights in the hearts of men. Word that Cleburne had taken personal command of the brigade quickly swept through the lines, calming frayed nerves and cementing confidence.

He pushed on north, with the three Alabama regiments advancing in a sturdy line and the two Mississippi regiments held back as a reserve. The Yankee regiments facing them, disorganized and dispirited though they were, fought with a grim stubbornness, knowing they had little space left in which to retreat. Peachtree Creek was less than a quarter of a mile away.

"Which direction to Collier's Bridge?" he asked Hanley, who was riding close behind him. Like him, Hanley had ridden over the ground the day before the battle to fully acquaint himself with the terrain.

"To the north and slightly west, I think!"

"Push on, men!" Cleburne urged. "The creek is not far! Push on!"

Thirty minutes later, after vicious fighting, Collier's Bridge was in Confederate hands. When the fighting subsided, the ground on the south bank was littered with dead and wounded men of both sides. His own troops had suffered heavily and expended a great deal of their remaining ammunition, but Cleburne beamed with pride as the hooves of Red Pepper thumped onto the sturdy wooden planks of the main bridge over Peachtree Creek.

"Prepare for defense!" Cleburne shouted. "The Yankees are going to try to get the bridge back!"

Cleburne was convinced that a counter attack was imminent. He certainly would have tried to retake the bridge had he been in the same position as the Yankees. The bulk of the Army of the Cumberland was still trapped on the south side of Peachtree Creek. Although they had erected a few bridges themselves that morning after they had first crossed the creek, Collier's Bridge remained the easiest place for them to escape to the north bank. Union forces would be drawn to the bridge as though it were a magnet.

"Hanley! Ride as fast as you can to General Clayton, or any other commander! Tell them that we have taken Collier's Bridge and that reinforcements must be sent immediately!"

"At once, sir!" He saluted and rode off. Cleburne was happy to see him go, for he would be much safer away from the bridge than he would have been had he remained.

He ordered the two Mississippi regiments to the north side of the bridge, to protect against any attempt by the Union forces there to retake it from that side of the creek. He then ordered his men to cut down trees to create a barricade on the south side, but only three or four axes were available and no trees had been successfully cut down when the shout came.

"Here they come!" an Alabama lieutenant called as he ran back from the thin picket line Cleburne had sent out. "Thousands of them! All headed this way!"

"Nowhere to run, boys!" Cleburne shouted out. "But if we are to die, let us die like men!"

The men cheered, but Cleburne felt apprehensive. His motley collection of soldiers probably numbered just a bit over a thousand men. For all he knew, they were about to be assailed by ten thousand Yankees.

But Cleburne had been in tight spots before. He figured the odds were only slightly worse than those he had faced at Ringgold Gap, when his small division had held back the entire Yankee army for hours. His confidence was buoyed by the fact that the Yankee troops about to attack him would be undisciplined and probably panic-stricken because of what they had already been through during the course of the day. Undisciplined soldiers did stupid things.

As the first Union soldiers came into view through the trees, Cleburne's belief was born out. They were not organized into proper lines at all, but were simply an enormous mob rushing toward the bridge in a human wave attack. Cleburne speculated quickly that they must be the remnants of a Union division that had been broken somewhere to the south, probably by Cheatham's men, and were now simply running as fast as they could to gain the north side of the creek.

He noticed the looks of terror on the faces of many of the Yankees when they realized that the bridge was occupied by Confederate troops. Many of them paused uncertainly, only to be shoved forward again by the men pressing from behind. Few officers seemed to be present. None of the Yankees halted to shoot.

Cleburne gave the order to fire. The few surviving officers repeated them up and down the line, and the Southerners unleashed a torrent of musketry into the terrified mass of Unionists. With such a large target, Cleburne's men couldn't miss. Scores of Yankees went down in the first few seconds, the wounded rapidly being trampled by the feet of their comrades. Cleburne tried not to listen to their screams.

"This is easier than wringing a chicken's neck!" someone near Cleburne shouted.

Suddenly, Cleburne saw a mounted Federal officer emerge from the woods. His formidable-looking black horse reared up as they saw the Confederate blocking position, which the officer coolly surveyed for a moment. Cleburne couldn't tell if he was a major, colonel, or maybe even a general, but the look on the man's face was not one of fear. It was one of both rage and determination.

"Form up!" the Union officer shouted in a thunderous voice. "I don't give a damn what regiment you belong to! Form up!" Cowed by the ferociousness of his words, which Cleburne could clearly hear even a hundred yards away, the frightened bluecoats rallied around the man and his horse.

"Right!" he said, satisfied. He drew his sword and pointed it straight ahead. "Now, charge!" The last word was shouted with a force Cleburne had never heard before. The man kicked his horse into a gallop and the mass of Union men surged forward. Cleburne had never seen an avalanche before, but he imagined that this was how it felt to be standing at the bottom of a mountain while one comes directly at you.

The Confederates fired furiously. The Union officer leading the attack was killed instantly. At such close range and with such a large mass of men as their target, every bullet they fired killed or wounded someone. But the sheer size and momentum of the enemy continued to drive forward.

Cleburne pulled his pistol out of its holster and blazed away, firing six shots in quick succession. As the Yankees reached the base of the bridge, hand-to-hand fighting erupted. Men jabbed at one another with bayonets, swung the butts of their rifles as clubs, or dropped their weapons altogether to grapple with their bare hands and teeth. Quite a few of his men carried bowie knives, which now did bloody work. Officers, what few there were, slashed with their sabers and fired away with their revolvers. For just a moment, the roar of musketry slowed and be replaced with the clanging sound of metal against metal that might have characterized a medieval battle.

Private John Hatch, who had faithfully followed Cleburne all day while bearing the divisional flag, had set the flag down to take his own place in the firing line, taking up a rifle from one of the fallen. As Cleburne watched, a bullet tore through Hatch's neck. He dropped his weapon and fell backwards with a pathetic cry, but was held up by the press of men behind him, who were pushing forward to discharge their rifles into the Yankee ranks. Hatch instinctively tried to stop the bleeding by holding his hand up to his neck, but it was no use. Every time his heart beat, a thick shower of blood spewed forth. Hatch panicked and began to flail about with his other arm, but his comrades ignored him, intent on the battle. As Cleburne watched helplessly Hatch sank to the ground and fell forward. Almost immediately, another soldier stepped on him, pushing his still moving body into the soft ground.

A shearing pain tore through Cleburne's left leg, just a few inches above the knee. He cried out in pain and clutched at his leg, remaining on his feet only with difficulty. Glancing down, he saw the fabric of his pants torn and blood seeping out from between his fingers. The wound did not appear serious, as the bullet had just grazed his skin. A mere inch farther to the right and the bullet would certainly have shattered the bone. That would have meant at least the loss of his leg and very possibly an excruciating death. He tried to force the pain from his mind and focus on the battle.

Cleburne's men maintained their discipline. Some of them, without orders, stepped back from the line and began reloading rifles to pass toward the men in front. This allowed at least a low level of fire to be maintained during the harrowing minutes of hand-to-hand combat. As he viewed the fighting, Cleburne struggled to reload his pistol. He noticed some of his men falling after being struck by bullets in their side. Glancing left and right, he was horrified to see the banks of Peachtree Creek crowded with Union soldiers as far as the eye could see. The shouting and screaming he could hear was almost as loud as the continued firing of muskets and the smacking sounds of rifles butts being swung against one another.

Another sound suddenly rolled across the creek valley. He strained his ears to make sure he actually was hearing it and that it was not just a trick of his mind. But yes, he could hear the high-pitched yipping of the Rebel Yell. Thankfully, it was coming closer. Relief was near.

A few Yankees now abandoned the idea of pushing over the bridge and, throwing away their weapons and kits, jumped down into the ravine of the creek. It was a drop of about eight or nine feet, but the chance of getting hurt seemed an acceptable alternative to staying at the bank to be shot or captured.

Cleburne fired off his last round. He stepped back from the firing line, knowing that he could do nothing more to influence the course of the battle. The incoming fire seemed to be slackening in any event. He glanced westwards, looking up the basin of the creek for several hundred yards, and saw the most horrible and terrifying sight he would ever witness in his life.

The first few dozen Yankees who had jumped down into the basin ran across to the other side, splashing through the waist-high Peachtree Creek as they did so. As they began to struggle up the high and steep north bank, gripping exposed tree roots and rock outcroppings in an effort to pull themselves upwards, more Federal troops dropped down into the basin in an effort to do the same thing. Panic-stricken, they grabbed at the feet of the men above them, inadvertently dragging many of them back down into the basin. Only a very few were able to pull themselves up the bank and run off northwards toward safety.

More and more Federal troops were dropping into the basin and attempting to escape by scaling the north bank. Some went unwillingly, knocked into the ravine by the crush of men cramming the bank of the south side, some of whom were still firing back at the advancing Confederates. Finally, as if a dam had suddenly broken, hundreds of Union troops seemed to simultaneously realize that their only hope for escape was to get into the ravine, cross it, and scurry up the other side. The result was a tragedy of nightmarish proportions.

To Cleburne, it seemed like Peachtree Creek had suddenly become a roaring river of blue-coated men, all of them scrambling wildly to get up the bank and shouting in confusion. A few lucky ones made it. Most did not. Crammed into a small and confined space, they got in each other's way, hindered one another's movements, and turned the basin of Peachtree Creek into a confused mass of screaming, terrified men.

They were right to be terrified, because as the south bank of the creek slowly emptied of Federals, it filled with Confederates. After hours of brutal battle, there were no longer any qualms about the morality of shooting defenseless men. Officers ordered their soldiers to pour fire down into the basin, and volley after volley of musketry raked the mass of Yankee soldiers. Most of the blue-coats had thrown away their muskets to ease their escape, so there was scarcely a shot fired in return.

The screams of the Yankees were like nothing Cleburne had heard in more than three years of war. They were not just the shrieks of the wounded, but the terrified cries of men who knew they were about to die and could do nothing about it.

Not all the dying in the ravine was caused by Confederate bullets. In the rush to get across to the north bank, many unlucky

Federal soldiers found themselves shoved under the waters of the creek by the weight of their comrades. There, they flailed about even as other men ran over them, unthinkingly pinning them down until they stopped moving, either drowned or crushed.

The south bank of Peachtree Creek seemed to be in flames for hundreds of yards, as the Confederate soldiers fired again and again into the terrified, huddled masses of Yankee troops. Almost without thinking, they fell into a dreadful routine, reloading and firing again and again.

Cleburne could hear voices crying from the ravine.

"Please don't shoot!"

"We surrender!"

Many of the blue-coats were raising their hands, but most were still stubbornly trying to scale the bank to safety, and so the shooting went on. Frenzied Southern officers were shouting to their men.

"Keep firing!"

"Kill them all!"

Cleburne had seen combat do this to men; the nightmare of battle had transformed them into animals.

There were no longer any Yankees trying to push over the bridge. The men of Lowrey's brigade lined the sides of the structure and blazed away to both the east and west, adding their fire to the slaughter. Cleburne stood and watched in horror as the scene of butchery unfolded as far as he could see. A few minutes before, Peachtree Creek had been a clear trickle of crystalline water, but now was rapidly filling with blood to the point where it was turning purple.

He wanted to shout for the firing to cease, but something held him back. Every enemy soldier they killed was a victory for the Confederate cause and would mean one less rifle trying to kill his own men. He thought of his friend Govan, out there dead on the field somewhere. He did not want to see what he was seeing, but it was war. How could it have been otherwise?

Cleburne couldn't tell how long the slaughter lasted. Ten minutes? An hour? It seemed to last forever. At last, some officers managed to regain control of their men, calling on them to hold their fire and yelling across the ravine for the trapped Yankee soldiers to come back to the south bank and surrender. Many did, but others continued their efforts at escape. Using piles of their own dead and protesting wounded as grotesque staircases, they ascended the steep bank and ran off to the north. Perhaps exhausted from all the killing they had done, the Confederates no longer fired on them.

The noise gradually faded from that of a storm of screaming and gunfire to a pathetic collective moan of thousands of wounded men. For as far as eye could see, Peachtree Creek was choked with the bodies of dead and wounded Union soldiers.

July 20, Night

"It's over," Mackall observed.

Johnston nodded, patting Fleetfoot tenderly on the neck. The sound of musketry and artillery had continued to roll over the ground south of Peachtree Creek even as the sun vanished beneath the western horizon. But they had begun to fade with the coming of night and now had almost vanished altogether. Johnston was glad of it. There had been more than enough killing for one day.

For the past half hour, staff officers he had sent to Stewart and Hardee had returned. The tidings they brought were beyond Johnston's wildest dreams. Although both corps had suffered heavy casualties, they had essentially obliterated the Union divisions facing them. Both corps commanders were reporting that thousands of Union prisoners had been taken, as well as vast quantities of artillery, battle flags and other prizes of war. The ground south of Peachtree Creek, according to Stewart's message, was so covered with Yankee dead that a man could walk two miles stepping from one corpse to the next, without his feet ever touching the ground.

Cleburne's brilliant breakthrough in the center had marked the turning point of the battle. By punching a hole in the Union line and sending his brigades crashing into the exposed Federal flanks and rear, Cleburne had unhinged the entire Army of the Cumberland and allowed the other divisions to drive forward as well. Stewart and Hardee had continued to push north until the Army of the Cumberland was backed up against Peachtree Creek, where untold thousands of Northern soldiers had been slaughtered.

There were many things Johnston did not know. He could not tell how much of the Army of the Cumberland had successfully escaped to the north bank of the creek, nor did he know the whereabouts of McPherson and Schofield. These questions would need to be answered before he could devise his next course of action.

Dispatches from Hood said that McPherson's army had drawn itself up in battle lines as if to attack, but had subsequently marched away to the north. Nevertheless, Hood was still petulantly demanding reinforcements. Reinforcing Hood made a certain amount of sense, as it was possible that Sherman might attack on his front the next morning. Consequently, Johnston had ordered Hardee to send Bate's division to Hood. This unit had emerged from the battle with its organization more intact that the other divisions. Clayton's division, which technically belonged to Hood's corps, was far too disorganized to be quickly assembled for a march to the southeast.

Johnston's body told him that he was tired and needed sleep. But his heart and mind were all afire. He was consumed by the knowledge that he had won the Confederacy's greatest victory of the war. He clicked Fleetfoot into a walk, heading north in the fading twilight, with no particular destination in mind. He felt the need to be near his soldiers, to bask with them in the aura of the victory that they had achieved together.

As he rode forth, he saw the lead elements of Bate's division marching southwards in column, away from the battlefield. They were led by men bearing torches, with other torches interspersed among the column itself. It was one of his finest divisions, composed of tough and brave soldiers from Kentucky, Florida, Tennessee, and Georgia. They had fought very well throughout the day and had to have been exhausted, yet they marched with a swagger and confidence that told Johnston that they were ready to follow any orders he might see fit to give them.

When they saw Johnston approach, the men began to cheer. Some took off their hats and waved them wildly. The marching column, without any orders from their officers, halted in its tracks as the men continued cheering.

He doffed his hat to the column, which caused the shouting to escalate. The men broke ranks and began swarming around Johnston. They shook their rifles in the air, reached out to shake his hand, shrieking the Rebel Yell as loudly as their throats could bear it. Johnston had not expected this and was momentarily apprehensive, for he distrusted large and undisciplined crowds. Underneath him, he could feel Fleetfoot tense, as the horse did not understand what all the clamor was.

The men didn't notice. If they had noticed, they wouldn't have cared. The men continued chanting their favorite nickname for Johnston so loudly that it must have been heard for a mile around.

"Uncle Joe! Uncle Joe! Uncle Joe!"

His heart soared. He stood up in the stirrups, raising his hat over his head and waving it about frantically, not wanting the moment to end. He had won. He had beaten Sherman. He had shown Jefferson Davis, Braxton Bragg, and John Bell Hood how wrong they were. He had proven himself worthy of the trust and devotion his men had always shown him. The cheering went on and on and he drank it in as though it were wine.

He didn't want to get carried away. He remembered how Roman generals celebrating a triumph were assigned a slave whose sole job it was to whisper in their ears that they were mortal.

He put his hat back on his head and took firm hold of the bridle. Kicking his horse into a brisk walk, he passed through the crowd of troops, continuing to wave. They kept cheering, but slowly returned to the ranks of their marching column. Fifteen minutes after they had charged forward to cheer their general, they resumed their march to the southeast.

The war was not over. Johnston knew that the coming months would bring more challenges and probably more bloody battles. He also knew that he would cherish the memory of the Battle of Peachtree Creek for the rest of his life. And so would the Confederacy.

Chapter Seven

July 20, Night

Sherman sat heavily in the saddle, riding slowly westward through the darkness, his shoulders drooping, his usually ramrod-straight posture beaten down by the events of the day. Schofield, McPherson and a small army of staff officers behind him kept their distance. They felt it was better for Sherman to be left alone.

Sherman felt nauseated, like a strong fist was clutching his stomach. He also felt dizzy and had to grip his saddle tightly with his legs to maintain his balance. He tried to focus his thoughts and recover his composure, but found himself unable to do so. He could tell that his hands were shaking and hoped that the men trailing behind him were far enough away that they would be unable to see it.

With his trembling hands, Sherman pulled out his pocket watch and held it up against the light of the lanterns and torches carried by some of the escort troops. It was nearly midnight. The day that was ending had been the most disastrous of his life and he was glad it as finally coming to an end.

He remembered from his West Point history classes the names of the decisive battles of history. Cannae, Hastings, Blenheim, Saratoga. The names of the defeated commanders in those battles were remembered with disgrace and dishonor. Was the name of Sherman to be counted now among the great losers of military history?

He found himself thinking of his miserable early service in the war, when he had effectively been kicked out of the army under suspicion of insanity. He recalled the seemingly endless days he spent in bed at his home in Ohio, tenderly cared for by his wife after he had attempted suicide. The demons which had tormented him then were now reaching for him again, their dark hands gripping him and attempting to pull him down into purgatory.

He felt his mind going.

Sherman closed his eyes tightly, then forced them open again. He told himself that he had to remain calm, maintain his composure, in this the greatest of all possible tests. He willed his mind away from the demons and tried to focus on military realities. If he failed, he knew his mind would fall apart.

He wasn't sure whether General Thomas had been killed or been captured. Sherman certainly hoped he was alive, but it made no difference from a practical point of view. What mattered was that what was left of the Army of the Cumberland didn't have a commander. Despite how much Sherman personally detested General Hooker, he had to admit that he had done a credible job rescuing as much of the Army of the Cumberland as he could after Thomas had disappeared.

But what remained of the Army of the Cumberland? When the morning had begun, it had been a strong and confident force of over sixty thousand men, the heart of the combined Union armies of the West. In less than twelve hours, it had been reduced to a shattered body perhaps half that size. Many of its men had lost their weapons and all were traumatized by their disastrous defeat.

In addition to General Thomas, a great many division and brigade commanders had also been killed, wounded, or captured. The staff officers he had sent to investigate had come back with stories of captains being the highest-ranking officers in many regiments, and of entire units so demoralized that the mere appearance of Confederate infantry might cause them to break and run. Several regiments had simply vanished from the face of the earth.

It would obviously be some time before the Army of the Cumberland would be in any condition to engage the enemy in battle again. Until that could happen, Sherman was left with the two armies commanded by McPherson and Schofield. Their combined strength was only about forty thousand men. Sherman was suddenly struck by the fact that, in terms of effective troops, it was entirely possible that Johnston now outnumbered him.

He turned around in the saddle and called for McPherson and Schofield to come up to him. A moment later they were by his side.

"We've had the devil's own day, haven't we?" Sherman began quietly.

"That's one way to put it," McPherson said glumly.

"We shall withdraw our forces to the north side of the Chattahoochee," Sherman said.

The two army commanders exchanged glances. "Are you sure that is wise, sir?" McPherson asked.

"We have no choice. The Army of the Cumberland is a wreck. Your two armies are all we have left. We know the rebels will receive heavy reinforcements from Virginia in the near future, if they haven't already received them. We must put the river between us and the rebels. The sooner the better. If we don't, we risk total destruction."

"I am not sure that this would be the best course of action," McPherson said with conviction. "A retreat would be an acknowledgement of complete defeat, which would have very bad effects on the morale of the troops who were not involved in today's disaster."

"We must also consider the negative political impact such a retreat would have on public opinion in the North," Schofield pointed out.

"Indeed," McPherson said emphatically. "Perhaps the Army of the Cumberland can be withdrawn to the north side to rest and refit, while Schofield and I remain on the south side. We can hold a lodgment near our initial crossing points, and when the Army of the Cumberland is ready for battle again, it can cross to the south side and we can resume the offensive."

Sherman sat mutely, staring off into the distance. He didn't respond to his subordinates for nearly a minute, causing McPherson and Schofield to exchange concerned glances with one another.

"General Sherman? Are you all right?"

"Yes, I'm fine," Sherman replied, even as he continued to stare steadily southward. "My orders stand. We will withdraw to the north bank of the river. I expect that we shall soon he outnumbered. We must avoid being trapped with the river at our backs."

"The rebels could not have gotten off lightly today," Schofield said. "And we have no certain intelligence that they are going to be receiving reinforcements. In all likelihood, we still outnumber them. Retreating to the north bank of the Chattahoochee will make it much more difficult for us to resume the offensive against Atlanta after we have recovered our strength. We shall have to cross the river all over again."

"Forget about Atlanta!" Sherman snapped loudly. "We must look to the safety of our own armies, not Atlanta!" His body physically jerked as if struck by an electrical jolt, causing his horse to rustle with uncertainty.

McPherson and Schofield were stunned and said nothing. Neither of them had ever seen their commander lose control in such a manner. It was as if they were looking at a different man then they had known that morning.

Sherman shook his head. "No, we must retreat back across the river. It's our only choice. If we stay on the same side of the river with the rebels, we will only risk another defeat, perhaps even greater than the one we have already suffered."

For the first time, Sherman turned and actually looked at his two principal subordinates. "I will issue you specific orders in a few hours. For now, return to your commands and take up positions to protect the remnants of the Army of the Cumberland in the event that the rebels resume their attack at daylight."

"Yes, sir," both men responded simultaneously. They clicked their horses into a walk and ventured out into the night, trailed by their respective staff officers. Sherman was left alone under the starry night, with no defense from the demons.

*   *   *   *   *

President Davis turned in his bed restlessly, trying to find a comfortable position. Sleep had never come easily at any point in his life. But the stresses and worries which daily bore down on him now made it even more difficult, and he counted himself lucky if he got more than five hours of uninterrupted sleep on any given night.

Retiring to bed was never pleasant to begin with. While in his office, he was always distracted by the business of running the war and attending to the administrative duties of being the chief executive of a fledgling nation. In his bedroom, though, those distractions were gone.

Instead, he often found himself unable to shake from his mind the image of the face of his little son Joseph, the purest and most beautiful boy he had ever beheld and the pride of his life. Only three months before, five-year-old Joseph had been taken away by God.

He remembered the day perfectly, as hard as he tried to forget every detail. He had been working at home, preparing to deliver his third annual message to Congress, while his wife Varina had been preparing his lunch. They had just been about to sit down at the table when one of their slaves had run into the room, screaming that Joe had fallen from the second-story balcony on which he had been playing.

He was outside by his son's side moments later, but it was too late. The son still breathed as Davis had knelt over him and prayed, but the breathing ceased within a few minutes. Varina was unable to stop screaming in anguish for the rest of the day. Davis himself ignored the urgent messages about imminent Union offensives in both Georgia and Virginia, instead locking himself in his room and shedding bitter tears.

Davis had buried his son the next day, and the day after that, he delivered his annual message to Congress. The war wouldn't pause in order to give him time to grieve. God demanded that it go on, and Jefferson Davis obeyed.

The tossing and turning continued, as the President tried to escape the imploring gaze of his dead son and find the peace of sleep. He was just about to slip into blessed unconsciousness when he was awoken by a loud pounding on the front door. Davis shot bolt upright in his bed, then angrily tossed the sheet aside and stood up. The last tolling of the clock bells outside had indicated eleven thirty, and if a message for him had arrived so late, it was bound to be important.

"What is it?" Varina asked, still half asleep.

"Someone's at the door." He tenderly touched her beautiful dark hair. "Go back to sleep. I shall return in a moment."

Wandering downstairs in his nightgown, guided by the flickering light of a candle, he soon reached the front door. It was open, and Davis saw his house slave, Mary Bowser, talking with a young-looking man in a lieutenant's uniform. They exchanged words quietly, no doubt concerned about accidentally waking the household.

Mary saw him coming. "I was just about to wake you, master. This gentlemen from the War Department says he has an important message for you."

"Thank you, Mary. You may return to your quarters." With a slight bow of the head, the female slave departed.

"I am very sorry to have to disturb you after you must have retired, Mr. President," the lieutenant said. "But we have received a telegram from General Johnston in Atlanta. Secretary Seddon was quite adamant that the news needed to be communicated to you at once." He held forth the telegram.

Davis took a deep breath. He had gone back-and-forth innumerable times over the last few days about whether he had made the right decision when he had listened to Lee and kept Johnston in his place as commander of the Army of Tennessee. He supposed he was about to find out.

President Davis,

This afternoon, when the enemy was crossing Peachtree Creek, I attacked him with the corps of Stewart and Hardee. By the grace of God and the valor of our soldiers, I can report that we have won a complete victory. We have captured upwards of ten thousand prisoners and killed or wounded perhaps a good deal more. The Army of the Cumberland has been effectively destroyed as a fighting force.

We have also taken from the enemy sixty-two pieces of artillery, over forty-five battle flags, a large quantity of small arms and many other supplies. I can also report that Major General George Thomas is among those captured.

Our own loss was not light. Eight thousand of our men were killed or wounded, though very few captured.

The enemy is now withdrawing northwards, his condition unknown. I shall report in greater detail shortly.

General Johnston

Davis caught his breath. "Lieutenant!" he shouted. "Hold this candle more closely to the paper!" He practically shoved the candle toward the surprised officer, who did as he was told.

Davis read the telegram a second time, and then a third. He half-expected the words to change in the midst of his reading, but they remained the same. He wasn't dreaming. For nearly three minutes,

Davis said nothing, then he looked up at the messenger, whom he didn't recognize.

"Son, do you know what this message says?"

The man smiled. "I do, sir. We received it in the telegraph office less than an hour ago. I was sent out to deliver this message to you the moment Seddon read it."

Davis found the report difficult to believe. An entire Federal army routed? Ten thousand prisoners, among them the arch-traitor George Thomas himself? Sherman retreating to the north, away from Atlanta? It all seemed too good to be true and Davis had long since learned not to trust such news. Too many times he had been deceived by initial positive reports, like that sent by Beauregard after the first night of the Battle of Shiloh or by Bragg after the first night of the Battle of Murfreesboro. He wasn't going to be deceived again.

But there was a firm tone, a sense of finality, to the telegram Johnston had just sent him. Johnston would not have sent such a detailed and concise message without having a firm foundation on which to base it. The specific numbers of reported prisoners, not to mention captured artillery pieces and battle flags, also spoke to the veracity of the report. Considering the bad blood between them, it seemed nonsensical that Johnston would have sent such a message had he known, or even suspected, that the next morning would reveal it all to have been a fantasy.

Davis suddenly realized that he hadn't spoken to the lieutenant for at least five minutes, and that the man was patiently waiting for him. He probably didn't mind, for how many officers of the Confederate Army got an opportunity to see their President react to news of one of the most decisive military victories ever won on the soil of North America?

"Forgive me, Lieutenant," Davis said, embarrassed.

"That's quite all right, Mr. President."

"Give me a moment and I will give you a message to send to General Johnston."

"Of course, sir."

He strolled back to the small room he used as his working space when he was at home, sat down at his desk, and prepared to write. But what could he say? He and Johnston despised one another. To congratulate a bitter enemy, no matter what the actual achievement, seemed almost impossible.

Senator Wigfall would have a field day, Davis realized. Indeed, all his political foes would likely pounce on him, telling every newspaper editor in the land that if Davis had only appointed Johnston to command the Army of Tennessee earlier, the disaster at Missionary Ridge back in November would never have taken place and Confederate independence would have long since been secured.

He shook his head. Now was no time to think about such matters. The Confederacy had won a victory, perhaps the greatest victory in its short history, perhaps a victory of such magnitude that its independence would finally be won after so much blood and suffering. Whatever faults others might identify in the Confederate president, at this moment he was more than equal to the occasion and would rise above them.

He dipped the pen in the inkpot and begin to write.

*　　　　*　　　　*　　　　*　　　　*

The headquarters of the Army of Tennessee had already assumed an air of wild celebration, greater than it had ever known before. As Johnston reined in before the Niles House he could see that bonfires had been lit, casting burning embers into the heavens like offerings to the gods. Banjos and brass instruments had been produced and festive tunes like "The Bonnie Blue Flag" and "Dixie" could heard for half-a-mile around. Men were dancing around the bonfires like wild Indians. The smell of whiskey permeated the air.

As he appeared, a half-drunken cheer erupted from the men in the yard of the Niles House. Some of them were members of his staff and other officers, men Johnston knew well. Others, however, were men he knew only slightly, various dignitaries from Atlanta or members of the Georgia state legislature. He chuckled to himself. A few days before, most of these men probably been loudly clamoring for his removal from command. Now they were cheering him as a hero.

He ignored them, but shook the hands of many of his staff officers as he dismounted his horse. He could smell the burning bonfires, the whiskey of the toasts being drunk, and he could hear the laughter of happy men. The excited conversations of officers as they recounted their own heroics of the day to one another made it seem as though the war was a sporting competition.

"Where is General Thomas?" he asked the nearest officer.

"In your room, sir. We gave him dinner. Posted some guards outside the door."

Johnston nodded and walked inside. A few moments later, having climbed the steps to the second floor, he opened the door to his room.

General George Thomas, the Rock of Chickamauga, sat solemnly at the table. An untouched plate of roast beef lay before him.

At the appearance of Johnston, Thomas looked up sharply and rose to his feet.

"General Johnston," he said with dignity, raising his hand in salute.

"General Thomas," Johnston said, returning the salute. He didn't really know what to say next. "I do hope I am not disturbing your dinner?"

Thomas shrugged. "I'm sure you will understand if my appetite is less than it normally is. Besides, I doubt the other prisoners you have taken today are eating this well."

"Your men are being treated properly, General. Of that I can assure you. They are being fed from the rations we captured during the battle. I know you must be hungry. Please eat."

Reluctantly and ever so slowly, Thomas picked up a knife and fork and began eating.

Johnston went on. "I want you to know that I will do everything I can to make sure your captivity is comfortable. It may be some time before you can be released. If I am not mistaken, the United States holds no Confederate officer of equivalent rank to you, which obviously makes a prisoner exchange complicated."

"That makes no difference, as General Grant has terminated prisoner exchanges in any event," Thomas said.

"Yes. A regrettable order, I must say. And an inhumane one."

Thomas drew his head back. "It was the decision of your so-called government in Richmond to treat captured black soldiers as if they were escaped slaves that prompted Grant's decision. Perhaps if your man Forrest had not seen fit to butcher hundreds of black Union troops when he captured Fort Pillow, after they had surrendered, the order could have been avoided."

Fort Pillow was a topic that Johnston certainly did not wish to discuss. "I can say nothing on the subject of Fort Pillow. I myself am not fully acquainted with the details of the engagement."

Thomas grunted again. He was upset, but Johnston couldn't blame him. Had he been in Thomas's position, he would have been mortified as well. For a moment, he tried to imagine how he might have reacted if he had fallen prisoner to the Yankees.

Johnston sat down across from Thomas. A servant brought in a plate of roast beef for him and he began to eat as he talked. "I have sent a telegram to Richmond to inquire as to your future circumstances. As you are the highest-ranking Union officer yet captured in the war, I am sure you will be accorded special consideration."

Thomas shook his head firmly. "No special treatment. I refuse to be treated any differently than any of the other officers you've captured, no matter their rank."

"I will inform you of my government's position as soon as they make it known to me. And I shall certainly convey your request, which does great credit to your character. They may be predisposed to grant it, as your status as a native Virginian who has fought against his state has given rise to a certain resentment toward you among many in the Confederacy."

Thomas waved his hand dismissively and picked away at the roast beef and sweet potatoes. Next to it stood a glass of water. Johnston walked over to a counter and pulled out a bottle of wine.

"Would you drink a glass of wine with me, General Thomas? It has become more expensive due to the blockade your navy imposes upon us, but it is not yet entirely unobtainable." Without waiting for a reply, he poured two glasses and sat back down.

Thomas swallowed his food and looked at the glass for a few seconds before picking it up and sipping. "I might as well. Today I have seen my army destroyed. While a glass of wine will not undo what has happened, I suppose it cannot hurt. And as for those who think I betrayed my state, I will merely reply that they betrayed their country."

"My country is Virginia. The same was true of you once, as I recall."

Thomas set his wine glass down and looked Johnston hard in the eye. "You took an oath on the field at West Point to protect the United States and the Constitution, yet you broke your oath and instead became a servant of the radical fire-eaters who tore our country apart in the misguided fear that Lincoln would act against slavery."

"You are aware, sir, that I do not own slaves. I have never have done so and never will. I consider the institution distasteful."

Thomas laughed. "You command an army that is defending the institution of slavery, whether you admit it or not. Your victory today is slavery's victory. But the pro-slavery fire-eaters, in bringing on the war to begin with, will prove to be their own worst enemies. For I believe the Union will yet emerge triumphant and slavery will be destroyed."

"The South did not secede because of slavery," Johnston said, as much to himself as to Thomas.

The Union general laughed. "I suggest you reread the manifesto that the South Carolina legislature published when they passed the ordinance of secession back in 1860."

Johnston shifted uncomfortably. He had read the manifesto, which justified the secession of South Carolina almost exclusively on the grounds of protecting slavery. Many other Confederate states had issued similar public statements when they had seceded, though his own state of Virginia had not.

"I did not join the Confederacy to defend slavery," Johnston offered. "I did so because I believed that the federal government was increasingly encroaching on the rights of the sovereign states." He unbuckled the sword from his belt and held it up for Thomas to see. "My father carried this sword throughout the Revolution. I joined the Confederacy for the same reason he joined the patriots who fought against the British."

Thomas frowned and shook his head, as if he were a teacher speaking to a disobedient student. "You cannot compare your misguided struggle to that of our Revolutionary forefathers. The patriots of old had no recourse but revolution, because they were not represented in Parliament and had no influence over the government that controlled their destinies. The Southern states had representation in Congress up until the moment they seceded from the Union. Revolution is only acceptable in the face of tyranny. You faced no tyrant."

"What good does that representation do when we are sure to be outvoted on every issue, due to the increasing population of the North and the smaller population of the South? And, in any event, what right does a lawyer from Boston have to dictate to a Southern planter how he will behave? Or a President in Washington City, for that matter?"

Thomas sat back in his chair and sipped on his wine. "I suppose, General Johnston, that we can engage in a discussion about political philosophy and constitutional history until doomsday, but you and I both know that neither of us will ever change the mind of the other. I have never been a political man in any event. For me, the only thing that matters is that I took an oath at West Point to uphold the Constitution. I kept my oath, though doing so tore my heart in two. You broke your oath and now wage war on the very government you once swore to protect. And for that, sir, I shall pray to God for the salvation of your soul."

Johnston took a long sip from his wine glass, the last statement from Thomas having firmly ended the conversation. The Union general went back to his roast, not caring about whether he was being polite. He thought about what Thomas has said to him, but he had had a sufficient number of such conversations when secession had taken place in 1861. Right or wrong, Joseph Johnston was with the Confederacy.

He stood up. "I will have proper quarters prepared for you, General Thomas. I shall also send a message to General Sherman under a flag of truce to inform him that you are alive, so that he may in turn inform your wife. When my government communicates to me its intentions regarding your confinement, I shall inform you."

"Thank you."

"Do you wish me to send a message to your family in Virginia?"

Thomas thought for a moment. "No, thank you."

Johnston nodded in understanding. "This war is hard on everyone."

"I have read in the newspapers that many prominent Southern politicians and officers have said that I should be hanged if captured. Should I have my will updated?" His voice betrayed not the slightest hint of fear, but only bitter humor.

"I am not aware of any such comments, though you and I both know that many of our fellow Southerners have a tendency to be rather melodramatic. Rest assured, if any such orders arrived, I would refuse to follow them."

"Of that I have no doubt. Unlike General Forrest, you are an honorable man. I apologize for being rude, for you are being most gracious."

"There is no need to apologize, General Thomas. In your position, I would feel much the same way."

There was a soft knocking on the door, and a moment later Mackall appeared. He handed Johnston a message.

"Telegram from the President, sir."

Johnston smiled, relishing the moment. He took the paper and read it quickly. It was short and to the point.

General Johnston,

I offer you the thanks of a grateful nation for the great victory you have achieved over the enemy. Please express my deepest appreciation to the men and officers of your army. I look forward to receiving your full report.

President Davis

Johnston laughed softly. He knew the President would be happy with the news, but he also knew that there was a part of the chief executive that hated having to thank him for it. Receiving such a telegram was a delightful combination of business and pleasure.

*   *   *   *   *

July 21, Morning

Lincoln sat at his desk in his White House office, scribbling comments in the margin of the latest letter from Henry Raymond. Messages from the Republican National Committee chairman were now arriving on a near daily basis. Outside the door, Lincoln could hear one of his private secretaries, John Nicolay, arguing with someone who clearly thought they should be allowed in to speak to the President, but whom Nicolay did not consider important enough to be admitted. It was a familiar sound.

The letter from Raymond bothered Lincoln considerably. According to what it said, Republican leaders across the North were sending worried reports to him, telling of large Democratic rallies being held not only in all major cities but increasingly in the smaller towns and rural areas, too. Clement Vallandigham and other Copperheads were crisscrossing the country, speaking to bigger crowds every day.

Even worse was the growing potential for violence. If Raymond's letter was to be believed, and he had always been a trustworthy correspondent, mobs of anti-war Democrats were routinely harassing draft officers and trashing the offices of pro-Republican newspapers. It seemed to Lincoln that these disturbances were just the early rustles of the wind. As the election approached, they could well build into a hurricane.

Lincoln pulled out some paper to begin drafting a reply to Raymond, when he heard another muffled voice outside the door. It sounded like Stanton, but he couldn't make out the words. There was a hurried conversation in anxious voices between Stanton and Nicolay and then a soft knocking on the door.

"Mr. President? Secretary Stanton is here to see you." A few moments later, the Secretary of War slid into a chair across from the President, and Nicolay had firmly shut the door.

"Mr. President, I am afraid I have some very bad news to report."

"Not another setback in front of Petersburg, I hope," Lincoln said.

"No, sir, not at Petersburg, but in Georgia. And I'm afraid the word `setback' does not do justice to the magnitude of what happened yesterday."

Lincoln took a deep breath, set down his pen, and steeled himself. His Secretary of War was not one to mince words. For nearly half a minute, Stanton said nothing, clearly searching for the right words to convey the news.

The President eventually got tired of waiting for Stanton to speak. Lincoln said, "Edwin, I have endured Bull Run, Fredericksburg, Chancellorsville, Chickamauga, and a host of other terrible defeats. If we have suffered yet another such blow, I shall endure it again. So, out with it."

"Very well, Mr. President. We received a cable from General Sherman this morning. Yesterday, while the Army of the Cumberland was in the process of crossing a difficult creek and was separated from the rest of our forces by a gap of several miles, it was attacked by the bulk of the rebel army and was disastrously defeated. Ten thousand of our men were taken prisoner, including General Thomas himself, and more than ten thousand killed or wounded. We also lost vast amounts of critical supplies and artillery. The Army of the Cumberland has been shattered. It is our worst defeat since the commencement of the war, Mr. President."

The words seemed to hang in the air. Lincoln's face had betrayed not a sign of reaction as Stanton spoke, but his heart had begun pounding within his chest. He had striven so hard and suffered so much over the past three years to preserve the Union and destroy slavery. When the great spring offensive had been launched in May, he had felt that he could almost grasp the victory that would make right all that had gone wrong in his country and make his own sufferings and those of his fellow countrymen meaningful.

Stanton continued, relaying the details of the defeat at the Battle of Peachtree Creek as far as he knew them. Lincoln felt like a man being pushed ever closer to the edge of a cliff. The victory for which he had striven so hard and so long felt like it was slipping away.

Stanton finished talking, and waited for a response. Lincoln silently shook his head for nearly thirty seconds before he said a word.

"Edwin, I wonder if I would have willingly given up my own life to spare the country the news you have just told me."

"There is no need to be melodramatic, Mr. President."

"That is easy for you to say. If I understand what you're telling me, we may have just lost the war."

"No, sir," Stanton replied quickly, seeing the need to reassure the President. "Despite this catastrophe, our army outside of Atlanta still outnumbers the rebels. We have recovered from defeats in the past. We can recover from this one as well."

"Can we?" Lincoln said, rising to his feet. He turned and looked out the window. He had to fight off the instinct to tear out his hair in rage and despair. "The people are wild for peace. The treasury is nearly empty. The election is less than four months away. The Democrats are telling every crowd that will listen to them that our war effort is a failure and that victory is impossible. It seems like rebel bullets may have just proven the Democrats right."

"Mr. President, it is a terrible defeat. I shall not sugarcoat it. But rest assured, we can recover. We can reinforce Sherman, he can still capture Atlanta, and all will be set right."

Lincoln didn't respond, but put his hands behind his back and stared out the window into the city of Washington. He could already envision what the newspaper headlines and the editorials were going to be saying in the coming days. He could imagine the glee that Vallandigham and his ilk would feel when they got the news, if they hadn't already.

"In late 1862, Edwin, when our party did so badly in the congressional elections, the word 'Fredericksburg' was on everyone's lips. Now, surely, 'Peachtree Creek' will be their watchword."

"Perhaps, Mr. President. But remember that the Union is as strong today as it was yesterday. We can still win the war."

Lincoln nodded slowly, continuing to look out the window. "Get your bags packed, Edwin. You and I are taking a trip."

Stanton's eyes narrowed. "Where to, Mr. President?"

"We're going down to see General Grant in Virginia. After such a calamity, I feel the need to speak to my commander-in-chief."

*   *   *   *   *

July 21, Noon

General Johnston was hunched over his desk, reading reports from the cavalry patrols that had been sent out at dawn. According to the horsemen, the remnants of the Army of the Cumberland were continuing to fall back to the north. They were still in some disarray, but had managed to reorganize somewhat during the night. This didn't surprise Johnston, who thought it was inevitable. The Army of the Tennessee and the Army of the Ohio had apparently marched all night and taken up a strong position running from east to west north of Peachtree Creek, covering the retreat of the Army of the Cumberland.

He shook his head. Normally, after such a decisive victory, a rapid pursuit would be called for. The Union bridges across the Chattahoochee were tantalizingly within reach. If Johnston could capture them, Sherman and his entire force would be trapped on the south side of the river.

However, the armies of McPherson and Schofield had not been involved in the previous day's fighting. To capture the bridges, his men would have to punch through the forty thousand Yankees of those two armies. Hardee and Stewart had both suffered heavy losses during the battle and their divisions had inevitably become disorganized. The men were exhausted. The two divisions of Hood's corps that had remained unengaged were nowhere near strong enough. To Johnston's mind, it was not prudent to continue the attack. If he fought a battle against McPherson and Schofield and lost, all the fruits of victory gained the previous day might be lost as well.

If the reports being sent back by Wheeler accurate, Union forces were making preparations to withdraw north of the Chattahoochee River. Johnston couldn't tell if Sherman was really intending to make a major strategic retreat or if he was simply keeping his options open. The best logical course therefore would be to close up to the Union positions and await events. If the Yankees did try to retreat across the river, he might have the opportunity to attack them when their forces were divided.

Johnston had set down the cavalry reports and was about to pick up a paper from his chief of artillery on the Yankee guns that had been captured the previous day. He looked up when he heard Mackall say something not entirely unexpected.

"Sir, General Hood is approaching."

"He knows that the meeting of senior commanders is not for another two hours, yes?"

"I told him myself, sir. I do not know why he is arriving early."

Johnston grinned. "I do."

A minute later, the one-legged warrior hobbled in. The look on his face was one of fury. Immediately a blanket of tension fell over all the staff officers in the headquarters.

"General Hood," Johnston said as Hood walked toward the table. "I expected you to arrive at two o'clock. To what do I owe this early arrival?"

The seething look on Hood's face could have only one cause. Johnston knew immediately that Hood was incensed about having missed out on the glory of the previous day's victory. In any army filled with so many prima donnas, such behavior was all too common, though that made it no less childish. No doubt compounding Hood's anger was the simple fact that Johnston remained in command of the Army of Tennessee. Hood had clearly expected his and Bragg's machinations to have brought about Johnston's removal and Hood's elevation to command.

Hood stood himself up as straight as was possible on his peg leg. "General Johnston, I demand to know why I was not assigned to lead the attack on the Army of the Cumberland yesterday!"

"General Hood, please calm yourself. Your corps played a critical role in guarding the army's right flank against any possible intervention by the forces of Schofield and McPherson. Had it not achieved its objective, our victory could not have been won."

"Don't talk to me like a child, Johnston. You robbed me of one of my divisions and then had me sit out the entire battle with a mere two divisions, who simply stood in their positions all day and did nothing. And when McPherson appeared on my front in greatly superior numbers, you denied me reinforcements!" Hood's face had curled into a scowl and he was making no attempt to keep his voice down. Throughout the headquarters, the staff officers watched the unfolding scene in rapt fascination.

Johnston could smell whiskey on Hood's breath, though that only partially explained the man's irrational behavior. Hood was an angry man, and while he was no Nathan Bedford Forrest, he could easily lose his temper at sufficient provocation. Johnston felt himself to be in no danger, for he knew that if Hood attempted to draw his pistol, half a dozen staff officers would immediately tackle him to the ground.

Johnston stood calmly, folding his hands behind his back. "The positions occupied by the various corps of the army, when the opportunity to attack presented itself, was purely coincidental. Had we had a better chance to attack on the eastern side of the city than on the northern side, your corps would obviously have been in the forefront of the attack."

"You could have countermarched my men through the city and to the north, while Stewart or Hardee had moved to replace my divisions on the east side!"

Johnston shook his head calmly, though such a ridiculous suggestion more properly merited laughter. "There was no time for such movements, which would have necessarily entailed much confusion, and I can see no advantage that would have been gained to compensate for it. Stewart and Hardee were both every bit as qualified as you were to lead the attack."

"Damned if they were!"

"Your forget yourself, General Hood. I shall not tolerate insults to brother officers."

"I will say whatever I damn well please!"

Something snapped in Johnston at that instant. His voice remained calm, but he no longer felt that he was bound by decorum. Uncouth bumpkins from the frontier simply did not speak with such insolence to Virginia gentlemen. Hood was a man who had willingly subverted the operations of the army, placing his men and the fate of the country at risk, merely to serve his own personal ambitions. Such men were simply not entitled to the respect accorded to gentlemen.

"I know you will say whatever you please," Johnston replied in ice-cold tone. "You certainly say what you please in your secret letters to President Davis and General Bragg, do you not?"

Hood's angry scowl vanished, replaced by an expression of stunned shock. It was as if he had been punched in the stomach. He required an awkward five seconds before he remembered to close his mouth. He let out a deep breath, and stared Johnston deeply in the eye.

"Private letters between friends are no concern of yours," Hood said.

"Perhaps if you had confined the subject of your letters to purely personal matters, you would be correct. But it has been made known to me that these letters of yours contained repeated criticisms of my command of this army. These comments included several verifiable falsehoods, such as assertions that you had counseled me to take the offensive on occasions when you and I both know you actually counseled retreat."

Hood did not reply, but his gaze fell away from Johnston's eyes and to the floor.

Johnston went on. "You must be aware, General Hood, that communicating with the civilian government without your commander's knowledge or permission is an act of insubordination meriting a court martial."

For nearly thirty seconds, Hood simply shook his head, pursed his lips, and breathed heavily. When he looked up, the surprise and sadness had vanished, replaced once again by fury and rage.

"General Johnston, you shall pay dearly for your treatment of me."

One corner of Johnston's lips went up in a sneer. "Return to your command, General."

Without another word and without pausing to salute, Hood turned and walked directly toward the door.

"General Hood?"

He looked back. "What?"

"There will be no more of these secret letters. If you wish to make your views known to the government, you shall do so through the proper channels and only with my permission. Is that clear?"

Hood looked at him silently for a second, but did not respond. He turned and walked out the door without another word. A few minutes later, having been strapped into the saddle by helpful staff officers, he rode off.

Mackall walked up beside Johnston. "Shall I prepare papers for a court martial?"

"No. Not yet, at least. Perhaps it will blow over, now that my command of this army is secure. Keep an eye on him, though. In the meantime, let's turn our attention to Sherman."

*   *   *   *   *

July 21, Afternoon

The 7th Texas had covered itself with glory during the Battle of Peachtree Creek. They had spearheaded the drive of Granbury's Brigade that had broken through the Union lines at the critical moment of the battle, captured a four-gun enemy battery and two battle flags, and ended the engagement by taking the commander of the opposing army prisoner. Few regiments on any battlefield in history could have matched such an achievement.

The price they had paid for their glory was high. The 7th Texas had been shattered. Going into the Battle of Peachtree Creek with slightly more than a hundred men, it had come out of it with just seventy. Although Collett had emerged unscathed, one of the regiment's lieutenants had been killed and the other seriously wounded. The Lone Star Rifles, in particular, had suffered heavily, with only eleven men still standing when the battle had ended.

McFadden wiped sweat away from his forehead as he pushed the shovel into the earth yet again. While details had been sent out to collect as many of the bodies of their fallen comrades as could be found, the rest of the regiment was busying itself digging a burial trench.

"Take a break, James," Captain Collett said. "You've earned it, if anyone has."

McFadden shook his head. "Thanks, sir, but no. We owe it to our boys to get this done as quickly as possible."

"Suit yourself."

He went back to digging. Slowly, the bodies of their comrades were brought in and laid respectfully next to the trench as quietly as possible. The work went on for some time. After a few hours, the details were back with seventeen bodies. The remainder would likely be buried in those trenches reserved for unidentified men.

They carefully lifted the bodies into the trench. When this was completed, the 7th Texas mustered in a line facing them.

Stokely Chaddick, the chaplain of Granbury's Texas Brigade, arrived to officiate. He pulled out his Bible and gazed over the sad faces of the surviving members of the 7ᵗʰ Texas. Aside from a few muffled coughs, there was complete silence. Chaddick read Psalm 23, which did not surprise McFadden. It was the verse almost always used on such occasions. He read the names of each of the soldiers and spoke of their Christian devotion. McFadden knew that was untrue in many cases, but of course it would have been impolite to say so.

The service ended quickly. Chaddick made his apologies and departed, for he had other funeral services to officiate. McFadden and some of the others began shoveling the refuse dirt back into the trench, covering the bodies of their friends. When it was over, McFadden set his shovel down, sat down with his back to a tree, and promptly fell asleep.

He didn't know how long he slept, but some time later he was awoken by a gentle shaking of his shoulder.

"Jim? Wake up, Jim." It was Collett's voice.

"What is it?" McFadden asked angrily, still half asleep.

"General Cleburne is here to see you."

Those words woke McFadden up as though someone had thrown a bucket of water in his face. His eyes opened. Cleburne was standing before him, patiently waiting. He scrambled to his feet, quickly brushed himself off, and saluted.

"Sorry, sir."

"That's all right, McFadden. I just came by to give your regimental commander this." He pulled a piece of paper out of his coat pocket and handed it to Captain Collett.

"What is it?" McFadden asked.

"Orders. Captain Collett has been promoted to major and you have been promoted to lieutenant. You'll receive official confirmation from the War Department just as soon as they take care of the paperwork."

His eyes widened. "Lieutenant?"

"Don't be surprised, McFadden. You personally captured the highest ranking Union officer yet taken prisoner by the Confederacy. And your record up to this point has been stellar. Honestly, I do not know why you were not made an officer some time ago."

"I have offered to send in McFadden's name for promotion to lieutenant on previous occasions, sir," Collett said. "He has always declined the honor."

"Has he?" Cleburne said. "Why is that?"

Collett looked at McFadden, silently telling him to answer their division commander. McFadden, still not fully awake and stunned by what Cleburne was telling him, could not find any words to say. He didn't really know the answer anyway.

Cleburne waited a few moments before going on. "Well, not this time, son. As the commander of your division, I am not offering you a promotion. I am ordering you to take it. Is that clear, Lieutenant McFadden?" Cleburne's voice stressed the new title.

"Completely, sir."

"Very well." He extended his hand. "Congratulations."

McFadden shook his hand and was surprised by the strength of the Irishman's grip. "Yes, sir. Thank you, sir."

"Three cheers for Major Collett and Lieutenant McFadden!" someone shouted.

The men of the 7th Texas cheered heartily and applauded as Cleburne handed McFadden an officer's sword and lieutenant stripes to be sewn into his uniform. McFadden had a bemused look on his face, which the men found quite funny.

Cleburne departed, and the rest of the regiment went back to its business. Private Montgomery walked up to McFadden.

"Congratulations, Jim."

"Thank you, Ben. Not really sure if I want it, though."

"You'll make a fine officer. You led the Lone Star Rifles well enough."

"A company is one thing. Now I'm going to be in charge of half the regiment."

"Couldn't ask for a better man."

McFadden shook his head. "I hoped that I had turned down Collett's offers to send in my name often enough that people would stop thinking about making me an officer."

"Well, you were the one who captured General Thomas. The whole army's talking about you. Your name is in the papers. Hell, I bet Jefferson Davis and Robert E. Lee have heard of you by now."

"Dear God." The thought of fame, even if it was temporary, frightened McFadden more than any number of Yankee rifles.

Montgomery smiled mischievously. "Another person who has certainly heard about what happened is that lady friend of yours down in Atlanta. Annie, is it? Her father, too, I would guess."

His head jerked up. It had not occurred to McFadden that his capture of Thomas and his sudden distinction would have any impact on his developing relationship with the Turnbow family. Before he could stop himself, he wondered if Annie would be impressed by what he had done. He also wondered whether her parents might consider him more worthy to court their daughter now that he was an officer with a great martial deed to his credit.

These thoughts vanished instantly when he suddenly realized that the Turnbows were no doubt wondering whether he had even survived the Battle of Peachtree Creek. He had not thought to contact them to let them know he was alive. He had lived for years effectively cut off from society outside of the 7th Texas itself. It was strange to think that people outside his unit knew of his existence, much less actually cared about his well-being.

The first thing McFadden did upon becoming a Confederate officer was sit down to write a letter to Annie Turnbow.

The corps commanders arrived at the Niles House one by one. First Hardee, then Stewart, then Wheeler, and finally Hood. Johnston had decided to act as though his previous conversation with Hood had not taken place, and his face positively beamed as he greeted his subordinates with firm handshakes and warm pats on the back. The atmosphere at the headquarters of the Army of Tennessee remained festive, with laughter and smiles all around.

Johnston happily showed the four generals some of the Union regimental battle flags that had been captured the day before, as well as the pile of swords taken from Union officers who were now Confederate prisoners.

"All in a good day's work, eh, General Johnston?" Hardee said.

"Indeed, William. I think these trophies prove that we won the greatest victory yet in our war against the Yankees yesterday."

"Amen," said Stewart with a smile.

"Come in, gentlemen. We have much to discuss."

The five men strolled through the Niles House foyer toward the dining room, which had been made the de facto conference room of the headquarters. Johnston glanced carefully at Hood, whose face held a stony expression. He did not meet the gaze of any of his comrades. Johnston wished that he had the ability to read Hood's mind.

Mackall was already in the dining room, trying to scrawl the latest known movements of the enemy onto the ever-present map of the Atlanta area laid out on the table. Johnston waved them all closer to the map table, and the men crowded around it. Mackall started giving a general update.

"The Army of the Cumberland, or what is left of it, has fallen back to the north in confusion. Our scouts report that it is still in considerable disarray, with units largely intermingled."

"My boys are hassling them," Wheeler said, his voice eager and happy. "I would bet on us bringing in another couple hundred prisoners before this day is over."

"Excellent, General Wheeler," Johnston said. "Go on, General Mackall."

"The two armies of Schofield and McPherson have been moving north and west since last night and are now in the process of interposing themselves between us and the remnants of the Army of the Cumberland."

"That makes sense," Hardee said. "It's only natural for Sherman to use his remaining effective troops to protect those that we routed yesterday."

"Where are they now, General Mackall?" Johnston said.

The chief-of-staff thumped the map. "According to the information General Wheeler has provided me from his scouts, it appears that Schofield's troops have reached the Chattahoochee River here, just north of where it intersects with Peachtree Creek. McPherson's force is on his left flank. Their line is extending from the river almost due east. They marched all night to get into this position and since early this morning have been cutting down trees to create fortifications."

"So, even if we could reorganize our men quickly enough, move them north of Peachtree Creek and attack the Yankees before the end of the day, any assault would likely be repulsed," Hardee said.

"Yes," Johnston replied. "And with great loss. We will not squander our hard-earned victory with any reckless actions. For the moment, the threat to Atlanta is at an end. We must remain wary, however, for the Yankees are far from finished."

"What shall be our strategy, then?" Wheeler asked.

Johnston tapped the map in the location of the new Union line. "We shall close up on the enemy position, catching any stragglers we can in the process. Stewart on the left, Hardee on the right, with Hood in reserve. Our left flank will be on the Chattahoochee River. General Wheeler, your cavalry will cover our right."

"Of course, sir."

"In the event of any surprises, the Georgia Militia will remain in the defenses around Atlanta, which shall continue to be improved. Two thousand of the militiamen have been detailed to guard the Yankee prisoners, freeing up our regular troops. General Wheeler, you will assign two of your brigades to closely monitor the Chattahoochee River between the new Federal line south to the ford at Campbellton, immediately reporting to me any Federal movements which might be detected on the other side."

"Yes, sir."

"I have no intention of throwing our men uselessly against their entrenchments, gentlemen. And I am well aware that the armies of Schofield and McPherson represent forty thousand fresh Union troops who remain unscathed by yesterday's victory. Caution is called for. But neither do I intend to give the Yankees any rest. We obviously have the advantage for the moment. So we will probe their defenses and harass them with artillery fire. Thanks to the Yankee quartermasters, we now have a large surplus of ammunition."

The men around the table laughed with some surprise at the joke. Johnston was not particularly known for his sense of humor.

"In the meantime, I have just sent a telegram to President Davis, requesting that he unleash Forrest's cavalry against Sherman's supply lines in Tennessee."

"Correct me if I am mistaken, General Johnston," Hardee said. "But have we not already requested this course of action from the President, only to be repeatedly denied?"

"Yes, indeed," Johnston answered. "But the President has always maintained that the reason Forrest could not be ordered into Tennessee was because Federal troops stationed in Memphis posed too great a risk to Mississippi and Alabama to allow Forrest to leave the area."

"I can see the logic behind his reasoning," Stewart said. "Do you believe our victory of yesterday has changed the equation?"

"I do," Johnston said. "Sherman will be stripping troops from all areas in order to make good his losses of yesterday. I would suppose that at least some of these troops will have to be drawn from West Tennessee, meaning that the pressure on Mississippi and Alabama will be correspondingly reduced. Hopefully, it shall be reduced to the extent that Forrest will be able to launch an operation against Sherman's supply lines in the manner I have outlined to the President."

"I suppose that makes sense," Hardee said.

Johnston went on. "If Sherman elects to remain on the south bank of the Chattahoochee, we shall look for a favorable opportunity to engage him in battle, most likely by seeking to turn his left flank. If he withdraws to the north bank, we shall endeavor to ensure that he cannot again cross to the south bank. In either case, assuming that Forrest can get onto Sherman's railroads and cut him off from his supplies, we can continue to hold Atlanta indefinitely. Victory will be ours."

The meeting broke up shortly afterwards and the generals dispersed to their commanders. Throughout the entire meeting, Hood had neither said a word nor made eye contact with anyone else. Johnston watched him go with considerable unease.

*　　　　　*　　　　　*　　　　　*　　　　　*

July 22, Evening

Marble sat quietly at a reserved table at Delmonico's, reading through that day's edition of *New York World* while he waited. The headlines he had chosen for his paper the previous evening had been anything but subtle.

CATASTROPHE IN GEORGIA!
SHERMAN'S ARMY UTTERLY ROUTED!
UNION CASUALTIES ENORMOUS,
REBEL LOSSES LIGHT

He smiled. His copy editor had first wanted to use the term `disaster' to describe the defeat at Peachtree Creek, but as they had been using that term rather too often to describe General Grant's operations in Virginia and Marble feared his readership was growing tired of it. Besides, 'catastrophe' somehow sounded bigger and more significant than 'disaster.'

The paper boys had been busy hawking the edition on every street corner in New York City throughout the day. Sales had been brisk, better than on any day since the Battle of Gettysburg. Within the paper was perhaps the most venomous editorial Marble had yet printed against the Lincoln administration, damning the President for the conduct of the war and laying all blame for the defeat in Georgia squarely at his feet.

Marble took a sip from his glass of wine, just as he noticed George McClellan finally arriving at the door. He raised his newspaper until the former general noticed him. An instant later, McClellan slid into the chair across the table.

"Momentous news from Georgia," McClellan began.

"It changes everything. Did you read my paper this morning?"

"Of course. The accounts of the fighting sent back by your reporters do not make for pleasant reading. So much incompetence! So many casualties! Your editorial denouncing the Lincoln administration, however, was quite enjoyable. And right on the money, if I may say so."

"You may," Marble said with a grin. The waiter approached. Marble ordered the famous Delmonico steak without much thought. He had had it many times during his visits to Delmonico's and always enjoyed it. McClellan perused the menu for several minutes, torn between a lobster dish and an Alsatian glazed ham, before finally deciding upon the latter. Marble ordered a bottle of Burgundy to accompany the dinner.

"So," Marble said as the waiter walked off. "What is your take about what has happened in Georgia?"

"I could have predicted it," McClellan said. "I know Johnston well. He and I were friends before the war. I fought against him during the Peninsular Campaign in 1862 until he was wounded. A dangerous and crafty man, I must say. Sherman got careless and paid the price. I would not have been so imprudent had I been in command."

Marble nodded. "Needless to say, these events will have a great impact on your presidential campaign."

"Without doubt. If anything good is to come of this bloody fiasco, it must be that it shall help the people see what a bumbling fool they have as their chief executive and how desperate is the need to replace him with someone more competent."

"That is what my newspaper is trying its damndest to achieve. My friends at the *Chicago Times*, the *Detroit Free-Press*, and dozens of other papers are doing the same. Clement Vallandigham and his friends are moving heaven and earth, crisscrossing the country and speaking to every crowd they can gather. We are steadily eating away at the strength of the Republican Party and the Lincoln administration throughout the country."

McClellan's face clouded a bit. "I do not like Vallandigham. He seems to believe we should give the South everything they ask for on a silver platter. I find the idea of being indebted to him to be extremely unpleasant."

"As the saying goes, the enemy of my enemy is my friend. Vallandigham is the enemy of Lincoln. Lincoln is your enemy. Therefore, Vallandigham is your friend."

McClellan shrugged. "Put that way, I cannot but see your logic. The most important thing to me is that Lincoln is defeated."

The waiter arrived with their dishes and refilled their glasses of wine. For a few minutes, the conversation became muted as the two men plunged into their delicious meals. Delmonico's had enjoyed its reputation as the finest restaurant in New York City for decades and the taste of the food proved that it was completely deserved.

"How do we stand electorally?" McClellan asked. He tried to sound nonchalant, but Marble could tell that the former general's mind was buzzing with anticipation regarding the answer he was about to receive.

"Very well," Marble said with a smile, sipping from his wine glass before going on. "New York is all but locked down for you. It shouldn't come as a surprise to you that New Jersey, your home state, is also as good as won. We have no doubt that the border states of Kentucky, Delaware, and Maryland are leaning heavily in your favor."

McClellan did the math in his head. "That would give us sixty-two electoral votes."

"Yes. More than half of the one hundred and seventeen votes that will be required for victory. But my sources in Pennsylvania, Michigan, Minnesota, Indiana and even Illinois are continually sending me very positive news. With this latest disaster yet again demonstrating the incompetence of the Lincoln administration, the situation for us can only improve."

"If we add the states you just mentioned to the ones you have already asserted are definitely in our column, our total would come to 121 electoral votes."

"Four more than needed to win the Presidency, General McClellan. And that's only counting the states which are either certain to vote for you or are likely to do so. You cannot discount the possibility of surprises. I'm even hearing rumblings from Connecticut and Rhode Island of unexpected Democratic strength."

"Well, this is very pleasant news," McClellan said, smiling for the first time and taking a sip of his Burgundy. "It also matches what I am being told by other people who are well-informed on political matters. Governor Seymour shares your confidence that we will win New York. And Chairman Belmont has written numerous letters to me outlining, as you just did, the likelihood of most of the Northwestern states falling into line as well."

Marble nodded. "I am glad you are able to verify what I say with other sources. As a newspaper man, I more readily trust many people saying the same thing than a single person saying one thing. And what everyone is telling me is that you shall be the next President of the United States."

McClellan smiled and went back to his glazed ham, eating it with more gusto than he had before.

*   *   *   *   *

July 22, Night

Sherman leaned against a tree, smoking a cigar and gazing off to the southeast. He was still south of the Chattahoochee River, with Atlanta a mere five miles away. For all the chance he had of reaching the city, it might as well have been on the far side of the Moon.

Three days before, Sherman had commanded a great host of soldiers more than a hundred thousand strong. Following the disaster at Peachtree Creek, its numbers had been reduced to perhaps seventy-five thousand men. Sherman figured that only about half of them could be considered reliable.

The Confederate army, by contrast, was no doubt flush with victory, largely reequipped with captured cannon and muskets, and possibly receiving large reinforcements from Virginia. Sherman couldn't be sure how much the enemy had suffered in the recent battle. Nor could he be sure whether or how many troops from Lee's army were actually arriving. All Sherman knew was that he needed to put the Chattahoochee River between him and Johnston.

As he had ordered, the armies of Schofield and McPherson had taken up position in a line running from east to west a few miles north of Peachtree Creek. Behind that line, the shattered remnants of the Army of the Cumberland were withdrawing across the Chattahoochee.

Off in the distance, Sherman could hear scattered musket fire and the occasional boom of artillery. The rebels had been harassing his men all day, as if to mock them for their recent defeat. It stung to realize that many of the cannon now shelling his men had been captured from him during the battle two days before.

"Cump?" said a voice from behind him. He recognized it as McPherson, though he had not previously heard his subordinate approach.

Sherman did not want to talk to McPherson. Indeed, he did not want to talk with anyone at all. All he wanted was to be left alone until his entire army was safely on the north bank of the Chattahoochee River. A feeling of intense and indescribable exhaustion swept over Sherman. He realized that the last thing he wanted to do at that moment was to speak to another human being.

"Cump?" McPherson asked again. "Are you all right?"

With an enormous amount of will, Sherman was able to answer. "Yes. I'm fine."

He heard McPherson walk a bit closer, though his subordinate seemed careful to keep his distance. "My army continues to hold its position. The enemy is mounting only weak sorties. Probing attacks, seems like."

Sherman replied with a grunt.

McPherson waited a moment before going on. "Schofield is reporting more or less the same situation on the right. Johnston's men have closed up to our positions, but they seem to have no intention of making a determined attack."

"Very well," Sherman said.

"Cump, it seems to me that Schofield and I would be able to hold our positions on the south bank of the river even against a heavy attack. Our men are well dug in now."

"No. You shall continue your retreat across the river as previously ordered. I have already had one army shattered on the south bank of this damned river. I shall not risk losing the other two." Sherman did not turn to look at McPherson while be spoke, but continued to gaze off to the southeast.

"Perhaps it is not that great a risk," McPherson said. "Together, Schofield and I can put forty thousand men in the field. Considering that Johnston must have suffered heavy losses two days ago, I reckon we still match his numbers even if we do not count the still intact units of the Army of the Cumberland."

Sherman shook his head. "Grant sent me a telegram a few days before the battle, telling me that Lee was likely sending Johnston twenty-five thousand reinforcements. Indeed, it may have been the arrival of the first of these units that encouraged Johnston to attack in the first place. In all likelihood, General McPherson, we are outnumbered by the enemy, with our backs to a formidable river, and the morale of our men is at rock bottom. To remain on the south bank risks turning what is already a complete disaster into an even worse catastrophe."

McPherson waited some time before responding. "Well, what are your orders, then?"

"The same as they were before. You and Schofield are to hold your positions until the Army of the Cumberland has completed its withdrawal across the river, then withdraw yourselves, destroying the bridges as you do so. It is a very simple order. Obeying it should be no trouble."

"Of course," McPherson said, his voice uncertain. He cleared his throat to indicate a new topic. "Can I assume that you will be appointing General Hooker to command of the Army of the

Cumberland? He is the senior corps commander, after all. Though I don't like him any better than you do, I have to admit that he has done a decent job of cleaning up the disorganization."

A look of confusion clouded Sherman's face. Over the previous two days, he had often dwelt on the fate of Thomas, until a message from Johnston arrived under a flag of truce confirming that he was a prisoner, uninjured and safe. Sherman knew that he should had communicated this information immediately to the War Department, to say nothing of Thomas's wife, but he still had yet to do so. It would require nothing but a few words to a staff officer, yet Sherman found that he simply couldn't get his mind to do it.

Worse, Sherman suddenly realized that he had not yet given the question of who was to command the Army of the Cumberland a moment's thought. He was seized by a moment of silent terror. If he was unable or unwilling to give proper consideration to an issue of such great importance to the campaign, how could he judge himself fit to command all of the Union armies in the Western Theater?

Again, the memories of late 1861 came roaring back, like a fire he thought had been extinguished that suddenly exploded back into life.

"Cump?" McPherson asked, concerned.

"Yes?"

"Are you going to leave Hooker in command?"

"No," Sherman said, shaking his head. "No, I don't think I am. I shall give command to General Howard."

"Very well," McPherson said, sounding slightly unconvinced. General Oliver Howard was a fine Christian gentleman, but his performance as a corps commander in both the Army of the Potomac and the Army of the Cumberland had been little short of disastrous. "I imagine that General Hooker will be less than pleased when you inform him of your decision."

"Hooker may go to the devil, for all I care. That man shall never be at the head of an army under my command. Now, General McPherson, is there anything else?"

McPherson waited a moment, staring at his commanding general with a look of great concern.

"Well?" Sherman said.

"No, sir. Nothing else."

"Good. Now return to your army and continue to carry out my orders as planned."

McPherson saluted and slowly turned to leave. He waited for Sherman to face him and return his salute. But he never did, continuing to puff away on his cigar and stare off into the distance.

*   *   *   *   *

July 23, Morning

Thomas shifted uncomfortably on an old rickety chair that seemed likely to fall apart at any moment. Throughout the dusty and poorly-ventilated warehouse, dozens of other captured Union officers either stood about in quiet conversation or lay on moldy blankets on the floor, trying to get some sleep. Although it was still morning, the heat was already stifling.

There were well over two hundred prisoners in this warehouse alone. Most were lieutenants and captains, although there were also a large number of majors and colonels. Thomas was the only general in the warehouse, but conversations with other prisoners revealed that at least three other generals had been taken prisoner during the battle, which meant that there were probably other buildings nearby, similarly stuffed with captured Union officers.

Thomas himself had arrived only the night before. For the first two days of his captivity, he had been held in a small house near Johnston's headquarters, guarded by a squad of Tennessee infantrymen. He had been visited by many Confederate generals he had known in the peacetime army before the war. Some had been gracious and kind, but others had been sarcastic and mocking, dwelling on his perceived betrayal of the South.

To all such snide comments, he had made the same response he had made to General Johnston the night of his capture. He had sworn an oath to protect the United States and its Constitution, and he stood by his oath. His Confederate counterparts had violated their oath, and for that he would pray to God for the salvation of their souls.

Two days later, General Johnston had sent him a note. Richmond had acceded to his request to be treated no differently than any of the other officers who had been taken prisoner. He had been immediately transferred to the warehouse, with his guards hinting that a movement to yet another new location was imminent.

The prisoners had pieced together a general picture of exactly what had happened to their army during the Battle of Peachtree Creek. Although Thomas noted how studiously polite and deferential they were to him, given his status as their superior officer, he could not help wondering about the occasional side glances he saw cast in his direction. He couldn't blame them if they laid responsibility for the catastrophe squarely at his feet. In their place, he would probably have done the same.

The prisoners had been forbidden to come within ten feet of the walls of the warehouse. Lining the walls were three or four dozen rebel guards, loaded muskets on their shoulders. Most were old men

- 279 -

and young boys, which told Thomas that they were of the Georgia militia rather than the Army of Tennessee. Attempts to start conversations with these men had usually been met with angry warnings not to do so.

The guards had initially spent a lot of time loudly taunting Thomas, calling him a traitor, a coward, and a fool. He had done his best to ignore these insults, but this had only sparked a desire on the part of the guards, who were every bit as bored as the prisoners, to see who might be the first to get some sort of response from the Unionist Virginian. Eventually, a group of fellow prisoners had stood together around Thomas, forming a human wall that blocked their commander from the sight of the guards. Eventually, the rebels lost interest in the game.

There was a sudden murmuring among the prisoners closest to the warehouse double-door, which was big enough to accommodate a horse and wagon. Thomas was at the far end and could not see what was happening. A few minutes later, though, the doors swung open, flooding the warehouse was so much light that Thomas and many other prisoners had to momentarily shield their eyes. Outside, a long line of rebel soldiers was visible. An officer entered the warehouse.

"Attention, prisoners!" he grandly announced. "You are being transferred to a train for transport out of Atlanta! Be advised that you must follow the directions given to you at all times! Anyone who attempts to escape will be shot! Furthermore, if anyone does manage to get away, one of your fellow prisoners will be shot in your place! Is that understood?"

"Where are we being sent?" a Union major asked.

"Macon, about a hundred miles south of here. That's the last question I shall answer."

Thomas did not find this surprising. Up until quite recently, most high-ranking Union prisoners were sent to the infamous Libby Prison in Richmond. But a dramatic escape of several prisoners and the near approach of the Army of the Potomac had persuaded the rebel authorities to close Libby Prison down. If he recalled correctly, captured Union officers were now being sent to a special prison camp not far from the hellhole at Andersonville.

Thomas listened to the chatter among his fellow prisoners, who were discussing whether a cavalry raid on the prison camp in question might set them free. He doubted it. The rebel horsemen had proven superior to their Union counterparts at every stage of the campaign to date and the rebels would obviously be guarding their prison camps very carefully. Besides, even if Union cavalry did liberate the camp, how would the freed prisoners find their way back to friendly territory?

Over the next hour, the prisoners were led out of the warehouse in groups of twenty, marching in single file. Thomas went with the third group. Rebel guards marched on either side of them, watching them carefully and gripping their muskets tightly. They turned to the left as they exited the warehouse and began walking down the street.

On one side of the road stood a crowd of angry-looking women, with some older men and even some children mixed in. As he marched past them, Thomas could hear the shouts and jeers. The fury of rebel soldiers in battle was bad enough, but it was as nothing compared to the infinite hatred of the women of the South.

"Yankee pigs!"

"Scum of the earth!"

"Bastards!"

Some of the women in the crowd recognized Thomas and screamed out insults personally directed toward him, accusing him of betraying his state, betraying the South, betraying his family. One old man cried out that he hoped his captors would hang him from a sour apple tree.

A Union captain began to shout back a response to one of the abusers, only to have a guard violently slam the butt of his rifle into his knee, causing him to crumple instantly down onto the dusty road. The women laughed and applauded. Two fellow prisoners helped the man back onto his feet and he kept stumbling down the street toward their destination.

"Stand tall, men!" Thomas roared, unable to restrain himself any longer. "You are soldiers of the United States! Stand tall!"

As they kept moving down the road, the immense red brick structure known simply as the Car Shed loomed up ahead of them. The piercing sound of a train's steam whistle came over the Union prisoners like a portent of doom. Every mile the train carried them southwards would be a mile deeper into the hated Confederacy, a mile farther away from their comrades, a mile farther away from freedom.

They were herded into three different boxcars, stuffed inside in such great numbers that it was difficult for any man to sit down. The only ventilation was provided by small cracks between some of the boards. As he clambered up the ramp used to move cattle into similar cars, Thomas reflected that it was going to be a long and uncomfortable journey.

Four days before, he had been the commander of one of the most powerful armies on the planet. Now, he had been reduced to the level of a cow.

July 23, Noon

President Davis did not enjoy holding receptions at the Executive Mansion. He was a man much more comfortable working alone in his study than making small talk with people he considered idiots. Following the victory at the Battle of Peachtree Creek, however, it seemed necessary to schedule a special victory celebration. Failing to do so might have offended polite society, which Varina had assured him would have been a disaster too terrible to contemplate.

Davis stood as ramrod-straight as possible, shaking hands with a never-ending line of guests. There were numerous Confederate officers either temporarily on leave in Richmond or recovering from war wounds. There were members of Congress who smiled and chatted pleasantly with Davis and his wife, even though he knew they were doing everything they could to undermine his leadership when they were not actually in his presence. There were also many well-to-do Richmond merchants and bankers, quite a few of whom were in the highly-lucrative blockade running business.

The crowd congregated in the main reception room. Fine champagne was being poured in quantities that would have made many a wealthy family in Paris blush with embarrassment. The main dinner course was a baked ham drenched in a maple syrup glaze, which was among the most delicious things anyone had eaten in some time. In addition, fresh oysters and roast chicken filled the plates of guests. It was not as elegant a reception as would have been expected before the war, but it was certainly one of the finest parties the city had seen for some months.

Davis knew he himself was unlikely to have an opportunity to sample any of the fine food, as he would almost certainly be trapped in the receiving line for the duration of the levée. He didn't particularly mind. The soldiers fighting outside of Petersburg and Atlanta were making do with a few handfuls of cornmeal and a few bits of meat every week, so Davis felt that he could certainly forego fine food for a few hours.

A brass band made up of musicians from the Army of Northern Virginia was playing patriotic tunes outside, loudly enough for everyone to hear them but not so loudly as to interfere with conversation. Upon hearing *The Homespun Dress*, Davis couldn't help but let out a sarcastic chuckle, for as he looked at the female guests in his home, he saw little evidence of homespun clothing. Nearly all the fashionable dresses had been imported through the blockade from France.

The guests were bubbling with laughter and animated conversation, which created a hum rivaling the sound of the brass band. After they had gone through the receiving line to shake hands with the chief executive, they roamed throughout the first floor rooms of the mansion, as a staff of liveried slaves circulated among them with trays of champagne flutes.

The news of the tremendous victory at Peachtree Creek had fallen like a thunderbolt upon the Confederate capital, vastly improving morale among the civilian population. Combined with the relief felt at Lee's successful halting of Grant's offensive and the rumors of Jubal Early's heroic exploits in Maryland, the triumph of the Army of Tennessee had seemingly washed away the disillusionment which had set in after the defeats at Gettysburg and Vicksburg the previous year. The people of the Confederate capital seemed to have regained a belief in victory.

The sound of a hearty belly laugh shook the President from his thoughts. He instantly recognized the laugh and a rare smile came to his face as he saw the man who had just entered the house. Davis's countenance was normally compared to granite, but if there was one man in the world who could chisel it away, it was Judah Benjamin, the Confederate Secretary of State.

With some difficulty, Davis made an excuse and liberated himself from the receiving line, walking over toward the table nearest the front door, on which were trays of sorbet. Davis happily took a glass of champagne from a passing slave, and extended his hand to Benjamin with relief.

"Hello, Judah! I am delighted that you have been able to join us today."

Benjamin's smile rarely left his face, but it was today more animated than was normally the case. "I would not have missed this event for anything, Mr. President. For one thing, we have a great victory to celebrate. For another, it seems that your residence is the only place remaining in Richmond were one can obtain a decent meal, aside from Mr. Trenholm's house." As if to illustrate the point, Benjamin took a sip of his champagne. "What is the main course today?"

"Ham," Davis said apologetically. He declined to describe the delicious glaze everyone was talking about. "There is, however, some wonderful roast chicken."

"Well, I shall certainly partake of that in a few moments." He glanced around at the guests. "Many lovely ladies seem to be present. A delight for the eye."

His own eyes were sparkling as he said these words. Benjamin's wife had lived in France for many years and the Secretary of State was rumored to be quite the ladies man. Whether this had anything to do with his exotic background as a Jew from the Caribbean was open to speculation. Davis also considered the possibility that his apparent wandering eye was a calculated deception, as more than one confidential source had told him that his Secretary of State in fact preferred the intimate company of men.

"What news of the war?" Benjamin asked.

Davis paused a moment before answering. "There is some, my friend, which I was planning to discuss with you after the reception. However, as my hand is positively aching from shaking the hands of so many guests, I feel a strong desire for a reprieve. Shall we retire to the library for a few minutes?"

Benjamin nodded. He was careful to obtain a new glass of champagne before following Davis into the library. The guests in the room had quietly cleared out when it became obvious that the President and the Secretary of State had business to discuss. The door was closed and a slave was posted outside it to ensure that the two men would not be disturbed.

"General Hood telegraphed me this morning. He has requested a transfer to the Trans-Mississippi Department."

"Has he?" Benjamin said. "Why would he do that?"

"I do not know, but I would assume that he does not wish to remain under the command of General Johnston. He had to have known that we were planning on appointing him to Johnston's place. Now that's clearly impossible. I can understand a man in his position feeling awkward."

"That's certainly true. Johnston is the man of the hour. If the public discovers how close we came to removing him from command, the political consequences would be unfortunate."

Davis nodded, agreeing but not wanting to say so in words.

Benjamin went on. "I would advise you to grant Hood's request. He is a Texan, after all. His presence in the Trans-Mississippi might do some good."

"Yes, that would be very fitting. I have also sent Bragg to inspect our coastal defenses at Mobile," Davis added.

Benjamin said nothing, careful to avoiding commenting directly. Bragg, as the man who had been at the forefront of the effort to remove Johnston, would not be as much of a political hot potato as Hood, but still might prove compromising.

Davis removed a piece of paper from his breast pocket, unfolded it and handed it to Benjamin. "The latest telegram from Johnston. He again requests that I send Forrest into Tennessee to attack Sherman's supply lines."

Benjamin let out an exasperated sigh as his eyes scanned the paper. "Overly flowery language, as I have learned to expect from Johnston. I had hoped that his victory at Peachtree Creek would have given Johnston more confidence in his ability to defeat Sherman without anyone else's help. Yet here he is, continuing to call for Forrest."

"True enough," Davis said. "Nevertheless, I have decided to acquiesce to his request."

Benjamin looked at him in surprise, his perpetual smile vanishing for just a moment. This caused Davis to laugh. It was not often that the Secretary of State was caught off guard.

"Why give Johnston what he wants now when you didn't do so before?" Benjamin asked. "Having defeated Sherman, it seems to me that any assistance to the Army of Tennessee would be less necessary, not more so."

"Again, true enough. But Forrest now has greater freedom of action."

"How so?" Benjamin asked.

"Before Peachtree Creek, there were sound military reasons against ordering Forrest to attack Sherman's supply lines. Now that the enemy forces in the West have received such a mauling, the situation has changed. The bulk of Union forces around Memphis will likely be ordered to Georgia to reinforce Sherman. The threat to Mississippi is therefore lessened, and Forrest can operate against Sherman's supply lines without fear of placing our own territory in jeopardy."

"That makes sense. You are aware, however, that Johnston will see this as you finally caving in to his demands. He may therefore demand more of you in the future. And Senator Wigfall and his cronies in Congress will also use this decision as a means to undermine your administration."

A scowl crossed Davis's face. "I confess I had not considered that."

"If I may make a suggestion, Mr. President?"

"Of course."

"I recall from discussions at our cabinet meetings that you have often pressed Johnston to launch a raid on the enemy supply lines using his own cavalry, yes?"

"Correct. General Wheeler, the army cavalry commander, wrote to General Bragg and claimed that he had asked Johnston for permission to do so, only to be turned down."

"That being the case, why not inform Johnston that you will agree to dispatch Forrest into Tennessee if, and only if, he agrees to send a significant portion of his own cavalry to attack the Yankee railroads as well? Surely the changed military situation should give Johnston the same sort of increased freedom of action as it gives Forrest, yes?"

Davis mulled the idea in his mind for several seconds, slowly nodding. "You're suggesting a sort of unspoken gentlemen's agreement between me and Johnston? I agree to his request that I send Forrest, if he agrees to my request that he launch a raid of his own? What good would that do?"

"It would pull the fangs from Wigfall and his political allies. Don't you see? They cannot accuse you of being negligent in waiting this long to order Forrest into Tennessee if it has taken Johnston, their hero, the same amount of time to do exactly the same thing."

"They have always been hypocrites," Davis spat.

"Of course. But this would give you the ammunition you need to make a full reply in the newspapers, if it comes to that." Benjamin had long experience in the art of obtaining political cover. The Secretary of State was himself a frequent target of the editorial pages of the Confederacy, largely because of the South's pervasive anti-Semitism.

"It would provide shield us from political sniping, while achieving the military results we require. A fine idea, Judah."

"Wigfall will soon find another club with which to beat you over the head, Mr. President," Benjamin said.

"Certainly, but not immediately. By dispatching Forrest now, we can hope to silence our critics within the Wigfall faction, at least temporarily. And we only need them to stay quiet for a few more months."

Benjamin nodded in understanding. "The Northern election. The defeat of Sherman will greatly aid the cause of the Peace Democrats."

"Indeed, it shall. Now, what impact do you think Peachtree Creek will have on our diplomatic relations with Europe, such as they are?"

"It will have little overt impact, I must admit," Benjamin said with a sigh. "They shall not formally recognize us as an independent nation unless and until the United States does so. Lincoln's Emancipation Proclamation saw to that, for no European state will oppose the North if the people believe it is fighting to abolish slavery. But our victory shall certainly increase our credit among the British, French, and Dutch bankers, increasing the value of our bonds and helping our financial situation. It may also make the British a little more willing to look the other way as we outfit commerce raiders in British ports. With our ability to attack Northern merchant shipping reduced by the recent loss of the *Alabama*, being able to outfit some new commerce raiders has become more necessary."

Davis nodded, not commenting on the admiration Benjamin's voice betrayed when he mentioned the Emancipation Proclamation. Like himself, Benjamin was no abolitionist, but he knew a political masterstroke when he saw one. Besides, neither Davis nor Benjamin were fanatics on the issue of slavery. Both had privately acknowledged to one another that the South's peculiar institution was eventually doomed, no matter how the war turned out.

"Is there anything that can be done to improve our standing with the British, in light of our recent success?"

Benjamin tugged on his beard, thinking for a moment. "We should certainly not tarry in taking advantage of this victory. The British people are fickle. They love an underdog who seems to be doing well, slavery or no slavery. Peachtree Creek will provide us with at least a temporary shift in British public opinion back in our favor."

"I agree," Davis said. "But what shall we do to take advantage of it?"

"Let me send Mr. Mason back to London," Benjamin said. "While I do not believe he will perform any better than he has previously, the news of his return will send a message to the British that we are anxious to be on better terms with them. In light of Peachtree Creek, the members of Her Majesty's Government may be willing to listen to him more than they have in the past."

Davis nodded. James Mason had been appointed as the Confederacy's representative to Great Britain not long after the war had begun, but he had never been able to obtain significant concessions from the British. The year before, in exasperation at Britain's unwillingness to recognize the Confederacy, he had left London for the more congenial environment of Paris.

There was a soft knock on the door, and a moment later Varina Davis, the beautiful and willful First Lady of the Confederacy, entered. "My dear, you're neglecting your guests. Surely the pressing issues the two of you are discussing can wait until the next Cabinet meeting?"

"Indeed, they can," Benjamin said with delight, his general animation increased as if by electricity at the presence of a female. "I find to my dismay that my champagne glass is empty and I also would like to sample some of this roast chicken I have been hearing about."

As the band outside struck up *The Bonnie Blue Flag* for the third or fourth time, Davis and Benjamin rejoined the party.

Chapter Eight

July 24, Morning

"Make way!" the captain of the detail shouted to the work crew on the dock. "Make way for the President!"

Lincoln tried to conceal his embarrassment as he walked down the gangplank onto the dock. They were at City Point, Virginia, where the James River met the Appomattox. Although it had been but a tiny hamlet before the war, Grant had designated it his headquarters for the ongoing Siege of Petersburg. As the logistical nerve center of the enormous Army of the Potomac, it had been rapidly transformed into the busiest seaport on the planet.

Hundreds of dock workers, all of them black, were straining their eyes and jostling for the best positions to get a look at Lincoln. This was probably the only time that any of these men were ever going to see a genuine President of the United States, so he didn't begrudge them.

"God bless you, Father Abraham!" one of the black laborers shouted out as Lincoln's feet left the gangway and he stepped onto the dock. His words were immediately followed by a chorus of exclamations and cheers from the rest of the dock workers.

Stanton lumbered along behind Lincoln, afraid he would lose his footing and fall unceremoniously into the James River. When his feet were firmly planted on the dock, the look of relief on his face was obvious.

Lincoln gazed uncomfortably into the crowd of blacks, who continued cheering. He doffed his hat to them, causing the cheering to rise to a fever pitch. One man very close to him got down on his knees.

"No," Lincoln said loudly. "Stand up, young man. You must kneel only to God."

"Thank God for you, Father Abraham!" the man said as he rose to his feet.

With relief, Lincoln and Stanton were escorted to a waiting carriage. As the driver snapped his whip and they moved off, Lincoln cast a glance backward, where the crowd was still staring at him as he faded from their sight.

"I always feel rather awkward in such situations," Lincoln said. "It's as though I am an exhibit from one of P. T. Barnum's freak shows."

"All the dock hands are former slaves from nearby plantations," Stanton replied. "Before we rescued them, they were treated like beasts of burden, driven by the whip and lash. But now they are free men earning a fair wage for the work they do. They give you credit for it. And rightfully so, if you ask me."

"When this war began, I said in all honesty that my sole objective was to preserve the Union," Lincoln said. "I had no intention to interfere with slavery, repugnant though I have always thought it to be. The Emancipation Proclamation was a mere political maneuver. But seeing the looks in the eyes of those men, as I have seen in the eyes of so many over the last year-and-a-half, I begin to realize the critical moral imperative of what we are doing. And, for that matter, what remains to be done."

"Yes," Stanton said. "We have reached the point of no return. The Union cannot be preserved if the institution of slavery remains. It must be destroyed root and branch, as thoroughly as Carthage was destroyed by Rome."

Lincoln sighed. "If only the Democrats would understand that, we would all be much better off. They are badly deluding the people by suggesting that the Southerners will rejoin the Union if only we tell them that they can keep their slaves. I have lived a politician's life and I have never seen such an irresponsible action in any campaign."

"The people are wise enough to see through their lies," Stanton said.

"I hope so."

Stanton turned his attention to some papers in his lap, so Lincoln stopped talking and gazed out the window of the carriage as they rode northward along the docks toward Grant's headquarters.

To their right, all along the waterfront, dozens of enormous, three-masted vessels were being unloaded. Legions of black laborers hauled down crate after crate, which contained food, ammunition, medicine, shoes, clothing and all the other supplies required by the Federal army besieging Petersburg. The scale of the enterprise stunned Lincoln. Even during his visits to the great port cities of New York, Philadelphia, and Baltimore, he had never seen such an immense manifestation of logistical power.

To their left, there was an immense city of tents and newly-constructed wood cabins, where untold thousands of Union servicemen toiled away in a veritable beehive of productive activity.

Lincoln smelled the aroma of baking bread as they swept past the bakery which, if the stories were to be believed, turned out over a hundred thousand loaves of bread a day. He could see hospitals, sutler's stores, warehouses, stables, and buildings housing nearly every other conceivable kind of activity.

As their carriage followed the bank of the river and veered in an eastwardly direction, Lincoln looked to the right again, gazing out over the James River. In the distance, he could see a line of Union ironclads, arrayed like sentries across the river, guarding against any attack on City Point by the small fleet of rebel ironclads that was stationed at Richmond.

Lincoln shook his head in wonder. As President, he commanded all of this vast effort, wielding a power greater by several orders of magnitude than any of his predecessors in office. Seeing the awesome display of the Union's logistical might with his own eyes gave him a renewed confidence. With such power at his disposal, surely he could still turn the tide of the war and achieve victory, thus saving the Union, destroying slavery and ensuring that the United States fulfill its historical destiny.

After a ride of about fifteen minutes, the carriage pulled up in front of an attractive manor which was called the Eppes House. It served as Grant's headquarters. As he and Stanton were getting out, General Grant himself appeared at the front door, smoking a cigar. A dozen or so staff officers stood at attention and saluted when Lincoln approached.

Grant stepped forward and shook his hand, not bothering to take out his cigar.

"Welcome to City Point, Mr. President."

"Thank you, General Grant." To Lincoln, the general looked like the least pretentious man he had ever seen. Judging from his muddy boots and slightly disheveled uniform, he hadn't made the slightest effort to clean himself up before Lincoln's visit. He found this contrast to the vanity of other generals, especially buffoons like George McClellan or Joseph Hooker, quite refreshing. Grant, Lincoln had long ago decided, was his kind of man.

Grant gestured to the door. "Shall we?"

After ten minutes of brief introductions and handshakes with various staff officers, the three men sat down at a cleared table where a coffee service had been prepared in advance. Grant poured the coffee himself. The conference began.

For some time, the three men discussed the excitement caused by General Early's raid on Washington. Lincoln was pleased to see that Grant was as angered by the incompetent Union response as he had been. The general promised a major shakeup in the command structure around the capital to make sure such an event did not happen again. As the discussions moved on, Grant gave Lincoln and Stanton some of the details of the plan to blow a hole in Lee's trenches by means of a gigantic explosive mine. Lincoln thought the plan interesting and stated his hopes that it would succeed.

After awhile, Lincoln brought the meeting to its main point.

"General Grant, if we might discuss the situation in Georgia?"

The general took a deep breath and nodded. "I'm not a man who whitewashes things. The reverse General Sherman has suffered is very serious, indeed. It threatens the successful outcome of the present campaign, not only in Georgia but throughout the country."

"True," Lincoln said.

Grant went on. "I had thought that the rebel army under Johnston had been so reduced in strength that it was incapable of offensive action. Obviously, I was wrong. Sherman, too. To be proven wrong in such a dramatic fashion came as an unpleasant shock."

"Yes, yes, General Grant," Stanton said impatiently. "But I do not think it worth our time to muse over the past. Like it or not, the disaster has happened. We are here to discuss how to rectify the situation. Do you believe we should send reinforcements to Sherman?"

"Well, it's a difficult question," Grant said. "After such a defeat, it only makes sense to send Sherman reinforcements to make good his losses."

"It's not just that," Stanton said. "There are political matters to take into consideration. The defeat in Georgia is the greatest disaster we have suffered at least since the Battle of Chancellorsville. The newspapers are talking of nothing else. The Democrats are having a field day. Even setting aside all military matters, pure politics demands that we avenge the defeat. That can only be done by defeating Johnston, which means we must send reinforcements to Sherman."

"Naturally," said Grant. "But sending reinforcements to Sherman will necessarily curtail our operations in other theaters. To build up the strength of both Sherman's force and my own force for the campaigns which started in May, the subsidiary theaters of war have been largely stripped of troops already."

"What of those forces of ours between the Mississippi and the Appalachians which are not already concentrated in Sherman's army?" Lincoln asked.

"General Sherman has informed me that he is already in the process of ordering many of those brigades to his assistance at once."

"You disagree?" Stanton asked.

Grant shrugged. "I'm inclined to trust Sherman's judgment. But it may weaken the forces protecting our railroads in Tennessee, and will probably not represent a decisive increase in the size of Sherman's forces. It also may allow the Confederates to dispatch reinforcements of their own to Johnston."

"What about the less important theaters of war?" Lincoln asked. "The Trans-Mississippi, perhaps? Or our forces stationed along the Carolina and Florida coasts?"

Grant shook his head. "Our forces in those theaters are now primarily garrison troops, sufficient to hold the ground we have gained but with little else to spare. If we withdraw troops from either of those theaters, we risk allowing the rebels to regain the initiative in those areas. It would become more difficult to maintain the blockade, and we might also risk the restoration of enemy communications across the Mississippi River. In any case, it would also take months to redeploy forces from those areas to Georgia."

"We don't have months."

"I know."

For a moment, Lincoln had a horrifying image in his mind of George McClellan sitting down at a negotiating table with Jefferson Davis. "So," he said, "If a sufficient number of troops are sent to Sherman in time for them to do any good, they must come from the Virginia theater?"

"Yes, Mr. President. But that, of course, raises other problems."

"Such as?" Stanton said.

Grant took a long puff on his cigar and sat back in his chair, thinking deeply. Nearly a full minute later, just as Lincoln and Stanton were beginning to become uncomfortable at the silence, Grant spoke.

"I have Lee's army pinned down here on the Petersburg front, but we lack the strength to break through his lines. Our plan to blast a hole in the enemy's defenses by detonating a mine may work, but I wouldn't count on it. If we dispatch forces from here, we must accept that the current stalemate in Virginia will continue indefinitely."

Lincoln nodded soberly. It wasn't what he wanted to hear, but at least he was convinced it was the unvarnished truth. He waved for Grant to continue.

"As you know, we currently have significant forces chasing Early's small army in the northern Shenandoah Valley. Maybe they'll catch him, but I rather doubt it. I was hoping to use two corps of infantry as the main body of a new force to launch an offensive that would clear the Shenandoah Valley of rebels once and for all."

"That would be of great significance," Stanton said. "Not only does rebel possession of the Valley allow them to launch raids against Washington whenever they please, but the farms of that region are critical to supplying Lee's army at Petersburg."

"Indeed. But with the disaster at Peachtree Creek, I am considering whether one of the two corps I have been intending to send against Early might be of better use with Sherman in Georgia."

"So you're saying that we can send reinforcements to Sherman in time to be of use, but only at the cost of allowing Early to continue to threaten us from the Shenandoah Valley?"

"That's about the size of it, Mr. Stanton."

Lincoln sat back in his chair and considered all this. With the Northern people increasingly war-weary, and even more so now that the full extent of the disaster at Peachtree Creek was sinking in, a dramatic victory was essential if the war effort was to continue. With the Democrats asserting to everyone who would listen that the war effort had failed and was only resulting in useless casualties, only a big victory would do.

"So, General Grant," Lincoln finally asked. "If the choice is between sending reinforcements to Sherman or launching an offensive against Early, what is your recommendation?"

"I would recommend dispatching the Sixth Corps, a powerful infantry force of three divisions, to Sherman's army without delay. This means we won't be as strong in the Shenandoah Valley as I would like, but such are the fortunes of war. I would also recommend an appeal be made to the governors of the states north of the Ohio River to send as many militiamen as they can raise into Kentucky and Tennessee, to guard the rail lines. This will free up regular troops that Sherman can then bring down as reinforcements for his main force."

"A wise plan," Stanton admitted. "The Sixth Corps was brought to Baltimore and Washington to protect those cities from Early's raiders. If they set out in the next few days, our rail network would have them in Georgia within a few weeks. That would add more than ten thousand men to Sherman's numbers, making good many of his Peachtree Creek losses."

"Exactly," Grant said.

Stanton went on. "And with the new draft coming later this month, we can hopefully muster additional regiments that can be sent to Sherman's aid."

Grant tilted his head and shrugged. Clearly, he had little expectation that the coming draft would produce much in the way of new troops.

Lincoln looked at Stanton, and then back to Grant, who nodded soberly, still puffing away at his cigar. "Very well, then," Lincoln said. "It is decided."

Stanton cleared his throat. "There is another matter I wish to discuss with General Grant before we take our leave. In the wake of the defeat at Peachtree Creek, there has been some talk about whether our armies in the Western theater would be better off with a different commander."

Grant immediately shook his head. "I trust General Sherman as I trust no other man. I cannot think of any other officer who would be qualified for such a responsible position."

"I mean no offense," Stanton said. "And I share your confidence in Sherman. But over the last week, there have been renewed rumors about the stability of his state of mind."

"The events of late 1861 are in his past. No, I will stand by Sherman. He is the only man I can trust in such a high position."

Lincoln nodded, impressed by Grant's conviction. He and Stanton had carefully discussed how to broach this sensitive subject to Grant, knowing the close friendship between him and Sherman. The waters had been tested. For the moment, Sherman would stay where he was.

"Mr. President, you requested the opportunity to visit with some of the enlisted men in the camps. I have prepared a cavalry escort for you and an itinerary for the rest of the day."

"I would like to visit some of the regiments made up of colored soldiers, if that is possible," Lincoln said.

"I'm sure that can be easily arranged."

"And visits to regiments from Pennsylvania and Indiana would also be much appreciated." Lincoln wanted those men writing home to their fathers how much they admired their President. It might change a few votes on Election Day.

"Of course."

"Thank you, General Grant." The men rose from their chairs and shook hands. "I frankly tell you, my friend, that I take great comfort in knowing that my armies are under capable leadership."

Grant smiled. "Not nearly as much heart as I take in knowing that the country as a whole is under capable leadership. A situation I trust shall continue past November."

Lincoln shrugged. "It is up to the people. We shall see."

* * * * *

July 25, Morning

Despite the heat and humidity, Johnston relished being outside. In the days since the battle, he had felt himself increasingly confined to his headquarters at the Niles House and had felt the need to get on his horse and out among the troops. More importantly, he wanted to see the situation on the front lines for himself. He rode across the battlefield of Peachtree Creek, accompanied by Mackall, the army standard bearer, and a small escort of cavalry.

"Clear the road!" the officer commanding the escort shouted to a marching regiment. "General Johnston is coming through!"

At the sound of his name, the men of the regiment burst into a cheer. They turned off to the side of the road and began waving their hats in the air.

"What regiment is this, General Mackall?" Johnston said.

"The 16th South Carolina, sir. Gist's Brigade."

"Right," Johnston said. He stopped his horse for a moment, stood up in the stirrups, and spoke loudly. "You men fought well at Peachtree Creek, men! I am in your debt! The country is in your debt!"

"Three cheers for General Johnston!" one man from the ranks offered. The men lustily offered up their three cheers, and Johnston waved as he kicked his horse back into a trot.

The battlefield remained strewn with the debris of war. Although several days had passed since the battle, not all of the dead had yet been collected for burial. The regiments of the Army of Tennessee had buried their own soldiers, but those of the enemy had been left to the birds and wild hogs. Johnston frowned. He had no hatred for the Yankees and thought that all brave and worthy men deserved a proper Christian burial. He made a mental note to stress to his staff the need to gather and bury the Union dead.

Broken bits of discarded weapons, empty haversacks that had been cast aside, and overturned wagons with shattered wheels were also everywhere to be seen. Johnston's quartermasters, to say nothing of the ordinary soldiers themselves, had done a thorough job collecting anything useful from the wreckage of the battlefield, but that still left a lot of refuse to be done away with only by time and nature.

They reached Collier's Bridge, where Cleburne and one of his brigades had fought heroically against overwhelming odds and thereby blocked the retreat of the Army of the Cumberland. The bridge had been repaired and strengthened by the engineers using some of the bridging equipment captured from the enemy and it now served as the primary conduit for the Army of Tennessee as it moved northwards in pursuit of its defeated foe.

Without a word, Johnston and his entourage took their horses off the main road and rode along the south bank of the creek. What Johnston saw as he gazed down into the stream was like something out of Edgar Allen Poe's worst nightmare. The sight of unburied Union dead on the battlefield had been disturbing enough, but Peachtree Creek looked like a grotesque human abattoir. The creek bed was simply choked with blue-clad corpses. The birds were happily feasting. The stench was overpowering. He pulled his handkerchief out and held it over his face.

The water was considerably higher than it had been when Johnston had first surveyed the creek weeks earlier. All of the dead bodies were acting as a dam, impeding the flow of the stream and raising its height. More disturbingly, they had added a purplish color to what would have been crystal clear water.

Johnston had been a soldier all his life. He had fought against the Seminoles in Florida three decades before. He had served with Winfield Scott in the war against Mexico in the 1840s. He had commanded armies of the Confederacy for three years. In a lifetime of war, Johnston had never seen so many corpses collected in so small a place. Despite the heat, he shuddered. Somewhere behind him, he heard a man of the cavalry escort beginning to vomit.

He turned his horse back to the main road, followed with relief by his escort. A few minutes later, they crossed Collier's Bridge and continued northward. The road was crowded with Confederate soldiers.

"Look at their feet," Mackall said, somewhat absent-mindedly.

Johnston immediately noticed what had caught Mackall's attention. A week earlier, perhaps half the men of the Army of Tennessee had gone barefoot because the Confederacy lacked the resources to provide them with shoes. Now, however, nearly all of them were sporting solid footwear, taken from Yankee prisoners and Yankee dead. Johnston also noted an improvement in the quality of the trousers the men were wearing, no doubt for the same reason.

As they continued northward and approached the front lines, the number of troops grew gradually larger. A strange combination of music and scattered musketry filled the air, as well as the occasional boom of a cannon. It was the sound of heavy skirmishing rather than the sustained roar of a full-scale battle, but the men who died in such fighting were just as dead as anyone else.

Johnston sent off one of the escort to locate General Hardee, then stood his horse off to the side of the road to wait. Regiments from Mississippi, Georgia, Tennessee and Florida passed by him within the space of twenty minutes. The regiments continually cheered him as they passed, and he had to repeatedly doff his hat in return. He didn't enjoy doing this, as he was very sensitive about his baldness, but the men deserved a proper acknowledgement of his respect and admiration.

Hardee approached, followed by a single staff officer and his corps standard bearer. He had the look of a man who was tired but quite pleased with himself.

"Good morning, General Hardee."

"Morning, sir."

"How are things up front?"

"Fine," he said. "Nothing much happening. The Yankees aren't budging from their trenches, but they aren't making any effort to push us back, either."

Johnston nodded. "My guess is that McPherson and Schofield are still covering the withdrawal of the Army of the Cumberland across the river. That's what our scouts have been telling us, at any rate."

"It's been five days now. Surely the Army of the Cumberland has completed its retreat, or nearly so. I think we may expect McPherson and Schofield to pull back this evening."

"You think Sherman intends to pull all his forces back to the north side?" Johnston asked.

Hardee hesitated a moment before answering. This didn't surprise Johnston. During the long retreat from Dalton, Johnston had relied much more on the advice of Hood than that of Hardee, a decision he now bitterly regretted. He had resolved to seek Hardee's opinion more often and his corps commander was obviously somewhat unused to this sort of treatment.

"He might," Hardee said. "If I were Sherman, I would try to maintain a lodgment on the south side of the Chattahoochee, reform the Army of the Cumberland on the north side, and return to the offensive when it was again ready for combat."

"Possibly," Johnston said. "If that does turn out to be Sherman's intention, what course of action do you think we should follow?"

Hardee's eyebrows went up, but he was clearly gratified to be asked. "I think we should endeavor to drive McPherson and Schofield into the river. We have about fifty thousand men to their forty thousand. Their left flank is refused, but still vulnerable. Destroying the enemy bridgehead on the south bank would eliminate any possibility of the Yankees taking Atlanta."

Johnston considered this for a few moments, before shaking his head. "Your logic is sound, but such an attack would necessarily entail great loss of life and might well fail. No, it's too great a risk."

Hardee nodded. "Very well, sir."

"I see no reason to change our present course. We can continue to harass them with skirmishers and artillery for the time being. If Sherman does intend to remain on the south bank, we can block any attempt by him to resume the offensive. If he intends to withdraw to the north bank completely, we can be ready to exploit any opportunity for an attack which might present itself."

Hardee grunted.

"You disagree?" Johnston asked. "Please speak freely, General Hardee. I value your opinion highly."

"Very well," Hardee said. "I would fear entering into something of a stalemate with the enemy. As time passes, more and more of the divisions of the Army of the Cumberland will recover from the mauling they got at Peachtree Creek."

"I agree, but I do not see how we can again strike at the enemy with any probability of success. I do not fancy launching our boys in a frontal attack against the prepared defenses of McPherson and Schofield."

"Neither do I. Nevertheless, it is my conviction that we must force the enemy to react to our movements, rather than await the movement of the enemy."

Johnston wondered if Hardee's words were an implied criticism of his strategy during the long retreat south from Dalton. If so, he did not much mind. He was glad that Hardee felt more comfortable expressing his opinion. Besides, the strategy of withdrawal that so many people had strongly criticized had eventually led to the victory at Peachtree Creek. As far as Johnston was concerned, that success was answer enough to his critics.

A courier rode up to the two generals. "Telegram from President Davis, sir."

General Johnston,

I have received your request that General Forrest be sent to attack the enemy railroad in Tennessee. It seems to me that such an operation would have a greater chance of success if it were combined with an attack on the enemy railroad in north Georgia, to be undertaken by a force detached from the cavalry of your own army. What think you of this proposal?

President Davis

Johnston laughed softly, then passed the paper over to Hardee.

"You want my opinion on this?" Hardee asked after he finished reading.

"By all means."

"We have more than enough cavalry with this army to screen our movements and scout out the positions of the enemy. Sending a few thousand troopers against the Western and Atlantic Railroad would not seriously impede our operations."

"In the absence of these men, Sherman might send his own cavalry to attack our rail connections with Macon or Augusta."

"Possibly, but I would reckon it is more likely that he would send them off in pursuit of whatever force we have sent against the railroad. And if Forrest is on the loose in Tennessee at the same time, he will have to dispatch cavalry to that quarter as well."

Johnston nodded, even as another thought entered his mind. Wheeler had betrayed him no less than Hood. Dispatching Wheeler with a force of cavalry against Sherman's supply lines might not only be an effective military maneuver, but would free him of another subversive within his own ranks.

He turned in his saddle. "General Mackall?" he called. The chief-of-staff immediately clicked his horse into a walk and approached his commander.

"Yes, sir?"

"Return to our headquarters and send a message to General Wheeler. I wish to speak with him tomorrow morning."

Mackall's eyes narrowed in confusion, but the expression on Johnston's face told him that all would be made clear in the near future. "Of course, sir." He saluted, turned his horse, and was soon trotting away to the south.

Johnston turned back to Hardee. "I wish you a good day. Please report to me any unusual movements by the enemy, or anything else you consider important." He extended his hand, which Hardee took in a firm grip. The two men then saluted. Trailed by his entourage of staff officers and escorts, Johnston turned and headed southwest, as we wished to investigate the situation along Stewart's lines as well.

*　　　　　*　　　　　*　　　　　*　　　　　*

July 25, Afternoon

Sherman had transferred his headquarters to the north bank of the Chattahoochee River, moving himself and his staff into a moderately sized house near Vining's Station. Although the river now separated him from the enemy army, he could still hear the occasional booming of Confederate artillery. He sat alone in a quiet room, staring down at a telegram just received from General Grant.

General Sherman,
Be advised that the Sixth Corps has been ordered to move by railroad from the vicinity of Washington City to Chattanooga, where it shall come under your command. When it arrives, it shall add more than ten thousand men to your forces. This should go some way to replenishing your strength.
General Grant

Sherman nodded slowly. He knew little of the formations serving in Virginia, but everything he had heard about the Sixth Corps was positive. The previous year, after the rebel victory at Chickamauga, reinforcements had been sent to Tennessee from Virginia, taking about two weeks to arrive. Logically, the timetable should be more or less the same this time around. Sherman didn't immediately know what he would do with the Sixth Corps when it arrived, but he could think on that question later.

Aside from the telegram from Grant, the pile of papers on his desk included reports on everything from the state of the Army of the Cumberland to the security of his line of supply back to Louisville. He hadn't read them yet, for try as he might, he couldn't make himself read them. He feared that if he read the bad news it would somehow become magnified and morph into something even worse.

He stared down at the map. What was left of the Army of the Cumberland had completed its crossing to the north bank of the Chattahoochee. Sherman had issued orders that McPherson's Army of the Tennessee was to go next. The Army of the Ohio under General Schofield would serve as the rear guard, holding the line of entrenchments until the last man of McPherson's force was across before retreating themselves.

He knew he was handing Schofield a very dangerous mission. For at least a day, the fifteen thousand men of his small army would have to maintain their lines against nearly four times that number of Southern soldiers. Even with the strongest entrenchments, those odds were not good. Sherman could only hope to deceive Johnston long enough to extract Schofield under cover of darkness. The critical objective was to get all his troops onto the north bank of the Chattahoochee as quickly as possible. If that required the sacrifice of Schofield and his fifteen thousand men, so be it. After all, it would be a smaller number than had been lost at Peachtree Creek.

Suddenly, Sherman could hear an angry voice arguing with one of his staff officers on the other side of the door. A moment later, the door violently shot open and Joseph Hooker stormed into the room, his face a mask of anger.

"What do you mean by this?" Hooker demanded, waving a paper in Sherman's face.

Sherman didn't rise from his chair and appeared entirely unconcerned. "I assume that what you have there is the order I have issued this morning appointing General Oliver Howard to command the Army of the Cumberland and returning you to command of Twentieth Corps."

"This is unacceptable, Sherman! Unacceptable! I am the senior corps commander in the Army of the Cumberland and I am entitled to the command of the army!"

Sherman knew that Hooker personally despised Howard. One could argue that he had good reason. Howard had been a corps commander in the Army of the Potomac when Hooker had commanded it. It had been Howard's corps that had been surprised and routed by Stonewall Jackson's famous flank attack at Chancellorsville, leading to Hooker's defeat and humiliation.

"I understand your concerns, General Hooker. But I am required to make decisions based on what is in the best interest of the war effort and I believe that the Army of the Cumberland is best served with General Howard at its head."

"But my commission as a major general predates that of General Howard by six-and-a-half months!"

Sherman found this statement ridiculous. Hooker was probably the only general in the army who knew by precisely how many months he outranked all those below him. Before he could stop himself, Sherman laughed at the absurdity of it all.

Hooker's face turned a fiery crimson. "How dare you laugh at me!" Unsettled staff officers were watching from the open door, nervous that the altercation might descend to violence at any moment.

Sherman regained his composure and stopped laughing. "I apologize, General Hooker. But my orders stand."

"Are my services in rescuing the Army of the Cumberland from total destruction to be ignored?"

"I thank you for your efforts, as does the entire army. But as I said, my orders stand."

For a long minute, there was total silence. Sherman remained seated, while Hooker continued to glare down at him in fury. Then, the corps commander ostentatiously stood bolt upright. "General Sherman, I request to be relieved from duty with this army. Honor and self-respect alike require me to leave an army in which rank and service are ignored."

Sherman wanted to laugh again, but successfully restrained himself. Hooker clearly expected him to back down and submit to his elevation to permanent command of the army. But if Hooker thought that Sherman somehow considered him irreplaceable, he was mistaken. To the contrary, the vain and arrogant soldier had just provided Sherman with enough rope with which to hang him.

"Very well, General Hooker. Your request is accepted. Please turn over your corps to the senior divisional commander. I wish you a safe journey northwards, sir."

Hooker's mouth dropped open in surprise. The idea that Sherman would actually accept his request to be relieved had clearly not occurred to him. Sherman, inwardly delighted at this turn of events, simply picked up a report on the current status of the Western and Atlantic Railroad and started reading. Hooker stood there silently for nearly a minute, glaring down at Sherman, until he looked up again.

"Was there something else, General Hooker?"

"I promise you, Sherman. You will pay dearly for this."

"Nothing else, then? Very well. Good day to you."

Without another word, Hooker turned and walked out of the tent.

For the first time since the full extent of the disaster at Peachtree Creek had been made clear to him, Sherman smiled. What he couldn't have known was that he had set in motion another chain of events that he would soon come to bitterly regret.

*　　　　　*　　　　　*　　　　　*　　　　　*

"Present arms!" McFadden shouted.

The men raised their Enfield rifles so that they were held directly in front of their bodies.

"Shoulder arms!" he ordered.

The men now positioned their weapons so that they were resting on their left shoulder and held by their left hand, while their right arm went back to their sides.

"Order arms!"

The men now clasped the butt of their muskets with their right hand, then just below the barrel with their left, lowering their weapons until the butt was just a few inches over the ground.

Drilling the men had proven to be an unexpectedly odd experience for McFadden. As a private and then as a noncommissioned officer, he had gone through drill countless thousands of times. With his recent promotion to lieutenant, however, he was actually the one barking out the orders and watching as the men obeyed.

The five companies he was drilling collectively numbered less than fifty men. Though this amounted to half of the 7th Texas, it was less than what a single decent company would have mustered at the beginning of the war. Such had been the ravages of disease and battle.

He moved the men from a line of battle into a marching column and back again, shouting the orders as though he had been conducting drill since the beginning of the war. He found that it was rather easy for him to step into the shoes of an officer, simply speaking aloud what he had been telling himself in his own head all along. The troops themselves had done drill so many times since they had joined the regiment that they now did it with flawless precision and in perfect order. It was not unlike willing one's own hand or foot to do a certain thing and simply seeing it happen.

Cleburne's division, on account of the heavy casualties it had sustained, had been withdrawn from the front line for a few days of resting and refitting. They had been marched to the east side of the city, away from both the fighting and the stench of the Peachtree Creek battlefield. McFadden was delighted with this, as it allowed him to adjust to his new position as an officer without simultaneously dealing with the stress of combat. From what the rumor mill said, there was a good deal of sharp skirmishing up north, but no serious fighting. McFadden and his fellow Texans assumed they would be sent into the fray soon enough.

"Who the hell is that?" Pearson asked.

"Quiet in the ranks!" McFadden shouted angrily. Whether he was a sergeant or a lieutenant, McFadden was convinced that Private Pearson would always be the bane of his existence.

But he could see that the eyes of the men in the ranks were fixated on something behind him. He turned to see what it was and received the surprise of his life when he saw a wagon coming up the road. Annie Turnbow was sitting in the front, with the male slave McFadden had encountered at the Turnbow home sitting beside her and holding the reins. Being led behind the wagon was the fattest cow that McFadden had seen in some time. He could hear the cackling of chickens in the back. There were also some crates containing leafy vegetables.

There was a sudden stir in the ranks and several of the men licked their lips. For a moment, McFadden mistook their reaction as being due to the sight of Annie herself and was about to berate them for their lack of respect. He mentally kicked himself when he realized that their response was being caused by the close proximity of fresh beef and poultry. For men who had had nothing but barely edible cornmeal for the past several weeks, such priceless treasure was certain to be far more interesting than even the most beautiful woman.

The slave pulled the horses to a halt and Annie stood up, looking at him uncertainly.

"Lieutenant?"

"Yes, Miss Turnbow?" His heart leapt to see her, but he was unwilling to show any emotion in front of his men. It would have been unbecoming his status as an officer, but he had never been one to put his humanity on display in any event. He immediately realized the mistake he had made simply by saying her name. No doubt rumors of his visit to Atlanta would have spread throughout the entire regiment, spurred on by the talk of his own men who had seen him rescue Annie and her father in the first place.

"I have brought the food my father promised."

The men gave a hearty cheer at her words, which took her by surprise and caused her to smile. She was obviously not used to being a public hero.

McFadden turned back. "I said quiet in the ranks! One more sound out of you and I'll send this wagon to the nearest Georgia regiment!"

Such a deadly threat silenced the men instantly. Major Collett stormed out of his tent, where he had been working on his Peachtree Creek report for General Granbury, and marched sternly over to McFadden.

"What is going on here, Lieutenant?" he demanded.

McFadden nodded toward Annie and the wagon. "Mr. Turnbow of Atlanta has sent us a wagon of provisions, sir."

Collett took a hard look at the wagon. The cow trailing behind it, along with the chickens and vegetables inside, was probably more food than the 7th Texas had seen in a month.

"Dear God!" Collett said instinctively. "What possessed the man to send us all this?"

"Lieutenant McFadden saved my father's life, sir," Annie said. "And mine as well. My father wanted to provide these provisions as a way of saying thank you."

"Well, by God, we won't turn this gift down!" Collett said with a beaming smile. "Like manna from heaven, if you ask me."

The major quickly organized a detail of men to unload the wagon. Within a matter of minutes, a makeshift pen had been created for the chickens and the crates of vegetables were piled up next to the pen. Almost immediately, a debate began among the men as to whether they should eat the chickens right away or perhaps keep some on hand to provide fresh eggs. No such dispute took place regarding the cow, however. Before the unloading of the wagon had even been completed, the men had cut the animal's throat and commenced slaughtering it, delighted at the prospect of fresh beef for dinner.

"Where did your father get all this?" Collett asked.

McFadden answered for Annie. "Honestly, sir, perhaps the less we know, the better."

"I'll trust you on that, James. Just promise me that General Granbury or General Cleburne are not going to come down here and arrest me for pilfering."

McFadden laughed. "I promise, sir."

"So this is the lovely lady you saved from death?" Collett asked, looking at Annie.

"Yes," McFadden said simply. "This is Miss Annie Turnbow. Miss Turnbow, may I present Major James Collett, the commander of the 7th Texas Infantry."

They exchanged pleasant greetings. As they did so, McFadden noticed Collett giving him playful side glances, as though to express his surprise that Annie was as attractive as she was. He had heard the story of the river rescue from the men who had seen it happen, but had perhaps dismissed tales of Annie's beauty as the mere exaggerations of men who had not seen many women for a long time.

"Are you aware, Miss Turnbow, that Lieutenant McFadden here is now a hero?"

She glanced at him. "A hero?"

"Indeed," Collett continued. "He personally captured General George Thomas, commander of the Army of the Cumberland. He is the first soldier in the Confederate Army to have achieved such a distinction. In fact, few soldiers in history have such an honor."

"Is that so?" Annie said, looking at McFadden with surprise. "All of Atlanta knows that the traitor Thomas had been taken prisoner, but I had no idea that James himself was the one who captured him! Your letter only said that you had received a promotion to lieutenant."

"It did not seem important," McFadden said.

"Well, all of Atlanta will soon know McFadden's name," Collet said. "All of the Confederacy, by God!"

"I do earnestly pray to be saved from such a fate," McFadden said with deep sincerity. "Fame has never been something I desire."

"Desire it or not, it is what you shall have," Collett said.

"My parents will be very interested to hear this news," Annie said. "They shall be delighted to know that they have dined with the man who captured the South's most famous traitor."

Despite himself, McFadden could not help but wonder if his newfound status and fame, absurd though he thought it to be, would soften the feelings of Annie's mother toward him. If he had any intention of pursuing some sort of relationship with Annie, it would obviously be easier if her mother warmed to him.

"Miss Turnbow, would you do my regiment the honor of having dinner with us?" Collett asked. "Thanks to your father, we shall be enjoying fresh beef for the first time in several months. It would please us greatly to have you as our honored guest."

She looked slightly taken aback and glanced toward McFadden as if for reassurance. She then looked back at the slave, who was still sitting on the wagon.

"My man Jupiter will have to accompany me as a chaperone," she said. "My father would be upset otherwise."

"I see no problem with that," Collett replied. "Do you, McFadden?"

"None at all, sir."

The next few hours passed like a strange yet pleasant dream. As a sign of their gratitude for the gifts of the Turnbow family, the entire regiment drilled and marched back and forth on a short portion of the road, putting more effort into their steps than they would have even if they had been taking part in a grand review of the army. Annie stood and clapped, a smile on her face, while McFadden stood beside her. While no one ever actually said so, it was immediately obvious that Annie was McFadden's guest and that other men should not approach her. The slave Jupiter stood behind the pair, saying nothing but having a knowing expression on his face.

After the impromptu parade was over, with Jupiter still trailing behind, McFadden and Annie decided to take a stroll while the food was being cooked. The heat was still oppressive, but a somewhat overcast sky helped make it more tolerable.

"Why did you not tell me in your letter that it was you who captured Thomas?" she said after a few minutes of idle chit-chat.

"I thought it would seem arrogant, as though I were trying to impress you."

"Your parents raised you to be humble, did they?" she asked with a smile.

"Oh, they were Scottish. Hard work, dignity, self-education and not much else. Bragging was alien to their character."

"And to yours," she said. Without saying a word, she slipped her arm into his. This took him by surprise, but his heart gave a happy leap.

"I am surprised that your parents permitted you to come up to see the troops," McFadden said.

"My mother was opposed, but my father wanted me to go. He is intent on making sure that I grow into a capable woman who can take care of herself. He says that women will not be coddled by their menfolk in the future, now that the war has come and changed everything."

"He may be right."

"I bought all of this food at Ponder's shop on my own, I drove it all up here on my own, and I'll probably be doing it again. My mother may think me a weak and feeble child, but I'm not."

"On your own?" McFadden asked. He glanced behind him quickly. "Wasn't Jupiter with you?"

Annie looked confused. "Of course. But he's only a slave." She saw McFadden's uneasy look. "Oh, I'm sorry. I have not offended you, have I?"

"How's that?"

"I don't share all of my mother's views. On the slavery question, I lean more toward my father. But I cannot deny that one can often hear my mother speaking when I open my mouth."

"What are your father's views on the subject?" McFadden, asked, curious.

"He is not inherently opposed to slavery, but he does see each slave as an individual. His iron foundry is run with slave labor. But my father insists on paying the slaves for their labor. Not much, of course. Certainly far less than a white man would demand. But some of the slaves have earned enough to purchase their freedom from their owners. My father likes it this way, as it gives the slaves a greater incentive to work."

McFadden found this fascinating. He had never heard of any other Southern man doing such a thing. He remembered the strident anti-slavery talk he had heard from his mother while growing up and wondered what she would have thought of Mr. Turnbow's strange policy.

He did not think for a moment that Turnbow had adopted such a policy out of the goodness of his heart. He obviously employed the slaves for the very simple reason that they cost less to employ than white workers. But a deep moral good was still being accomplished. Would that be enough to save Robert Turnbow from the fires on Judgment Day? McFadden had no answer to that question, which he thought might well have been applied to most of the people in the Confederacy, himself included.

"May I ask you a question, James?"

"Of course."

"At dinner the other night, when my father asked you to say the blessing, it looked as though you could not do it. Why could you not?"

He took a deep breath. "It's been a long time since I spoke to God, Annie."

"How long?"

"More than two years now."

"Why?"

He took a deep breath. "I know you understand loss. You lost your brother at Seven Pines?"

"I did, yes. Did you lose someone in the war as well?"

He paused a moment. "I lost everyone."

"Everyone?"

"My brother was killed during the New Mexico campaign. I saw it happen."

"My God."

He nodded. "We were taken prisoner by an insane Yankee captain and his outfit. Really a criminal and his posse, I think. His men called him Cheeky Joe, because he had a big scar across his cheek. He was crazy, I'm sure. Like a minion of Satan let loose onto the Earth."

She said nothing but looked at him, her eyes wide.

"They decapitated my brother fifty feet away from me. I was bound with rope. There was nothing I could do."

"How did you get away?" she asked, breathless.

"They shot me and left me for dead. When I woke up, all that was left was my brother's headless body. I think they took his head as a trophy."

She shuddered at the thought. McFadden wondered if perhaps he had said too much, for such a subject was not proper for conversations with a lady. He had never told anyone the details of what had happened to him out on the New Mexico desert that dark day more than two years before. Somehow, he felt able to tell her these things that he had kept locked up for so long.

He went on. "I scarcely remember how I got back. I spent several days wandering in the desert, wounded and with no food or water. The sun baked me nearly to death. Maybe I even wanted to die. I collapsed several times, but kept waking up and kept going. Finally, after waking up yet again, I discovered that I had been thrown over the back of a mule. A retreating Confederate unit had found me and taken me with them."

"Thank God for those men," Annie said.

McFadden nodded. "Yes. Were it not for them, I would be dead."

She stopped walking and turned to him, looking him deeply in the eyes. "We have both lost a brother, James. There are no words to express the immensity of our loss. But that should not turn you away from God."

He shook his head. "I have not told you all."

"No?"

"No." He motioned for them to resume walking. Somehow it made it easier for him to talk. "Because of the war, the federal troops that had patrolled the Texas frontier had been withdrawn, and neither the Confederate government nor the Texas state government had deployed any troops of their own. The Comanche Indians took advantage of the situation and launched a series of raids. One of these raids targeted my family's farm."

"God help you," she said as though from reflex. Yet she continued to listen intently.

"When I returned home, the farm was a burned out shell. It could only have happened a day or so earlier, because some of the wood was still smoldering. I found the bodies of my father, my mother, and my two sisters. All of them had been pierced by arrows several times."

"God help you," she said again. "I had no idea."

"How could you? You've only just met me."

"Yes, but I could tell as soon as we met that your heart is filled with fire. Now I know why."

He said nothing in response, mulling this over. He wondered exactly what she meant by describing him as being full of fire and worried that she might perhaps be afraid of him. However, she seemed content to be walking along beside him.

"I understand, though, James," she said softly. "I really do. My heart is full of fire, too."

Their walk had taken them in an arching circle and now they found themselves approaching the campground of the 7th Texas once again. The men were roasting juicy pieces of beef over several campfires, while pots boiled happily with potatoes and other delicious ingredients inside them. When the men saw McFadden and Annie approach, they cheered and waved happily.

The next two hours were the most enjoyable McFadden had experienced in years. Annie ate dinner with the men of the regiment, who told her stories of their heroics during the Battle of Peachtree Creek and various other yarns from their time in the service. McFadden suspected that she saw right through their tall tales but still enjoyed the experience.

Private Montgomery produced his fiddle and the men happily danced around the campfire while Annie and everyone else clapped in rhythm. They sang songs, starting with *The Bonnie Blue Flag*, moving on to *Captain and His Whiskers* and then *Dixie*. Being men of the Lone Star State, however, they ended with *The Yellow Rose of Texas*. It was a happy time at the camp of the 7th Texas.

McFadden stood next to Annie, who was sitting on an empty ammunition crate. He was somewhat surprised to realize that he was smiling and clapping along with the rest of the men. It had been a long time since he had allowed himself to have fun.

He glanced over at Jupiter, who had gone back to the wagon and was waiting patiently. The slave was listening to the music, but his face was expressionless. McFadden wondered what was going through Jupiter's mind as he watched the frolics of soldiers fighting for a cause that, were it to succeed, would mean that he would remain trapped in a condition of perpetual servitude.

McFadden picked up half of a cooked potato and strolled over to the wagon. He held it up for Jupiter to take.

"Hungry?"

"Much obliged, sir," Jupiter said, taking the potato.

"Thank you for bringing Annie out here, Jupiter."

"You're welcome, sir." He paused a moment before continuing. "She's a special girl, Annie."

"Yes, she is."

"Mr. Turnbow, sir. He likes you, sir."

"Does he?" McFadden said, surprised.

"Yes, he does. I heard him say, sir."

"And you, Jupiter? Do you like me?"

The black man looked down on him with a bemused look on his face. "I think you're an odd one, Mr. McFadden. I like you just fine, but you sure are an odd one."

McFadden smiled, then turned and walked back toward the group around the campfire. Annie was standing, waiting for him.

"I should go," she said softly.

"Yes. Your mother will be worried."

"I don't much mind that," she replied playfully. "But it is getting late. We will need to head home before it gets too dark."

"Be careful on the streets of the city."

"Jupiter has a gun. I'm not concerned. And if the provost marshals harass me, all I need to do is mention my father's name."

McFadden smiled. "Well, I am very sorry to see you go. The last few hours have been most pleasant."

"Yes, they have." She leaned forward and lightly embraced him. Pulling back, she said, "Thank you again for saving my life."

"Thank you for bringing such delight to me and my men."

"I shall visit again. In the meantime, I look forward to your next letter."

He watched her go as she clambered aboard the wagon. Jupiter whipped the horses into a walk. The men of the regiment stood and waved as one as she vanished down the road, calling out their thanks for the food. But as she disappeared, her eyes were only on McFadden.

*   *   *   *   *

July 26, Morning

Reading the reports coming in from every source of information he possessed, Johnston still could not decide whether Sherman intended to withdraw completely to the north side of the Chattahoochee or attempt to maintain a bridgehead on the south bank. Until the intentions of his enemy became clear, Johnston was unsure exactly which course of action to pursue. All he could do was watch and wait.

Mackall entered the room. "Sir? General Wheeler is here to see you, as you requested."

"Good. Send him in."

Wheeler entered and saluted, a questioning look on his face.

"Sit down, General Wheeler. I have something very important to discuss with you."

Wheeler nodded nervously and took the seat. Johnston looked at him carefully. The cavalry general had treacherously sought to undermine him during the most critical days of the campaign. Such a betrayal was impossible to forgive. Had he had complete freedom of action, Johnston would simply have removed Wheeler from command and thought nothing more of the man.

But it wasn't that simple, for Wheeler still had the backing of President Davis and General Bragg. Although any danger that the authorities in Richmond would remove him from command had vanished with the triumph of Peachtree Creek, Johnston knew he still had to tread carefully. Still, by playing his cards correctly, Johnston was convinced he could simultaneously remove an impediment to his command of the army while ensuring that General Forrest would finally be unleashed against Sherman's supply lines in Tennessee.

"I recall that, on a few occasions during the retreat from Dalton to the Chattahoochee, you requested permission to take a force of picked cavalry in order to launch a raid on Sherman's supply lines."

Wheeler nodded. "Yes, I did. But you were of the opinion that my troopers were needed with this army in order to guard its flanks and scout the positions of the enemy."

"Indeed, and I was correct at that time. But the situation has obviously changed. Peachtree Creek has so severely damaged the enemy that his movements are not as free and wide as they were before, thus making the job of tracking him considerably more easy. Do you agree?"

"Yes, I agree."

"That being the case, I should like to reconsider your request. Do you think you could take a force of four thousand cavalrymen around the Union army, return to north Georgia, and cut the railroad bringing the Yankee supplies down from Chattanooga?"

Wheeler's eyes widened. He licked his lips as though he were anticipating a delicious meal. "Well, I would not have previously suggested the mission, General Johnston, if I hadn't been confident I could accomplish it. So, yes. I am confident I can do it."

Johnston spread a map of north Georgia over the table and the two men were soon poring over it. Because of the necessity of avoiding large concentrations of Federal troops, it was agreed that Wheeler's raiding force should quickly move far to the north of the old battlefields of New Hope Church and Kennesaw Mountain, striking at the railroad bridges spanning the Etowah and Oostanaula Rivers. Johnston stressed that the enormous railroad tunnel running through the aptly-named Tunnel Hill near Dalton had to be one of their primary targets.

For half an hour, Johnston and Wheeler discussed which regiments of cavalry should be part of the raiding force and which should remain behind with the Army of Tennessee. During these conversations, Johnston could almost forget his personal distaste for Wheeler, though this might have simply been due to relief that he would soon be gone.

"One more thing, General Wheeler."

"Yes?"

"You should be aware that General Forrest shall soon be ordered into Tennessee to attack the Union railroads in that state. In order to maximize the effectiveness of both operations, you should confine your own activities to the area south of the Tennessee River in order to avoid any duplication of effort."

Wheeler nodded. "Very well, sir."

Johnston wasn't sure if this particular order would be obeyed, as Wheeler had a well-deserved reputation for interpreting his orders with extreme looseness. But he didn't particularly care, for his hopes for severing the enemy supply line rested much more with Forrest than they did with Wheeler. As long as the insubordinate commander of his army's cavalry was out of his sight, and hopefully creating at least some trouble for the Yankees, Johnston was happy.

About ten minutes after Wheeler had departed, a telegram from the War Department arrived.

> *General Johnston,*
> *Please be advised that General Hood has requested a transfer from the Army of Tennessee to the Department of the Trans-Mississippi. The War Department has decided to grant this request with immediate effect. Please notify General Hood. You may select a temporary commander for Hood's corps from among your division commanders, although General Cleburne is not to be appointed under any circumstances. You shall be notified of Hood's permanent replacement when the decision has been made.*
> *Secretary Seddon*

Johnston found this message confusing on many levels. On the one hand, he was irritated to once again find that Hood was communicating with Richmond outside of the proper channels and even more irritated to learn that the War Department apparently found this behavior completely normal. He considered sending a note of protest about this, but knew it would do no good and would unnecessarily antagonize the President.

His annoyance was quickly swept away by delight at the import of the message. Since discovering Hood's treachery, Johnston had been puzzled as to what exactly he should do about it. Now, Hood was solving the problem for him. Clearly his anger at not being granted command of the army and at missing out on the glory of the Peachtree Creek victory had been too much for Hood. Rather than endure an embarrassing situation, he had decided to take himself out of the picture. To Johnston, who had just rid himself of Wheeler, it all seemed too good to be true.

He frowned again when he noted the end of the message, stipulating that the War Department would choose a permanent commander for Hood's corps rather than leave the decision to Johnston. Since he had first taken command of the Army of Tennessee, most of his personnel requests had been ignored by Richmond, which saw fit to appoint its own people. To see that this situation was continuing was not pleasing. Johnston highly doubted that Robert E. Lee was treated in such a slipshod manner.

He shook his head when he reread the proviso that Cleburne was not to be given the command, even temporarily. Hardee would be displeased no less than Cleburne himself. There was no doubting that Cleburne was the finest division commander in the Army of Tennessee. If it were up to Johnston, Cleburne would have been appointed to the command without much thought. Considering the critical role he had played in the Battle of Peachtree Creek, he certainly was entitled to it.

Johnston knew why Richmond refused to give Cleburne his due. The infamous, if still secret, memorandum Cleburne had presented in January calling for the emancipation of slaves and their enlistment in the army had poisoned Cleburne's chances for any future promotion. Had Cleburne been an ordinary division commander, that foolish piece of paper would have been the end of his career altogether.

Johnston began writing. Hood was notified that his transfer request had been accepted and ordered to turn over command of his corps to General Cheatham.

*   *   *   *   *

July 27, Morning

Lincoln let out a deep breath, even as the two men sitting opposite him continued their joint tirade against him. The conversation had become so heated that Lincoln felt compelled to raise his hand to quiet the men down. For just a moment, he was reminded of the more raucous court cases he had had as a lawyer back in Springfield, when the judge had to loudly pound down his gavel to silence the boos and hisses coming from the audience behind the attorneys.

"Senator Sumner, Congressman Stevens, if you will permit me to interrupt you for just a moment and get a word in myself, I can only try to reassure you that your concerns are unfounded."

"We require reassurance," Congressman Thaddeus Stevens said coldly, his face as unmoving as a block of granite. "With the recent reversals in Georgia and Virginia, and the success the Democratic Party seems to be having in molding public opinion, we fear the pressure to repudiate the policy of emancipating the slaves is increasing. More to the point, we fear that you are buckling under such pressure."

Lincoln shook his head, and tried to summon up an injured expression. "Believe me when I tell you, Congressman, that I am not buckling under the pressure to repudiate my abolition policy. I remain as firmly committed to emancipation as ever. Rest assured, there can be no peace between the North and the South unless and until the South agrees both to rejoin the Union and to abolish slavery. My proposals for the restoration of normal relations with the South include a requirement that the Southern states approve a constitutional amendment specifically prohibiting slavery in all its forms."

Senator Charles Sumner raised a pointed finger, like a professor interjecting during a presentation by one of his students. "Ah, but it is not simply the abolition of slavery we're talking about. If the South is brought back into the Union, whether by force or of its own free will, we shall have to protect the political rights of the freedmen, especially voting rights. Otherwise, the slavocrats will find ways to keep the blacks in subjugation."

"And I fully intend to protect the political rights of the freedmen, Senator Sumner," Lincoln said, sounding increasingly frustrated.

"Then why have you not yet announced a policy on the subject, Mr. President?" asked Stevens. Again, he was as unmoving as stone, which Lincoln never ceased to find disconcerting.

Lincoln sighed in exasperation. He had, of course, been harried by the abolitionist lobby since the moment the war began. He never ceased to be amazed at how otherwise intelligent and moral people couldn't understand political realities. At the time he had issued the Emancipation Proclamation, he had thought the abolitionists would give him some credit and allow him some breathing room. Instead, they had simply begun demanding even more, and had paid no attention to whether it was truly in his power to give it, or whether it furthered the war aims of the Union.

"Gentlemen, I have told you many times that I fully intend to protect the political rights of the freedmen at the conclusion of the war, including the right to vote. But in case you haven't noticed, we have not yet won the war. Stirring up public opinion on the issue will only cloud matters further at the present time. Why can we not agree that the war is to be won first, and only then get down to the details?"

Stevens answered. "Because with the ending of the war, the government will no longer have to ability to act through the use of war powers. Under the reconstruction plan you have proposed, we shall soon have Southerners again sitting in the Senate and the House of Representatives, who would be certain to oppose all meaningful efforts to secure and improve the conditions of the freedmen."

"But announcing such policies at the present time would have two profoundly negative effects," Lincoln protested. "First, it would stiffen rebel resistance and doubtless result in more of our brave men losing their lives. Second, it would lend credence to the Democratic charge that our government is fighting more for the abolition of slavery than for the preservation of the Union."

"Aren't we?" Stevens asked rhetorically.

Lincoln eyed him coolly. "We are fighting for two great causes, Congressman Stevens. One is the abolition of slavery. The other is the preservation of the Union. Neither can be achieved without the other."

"But as we have said, it is not just the abolition of slavery," Sumner interjected.

"Yes, I know. The protection of the political rights of the freedmen, as well."

"And not only that," Sumner said with greater force. "The property of Southern slaveholders must be appropriated by the government and redistributed to the freedmen. Free schools must be established for the young freedmen in the South, the funding being appropriated from the Southern states themselves. And any man who served this so-called Confederacy in any prominent political or military role must be forever barred from participating in politics. The power of the slavocracy must be completely crushed, so as to prevent it from ever rising again."

"I have heard you say these things many times before, Senator Sumner. Can you not see that such rhetoric merely makes the rebels stronger? It causes them to redouble their resistance to our armies and makes the cause of abolishing slavery all the more difficult."

"I am not concerned with the mundane matters of military policy, Mr. President," Sumner said in all seriousness. "I am concerned with what is morally right. And I have no sympathy for slaveholders."

"Nor do I, as you know better than most." Lincoln was making an unspoken personal plea. Despite their differences on matters of policy, Lincoln and Sumner had a personal friendship of considerable warmth. He recalled an evening dinner, not many months before, after which Sumner had read Lincoln several sermons by the celebrated Boston Unitarian preacher, William Ellery Channing. A long conversation on the evils of slavery had followed. Lincoln had thought he had made it perfectly clear to Sumner that their views on the moral imperative of emancipation marched in total lockstep.

"Mr. President," Stevens said, in a low tone that Lincoln had long since learned to associate with some grand yet subtle threat from the political giant of Pennsylvania. "You must be aware that many Radical Republicans are becoming increasingly willing to cast their votes in the upcoming presidential election to John Frémont, whose views on these subjects are more in keeping with ours."

"That would be the most self-defeating act in the history of American politics," Lincoln said with conviction. A few Radical Republicans, having lost all sense of political reality, had broken away from the mainstream party and nominated Frémont for president at a rogue convention in Cleveland. "As any child can clearly see, Frémont has no chance at all of winning the election. Support for him merely drains support away from the true Republican Party. In essence, anyone who casts a vote for Frémont, in actuality, casts a vote for McClellan, and thus for the perpetuation of slavery."

"I am merely stating facts, Mr. President," Stevens replied.

"Yes, facts," Lincoln said, his voice more tired than it had been. "If you'll permit me, gentlemen, allow me to state certain facts as I see them."

"Certainly, Mr. President," Sumner replied. Stevens merely bowed his head, deigning to grant Lincoln permission.

"We have recently suffered a serious military disaster in Georgia. Our offensive against Richmond has completely stalled. The people are war-weary. The treasury is nearly empty. We are rather like a man walking across a frozen lake, uncertain as to the thickness of the ice beneath his feet. Would it not be wiser for us to wait until we are on more solid ground before we begin to jump up and down?"

"An amusing analogy," Stevens said in a voice that sounded anything but amused. "But let me remind you, Mr. President, that the human beings held in bondage in the South have been waiting for their freedom for two-and-a-half centuries."

"That, of course, I know," Lincoln said. For a moment, he remembered the looks on the faces of the black dockworkers at City Point. Each face had had hopes and dreams, aspirations and fears, as real as those of any rich Southern planter or wealthy New England shipping tycoon. For whatever reason, it seemed that God had chosen Abraham Lincoln as the instrument of their emancipation, but he couldn't comprehend why, nor could he fully comprehend how he was to do so. After all, he could no more alter political reality than he could repeal the law of gravity.

Lincoln found himself wondering what would happen if he simply gave in to Sumner and Stevens. What if their extreme views on how the South should be treated were simply adopted as a national policy by his administration? He shook his head. If he did such a thing, the occupied area of the Confederacy, as well as the border states of Kentucky and Missouri, would erupt in violent resistance. Thousands of Union officers and tens of thousands of enlisted men would throw down their weapons and refuse to fight. There would be riots in the streets of New York and Chicago by disgruntled factory workers fearful of freed slaves swamping the Northern labor force. The Southerners would be inspired to even greater feats of resistance to Yankee power. In such a scenario, the Democrats would win the November election in an unprecedented landslide.

"Gentlemen," Lincoln said, his voice betraying immense fatigue. "I thank you sincerely for coming to the White House to share your views on these subjects. I can only plead with you to remember that we are on the same side and that winning the war against the South is a prerequisite for all else that you hold so dear."

Senator Sumner and Congressman Stevens rose to their feet as Lincoln did. Handshakes and brief expressions of thanks were exchanged. A few moments later, the two giants of abolitionism left the office. Lincoln sank back into his chair.

He knew that, on a moral level, Sumner and Stevens were absolutely correct. Slavery was an evil that had to be eradicated and those who denied freedom to others did not deserve it for themselves. But the President of the United States had to operate in the real world. He had to deal with military and political reality. With that thought, he picked up and began reading a report about the conditions of the prison camp at Point Lookout, which had recently caused some controversy.

*　　　　*　　　　*　　　　*　　　　*

July 27, Evening

"You wished to see me, sir?" Hardee asked.

"Yes, William," Johnston answered. "Please sit down. How are things with your corps?"

"Fine, I suppose," Hardee said, sitting back comfortably in his chair. "Little activity aside from some heavy skirmishing. But our scouts who have penetrated the Union line report that the Army of the Cumberland has almost fully withdrawn to the north bank of the river."

"What's left of it," Johnston said, unable to suppress a grin.

Hardee smiled. "Quite so."

"McPherson and Schofield will follow, I imagine. Make sure your men are ready to advance at a moment's notice."

"They are, sir. Have no doubt."

"Good. Now, I've asked you to come because there is an urgent matter about which I need your advice. I received a telegram from Richmond yesterday. General Hood has requested a reassignment to the Trans-Mississippi."

"What?" Hardee asked, incredulous.

"It seems that General Hood would prefer not to remain with the Army of Tennessee. I confess I do not know why. The answer to that question can only be provided by Hood himself."

"I am shocked," Hardee said. "I had no idea he had any desire to leave the army."

"Nor did I. Alas, that is not what I wished to discuss. We must decide which division commander we shall promote to take Hood's place, at least until Richmond sees fit to appoint a permanent replacement."

Hardee rubbed his chin for a moment. "The answer is obvious, sir. Cleburne. I can think of no better man than Patrick Cleburne. His record should speak for itself and a man more devoted to the cause of Southern freedom has not yet been born."

Johnston nodded slowly. "Regrettably, there's a problem."

He slid the telegram from the War Department across the desk. Hardee's eyes narrowed as he picked up the paper and quickly read through it. Johnston saw the expression on Hardee's face change instantly to one of anger. He tossed the paper back onto the desk and shook his head.

"It's not right," he said sadly. "It's just not right."

"I know, William. Believe me, I know."

Hardee's voice now became flustered. "Cleburne is the best division commander in the Confederacy. He has fought gallantly in every major battle of the Army of Tennessee since the beginning of the war. He saved the army at Ringgold Gap. His performance at Peachtree Creek was perhaps the best rendered by any division commander on either side in any battle since the beginning of the war."

"I agree with you completely, my friend."

"Then why must I go back to him and tell him that, in spite of his outstanding record, he is to be passed over for promotion yet again?"

Johnston sighed. "I will tell him, if you like."

Hardee shook his head. "No, I'm his immediate superior. I'm also his friend. I'll tell him. But can I at least tell him why?"

"To be honest, your guess is as good as mine, William. Is it because he did not graduate from West Point? Is it because he is a foreign-born Irishman?" He paused for just a moment. "Or is it because he advocated freeing the slaves and enlisting them in the army?"

There was a long silence. Hardee pursed his lips and said nothing for some time. Johnston waited patiently. "So, that's it, is it?" Hardee finally asked.

"Only Jefferson Davis knows for certain. But I think so, yes."

Hardee shook his head again. "Not fair. Cleburne was only saying what he honestly believed."

"His logic was perfectly reasonable, if you ask me. Were the slaves to serve as soldiers in our armies, we could face the Yankees with armies equal in strength. Moreover, if the Confederacy were not a slaveholding nation, we would long since have obtained official diplomatic recognition from Britain and France, with all that entails."

Johnston spoke with conviction he did not entirely feel, for though he was no friend to slavery himself, he thought Cleburne's plan had been naïve and hopelessly impractical. He recalled the raucous meeting of the senior officers of the army that had taken place in January, seemingly a lifetime ago, at which Cleburne had pitched his idea. Some of the generals present, including Hardee, had endorsed Cleburne's plan, but most had opposed it. Indeed, General Walker had bitterly denounced the idea and had come close to accusing Cleburne of treason. Whatever its merits, Johnston had recognized the memorandum's potential for stirring up strife within the ranks of the Confederacy. It was just as well that, upon learning of Cleburne's memorandum, President Davis had promptly ordered all discussion of it terminated.

"Well, we must obey the orders of the War Department," Hardee said reluctantly. "It will be hard on Cleburne, though. He burns for advancement, and no man is more deserving."

"You and I are as one on this question, William. However, since Richmond has made its wishes known, whom do you advise I appoint to take over Hood's corps?"

"If it is not to be Cleburne, then I suppose the honor should fall to Benjamin Cheatham," Hardee replied. "He's a good soldier and very popular with the army. His performance in battle has always been good. At Peachtree Creek he was second only to Cleburne in his contribution to victory."

"I agree," Johnston said. "Cheatham it shall be."

In truth, Johnston had already decided to promote Cheatham and would have done so even had Hardee recommended someone else. But he was happy to allow Hardee to think he had been the deciding factor. With so many enemies within his own ranks, Johnston knew he needed friends.

July 28, Morning

By the standards of the giant armies waging war against each
another in Virginia and Georgia, the Confederate encampment
outside the town of Tupelo in northern Mississippi was not
particularly large. The few acres of tents, most of them captured from
the enemy, sheltered only about 3,500 rebel horsemen, all trying to
find some relief from the oppressive Mississippi summer. It wasn't
the size of the force that made it formidable, so much as its
commander.

That commander sat quietly in his headquarters tent, reading
a Louisville newspaper only four days old, smuggled in earlier that
day by a spy. In his mid-forties, he was tall and exceedingly well-
built. He bore scars of numerous wounds, some inflicted by the
Yankees, others by his own kind.

Nathan Bedford Forrest didn't smile very often. Neither did
anyone who happened to be in his presence. That was probably just
as well, for on those rare occasions that Forrest actually did smile, its
effect was to freeze the blood in a man's veins, as if Satan was making
a joke at their expense.

He had earned his reputation and did his best to quietly foster
it. This was not because he particularly enjoyed it. He was not one of
the flamboyant dandies of the Confederate cavalry like Jeb Stuart or
John Hunt Morgan. He couldn't have cared less for newspaper
headlines in and of themselves. Rather, he built his reputation
because he knew that it gave him an advantage in battle. When
Yankee soldiers heard rumors that Nathan Bedford Forrest and his
deadly troopers were approaching, the fear in their hearts rendered
them half defeated before he and his men even appeared over the
horizon.

Some of the stories which were told about him, such as the
allegation that he had killed more than two dozen Union soldiers in
hand-to-hand combat, were quite true. Others were more fanciful. It
was said that he could cause birds to fall dead out of the sky merely
by looking at them, that he never slept, that wolves obeyed his
commands, and that his horse King Philip exhaled fire and had red-
glowing eyes. There were other stories, even more far-fetched and
even more frightful.

Forrest was not concerned with such stories now. He tossed
down the paper in frustration, for it contained no details about the
recent battle he had fought against Union forces just west of Tupelo,
two weeks before. While the battle had been tactically inconclusive,
the Yankees had hurriedly retreated to their stronghold of Memphis
in its immediate aftermath. Forrest had hoped to glean some
information about the condition of the enemy forces from the

newspaper article, but the editors were more concerned with the fighting taking place in Virginia and Georgia.

Forrest was gratified, though, to get further details about the Confederate victory at Peachtree Creek. He had to admit his surprise at the sudden turn of events. While Johnston handled his army with a certain level of skill, he was far too cautious a general for Forrest's taste. Nevertheless, he had inflicted a decisive defeat on Sherman, which was all Forrest cared about. As far as he was concerned, the more Yankees in Hell, the better. Moreover, success in Georgia might weaken the enemy in West Tennessee, allowing him to mount the raid against Sherman's railroads that he had been dreaming of for weeks.

His own command was in good shape, which made him very proud. He had beaten back everything the Yankees could throw at him, fighting them to a draw in the recent battle outside Tupelo and, a month before, utterly smashing a superior Union force at the Battle of Brice's Cross Roads.

These thoughts were still rolling through Forrest's mind when a staff officer entered the tent.

"General Forrest, excuse me, sir."

"Yes, Captain. What is it?"

"We've received a telegram from the departmental headquarters. Here it is, sir." The man passed the paper over to Forrest, then quickly saluted and exited the tent. Forrest grabbed the paper and quickly read it.

General Forrest,

The victory recently achieved over General Sherman in Georgia renders it more desirable that we cut the enemy supply lines. You are thereby directed to operate with your force against Sherman's railroads in Tennessee. You may operate as you see fit, but your command is to remain north of the Tennessee River. If at all possible, destroy the bridge over the Tennessee River at Bridgeport, Alabama.

Secretary of War Seddon

It was the order Forrest had been waiting for. Within thirty seconds of reading the telegram, Forrest was outside the tent, barking orders at his three brigade commanders. Less than ten minutes later, the quiet camp had turned into a maelstrom of activity, the men quickly folding up their tents and rolling up their blankets, saddling their horses with a speed and coordination possible only for men who had practically lived on horseback for the previous three years. In only half an hour, what had been a well-laid out military encampment had entirely disappeared, replaced by 3,500 Confederate cavalrymen mounted, armed, and ready for action.

While all this was going on, Forrest hurriedly conferred with his brigade commanders, tracing out his proposed route of march on a map. The details would be worked out later, Forrest said. What was important now was speed and an early start.

Forty-five minutes after Forrest had been handed the telegram, officers shouted orders to their men and the entire mounted force began trotting northeast.

*   *   *   *   *

July 28, Evening

"I shall make no complaint," Cleburne said stoically. "Please convey my congratulations to General Cheatham, who very much deserves this promotion."

Hardee looked at his friend warmly. "Again, as was the case when we needed to find a replacement for General Polk, I told General Johnston that you were the best possible choice. But because Cheatham's appointment as a major general precedes you, it was thought best that he take up the position."

"You need not sugar-coat it, my friend. It is about much more than seniority. I am not a West Pointer, but then neither is General Cheatham. If you ask me, my lack of promotion is due to my memorandum on recruiting freed slaves into our army."

Hardee nodded. "I won't deny the truth of it, my friend. I just hope that you do not see Cheatham's appointment as a reflection of Johnston's opinion of you. He believes you are quite possibly the greatest division commander in the Confederacy."

Cleburne shrugged and reached for the mug of coffee which sat next to his plate of roast beef. Outside, the warm humidity of the Georgia evening did not seem to dampen the spirit of the men, who continued to play their banjoes and sing around their campfires.

"How are things in your division?" Hardee asked.

"Fine, I suppose. The men are rather bored, I think. The rumors are circulating about Wheeler's raid against the railroad."

Hardee shrugged. "I expect nothing good to come from that. Wheeler is good in a fight, but honestly worth little when it comes to anything as complicated as tearing up railroad track."

"What does Johnston expect?"

"Nothing, most likely. I frankly think he sent Wheeler off north just to get rid of him, rather than out of any expectation that his raid will be a success. No, Johnston is trusting in General Forrest for that."

"We'll see," Cleburne said.

"Have you had any word from Susan?"

"Yes," Cleburne said, his face brightening at the mention of his fiancée. "A letter from her arrived just yesterday. Mobile is apparently in consternation at the prospect of an attack by the

Yankee navy, which might be a prelude to an effort to capture Mobile itself."

"Where will she go if they do attack?" Hardee said, concerned.

"Montgomery, most likely. I would prefer for her to come to Atlanta, so that we might get to actually spend some time together. But if Sherman attempts to cross the river again, the fate of Atlanta would again be uncertain, and I will not permit Susan to be placed in a potentially dangerous situation."

Hardee laughed. "You are a gentleman, Patrick. Rest assured, you and your love will have ample time to spend together when the war is over. The whole rest of your lives, in fact."

Cleburne reflected on the uncomfortable fact that such optimism depended on him surviving the war. That was something of which Cleburne himself was not at all confident. The leg wound he had suffered at Peachtree Creek had been minor, but still burned and would keep him limping for at least another week. He had been in the thick of the fight for much of the battle, mounted on a horse and obviously a high-ranking officer. How many bullets had been fired at him he could not possibly know. By all rights, he should have been killed, yet he had passed safely through.

It had been far from the first time. In the midst of a small battle during the invasion of Kentucky, an enemy bullet had sliced through his cheek and knocked out two of his teeth. The wound had appeared worse than it actually was, but Cleburne was well aware of the fact that he had come within an inch of having his head blown off. He also had suffered a minor wound at the Battle of Perryville. No one had to tell him that he was as vulnerable as anyone else.

Cleburne found himself wondering how long his luck would hold. He then chastened himself for asking such a stupid question. Obviously, God would not have brought Susan Tarleton into his life if He intended for him to die on some blood-soaked battlefield before they even had a chance to be married.

"Remember Bleak House?" Hardee said with a smile.

"How could I forget?"

"Not even seven months ago," Hardee said wistfully. "It seems like a lifetime."

The memory of those heady days came rushing back to Cleburne like a deluge. Some time before, Hardee had become utterly smitten with an Alabama lass half his age, the refined and beautiful Mary Lewis, and had impulsively asked her to marry him. Besotted by the handsome general who professed such an intense love, Mary had accepted. A wedding had been hastily arranged at the wealthy estate of the bride's father, which took its ironic name from the recent novel by Charles Dickens.

Hardee had asked Cleburne to serve as his best man and Cleburne had happily accepted. It had been the first leave of absence he had taken since the beginning of the war, two years earlier.

Cleburne had expected to enjoy himself, happy to leave the stress of command and the disappointment of the failure of his infamous memorandum behind him for at least a few days. He could not have known the magical delight into which he was about to be plunged.

In the midst of a dreary and uninviting central Alabama countryside, Bleak House Plantation belied its name by being beautiful, warm, and inviting. It was a center of culture and refinement where the latest artistic and intellectual trends of London and Paris were discussed. Abandoning his teetotal habits for once, Cleburne had sipped champagne while marveling at the strange but beautiful pieces of French art that had graced the walls of the house, some of which had arrived just before the outbreak of the war.

The wedding itself had been a divine event. Cleburne had presented himself in a fine dress uniform of Confederate gray and with a ceremonial sword, both of them gifts from the men of 15th Arkansas Infantry, which he had commanded at the beginning of the war. He flattered himself if he thought that he appeared half as dashing as the other officers involved in the ceremony.

It was there that General Patrick Cleburne had met the lovely Susan Tarleton.

He had been the best man; she the maid of honor. From the first moment he had looked upon her, he had been struck down by the intensity of her gaze. She had heard of the gallant Cleburne, of course, for everyone in the Confederacy had heard of Cleburne. Still, he found it astonishing that she even deigned to notice him. Such beauty, such intelligence, such vivaciousness, such coyness; he felt that they were not to be found in any other female on Earth. Patrick Cleburne, who would have never surrendered to the enemy, had surrendered to Susan Tarleton at first sight.

The days that followed seemed like something out of a romantic poem from Elizabethan days. A beautiful steam paddleboat had carried the wedding party down the Tombigbee River from Bleak House to the city of Mobile. Bachelors were being struck down without mercy, as two of the groomsmen announced their engagements to members of the bridal party not long after.

Cleburne had spent every moment with Susan, walking the decks of the steamboat as they passed through some of the most beautiful countryside in the South. He didn't talk much about the war, but rather his life before it and his dreams for his life after it. He was delighted to find that she didn't hold his Irish birth against him, nor the fact that he had once been a humble enlisted man in the British Army. Indeed, she seemed captivated by the story of his rise from humble beginnings and his determination to make a name for himself in the Confederacy.

Once they reached Mobile, there had been a whirlwind of dinner parties and official events. Cleburne had spent the time with Susan and her family, for it had become obvious by this point that he was pursuing Susan with a view to a marriage proposal. The main newspaper in Mobile considered his presence in the city worthy of a lead story and he had been the guest of honor at a grand review of the Mobile garrison. Cleburne hoped that Susan and her family had been impressed.

His idyllic visit to Mobile had not lasted long. Soon he had returned to the Army of Tennessee, then encamped at Dalton waiting for Sherman to launch his spring offensive. But a steady stream of letters had passed between Cleburne and the object of his affections, each more ardent than the last. Only a few weeks passed before Cleburne had prevailed upon Hardee and Johnston for a few days of additional leave. He had dashed back down to Mobile and, within days, he and Susan were engaged.

"I went on that trip intending to help you gain a wife," Cleburne said with a smile. "I did not expect to acquire one myself."

"You did me the honor of standing beside me as I was married. Introducing you to your future wife was the least I could do in terms of compensation."

"I am looking forward to having you stand by my side on my wedding day, you know."

Hardee smiled and slapped Cleburne's shoulder. "I am deeply honored, my friend. And I shall look forward to the wedding with great pleasure. Indeed, if the trip we take for your wedding is even a tenth as pleasant as the one we took for mine, it shall be well worth it."

"I very much wish this campaign were over," Cleburne said. "If it were, we could depart for Mobile tomorrow. Susan and I could be married within a week."

"Alas, duty."

"Yes, duty. Sometimes I do not care for it."

"You're a liar," Hardee said. "You are duty manifested in human form. I don't doubt your love for Susan, but you could no more leave this army, leave your division, than you could cut off your own legs."

Cleburne grunted and said nothing.

"Cheer up, my friend. The war will be over after the presidential elections in the North. We shall have succeeded in establishing the independence of our nation, and you can live out the rest of your life with your beloved. Whether you go home to Arkansas to practice law again or decide to remain in the army, you shall have a loving wife by your side."

Cleburne shook his head. "I pray so, but it's best not to tempt fate. A lieutenant in my division was killed at Peachtree Creek only hours after learning that he had become a father. I shall make Susan my wife this fall, peace or no peace, but I shall not dream of the future until the last shot of this damnable war has been fired."

July 29, Evening

"Where the hell did they go?" Pearson asked.

McFadden shook his head. A few minutes before, fire from Federal skirmishers had been smacking into the ground all around the small depression in which they had been sheltering. Now the fire had abruptly ceased and, carefully poking their heads up over the rim of the hole, they could see no enemy. There had been a cacophony of shouted voices from the other side shortly before, which conceivably had been the voices of officers ordering their men to retreat.

"Lieutenant McFadden!" Collett called. He was behind the cover of a tree about twenty yards away. "Do you see anything?" His tone indicated that he still took a sort of amused pride in calling McFadden by his new rank.

"Nothing, Major," McFadden called back.

Collett inquired of the rest of the men and received the same reply from everyone. He began barking out orders. Very carefully, the Texans emerged from their cover and warily stepped forward, ready to drop back onto the ground at the first sound that might indicate the presence of an enemy. It was possible, after all, that the Yankees were luring the men of the regiment into an ambush.

Forming a rough line in skirmish order, with gaps of several yards between each man, the 7th Texas began slowly edging forward. McFadden guessed that the other regiments of Granbury's Brigade were doing the same on either side of them. Beyond that, McFadden wouldn't venture to guess what was happening.

The last two days had seen constant skirmishing with the Yankee picket line, which the enemy had pushed out several hundred yards in advance of their fortified positions. Since moving back onto the front line from their temporary hiatus, the Texans had lost three killed and several wounded in these low-level fights. The skirmishing had never amounted to a full-scale battle and the regiment had not been called on to participate in any full-scale assault on the enemy line.

In the meantime, the 7th Texas had been reorganized to take into account the heavy losses in officers and men it had sustained at Peachtree Creek. Four companies had been abolished and their men incorporated into the remaining six. McFadden, with his new rank, had been given overall command of three of these companies, including the Lone Star Rifles. The other three companies were now under the command of Lieutenant William Huff, who had been promoted and brought in from another regiment.

The biggest adjustment McFadden had had to make was getting used to having an officer's sword tied around his waist. It was always hitting against his foot, which he found very annoying. He also had been required to trade in his Enfield rifle for a Colt Navy revolver. Although he could now fire six shots without reloading, he was finding the pistol difficult to operate and had not yet fully mastered the reloading process despite many hours of practice. He had asked Collett for permission to continue using his Enfield rifle but had been turned down. It would not have been proper for an officer to use a rifle, Collett had explained.

The sun had vanished over the western horizon, but the twilight continued to glimmer. Diffused by branches of the thick pine trees that surrounded them, it illuminated the area in almost frightening grayish light. With the disappearance of the sun, the temperature began to drop and, as an hour passed, it gradually became almost pleasant.

"Something up ahead, Lieutenant!" one of McFadden's comrades whispered harshly. "Looks like a trench line!"

The men tensed, quietly taking cover behind the nearest trees and aiming their Enfields forward. McFadden strained his eyes and was able to make out through the underbrush the unmistakable sight of a line of prepared fortifications, complete with a trench, parapet, head-log, and abatis. But there was absolutely no sign of the enemy. All was silence.

Using hand signals, Collett ordered two men to move forward stealthily. Private Thompson and Corporal Anderson, two men with a reputation in the regiment for being absolutely unshakeable, crawled ahead. McFadden said a silent prayer for the two brave men as he watched them go, for he expected the Federal trench line to erupt in musket fire at any moment. If that happened, Thompson and Anderson would have no chance to survive.

"Nobody here, Major!" Thompson called after crawling up to the parapet and peering beneath the head-log. "They've lit out, looks like!"

"Okay, let's go in," Major Collett said. The Texans strolled forward, climbed over the parapet and down into the enemy trench. Rather to their surprise, they found that the enemy had left behind haversacks half full of rations, canteens filled with water, and even a few muskets. They were strewn about haphazardly.

Collett looked around with the measured stare of an officer. "Looks like they left in a hurry." Some of the men stopped for a moment to stuff hardtack into their mouths, while the regimental quartermaster quickly began collecting the discarded muskets and other useful supplies to send back to the rear.

Suddenly, the sound of a distant but clearly enormous explosion startled the men of the 7th Texas. It came from the direction of the Chattahoochee River, perhaps another mile away. McFadden felt the ground shake beneath his feet. Barely two minutes later, there was another explosion of roughly the same size from the same direction.

"The Yankees are blowing up their ammunition!" Collett shouted. A shiver of excitement ran through the men, for everyone knew that the Yankees would only be doing this if they were evacuating the south bank of the Chattahoochee.

All was suddenly activity. General Granbury rode up and had a hurried discussion with Collett. All pretense of stealth vanished at once, with buglers blaring their instruments and drummers pounding their drums. The 7th Texas formed up and abandoned their skirmish order in favor of a battle line. The rest of the brigade formed up tightly on either side. Less than ten minutes after the sound of the first detonation, the order to march was given and the brigade stepped off.

"What's going on, Jimmy?" Montgomery asked, apprehensive.

"If the Yanks are abandoning their hold on the south side of the river, we can bet General Johnston wants to catch as many of them as possible before they get away. Probably scoop up some loot, too."

"I don't much like the idea of fighting in the dark. I'd just as likely trip on a rock and break my neck as get shot by a damn Yankee."

As they moved forward, the sound of scattered musketry was heard all around them, as well as confused shouting by men with Northern accents. McFadden judged from the sound of the firing that other Confederate units were advancing to the river as well. He feared that his unit might be struck by friendly fire in the confusion and darkness. He called out for his men to be careful on their flanks. Somewhere ahead of him, McFadden could see the yellow flickering of large fires, although he could not tell what was burning.

An hour after leaving the abandoned enemy trench, having gone about a mile, the men of the 7th Texas emerged from the thicket onto the banks of the Chattahoochee River. Off to their left, only a few hundred yards away, they saw a surrealistic line of flame spanning the entire width of the river. McFadden quickly realized that it was one of the pontoon bridges, set ablaze by the retreating enemy. Presumably there had not been enough time to dismantle the thing.

All around them were the shattered remnants of a disorderly retreat. Broken wooden crates spilled their contents out onto the muddy ground. Several horses, their owners long gone, stood about in confusion, waiting for some human to tell them what to do. Small fires burned every hundred yards or so, as the withdrawing Federals had clearly made some effort to destroy the supplies which they could not take with them.

On the bank, directly in front of the 7th Texas, Yankee troops were jumping onto half a dozen small boats and frantically trying to push off for the northern bank.

"Stop, you bastards!" Collett shouted, waving his sword. "Stop or we'll shoot!"

Without being told, McFadden's men raised their muskets.

"Let's get the hell out of here!" one of the Yankees shouted. They continued pushing their boat into the river, and two oars appeared on either side.

"Fire!"McFadden yelled. Instantly the tiny flotilla of small boats was peppered by musket fire from dozens of men. Many Yankees were hit and fell into the river or onto the bank with pathetic yelps of pain. The men in two of the boats stopped rowing and held up their hands, but the other four gamely continued on and were soon out of reach.

"Put out those fires!" Collett was yelling. "Stop shooting at the boats and put out those fires! We've got to save all the supplies we can!"

Their commander was gesturing frantically to the piles of wooden crates that continued to burn, illuminating the darkness with a sinister yellowish glow. Men grabbed discarded blankets and uniform coats from the ground and began beating at the fires.

"Row, men! Row!" a dark voice was shouting from one of the boats.

The sound of the voice caused McFadden to freeze. Everything else suddenly became entirely unimportant while his brain processed the awful memory. He had heard the voice before, years earlier, in the desert of New Mexico. The sound of it was burned into his brain as if from a branding iron. Instantly, McFadden's heart began pounding with the force of a steam engine. He jerked his head to the sound of the voice. McFadden could see the man's face against the yellow glow of the fires on the riverbank. Even from a distance, he could see the mark on the man's left cheek.

It was Cheeky Joe.

He looked up and saw McFadden gazing at him in shock. McFadden was certain that he could see recognition in the man's eyes. For one endless moment, the two men stared at each other across the waters of the Chattahoochee River.

McFadden raised his revolver and fired, but the bullet passed harmlessly through the side of his enemy's uniform coat. He fired again and again until all six bullets had been expended. Joe stood tall in his boat, as if welcoming the fire and yet remaining unharmed. McFadden thought he could hear sinister laughter coming from the boat.

"Shoot him!" McFadden screamed to his men. "Kill him!" But his men had all put down their weapons when they had been ordered by Collett to put out the fires.

"What the hell's the matter with you, McFadden?" Collett called out. "Forget the boats and help us put out these damn fires!"

"No!" McFadden cried. He pulled out another set of cartridges and struggled desperately to reload his pistol. He wished more than anything that he had his Enfield rifle, which he could have reloaded in fifteen seconds and which had a much longer range than his pistol. He thought about picking up one of the rifles set down by one of his men, but that would have taken several seconds and he would have had to seize an ammunition pouch off someone, too.

His hands fumbled and the cartridges fell out onto the river bank. McFadden glanced up and saw the boat quickly vanishing into the darkness in the middle of the river. He screamed in rage at his powerlessness. The boat faded from sight. For a few haunting seconds, the sound of Cheeky Joe's laughter seemed to echo across the Chattahoochee River.

The remainder of the regiment was busy putting out the fires. A few enterprising soldiers tried to organize a water line from the river using a few buckets they had found lying around. Although most of the Union crates went up in smoke, they were able to salvage some boxes of food, horse tackle, and various other kinds of useful gear.

McFadden ran over to a wounded Union soldier laying on his back at the water's edge. He grabbed the collar of his uniform coat and yelled into his face.

"What regiment are you?"

The man winced against the pain and did not immediately answer.

"Tell me! What regiment are you?" McFadden drew his sword and put it up against the man's throat. "Tell me what regiment you are or I'll kill you!"

"Lieutenant!" Collett shouted in surprise and alarm. "What the hell are you doing?"

McFadden ignored him. "Tell me!" McFadden screamed at the Yankee soldier. The fiery rage in his eyes was more than enough to terrify the bluecoat.

"118th Ohio," came the meek response.

McFadden shoved the Yankee painfully back down onto the ground, causing him to cry out in pain. He sheathed his sword and turned away from the river, raising his hands to the sides of his head. He screamed forth a primal yell of pain and hatred that the rest of the regiment found frightening. Then, he fell down onto his knees.

"Go about your business, men!" Collett shouted to the regiment. They finished putting the fires out and began the task of collecting anything usable from the wreckage. They glanced over continually at McFadden, curious looks in their eyes.

Collett walked up to him and cautiously put his hand on McFadden's shoulder.

"Who was that man, James? The one you were shooting at?"

McFadden waited a few moments before replying. The answer, when it came, was simple.

"It was the Devil, Major. God help me, but it was the Devil."

Chapter Nine

July 31, Morning

Lincoln nodded to Major Eckert as he entered the telegraph room, but said nothing as he hurried over to the drawer of telegrams and sifted through the first several sheets. He knew what he was looking for, as the rumors of the disaster which had befallen Grant's army in front of Petersburg were on the lips of every person in Washington that morning.

Lincoln's face glazed over with disappointment and frustration as he read. The enormous mine which Grant had told him about during his recent visit to City Point had finally been set off. According to the reports, the initial phase of the operation had gone well. The mine had blown a gigantic gap in Lee's fortifications, killing hundreds of rebel soldiers instantly. But everything thereafter had gone disastrously wrong, with the local commanders displaying an unprecedented level of incompetence.

Lincoln's despair deepened further the more he read. The explosion had formed an enormous crater, into which the assault force had inexplicably charged. There, they had become trapped. Enemy troops massed along the rim of the crater and drenched the Union soldiers with concentrated musket and artillery fire, inflicting heavy casualties. Unable to make any headway, the attack had been called off. It seemed to have been less a battle than a slaughter.

Reading another telegram melted Lincoln's sadness and replaced it with anger. A division of black troops had been part of the operation and by all accounts had fought with great gallantry. But numerous eye witnesses had reported that hundreds of the black soldiers had been killed in cold blood by the rebels as they had tried to surrender.

"Another disaster, Mr. President," Stanton said. The Secretary of War had quietly entered the room while Lincoln had been reading.

"Worse than a disaster, Edwin. A disaster caused by incompetence. The fortunes of war may occasionally present us with unavoidable defeats, but to lose so many brave men and squander such an opportunity because of the ineptitude of our own officers?"

"Apparently, the commander of the assault force didn't even lead his men into action. He remained behind the lines in a bombproof shelter, drunk as a sailor."

"It's like the girl left us the key to her hotel room and we were too stupid to notice it." Lincoln angrily shoved the telegrams back into the drawer and slammed it shut. "Defeat is one thing. Disgrace another."

"It is very bad, Mr. President. I wish I could put it some other way, but I cannot. Combined with the final evacuation of the last of our troops from the south bank of the Chattahoochee, I can't help but see nothing but gloom on our military horizon."

Lincoln sighed. "Less than two weeks after the catastrophe at Peachtree Creek, we have experienced yet another humiliating defeat. Imagine how the public will react. The Democrats are making the case that we are not fit to run the war. Any Ohio farmer or Pennsylvania shopkeeper who reads the newspapers could be forgiven for agreeing with them. Our chances in November seem to be slipping farther away every day."

Suddenly, Lincoln felt a wave of grief and guilt sweep over him. The fact that his first thought upon hearing the news of the battle near Petersburg was one of politics stabbed at his heart. He tried to put himself in the place of the terrified soldiers crammed into the bed of Peachtree Creek or the crater at Petersburg, panicked and unable to flee as the rebels standing above them slaughtered them like sheep. Unconsciously, his hand went up to his head, as if he were nursing a horrible headache.

"Mr. President? Are you all right?"

"As well as can be expected, Edwin. The war is eating me alive, but I must press on." Stanton grunted, and Lincoln continued, steeling himself to ask the next question. "How many men did we lose?"

"About four thousand, Mr. President."

Lincoln nodded. Part of his mind did quick calculations as to how the loss of four thousand men would affect the military situation around Petersburg. Another contemplated the fact that the mothers and wives of four thousand men would soon be getting the telegram they all so dreaded to receive.

"You'll send me a full report when you have all the information?"

"Of course, Mr. President. And while I hate to give you more bad news, I have to report that the Pennsylvania town of Chambersburg was burned by rebel cavalry yesterday."

"I heard about that. I assume it was Early's men?"

"It was."

The President nodded. "The Democrats will now begin attacking us by saying that we cannot even defend our own towns and cities. And they will be correct."

"I also have the response from General Grant regarding your proposal that Indiana troops be furloughed home in order to vote in the upcoming elections."

Lincoln's eyes lit up briefly. Indiana was one of the few states that did not allow its soldiers to cast absentee ballots, and acting on the assumption that serving soldiers would be more likely to support the Republican ticket than that of the defeatist Democrats, Lincoln was hoping that a sufficient number of Indiana troops serving in the army might be allowed to return home briefly in order to vote. Lincoln felt that Indiana would be one of the most closely contested states in the election, where even the swing of a few thousand votes might decide the outcome. The more troops from the Hoosier State that could be temporarily sent home to vote, the better.

"Well?" Lincoln asked. "What did he say?"

"Grant tells me that there are only half a dozen Indiana regiments serving with the Army of the Potomac in Virginia. The vast bulk of Indiana units are serving with Sherman in Georgia. While those men fighting in Virginia can be easily furloughed, those fighting under Sherman's command are needed at the front."

"In other words, rather than an additional ten thousand voters who would likely favor us at the polls, we might expect a thousand or so?"

"Yes, Mr. President," Stanton replied, glumly. "I apologize for being the bearer of so much bad news today."

"Not your fault," the President said simply. The idea of furloughing Indiana troops in order to impact the election in that state had been worth a shot, but it was only one of a multitude of political tricks whirling about in Lincoln's mind.

Among other things, Lincoln was considering having the military governors of the recovered areas of Tennessee, Arkansas, Louisiana, and Florida quickly form loyal governments in those otherwise rebellious states, which would be controlled by the Republican Party and whose electoral votes could be counted in his column on Election Day. He had already issued a proclamation declaring martial law throughout the states of Kentucky and Missouri in order to combat Southern guerrillas and, if he so choose, he would be able to turn a blind eye to any use of military force by his officers to promote his candidacy in November. Those were just a few of the aces he was shoving up his sleeves for when he needed them.

Lincoln had been a politician too long to expect that his Democratic opponents were not going to indulge in some clever political chicanery of their own. If his correspondents in New York City telling the truth, Democrats with deep pockets and connections on Wall Street were buying up all the gold they could get their hands on, their aim being to drive up the price of gold so much that it would depress the value of United States currency. The voters, so the instigators of this plan expected, would blame the resulting inflation on President Lincoln and therefore be more inclined to vote against him on Election Day.

He chuckled softly. In an ideal world, of course, such schemes would have no part in political discourse. Unfortunately, as Lincoln was painfully aware, the world in which he lived was far from ideal.

*   *   *   *   *

August 1, Afternoon

Thomas looked sullenly around at Camp Oglethorpe, which would be his home for the foreseeable future. He nearly gave in to despair. A stockade enclosed a few acres of ground, in which several wooden huts had been constructed. All looked flimsy and likely to fall apart at the first rain. Although a few tall trees near the center of the stockade provided a small amount of shade, the heat was so intense that they might as well have been inside an oven. The humidity made it all the worse.

Within the camp, large numbers of Union officers milled about like chickens in a coop. Camp Oglethorpe, near the town of Macon in central Georgia, had been designated as the main prison camp for captured Union officers since the near approach of the Army of the Potomac to Richmond had forced the rebel authorities to close the infamous Libby Prison a few months before. Within the small acreage of the camp, some four thousand officers were being held.

He was being escorted by Confederate Captain George Gibbs, who was the commandant of the prison camp. Thomas had taken an instant dislike to him.

"This will be your cabin," Gibbs said. "You will share it with seven other officers."

Thomas looked inside. "This space would be insufficient for four men! How do you expect eight men to sleep in such a small space!"

Gibbs shrugged. "I'm sure you'll figure it out, Thomas. Not my problem."

Thomas growled in anger, but there was nothing he could do. Over the past week, he had been forced to endure humiliation after humiliation from young Georgia militiamen barely old enough to have pimples on their faces. Thomas felt nearly broken, but could not admit defeat just yet.

The train ride from Atlanta to Macon had been miserable. The rails themselves had clearly been in bad need of repair, for the trip had been so full of jolts and near-derailments that the nerves of many of the officers in the boxcars had been all but shattered. It stood in stark contrast to the comparatively smooth and easy journeys they had all enjoyed on Northern railroads. There had been next to no ventilation in the boxcars and the men had suffered brutally in the stifling heat.

The train on which Thomas had traveled had frequently been pushed to the sidings. Trying to see what he could through tiny cracks between the boards, he had observed several trains traveling north on the tracks toward Atlanta from Macon. One of them had been carrying a battery of artillery. The idea that the rebel army defending Atlanta was being strengthened made Thomas furious and also increased his feeling of powerlessness.

By the time the train carrying Thomas had arrived in Macon, two of the prisoners in it had died, one lieutenant and one captain. According to the Southern doctor who had quickly examined their bodies, both had died of dehydration. Although the doctor himself had seemed conscientious about his work, the rebel soldiers standing nearby had made mocking comments about the two dead men as they had carted their bodies away for burial. The other prisoners had looked on, helpless.

They had been held in a barn for a few days, with the rebels saying that they could not enter the camp itself until they had been properly processed. With undisguised schadenfreude, the guards explained that they were experiencing delays on account of the sheer numbers of Union officers that had been taken prisoner at Peachtree Creek. It had not been until that very morning that Thomas and his companions had finally been herded into the stockade of Camp Oglethorpe. Considering the stories of how smallpox and cholera swept through the camp with grim regularity, many wondered if they would ever get out alive.

Gibbs unenthusiastically told them other necessary details about the camp, including where they were to draw their rations. He warned them against going too close to the stockade, as the militiamen serving as guards had orders to shoot men who came too close. After a few minutes, he took his leave. Thomas was pleased to see the man go, as he had been insufferably arrogant.

Thomas was soon swarmed by other prisoners, all asking for details about how he had been captured. Many had been captured during the previous year, including several who had fallen into rebel hands at Chancellorsville, Gettysburg and Chickamauga. These men were particularly desperate for news of the war, especially concerning the fates of friends and relatives who were also in uniform.

"George!" a familiar voice called.

Thomas turned to see General Truman Seymour. For the first time in many days, a smile crossed his face. When Thomas had been a cavalry and artillery instructor at West Point during the early 1850s, Seymour had been a professor of drawing. Thomas quickly recalled many nights of good conversation over good wine at the Seymour household. According to the newspaper accounts Thomas had read, Seymour had been taken prisoner by Lee's men during the Battle of the Wilderness, three months earlier.

"They got you, too, did they?" Seymour said, mixing bitterness with a good natured attempt at humor.

"Afraid so. Not just me, but practically my whole army." He spent the next few minutes describing the debacle at Peachtree Creek.

"Dear God," Seymour said when Thomas finished.

Thomas shook his head. "I am ashamed, I don't mind saying."

"Don't be so glum," Seymour said. "Even good generals lose battles. When I commanded our forces in eastern Florida, the rebels beat me badly at the Battle of Olustee. I lost nearly a quarter of my army and we had to run helter-skelter back to Jacksonville with our tails between their legs."

"I heard," Thomas said. "But Peachtree Creek was a defeat of such magnitude that the outcome of the war may turn on it. The South has always looked on me as a traitor and now the North will look on me as a fool."

"No," Seymour said firmly. "Your friends know better. In any case, we have more important things to worry about."

"Like what?"

Seymour grinned. "Like getting out of this damn place."

*   *   *   *   *

August 2, Morning

Manton Marble had expected the trip to be a waste of time and had not really wanted to go. However, the telegram he had received was so intriguing, and the conversation thus far was so revealing, that even the endless hours on the train to Cincinnati now seemed well worth it.

"So, you're saying he's really crazy? Not just as an exaggeration, but genuinely insane?"

Across the table in the middle of the hotel room, nursing a larger-than-average glass of whiskey, General Joseph Hooker nodded sternly. "No doubt about it. I think Sherman is genuinely out of his mind. It would be better for him to be incarcerated at Bedlam than for him to remain in command of our armies in the West. The man's mental state is such that he is not fit to lead a company of infantry, let alone three entire armies."

Marble was already imagining the headlines the *New York World* could run with the information Hooker was passing on to him. Certainly, people would say that Hooker was obviously not an objective and reliable source, but the people who bought his newspapers wouldn't care and it would further solidify the opposition to the Lincoln administration.

He let out an exasperated sharp breath. "So, Lincoln literally chose a madman for the second most important military position in the country?"

"That's about the size of it, Mr. Marble," Hooker replied.

"I remember reading the stories about his mental instability back in late 1861. I believe it was a newspaper of this very city, the *Cincinnati Commercial*, which used the word 'insane' to describe him. I reserved judgment then, but I am listening with great attention to what you are saying. Please go on."

Hooker took a sip of whiskey before he spoke. "The man talks to himself, all the time. His staffers are embarrassed by it when a high-ranking subordinate overhears it. He babbles on and on, endlessly, usually making no sense. Even his written orders often seem utterly incoherent."

"How did the campaign progress at all, then?"

"By fits and starts. More by luck than anything else. We could have crushed Johnston's entire army at Snake Creek Gap, in the very first days of the campaign, had Sherman's mental incompetence not gotten in the way of things. And it was his insanity that led us into the trap at Peachtree Creek. The man's crazy, sure as hell."

As Hooker continued to describe additional episodes demonstrating Sherman's insanity, Marble jotted down notes on a small pad. He hadn't asked Hooker's permission to do so when the conversation had begun, but the general had raised no objection. And since Hooker had been the one to initiate the meeting, it was obvious that he wanted the views he was expressing to find their way into the press. The *New York World* was certainly the best-positioned paper to do so.

"Who can corroborate this?"

Hooker shrugged. "The only general in the West who had a mind of his own was General Thomas, who I imagine is now in some godforsaken prison camp. All the others owe their positions to Grant and Sherman. I doubt any of them would be willing to say anything critical about Sherman publicly, as it would cost them their positions."

"I've heard people say that the officers of the Army of the Tennessee, the ones who served under Grant and Sherman at Shiloh and Vicksburg, have basically taken over the whole army. That the men of the Army of the Cumberland have essentially been sidelined."

"It's true," Hooker said with conviction. "Look how Sherman was promoted over both Thomas and myself to command the combined Western armies, despite the fact that we both outrank him. It's really shocking, when you think about it. Completely unjustified and unfair."

Marble jotted all this down, thinking about what great copy it was going to make. The Lincoln administration had long been under fire for its management of the war effort. The massive casualties of Grant's operations in Virginia, combined with the disastrous defeat of Sherman at Peachtree Creek, had raised these voices to a fever pitch. Once the *New York World* ran the exclusive story about Sherman being genuinely insane, the political pillars shoring up the administration would be one step closer to crumbling.

"Tell me, General Hooker. What caused our defeat at Peachtree Creek?"

"Sherman got careless and overconfident. As usual, he had the Army of the Cumberland doing his dirty work by advancing on Atlanta from the north, while his beloved Army of the Tennessee was gallivanting off to the east of the city, much too far away to come to our support when the rebels attacked."

Marble jotted this down. It seemed inappropriate to question Hooker on his own handling of the troops, as that didn't fit into the narrative Marble was already envisioning.

"Do you think that Sherman's mental instability contributed to the defeat?"

"Oh, absolutely. As far as I can tell, it was the main cause of the disaster."

Marble nodded and kept writing. Without asking, he poured Hooker another glass of whiskey.

The interview, Marble soon learned, had only just begun. Hooker was a typical blowhard and he went on for quite some time. The more whiskey Marble poured for him, the more animated the general became. Juicy bits of information concerning Sherman's lack of mental stability, Grant's favoritism and pandering, Lincoln's utter mismanagement, and a whole host of other subjects flew from Hooker's mouth in a torrent of words.

"What is your opinion on the current presidential election?" Marble asked at one point.

"Lincoln and McClellan can both go to the devil, for all I care. My horse could manage the war effort better than Lincoln. As for McClellan, the less said about him, the better. I could have won the war at the Battle of Antietam single-handedly if McClellan hadn't been such a blundering idiot."

Eventually, after nearly three hours of conversation, Hooker was virtually asleep in his chair. Leaving him there, Marble got up and quietly left the room. In his notebooks, he was sure, was enough journalistic ammunition to inflict a devastating blow against Lincoln's chances for reelection.

*   *   *   *   *

August 3, Morning

"You can't be sure that it was him," Collett said, trying to sound reassuring.

McFadden, sitting on the edge of his cot, shook his head forcefully. "I saw his face. I heard his voice. It was Cheeky Joe, no doubt."

"I was there, too, you know," Collett said. "It was dark and confusing. There was lots of noise, men shouting and fires burning. The man you saw was fifty yards away at least, moving away from the light of the fires. Honestly, Lieutenant, you might have been mistaken."

McFadden wanted to believe his commander was right. With Collett having seen him temporarily lose control on the banks of the Chattahoochee, McFadden had decided to tell him the whole story. Having already told Annie, it was somehow easier to tell a second person. Moreover, there was a new level of trust between him and Collett, now that they were both officers.

Was it possible that Collett was right and that he had honestly been mistaken? Could the man he had seen in the pontoon boat have been someone other than Cheeky Joe? Collett was correct when he said that the scene had been dark, noisy and confusing. Could his memories of that nightmarish day in the desert have been twisted by the torment he had endured? Could he honestly trust his own senses?

But his face had been unmistakable. Although it had been years since he had seen Cheeky Joe, his face had been so deeply burned into McFadden's mind that he was sure he could not have forgotten it. No, he was certain that the man he had seen on the river was the same man who had brutally tortured him and his brother before killing his brother and leaving him for dead. While his rational mind might have its doubts, another part of his mind had never been more certain of anything.

"I don't suppose you might put it out of your mind for the time being?" Collett suggested. "We have an inspection tomorrow, you know. I'm going to need your companies looking their best, because I'd rather be sent to the Yankee prison at Point Lookout than leave General Cleburne disappointed."

McFadden forced a smile. "Of course, sir."

"You'll give me your report on the engagement on the bank of the river when you get a chance?"

"I should have it finished by the end of the day, sir."

"No need to rush. Take it easy for the rest of the day, James. The last few weeks have been a chaotic time for you, what with your promotion, all the hubbub about capturing Thomas, all the stuff with your lady friend. Maybe you just need to rest."

"I'm all right, sir."

"Well, consider it an order. Take a rest. Write another letter to Miss Turnbow. Read more in that book her father lent you about the Russian fellow."

"Kosciuszko was Polish, sir."

Collett held his hands up helplessly. He could not have told a Pole from an Indian. Without another word, he turned and left the tent, leaving McFadden alone.

McFadden turned and lay down on the cot, his hands already fumbling for the Kosciuszko biography. He had begun reading it just before the Battle of Peachtree Creek and, rather to his surprise, had found it very interesting. Perhaps if he could lose himself in the pages of the book, he could push Cheeky Joe, or whoever the man on the river had been, out of his mind.

Poring over his father's library as a young man, McFadden had read Plutarch's *Lives of the Noble Greeks and Romans* over and over again, imagining countless adventures with Alexander the Great, Julius Caesar, and other great men of the ancient world. He had also read his father's biographies of Napoleon Bonaparte and the Duke of Wellington and several books on the heroes of the American Revolution. These men had been the heroes of his boyhood, riding alongside him in his dreams.

As he plunged into the life of Thaddeus Kosciuszko, he felt the same exhilaration he had experienced as a child reading about the lives of his heroes, learning their stories for the very first time. As McFadden had read, Kosciuszko had left his native Poland and come to fight alongside George Washington during the American Revolution after having been inspired by the words of the Declaration of Independence. McFadden found him particularly interesting because, unlike Alexander, Caesar, or Napoleon, he fought not for his own glory but rather for the pure ideal of liberty. In doing so, Thaddeus Kosciuszko achieved a glory greater than that won by any combination of kings or emperors.

He was grateful to Robert Turnbow for giving him this book, but he could not deny that it made him somewhat uneasy. He weighed his own struggle and that of his comrades against that of Kosciuszko and found it wanting. After all, any man worth his salt would take up arms to defend his home and family from hostile invaders. But what kind of man would abandon the comforts of his own hearth and home and travel to a distant land to fight for the freedom of others?

McFadden was able to read perhaps thirty more pages, carrying the story through Kosciuszko's participation in the Battle of Saratoga, before he found his attention being drawn back to the image of Cheeky Joe on a boat, escaping across the Chattahoochee. He struggled for a few minutes to get into the book, but could not.

He set the book down and picked up the last letter he had received from Annie. She had written it three days before and it had arrived the previous day. Their correspondence had developed to the point where they were exchanging two or three letters a week. The fact that they were only a few miles apart made writing to one another fairly easy. Some of the other Texans in the regiment were beginning to express, in a good-humored manner, a certain jealousy about McFadden receiving so many letters.

Their relationship was growing. Annie had come up to visit the regiment three times now and she had written of her intention to come for a visit the next day. On each occasion, she had brought much-appreciated fresh produce from the mysterious slave named Ponder. The 7th Texas had begun sharing some of their bounty with the other units in the brigade, so as not to create too much resentment.

The letters that crossed between them were becoming deeper and more meaningful. They continued to discuss their favorite literature. Annie had asked McFadden about Scotland and what he knew about the country's history. She had also asked him, in an oddly forward manner, what he intended to do after the war was over. He had had trouble crafting a proper response to this question, for he himself did not know the answer to it.

Try as he might, though, McFadden could not focus on Annie's letters. He could not focus on anything, in fact, except the face of the man in that rowboat on the river. What if McFadden was right and it had been Cheeky Joe? The wounded Union soldier nearby had told him that the unit they had driven off had been the 118th Ohio. Like every other regiment in Sherman's army, they were now safely back on the north bank of the Chattahoochee River. Wherever his enemy was, he was beyond McFadden's reach.

He didn't want to think about Cheeky Joe. For more than two years, the man had stalked his dreams. Then Annie Turnbow had begun to relight a different kind of fire inside of him, a fire that promised to lift him up into a bright and happy future, rather than drag him down into the dark regions of terror and revenge.

He laid down on his cot. Perhaps a nap would do him good. He began to think that Major Collett had been wrong in asking him to take some time to rest. Had he been busy with his new duties as one of the regimental officers, it would have been easier to turn his mind away from Cheeky Joe. After all, Annie was supposed to be coming up for another visit soon, this time accompanied by her father. It would not do for McFadden to be distracted by what, in all probability, had just been a case of mistaken identity.

But try though he might, McFadden would not fall asleep, nor could he convince himself that he had mistaken the man's identity. Not for a single minute.

*   *   *   *   *

August 3, Evening

Hood stared unhappily down at the desk in front of him. He had finished three letters in the past three hours and was now about to begin a fourth. Writing was always uncomfortable for him, as his useless left arm was unable to hold the paper down. Still, he had learned to manage.

He noted that the sunlight coming through the window was beginning to fade. Glancing about, he saw only three candles in his room. Irritated, he pounded on the wall in front of him. A few moments later, the door was opened by a lieutenant, one of the two staff officers traveling with him.

"Yes, sir?" the man asked.

"This miserable excuse for a hotel has provided me with only three candles. Kindly ask the owner for more."

"At once, sir." The man saluted and was gone.

Hood shook his head. He was not much impressed with the town of Opelika, Alabama, just over the border from Georgia, and the hotel in which he was staying also seemed a model of mediocrity. But at least they had provided him with a decent bottle of Tennessee whiskey, which had helped him with his writing.

He looked down at the three letters he had already finished. The first had been to General Bragg, who had gone down to Mobile to inspect the coastal fortifications there. Although the bulk of the letter was a rather dry description of the progress and anticipated future course of Hood's journey to the Trans-Mississippi, the letter had ended with a suggestion that Bragg and Hood might meet before the former returned to Richmond and the latter had moved on to the west.

Obviously, Bragg would see that the last portion of the letter was what the letter was actually about. Hood needed to discuss matters with Bragg, for he wanted to discover why he had not been appointed to replace Johnston. It had seemed clear to Hood that this had been the plan on which they had agreed during their meeting outside Atlanta. Any hope of becoming the commander of the Army of Tennessee was clearly now at an end, but Hood felt he deserved a proper explanation from Bragg.

The second letter had been to President Davis, in which Hood had described his vision of a campaign in the Trans-Mississippi. General Kirby Smith was the overall Confederate commander west of the Mississippi River, but it was Hood's understanding that he would be placed in command of the troops in Arkansas. Hood's suggestion was for a large force of Confederate cavalry to raid into Missouri while a force of Texas infantry, under his own command, launched an offensive to recapture Little Rock. With Union forces likely to be diminished by the need to reinforce Sherman in Georgia, such an offensive had a chance of success.

He knew that President Davis was not entirely pleased with Smith's performance in the Trans-Mississippi. The thought had already entered Hood's mind that, having failed to obtain command of the Army of Tennessee, he might now aspire to command in the far west. It was worth thinking about, in any event. Whatever happened, Hood felt some satisfaction at moving closer to Texas, his adopted state.

The only drawback to his current plan was that it was taking him farther away from Sally Preston. The third letter he had written, which he had actually begun on the train the day before, had been addressed to her. Of course, he could not openly describe to her the machinations he had attempted to get Johnston removed from command and have himself appointed in his place. Nevertheless, the simple act of writing to her acted as a tonic to his disappointment, smoothing over the turmoil that his spirit was having to endure.

He had sacrificed his honor as a Southern gentlemen in undermining Johnston's command. The letters he had written to Bragg and Davis criticizing Johnston's leadership had been sordid and ignoble. He knew that. Even worse, he had botched the attack at Cassville when it had had a chance of success. He had done it again at New Hope Church a few weeks later. He had advocated retreat from defensive positions he suspected could have been held. If he were being honest with himself, John Bell Hood had to admit that he had jeopardized the success of the Army of Tennessee and potentially the very survival of the Confederacy in his quest to obtain high command and military glory for himself.

The letter he had written to Sally had described his request for a transfer to the west as a routine matter. In fact, he had suggested that General Smith had asked for his presence on the other side of the river, though this was as false as many of the other claims he had made in his recent letters.

He was about to begin his fourth letter of the day, addressed to Senator Benjamin Hill and requesting him to describe his recollection of the meeting of the Army of Tennessee high command on July 1, when there was a knock on the door.

"Yes?" Hood said, more loudly than necessary.

The door opened and the lieutenant appeared, bearing a dozen or so candles.

"Here you are, sir," he said, placing them carefully on the side of the desk.

"Thank you," Hood said, anxious for the man to depart.

"And this came for you, sir," the officer said, handing Hood an envelope.

He took the envelope and wordlessly waved the man away. He left the room and shut the door seconds later. Hood tore open the envelope, finding two smaller envelopes inside as well as a single letter. He quickly opened the letter and began reading.

General Hood,

I have received your two most recent letters addressed to my daughter. These two letters are hereby respectfully returned unopened. Please be advised that any letters I receive from you addressed to my daughter in the future shall likewise be returned to you unopened. I thank you for the attention you have paid to my daughter up to this point, but it is no longer welcome.

Sincerely,

John Preston

Hood did not need to read the letter twice to see in an instant that whatever hopes he had entertained of making Sally his wife had been utterly destroyed. He had to restrain himself from bellowing out in rage. He stood as best he could, grabbing his crutch and clambering back and forth across the short length of the room, clutching the letter in his hand and crumpling it into a tight wad.

He went back to the desk and grabbed the bottle of whiskey, quickly pouring himself a large glass. He unfolded the letter and read through it one more time, desperately trying to see if there was some word or phrase he had missed which might give him some sort of hope. But he knew there was none. Sally's father had spoken decisively and unambiguously.

After taking a large swig, Hood slammed the glass down onto the desk and clutched his hair, his face curling into a mask of wrath. In the innermost recesses of his mind, he knew that Sally shared the elitist prejudices of her parents. That glaring fact was what had driven him to seek command of the Army of Tennessee in the first place.

He thought of her face, her sparkling eyes, her flowing hair. For just a moment, he imagined how her comely body would have felt when he would finally have been able to take her to his bed. He thought of her laugh, and how impressed all the aristocrats in Richmond would have been had he arrived at their stuffy dinner parties with her on his arm. No one would ever have spoken of John Bell Hood in a mocking manner again.

That dream was now dead.

Hood threw his whiskey glass against the wall, where it shattered violently. Fortunately, there was another glass on the desk, so Hood was able to quickly pour himself another drink. He had a feeling he would need many more before the night was over. He might even have to send one of his staff officers to obtain another bottle before too much longer.

Hood's mind fixated on Joseph Johnston as the cause of all his pain and fury. The mental image of the puffed-up, arrogant, disdainful man, riding about on his horse as though he were Robert E. Lee, made Hood furious. Had Johnston been standing before him at that moment, Hood would simply have pulled his revolver out and shot the man down like the dog he was.

Somehow, Johnston had discovered that Hood had been writing to Bragg and Davis behind his back. Hood was determined to find out how that happened and who was responsible. It should have been no business of Johnston's that he was writing letters to the President and his military advisor. Besides, if Johnston had adopted a manly military posture from the beginning of the campaign, those letters would not have been necessary. Johnston really had no one to blame but himself, as far as Hood was concerned.

Hood had been seen as the most daring and aggressive commander in the Army of Tennessee, if not the whole Confederacy. Yet when he had finally turned to attack the Yankee hordes threatening Atlanta, Johnston had pushed Hood out of the action entirely, positioning him out on the right flank where there had been no action. The plaudits had been won by Hardee, Stewart, Cleburne and Cheatham, with nothing but the dregs left for poor John Bell Hood to gather. He had no doubt that Johnston had kept him out of the fight purely as an act of retribution. That was something no honorable man could forget or forgive.

Hood was certain of one thing. Joseph Johnston would pay. And Hood already knew which instrument of vengeance he would use.

*   *   *   *   *

August 4, Morning

"General Forrest, the blockhouse is waving a white flag."

Forrest laughed with disdain. It seemed that the men Sherman had detailed to guard his railroads in Tennessee were mostly militiamen of the type mustered into service for a mere hundred days and sent down by the governors of the individual northern states. Had he been up against hardened veterans, Forrest would have expected a better fight, but he figured that all seasoned troops had been sent down into Georgia to reinforce Sherman.

"Good," Forrest told the staff officer, who bore the rather unfortunate name of Major J. P. Strange. "Have the men cease fire, then send over a reliable man to again demand that the Yankees surrender. If they balk, tell them to send a man to talk to me directly."

"Yes, sir." Strange saluted and rode off to carry out his orders.

Forrest thought the whole display was pathetic. The much-vaunted blockhouses had proven to be, if not exactly paper tigers, at least highly overrated. They had proven vulnerable to the four twelve-pounder artillery pieces he had brought with his raiding force. The moment he had appeared with a thousand men, the troops guarding the railroad bridge had retreated inside the blockhouse to wait for reinforcements. In response, he had simply had his artillery officer set up position at a convenient location and start pummeling the blockhouse with twelve-pound shells. He had plenty of ammunition, and eventually the walls of the blockhouse had been crumpled like matchsticks under the remorseless fire of his guns.

Ostensibly, the blockhouse was only supposed to protect the garrison of this particular railroad bridge until reinforcements arrived to drive away any Confederate raiding force. Forrest had thousands of his troopers swarming the surrounding twenty or thirty miles of territory, spreading confusion and havoc in all directions. If any large Union force was in the region, it would have little idea where to go or what to do.

He sat on his immense horse, King Philip, and waited. Studying the blockhouse with his field glasses, he could see that it had been reduced to a wreck, with so many gaping holes in its walls that the Yankee soldiers trapped inside were completely at his mercy. If he ordered his cannon to resume firing, they would all be killed in a matter of minutes.

Forrest raised his field glasses above the blockhouse and gazed for a time at his target: the Central Alabama Railroad bridge over the Duck River just north of the town of Columbia, Tennessee. It was an important link in Sherman's supply line and destroying it would certainly strike a blow for the Confederacy.

He closed his eyes for just a moment, quickly thinking over the entire situation. The greatest Union supply base in the entire Western theater of war was at Nashville, which was protected by immense fortifications and a substantial garrison. It was impregnable, and enough food, fodder, and supplies had been accumulated there to provide for Sherman's army for many months. He couldn't capture the city, and riding into Kentucky to break the railroad north of Nashville would do no immediate good.

If any useful damage was to be done to Sherman's supply line, it would have to be done south of Nashville. Between Nashville and Chattanooga, the second biggest Union supply depot in the West, ran two different railroads. Breaking one of them would be a significant achievement, but so long as the other railroad remained in operation, their task would be incomplete. Considering how quickly Union construction crews would be able to repair the damage Forrest and his men could do, being able to break both lines and keep them broken seemed unlikely.

As he was enmeshed in these thoughts, Major Strange rode up to him, with a Union officer clinging to him on the back of the horse. The two men dismounted, but Forrest remained on King Philip. He raised his hand in a salute to the Union officer, whose uniform indicated the rank of major.

"Major," he said simply. "I am Nathan Bedford Forrest."

The Yankee major saluted. "Major George Foster. I am the commander of the blockhouse." His tone betrayed apprehension, but not fear.

"In that case, I demand your immediate and unconditional surrender."

"I am prepared to discuss terms, General. My men are colored soldiers. I would like your assurance that they will be treated properly as prisoners-of-war in accordance with the accepted rules of warfare."

Inwardly, Forrest grinned. The killings at Fort Pillow had been a nasty business, but as far as Forrest was concerned their impact had been quite beneficial. His men had gotten out of hand and had slaughtered over a hundred black Union soldiers, either while they were trying to surrender or immediately afterward. Major Foster was clearly concerned that the same fate would now befall the men under his command.

"I repeat that you must immediately and unconditionally surrender. If you don't, I will have my guns start firing again. You have no protection. If you don't surrender, all of your men will surely die. And yourself as well."

"I have no more desire to die than anyone else, General Forrest. But I know what happened to the garrison at Fort Pillow. If I am to die, I would rather go down fighting than being slaughtered like an animal. I'm sure my men feel the same way."

Forrest generally considered white officers in command of black troops to be little better than pond scum, but he had to admit that Major Foster was a brave man.

"There are no terms to discuss, Major. Either you surrender immediately and unconditionally, or my gunners will resume firing. If I do resume my attack, no mercy will be shown to you or your men. I'll give you five minutes to make up your mind."

The five minutes must have seemed endless to Major Foster. Forrest simply sat on his horse and gazed down at the shattered blockhouse.

Forrest took out his pocket watch, checked the time, and put it back. "Time's up. What's it going to be?"

"You leave me little choice, General Forrest. I therefore surrender my command."

Forrest smiled. "Major Strange, take down the names of all white officers and men for proper processing."

"And my colored soldiers?" Foster asked anxiously.

"For now, I'll put them to work tearing up the railroad south of town."

"If they are to be considered prisoners of war, then the commonly accepted rules of warfare prohibit their being used for unpaid manual labor."

Forrest laughed at that. "Almost all of them are escaped slaves and have no right to be considered genuine prisoners of war. You're lucky I don't simply give my men permission to kill them."

Forrest honestly didn't know what he would do with the soldiers. He couldn't simply have them killed in cold blood, because the blockhouse had willingly surrendered before being stormed. Ordinarily, he would detail an escort to take them south and try to locate their owners so that they could be returned to the plantations. They were, after all, valuable property. But Forrest didn't want to weaken his raiding party. Had they been white soldiers, he would simply have paroled them, releasing them by having them sign a pledge not to take up arms against the Confederacy. However, to do that with black prisoners would be an acknowledgment that they were on equal footing with white troops and that was an idea to which Forrest could never subscribe.

Forrest, along with Major Strange and Major Foster, walked down to the blockhouse, where Foster announced the surrender to his men. A few minutes later, a line of Confederate troops had formed up outside, their guns at the ready as they glowered menacingly at the black soldiers as they walked out in a single-file line. Unsurprisingly, the prisoners looked somewhat bewildered and many were frightened that they would be shot down at any moment. Others, however, looked more angry than anything else. Perhaps they had disagreed with Foster's decision to surrender.

A few of the Confederates pilfered the blockhouse, but there was nothing of any value inside. The black troops were made to remove their shoes and turn out their pockets for any valuables. Then, with angry voices, the Confederate guard ordered them to march off to the south, where they would soon be put to work destroying the railroad tracks.

After the blockhouse had been cleared, Forrest rode to the bridge over the Duck River. The waterway wasn't huge, but it was certainly big enough to be a formidable natural barrier. Once the bridge was gone, it wouldn't be quick or easy for Yankee engineers to build a replacement. It would also require an expenditure of significant resources.

Forrest was happy to see that some of his more enterprising officers hadn't bothered to wait for orders, but were already hard at work on the demolition of the bridge. Men were carrying kindling and dumping it onto the bridge, mostly planks and fence-posts taken from the town. Others were soaking bunches of cotton in turpentine and stuffing them into the kindling all along the bridge's length. Beneath the structure on the riverbank, men were hacking away at the support beams, weakening them so as to increase the odds of a complete collapse when they set the bridge on fire.

He watched his men go about their work, rarely calling out any orders. His command was a well-oiled machine when it came to this kind of work, for Forrest and his men had been burning bridges and wrecking train tracks since the opening days of the war.

After an hour, all was ready. He gave the order, and one of his men tossed a torch onto the nearest bunch of cotton. It ignited immediately, and with astonishing speed a trail of fire seemed to shoot across the bridge like a phantom train. The kindling went up at once, and within minutes the wooden rail ties beneath it were also aflame. As a manifestation of destruction, it was darkly beautiful.

He had details of men standing by with buckets of water, to ensure that the flames did not spread to the homes of Columbia itself, but it turned out that there was no need for them. Less than thirty minutes after the torch had been tossed onto it, the Duck River Bridge of the Central Alabama Railroad collapsed into the river, to the cheers of Forrest's men.

*   *   *   *   *

August 4, Evening

"Two thousand?" Johnston asked, incredulous. "In just the past two weeks?"

"Yes, sir," Mackall said happily. "It seems that news of Peachtree Creek, along with your announcement of a general amnesty, has persuaded many deserters to return to the colors."

Johnston nodded sharply, anxious not to appear too satisfied. "Please prepare a circular for distribution to all regimental commanders, stating that they are not to mistreat returned deserters in any way. My offer of amnesty meant exactly what it said."

"I shall have the circular drawn up at once, sir."

Johnston nodded again. It would not be completely effective, of course. There would be many regimental commanders who would go out of their way to give returned deserters unpleasant tasks. In combat, many captains and majors might think less of placing returned deserters in positions of danger than they would other men. But if the deserters were willing to return to the colors and endure the scorn of their comrades, Johnston would give them a chance to prove themselves worthy of his trust. He hoped his officers would do the same.

The return of so many deserters was enough on its own to bring a smile to Johnston's face, but his recent success on the battlefield had also resulted in increased enlistment of Georgia militiamen. Seven thousand of those old men and young boys now manned the defenses of Atlanta and vital points along the railroads that webbed out from the city. Although they would not have been much use in a stand-up fight, they could at least protect strongly fortified posts and thereby free up veteran troops for use against Sherman. They were also useful in guarding the vast number of Union prisoners.

Further bolstering the Army of Tennessee was the arrival of a brigade of reinforcements made up of regiments which had been serving in the coastal regions of Florida and Georgia. Taken together, all of this had boosted the strength of the army to roughly sixty thousand men.

Johnston still wasn't satisfied. Determined to increase the strength of his army by any means possible, Johnston had also dispatched some of the Georgia militia units to scour the plantations south of Atlanta and bring back as many able-bodied slaves as possible. He intended to put these black men to work digging fortifications, serving as cooks and teamsters, and performing other menial tasks. The white men thus relieved could be added to the muster rolls of the infantry regiments.

Johnston thought this move was only common sense, but he knew that many politicians in the Confederacy would be uncomfortable with it. They saw it as the beginning of a slippery slope toward enlisting slaves directly into the army as combat soldiers, which could only be done if they were promised their freedom. He smiled, wondering what those politicians would have thought had they known about General Cleburne's radical proposal to do just that.

"Has there been any word from our friends across the river?" Johnston asked Mackall.

Mackall chuckled slightly. "They seem to be completely inert, according to the latest information we have from General Jackson." Since Wheeler had vanished into north Georgia with four thousand troopers on his mission to disrupt Sherman's supplies, command of the cavalry of the Army of Tennessee had fallen to General William Jackson, the senior officer among the remaining cavalry divisions.

"Have we hurt Sherman that badly?" Johnston asked, mostly to himself. "It's been more than two weeks since the Battle of Peachtree Creek, yet our enemies still seem unable or unwilling to take action."

"Perhaps our cavalry is succeeding in their attacks on the enemy supply line?" Mackall offered. "If Sherman is worried about food and ammunition, he certainly would not likely want to risk mounting any major operation against us."

"Possibly. But I expect any attack on our enemy's supply lines to require time to take effect, even if it is completely successful. Sherman has built up large supply depots at Allatoona and other locations south of Chattanooga and can draw on them for sustenance for some time after his lines are cut. It's a mystery, William. It's as if we're dealing with a different man now than we were before Peachtree Creek."

*   *   *   *   *

Sherman was finding the words coming out of Oliver Howard's mouth to be increasingly annoying. Indeed, the constant stream of bad news was causing Sherman to wonder whether he might have made a mistake in appointing Howard to the command of the Army of the Cumberland after all.

"Surely it's not that bad, General Howard."

"I'm afraid it is that bad, General Sherman. At least a hundred men deserted from the Army of the Cumberland in just the last twenty-four hours. That brings the total for the last week to nearly a thousand men. The morale of the men has not recovered from their defeat at Peachtree Creek and the retreat across the river has only made the situation worse."

"The decision to retreat across the river was taken by me, General Howard," Sherman said sharply. "If I desire your opinion as to the wisdom of my decision, I shall ask for it."

Howard, stung by such uncharacteristically unfair criticism from Sherman, glanced for support over to McPherson and Schofield, who tensely stared down at the floor and refused to meet the eyes of either man.

The scene within the headquarters was tense. Sherman remained seated behind a table strewn with maps, while his three senior commanders stood on the other side, holding their hats like penitent men come to seek the blessing of the local bishop. All around them, staff officers pretended that they were not listening to the conference.

Sherman looked at McPherson. "I trust, at least, that the brave men of the Army of the Tennessee are remaining true and steadfast, as opposed to the shaky men of the Army of the Cumberland?"

"Desertions have increased among my forces as well," McPherson said in as neutral a tone as he could manage.

"Have they?"

"Yes, they have. We might as well face facts. Desertions have been on the rise in all three of our armies since the disaster at Peachtree Creek. The news of the defeats in Virginia are only making the situation worse. Our boys don't have the stomach to keep fighting in a war they are increasingly convinced is simply not winnable."

"Well then, firm measures must be taken to clamp down on desertions. I want ten captured deserters from the Army of the Cumberland, and five each from the other two armies, to be tried by court martial and, if found guilty, executed by firing squad. Make sure that brigades are called out on parade to witness the executions themselves. I will also prohibit the further distribution of newspapers, as they only contain bad news these days."

The three army commanders glanced at one another in considerable discomfort. Schofield was the one with the courage to speak up first. "General Sherman, are you sure that is wise? Such draconian measures might further inflame the situation and actually increase the number of desertions."

"As I said to General Howard a few minutes ago, if I desire your opinion on my orders, I shall ask for it."

"But it's not just the issue of desertions, General Sherman," McPherson said. "Many of our regiments are coming to the end of their enlistments. They signed up in 1861 to serve for three years and those three years are up. A lot of these units are simply leaving the morning the terms of their enlistments are up and there's not a damn thing we can do to stop them. Morale being what it is, these men are not reenlisting."

"General Sherman," Howard said with great graveness. "Our losses at Peachtree Creek, combined with the increase in desertions and the expiration of the enlistments of so many of our regiments, have reduced our total force to roughly seventy-five thousand men. We can only expect that further desertion and the expiration of enlistments will continue to weaken our forces in the weeks to come."

These words seemed to cast a cloud over the meeting. No one needed to be reminded that the Union host which had swarmed over the Chattahoochee River a month before had numbered well over a hundred thousand men. Nor did anyone need to be reminded they now had scarcely any numerical advantage over the rebels. The idea that they might cross the river once again, defeat Johnston's army, and blast their way through Atlanta's formidable defenses before the election in November seemed utterly impossible.

Sherman looked back at them sternly. "General Grant has ordered the Sixth Corps transferred from Virginia to Georgia. Its lead brigades have already arrived in Nashville. When they arrive here, they shall add between ten and fifteen thousand bayonets to our force."

"I should have liked more than a single corps sent to us," McPherson said. "As it is, fifteen thousand men will not make good the losses we have sustained."

"You think I don't know that?" Sherman snapped.

A courier from the telegraph tent arrived. "I'm sorry, excuse me, sirs. But these messages have just arrived."

Sherman impatiently gestured for the lieutenant to hand him the two telegrams, which he quickly read through. The three army commanders stood quietly for a time, waiting to hear whatever the news was.

"Well, it seems that a rebel raiding force has destroyed the bridge over the Duck River at Columbia, Tennessee."

"What about the garrison?" Schofield asked.

"They surrendered to the raiding force."

"That sounds like Forrest," McPherson said.

"If it is Forrest, God help the black troops who made up the garrison," Howard said. "If he has had those men killed in the same manner that he had the garrison at Fort Pillow killed, he will yet again demonstrate that he is a despiser of God and all true Christian virtues."

Sherman reflected with some amusement that Howard intended for his comment to be taken literally, as he was by far the most religious officer in the Union army. Sherman, himself a freethinker despite the agony it caused his devoutly Catholic wife, thought such statements of piety to be mildly ridiculous. He didn't care, though, so long as Howard carried out his orders with reasonable efficiency.

"So, Forrest is on the loose against our railroads in Tennessee?" Schofield asked, despondent.

"It gets worse," Sherman said, holding up the second telegram. "Reports from our outposts and garrisons along the Western and Atlantic Railroad through northern Georgia are saying that small rebel bands have been firing on trains coming south from Chattanooga, that several of our blockhouses have been attacked and a few miles of railroad torn up near Resaca and Dalton."

"That makes no sense," Schofield said. "Forrest cannot be in both Tennessee and Georgia. Even he can only be in one place at one time."

"It's very simple, gentlemen," Sherman said. "We have two raids underway against us. Forrest is attacking our supply lines in Tennessee, while Wheeler attacks them here in Georgia with the cavalry of the Army of Tennessee itself."

"My God," McPherson said. "Forrest and Wheeler? A single raid is a serious enough problem on its own, but two simultaneous raids represent a mortal danger to this army. If they succeed, we shall be completely cut off from our sources of supply."

"They shall not succeed," Sherman said. "All along the railroad, stretching back to Louisville on the Ohio River, strongly fortified posts are guarding key points, as well as crews and equipment standing by to repair any breaks. If the rebels succeed in damaging the line, a break will only be temporary."

"But if both Forrest and Wheeler are on the loose in our rear areas, our resources might be stretched very thin, indeed," Schofield pointed out. "Many of the men guarding our supply lines have been called down to the front in order to replace the men we lost at Peachtree Creek."

"If needs be, we shall detach forces from the Sixth Corps as they arrive to shore up the defense of our supply lines."

"At the cost of reducing the strength of our reinforcements before they reach the front lines," McPherson pointed out.

"I am aware of that, General!" Sherman snapped. "Do you think I can just wave my hand and make more soldiers magically drop down from the sky? Not even President Lincoln can do that. General Howard here may believe in manna from heaven, but I do not."

The insult brought another awkward silence to the meeting.

Sherman exhaled sharply. "I know you are all tired. I know you are all frustrated. Return to your commands and carry out my orders regarding the need to clamp down on desertions. In the meantime, I shall prepare a plan for dispatching some of our cavalry northward to keep Wheeler off our railroad here in Georgia. Our forces in Tennessee are adequate to deal with Forrest, and can be reinforced by the arriving Sixth Corps if needs be."

Schofield and Howard muttered a farewell and departed. McPherson lingered just long enough to say something further.

"Cump? Are you all right?"

Sherman glared up at his friend. "Worry about yourself, James, and allow me to worry about myself."

McPherson nodded, saluted, and left, leaving Sherman alone in more ways than one.

*　　　　*　　　　*　　　　*　　　　*

"Gentlemen," President Davis said as he looked at the two men sitting across the desk from him. "I am almost reluctant to say it, but I believe that we are winning."

Secretary of State Benjamin nodded happily, while Secretary of War Seddon remained impassive. Judging by the look on the latter man's face, Davis concluded that Seddon was not feeling entirely well, a far from uncommon occurrence.

Davis went on, waving at the military map on the wall. "In just the last week, we defeated the Yankee attempt to blast through our lines with that mine at Petersburg and drove the last Yankee troops back to the north bank of the Chattahoochee River. Not only that, we have just received word from General Early that his men have made a successful raid on the Pennsylvania town of Chambersburg and have struck the Baltimore and Ohio Railroad at various points."

"We have, indeed, been showered with good news of late," Benjamin said. "Furthermore, judging by the Northern newspapers I have been perusing over the past few days, the domestic situation in the North should also give us cheer."

"How's that?" Seddon asked.

"The price of gold continues to rise in New York, indicating that inflation is continuing to bring economic pain to the Northern people. The value of the Yankee greenback has been badly hit by their recent military defeats. Opposition to the draft is still increasing, with many demonstrations in the big cities virtually turning into riots. The numbers of people going to hear Democratic orators denounce Lincoln continues to rise. Vallandigham spoke to a crowd of ten thousand in Philadelphia just a few days ago, if the *New York World* is to be believed."

Seddon nodded. "So long as Lee can maintain his lines at Petersburg and Johnston can maintain his position along the Chattahoochee River, I see no real prospect of a major defeat before the Northern presidential election."

"Very good," Davis said.

"Our spies indicate that many Yankee divisions, including some of those which were sent to protect Washington from Early last month, are being sent to Georgia to reinforce Sherman," Seddon said. "Might I suggest that we press upon General Early the need to continue launching raids into Maryland and Pennsylvania in order to ensure that as many Yankee troops as possible remain in the vicinity of Washington?"

"Of course. The more Yankee towns that receive the treatment of Chambersburg, the better."

"I shall send the telegram to him immediately upon my return to Mechanic's Hall." Mechanic's Hall was the building that housed the Confederate War Department.

"Have we heard anything from Forrest or Wheeler?" Davis asked.

"Nothing," Seddon replied. "General Johnston informed us a week ago when Wheeler set out for north Georgia, taking four thousand cavalry with him. I have heard nothing further from Johnston on the subject. Forrest, upon receiving his orders, immediately departed and has not yet sent back any word. It is as if they both disappeared."

"You cannot expect either of them to be in communication with us during their raids," Benjamin said. "But according to the Yankee papers, Forrest has already inflicted some damage on the railroads in central Tennessee."

"General Johnston is also requesting additional reinforcements." Seddon said sourly.

"Again?" Davis asked. "We already sent him the equivalent of a brigade from the Atlantic coast, did we not?"

"More than that, Mr. President. Four thousand men, more or less. We have also sent him additional heavy artillery from the coastal fortifications protecting Mobile, in order to reinforce the defenses of Atlanta. I do not see how we can spare any additional troops from other theaters in order to reinforce Johnston further."

"Send him a telegram to that effect, if you please. Tell him that we have already sent him all that we can spare. Considering the damage the Yankees have suffered, he should surely be able to deal with Sherman with the forces he already has."

Davis paused for a moment and rubbed his chin, thinking deeply. He glanced up at the map and stared hard. He turned back to Seddon.

"If these reports of Yankee reinforcements moving from Virginia to Georgia are true, how long would it take for them to arrive?"

Seddon shrugged. "When they sent reinforcements last year in the wake of our victory at Chickamauga, I believe it took them two or three weeks. I would assume that it will take them roughly the same amount of time now."

Davis nodded. "If Sherman has been so badly damaged, why cannot Johnston assume the offensive? If he could cross back to the north bank of the Chattahoochee, could he not flank Sherman out of his present position and force him back northwards toward Chattanooga?"

Seddon thought for a moment. "I am not sure. I suspect Johnston will say it is impossible, were we to ask him."

"If it we are to do it, it would obviously be best for us to attack before heavy Union reinforcements arrive."

Benjamin nodded. "A concession to common sense."

Davis looked back over to the map. "If we could regain our lost territory in northern Georgia, it would be yet another nail in the coffin of Lincoln's reelection chances. As has been the case with all our victories in recent months, it would increase the confidence of the people and the value of our currency. If Sherman has truly been as badly damaged as Johnston claims, it should be an easy matter to force him to retreat northwards." The President's voice became more animated the more he spoke.

"True enough," Benjamin said. "I cannot comment on the military aspects. If I were you, I would consult General Bragg."

"Bragg is not scheduled to return from his inspection trip for several more days, Mr. President," Seddon pointed out.

"Well, when he does, please tell him that I wish to meet with him at once. And as for Johnston's constant requests for additional reinforcements, I can only say that I am tired of all his complaining."

"I would let it slide," Benjamin suggested with a smile. "Keep in mind that when the war is brought to a successful conclusion you need not trouble yourself about him ever again. Indeed, when you eventually take leave of political life and have no more obligations or responsibilities, you can write your memoirs and skewer General Johnston to death for all the public to see. Senator Wigfall, General Beauregard, and all the others who have troubled you, too."

Davis's face lit up at those words. Clearly, he had not considered the possibility and a rare smile formed on his face as he thought about it. He quickly turned back to the conversation. "What else, Mr. Seddon?"

He handed over a small collection of papers. "Recommendations from Lee and Johnston regarding promotions and such."

Davis sighed, knowing that the paperwork would consume most of the evening. He would be lucky if he got home before Varina and the children had gone to sleep. Other chief executives might have left such routine tasks in the hands of subordinates, but Davis felt strongly that such matters required his personal attention. Ten minutes later, just after Seddon and Benjamin had left, Davis called out to Mr. Harrison, asking for a cup of strong coffee.

*   *   *   *   *

August 5, Evening

"Well, what do you gentlemen think of this?"

Marble tossed a copy of the *Chicago Times* onto the table, around which a dozen of the nation's most powerful Democrats were arrayed, smoking cigars and drinking brandy, lounging in fine red leather chairs. They all leaned forward to read the headline.

GENERAL SHERMAN INSANE!

There was a light chorus of satisfied laughter. A few of them clapped lightly, while others raised their snifters in a toast.

Marble glanced anxiously at Clement Vallandigham, who was perhaps the most important man in the room, as far as Marble's immediate objectives were concerned. As informal as it was, the personal contact between Marble and Vallandigham had already emerged as the *de facto* link between the McClellan campaign and the Peace Democrats who looked to Vallandigham as their leader. Marble knew he would have to tread carefully with him. Getting too close would open McClellan up to charges that he was pro-Confederate, while keeping Vallandigham at a distance could disillusion the Peace Democrats and cause many of them to stay home on election day. He would have to walk a fine line.

Marble gestured down at the newspaper. "This is on every street corner in Chicago now. My own *New York World* is running with it for tomorrow's edition. Within a few days, every major city in the Union will have at least one newspaper leading with this story."

"It certainly will increase the appeal of our message that the Lincoln administration has been incompetent in its management of the war effort," said Vallandigham.

"Indeed. It will also increase pressure on Lincoln to replace Sherman with another commander. This began, of course, in the immediate aftermath of Peachtree Creek, but Grant has been firm on retaining him. If we play our cards right, we can use that particular issue to further fan the flames of discontent."

"Well done, Marble," said Governor Seymour. When he spoke, the others fell silent. The chief executive of New York state was unarguably the most powerful man in the room. "Well done, indeed. This will divert attention away from the vicious attacks the Republicans have been making on me of late."

"That is something to which I can certainly relate," said John Mullaly, editor of the New York newspaper *Metropolitan Record*, whose readership was overwhelmingly Irish Catholic. "I spent a night in jail last week, after federal troops hauled me out of my own house for what they called 'advocacy of draft evasion.' As far as I am aware, no such charge exists on the law books."

"It could get worse," Marble warned. "The more desperate Lincoln gets, the more reckless and unconstitutional his actions may become. More than a few Democrats have been tossed in jail and several newspapers shut down."

Mullaly sneered. "So long as the draft falls disproportionately on poor Irish Catholics, while rich Protestants are allowed to hire substitutes, I shall resist it. That, and this damn fool bloody war!"

"The Irish community must be continually reminded that Lincoln is their enemy," said Vallandigham, whose heavy consumption of alcohol throughout the evening had not impaired his mental abilities in the slightest. "He is willing to recklessly throw them into the slaughterhouses of Virginia and Georgia merely to free slaves who will just compete with the Irish for jobs after the war. Are the Irish Catholics of America to dig their own graves?"

Marble nodded, filing away the last sentence in his mind for use in a future editorial, as it sounded lovely.

"And how is our prospective candidate?" Vallandigham asked, his voice not entirely free of sarcasm. While it seemed clear that the Democratic Party was rallying around General McClellan to be their candidate for the Presidency, Vallandigham had not come on board to the idea until very recently, preferring a person more openly determined on a cessation of hostilities.

"He is well," Marble said. "As we have long planned, he is sitting tight in New Jersey. We will release letters from him when necessary, and possibly send him to make a speech in a critical city or state if the situation warrants it, but otherwise his position will be that his dignity precludes him from actively campaigning for office."

Everyone around the room nodded. Such had been the accepted American political tradition since the earliest days of the Republic.

"And what of Fremont and his crazy abolitionist friends?"

Marble laughed before replying. "The fools are playing right into our hands. They have termed themselves the "Radical Democracy" party, or some such thing, and are making speeches all over the Midwest saying that Lincoln is being too soft on the Confederacy and must act more aggressively to free the slaves. They seem to think that Fremont actually has a chance to win the election."

There was a chorus of laughter throughout the room. "Playing into our hands, indeed," Seymour said. "I would hazard a guess that Fremont shall not win a single state, although he may have a chance at Kansas. Every vote for him is one less for Lincoln and, in effect, one more for us. In some states, support for Fremont may be the decisive factor that pushes the state into our column on Election Day."

Marble nodded. "Our prospects in the upcoming election appear excellent and seem to get better with every passing day. I'd like to go around the room and ask for a general summary of how you think things are proceeding in your own states. Perhaps I could start with you, Governor Seymour?"

"If New Yorkers went to the polls today, I have no doubt that we would emerge victorious. Tammany Hall completely controls the election in New York City itself, and will have no trouble getting the Irish immigrants to the polls. As for the upstate region and the other cities, I think we will at least match the Republican vote. Overall, I would guess we will gain upwards of 60% of the vote in the state overall."

Marble nodded. "Senator Bigler? How are things looking in Pennsylvania?"

"I wish I could be as sanguine as Governor Seymour," Bigler began. "In the mid-term elections last year, the Republicans routed us completely. Still, with the defeats suffered by Grant and Sherman, and the heavy losses that Pennsylvania troops in particular have suffered in recent months, the winds are changing. I would call myself cautiously optimistic. With a little luck and a lot of work, we can pull Pennsylvania into the Democratic column."

Again, Marble nodded. Bigler was generally a pessimist in any event. If he was even slightly hopeful, then the situation in Pennsylvania was likely to be very good for the Democrats.

"And Indiana? How fare we there, Congressman Voorhees?"

"Quite well, I think," replied Daniel Voorhees, second only to Vallandigham himself on the list of Lincoln's political enemies. "A large proportion of the prisoners captured by the Confederates at Peachtree Creek were Indiana boys, and the disaster has significantly increased opposition to the Lincoln administration. If we held the vote today, I would expect a win."

"Which brings us to Ohio. Mr. Vallandigham?"

Clement Vallandigham smiled an impish yet faintly threatening smile. "I have been giving speeches across the state. Every week, the crowds get bigger and more supportive. It's like dry grass being lit on fire. The Democrats are clearly in the ascendant in Ohio. You can take that to the bank."

"So, assuming we win the border states and McClellan's home state of New Jersey, as well as New York, Pennsylvania, Ohio, and Indiana, we get..." He tried to do the math in his head.

"One hundred and twenty-one electoral votes," Governor Seymour answered. "Four more than the one hundred and seventeen needed to win the election. And that is assuming that the Republicans win absolutely everywhere else, an eventuality I find very unlikely."

"Governor Seymour is right," Voorhees said. "Too many other states are up for grabs. Minnesota, Connecticut, and even Lincoln's own state of Illinois could conceivably end up in the Democratic column come November. If you ask me, it's beginning to look as though we can win the election if we show up with a pair of aces, whereas the Republicans will need a straight flush."

People around the room nodded in agreement. Bigler, however, did not, and when he next spoke his voice was filled with caution.

"I would remind you all, my friends, that the military situation can change in the blink of an eye. Yes, this week's newspaper headlines are about rumors of Sherman's insanity. Suppose next week's headlines are reporting a major Union victory against Johnston or Lee? You must agree that it is not outside the realm of possibility."

Vallandigham scoffed. "If Lincoln continues to put Grant against Lee and Sherman against Johnston, I would expect nothing other than continued Union disasters."

Bigler shrugged. "Perhaps so. But if the Union obtains a significant victory anywhere, the tide which now seems to be for us could quickly turn against us. The people are very fickle, you know, and their opinion is apt to change very quickly."

Chapter Ten

August 6, Evening

Lincoln didn't like what he was reading. All the major newspapers, with the exception of a few in Boston, were running with the story that Sherman had lost his mind. The fact that the source for the story was the obviously biased and unreliable Joseph Hooker was being conveniently ignored. The Democratic papers, naturally enough, were simultaneously running editorials condemning his own management of the war.

The last words of Manton Marble's editorial in the *New York World* were especially stinging: *Only a deranged lunatic would keep a madman in command of one of his principal armies.*

Lincoln dropped the paper in disgust. He reflected silently that perhaps it would have been better had James Madison not enshrined freedom of the press in the Constitution. The charges of insanity against Sherman would not only quickly reach the men at the front and further reduce their shaky morale, but would also further damage Republican hopes in the fall election. Every letter he received from state party leaders told the same story. Unless there was some sign of military progress in the very near future, the Republicans were going to lose the election by a heavy margin.

Even friendly Republican papers, such as Henry Raymond's *New York Times*, were now calling on Lincoln to remove Sherman from command. But a tactful telegram to Grant on the subject, sent immediately after the story had hit the papers, had only elicited the response that Sherman continued to enjoy Grant's complete confidence. Using his presidential powers, of course, Lincoln would be fully entitled to fire any general, or for that matter any captain or lieutenant, that he saw fit to fire. He did not need Grant's permission. However, peremptorily removing Sherman without Grant's consent might risk a serious rift with Grant. Lincoln knew how much the successful outcome of the Union war effort hinged on his personal relationship with the general down at Petersburg.

A soft knocking on the door caused Lincoln to look up. "Come in!" Lincoln shouted, the irritation clear in his voice.

It was Stanton, which wasn't a surprise. No one visited him in the White House more than the Secretary of War.

"Ah, Mr. Stanton. How are you this evening?"

"I imagine I am rather like you, Mr. President."

"Which is to say, poorly and in a bad mood?"

"That about sums it up, Mr. President."

Lincoln held up a copy of one of the newspapers. "The Democratic press is having a field day with Hooker's comments about General Sherman's alleged insanity."

"I have read them. Indeed, that is why I am here."

"What are we to do? Truth be told, I myself am greatly concerned about Sherman's state of mind. Since his defeat at Peachtree Creek and his retreat across the Chattahoochee, he has done nothing at all. He seems as stunned as a duck hit on the head."

"Grant still has confidence in him," Stanton replied as he took his seat across from Lincoln.

"Indeed. The two men are like brothers. I can respect that, but I am beginning to have my doubts about Sherman. And I worry that Grant's loyalty to Sherman, while admirable from a personal point of view, may be misplaced."

"You are the President," Stanton said. "You can replace Sherman with a word."

Lincoln nodded. "I know. But in dealing with military questions, I must walk on a political tightrope."

"If we replace Sherman now, it will look as though the anti-administration newspapers have been right all along. It would make us appear incompetent before the public, further damaging our chances in the upcoming election."

Lincoln pursed his lips and shook his head. "True. On the other hand, if we keep Sherman in command of our forces in the West, we may suffer yet another reverse in Georgia. The Democrats would trumpet to the public that I am at fault for foolishly putting a crazy person in command of one of our most important armies and then keeping him there despite a public clamor for his removal."

"You have replaced commanders before, in spite of political pressure to keep them in place. McClellan himself comes to mind. Also General Rosecrans."

"But that was not three months before what may be the most important election in American history. An election which may well determine whether America is to be one nation or two."

At that moment, there was another knock on the door. Upon calling for the person to enter, Lincoln looked up and saw his Navy Secretary, Gideon Welles, walk into the room. He had a beaming smile on his face, evident even through the enormous white beard that seemed to cascade off his face like a waterfall.

"Good evening, Mr. Welles," Lincoln said warmly. "This is an unexpected pleasure. If I may judge by the expression on your face, you have good news to share with me. I must say that receiving some good news for a change would be quite a tonic."

"I do have good news to report, Mr. President," Welles said. "Stupendous news, in fact. We have just received a telegram from Admiral Farragut."

Lincoln nodded quickly, anxious to hear what had happened. "If I recall correctly, his fleet is currently on blockade duty in the Gulf of Mexico."

"Yes, Mr. President."

"And what news do we have from the good admiral? Out with it, man!"

"I am delighted to report that Admiral Farragut successfully entered Mobile Bay yesterday with a fleet of eighteen warships. He fought and won a fierce battle with the rebel fleet there, destroying or capturing every enemy ship. He is now in the process of reducing the coastal forts and expects to complete this task within days."

Lincoln sat back with a wide smile on his face, a heavy weight having fallen off his shoulders. "So, if I am understanding you correctly, we have successfully closed off one of the principal routes of enemy blockade runners."

"Indeed, Mr. President."

"Losses?"

"One of our ironclads, the *Tecumseh*, was sunk by one of those barbaric torpedoes. The other ships lost a few hundred men in killed and wounded. But we destroyed two enemy ships and captured the ironclad *Tennessee*."

"Good. Very good, indeed." Lincoln slapped his thigh and allowed his lips to curl into a smile. "I regret the loss of the brave men of the *Tecumseh* and the other vessels, of course, but no victory is without its cost."

"It is a great and important victory, Mr. President," Stanton said with conviction. His normally dour expression had lit up upon hearing Welles relay the details of the battle. "I must say, this is the first bit of good news we have heard in weeks!"

Lincoln rubbed his chin. "A victory in a dramatic naval battle, especially one that inflicts such damage on the enemy, will certainly do much for the morale of the people. The papers love this sort of thing."

"Quite so," Stanton said. "Of course, the strategic results are all very well, but this event will prove very important in terms of politics. We must use this victory in such a way as to influence public opinion as to the course of the war."

"How do you suggest we do this, Mr. Stanton?" Lincoln asked.

"I shall immediately send telegrams to the editors of all major newspapers which are friendly to our administration, giving them full details of the recent victory, including any particularly dramatic anecdotes which may have taken place during this engagement. If they do their job right, we can expect that citizens throughout the Union will soon be seeing headlines describing a major Union victory, rather than a major Union defeat."

Lincoln nodded. "Yes, that would be very well done. In the meantime, I shall write to all Republican state leaders, reminding them to trumpet the news of Mobile Bay whenever they hear any suggestion of a lack of military success."

Welles chimed in. "I can compile a report as to the impact we think the seizure of Mobile Bay will have on the Southern war economy and arrange for the report to find its way into the hands of friendly editors. That would ensure the story will last longer than it otherwise would."

"A fine idea," Stanton said.

Welles wasn't done. "I'll also make sure that all the reporters and editors understand that the *Tennessee* was quite possibly the most powerful warship afloat anywhere in the world. It will make our capture of the rebel vessel appear all the more dramatic and impressive."

"Indeed," Lincoln said with an appreciative nod. He went on. "Gentlemen, you have made me a very happy man this evening. Since the sad events of Peachtree Creek at Atlanta, the rebel raid on Washington City and the disaster of the Crater at Petersburg, I have been on the hunt for good news. I thank you for bringing my search to a successful conclusion."

After a quick round of thanks and congratulations, Stanton and Welles departed, leaving Lincoln alone. He went back to reading the newspapers, considerably more pleased than he had been half an hour before.

*　　　　*　　　　*　　　　*　　　　*

August 7, Noon

"Have you read this?" Johnston asked, holding up a telegram for Mackall to see. The tone of his voice was one of incredulous amusement.

"The latest message from the War Department, I assume?"

Johnston shook his head. "If Jefferson Davis seriously thinks that this army can cross the Chattahoochee and launch an attack on Sherman, than I can only conclude that the man has gone out of his senses. Dear God, he even suggests that we might drive the enemy back toward Chattanooga!"

"Davis is building a castle in the sky, clearly."

"Please draft a reply to Richmond, concisely explaining why such an offensive is inadvisable." He paused and considered. "No, don't say 'inadvisable'. Say 'impossible'. We must force them to see that such an offensive is simply beyond the realm of possibility."

"Of course, sir. Perhaps you might summarize?"

Johnston laughed lightly. "Happily. The Army of Tennessee cannot possibly cross the river and attack Sherman for a number of reasons. First, despite the losses the enemy suffered at Peachtree Creek, their army still outnumbers our own. It must be remembered that we suffered heavily at Peachtree Creek, too. Second, attempting to cross a major river in the face of the enemy is a difficult military operation even under the best circumstances. To do so here would risk having our army defeated in detail, thus squandering all we gained as a result of our recent victory."

Mackall nodded, taking notes. "Sounds logical, if you ask me."

"Logic does not often enter the mind of our illustrious President, my friend. Now, to continue. We lack sufficient bridging equipment to build more than one or two pontoon bridges over the Chattahoochee. Even if we were somehow able to seize a bridgehead on the north bank, it would take many days to cross over a force large enough to hold its own against Sherman's forces."

Mackall continued writing and Johnston continued.

"Attempting to cross back to the north bank of the river to fight a major battle against Sherman would obviously entail moving the vast majority of our troops away from the railroads for several days. We lack sufficient wagons and horses to carry enough food and ammunition for an extended operation."

"All good points, General."

"Finally, having sent Wheeler to raid the Western and Atlantic Railroad far north of our present position, roughly half of our cavalry is now absent from this army. If we were to somehow succeed in crossing the river, and if we were to somehow supply our troops with food and ammunition, we would be fighting a battle with our eyes closed. We would lack sufficient cavalry to properly scout the enemy positions and screen our own flanks."

"Well, that should give me sufficient material with which to draft a persuasive message," Mackall said.

"Let me see it before you send it," Johnston said. "I want to make it perfectly clear to our friends in Richmond that any talk of an offensive is simple lunacy. Dear Lord, can they not be satisfied by the victory we obtained at Peachtree Creek?"

The conversation was interrupted by a messenger who entered and quickly handed Johnston a telegram. As he read it, his face darkened.

"What?" Mackall asked.

"Message from General Taylor. It seems the Yankees have seized Mobile Bay. Their fleet destroyed all our vessels in the bay, including the *Tennessee*, and is now proceeding with siege operations against Fort Morgan. Taylor says that its fall is only a matter of time."

"I was under the impression that the *Tennessee* was invincible, sir."

"It would seem not, William. Taylor is now concerned that the Yankees will follow up with an attack on the city of Mobile itself."

"Bad news, obviously. How might this affect us?"

Johnston shrugged. "A few batteries of heavy artillery have been sent to us from Mobile. In light of this news, Richmond may order us to send them back. Beyond that, I would imagine that any hope of further reinforcements is ended. If any troops can be spared, Richmond will likely send them to Mobile. Indeed, Davis may well demand that we send troops to Taylor's assistance."

"If he does, would you expect him to at least have the sense to drop his demand for an offensive against Sherman?"

Johnston laughed bitterly. "You're talking about a man who has less sense than a fence post, William. I would not be all that surprised if his next telegram includes an order for us to launch an assault on the moon."

*   *   *   *   *

August 8, Night

"I did everything I could on your behalf," Bragg said. "I want that to be clear. I told President Davis directly that Johnston should be removed and that you should be put in his place."

Hood nodded as he sipped his ale. "I believe you."

Not wanting to attract attention, neither Bragg nor Hood were in uniform. Neither were any of the other men packed into the ale house off Court Square near the center of Montgomery, busy swilling beer and smoking cigars. The large number of able-bodied men who might have been serving in the ranks troubled Bragg, but he reminded himself that Montgomery was a center of production for Confederate war material. Presumably, most of these men served their country by working in the iron foundries or powder mills. Without their labor, Southern soldiers would be going into battle without weapons.

They were cloistered together in a corner table, their conversation illuminated by the flickering light of a single candle. Bragg, a teetotaler, was drinking apple cider that the disapproving bartender had pushed on him. Hood was finishing his third ale.

"And now that bastard has won his big battle," Hood said angrily. "Davis can't replace him now, by God. He still has no business running an army, but he won't be replaced. The people wouldn't like it. Politics and such."

"That's true."

Hood shook his head. "Johnston just got lucky is all. Thomas and Sherman made a stupid mistake. Johnston didn't do anything brilliant. Any child could have done the same thing and gotten the same result. I would have beaten Sherman far more thoroughly than Johnston did."

Bragg nodded.

Hood's mouth turned into a furious frown. "And I'll tell you what, Bragg. If Johnston hadn't been so lucky, the Union army would have smashed right into Atlanta from the east, because that fool had stripped me of nearly half my corps! You should have seen it. I was left alone with ten thousand men against forty thousand Yankees. It's a damn miracle that the battle did not end in complete disaster."

"You will include these details in your official report, I assume?"

"Of course. But that's not the only thing."

Bragg took a sip from his cider. "Go on."

"When the battle was over, the Yankees were helpless. I had two good divisions that had barely fired a shot all day, along with several batteries of horse artillery. Wheeler had three brigades of cavalry that had been uncommitted. But Johnston would not let us pursue the beaten enemy. He let them escape."

"Is that so?" Bragg asked.

"It is, sir. And since the Yankees were all south of the Chattahoochee River, we could have captured the whole damn lot of them had we undertaken a vigorous pursuit. But Johnston didn't. And I shall include that in my report, too."

Bragg nodded. He himself had come under furious criticism from Hardee and other generals in the Army of Tennessee for failing to pursue the defeated Army of the Cumberland after the victory at Chickamauga. He had always considered this an absurd insult to his leadership, for his own army had been almost as badly damaged from victory as the Yankee army had been from defeat. If what Hood was saying had any truth to it, however, Johnston had had sizable forces still at hand with which he might have pursued Sherman and won an even more decisive victory.

Resentment suddenly burned in Bragg's soul. It was a familiar feeling, but one he had been experiencing much more often of late. For the past two-and-a-half weeks, the headlines of every major newspaper in the Confederacy had been trumpeting the genius and daring of Johnston. They had also been fawning over Hardee and Cleburne, celebrating as heroes men Bragg considered nothing but villains.

Those men in the Army of Tennessee who were friendly to Bragg, by contrast, were receiving no credit whatsoever for the victory at Peachtree Creek. General Walker's division had done fine work, but few accounts mentioned his name. Wheeler had had virtually no part to play, and Hood's corps had been left out of the fighting altogether.

The Battle of Peachtree Creek may have been a victory for the Confederacy. For Braxton Bragg, however, it felt more like a defeat.

He looked across the table at Hood, who had just started his fourth ale. No doubt Hood felt the same as he did. All of Richmond had been swirling with rumors of Hood's impending promotion to command the Army of Tennessee in the days leading up to the battle. The moment news of the victory had shot through the telegraph wires, however, most of those who had been vilifying Johnston and looking with hope to Hood's ascension immediately reversed themselves, claiming how relieved they were that Johnston had remained in command.

"Are you confident in being able to reach the Trans-Mississippi?" Bragg asked.

Hood nodded. "I'll go from here to Meridian by train. General Taylor has told me that it will be fairly easy to avoid Yankee gunboats on the Mississippi by crossing in a small boat at night. I'll then report to General Smith at Shreveport. It is my understanding that I will be put in command of our forces in Arkansas."

"Hopefully you will be able to achieve some good out there. Most of our efforts have not been as successful as we would like."

"I should like to recruit additional soldiers from Texas as well."

"Well, your reputation among your fellow Texans is well-known. I am sure that many new recruits will come to the colors if they learn they are to serve under your command."

"We'll see, I suppose." He took a quick sip of his ale. "And you? Are you to return to Richmond now?"

"Yes, my inspection tour of the area is complete. A pity my warnings about the weaknesses of the defenses of Mobile Bay came too late. Ah, well, there's nothing to be done about that now. Elsewhere, our forces seem strong enough. So many Yankee troops have been sent to reinforce Sherman that their ability to launch incursions into Mississippi and Alabama has been sharply reduced."

"Well, that's good."

"It is, yes."

Hood paused and took a deep breath before speaking again. "When you go to Richmond, I wonder if you might do something for me."

"Certainly. What is it?"

He pulled out a large, fully stuffed envelope. "This contains a copy of the infamous memorandum General Cleburne authored a few months ago. The one which advocated that the government free negro slaves in order to enroll them in the army."

Bragg pulled back as though the envelope were made of fire. "President Davis has strictly ordered that no discussion of that memorandum be permitted."

"I know. But there is information which I think President Davis needs to know. Information which has not yet been brought to his attention."

"I thought this whole devilishness had been put behind us. Cleburne is a fool. That proposal should never have been conceived, much less written. And what is this new information you are talking about?"

Hood looked into Bragg's eyes. "General Johnston is a supporter of Cleburne's proposal. A strong one, as a matter of fact."

Bragg furrowed his brow. "Johnston's a secret abolitionist?"

Hood nodded. "I believe he is. You are aware that he himself does not own slaves and I have been told that his wife secretly holds abolitionist sentiments."

"What evidence do you have?"

"About his wife, nothing. Only rumor and hearsay. But about Johnston's support of Cleburne's proposal, I have signed affidavits from officers who were present at the meeting in January where Cleburne pitched his proposal. They confirm that Johnston spoke strongly in support of freeing the slaves and enlisting them into our army."

"Which generals?"

"Joseph Wheeler, William Walker and Patton Anderson. Furthermore, these men say that General Hardee was also an enthusiastic backer of Cleburne's scheme."

"That's no surprise. Hardee and Cleburne are like brothers."

Hood dismissed the remark. "General Bragg, I feel it my duty as a responsible officer to bring to the attention of the President and the Secretary of War the fact that General Johnston and General Hardee support this abolitionist scheme. Such men are not fit to command troops of the Confederate army. Protecting our peculiar institution, after all, is the reason the Confederacy was established in the first place."

Hood was not a subtle man and Bragg could see immediately what he was doing. But it didn't matter, so long as Hood's actions served Bragg's own purposes. He reached across the table and took the envelope.

"I will examine these papers. If I see fit, I shall show them to the President and the Secretary of War."

"Thank you, General Bragg."

August 9, Morning

Colonel Edgar Robertson, commanding the Union garrison protecting the town of Bridgeport, in extreme northeastern Alabama, was feeling impatient. He was anxious to drive off the small rebel raiding party that was trying to tear up railroad track west of town, so that he could get back to Bridgeport in time for an appointment he had made with a particularly skillful prostitute named Faye. He had visited her twice before and enjoyed himself thoroughly on both occasions. She certainly helped relieve the boredom of garrison life and, as the saying went, no man in the Northern army was married south of Nashville.

Had Robertson known that he had entered the last hour of his time on Earth, he might have spent the final minutes of his life engaged in thoughts of a less impious nature.

He walked near the middle of the column of a thousand infantrymen, which he had led out from Bridgeport about two hours before. If the reports he had received were accurate, the Confederate guerrilla band, numbering perhaps a hundred men, was only about three miles west of the edge of the town's fortifications. The thousand men he had brought with him represented nearly half of the garrison, and Robertson figured that they would be more than adequate to deal with the situation.

Bridgeport was one of the key transportation links in the long lines of communication and supply that extended from the farms and factories of the North all the way down to Sherman's army outside Atlanta. Running south from the great Union base at Nashville, two large railroads converged on Bridgeport, crossed the wide chasm of the Tennessee River on one of the longest bridges in the area, then ran a few dozen miles on a single track to the Union base at Chattanooga. The bridge at Bridgeport, therefore, was one of the few critical chokepoints in Sherman's supply line, where a break could have extremely serious repercussions.

Bridgeport was especially important to Sherman's campaign because the lead elements of the Sixth Corps, dispatched from Virginia to reinforce the Union armies in the West, would soon be passing through. Thousands of Northern soldiers were now crowding the rail depots in Nashville and Tullahoma, waiting to continue south and being delayed by the damage that had been done by Forrest's raiders. Colonel Robertson was not concerned, feeling confident that Forrest had long since scurried back to his Mississippi lair.

Robertson heard some firing up toward the front of the column, and jogged ahead to see what was happening. Most likely, the men at the head of the column had encountered the rebel raiding party. Then again, some of the boys might simply be taking potshots at a deer or other kind of animal. Since they were mere hundred-day men of the Indiana militia, there hadn't been much time to instill a sense of discipline in them.

Upon arriving at the head of the column, Robertson squinted in confusion. Through the glare of the August sun, he could see that the rebels had erected a makeshift barrier perpendicularly across the railroad tracks by piling up some logs and railroad ties. That didn't make any sense. Any train would smash through such a flimsy obstacle as if it weren't even there. Why would a small band of guerrillas try to set up defenses if they expected to be attacked by a large force of infantry? The defenses were far too puny to protect them, and the only logical thing they could do would be to flee.

From behind their improvised barricade, the Southerners began firing into the lead ranks of his column. Clearly, the fools intended to stay and fight. This annoyed Robertson, as it would perhaps take over an hour to drive them off now, and he was anxious to get back to Bridgeport and into the sensual embraces of Faye. He shouted orders for his men to halt and prepared to deploy them in a line of battle. Perhaps the rebels would see reason and run away.

So fixated was Robertson on the barricade in front of him that he didn't notice the scattered movements within the trees on the north side of the railroad, to the right of his column. A more diligent officer would have sent flankers into the woods to make sure they were empty of potential enemies, but Robertson had forgotten to do so.

The first hint that Robertson or any of his men had that they were facing more than a small band of rebel guerrillas came when the woods along the north side of the railroad, for a distance of nearly a quarter of a mile, erupted in a ferocious volley of musket fire.

Scores of Union men were killed instantly. Cries of surprise and horror blended with the screams of agony from wounded men, and the disjointed Union column buckled in confusion, like a whale being attacked by a host of sharks. Most of the officers had gone down with the initial volley, as Forrest always instructed his men to pick them off first. A rather bored and lackadaisical band of militiamen a moment before, the Union column was instantly transformed into a mass of terrified humanity.

Some men began to fire back, but they could not see their opponents very well, as they were largely concealed in the trees and brush. Heavy fire continued to pour into the Union ranks. Perhaps one minute after the first shot was fired, the sound of bugles could be heard and with a deafening Rebel Yell the Confederate force charged forward.

Robertson struggled to control his own terror. He suddenly realized he was shouting incomprehensible orders that made no sense and shut his mouth. Consciously or not, he made a quick decision. His men would have to fend for themselves as best they could, for if he had any hope of remaining alive, he would have to focus only on his own escape.

As he turned and ran toward the woods on the south side of the railroad tracks, away from the oncoming wave of Confederate soldiers, he was stunned to find himself confronted by a tall figure on a dark horse, who held a pistol in his left hand and a saber in his right, while holding the reins of his horse in his teeth. Robertson was paralyzed with fear, and froze.

Nathan Bedford Forrest unceremoniously skewered Robertson, his sword penetrating right through the Yankee's ribcage and into his left lung. He twisted the sword, eliciting a pathetic sound that was more like a gurgle than a cry of pain. It was the twenty-seventh time Forrest had personally killed a man since the start of the war, so while he still watched with interest as the man's eyes glazed over and the life seeped out of his body, the phenomenon no longer held the same fascination for him that it had the first time he had seen it, three years before.

Tossing the body aside, Forrest kicked King Philip into a walk and strode onto the railroad track. Surveying the scene, he could see that the battle had ended almost before it had begun. While a few brave men had tried to resist, most of the Yankees had immediately bolted into the woods to the south the moment his men had charged out of their concealed position. Hundreds of others had meekly thrown down their rifles and put their hands up. Forrest thought the behavior of the Northern men pathetic, but it certainly made his task much easier.

Major Strange rode up to him, his face flush with the excitement that always came with a successful ambush.

"How's it going?" Forrest asked.

"Two hundred prisoners, or thereabouts. About a hundred Yankees dead. The rest of them, maybe five hundred or so, ran off into the forest."

"They won't cause any trouble. We'll send a couple of companies to keep them running and maybe grab a few more prisoners. In the meantime, leave enough men here to process the prisoners and get the rest of the boys back in the saddle. Let's head to Bridgeport."

Strange saluted and dashed off. Forrest walked King Philip eastward along the railroad, gazing silently at the human wreckage his surprise attack had inflicted. It had been a textbook operation, with the decoy force drawing roughly half of the Union garrison at Bridgeport, so that it could efficiently be chopped to ribbons. Now reduced to perhaps a thousand frightened Yankee soldiers, the defenders of Bridgeport would find themselves surrounded by nearly four times that many Confederates. And while the Yankee defenders were inexperienced militiamen, Forrest's troopers were perhaps the most experienced veterans in the world.

Had the Union commander not been deceived and kept his men within the fortifications, Forrest's task would have been much more difficult. Even if inexperienced, two thousand militiamen could probably resist a direct assault by thirty-five hundred veterans if they were protected by the substantial earthworks and redoubts that ringed Bridgeport and protected its critical bridge over the Tennessee River. By cleverly reducing the garrison by half, and instilling the survivors with terror, Forrest had effectively leveled the playing field.

Forrest barked out orders to his staff officers. His three brigades were to remount and converge on Bridgeport from three directions, cutting the telegraph wires as they did so. He had left the telegraph wires undisturbed up until now, for fear of unduly alarming the Bridgeport garrison. Once the town was surrounded, he would demand its surrender.

The next few hours passed quickly and relatively easily. His three brigade commanders had been with him long enough that they carried out their orders as easily as his own arms and legs obeyed his very thoughts. The ambush had been carried out just after ten in the morning, and by four in the afternoon, all of Forrest's brigades were in position and the telegraph lines had been cut. The Union garrison of Bridgeport was on its own.

Forrest sent forward an officer with a white flag and, after about fifteen minutes of haggling, the cowed Union commander agreed to surrender on the basis that his men would be paroled rather than become prisoners-of-war. Forrest scarcely cared. It was the bridge that he cared about, not the garrison.

While Major Strange and the Union commander sat down at the table and worked out the terms of the parole of the garrison, Forrest set his men to work burning the bridge. Being far longer than the one over the Duck River which he had wrecked at Columbia, it required quite a bit more time for the work to be completed. But the end result was the same. As the sun was beginning to dip below the horizon, the torch was thrown onto the cotton bales and dry timbers, and within a few minutes, the bridge was aflame from one side of the Tennessee River to the other.

*   *   *   *   *

August 11, Morning

Vallandigham was tired. The schedule of his speaking tour was punishing both physically and mentally. Most of the sleep he had gotten over the past month had been fitfully experienced while sitting in the seat of a shaky train. He had made so many speeches that he could feel his voice beginning to weaken and he was worried that he might be forced to take a few days off in the near future.

He was about to make what would be his fourth speech in New York City since his return from Canadian exile. He was anxious to get it over with, so that he could head back to Ohio and focus his energies on defeating the Republicans in his own state. However, following the previous week's meeting of prominent Democrats and a quick side trip to make a well-received speech in Philadelphia, Vallandigham had decided to return to New York for one final speech at the urging of Governor Seymour. The Governor, Vallandigham realized, was as worried about his own reelection prospects as he was about defeating Lincoln, but that didn't matter so long as the Democrats continued to present a united front.

Vallandigham looked out at the crowd, packed into an area of Central Park in front of a large stage that had been set up by some Tammany Hall people. It was a considerably larger crowd than he had spoken to previously in New York City and he thought it might even be a bigger throng of people than the one he had just addressed in Philadelphia.

He had given his stump speech so many times that he no longer even had to think about the words. They simply flowed out of his mouth like water from an overturned bucket. He thought for a moment and realized he had just reached the portion of his speech where he discussed the high inflation that was sweeping the economy thanks to the flawed monetary policies of the Lincoln administration and the massive debt it was accumulating in order to pay for the war.

"If we continue down this path, what will become of you? If the necessities of life which cost you five dollars today cost you six dollars a month from now, and ten dollars six months from now, how will you survive?"

The uncomfortable stirring he sensed in the audience was expected, for he had seen it many times. Most of the people who came to hear him speak were common laborers, many of whom were fresh off the boats from Ireland, Germany, or southern Italy. They were more concerned with putting food on the plates of their children than with abstract notions of preserving the Union or abolishing slavery. Freed slaves, after all, were potential competitors for jobs. Vallandigham had been in politics long enough to have learned that nothing motivated people more than fear and self-interest. He was playing up both of them.

As his speech continued, he noticed something which he had not noticed before. Off to the left side of the crowd was a group of perhaps two dozen men wearing the blue uniforms of Union soldiers. Vallandigham tensed. He knew he was in no danger of being arrested by the New York City police, who were controlled by Tammany Hall and sympathetic to Vallandigham in any event. Soldiers, on the other hand, would follow the orders of their commander, and their commander would follow the orders of President Lincoln.

Vallandigham kept speaking automatically, moving on to the portion of his speech in which he spoke about the enormous casualties which had been suffered by Grant in Virginia and Sherman in Georgia. In his mind, he wondered if his time was finally up. Lincoln had had him arrested once already and the stakes were obviously much higher now than they had been then. Vallandigham told himself that he was likely to be spending the night in jail rather than on the train back to Ohio.

Even as his mind raced, he continued talking. "Since May, one hundred thousand brave Union men have died thanks to the incompetence of General Grant and General Sherman." He pronounced the word *general* with heavy sarcasm to lay emphasis on their ineptitude and stupidity. "If laid end to end, the line of corpses would stretch more than one hundred miles!"

The stirring of the crowd increased. Many of their friends and family members were serving in the army and any of the men might be drafted into service at any moment. Vallandigham went on, reminding his listeners that Lincoln had just issued a call for four hundred thousand new recruits and had made it clear that the men would be brought forth by a draft if an insufficient number of volunteers was forthcoming.

"And who is it that will be sent to die in the trenches around Petersburg or along the banks of the Chattahoochee? Will it be the rich Boston merchant who prattles on about abolition while purchasing a substitute so that he will not be drafted himself? No! It will be you and your kin who will be sent into the slaughterhouse! It will be you and your kin who will be sent to die!"

The crowd began chanting. "We won't go! We won't go!"

At a wave from a man who was apparently their commander, the small group of Union soldiers began to move toward the stage. Vallandigham saw them coming, and realized in an instant what was happening. They would attempt to arrest him on a charge of interfering with the draft.

He kept speaking, making a comment about how many Union soldiers were languishing in Southern prisons such as Andersonville. But he kept glancing to his left, where the first of the Union soldiers were climbing up onto the stage. Some of the Tammany Hall men attempted to stop them and Vallandigham could hear shouted arguments. The ruckus also quickly drew the attention of the crowd.

"No!" the audience roared. "No!"

The Tammany Hall men were shoved aside, and Vallandigham was dismayed but not surprised to see the soldiers holding them at bay with bayonets. The officer, a captain by the look of him, marched straight up to him.

"Mr. Vallandigham, you must come with me immediately."

"Am I under arrest?"

"You must come with me at once."

"I do not wish to go with you," Vallandigham said sternly.

"You have no choice."

"What you are doing is illegal. The Constitution protects all citizens from arbitrary arrest."

"If you do not come willingly I shall be compelled to use force."

Vallandigham looked out into the crowd, seeing thousands of anxious and furious faces. He was paralyzed with indecision. He knew he had but to shout for help and his supporters would storm the stage to prevent his arrest. But that would lead to violence, almost certainly costing the lives of many of the people in the crowd. The soldiers might number only two dozen, but they were all armed with loaded muskets. In fear of their own lives, they would likely fire into the crowd. Unscrupulous he might have been, but Clement Vallandigham had no wish to see anyone get killed.

"Very well, young man. I shall come with you, but only under protest." The officer nodded quickly, then jerked his head toward the left of the stage. A chorus of boos and angry shouts echoed from the crowd.

Having made his decision, Vallandigham instantly saw the matter taken completely out of his hands. The Tammany Hall men had continued to argue with the soldiers by the side of the stage as he had conversed with the captain. Vallandigham could not hear what was being said, but matters had obviously become quite heated. One Tammany Hall enforcer, not used to being ordered around, shouted something vulgar into the face of one of the soldiers before violently pushing against his chest. The soldier fell over backwards and one of his comrades stepped forward, knocking the Tammany Hall man to the ground by smashing him over the head with the butt of his musket.

"No!" Vallandigham shouted, seeing what was about to happen.

One of the Tammany Hall men, clearly used to the kind of violence that characterized the gang warfare of the Five Points district of the city, pulled out a revolver and calmly shot the soldier who had clubbed his comrade. One of the soldiers instantly raised his musket and shot the Tammany Hall man dead.

At the sound of gunfire, the crowd promptly panicked. The screams of terrified women filled the air and people begin scattering in every direction. Among the teeming multitude were several dozen Tammany Hall enforcers, placed in the crowd originally to clap and cheer the speaker when they felt the crowd needed encouragement. Seeing the situation on the stage, they ran toward the sound of shooting rather than away from it, determined to come to the rescue of their fellows. Seeing what looked like part of the crowd surging toward them, several of the Union soldiers raised their rifles and fired.

Vallandigham dashed forward, waving his arms and screaming for the firing to stop. The shots were now coming fast and furious. In answer to the blasts coming from Tammany revolvers in the crowd, the soldiers were reloading and firing again. The bullets whizzed back and forth at random, striking civilians who were desperately trying to escape the chaos. Terrified screams and confused calls filled the air.

"Stop!" Vallandigham called as he reached the group of Union soldiers and grabbed the barrel of one of the muskets. "Stop shooting!"

As Vallandigham instinctively tried to interpose himself between the Tammany Hall men in the crowd and the overeager Union soldiers on the stage, a bullet struck him in the forehead, tore through his brain, and killed him instantly.

*   *   *   *   *

August 13, Evening

It was the fourth time McFadden had come to the Turnbow home for dinner. His sense of awkwardness had faded with each visit and this evening he actually found himself feeling comfortable as he took his seat at the table. The slave cook Mattie had prepared roast beef and potatoes for the evening, which were very good. Even better, Robert Turnbow had opened what he described as an excellent bottle of wine. McFadden, whose alcoholic experiences were mostly confined to strong and simple whiskey, could not tell a good wine from a bad wine, but he took Mister Turnbow's word for it.

As far as McFadden knew, wine was not produced in North America, which meant that Mister Turnbow was serving a bottle saved from before the war or one which had been brought through the blockade at great expense. Either way, it made McFadden feel appreciated that his host would go to so much trouble on his account.

McFadden had brought with him a letter signed by every member of the 7th Texas Infantry, expressing their gratitude for the interest the Turnbow family had shown in their well-being. The three large shipments of produce and meat that Annie had brought up to the regiment since the Battle of Peachtree Creek had been deeply appreciated. There had even been enough to share a portion with some of the other regiments in Granbury's Texas Brigade, which had been expressing some jealousy at the good fortune of the 7th.

Annie had brought the provisions herself on each occasion, escorted by the slave Jupiter. As the men of the regiment had happily unloaded the provisions, Annie and McFadden had strolled together through the brigade encampment, quietly talking and simply enjoying one another's company. Although he had never openly declared the fact, even to himself, it had become obvious to everyone that McFadden was courting Annie.

Teresa Turnbow's attitude toward him had notably shifted. The first evening he had joined the Turnbows for dinner, Annie's mother had treated him with a disdain that she had not bothered to conceal. Since then, however, he had been promoted to lieutenant and had become a hero of the Confederacy due to his capture of the traitor George Thomas. She had positively fawned over the officer's sword he had worn to dinner and had treated him more like a beloved son to be embraced than a contemptible provincial to be ignored.

McFadden saw through her at once and still felt little warmth toward her. People like Annie's mother were like weather vanes, ready to change their attitudes in an instant if it suited their own purposes. But if Teresa's remarkable about-face made it easier for him and Annie to grow closer, McFadden was not about to complain.

"Have you finished the book about Thaddeus Kosciuszko yet?" Mister Turnbow asked, taking another sip of his wine.

"Not yet," McFadden answered. "My duties with the regiment leave me precious little time to read. I am slightly over halfway finished. But I am enjoying it very much."

"His life reads like a novel, doesn't it?"

McFadden nodded. "Yes, I would say so."

"Many figures from history often seem to be drawn from the pages of a fictional story. Kosciuszko certainly seems like one of those."

"His lifelong struggle in defense of liberty is deeply inspiring," McFadden said. "I find in his story an example I believe we Southern men should set for ourselves."

"A sound idea."

"I have also been struck by the similarities between the Polish struggle against Russian domination and the Scottish struggle against English domination."

"Hmm," Mister Turnbow said. "I confess I never considered that."

"Is it true that the Yankees will be bringing in negro soldiers to replace their losses at Peachtree Creek?" Teresa Turnbow asked.

"There are rumors that say so," McFadden said. "Anything is possible, I suppose."

"Barbarism!" she spat. "Sheer barbarism! Giving weapons to negroes! Do the Yankees have no shame at all?"

McFadden tilted his head slightly in confusion. The 7th Texas had never yet encountered black Union soldiers, but he had heard men from other regiments speak of fighting against them around Charleston and at various points in Tennessee. The men relating these stories had always spoken of the black Union soldiers with nothing but contempt, but McFadden had often detected a trace of fear in their voices. Considering the heavy casualties the

Confederates had sustained in these engagements, no one could deny that the negro soldiers could fight as well as the whites.

To him, it did not much matter if the enemy in the ranks across from his regiment was white or black. What mattered was that they were trying to kill him. If he wanted to stay alive, therefore, he had to try to kill them first. If anything, he felt less enmity for the blacks in Union service than he did for the whites. After all, who could blame a slave for wanting to fight for his freedom? In their place, McFadden knew he would have done the same thing.

The man who had tortured and killed his brother had not been a black man.

He tensed, angry that the mental picture of Cheeky Joe had intruded upon his time with Annie and her parents. His mind had remained tormented over the question of whether the man he had seen on the boat in the Chattahoochee had been Cheeky Joe or not. Major Collett was still encouraging him to dismiss the idea and focus on his regimental duties, but this task was almost an impossibility.

The only thing which could banish Cheeky Joe from McFadden's mind, even if only temporarily, was Annie.

"James?" Annie asked.

"I'm sorry?" he said, startled out of his thoughts and back into the conversation.

"Father asked you about your regiment's deployment."

"Oh. I apologize. Our deployment?"

Robert Turnbow nodded.

"Our brigade has rotated back and forth with other units from Cleburne's division, doing picket duty along the river. Generally, General Cleburne positions two of his brigades along the river at any one time, with his third brigade in reserve. Because of the heavy casualties the Texas Brigade sustained in the Battle of Peachtree Creek, we have been granted more time in reserve than the other two brigades, allowing us more time to rest and refit."

"When will you go up to the river again?"

"The day after tomorrow."

"Is it dangerous?" Annie asked.

"Not especially. The river itself prevents any tactical advance by either side, so we and the Yankees opposite us can usually come to an agreement that neither side will open fire. In fact, there is often trading between the two sides, with Southern tobacco being exchanged for Northern coffee."

"Really?" Annie asked. "Trading with the Yankees?"

"I know it sounds absurd, but I can assure you it does happen from time to time."

McFadden himself did not approve of any sort of friendly intercourse with the enemy, but neither did he refrain from drinking the coffee the regiment sometimes acquired as a result of the illicit trade. If they did not have access to coffee from the Yankees, they had to drink the bizarre Southern concoction brewed from a combination of ground peanuts and roast corn.

"I am willing to bet that Prince Ponder gets his supplies of coffee from the Yankees," Mister Turnbow said. "Exactly how he does it, I could never guess. But he always seems able to supply it, albeit at a high price."

Teresa sighed. "Everything is expensive these days. How the poor manage to survive is a mystery to me."

"Yes, well, the war is hard on everyone."

"Annie tells me that she has greatly enjoyed her visits to your encampment," Mister Turnbow said. "Isn't that so, Annie?"

She smiled slightly and nodded. "James and his men have been very gracious during my visits. When I have remained for dinner, they have regaled me with singing and dancing, as well as stories about life in the army."

Teresa's face clouded slightly. "Robert, do you really think it is appropriate for Annie to be associating with enlisted men of the army?"

"My dear, why speak so sourly about the brave defenders of the Confederacy?"

"It is not their bravery I am concerned about. It simply seems socially unsuitable for a girl of Annie's upbringing to be socializing with enlisted men."

"Nonsense. Besides, James is always at her side during her visits. Is that not so, James?"

"It is so, sir."

"Well, that is enough for me," he said with a smile. "James already saved Annie's life, after all. Surely he is capable of escorting her around the encampment."

Annie smiled. "Not only does James keep me safe, but he is also very pleasant company."

"Thank you," McFadden said, genuine and deep respect in his voice. Receiving even a simple compliment from Annie warmed McFadden's heart.

"Would it not be best to simply have Jupiter deliver the produce himself?" Teresa asked. "That way Lieutenant McFadden would not be burdened with the task of escorting Annie about."

"It is no burden at all," McFadden said instantly. He momentarily considered that perhaps he had spoken too eagerly, but dismissed the thought and went on. "Annie's presence is of great comfort to my men. It reminds them that the people think about them and are concerned for their welfare. I think also that Annie's presence reminds them of the wives many of them left behind in Texas, whom they pray they will one day see again."

Neither Robert nor Teresa responded to the final words. McFadden felt a sudden rush of terror. His face flushed. How could he have been so foolish as to mention the institution of marriage while talking about Annie? He had not known the Turnbow family existed two months before and he had probably seen Annie herself no more than a dozen times.

He told himself that he was worrying too much. There was no reason to think that either of Annie's parents saw his words in an untoward way. Besides, he was no longer a mere sergeant but a respected officer. He had to believe that the time he had spent with the Turnbows had persuaded them that he was more than simply a roughhewn man from the Texas frontier.

Looking across the table, he saw that Robert Turnbow had a curious grin on his face. He could not imagine its cause, but it still comforted McFadden, for Turnbow's expression was not the look of an offended man.

Mattie and Jupiter came into the room with dessert, which turned out to be a delicious pecan pie. Conversation shifted toward a discussion about the upcoming election in the North and whether Britain might recognize the Confederacy, subjects on which McFadden felt uncertain. Then, the talk shifted direction in a way McFadden had not expected.

"What do you think you will do when the war is over, James?" Teresa asked.

This caught McFadden by surprise and it took him a moment to answer. "I confess I have not given the matter much thought," he said, feeling somewhat awkward. "The knowledge that I might well not survive the next battle casts a shadow over such thoughts. One does not wish to tempt fate."

"I'm sorry," she said.

"No, it's all right. It is something I should think on more. I still own my family's farm back in Texas, though I have no idea what condition it is now in. I suppose I would return there when the war is over and put it back into proper shape. Beyond that, I don't know."

"Have you ever considered entering the ministry, like your father?" Mister Turnbow asked.

"Not especially."

Robert glanced quickly at his wife, then back to McFadden. "You might remain here, you know. Here in Georgia, I mean. You're an intelligent, well-read man. You may lack a university education, but that should be no obstacle to a man of your obvious talents."

"I would have no idea what I would do here in Georgia, sir."

"Well, I could always use a good man to help me run the iron foundry. I expect business to be good after the war, as there will be a great need to repair all the railroads that have been torn up by the Yankees. Your experience as a sergeant and now as an officer is surely teaching you how to manage men."

McFadden was initially not sure if he had heard Turnbow correctly. "Are you offering me a position at your foundry, sir?"

"I suppose I am, James. Think on it, will you?"

"I will, sir," McFadden said immediately, not sounding nearly as taken aback as he actually was.

"Very good." Robert glanced up at the clock. "The sun will be going down soon. You need to get back to your encampment, don't you, James?"

"I do, sir, yes."

Robert rose from the table, prompting McFadden to so the same. Annie and her mother both stood and gave graceful curtsies, to which McFadden responded by awkwardly bowing his head. He had no idea if this was the proper response or not, but Annie apparently found it amusing as she playfully grinned at him.

After exchanging farewells with Annie and her mother, McFadden was walked to the front door by Robert. Somewhat to his surprise, Mister Turnbow stepped outside with him. The sun was now setting, but the air was still quite hot.

"James, I must ask you a question which I am sure you have been expecting."

McFadden's eyes narrowed in confusion. "I am not sure I understand you, sir."

"Respectfully, what are your intentions toward my daughter?"

He waited a moment before replying, suddenly feeling more fear that he had felt even when facing a line of leveled Yankee muskets. The father of a woman with whom one was falling in love was certainly not to be trifled with. If that man happened to be as formidable a figure as Robert Turnbow, the rule was doubly true.

McFadden finally answered. "I am very fond of your daughter, sir."

Turnbow arched his head slightly to the side. "How fond?"

He struggled to find an appropriate answer. His mind raced, his heart pounded, but he simply could not conjure up the right words.

It was Turnbow who broke the awkward silence. "Fond enough to ask my permission to court her?"

He paused only a moment. "Yes, sir."

Turnbow smiled, patting McFadden gently on the shoulder. "I am glad of it and you have my permission. I like you very much, James. Whether my daughter likes you as much remains to be seen. But she is fond of you and I invite you to win her heart if you can. You are one of the few genuinely good men I have met since this damn war began."

"I thank you with all my heart, sir."

*   *   *   *   *

August 15, Afternoon

He read through the telegram once again.

> *General Sherman,*
>   *The flow of events, both military and otherwise, make it exceedingly necessary for us to obtain a significant military victory in the vicinity of Atlanta. That being the case, I have decided to send three additional infantry divisions to reinforce you. Combined with the already dispatched Sixth Corps, this should increase the forces under your command by roughly twenty-five thousand men, being the same number of troops lost during the Battle of Peachtree Creek.*
>   *If a renewed offensive against Atlanta is not advisable, would it not be possible to maintain your position north of the city with a portion of your force while dispatching one of your three constituent armies, perhaps the Army of the Tennessee, into central Alabama with a view to seizing control of the rebel cities of Selma and Montgomery?*
>   *Please advise me immediately as to your future course of action.*
> *General Grant*

Sherman folded up the paper and set it gently on his desk. He then stared at it for some time. Over the course of a few minutes, a feeling of rage filled him. He felt abandoned and betrayed by the man he thought had been his friend. Did Grant seriously expect that dispatching a few measly divisions of reinforcements would make any difference? Sherman had no doubt that an even larger number of enemy reinforcements were arriving for Johnston, who might be expected to launch an attack north of the Chattahoochee at any moment. If that happened, Sherman expected to have little choice but to retreat back to Chattanooga, if not further.

The fact that Grant was trying to prod him into an ill-advised attack on Atlanta or Alabama was, as far as Sherman was concerned, a grievous insult. Indeed, it was nothing less than an attempt to brand him a coward. Did Grant seriously think that Sherman would not have already done such a thing if it were at all possible?

Moreover, Grant's telegram made no mention of the fact that Forrest and Wheeler were both chopping away at his supply line, tearing up his railroads as though they were made of spaghetti rather than iron. Sherman couldn't force his mind to do the calculations necessary to figure how long it would be before his men began to starve, but he imagined that it couldn't be very long.

There was a soft knocking on the door.

"Come in!" Sherman said sharply. McPherson quietly entered.

"You wanted to see me, Cump?"

"Yes. I understand that my orders to execute five deserters from the Army of the Tennessee have yet to be carried out. What is your explanation?"

"Four of the men have been shot," McPherson answered, his voice unsuccessfully attempting to hide the disquiet he felt. "The fifth man has yet to be executed because doubts have arisen as to whether he actually deserted or had simply gone off to forage for supplies."

Sherman grunted. Without a word, he passed Grant's telegram across the table. McPherson picked it up and read it, as Sherman watched his face for the signs of anger and dismay he hoped and expected to see. To his disgust, McPherson's face lit up with delight.

"This is excellent news, Cump!" McPherson said with enthusiasm, affectionately slapping the paper with his free hand. "With an additional corps, we can get the campaign back on the move once again!"

"You think so?" Sherman asked.

"Absolutely. And I think Grant's concept of an advance into Alabama is an intriguing idea. My army, with some reinforcements, could simply advance down the north bank of the Chattahoochee until it is within striking distance of Selma and Montgomery. We could move rapidly and live off the land, just like we did during the Vicksburg campaign. Both cities are critical enemy industrial centers. Capturing them would be a tremendous victory!"

"Really?"

"Of course! With the enemy forces all bunched up around Atlanta south of the Chattahoochee, there is really nothing to prevent a large force such as the Army of the Tennessee from moving from here into Alabama. The capture of Selma or Montgomery would greatly strengthen morale both within the ranks and on the home front and would certainly assist the present administration in its reelection prospects."

Sherman thought the eagerness being displayed by McPherson was akin to that of a child presented with a new toy. "Have you taken leave of your senses, man?"

McPherson's eyebrows shot up and his head jerked slightly backward. "I'm sorry?"

"You are talking nonsense!" Sherman said with energy. "Six divisions of reinforcements is hardly sufficient! The enemy has probably received much more than that already, and could cross the river at any moment! The enemy cavalry is tearing our supply line to pieces! If we can make it back to Chattanooga with a thousand men remaining, we should count ourselves lucky!"

The look of enthusiasm on McPherson's face vanished in a flash, replaced by a look of horrified concern. "Cump, I have heard nothing of any enemy reinforcements, nor have I heard-"

"You will address me as `General', young man! Do you understand me properly?"

McPherson was utterly taken aback. He and Sherman had become close friends over the years they had served together and informality between them was a matter of course. But the personal snub was nowhere near as frightening to McPherson as his chief's clearly tenuous grip on sanity.

Sherman continued on, waving his arms in exasperation. "And how dare Grant try to provoke me into launching an attack on Atlanta? Does he want my men slaughtered under the guns of our enemy like they were at Kennesaw Mountain? Or, dare I say, like his own men were slaughtered at Cold Harbor? And this talk of mounting an offensive into Alabama is the sheerest lunacy! How would he expect me to keep such a force supplied?"

"If the Army of the Tennessee brought along sufficient ammunition in its wagon trains, it could subsist from the countryside as far as foodstuffs are concerned, just like we did during the Vicksburg campaign. It would also force Johnston to detach strong forces from his present position in order to block our advance." McPherson said this cautiously, knowing its logic but not knowing if its logic would be appreciated.

Sherman pointed his finger directly at McPherson. "When I ask you for information, you shall provide it to me. But I shall never ask for your advice on military matters, so do not presume to give it to me."

"Of course, sir." There was nothing else McPherson felt he could say.

"Return to your command. Shoot that deserter. If you feel it necessary, find a different deserter and shoot him instead. But I will have examples made."

McPherson nodded. "Yes, sir." He paused for a few moments, considering whether he should say what he wanted to say. "General Sherman, are you all right?"

Sherman looked up at him icily. "Am I all right? Am I all right, you ask? You always ask me that! What the hell kind of question is that? Are you in league with Joseph Hooker now?"

"You know that I detest that man just as much as you do," McPherson said, resentment creeping into his voice. "What he has done to you by going to the papers with his false and slanderous stories offends me every bit as it does you."

"Does it now?" Sherman said sarcastically.

McPherson waited a few moments before speaking again. "Was there anything else, sir?"

"No. Return to your command."

"Yes, sir." McPherson saluted stiffly, turned and walked out the door. Sherman didn't bother watching him go, instead reading through Grant's telegram once again.

*   *   *   *   *

August 16, Night

Nightfall had only made the rioting worse. From the roof of the building housing the offices and printing press of his newspaper, Manton Marble watched as New York City burned all around him. He was equally aghast and enthralled by what he saw. He had been an eyewitness to the devastating draft riots which had wracked the city the previous year, but it had quickly become apparent to him that the disturbances now engulfing the city made the unrest of 1863 appear trivial by comparison.

Next door, a mob was busy ransacking the offices of the pro-Lincoln *New York Times*. Though he was not exactly displeased to see a rival newspaper receive such treatment, Marble was somewhat worried lest a fire start and spread to the *New York World* building. The rioters were leaving his own newspaper alone, deterred by the armed guards he had posted on the ground floor and the fact that his paper was well known to be opposed to the Lincoln administration.

If what he was hearing from his reporters in other parts of New York City was true, the entire metropolis was dissolving into chaos. The houses of prominent Republicans were being attacked, gangs of Irish immigrants were venting their racial hatred by killing blacks on the street in horrific fashion, and stores and warehouses were being looted indiscriminately in every ward. The veneer of public order had completely fallen apart. Marble could see ugly red glows off to the north and northwest, indicating that much of New York City was on fire.

One of Marble's errand boys, those young men who did favors and occasional reporting for him in the hopes of one day being a major player at the newspaper, came running breathlessly up to him, having charged up the stairs from the ground floor.

"Mr. Marble! Mr. Greeley is here!"

"Is he?" Marble said with a grin. Greeley, the eccentric but fervently Republican editor of the *New York Tribune*, was one of Marble's most devoted enemies in both politics and the newspaper business. "What is he doing here?"

"Don't know, sir."

"Well, send him on up."

Marble turned and gazed out over the city again as the errand boy ran back downstairs. A few minutes later, Greeley arrived on the roof.

"I hope you're proud of yourself, Marble," he said harshly.

- 386 -

"I don't know what you're talking about. What are you doing here?"

Greeley's face was a synthesis of anger and despair. "It seems that the *New York World* is magically immune from the attentions of the rioters, though all Republican newspapers in the city are being attacked. If I want to save my own skin and avoid being hanged from a lamppost, I have little choice but to come here and ask for your protection."

"You have it," Marble said, nodding. He honestly couldn't have cared less if Greeley were hanged by the mob or not. Indeed, he would have found such an event worthy of several good jokes. But having one of his archenemies come and throw himself upon his mercy gave Marble a sense of satisfaction.

"I hate having to ask you for it, thought, especially since all this is your doing."

"I am insulted, sir. How can a mere newspaper man like me be responsible for these riots?"

"That story you ran the day after the shooting in Central Park!" Greeley spat. "The `Manhattan Massacre' is what you called it! You said that the soldiers murdered Vallandigham and then fired into a peaceful crowd without provocation!"

"That is what happened, according to my reporters."

"Hogwash! You just want to paint the administration with a tar brush and to sell newspapers! And if the city is burned to the ground as a consequence, you don't care a damn!"

"Did I send an angry crowd to attack the provost marshal's headquarters the day after the shootings? Did I organize the funerals of the victims? No, I did not. These are real people we're talking about here, Greeley. People who were killed by Union soldiers for no reason other than that they were attending a Democratic Party rally. You can't argue with the facts."

The part of Marble's mind which still respected the truth told him that Greeley might be correct. Exactly what had happened during the incident in Central Park was unclear, but it did seem that there were armed Tammany Hall men shooting at the soldiers at some point. Still, Marble had felt no particular compunction in failing to mention this fact in the story the *New York World* had run. The patriots of old had acted in precisely the same manner when the Boston Massacre had taken place, after all.

The story he had run had suited his needs. The image of government soldiers murdering one of the President's most vocal political opponents before firing into a peaceful crowd had quickly flashed across the country. The story he had written for the *New York World* had been reprinted almost word for word by the *Chicago Times*, the *Cincinnati Inquirer* and other Democratic newspapers across the North. Just as the story of Sherman's insanity was beginning to fade from the front pages, the story of the Manhattan

Massacre appeared. It, and the resulting riots in New York City, would obviously dominate the headlines for at least the next several days.

"You should be ashamed of yourself, you son of a bitch," Greeley was saying. "You have on your hands the blood of all the people who have been killed in this chaos. I shall pray to God to have mercy on your soul."

Marble simply shrugged. He couldn't possibly have cared less what Greeley said, nor was he paying attention to him any longer. He gazed out over the city as though it were a stage, feeling as though he was the playwright and the flames were his actors.

*   *   *   *   *

August 17, Afternoon

The confines of the office seemed even more stuffy than usual as Davis listened to George Trenholm, who had just recently joined his Cabinet as the new Secretary of the Treasury. What he was hearing did not make him happy.

"How bad is it?" Davis asked. "Summarize, if you please."

"It's bad, Mr. President. Very bad. According to my latest information, a barrel of flour which cost eight dollars at the commencement of the war now costs, on average, about four hundred and twenty-five dollars. People are paying five dollars for a pound of coffee, whereas when the war began it would have cost less than twenty cents. Potatoes cost seven times more today than they did two years ago, and a pound of beef that cost fifteen cents in late 1861 is today going for more than two dollars. The same is true for all other commodities, Mr. President."

"Not cotton or tobacco," Davis pointed out.

"True. But people can eat neither cotton nor tobacco."

Davis sighed and slowly nodded. He was far from unaware of the suffering endured by the civilian population on account of the inflation that was ravaging the Southern economy. For a moment, he recalled the day in the spring of 1863 when he had had to clamber atop a wagon in the Richmond streets and give an impromptu speech to calm an angry mob of women who were desperately seeking bread.

"Can you at least tell me that our currency fares better?"

"I wish I could, but I cannot," Trenholm replied. Unlike the other Cabinet members, Benjamin aside, the new Secretary of the Treasury was displaying an annoying habit of telling Davis the bad news.

"Out with it, then."

"Very well. At present rates, a Confederate dollar is worth only four percent of a dollar in gold."

"But that's worse than it was three months ago!" Davis exclaimed.

"Indeed it is, Mr. President."

"Surely the victory at Peachtree Creek would cause people to have more faith in Confederate currency!"

"Perhaps, but you must remember that the Union has since won their naval victory at Mobile Bay."

"I know that. But the Battle of Peachtree Creek was far more important than the Battle of Mobile Bay."

"I'm not qualified to comment on matters of a military nature, Mr. President. But as great a victory as Peachtree Creek was, it has no apparent economic consequence. By contrast, the Union closure of Mobile Bay represents a severe economic blow to our Confederacy. Mobile, like Charleston and Savannah, is now closed to blockade runners. Galveston remains open but is cut off by Union control of the Mississippi River. This leaves Wilmington in North Carolina as the single port through which we can export cotton and import foreign goods."

Davis nodded quickly. He made a mental note to ask Secretary Seddon about conditions at Fort Fisher, which guarded the sea approaches to Wilmington. He also considered inquiring of General Lee as to whether it might be possible for some troops to be spared from the Army of Northern Virginia to reinforce the garrison of the fort.

Trenholm was still talking. "The closure of Mobile Bay is about more than just hindering our ability to bring in hard cash through the sale of cotton. The government securities we have on sale in the bond markets of London, Paris and Amsterdam are only fetching the prices they are because they are backed by cotton. Even if we are unable to keep up the interest payments, the bond holder can still redeem them in cotton. But this only matters if the holder is actually able to take physical possession of the cotton."

"And the closure of Mobile Bay makes it much more difficult to do that than was previously the case."

"Exactly, Mr. President. This means that the bonds will decrease in value, and our currency with them, despite our recent victory at Peachtree Creek."

Davis looked down at the desk and shook his head. He was no economist, but had assumed that the rise in confidence following their great victory would help stabilize the value of Confederate currency and therefore limit the rise in commodity prices that was slowly strangling the country's economy. To learn otherwise was extremely discouraging.

If prices for foodstuffs and other necessary items continued to increase, morale on the home front would become increasingly worse. Davis could imagine how the men in uniform were being affected by receiving desperate letters from their families at home, describing how hard it was simply to obtain enough food for the children. At best, the spirits of the men would suffer. At worst, they might be tempted to desert.

Could he blame them if they thought about deserting? He tried to imagine how he would react if he were in the army and received a letter from Varina telling him that the family was in desperate straits. Like any man, his first instinct would be to abandon the colors and go to his family with all speed, doing whatever he could to protect and provide for them. If anything was more important than a man's duty to his country, it was his duty to his wife and children.

Immersed in these thoughts, he suddenly realized that Trenholm was still talking.

"I'm sorry, Mr. Secretary. Could you repeat what you just said?"

"I was saying that the latest figures regarding the blockade runners, which I have from Mr. Mallory, are equally discouraging. Not only is Mobile Bay now closed to us, leaving Wilmington as our last major open port, but the Yankee blockaders are becoming increasingly effective. When the war started, only one out of ten blockade runners was captured. Today, however, the figure is one out of three. The increased possibility of capture is making British sea captains increasingly reluctant to even make the attempt, as the higher insurance premiums they must pay are making the business less profitable."

Davis nodded. If anyone knew the economics of blockade running, it was Charles Trenholm. It was through blockade running that he had made himself the wealthiest man in the Confederacy before accepting Davis's offer to become the Secretary of the Treasury.

"Surely the legislation that Congress passed to regulate blockade runners earlier this year is helping to alleviate the situation?" The law had specified that at least half of the cargo space on every blockade runner had to be placed at the disposal of the government. It had been an attempt to reduce the quantity of luxury goods such as wine and perfume in favor of military supplies and basic foodstuffs. The former, needless to say, generated significantly higher profits than did the latter.

"The new law might be effective, if only we could enforce it. But most captains, to my knowledge, are completely ignoring the legislation. We could prosecute them, I suppose, but if we did that most of them would just get out of the blockade running business altogether, which would gain us nothing."

The President sighed in exasperation. Legislation which seemed so simple on paper was all too often ephemeral when applied to the real world. It was like trying to eat soup with a fork.

'Very well, Mr. Secretary. I thank you for your report. Please summarize any recommendations you have as to how we might improve our financial situation and submit them to me in writing before next week."

"Of course, Mr. President." Trenholm rose, bowed, and walked out the door, leaving the President alone.

Davis slowly shook his head. What Trenholm had told him was not especially surprising, but this made it no less dispiriting. The Confederacy might win a dozen battlefield victories as decisive as Peachtree Creek, but if the war went on the economy that supported the war effort would eventually collapse. Inflation and the growing lack of basic necessities were like an acid that was dissolving the Confederacy from within.

Since the defeat at Gettysburg and the fall of Vicksburg, Davis had known that the only way for the Confederacy to gain its independence would be to outlast the North until a peace party was voted into power. They had only to hold on for three months longer. With the Southern economy rapidly falling to pieces, he wondered if they had that much time.

*   *   *   *   *

August 18, Noon

To Grant, the sound of the guns bombarding the Confederate trenches at Petersburg rolled over the central Virginia countryside like the thunder of a distant but approaching storm. He didn't hear the louder, clanging sound of rebel return fire, which didn't surprise him. As low on gunpowder as they were, the enemy didn't respond to his regular artillery barrages unless they felt they had to.

Sitting under a tree just outside his headquarters at City Point, Grant paid no attention to the sound of artillery in any event. He was focused on the shocking telegram he held in his hands.

General Grant,

We send this message to you with the greatest reluctance, but we feel that the duty we owe to the nation requires it. It seems to us that General Sherman has suffered some sort of mental breakdown that has incapacitated him and rendered him unfit for command. The symptoms appear to resemble the same malaise from which General Sherman suffered in late 1861. He seems not to comprehend the true nature of the military situation, imagining it to be far worse than it is. We fear for the well-being of our commander no less than we do for the good of the service. Having had discreet discussions among ourselves, we feel compelled to bring this matter to your attention and we trust that you will take any necessary and appropriate action.

General James McPherson
General John Schofield
General Oliver Howard

Grant folded the telegram and put it in his pocket. Shocking though it was, no member of Grant's staff could have told it from the expression on their commander's face, which remained as serene and unconcerned as ever. The contents of the message were what he had greatly feared and hoped against hope would not happen. Now, he had to make what would be one of the most difficult decisions of his tenure as general-in-chief of the Union armies.

Ulysses S. Grant trusted William T. Sherman as he trusted no other man. But he also knew him better than any other man. He remembered the dark days of late 1861, when Sherman had very nearly been forced out of the army under suspicion of insanity. He knew, from countless midnight discussions with Sherman throughout 1862 and 1863, about the dark depressive states into which he could fall, to say nothing of his suicide attempt.

During his service as Grant's subordinate at Shiloh, Vicksburg, and Chattanooga, Sherman had successfully regained his self-confidence. His strength had endured such setbacks as the failed attack at Kennesaw Mountain. Despite this, Grant could well imagine the damage inflicted upon Sherman's mind by the disastrous defeat at Peachtree Creek. The renewed charges of insanity in the papers brought on by the interview with Joseph Hooker had only made it worse. Such misfortunes could break the mind of any man.

Looking down at the three names signed to the bottom of the telegram, Grant focused in particular on McPherson. A brother-in-arms, McPherson had served with both Grant and Sherman since the beginning of the war. Sherman alone excepted, McPherson was the man in the army Grant most admired and trusted. He would not have attached his name to such a message unless he had seen the evidence with his own eyes and had absolutely no doubt that the essence of the telegram was true.

The fact that the two other army commanders serving under Sherman had attached their names to the telegram was also quite telling. While he did not know either Schofield or Howard particularly well, he knew that they would not have advanced to the level of army command had they been fools. If all three of them were of the same mind on the subject, then the situation had to be truly grave.

The facts on the ground confirmed what the men said. Nearly three weeks had passed since Sherman's forces had withdrawn to the north bank of the Chattahoochee. The reinforcements being sent from Virginia were soon to arrive, despite the annoyance of the rebel raids on the railroads in Tennessee and Georgia. Yet Sherman had communicated no clear plan and had not undertaken any significant operation. It was as if he had become paralyzed.

For a long time, Grant sat silently. He smoked a cigar and, as he was wont to do when faced with a difficult decision, whittled away on a short stick with a knife. He went over in his mind, again and again, the likely consequences of varying courses of action he might take in light of the information he had just received.

Finally, after a long time, he made his decision. He rose from his chair, walked into his headquarters, and called for writing materials.

*   *   *   *   *

August 18, Afternoon

"Wheeler dead?" Johnston repeated, shocked despite himself.

"Yes, sir," the officer standing before him said sadly. He was Captain Jefferson Leftwich of the 8th Tennessee Cavalry Regiment, one of the units which had gone north with Wheeler on his grand raid against Sherman's supply lines. He had arrived at Johnston's headquarters at the Niles House only ten minutes earlier, covered in dust and with his head wrapped in a bloody bandage.

Johnston nodded slowly. "Give me the details, son."

The story which Leftwich proceeded to recount was not a pleasant one to hear, but neither did it particularly take Johnston by surprise. He had heard nothing from Wheeler since the cavalry general had departed the army with four thousand troopers on July 28. Not having had a very high opinion of Wheeler's abilities to begin with, he had not expected any useful results from the raid.

What had apparently happened was less a raid than a fiasco. Rather than strike at the most vulnerable sections of the Western and Atlantic Railroad, Wheeler had gone looking for a fight, directing his men to attack the strongly fortified blockhouses Sherman's engineers had constructed to protect bridges and other important points. Instead of avoiding Union cavalry brigades, Wheeler had actively sought them out in his quest for combat. Although the Southern troopers had won some of these fights, on each occasion they suffered significant losses, became more disorganized, and lost valuable time.

As he listened to Leftwich go on, Johnston felt more and more disappointed. After tearing up a measly few miles of railroad south of the Etowah River, Wheeler veered northwards and attempted to attack the Union forts at Dalton and Resaca.

However, according to Leftwich, Wheeler had begun to lose control of his command by this point. He had never been a very strict disciplinarian, which was one of the main complaints Johnston had had about him, and had clearly failed to keep his units under firm control. Hundreds of Tennessee and Kentucky troopers had deserted and gone off to visit their homes. Other units fell to looting local communities on the excuse that they needed supplies.

"A damn disgrace," Mackall said upon hearing of the looting.

"Captain Leftwich," Johnston said firmly. "Before you take your leave, please give General Mackall the names of any looters you can specifically identify. They shall have charges brought against them at the earliest possible opportunity."

"Of course, General."

"Now, go on."

He did. Leftwich told of a foolhardy attack Wheeler had launched on an enemy fort near Dalton, which he had expected to be an easy victory because the men holding it had been black troops, recruited from among the freed slaves of Tennessee. But the black troops defending the post had fought bravely and effectively, holding their position without much trouble at all. Wheeler himself had been carried from the field, shot through the chest. According to Leftwich, he had lasted about two hours before he finally died, enduring agonizing pain before the end.

The remainder of the story was even worse. Of the four thousand men Wheeler had taken with him into northern Georgia, only a few hundred were on their way back to the Army of Tennessee. Leftwich was, as far as he knew, the first officer to make it back to friendly lines, and had taken it upon himself to report to Johnston as quickly as he could.

"You have done very well, Captain Leftwich. Now, return to your men and do what you can to get them in proper fighting trim. And please prepare a written report."

"Yes, sir." The young captain gave a stiff, professional salute, which Johnston returned with every mark of respect.

Throughout the interview, several staff officers had crowded around, interested to hear the account for themselves. Now that it was over, they scattered to return to their duties. Johnston leaned against one of the pillars on the porch, a surly look on his face, shaking his head.

"It's a shame, William. A fine force of four thousand cavalry, destroyed for no good reason."

"Indeed," Mackall replied. "I see no benefit from Wheeler's raid. Our scouts report that trains from Chattanooga have continued to arrive in Sherman's camp without any apparent trouble."

"The only benefit I can see from this disaster is that it may have drawn away Union cavalry forces which would otherwise have been employed against Forrest in Tennessee. Forrest, unlike Wheeler, has actually been able to accomplish some good. However, now that Wheeler is dead and his force scattered, it may be that Forrest will face increasing opposition."

Mackall nodded. "It is already clear that several brigades of the Sixth Corps arriving from Virginia have been deployed to garrison threatened points in Tennessee rather than be shipped on down the railroad to Sherman. Reconstruction of the bridge at Bridgeport is already underway, according to our sources."

"Astonishing," Johnston said with admiration. "Had we but a fraction of the material resources of the North, our independence would have been achieved long ago."

"Truth, indeed."

"Please send a message to General Forrest informing him of what happened to Wheeler's command. He will want to know, as it may affect his own operations."

"At once, sir."

"Wheeler was not married, was he?"

Mackall thought for a moment. "I don't believe so, sir."

"Double check. In any case, find out the name of his nearest living relative and draft a letter for me to send to them."

"I will." Mackall paused a moment before he spoke again. "Wheeler was among those plotting to remove you from command."

Johnston waved dismissively. "It makes no difference now. Whatever his flaws as a man and as a commander, he was a brave man who died defending his country."

Mackall nodded and strode off, leaving Johnston to his thoughts. He shook his head again. It was impossible to know how many of his troopers had been killed or captured in this foolish escapade. Some would have deserted and gone home, while it was likely that others would trickle back to the army either individually or in small groups over the coming weeks.

What was clear to Johnston was that half of his cavalry had been effectively destroyed. What impact this would have on the campaign was anyone's guess. Sherman had barely budged since he had withdrawn across the Chattahoochee three weeks earlier, and Johnston found his lack of activity very disquieting. True, thousands of Sherman's men had departed due to expired enlistments, but he was also receiving reinforcements from Virginia.

Johnston was worried. If Sherman now intended on making some sort of movement across the Chattahoochee to once again threaten Atlanta, the weakness of the Confederate cavalry would make it more difficult for such a move to be detected in time for it to be intercepted. It was still summer. There remained several months in the campaign season before winter would bring a halt to active operations. Johnston had no doubt that the enemy would make another attempt to capture Atlanta, though he had no idea where and how they would do it.

Worse, Johnston felt certain that President Davis would seek to lay the blame for the destruction of the cavalry and the death of Wheeler squarely on his shoulders. After all, Davis blamed Johnston for the loss of Vicksburg, the loss of northern Georgia, and just about every other Confederate setback. As far as Johnston could tell, Davis would have liked to blame him for the original sin of Adam and the damnation of all mankind. It would not matter in the least that it had been Davis, rather than Johnston, who had pushed for the dispatch of Wheeler.

He had defeated Sherman at Peachtree Creek. Hood had departed the army and now Wheeler had been sent to his eternal reward by a bullet fired from the gun of a freed slave. Still, Johnston felt certain that his most dangerous enemy remained determined to destroy him.

Mackall returned and held out an elegantly enveloped letter with a wax seal. "Just arrived from Atlanta, General. Mayor Calhoun requests the honor of your presence at a banquet this Saturday celebrating our victory at Peachtree Creek and the eviction of the enemy from the south bank of the Chattahoochee. This is your official invitation, or so I am told."

"Well, that's very generous of the honorable mayor," Johnston said, taking the invitation, slicing through the wax seal and quickly reading its contents. "Two days from now? I suppose that would be acceptable, barring any serious military developments. Please send Mayor Calhoun my regards and tell him I will attend."

"Very well, sir. If there happens to be any wine left over, I hope you would do me the favor of bringing it back for the headquarters staff to enjoy."

Johnston laughed. "Consider it done, my friend."

Chapter Eleven

August 19, Evening

"I don't which circle of hell Clement Vallandigham ended up in," Lincoln said with a wry grin. "Wherever he is, though, I have no doubt that he's having a good laugh at my expense."

Across the table, Secretary of State William Seward chuckled softly, pouring himself another glass of claret from an ornate decanter as he did so. Lincoln nodded when Seward held the decanter up slightly, whereupon another glass was poured for the President. Lincoln drank virtually no alcohol, but the wine Seward served was so fine that Lincoln usually indulged in a glass or two whenever he visited the table of his Secretary of State.

"Wherever traitors go, I should think," Seward answered. "Wasn't that the eighth circle?"

"The ninth, I believe." Lincoln thought about it for just a moment. "Yes, I am quite certain it was the ninth. That was where Dante found Brutus, Cassius, and Judas Iscariot."

Lincoln thought back to when he had first encountered Dante's *Inferno* as a teenager. He was momentarily transported back to the lonely youth on his father's farm in Indiana, with less than a year of formal education, seemingly condemned to live a life of obscurity and meaningless toil. His love of books and poetry had provided the only means of escape from the harsh realities of his existence.

Lincoln took another bite of the delicious roast beef that had been set before him, which had been tenderly cooked on a spit for hours while being flavored with rosemary and other herbs. Next to it was a dish of delicately stewed vegetables. It was about as far from the simple fare he had eaten in his youth as was possible to get. They had already completed a lovely first course of turtle soup and salad. If the previous evenings he had spent at Seward's home were any indication, Lincoln could look forward to a splendid dessert when the dinner was completed.

The President greatly enjoyed the evenings he spent at Seward's splendid home on Lafayette Square. Such nights were becoming more frequent as the stresses of his office increased as the war dragged on. In Seward's company, Lincoln found a companion with whom he could discuss poetry, philosophy, religion, and other subjects that had absolutely nothing to do with the war or the political issues of the day. It was a relationship that Lincoln could never have had with Stanton or any of his other friends in Washington. Moreover, since Mary Todd disliked Seward and refused to set foot in his house, as Seward's guest Lincoln could find a few precious hours of freedom from his complicated and frustrating marriage.

Seward was still talking. "In any case, you are correct. In death, Vallandigham may have the last laugh. I fear that he will do us more harm by getting himself killed than he would have done had he given a thousand additional speeches and written a thousand more pamphlets."

Lincoln nodded soberly, taking another bite of the roast beef. Ever since Vallandigham's death, in what even some Republican newspapers were now calling the Manhattan Massacre, the unscrupulous Copperhead politician had been held up as a martyr by the Democratic Party. Demonstrations against what was seen as his murder had been held from one end of the Union to the other.

"Did you hear about what happened in Cincinnati?" Lincoln asked.

"No. What?"

"It seems that the local Democratic Party machine held some sort of funeral *in absentia* for Vallandigham, which was attended by several thousand people. After they laid down the coffin, which contained God's knows what, Congressman George Pendleton made a speech which got the crowd so worked up that they marched to the local draft office and burned it down."

Seward laughed again with a soft bitterness. "I'd suggest that you have Congressman Pendleton arrested, but that would only strengthen the Copperheads. Incidents like this are breaking out all over the country now. I am only thankful that the disorders in New York were put down before they spread to other cities."

"Quite so," Lincoln replied. "I reckon I made the right choice when I ordered General Butler to the city with two brigades. The man might be a bumbling fool when it comes to generalship, being much more a politician than a soldier, but he knows how to secure and maintain order in a city. He proved that two years ago in New Orleans, by God!"

"We may have avoided the worst, Abe. But what is happening is quite bad enough. I read in the papers this morning that workers in several iron foundries and textile mills in Chicago have refused to continue working unless the men responsible for Vallandigham's death are brought to justice. The Democratic Party is determined to make as much hay as possible from Vallandigham's death. I hear that they are printing tens of thousands of copies of a new pamphlet containing a cartoon that depicts you cleaving Vallandigham's head in two with a giant axe."

A grin crossed Lincoln's face. "I should like a copy of that pamphlet, I would think. I might find it relaxing to look at such a picture when I find myself hassled by the pressures of my office."

Seward went on, ignoring what he interpreted as a joke. "All over the country, excepting only New England, crowds are attacking draft offices, newspapers that are sympathetic to our party, and even the homes of prominent Republicans."

Seward didn't add, because he didn't need to, the fact that supporters of the Republican Party were giving as good as they got, retaliating with their own brand of mob violence against Democratic targets. Public order throughout the Union was coming under strain.

Lincoln took a sip of wine. "I feel rather like Atlas, William. The weight on my shoulders is getting more and more unbearable. The draft is not achieving anything and is ruining us politically. Scarcely a man has volunteered this summer, even though we have increased the monetary bounty again."

"The young men of the North do not want to die in fiascoes like Peachtree Creek or the Crater, it would seem," Seward observed sourly.

"Yes, but compounding the problem is that so many regiments who enlisted for three-year terms back in 1861 are now going home. Since Peachtree Creek, Sherman's army has lost ten thousand men simply because of expired enlistments, nearly half the number of men they lost in that dreadful battle itself. I am told that desertion has increased in the armies of both Sherman and Grant in the past few months. Our armies are steadily melting away."

Seward nodded slowly, looking at Lincoln with profound compassion. "The sunlight seemed to break through the clouds with the news of Farragut's victory at Mobile Bay and the defeat of Wheeler's cavalry raid in north Georgia. But with the recent domestic disturbances, those successes have already been forgotten by the people. And now, my friend, I am afraid that I must add to your burdens."

Lincoln stopped in mid-chew for a moment. He straightened in his chair, put down his knife and fork, and savored the taste of the beef for a few more precious seconds before swallowing. "Well, out with it, William."

"I was visited by Lord Lyons today."

"And what did the noble representative from Her Britannic Majesty have to say?" Lincoln said these words with a heavy dose of sarcasm, as he found the ideas of nobility and monarchy absurd. But however nonsensical he found Lord Lyon's title to be, Lincoln respected Lyons as an individual and was certain that the British minister personally desired a Union victory.

"Lord Lyons wanted to inform me, unofficially, that Prime Minister Palmerston is preparing a proclamation formally recognizing the rebels as an independent government should we lose at the polls in November."

Lincoln put his elbows on the table, leaned his face forward into his hands, and let out the deepest sigh Seward had ever heard. He was silent for nearly two minutes before replying.

"Did he say why?"

"The thinking in London is that if the Democrats triumph in November and implement a cease-fire and open negotiations with the rebels, and if the rebels continue to be militarily successful in the present campaigning season, Southern independence is all but assured. In that case, any delay in establishing formal diplomatic relations might allow the French to get the diplomatic jump on them, thereby gaining better access to valuable cotton and tobacco, plus a lucrative export market. These gentlemen want England, not France, to reap the benefits of being the first to recognize Southern independence."

Lincoln shrugged, then picked his fork back up and went back to his roast beef. "It is a disappointment, to be sure. But we're already doing all we can to win the war. We may as well act as though we never heard this news."

Seward nodded. "Very well, Mr. President."

"Please ask him not to mention this to anyone else, though. If it got into the papers, it would not encourage the rebels, but it would also hurt the value of greenbacks and contribute to further inflation. The Democrats are already doing their damndest to devalue our currency by manipulating the gold markets. I'd rather not have more coal thrown onto that fire."

"Of course. Lord Lyons has always been a discreet man."

"And now, my dear William, in the spirit of reciprocity, I shall answer the bad news you have delivered with some bad news of my own."

Seward leaned forward and rang a bell that sat on the table. In less than five seconds, the door to the dining room opened and a black servant appeared.

"Yes, Mr. Seward?"

"More wine, if you please, James. And there's no need to be frugal."

"Right away, sir." With a short, sharp bow, James vanished.

Seward turned back to Lincoln. "Allow me to improve my defensive fortifications before you give me your bad news, Mr. President."

Lincoln rolled back his head and laughed in that enormous and all-consuming manner which so delighted all who saw it. James appeared a moment later with another ornate decanter filled with red wine.

"The Haut-Brion, Mr. Seward?"

"Excellent choice, James. I'll pour, thank you." James bowed again and vanished. "Mr. President, now that we shall be well-fortified, what is this bad news of which you speak?"

"I received a letter from Raymond yesterday."

"Oh? I had heard that he made good his escape from the mob in New York City."

"He did, though his printing presses were all destroyed."

"What did he say in this letter, which has disturbed you so? He sends you letters regularly, after all."

"He made the suggestion, shocking to me, that we quietly approach the leaders of the so-called Confederacy and make an effort to reach a compromise peace. He said we should ask them to accept the authority of the federal government in exchange for a guarantee that the Emancipation Proclamation will be revoked. He also suggests that we stop our efforts to get the amendment abolishing slavery through Congress."

A scowl appeared on Seward's face. "I thought Raymond was one of us," he said bitterly.

"He is," Lincoln replied. "He is as staunch a Union and anti-slavery man as any of us, which is why his letter pained me so much. If he has lost faith, if he suggests that we should negotiate with the rebels and drop emancipation as a condition of peace, then how many others must feel the same way?"

"Quite a few, no doubt. How can we expect to win the election in such circumstances? The tide is setting strongly against us."

For one long and sober moment, neither man spoke. Then, as if in answer to a silent prayer for something to lighten the mood, James again appeared at the door bearing a covered silver platter. He set it before Lincoln and Seward and, in a single deft move, withdrew the cover to reveal beautifully crafted iced fruits and ice cream.

"I hope you enjoy this, Mr. President," James said. "The chef wanted to provide something extra special for you tonight."

"If tasting it provides even a fraction of the pleasure I gain from looking at it, I shall enjoy it heartily," Lincoln said.

As James spooned generous portions of the dessert onto the two plates, there was a soft clearing of a throat at the doorway. Seward pushed his chair back, walked over and was handed a message. He excused the messenger with a wave and, while walking back to the table, darted his eyes through the paper. Seating himself again, he passed it over to Lincoln.

"From the War Department."

President Lincoln,

Be advised that I have just this hour received a telegram from General Grant. He has decided to go to Georgia and personally take command of our armies positioned near Atlanta north of the Chattahoochee, leaving the Army of the Potomac in the hands of General Meade. He says that he shall be leaving City Point immediately and, if you so wish, he can stop in Washington for consultations before commencing his journey west.

Secretary of War Stanton

Lincoln's eyebrows popped up. "Well, this is certainly interesting."

"I should say so," Seward said. "I assume that in resuming personal command of our Western armies, Grant is effectively removing Sherman from command?"

"I suppose he might keep Sherman on hand as chief-of-staff or some such thing. If not, we can find him some position in the Trans-Mississippi, or simply ask him to return to his home until we have need of him. Better this way, I think. It will soften the political fallout. As it has been Grant's decision rather than mine, the Democratic press cannot honestly say that I cracked under pressure to replace Sherman."

"They shall say so in any event," Seward noted.

"Yes, but the people will not be so easily persuaded."

"I hope so, Mr. President."

"Alas, let us enjoy this enchanting dessert and finish this bottle of wine. After that, I shall leave you to own devices and hurry over to the War Department to try to get more details about what General Grant is up to."

*   *   *   *   *

Sherman was not surprised at the two telegrams he had received within a quarter of an hour of one another. The fact that their arrival had not been unexpected did nothing to diminish the pain.

He read through the first telegram again.

General Sherman,

Be advised that General Grant has decided to take direct command of the Military District of the Mississippi and is en route to your headquarters at Vining's Station at this time. Please turn over your command to General McPherson until such time as General Grant arrives. Report to Louisville and await further orders.

Secretary of War Stanton

Telegrams such as this had been sent to many Union generals since the beginning of the war. McClellan had received one after his pathetic failure to pursue Lee following the Battle of Antietam. Rosecrans had received one after his disastrous defeat at the Battle of Chickamauga. Burnside had gotten one after the one-sided fiasco at Fredericksburg, just as Hooker had after the humiliating defeat at Chancellorsville.

Sherman tried to take some comfort from the fact that none of those other generals had received what amounted to a message of apology from the general-in-chief.

General Sherman,

I hope you realize and understand that I am taking this step with the greatest reluctance and only after determining that I have no other choice. I sincerely hope that you do not conclude that this decision represents any lack of confidence in you on my part. Your friendship and personal esteem mean as much to me today as they did on the day we accepted the surrender of Vicksburg. Rest assured that you may continue to call on me for anything at any time and that I earnestly hope to be in your friendly company at the earliest possible moment.

General Grant

The gracious telegram from his friend and superior alleviated the pain he was feeling, but only slightly. The first telegram decisively confirmed, as only an official communication could, that he had abjectly and completely failed. Rather than be renowned as the conqueror of Atlanta and the destroyer of the slave-holding traitors of the Confederacy, he would only be remembered as the incompetent general who lost the Battle of Peachtree Creek, cost tens of thousands of brave Northern soldiers their lives, and allowed America to be torn asunder.

Sherman wrote out a response to the War Department acknowledging his receipt of the earlier message. He momentarily considered sending a message protesting the decision, arguing that he had done as well as could have been expected of any man. He just as quickly decided against it. To do so would be humiliating and would leave a permanent written record of his petulant response. Disgraced enough as he was, Sherman had no desire to magnify his shame any more than was necessary.

He sent a courier to the headquarters of the Army of the Tennessee, requesting that General McPherson come and meet with him at once. Though he hated himself for it, Sherman could already feel a wave of relief sweeping through him. The pressures of command were rapidly fading and he could sense the mental threads securing his sanity being strengthened. If losing his command was the price he had to pay to avoid falling into the abyss, he was willing to pay it.

It was slightly before midnight when McPherson finally appeared before him.

"I assume you've been notified?" Sherman asked, holding up the telegram.

"Yes, sir," McPherson answered simply.

Sherman saw that he was attempting to placate him, to make him feel better, to help him avoid the humiliation.

"You'll be in command until Grant arrives, which might take as long as a week."

"Yes, sir."

"It is a grave responsibility, having all the burdens on your shoulders."

"Of that I have no doubt."

"One can only know it fully when one has actually experienced it. Might I offer some advice?"

"Of course, sir."

"I would advise you to do nothing until Grant arrives to assume command. Hold our positions if the rebels seek to advance north, but otherwise wait for his instructions."

"That was what I had determined to do, sir."

"If Johnston does seek to attack north of the river, remember that he is a crafty and dangerous opponent. He will always be rational, yet will never do what is expected. You must be prepared to deal with him, for it shall be your duty to hold him in check until Grant arrives."

"What do you think Johnston shall do, sir?"

Sherman had not the foggiest notion of how to answer McPherson's question. Exactly a month before, Sherman thought he had had a measure of the old fox commanding the Army of Tennessee. Peachtree Creek had destroyed that illusion. Would Johnston remain idle on the south bank of the river? Would he cross to the north side and attempt to attack? Might he even attempt to do that which Wheeler had failed to achieve, and swing a portion of his army against the Union railroad and cut the Northern armies off from their supplies?

"I do not know," Sherman finally answered. "He is unpredictable. I thought I knew the man, but events have proven that I do not. You shall have to use your own judgment."

"And, if I may ask, what do you think Grant will do when he arrives?"

Sherman smiled and chuckled ever so softly. "I think Grant will achieve what I could not. At the very least, he will do his damnedest to try."

August 20, Evening

Johnston could not remember the last time he had enjoyed such a meal. Mayor Calhoun had certainly spared no expense or effort in putting on as lavish a display as he possibly could. Johnston estimated that at least a dozen chickens had been given up to the roasting oven and that the local farms must have been scoured mercilessly to provide the abundant vegetables covering the table. The excellent wine was no less impressive and Johnston made a note to inquire of Calhoun where he had gotten it. It might, after all, prove possible to acquire some for the headquarters mess of the Army of Tennessee.

As he sampled the delectable food, he looked around at the collection of distinguished men who had assembled in the large and elegant dining room at the Trout House, the city's finest hotel. All were there ostensibly to honor him and his army for their recent victory. Despite the fact that he was a high-ranking general and commander of the one of the two most important armies in the Confederacy, he admitted to himself that he felt intimidated in such company.

Directly across the table from Johnston sat Alexander Stephens, Vice President of the Confederate States of America. Though Stephens was in his early fifties, his skeletal body looked as though it had stopped growing when he had been a teenager, though the withered skin of his face certainly had continued aging. Despite his strange physical appearance, it was said that Stephens' intellectual powers rivaled those of any other man in the Confederacy. Having been denied a meaningful role in the Confederate government, Stephens had spent most of the war at his estate in Georgia. If the rumors were even half true, Stephens detested President Davis almost as much as Johnston did.

Next to Vice President Stephens sat Joseph Brown, Governor of Georgia. Johnston had worked closely with Brown on such matters as the operation of state railroads and the recruitment of the Georgia Militia. The governor's long white beard belied the fact that he was only in his mid-forties, though his eyes sparkled with a strange intelligence that one hesitated to trust too much. Johnston considered Brown a mediocre politician at best, though his loathing for President Davis was, as with Vice President Stephens, something Johnston could appreciate.

Next in line was the man Johnston was most delighted to see, Senator Louis Wigfall. Just returned from his visit to Texas, having narrowly avoided a Yankee gunboat when crossing the Mississippi, Wigfall was now on his way back to Richmond. It was the first time Johnston had seen his friend since the night following the Battle of

Kennesaw Mountain, where he had first warned Johnston of the machinations of Davis and Hood.

Mayor Calhoun, Vice President Stephens, Governor Brown, and Senator Wigfall were only four among two dozen distinguished guests. Some were members of the Georgia state legislature, while a few were members of the Georgia congressional delegation who happened to be home on visits to their constituents. Others were prominent merchants and businessmen from Atlanta's commercial community. Most of these men had been accompanied by their wives, who were wearing dresses that struck Johnston as oddly new and fashionable, considering the wartime hardships the South was experiencing. He couldn't help but wonder how many rifles might have been purchased for his men for the amount of money represented by those dresses.

Sitting to Johnston's right was his wife, Lydia. Throughout the campaign, she had bravely remained in Atlanta despite his occasional suggestions that she depart for some safer place. Johnston had always left the final decision to her and she had chosen to stay put. Despite their proximity, Johnston had seen his wife only on a few occasions since the campaign had begun, though he had written her on a nearly daily basis.

"You look radiant, my dear," Johnston whispered in her ear. It was true. Looking at her, he felt a pang of regret that their devoted marriage had remained childless.

"Do I?" she asked. "This dress is one I had left over from before the war. I fear these other ladies are wearing the latest fashions of Paris, having had them run through the blockade."

"Even the second most beautiful woman in the Confederacy does not possess so much as one-tenth of your beauty." She playfully slapped his arm.

Mayor Calhoun rose to his feet, tapping his wine glass with his fork to quiet the other guests. When this had been accomplished, he held forth.

"I wish to propose a toast to General Joseph Johnston, the commander of the Army of Tennessee, who defeated the Yankee hordes of Sherman and saved the city of Atlanta from certain destruction!" He raised his glass. Everyone around the table stood and raised their glasses. "To General Johnston!" Calhoun said.

"To General Johnston!" the room roared in reply.

As the guests resumed their seats, Vice President Alexander Stephens cleared his throat to speak. "That Johnston was the savior of Atlanta is not to be doubted. The question the history books shall ask is whether our victory might have come earlier and at a smaller price in blood had the chief executive of our nation pursued a proper political and military policy."

Johnston couldn't suppress a smile, as any criticism of the President was music to his ears. Despite himself, he could not resist responding. "Far be it from me to speak ill of the President, but I must say that his policies have certainly hindered the defense of Atlanta in many ways."

"Oh?" Stephens asked. "How so?"

"I believe that had the President seen fit to order Forrest into Tennessee back in June, when I first urged him to do so and when it might have actually done some good, we should have defeated Sherman before he had reached the Chattahoochee River. As it was, I had no choice but to fall back nearly to the gates of Atlanta before being able to attack him successfully."

"Intriguing," Governor Brown said. "As I recall, I myself sent many telegrams and letters to the President also asking him to order Forrest into Tennessee. As he seemed happy enough to do it following the Battle of Peachtree Creek, I am at a loss to explain why he failed to do so before the battle."

"I am distinctly not at a loss to explain it," Wigfall said gruffly. "If you ask me, Davis refused to order Forrest into Tennessee until it was too late to do any good because he actually wanted Johnston to be defeated. His petty vindictiveness toward General Johnston placed the Confederacy in great danger. It was in spite of the President that Johnston was able to emerge triumphant, and certainly not on account of any help the President provided."

Side conversations among the dinner guests had now largely stopped and everyone was suddenly fixated on the three-way discussion among Stephens, Brown and Wigfall. Johnston himself, feeling that he had perhaps said too much even with his single sentence, sat back and acted as though the conversation were about horse racing.

"The President's treatment of General Johnston is nothing new," Wigfall said. "He denied him his proper place in the chain of command back in 1861 and refused to properly support him on the Virginia Peninsula in 1862 and during the Vicksburg Campaign in 1863. Is that not so, General?"

Johnston heartily agreed, but felt it improper to say so. "Etiquette requires me to remain silent on such a question in such a public sphere as this."

Vice President Stephens went on, as though Johnston had said nothing. "General Johnston is far from the only general who has received such treatment from the President. Beauregard and D. H. Hill have as well."

"Such is the fate of any general who fails to acknowledge the omnipotent genius of the almighty Davis," Wigfall said, drawing laughter from around the table. Some of the laughter was hearty, while some sounded distinctly uncomfortable.

"His treatment of generals who earn his personal disfavor is bad enough," Brown said. "But look at the policies of his administration in Richmond! We seceded from the United States in order to escape the centralization of power in Washington, but we find ourselves paying taxes directly to Richmond and having draft officers from the central government swarm through our towns and farms to round up our young men for service outside our state. It's absurd."

"If I am not mistaken, the War Department has even established regulations dictating what blockade runners can and cannot hold as cargo," Vice President Stephens said. "Is it not so, Captain?"

He had addressed this question to an extremely well-dressed guest at the table, who had a warm and wry smile and an elegantly thin mustache. Johnston did not know who the man was, though clearly most other people at the table did. Since he had been addressed as a captain but did not wear a naval uniform, and because of the nature of the question, Johnston assumed that he was the captain of a blockade runner.

"The regulations require that half the space on each blockade runner be reserved for government cargo," the man responded.

"Does this not trouble you?" Wigfall asked.

The man shrugged nonchalantly, as though he considered the whole matter nothing more than an amusing game. "I am happy to bring in rifles and cannon if I am paid well for it. But in truth, the cargo I most enjoy running past the Yankees consists of fine dresses and perfumes for the ladies and good brandy and cognac for the men."

The table laughed heartily at this statement. Johnston thought it unpatriotic, yet found himself joining in the laughter nonetheless. The man smiled as he took another sip of wine, saying nothing more.

Wigfall spoke up again. "I have heard it said by many people that we have simply exchanged one petty tyrant in Washington for another in Richmond. Not a good tradeoff, if you ask me."

Johnston decided to interject. "I suppose that the necessities of war have required certain compromises. After we have achieved our independence, we can return to a proper and smaller form of government."

"The correct sentiment," Stephens replied. "But do you really think that President Davis, having accumulated so much power in his hands, shall happily give it up when the war is over? Is he really that sort of man?"

"I am not qualified to express any opinions on such political questions, Mr. Vice President."

"You do not give yourself enough credit, General," Governor Brown said. "History is full of men who excelled in the art of war and who later excelled in the art of politics. George Washington comes to mind."

"I cannot even see myself standing in the shadow of George Washington," Johnston replied.

"A pity," Stephens said. "After all, the Constitution limits the President to a single term in office. An election will have to be held in 1867. Davis will naturally attempt to choose his own successor in an effort to maintain his effective control over the Confederacy. Those of us who love liberty shall have to find a man of conviction to challenge whoever Davis puts forward. A general who has earned the love of the people by winning a dramatic victory over the Yankees would fit the bill nicely, I should think."

Johnston said nothing, looking down at his plate and carefully sipping his wine. Wigfall, Brown, and Stephens watched him intently, as did every other person sitting at the long table, but the general never looked up. Gradually, he resumed eating his food, ignoring the silence and all the eyes that were fixed on him.

Mayor Calhoun stood up and cleared his throat, having clearly decided to rescue Johnston by changing the subject. "I am happy to report that I have given permission for the Athenaeum to reopen. An acting troupe up from Savannah will be putting on Shakespeare's *King Lear* a week from today."

There was a happy chattering from the assembled guests, followed by light applause. Calhoun beamed happily. "I thought that there would be no better way to celebrate the salvation of the city than to begin the process of getting things back to normal."

Johnston pursed his lips. "Mr. Mayor, with all due respect, the threat to Atlanta is not yet over."

"What?" Calhoun said, still smiling. "Surely you're jesting, General Johnston. You shattered Sherman's army at Peachtree Creek and forced him to retreat north of the Chattahoochee."

"The Battle of Peachtree Creek took place a month ago. Despite the best efforts of my own cavalry and that of General Forrest, the enemy supply lines have not been cut. Even with their heavy losses, they continue to outnumber us, especially as they have been receiving heavy reinforcements from the Eastern Theater. There are yet many months remaining in the campaigning season. I regard another Northern offensive as inevitable."

Calhoun's smile had vanished as he listened to Johnston's words. Rather than continue the conversation, which would have required him to either contradict the general or to agree with his pessimism, he simply returned to his seat.

At that moment, the doors opened and a coterie of slaves entered with dishes of frozen custard. The awkwardness of the preceding minutes of conversation vanished as the guests plunged their spoons into the delicious dessert. Within moments, animated conversation again filled the Trout House dining room.

"Do you really believe Atlanta is still in danger, darling?" Lydia asked her husband.

"Sherman has been completely inactive for the past few weeks. I do not know why, but it cannot remain this way. Something is bound to happen in the very near future."

"As much as I cherish our friendship with the Wigfalls, I am displeased with Louis this evening. To speak of you as a potential political candidate? And in such a public sphere? It's not proper."

"Believe me, love. When this war ends, I intend to live out my days in peaceful retirement with you. I suppose I might pen my recollections of the events of this war, but you may rest assured that I have no political ambitions whatsoever."

"It pleases me to hear it, darling. If you ever express even the slightest interest in running for political office, I shall exercise my wifely right to veto."

Johnston laughed as he took another bite of the custard.

*　　　　*　　　　*　　　　*　　　　*

August 20, Night

There was no one in sight. The sound of his footsteps was strangely audible amidst the eerie silence of Richmond at night. Grace Street was home to many of Richmond's older and more elegant houses, mostly owned by those fortunate few who had inherited their wealth rather than made it themselves. Walking to the east, away from the center of the city, Bragg passed by the stately home of Miss Elizabeth Van Lew, an eccentric Union sympathizer everyone called "Crazy Bet". Insane or not, she would have long since been thrown in jail had Bragg had anything to say about it. He dismissed the thought as irrelevant to the matter at hand.

He was not wearing his habitual immaculate gray uniform. Instead, Bragg was wearing black civilian clothes. Although scarcely a soul was walking the streets, as it was approaching midnight, provosts on horseback occasionally rode by in their endless patrols of the streets. Recognizing him as a general, they would certainly stop to salute him. As it was, Bragg wanted to be as inconspicuous as possible.

As he walked down the street, Bragg knew he was taking a risk. John Daniel, editor of the *Richmond Examiner*, was one of the most ardent critics of the Davis administration, never letting pass an opportunity to lambast the President or disparage his policies. Among the favorite targets of the venomous pen of Daniel and his team of hack writers had been Bragg himself. That was an unforgivable sin in Bragg's eyes, made all the worse by the fact that Daniel had been a staunch defender of Joe Johnston since the beginning of the war.

There was, however, one cause to which Daniel felt an even stronger commitment than his crusade against Jefferson Davis.

Daniel was a passionate defender of slavery and white supremacy. That was what Bragg was now counting on.

Bragg turned north and began walking up 22ⁿᵈ Street until he came to St. John's Episcopal Church, famed as the location where Patrick Henry had made his "Give Me Liberty or Give Me Death" speech at the beginning of the American Revolution.

A man similarly dressed in dark civilian clothes stood beneath a tree off to the left of the church's main door. He was smoking a large cigar, but tossed it into the ground when he saw Bragg approach.

"Mr. Daniel?" Bragg asked uncertainly.

"So, it was not a joke," the man replied. "When I got your note, I thought either someone was playing a prank on me or that you had gone out of your mind."

"Why is that?" Bragg asked, walking up beside Daniel. He motioned for the newspaperman to walk over with him to a spot just beneath one of the church's windows, from which a faint glow was being cast by liturgical candles.

"Your note said that you had confidential information about a critically important story which you wished to share with me. No man has been treated more roughly in the pages of my newspaper than yourself, so why on earth would you want to help me?"

"My reasons are my own, Daniel." He held up the packet. "Do you want this or not?"

"I'm not sure. What exactly is it?"

"Proof that one of the Confederacy's most distinguished military commanders is in favor of the abolition of slavery."

Daniel's face immediately became dark and angry. "Who?" he quietly demanded.

Bragg didn't answer directly, instead passing over the packet. Daniel opened it and withdrew the first few sheets. As the editor started reading, Bragg went over his mental calculations once again. The written statements and other pieces of evidence given to him by Hood, of which Bragg had made several copies, revealed the full extent of the proposal by General Cleburne to emancipate slaves and enroll them as soldiers in the Confederate Army. Cleburne's politics were generally unknown and he was not seen by the public as either for or against the President. If Daniel were provided with the text and background of the proposal, he would have no compunction against snatching up his pen and cutting Cleburne to ribbons in the face of the public.

"Patrick Cleburne?" he asked, incredulous.

"None other, I'm afraid. As you'll see from the included papers, he convened a meeting of the high command of the Army of Tennessee back in early January, not long after Joe Johnston took command of the army. There he laid out his proposals to free as many slaves as possible and enroll them as soldiers in the army, freeing their families as well."

As Daniel continued reading, a look of disgust came over his face.

"This man speaks as though the negroes could fight in battle as well as white men!"

"I know," Bragg replied. "It's disgraceful. Quite disgraceful, I must say."

Daniel shook his head. "He's a foreigner. He doesn't understand the ways of the South. Still, for such a successful general to be suggesting such things! It is an absolute abomination!"

"Keep reading," Bragg said. "I think you will find something even more surprising."

Daniel glanced up suspiciously at Bragg for a moment but continued to leaf through the papers. A few minutes later, his eyes widened in shock.

"Johnston!" Daniel exclaimed. "Johnston backed Cleburne's proposal?"

"So it seems," Bragg replied. He knew that this was the most delicate moment of the exchange. Because he was held in such high esteem by Senator Wigfall and other prominent politicians who opposed the Davis administration, Johnston had become the darling of the *Richmond Examiner* editorial pages. Some idiotic columns in the paper had even described Johnston as equal in military skill to Robert E. Lee. Daniel would be reluctant to print anything that put Johnston in a bad light, but the copies of the affidavits of Hood, Walker, and others that implicated Johnston, as well as Hardee, would hopefully persuade him.

"To think that I defended Johnston in the pages of my newspaper, while all along he was a damned abolitionist!"

"I didn't know there was another kind of abolitionist," Bragg said with what amounted to a smile. "I trust that these papers shall be put to good use in the pages of the *Richmond Examiner*?"

Daniel looked up from the papers and stared Bragg deeply in the eye, silent for several moments. "Why are you doing this, Bragg?" he asked skeptically. "You have it in for Cleburne and Johnston?"

"I have no personal motive. Before I received this information, I had nothing but respect for both Cleburne and Johnston. But having been given this information, I feel it only fair that the public be made aware of it. My sense of duty demands it."

"I don't believe that for a moment," Daniel scoffed. "Still, provided these papers are genuine, you are correct that this matter must be brought to the public's notice as quickly as possible."

"They are genuine," Bragg said firmly. "On that you have my word."

"But where did you get them? You were no longer in command of the army when this meeting is said to have taken place."

"No. But many of the men who attended the meeting remain my friends."

Daniel nodded absently, turning his attention back to the papers. "May I keep these?"

"By all means."

"Well, I never thought I would hear myself say this, but thank you, General Bragg."

Bragg didn't reply, but merely grunted as he started to walk back the way he had come.

*   *   *   *   *

August 21, Morning

McFadden sat in one of the back pews, Annie just to his right and her parents farther down. Central Presbyterian Church was packed with families and with army officers who, like McFadden, had been granted leave for the day to attend services in the city. On the pulpit, the Reverend John Rogers was giving the sermon, reading from the Book of Exodus.

"'And Moses said unto the people, Fear ye not, stand still, and see the salvation of the Lord, which he will show to you today. For the Egyptians whom ye have seen today, we shall see them again no more forever.'"

"Not very subtle, that Reverend Rogers," Annie whispered to McFadden. "Obviously the Egyptians are the Yankees."

Teresa Turnbow harshly shushed her daughter, causing McFadden to grin.

"The Israelites were freed from the Egyptian yoke," Rogers was saying. "God helped the Israelites so long as they remained His people. If we ourselves are to ever be freed from the Yankee yoke and the scourge of Northern aggression, we must be God's people no less than were the ancient Israelites!"

Glancing to his right, McFadden saw Teresa nod her head while Robert pursed his lips. Clearly, Annie's mother agreed with the preacher's point and her father did not.

McFadden had heard more than one preacher compare the Yankees to the biblical enemies of Israel. Stokely Chaddick, the chaplain of Granbury's Texas Brigade, did so on a regular basis at his Sunday services. McFadden wasn't sure whether or not he agreed with the analogy himself, for after coming back from New Mexico he had not given the political or philosophical issues surrounding the war much thought. He had stayed in the army because he had not known what to do with himself and he had fought against the Yankees simply because he wanted to fight.

His conversations with the Turnbow family had begun to awaken his mind and forced him to ask himself what, exactly, he was fighting for. He could easily have been killed in a dozen different battles or died of one of the innumerable diseases that stalked the army camps. Shouldn't the cause for which he was putting his life in peril be worthy of his sacrifice? What about the sacrifice of so many thousands of other men?

The war was about slavery. McFadden was too intelligent and too honest to deny that. He doubted if more than one out of ten men in the 7th Texas had ever owned a slave, but had there been no slavery, there would have been no war. To admit this was simply a concession to the obvious. But the fact that slavery was the cause of the war did not mean that slavery was the reason for which he fought. He certainly would never put his own life on the line to defend the right of rich men to keep their slave property, especially since such men cared nothing for people like him.

So why did he fight?

Whatever the cause of the war, the Yankees had invaded the South. They said they were doing it to free the slaves and preserve the Union. They might even be sincere when they said this. But it didn't matter to McFadden, for it didn't change the fact that they had invaded the South, burned its farms and towns, forced its people to become refugees, set up armies of occupation, and subjected the people to all manner of shames and humiliations.

He had not cared much about these things before. He had fought because he wanted to fight. But he cared about them now, for the people of the South had become real to him again. Annie Turnbow was why he fought now. To protect her from the Yankees, he would happily surrender his own life.

Reverend Rogers was still talking. "Sitting amongst us here, in this very church, are many of the men who serve as fingers of the fist of God. Our brave soldiers, fighting to defend all that we hold dear just as the Israelite warriors did so long ago, we thank you. We pray for you. We ask that you remain strong, that you remain faithful, that you remain committed. We place all our trust in you as you go forward to smite the Northern invaders and drive them from our land."

McFadden shifted uncomfortably as he heard these words, feeling the sidelong glances of the Turnbow family. Whatever else he was, McFadden did not consider himself a hero. The minister's words made him feel uneasy.

After having gone on for what McFadden felt was rather too long, Reverend Rogers finally came to a conclusion. Gratefully, the congregation rose from their pews and the gentle chatter of greetings and conversation filled the church as people drifted toward the doors. A few minutes later, McFadden and the Turnbows were on the street, walking back to the Turnbow house. The slave Jupiter, who had been waiting outside the church, wordlessly joined them, keeping a respectful distance. It was a clear, hot day, with scarcely a wisp of white clouds visible in the sky.

"I thought it was a nice sermon," McFadden said.

"John Rogers is a good preacher," Robert Turnbow said. "But then, I suppose you would be a better judge than I, being the son of a preacher."

"He speaks very well." McFadden thought that a fair enough compliment. In truth, he felt his father had been a more much effective preacher, but he couldn't discount the possibility that he was biased.

"How is the book coming?" Robert asked.

"The Kosciuszko biography? Quite well, thank you. I think I may finish it soon."

"I look forward to discussing it at more length when you are finished."

"As do I."

"Lieutenant, would you mind escorting Annie back to the house?" Teresa asked. "Robert and I want to pay a visit to a friend who has been ill."

"Certainly, ma'am," McFadden replied.

With a happy nod, Robert took Teresa by the arm and turned right down a side street. Annie and McFadden continued back toward the house, with Jupiter following a short distance behind. Without a word, Annie slipped her arm into McFadden's.

"Mother hasn't spoken about any ill friend," Annie said.

"No?"

She grinned. "I think that Father has persuaded her to allow us some time together."

"Well, deception or not, I thank her for it."

"How are things in your regiment?"

"We're going up to the picket line again soon." Annie's expression became apprehensive and he hurried to reassure her. "There's nothing to worry about, my dear. There is no fighting on the picket line. We and the Yankees mostly just watch each other and sometimes toss insulting remarks back and forth."

"Strange," Annie said, shaking her head. "An unusual war."

"That is the truth."

"I have read in some of the papers that Poland has risen up against the Russian Empire again."

"Has it?" McFadden asked, interested. "I hadn't heard." He had enough trouble keeping track of the events in America to concern himself with anything going on in Europe.

She sighed. "It's happened before. As always, the Poles have no chance. They don't have an army. They don't have any leadership. The British and French won't help them."

"There may be hope. Men fighting for their freedom can accomplish amazing things." He thought of the feats of courage he had seen from the men of the 7th Texas on a dozen different battlefields. "Besides, Poles are brave fighters. That's one thing I've learned from reading your father's book about Kosciuszko."

She smiled. "He is very happy that you are enjoying it so much. So am I, for that matter."

"Why you?"

"I think the more you know about Poland, the more you know about me. And the more you know about me, the happier I am." Her voice was playful.

"Poland is in your blood, isn't it?"

"The same way Scotland is in yours, I should think."

"May I ask you a question, Annie?"

She looked at him. "Of course."

"You and your mother are Polish patriots, yet you attend a Presbyterian Church. It was my understanding that almost all Poles were Catholic."

"I think that my mother loved my father so much that she was willing to turn away from the holy church in Rome in order to marry him. So I was raised Polish and Presbyterian. An odd blend, I know."

"Not to me," McFadden said. "I like you just the way you are."

He was speaking the truth. The more he learned about Annie Turnbow, the more fascinating he found her. They had reached the point where they exchanged letters on almost a daily basis, while his visits to her parents' house and her visits to the regimental camp were also increasing in frequency. Having been granted permission by Annie's father to court her, McFadden found himself happier with every passing day.

Then he tensed. The thought of Cheeky Joe on the river intruded rudely into his mind. Even in the presence of Annie, he was unable to entirely rid his mind from the demon's grip.

"James? Is something wrong?"

"No, not at all." He continued walking with Annie, trying to focus his attention on her words. With a great effort of will, he forced the image of Cheeky Joe from his mind.

*   *   *   *   *

August 21, Afternoon

Thomas had settled into life at Camp Oglethorpe, albeit with the greatest reluctance. The Union prisoners had devised various means of keeping themselves occupied during their captivity. A group of men had formed that regularly put on amateur theatricals for the amusement of their comrades. One clever fellow had begun putting his fluency in French to good use by giving lessons in the language, accepting promises from his students to pay after their release. A debating society had also been formed, although the rebel authorities had prohibited any discussion of issues related to the war. Most of the debates had centered upon questions of history, such as whether Caesar had been justified in crossing the Rhine or whether William the Conqueror's claim to the throne of England had been legitimate.

None of this interested George Thomas. His mind was bent only on escape.

He was sitting on a bunk inside one of the cabins. It was not especially close to the fence line and therefore would hopefully not be seen as interesting by the prying eyes of rebel guards.

A colonel poked his head out of the hole that had been dug in the center of the floor. "Here," he said, handing Thomas a pewter cup filled with soil. "Put this with the other ones." The man's voice carried the tone of command and he stiffened momentarily when he remembered to whom he was speaking. "Sorry, General."

"It's all right," Thomas replied. "When it comes to digging this tunnel, consider yourself the general and me the private. After all, you have much more experience."

The colonel smiled and then disappeared back into the tunnel with the dexterity, if not the speed, of a groundhog dashing back into its hole. When actual work on the tunnel was not being conducted, the entrance to it was concealed beneath a square-shaped plank of wood that had been surreptitiously made from planks taken from other cabins. One of the beds was placed over the entrance as an added disguise. Although rebel guards inspected each cabin at least once a day, it had been noted early on that they were not particularly thorough. Being young and mostly uneducated, the militiamen most often simply glanced around and, seeing nothing amiss, moved on to the next cabin.

Even better, the guards had fallen into a lazy and predictable schedule, always inspecting the cabins an hour or so after lunch had been issued. The Union prisoners therefore found it easy to work on the tunnel during the night and morning hours, stop work and conceal the passage around noon, and then resume work immediately after the inspection had been conducted. As a precaution, however, they regularly practiced a method of rapidly closing the tunnel entrance and positioning the bed over it in the event of an unexpected visit from the guards. From what Thomas had been told, they had reduced the time necessary for concealment down to thirty seconds, although it meant that whoever was actually in the tunnel would have to remain there until the guards had left.

Wooden planks taken from other cabins had also been put to use as structural supports inside the tunnel itself. Using a long length of twine, the diggers estimated that they had already dug approximately seventy feet, with perhaps another fifteen to go before they reached beyond the fence line. They were now managing about a foot a day, with the refuse dirt quietly being discarded throughout the vast area of the camp in small quantities so as to avoid any suspicion. The tunnel itself was just about two feet high, though somewhat less in width. It would be an exceedingly narrow squeeze for those who would make the escape.

The problem of ventilating the tunnel had proven to be the most difficult challenge for the would-be escapees. Some had advocated that they simply ignore the problem and hope for the best, but the engineering officers had prevailed by pointing out that many of the men would likely pass out and suffocate while attempting to crawl through an unventilated tunnel. This would not only kill them, but block the passage for those behind them and probably lead to their deaths as well. As a result, the diggers had been forced to divert the path of the tunnel away from the most direct route toward the fence line in order to pass underneath another cabin, where a ventilation shaft was being driven downward. On the day of the escape, a small fire would be lit on the floor of the tunnel near the entrance, carrying the stale air within the tunnel upwards while fresh air would be sucked into the tunnel through the ventilation to fill the resulting vacuum. It was not the most elegant solution, and it added a considerable distance to the length of the tunnel, but it was the best the engineers had been able to devise.

The plan for the escape itself had been carefully crafted. On the chosen date, as soon as it was sufficiently dark, one hundred men chosen by drawing sticks would crawl through the tunnel, pass underneath the fence line, and make for the deep woods northwest of the camp. While this was happening, those privy to the plot who had not been selected would foment an apparent riot over poor rations, hopefully distracting the attention of most of the guards. If the initial one hundred successfully got away, those who remained behind could attempt to escape through the tunnel the following evening in the unlikely event that the earlier escape had gone unnoticed by the rebels.

General Seymour and the other officers involved in the planning of the escape had explained all of this very carefully to General Thomas. As Thomas was now the senior officer in the camp, they had officially requested his permission to continue their efforts. After pondering the matter, Thomas had decided to approve the plans as they already existed and urged the men to continue.

There was a knock on the door, three loud thumps following by four soft ones. This was the code indicating that it was safe to momentarily open the door without initiating the emergency concealment procedure. One of the other diggers stood up and let General Seymour in. The door was quickly closed behind him.

"How is it going, George?"

"I am learning the trade of a mole," Thomas replied with a smile.

"One gets used to it quickly, I have found."

"What's going on outside?"

"About a dozen new arrivals came in today, all from the Army of the Potomac."

"Oh. Any war news?"

"Nothing we haven't already heard. Some of them do have some greenbacks, though."

"Ah, that's good."

As officers, many of the prisoners in Camp Oglethorpe had been permitted to keep whatever cash had been on their person at the moment of their capture. Some money had been collected into a fund that would be used to try to bribe any rebel guard who somehow discovered the secret of the tunnel. Thomas did not think that this would work, but the small comfort it provided was worth the effort. There was little else on which to spend the money, after all.

"How far have we gotten today?" Seymour asked.

"We're approaching one foot for the day. A bit ahead of schedule."

"That's good. If our luck holds, the tunnel will reach beyond the fence line in a bit over two weeks." He paused for a moment, thinking. "You know, if our security remains tight enough, we might continue working for an additional week and push the tunnel farther beyond the fence line. Every inch closer to the woods we get, the higher the chance of a successful escape."

Thomas nodded. "I thought of that myself. We can discuss it at tonight's meeting."

The digger emerged from the tunnel and handed Seymour the next scoop of dirt. The man's face was so black with grime that Thomas thought he looked like a slave. He immediately disappeared back into the tunnel without a word.

Seymour leaned forward and spoke earnestly. "Whenever the attempt is made, I feel very strongly that you should go first."

"What makes you think I'll go at all? The odds of me drawing one of the hundred short sticks are no better than anyone else's."

"You're going no matter what," Seymour said with conviction. "You're the highest ranking officer in this place and you need to be at the head of your army."

Thomas shook his head. "No," he said firmly. "In here, I am a prisoner like anybody else. I will draw sticks the same as every other captive. What would people say if I pulled rank in order to escape while thousands of other officers remained in captivity?"

"But George, consider this. Your capture has been a tremendous propaganda victory for the rebels. Your escape would be the exact opposite. If you were to successfully get away and return to the head of your troops, it would have an electrifying effect on the morale of our soldiers and of the people at home."

Thomas considered this. He conceded that Seymour had a point, especially with the election scarcely two months away.

However, he refused to allow himself to rationalize his decision. He was only human and wanted to escape the prison camp as much as anyone did. But he would not do so in any manner he did not believe consistent with his personal honor.

"We'll talk about it later."

*   *   *   *   *

August 22, Morning

"You're certain?" Davis asked.

"The spy is a person who has always been accurate in the past," Secretary of War Seddon replied. "He is the same man who alerted General Lee to the correct position of the Army of the Potomac just before the Battle of Gettysburg. Obviously, such momentous news will soon appear in the papers. If the papers make no mention of it over the next few days, we will know that the information is incorrect."

Davis rubbed his chin. "Old Abe has finally decided to remove Sherman from command, eh? And replace him with none other than Grant to boot."

"A month too late, from his point of view," Secretary of State Benjamin said. "It will not help him politically. The accusations of Sherman's insanity have been filling many a Northern newspaper for weeks. By replacing him at this juncture, Lincoln will appear to the public as acknowledging the truth of these accounts and therefore proving himself an incompetent commander-in-chief."

Davis glanced up at the military map on the wall of his office. "Perhaps it was not Lincoln's choice. If I am not mistaken, Grant would have the authority as general-in-chief to make this decision on his own."

"Correct, Mr. President," Seddon answered.

Davis grinned and shook his head. As a fellow chief executive, he could not imagine giving any general, even Robert E. Lee himself, such unchecked power over military policy as Lincoln had apparently given Grant. It was his responsibility as President to direct the war effort of the nation. He didn't deny that Lincoln was an intelligent man, but Davis also thought that his counterpart in Washington often made incredibly foolish decisions.

"I don't believe that Grant's departure from the Army of the Potomac will greatly impact operations," Davis said. "With so many enemy divisions having been pulled out of Virginia and sent west, the pressure on Richmond and Petersburg has greatly lessened."

"True," Seddon said. "It seems that the Yankees have accepted the stalemate on the Petersburg front. We have little to fear in this quarter."

"Nor in the Shenandoah Valley," Davis said. Jubal Early's valiant army, recently reinforced by Lee, securely held the northern mountain passes of that region, with Union forces unable or unwilling to test their mettle against him. Federal forces which might have otherwise been sent against Early had already been dispatched to reinforce the Union forces near Atlanta.

"I may be ignorant of military matters," Benjamin said. "But it seems to me that if Grant has made the decision to take personal command of the Yankee army north of the Chattahoochee, it can only mean that a renewed Union offensive will soon take place there."

"Probably," Davis said, nodding sharply. "We know Lincoln needs a major victory if he is to remain in office. The dispatch of such heavy reinforcements and the assumption of personal command by Grant himself clearly indicates that the Yankees will attempt again to capture Atlanta." Davis scowled. "If Johnston had done what we asked him to do and launched an offensive when he had the chance, he might have dealt Sherman another stunning blow and driven him back toward Chattanooga."

"Indeed, Mr. President," Benjamin said, a familiar twinkle in his eye. "Johnston's list of reasons why he considered an offensive impossible sounded very much like a catalogue of complaints from a spoiled child."

Davis shook his head. "And with Grant now taking command in the West, and so many reinforcements arriving, it is as though we never won the victory at Peachtree Creek. Johnston's cowardice may cost us a great deal."

"I agree, and not simply in military or political matters, Mr. President," Benjamin said. "It may damage us diplomatically as well."

"Oh?"

Benjamin nodded. "Mr. Mason's latest dispatch from London carried interesting news. Parliament was prorogued on August 1, just a day after news of our victory at Peachtree Creek reached London. The Conservative opposition made a bid to topple the Liberal government of Prime Minister Palmerston by forcing a vote of no confidence."

"What does this have to do with us?" Davis asked tiredly. He had little time for foreign affairs and little love for anything having to do with the British.

"The Conservatives have been criticizing the Liberals for not being assertive enough on the international stage. Prussia has attacked Denmark over some minor border issue and the British government is sitting on its hands despite the fact that Prussia's aggression violates an earlier treaty the British pledged to uphold. Meanwhile, Russia is suppressing the latest uprising in Poland with great brutality, with Prime Minister Palmerston saying nothing about it."

"As I said, what does any of this have to do with us?"

"Bear with me, Mr. President. The Liberals won the vote of no confidence, but by a much closer vote than anticipated. Mr. Mason reports that the word in London now is that Palmerston is taking to heart the criticism about his perceived weakness on foreign matters and that he will be more inclined to flex Britain's muscles, as it were, in the coming months."

Davis leaned forward. Benjamin's conversation was finally becoming more interesting. "Flex its muscles in what way?"

"Our recent victories at Peachtree Creek and outside Petersburg, along with Jubal Early's raid on Washington City, certainly present firm evidence of our ability to resist the North's attempts to overwhelm us before the election. If Britain wants to demonstrate its ability to intervene around the world, an effective way to do this would be to finally put forth an offer to mediate the dispute between the Confederacy and the Union."

"Ah," Seddon said. "That would be most welcome."

"I'll believe it when I see it," Davis said. He had little faith in the British. Still, were the British to make an offer of mediation, it might well present the Confederacy with its independence on a silver platter. For Lincoln would obviously refuse the offer, which would in turn lead to unilateral British diplomatic recognition of the Confederacy. Like a row of dominoes falling down, this action would spark a declaration of war by the United States, bringing the world's superpower into the conflict as an ally of the Confederacy.

These musings were interrupted by a knock at the door. A moment later, Braxton Bragg entered.

"Have you gentlemen seen this morning's edition of the *Richmond Examiner?*" Bragg asked, his voice heavy with concern.

"No," Davis spat sharply. "What is that worthless rag printing this time?"

"See for yourself," Bragg said, passing a copy across the desk as he took a seat.

Davis took the paper, unfolded it with irritation, and scanned the front page headline. As he did so, his eyes widened and his face went ashen. "Oh God," he said simply. He dropped the paper on the desk and held his hands up to his face.

"What is it?" Seddon asked with alarm, looking back and forth between Bragg and Benjamin.

"Do you recall the misguided proposal by General Patrick Cleburne last winter that our government should free large numbers of slaves and enlist them as soldiers in the army?" Bragg asked.

"Of course," Seddon said. "I ordered all discussion about that matter terminated."

"Well, apparently someone saw fit to disobey those orders, for the *Richmond Examiner* has a front page story about it this morning."

Benjamin let out a deep, exasperated breath. "Anything but that," he said. "And anytime but now."

Davis lowered his hands. "It can undo us," he said. "This could not have happened at a worse possible time. If it had come out after the war, I would not care. But to come out now, when we must be as united as possible?"

"This will promote rancor and division within the Army of Tennessee," Seddon said. "I cannot see how it can be otherwise. Everyone will be asked where they stand on the question. Everyone will be forced to take a position for or against. Dammit, why were my orders not obeyed?"

"It won't just be the Army of Tennessee," Benjamin said, shaking his head. "Every officer over the rank of major across the whole Confederacy will be forced to take a stand. Every member of Congress, every governor, every member of every state legislature, will be at daggers drawn."

"The newspapers will speak of nothing else for the next week," Davis said.

"Cleburne's proposal threatens to undercut the very purpose of the Confederacy itself," Bragg said sternly. "As Vice President Stephens said at the outset of our revolution, our nation is founded upon the great truth than the negro is not equal to the white man. If Cleburne's proposal were to be adopted, and negroes were to be placed on an equal footing with white Southerners as soldiers of the Confederacy, does that not refute the very purpose of our nation?"

"Cleburne is not a native Southerner," Davis said defensively. "He is an Irishman. Understand me, I do not mean to question his patriotism, for he is a true hero to the South. But he did not grow to manhood among us. He perhaps does not fully understand the deep-rooted traditions of our people, especially those governing the relationship between the white and black races."

"Patrick Cleburne is many things," Seddon said. "But he is not a fool."

"I do not call him a fool. I only say that he is naïve."

"And what will become of Cleburne, now that his foolish proposal has become publicly known?" Seddon asked. "He is one of the finest division commanders we have. How many of his troops will now refuse to fight under his command? How many of his comrades in the Army of Tennessee will refuse to fight alongside him? How much pressure will now be brought to bear on us to remove him from command?"

"Cleburne is no ordinary soldier," Davis said. "He has fought gallantly in every major battle the Army of Tennessee has ever been involved in. Congress officially commended him for his action at Ringgold Gap, which probably saved the Army of Tennessee after the disaster of Missionary Ridge. It was his division which broke the enemy line at Peachtree Creek."

Seddon shook his head. "Cleburne would undoubtedly be a corps commander today if he hadn't written that damnable memorandum."

Benjamin leaned forward, his customary smile having long since vanished. "Mr. President, we must move to contain the damage from this. It is in the newspapers now. There is no keeping it under wraps. The story will spread across the Confederacy over the next few days. Congress will be asking questions. The state legislatures will be asking questions. We must devise a course of action."

"Yes, yes, of course," Davis sputtered. He thought for a long moment, then turned to Seddon. "Cable General Johnston. Inquire as to whether General Cleburne would be willing to retract his earlier proposal. It won't undo the damage, but at least it might limit it."

Bragg cleared his throat. "There's more to it than that, Mr. President. You have not had time to properly peruse the story. What is printed in the *Richmond Examiner* discusses the position of General Johnston on Cleburne's proposal at great length. General Hardee, too."

"Oh?" Benjamin said. "What does the story say about them?"

"The story quotes three general officers from the Army of Tennessee who maintain that both Johnston and Hardee are strong supporters of Cleburne's scheme. Joseph Wheeler, William Walker, and Patton Anderson, to be precise. I assume that Wheeler, God rest his soul, signed his statement before setting out on his unfortunate expedition."

"Johnston supports Cleburne's proposal?" Davis asked incredulously. "And Hardee? How can that be?"

"Dear God," Seddon said. "Half of Congress is probably flying into a rage at this very moment."

"No doubt," Benjamin added. "And the other half will be enraged that the first half is enraged. When we should be uniting together to fight against the Yankees, we shall instead be tearing away at one another's throats."

"You gentlemen are speaking as though the matter were hypothetical," Bragg said sourly. "It is in the papers. It will indeed come to pass. I will hazard a guess that despite the recent military success obtained by Johnston and Hardee, there will be a loud clamor for them to be removed from command."

"Removed from command?" Seddon said. "I would not be surprised if certain members of Congress will want Cleburne, Johnston and Hardee hanged from a sour apple tree."

Davis pursed his lips and shook his head, greatly wishing that the Yankee bullet which had wounded Joseph Johnston at the Battle of Seven Pines had instead taken his head off. It seemed to the President that everything Johnston did was poisonous. He thought of how his timidity had nearly led to the fall of Richmond in 1862, how his indecisiveness had caused the fall of Vicksburg in 1863, how he had failed to follow up on his victory at Peachtree Creek. Now there was this business of supporting Cleburne's proposal to free the slaves. It was all too much.

Davis looked at Seddon. "Mr. Secretary, there must be some sort of public inquiry about this. It will give us some cover with the papers. My earnest desire is that we can then leave it at that and hope the attention of the people goes somewhere else very quickly. If we're lucky, the newspapers will soon start focusing again on the election in the United States and will drop this story like a hot potato."

"I'll talk to the editors who are friendly to us," Benjamin said. "I'll let them know that we would prefer for this story to be brushed under the carpet as soon as possible."

Davis nodded sharply, though he doubted this would happen. He noted Bragg intently looking at everyone in the room, as though gauging their reactions to the news, but thought nothing of it.

* * * * *

August 24, Evening

The platform for the New York Central Railroad was packed with people. Clutching his carpetbag tightly for fear of being unable to retrieve it if he accidently dropped it, Marble struggled to make his way through the mass of humanity and board his train before it pulled away. All around him, the cacophony of talking and shouting people, along with an abnormally large number of crying children, was deafening.

After much effort, Marble managed to force his way to his train. Thankful that he had decided to pack lightly and didn't need to deal with the porter, he handed his ticket to the collector and quickly found his seat. Settling in, he exhaled in relief.

To get to Chicago, Marble had elected to take the train to Buffalo, go by steamer to Detroit, and then again by train to his final destination. Ordinarily, he might have ventured down to Washington City for consultations with congressional Democrats, then headed west on the Baltimore & Ohio Railroad. Unfortunately that line was now the frequent target of raids by rebel troops under Jubal Early and could not be relied upon. In any event, taking this particular route afforded him plenty of opportunities to meet with many prominent Democrats along the way. Indeed, as he looked at his schedule, Marble wondered if he would even have time to sleep, as every stop along the way would involve a meeting of some kind and every hour in transit would be crammed with necessary reading and preparation.

After an annoyingly long wait, the engine of the train finally began to hiss and sputter and the iron wheels began to roll. Beginning with a soft jolt, Marble's train slowly pulled away from the platform and started its long journey northward, eventually to turn to the west when they reached Albany. Now that his trip had finally begun, Marble began to relax. He removed a bottle of scotch and a glass from his carpetbag and took the first of what would be many drinks consumed during the trip.

All over the country, Marble knew, literally thousands of Democrats had either already started similar journeys or were soon to do so. In five days, the Democratic National Convention would begin in the city of Chicago and everyone knew that it would almost certainly be the largest political gathering of its kind ever to have been held in North America.

Like all other prominent Democrats, Marble knew that his party had taken a great risk in holding its national convention so late in the year. The presidential election itself was a mere seventy-six days away. The Republicans, for their part, had held their national convention in Baltimore back in June. Holding their convention so late would allow the Democrats precious little time to properly campaign after having settled on a candidate.

Still, Marble was satisfied that the potential advantages had been well worth the risks. By having such a late convention, the Democrats had hoped to be able to lay before the people yet further evidence of incompetence and stupidity on the part of the Lincoln administration in the form of more inflation and, more importantly, additional military fiascoes. The whole point of the election, after all, was to offer the Northern public a viable alternative to the Lincoln administration. As far as Marble could see, the gamble was paying off handsomely.

Since the opening of the spring campaign, virtually all the news from the war front had been bad. Grant's campaign against Lee in Virginia had resulted in horrific casualties, in excess of sixty thousand men, and had failed to take Richmond. Sherman's campaign against Atlanta had been similarly unsuccessful and had been topped off by the disaster at Peachtree Creek. Meanwhile, Jubal Early's raiders had nearly captured Washington City itself, had left several Pennsylvania towns in flames, and had beaten back every Union effort to push into the Shenandoah Valley.

Military failure was compounded by economic dislocation and social instability throughout the North. Inflation was increasing at a rapid rate, helped along by Wall Street financiers with Democratic sympathies who were buying gold as rapidly as they could. Although the riots that wracked New York City following the death of Clement Vallandigham had been put down by the troops of General Butler, there remained a simmering unease in the great industrial cities of the North. Low-level violence continued and major riots could potentially break out at any time.

The thought caused Marble to remember Vallandigham. As many Republicans had feared and many Democrats had hoped, the man's death was doing far more harm to Lincoln's chances of reelection than any speeches he would have given and pamphlets he would have written had he remained alive. The Manhattan Massacre was being held up from Maine to California as an example of the Lincoln administration's brutal and unconstitutional efforts to clamp down on dissent of all forms. Every Democratic newspaper in the country, and even some which normally aligned with the Republicans, had printed the names of all the civilians who had been killed in large block letters on the front pages, surrounded by borders of black.

Marble considered all these facts, juggling them in his head as though they were all numerical factors in some giant mathematical equation floating in an abstract Platonic realm. Assuming the Democrats played their cards right, they all added up to an overwhelming victory at the polls in November, a victory which would not only give them the White House but would give them control of Congress as well.

In order to play those cards correctly, the Democrats had both to nominate the right candidate and approve the right party platform. Like many others, Marble had been striving for many months to assure that their nominee would be George B. McClellan, who could hardly be accused of being a defeatist considering his long and well-known service in the first two years of the war. The platform had to call for a negotiated settlement to the war, while being phrased in such a way as not to disparage the great sacrifices the North had made up to this point. It would require a very delicate political balancing act.

Hours passed. The train left New York City behind and ventured into the vastness of the Hudson Valley to the north. Marble realized that he didn't much care how the convention turned out, or even how the war itself turned out. All that he cared about was helping the Democrats win the election. For with the Democrats in control of the federal government, his own power and influence as the editor of the *New York World* would be vastly increased and he would be in a position to dispense patronage to his friends and associates as he pleased. To achieve that aim, he would have been just as happy to kiss the ass of Jefferson Davis as he would have been to kiss the ass of every slave in the Confederacy.

Marble was immersed in these thoughts when a man slid into the chair directly across from him, wearing a sinister grin.

"Mr. Marble?"

Marble nodded. "I am. And who might you be?"

"My name is Alexander Humphries. I have written to you numerous times using only my initials."

"Ah," Marble said, a smile creeping onto his face. He had initially ignored the letters from A.H. when they had begun arriving a year or so before, until he realized that the information they contained about events within the Confederacy was soon corroborated by other, more verifiable sources. Afterwards, the letters he had continued to receive had allowed the *New York World* to achieve numerous scoops that other newspapers could only print the following day.

"Surprised to see me?"

"Of course. You have never suggested in any of your letters any intention of presenting yourself personally to me, and certainly not so unexpectedly as to appear in the seat across from me on a train. Come to think of it, how did you know on what train I would be travelling?"

Humphries shrugged. "As should be obvious from my letters, I am in a position to know a great many things."

"That's certainly true," Marble replied, not recognizing the danger that had just entered his life. "Your letters have been most useful to my newspaper. I thank you very much for them."

"You are most welcome. Our goals are the same. We both desire the defeat of Lincoln and the victory of the Democratic ticket."

Marble nodded, even as inwardly he eyed the mysterious person warily. He had no idea who Humphries was. His letters had demonstrated that he had inside knowledge of events within the Confederacy before they became known to many people in the North. The information he had fed to Marble was always useful as source material for stories that would be embarrassing to the Lincoln administration. There were many unscrupulous businessmen who ran cotton through the rebel lines to sell in the Union at an enormous profit, while selling grain to the rebel armies and bribing Yankee officers to look the other way. Marble assumed that Humphries was one of that sort, who also provided information to the *New York World* for unfathomable reasons.

"I assume that you didn't arrange to meet me on this train simply to exchange pleasantries," Marble said.

"Indeed not," Humphries replied. Without another word, he picked his carpetbag up from the floor and passed it over to Marble. The editor opened it and had to restrain himself from gasping. Inside were large clumps of greenback bills, carefully taped together. He flipped through one set of wrapped bills, finding that all of them were twenty dollar notes. After examining a second set, he concluded that all of the greenbacks in the carpetbag were also twenty dollar notes.

Marble looked across at Humphries. "How much?"

"Twenty-five thousand dollars," Humphries said, as calmly as if he were discussing the price of a loaf of bread.

"What the hell for?"

"You are headed to the Democratic National Convention and you are one of the country's most well-connected Democrats. Surely the money in that bag could prove useful in the upcoming electoral campaign, especially in states like Ohio, Pennsylvania and Indiana. Use it to pay for the printing of pamphlets. Buy liquor for the local drunkards if they agree to vote for the Democratic ticket. Toss a hundred dollars to the local judge to close the polling booths early if it looks like the abolitionists are voting too much. Do whatever you want with it, just as long as it contributes to the defeat of Lincoln."

Marble licked his lips. Twenty-five thousand dollars was a stupendous amount of money. If used properly and in the right places it could certainly prove useful to the Democratic cause. And if he was the man who would be dispensing it, Manton Marble's stature would certainly be on the rise. He was already one of the great up-and-comers within the party and having such largesse at his disposal would make his influence all the greater.

He was astute enough to maintain his skepticism. He looked across at Humphries. "Who are you?"

"Do you want the money or not?"

"How do you know I won't simply take the next steamer to Europe and take the money with me?"

"If you do, you'd be well advised to avoid encountering me in the future." The tone was neutral and polite, but the threat was obvious. "And I would expect you to provide me with an account of how the money was distributed, so that I may in turn present it to my employer to prove that his money is being well spent."

"And just who is your employer?"

Humphries said nothing in response, simply smiling in a way that Marble found slightly menacing.

Marble saw that he wasn't going to get anywhere on that line of questioning. It was clear that he wasn't a businessman. Most likely, he was a Confederate agent of some kind. But as long as Humphries choose not to answer him directly, Marble could honestly say that he did not know.

"How will I find you to provide you with such an account?" he asked.

"No need," Humphries said. "I'll pay you another visit. Just have the account ready and at hand when I do."

The train began to slow and, within five minutes, came to a complete halt. "All out for Kingston!" the conductor shouted. Without another word, Humphries rose from his chair, shook Marble's hand and stepped off the train. Staring out the window, Marble saw him disappear into the crowd.

He clutched the carpetbag containing the money. He had made the comment about taking the cash and fleeing to Europe in jest, but he could not deny that the temptation was real. So much money invested the right way could provide a comfortable life for Marble in Paris or London until he died of old age. However, Humphries had made clear that such a course would be extremely dangerous. Besides which, Marble had no particular desire to retire amid the luxuries of the Old World. His world was politics and power, and it seemed to him that his own interests would best be served by using the money in exactly the manner Humphries had laid out.

- 429 -

Marble spent the remainder of his journey contemplating how he would divvy up the money when he arrived in Chicago. It made for a pleasant trip.

* * * * *

August 25, Noon

Forrest leaned forward in his saddle, staring intently southwest at the ramparts of Fort Granger, on the north bank of the Harpeth River just outside the Tennessee town of Franklin. Around him, a cluster of officers wore stony expressions on their faces, while behind them nearly two thousand troopers waited patiently for the orders of their commander. King Philip neighed uncertainly for a moment and shook the bridles in his mouth, but quieted down almost immediately after his master gave him a few reassuring pats on the neck.

It had been a frustrating few weeks for Forrest and his men. After burning the vital Yankee bridge at Bridgeport in northern Alabama, the raiders had turned north back into central Tennessee, intent on further destruction of the enemy supply lines between Nashville and Chattanooga. The arrival of Union reinforcements from Virginia had largely thwarted Forrest's efforts. Strong Union forces were now in place across the key transportation routes. Since Bridgeport, the pickings had been slim.

Leaving nothing to chance, the Yankees had deployed the equivalent of two entire divisions along the stretch of railroad between the two cities. Worse, these troops were not the pathetic and poorly trained "hundred day men" of the various state militias. They had come from the Sixth Corps, which was made up of hardened combat veterans of the Army of the Potomac.

Forrest and his men were brave but not foolhardy. It was one thing to attack fortified posts held by Illinois militiamen who barely knew how to fire their muskets, but quite another to attack those same fortified posts when they were held by troops who had gone up against Lee's veterans. For more than two weeks, they had ridden up and down the length of the Union railroads passing through central Tennessee, constantly having to elude Yankee cavalry sent to intercept them while searching for a weak point that they might successfully attack. They had not found one.

However, Forrest thought his luck was about to change.

Despite occasional heavy fighting which had raged around it for the past three years, the town of Franklin had been blessedly spared by the war. The presence of large Union forces in the fortress city of Nashville, only eighteen miles to the north, had deterred any major Confederate force from venturing into the vicinity of Franklin.

Forrest had decided that the potential payoff of a lightning raid on the town was worth the risk.

Forrest had accepted roughly a week earlier that the mission of his raid had been changed by circumstances beyond his control. When he and his men had launched themselves out of northern Mississippi into central Tennessee, their goal had been to disrupt the Yankee supply lines that kept Sherman's armies in the field. Unfortunately, their best efforts had proven futile. The bridge over the Duck River at Columbia had been rebuilt with surprising speed. The miles of track torn up in various spots had also been put back into operation within a matter of days, if not hours. Even the immense span at Bridgeport would soon be back in service, according to Forrest's spies. From all the information available, he knew that supplies of food and ammunition were continuing to reach the Yankee forces north of Atlanta with scarcely any interruption.

Still, if his initial objective was not being achieved, Forrest knew that his actions were benefiting the Confederacy. By threatening the railroads, he was pinning down large numbers of enemy troops that would otherwise have been employed against the Army of Tennessee near Atlanta. That was a goal worth fighting for.

The bridge over the Harpeth River in Franklin was not a critical juncture of the enemy supply line, but destroying it would force the enemy to spend several days and considerable resources building a replacement. It would also cause them to send a large force of infantry and cavalry to chase Forrest away. While not decisive, it would still be a significant blow on behalf of the Confederacy.

Only the puny obstacle of Fort Granger stood in the way.

To Forrest's trained eyes, it didn't look like much. Although it had been built nearly two years before, the fort's dirt parapets looked like something a reasonably sized infantry force could have thrown together in a day or two. A few cannon bristled from the fort's walls, but they appeared to be no larger than twelve-pounders. Along the ramparts, he could see a scattering of blue uniformed men, the bayonets on their rifles flashing occasionally in the sunlight.

Major Strange was scanning the parapets of the fort with a spyglass.

"Black troops, sir," he said simply.

"No hard task, then," Forrest replied. "We can give these black bastards the same treatment we gave those who held Fort Pillow. If they don't give up before the shooting starts, of course."

Even as he said the words, his wishes were already being carried out. One of his three brigades had already occupied the town of Franklin itself, to the delight of the local citizens, and would commence burning the railroad bridge the moment the cannon in the fort had been silenced. His other two brigades had simultaneously taken up positions to the north and east of the fort, from which it could be most easily assaulted.

King Philip stirred again, sensing the possibility of a coming fight. Forrest didn't think it would come to that. After the pathetic showing of black troops against his men at Fort Pillow, and the speed with which black troops had surrendered to him at Columbia, he didn't think the outnumbered troops in Fort Granger would have much stomach for a fight.

"Come along, Strange. Have the color-bearer bring a flag of truce."

Strange nodded and wordlessly pointed to the color bearer. Moments later, the three men were cantering down toward the fort, the white flag fluttering in the breeze. Three men advancing under a flag of truce should surely not have appeared threatening to the garrison of the fort. It was always possible that some hot-headed fool would open fire anyway, but such were the uncertainties of war.

Forrest reined in a few dozen yards from the fort's rampart. A few hundred black soldiers glared down on him with a hatred he could scarcely comprehend, but he paid no mind.

"What white man commands you?" Forrest demanded.

"I do," an insolent voice with a New England accent replied. A white officer wearing an impeccable blue uniform, young but self-assured, appeared on the rampart. "I am Major David Easton, commander of the 13th United States Colored Troops."

Forrest sneered at the unit's name. He didn't think that giving a rabble of escaped slaves such a grand title was likely to make them any more effective in fighting. "I am Nathan Bedford Forrest."

"I know that," Easton replied, his rather calm expression not changing.

"I demand that you surrender Fort Granger immediately."

"Demand all you want. You shall not get it." Easton smiled after he said these words.

Forrest's eyes narrowed. He was not used to being spoken to in such a manner. For years, he had relied upon his fearsome reputation for ruthlessness to intimidate his opponents. Frustratingly, Easton did not appear to be intimidated.

"You do not have more than a few hundred men, Easton," Forrest said. "I've never heard of the rabble you call the 13th United States Colored Troops, so I am willing to bet that you and your negroes have never been in a fight. My men, though, number in the thousands and have fought on a hundred battlefields. You're hopelessly outnumbered and your men are no match for mine."

"My men are secure behind stout fortifications and are well supplied with artillery. Your presence has not gone unnoticed and I was able to send a telegraphic message to Nashville for reinforcements before you cut the telegraph line. I would guess that they would be here in less than an hour. Do you think you can overrun my position so quickly?"

"It took me less time than that to overrun Fort Pillow."

At those words, Forrest noticed a stirring among the black troops watching the conversation, not unlike a rustling of leaves in a breeze. They had all undoubtedly heard about what happened at Fort Pillow. He expected to see their faces melt into fear, but it did not happen. He could sense them tightening the grip on their rifles, gritting their teeth, and tensing their muscles. It was not fear these men were experiencing, but anger. In a part of his mind he scarcely acknowledged, Forrest found this unsettling.

"I have heard much about Fort Pillow," Easton replied. "So have my men. Why should we surrender if you intend to put my men to the sword? Or worse, send them back into slavery like you did with the garrison at Columbia earlier this month?"

Forrest was somewhat surprised that Easton might consider slavery a worse fate than death, but that was an abstract question for another time and Forrest set it aside in his mind. "I'm tired of talking to you, Easton. Are you going to surrender or not?"

"You and the bloody sons of bitches you have the dishonor of commanding can go straight to hell, Forrest. That is where you're headed, you know, as soon as you depart this Earth. In my opinion, I can hold this fort. If you want it, come and take it."

Without another word, Forrest turned his horse and cantered back to his own lines, concealing his anger beneath an impassive expression. To have had that Yankee speak to him in such an insolent manner in front of escaped slaves who were now bearing arms against the Confederacy was an affront that needed to be avenged as quickly as possible.

Arriving back in front of his officers, Forrest began barking out orders. Sharpshooters armed with Whitworth rifles began setting up their weapons. A few minutes later, they opened fire from a long distance, targeting officers and artillery crews. At the same time, Forrest's artillery, which had long since unlimbered and deployed, began hurling shot and shell at Fort Granger.

Forrest watched through his spyglass the impact of the shelling. At first, the federal cannon within the fort returned fire briskly. But in order to do so, the crews of the guns had to expose themselves Within a matter of minutes, several of them were picked off by his sharpshooters. After a time, Forrest had the satisfaction of seeing the federal artillery fall silent.

He readied his men. The horses were sent to the rear and the men deployed in skirmisher order. Unlike some other commanders, Forrest had never been so foolish as to arrange his men in massed formations to be hurled forward in a Napoleonic assault. Seeing no need to wait, Forrest ordered his bugler to sound the charge.

Still mounted on King Philip, Forrest watched as his men began moving forward at a jog, their carbines at the ready. His sharpshooters and artillerymen continued to pour fire into Fort Granger, hoping to keep the heads of the defenders down so as to limit their fire. As his men came within rifle range, several of the black troops raised themselves over the top of the parapet and began shooting. While the fire did not seem particularly brisk, Forrest could see several of his men fall. Onward they went, though, coming ever closer to the walls of the fort.

He kicked King Philip into a canter, following his men. The fire from the fort was become more intense, but it still seemed strangely fitful. No organized volleys were being delivered, which seemed to confirm Forrest's opinion about the fighting qualities of the blacks. His men were drawing nearer to the ramparts while suffering few casualties. He grinned. It seemed that this fight would be even easier than he had expected. He kicked King Philip into a full gallop, wanting to go over the top of the parapet with his men. If he was lucky, he might add to the tally of the number of men he had personally killed.

Reining in a few hundred yards from the fort, he slid off the saddle with ease and began jogging forward, leaving one of his aides to take his beloved mount to the rear and out of harm's way. Pulling out his pistol and saber, Forrest dashed forward to be with his men. They themselves were clambering into the shallow trench surrounding the fort's parapet. Forrest saw immediately how poorly designed Fort Granger had been, as the parapet was so high that the defenders could not lean over far enough to fire at their attackers without exposing themselves as well.

Seeing him leap into the trench, Forrest's men watched him carefully and waited for his command. From the base of the trench, his men would have to scamper up perhaps eight or nine feet at an angle of about forty degrees. Behind them, a loose line of men had paused at the edge of the trench, continuing to provide covering fire for their comrades. The cannon fire behind them had ceased, however, as his artillerymen did not want to risk hitting their own men.

Bullets were smacking into the ground near his feet, but Forrest paid them no mind. He glanced up and down the trench. Nearly a thousand men now crowded the base of the parapet, and there couldn't be more than a few hundred defenders within the fort itself. All they needed to do was go over the top of the parapet and Fort Granger would be at his mercy. They would slaughter the garrison, burn the bridge over the Harpeth River, and be on their way within an hour or so. Franklin would have yet another successful raid on his record.

"Ready?" he shouted to his nearby men. Even amidst the fire coming down on them, they nodded grimly. He glanced up and down the line one more time to make sure all was well, then raised his sword.

"Now!" he yelled.

With a ruthless and hearty yell, his men dashed upwards, clambering up the parapet. Forrest led the way, his men behind him. His expectations of an easy victory appeared to be confirmed when he saw the black soldiers turn and flee, leaving the top of the parapet virtually clear of enemy troops. A few of his men fell victim to the light fire they encountered, but not nearly enough to slow down the attack. Within seconds, he had scaled the parapet and dropped down inside the fort itself.

It was a trap.

Because of the height of the ramparts, Forrest had been unable to see the interior of the fort from outside of it. But now he saw a large inner space crowded with blue-coated black soldiers, numbering far more than he had expected and huddled in a long trench. Instantly, Forrest realized the danger into which he and his men had been led. Fort Granger was not held by a single small regiment, but by an entire brigade. There were more Union soldiers inside the fort than there were Confederate attackers. Worse still, the guns which had previously been withdrawn from the walls to escape the attention of his sharpshooters had been repositioned along the trench in the fort's courtyard, their muzzles now aimed squarely at the parapet near where he and his men were standing.

There was Major Easton standing behind the trench, a satisfied smile on his face. For just a moment, his eyes and Forrest's met. Easton had gotten the better of the Wizard of the Saddle, knew it, and relished it. For the first time in his life, Nathan Bedford Forrest knew fear.

"Fire!" Easton shouted.

The muskets of the black troops and the six artillery pieces opened fire simultaneously. A sheet of lead musket balls and canister fire tore into Forrest's exposed men just inside the parapet. Like a scythe running through a clump of dry grass, the Union fire cut down the Southerners in droves. Some of Forrest's men raised their weapons and fired back, but the black troops were protected by their trench while they themselves had no shelter on the inside of the parapet.

The soldiers on both sides of Forrest were instantly hit, but he himself remained unscathed. Though he was momentarily staggered by the dramatic turn of events, he recovered quickly. He could either order an immediate retreat or press on with the attack. Forrest would never retreat. He knew that he needed to get his men off of the parapet, for to remain there was certain death. He shouted over the din of federal fire for his men to charge forward toward the enemy trench. He then turned and shouted back to the men still outside the fort to bring everyone inside as quickly as possible.

It was a risk, Forrest knew. His men had now suffered grievous casualties and the psychological shock of falling into the enemy trap had badly shaken their morale. All could be made right, however, if his men could close the gap with their foes and engage them in hand-to-hand combat.

Forrest's men jumped down from the parapet and ran forward toward the trench, some pulling out bowie knives as they did so. The black Union troops were continuing to pour fire into them and Confederate soldiers fell with every step. It was a shaky and disjointed attack. Forrest could see instantly that the assault had lost its energy and momentum, yet he had no choice but to continue. To acknowledge defeat and withdraw was unthinkable.

Shaky or not, the interior of the fort was a small space and the Confederate troops closed the distance to their foes within a matter of seconds. Some dropped down into the trench and began hacking away with their knives, employing their bayoneted carbines as spears, or simply using their fists. The black Union troops did not flinch for an instant and gave as good as they got. A brutal hand-to-hand battle now raged inside Fort Granger, with the sound of fists punching faces, blades slashing flesh and the occasional gunshot whenever anyone had a chance to reload.

Forrest, watching the course of the fight from the parapet, shook his head. He was playing the enemy's game, for there were far more Union troops within the fort than Confederate troops. He and his men had been lured to Franklin like a mouse being lured to a piece of cheese. That was why all the other potential targets on the rail line between Nashville and Chattanooga had been strongly reinforced but Franklin had not. He was furious with himself. He had made a major error and the price he would pay would be the destruction of his command.

Over the sound of the fighting, Forrest began to hear a call going up from the black regiments. He was uncertain at first what they were saying, but after a few repetitions it became clear.

"Fort Pillow!" they were yelling. "Fort Pillow!"

At first, Forrest thought the cries were ones of fear and that the black troops were frightened that what had happened to their comrades at Fort Pillow was about to happen to them. But listening more carefully, Forrest began to hear another word being shouted in the chant.

"Fort Pillow! Revenge! Fort Pillow! Revenge!"

He jumped down from the parapet and ran forward, brandishing his sword. He fired his Colt revolver until its ammunition was exhausted, then cast it aside as he would not have the chance to reload it again until the fight was over. He wanted specifically to find Major Easton and put him to the sword, but he did not see him.

As he moved forward toward the hand-to-hand battle raging in the trench, Forrest suddenly found his way blocked by a black soldier who glared at him with a ferocious hatred. He was not all that large in comparison to Forrest, but he carried himself with a confident strength that Forrest found disconcerting. He carried a Springfield musket with a bayonet fixed on its end.

"Forrest!" the man bellowed. It was a challenge.

He didn't deign to respond. Speaking to the man, who by rights should have been working as a plantation slave, would have required Forrest to grant the man some manner of respect, which Forrest was not about to do. He was determined, however, to kill him.

Forrest charged toward the man, slashing down at him with his saber and shrieking like a banshee. But the black soldier raised his musket, holding the butt with one hand and the barrel with the other, blocking the sword. With a dexterity that surprised Forrest, he then swung the butt of his heavy weapon against the left side of Forrest's head. Pain screamed through his skull from the blow, which would have easily knocked a weaker man unconscious. Forrest staggered backward a few steps, blinked and shook his head to clear it, then came forward again.

With the chaos of the battle swirling around them, Forrest and his opponent fought their own duel. Forrest repeatedly slashed with his sword, but found his attacks blocked by the man's musket. The black soldier thrust back at Forrest with his bayonet, but as he did so Forrest let go off his saber and clasped the barrel of the musket as tightly as he could, attempting to wrest it out of his hands. Jerking the rifle off to the right, Forrest smashed his head forcefully into the nose of the black soldier, then threw him with such force that the man lost his grip on his weapon and was hurled down onto the ground.

Now wielding the man's own musket and bayonet, Forrest shrieked once again and attempted to run him through. He had been more than enough trouble. The soldier rolled out of the way and Forrest only planted the bayonet into the dirt floor of the fort. A second later, the man was back on his feet, smashing his fist into Forrest's face with such speed and force that several of Forrest's teeth were knocked loose and he immediately tasted his own blood. The man pummeled Forrest's face twice more, then raised his knee into Forrest's chest when he involuntarily hunched over in pain, striking with the force of a sledgehammer.

Forrest staggered and fell over, unable to continue resisting. The man rained down blow after blow, beating him in the head and chest. He retrieved his musket from the ground but, rather than run Forrest through with the bayonet, simply used it as a club to continue the beatings. Each blow felt to Forrest like it was being delivered by a giant. He didn't understand how a man of such average size was capable of such immense feats of physical strength.

Forrest felt his vision beginning to go black and his sense of balance going askew. He realized that he was losing his grip on consciousness. He tried to force himself to regain his senses, but his body refused to obey his mind. He now distantly felt the man's arms grip him from behind in a bear hug of tremendous strength, pinning his arms tightly to his sides and lifting him off the ground as if he were no more than a doll. Eventually, he felt himself thrown roughly down onto the ground against one of the fort's walls.

For a few minutes, Forrest was in a daze. As his mind began to clear, he sensed the pain caused by the terrible beating he had received. Several of his teeth were gone, his head throbbed so much he thought it would explode like a cannon shell. The slightest movement of either his left arm or his right leg caused so much pain that they had to be broken. With great difficulty, he opened his eyes.

Surrounding him were dozens of black Union soldiers.

They stood in silence, looking down at Forrest as a crowd might look down at an animal in a zoo. Forrest glanced around for any signs of his men, but there were none. The sounds of battle were long gone. Forrest figured his men had been defeated and had either retreated out of the fort or had all been killed or captured. That fact was almost as painful as the shattered bones in his arm and leg and the throbbing pain in his head.

Standing in the center of the rough semi-circle was the man who had defeated Forrest in hand-to-hand combat. The stripes on his uniform revealed him to be a sergeant and it was clear that the other soldiers regarded him as some sort of leader.

"Get rope," the sergeant said with a frightening bluntness.

"I am a general!" Forrest roared with anger.

"You are a criminal and a murderer," the sergeant replied, in a voice that surprised Forrest with its articulateness.

Forrest glanced around for Major Easton, no longer in search of revenge but rather in search of protection. In the distance, behind the line of threatening black troops, he could see what looked like a group of white Union officers, but they appeared to be processing Confederate prisoners and taking no interest in what was happening with him. Easton was among them.

"Major Easton!" Forrest shouted angrily. "I am entitled to the rights of a prisoner of war!"

"Did you respect such rights when you and your men captured Fort Pillow?" the sergeant asked impassively.

"Be silent, you negro bastard!" Forrest spat. He felt humiliated at having been goaded into speaking to the man.

Major Easton strolled over to Forrest, the sergeant, and the cluster of increasingly restive black troops. "What's going on here, Sergeant Bayard?"

"Nothing at all, sir," the sergeant said with an expressionless face.

"Your negroes say that they will hang me, Major! I am a major general in the Confederate Army and I expect to be protected."

Major Easton looked long and hard into Forrest's eyes. Then, he turned back to Sergeant Bayard.

"You say that nothing at all is going on here, Sergeant?"

"That's correct, sir."

"Very well, then. Carry on." With that, he turned and walked back to the line of Confederate prisoners.

"Major Easton!" Forrest shouted in angry protest. "Damn you, Yankee bastard! I hope you rot in hell!"

"You're the one who's going to rot in hell, Forrest," Bayard said.

They had dangled a rope from an iron pole designed to hold torches during the night. One man was busy tying its end into a noose, while two other soldiers walked forward and grabbed Forrest roughly by the shoulders. He tried to struggle, but his shattered bones prevented any resistance.

The man Easton had referred to as Sergeant Bayard looked at him impassively.

"It's Judgment Day, Forrest. I'm supposed to ask God to have mercy on your soul. I rather doubt He will."

The noose was wrapped around his neck. Forrest's heart pounded in his chest, terror filling every nerve in his body. He had cheated death so many times, but there would be no escape from this.

Two strong Union soldiers heaved on the rope from the other side of the pole. Forrest felt it snap tightly around his neck and jerk him violently off the ground. Instantly, his oxygen was cut off. He tried to reach up to grasp the rope with his hands, but to no avail. His feet jerked about uncontrollably.

The black soldiers gathered in an immense semi-circle around him did not gloat or cheer. They simply stood silently and still, watching the life fade from their tormentor's body. Forrest twitched and turned for several minutes, until his oxygen-starved brain gradually ceased functioning. Then, it was all over.

Chapter Twelve

August 27, Evening

Though he would never have admitted it, Grant was tired. It was never easy to get much sleep while traveling by rail. The few snippets he had managed to snatch during the long journey from Washington to Louisville and on down to Nashville had not been nearly enough. The hurried meetings he had held with General Meade and other officers before departing Petersburg, and the day he had spent closeted with Lincoln and Stanton at the White House before heading west, had only added to his fatigue. When he had finally arrived in Nashville shortly after dawn, he had quickly gone to his room at the St. Cloud Hotel and slept for two hours in order to have sufficient energy for the day ahead of him.

He had been delighted to learn of the death of Nathan Bedford Forrest while passing through Louisville. One of his earliest attempts to capture Vicksburg had been frustrated when rebel raiders, Forrest among them, had torn his supply lines to pieces. Now that Forrest was in his grave, he could be confident of going forth into Georgia with a secure railroad. More importantly, the strong infantry forces which had been deployed guarding the railroads could now be brought to the front and replaced by hundred-day men from Ohio and Illinois. It was an auspicious beginning for his return to the West.

Having awoken and spent ten minutes freshening up, he had gone downstairs and found a hearty breakfast of coffee, bacon, biscuits and gravy already prepared for him. He hoped that he would enjoy the meal, because the conversation that would accompany it was sure to be unpleasant.

On the other side of the table sat William Tecumseh Sherman, now the former commander of the Union armies in the West. He picked at his food unenthusiastically, an expression of profound and unsettled sadness on his face. Grant looked over at him, sipping his coffee, and tried to come up with words that would make him feel better.

"I meant what I said in my telegraph, Cump," Grant began. "The decision to come out here and take personal command has been the hardest choice I have had to make in this war. One of the hardest choices I have had to make in my own life, I don't mind saying."

"I know, Sam," Sherman replied tiredly. "I know."

"Had it been possible, I should certainly have asked for you to remain in Georgia as my chief-of-staff. But I was prevented from doing so. Not my choice, you understand."

"Politics," Sherman grunted. Neither he nor Grant had much time for politics or politicians. They were soldiers and obeyed orders. Sherman didn't bother to ask for details about what Grant was talking about, but he could imagine that Stanton or some other suit-wearing bigwig had made it clear to Grant that keeping Sherman on in any capacity would not be permitted, probably because of what the newspapers would say or because the governor of some big state might object. It didn't matter.

"Where are you going?" Grant asked.

"Washington," Sherman replied. "I've been asked to appear before the Joint Committee on the Conduct of the War. I suppose I am to be made a scapegoat for the disaster at Peachtree Creek."

Grant's face flushed. "I had no idea," he said. "I received the telegram from Senator Wade just last night."

"I shall use every means within my power to ensure that you receive a fair hearing. And I am sure the President will do so as well. The battle was lost due to bad luck, not because of any failings on your part. By rights, you should have been in Atlanta long ago."

Sherman shrugged. "I am to be crucified. There is nothing you or the President can do about it. It's all politics. You know how it is. Besides, the more blame they heap on me, the less that can be thrown against you and the President. It's all for the best, Sam."

Grant shook his head. "A damn disgrace. That's what it is."

"It's all for the best. And after my crucifixion, I shall go home to my wife and family in Ohio. I can't really imagine where else I would go. There, I shall lie low for awhile, at least until the war is over."

"And then?"

He shrugged again. "If you succeed, I can live out the rest of my days in the happy knowledge that, at least at the beginning of the conflict, I played some small role in ensuring the continued survival of the Union."

"The role you played at Shiloh and Vicksburg was critical. I would not have won without you." Grant took another sip of coffee, wishing it were bourbon. "Besides, I might well fail against Johnston."

Sherman looked at him carefully. "Your arrival will help restore the morale of the men. The reinforcements you have brought to the Georgia front will again establish a significant numerical superiority.   And the failure of the rebel cavalry raids on the railroads, especially the deaths of both Wheeler and Forrest, will ensure a steady flow of supplies to the army on the Chattahoochee. I believe that you will have a better chance of defeating Johnston than any other man possibly could. Better than me, by God."

Grant nodded.   He didn't doubt the wisdom of Sherman's words.   Much as he wished it were not so from the standpoint of personal friendship, the news of Sherman's departure and Grant's arrival had been greeted with great enthusiasm by the rank and file of the Yankee soldiers along the Chattahoochee. He had also ordered additional reinforcements from Missouri to join him in Georgia, judging that weakening the defenses of that state was worth the risk if it meant increasing the chances of victory at Atlanta.

If the information he had received was correct, despite the losses in battle and from expired enlistments, Grant estimated that he would soon be able to put about ninety thousand men in the field against Johnston's army, which numbered between fifty and sixty thousand. It was not as great an advantage as he had enjoyed over Lee in the recent campaigns in Virginia, but it was an advantage nonetheless.

Grant had never fought Johnston in a major battle, although elements of their respective forces had skirmished with one another on the edges of the Vicksburg campaign. He had carefully studied Johnston's tactics, read the reports of every Union general that had played a role in any battle against him, and felt he knew what to expect.   Besides which, Johnston could not possibly be as good a general as Robert E. Lee, and Grant had managed to fight Lee to a standstill in Virginia.

He pulled a cigar out of his pocket, lit it, and was soon puffing away. "I'll do my best, Cump. Maybe it'll be enough. Then again, maybe not. Either way, what else can we do?"

"Nothing," Sherman replied. "Nothing at all."

*　　　　　*　　　　　*　　　　　*　　　　　*

August 28, Morning

Marble stirred in his bed as he faintly realized that sunlight was coming through his window. Instantly he was awake, his mind already racing with thoughts of electoral votes to be won, deals to be made, and egos of restless politicians to be flattered. He kicked off the sheets of his bed and strolled to the window, thrusting apart the curtains and letting sunlight flood into his room.

Marble nervously glanced under the bedside table to make sure that the carpetbag he had been given by Alexander Humphries was still there.   There was absolutely no reason for him to have thought otherwise, but considering the amount of money the bag contained, he couldn't help but double check on it every few minutes. What was in that bag was going to be of great benefit to his future ambitions.

He looked out the window. From the top floor of the five-story Tremont House hotel, he could see the entire city of Chicago stretching out to the horizon. Although it was still early, he could tell that the city was already hard at work. Pillars of smoke from the city's innumerable factories rose lazily into the air. The streets below were crowded with buggies, wagons, horses and pedestrians. Out there, Marble knew, vast warehouses were crammed with agricultural produce and storefronts were filled with every sort of commercial product.

The sound of a steam whistle caused him to glance over at a train coming toward the center of the city from the west, riding on a track which Marble figured was probably owned by the Galena and Chicago Union Railroad Company. He laughed softly. So much attention was being given to Atlanta by the newspapers of both North and South, including his own, because three railroads converged there. In Chicago, no less than thirty railroads came together. Marble reflected for a moment that the industrial output of the city of Chicago by itself very likely exceeded the industrial output of the entire Confederacy.

As he looked down on the city, Marble found himself enthralled by the limitless possibilities of business and commerce. Thirty years before, the area within his vision had been nothing but empty prairie. Now, it was a city whose size and commercial strength rivaled that of the great metropolises of Europe. As the vast empty spaces of the American West lay open to the country, once they had been cleared of the pesky Indian tribes, Marble had no doubt that the success story of Chicago would be repeated time and again over the next few decades.

He was determined to be a part of it. Indeed, as he was yet a young man, he saw no reason why Manton Marble should not eventually rise to be the principal actor in the drama.

There was a soft knocking at the door. It was a black waiter bringing a dish of coffee and a copy of the *Chicago Times*. After the tray and paper had been set on the table, the man handed Marble a note before departing.

Dear Mr. Marble,
As you and I are both staying here at the Tremont, I wonder if you might give me the pleasure of your company at breakfast at nine o'clock in the main dining room.
Governor Horatio Seymour

Marble checked his pocket watch. It was a quarter past seven o'clock, so he had plenty of time. He sat in a chair beside the window, enjoying the coffee and reading through the newspaper for some time. He was fascinated to read about the proposal by the rebel general Patrick Cleburne to free the slaves and enlist them into the Southern army. Marble assumed that this would be the end of the Irishman's promising career, but he saw nothing about it that mattered much to him.

Aside from that item, nothing in the news seemed particularly momentous. Jubal Early's army had fought an indecisive battle with Union forces in the northern Shenandoah Valley and the U.S. Navy had opened another bombardment of Confederate coastal defenses in Charleston. In foreign affairs, some squabble was going on in Europe concerning an uprising against Russian rule in Poland, but that was no concern of Marble. He enjoyed his coffee and finished reading the paper, before spending some time freshening himself up for his breakfast with Seymour.

The dining room of the Tremont exuded elegance but, like everything else in Chicago, was characterized by its obvious newness. There was a feeling that the paint was still slightly wet on the walls and that the waiters had not been at their jobs long enough to have gained sufficient experience. Despite this, if the smells emanating from the kitchen were any indication, the chef and the staff preparing the food were more than experienced enough.

Marble slid into a chair across the table from Governor Seymour, who looked at him with a winning smile.

"Ah, Marble," he said simply. "I am glad you received my note."

"I thank you for your gracious invitation to breakfast, Governor." Seymour was already feasting on a plate of fried oysters. Partly to curry favor and partly because they looked delicious, Marble immediately ordered the same dish for himself.

"So," Seymour said as he folded up his newspaper and set it aside. "The train stations of the city are packed with Democrats from across the land. Yesterday the delegations from Pennsylvania and Ohio arrived. Fifteen thousand people are expected to attend the convention, rumor has it. Men from as far away as California and Oregon are coming."

"It is inspiring to see such an outpouring of support for the Democratic cause," Marble said.

"Do you agree that McClellan's nomination is assured?"

"It is, in all but name. The New York delegation will vote for you on the first ballot, in deference to your position as the favorite son of the state. But on the second ballot, they shall switch their vote to McClellan."

"I have no desire to be President. Not this year, anyway."

"Perhaps in 1872?"

"Perhaps." There was a pause. "Now, are there any other contenders?"

Marble shrugged. "No serious ones. Many of the delegations will, like New York, vote initially for a favorite son. But on the second ballot, I think we shall see the convention coalesce around McClellan."

Seymour smiled. "Just as we planned."

Marble already knew what he would do if any dark horse candidates unexpectedly emerged to challenge McClellan's nomination. Using the money provided by Humphries, a few select bribes would be paid and whatever support the dark horse had would rapidly collapse.

"If there are any difficulties, I believe they shall arise out of the committee which is writing the party platform."

"In what way?" Seymour said, happily picking at his oysters.

"There are still some Democrats who are not of the position that our platform should call for an immediate termination of hostilities. Granted, many of these voices have been silenced over the past few months as disaster has followed disaster on the battlefield, but they still represent a sizable fraction of the party. Perhaps as much as a quarter."

Seymour shrugged. "The people want peace. They are tired of the endless casualty lists. They are tired of runaway inflation. Our recent military defeats have surely convinced the vast majority of war hawks within our party that peace and negotiations are the only way forward."

"You shall have to convince any remaining war hawks to drop their opposition to opening negotiations with the South. As the presiding officer of the convention, you shall give the opening address. You will have the opportunity to achieve the result we need."

"I was intending to make my opening address, in effect, a eulogy for Clement Vallandigham."

"And so it should be. The message of our martyr was that the war is wrong, the war is useless, and the war is bringing the nation nothing but misery. Because he had the courage to say such things to the people, Vallandigham was killed."

Seymour nodded. "I see what you're saying. Ordinarily, I would object to exploiting the name of a man so recently killed for such a political purpose. But in this case, it is exactly what Vallandigham would have wanted."

"Yes, he would have. Furthermore, if I might be forgiven for making a political recommendation, the more prominent hawks remaining in the Democratic fold might be mollified if they were promised certain plum political positions, such as posts in the Cabinet."

"It's already being discussed. We are prepared to offer the position of Secretary of State to Governor Joel Parker of New Jersey and the post of Ambassador to France to Congressman Francis Kernan. A few other offers are on the table for other men. Feel free to spread the word that if those Democrats who have offered support for Lincoln's war effort will now simply shut up and toe the party line, they might receive some very beneficial rewards."

"I will happily do so," Marble said cheerfully. He would also spread his largesse.

Seymour snapped at a nearby waiter and ordered a bottle of champagne. "Will you join me in a glass, Manton?"

"Of course." Marble was never a man to turn down an offer of alcohol.

As he sipped his glass, Seymour inhaled deeply and smiled. "I think everything is coming together nicely, Manton. Our party shall be united behind a strong and respected candidate and shall have a platform calling for peace around which the people shall rally when the time comes. The Lincoln administration daily continues to display its incompetence. The presidential election is only seventy-two days away."

"Our prospects are indeed good, and they seem to be getting better. Barring any unforeseen event, I honestly cannot see any scenario in which we might fail."

*   *   *   *   *

August 28, Noon

Because he enjoyed inspections so much, Cleburne sometimes found it difficult to maintain the unsympathetic and stern expression for which the occasions clearly called. As he and Hardee walked down the length of the division, which was drawn up in a field in parade ground formation, they passed by each regiment in turn. Right now, the men they were passing by were the Arkansans of Warfield's Brigade. Each regiment stood tall and proud, as if they were competing with one another to earn the greatest admiration from their commanders.

The men looked tough, which was no surprise to Cleburne. Life in Arkansas made all men tough, as Cleburne knew better than most. He had made the state his home after immigrating from Ireland. He recalled the memorable day in 1856 when he and his close friend and political ally, Thomas Hindman, had been ambushed in the streets of Helena, Arkansas, by a gang of anti-immigrant fanatics following a political debate. The gunfight that had followed had left both Hindman and Cleburne lying on the street, badly wounded, although Cleburne had succeeded in killing one of their attackers. Arkansas was a rough place, but it also produced some damn fine soldiers.

"Your men appear to be in excellent condition, General Cleburne. You are obviously taking very good care of them." Hardee spoke these words loudly enough for several nearby soldiers to hear him, knowing that it would be good fodder for campfire discussions during the evening.

"Thank you, sir. But the credit belongs entirely to the men themselves."

"And to the Yankees, who kindly presented us with several thousand new pairs of shoes last month."

Cleburne chuckled. More than half the men in his division were sporting footgear taken from dead or captured Yankees after the Battle of Peachtree Creek or from the enemy supply depots captured when Sherman's men had retreated across the river. Some of the regiments were now equipped with new Springfield or Enfield muskets captured from the Yankees as well. Even better, four of the enemy cannon captured at Peachtree Creek had been assigned to Cleburne's division, allowing him to organize a new battery of horse artillery that gave him significantly increased firepower. All things considered, his division was in better condition than it had ever been since he had first taken command.

But it was not as big. Although the severe losses Cleburne had suffered at the Battle of Peachtree Creek had been partially made up by returned deserters and a paltry number of new recruits arrived from Alabama, the total strength of his division was only a bit over three thousand men. When the campaign had begun back in May, the division had fielded nearly twice that number. Far too many of his beloved men now lay in shallow graves scattered across northern Georgia.

Hardee and Cleburne passed by the last regiment of Warfield's Brigade. The next unit was Lowrey's Brigade, which was now commanded by Colonel Aaron Hardcastle as Lowrey was still recovering from the terrible wound he had received at Peachtree Creek. The men snapped to attention. Hardee and Cleburne exchanged salutes with the brigade officers. They then watched each regiment in turn go through its proper drill.

As they moved from one unit to another, Hardee began speaking in a more conversational tone, quiet enough so that the men could not easily hear him.

"Johnston has called for a meeting of senior commanders for tomorrow night."

"Has he?" Cleburne replied. "Well, I imagine he wants to discuss how Sherman's departure may alter the military situation."

"No doubt."

"And Grant will be the new commander."

"The men may be disturbed. They remember well that Grant commanded the enemy when we were routed at Missionary Ridge."

"Grant is not invincible. We beat him badly on the first day at Shiloh, you will recall."

"True. But he beat us the second day."

They continued to move from one regiment to another. Watching the men of one of the Mississippi regiments go through their drill, Cleburne found himself thinking of the years he had spent as an enlisted man in the British Army, before he had come to America. Although the discipline he had learned from that experience had served him well as an infantry officer, the memories were bitter ones. His regiment had been posted in Ireland and he had served essentially as a soldier in an army of occupation, keeping down his own people. He was happy when a new question from Hardee roused him from such unpleasant thoughts.

"Do you think Grant will be a more formidable adversary than Sherman?"

Cleburne thought for a moment, happy as always to be asked his opinion by his commander. "I believe so, yes. Grant proved during the Vicksburg Campaign that he is a brilliant and unorthodox commander. Whatever else we can say about him, Grant has certainly demonstrated in his recent battles in Virginia that he is a ruthless man who is not afraid to employ the sheer weight of numbers to achieve victory, no matter how many of his men get killed in the process."

"Rather more blunt than Sherman, I think. Wouldn't you agree?"

"Yes. If Sherman is like a French rapier, Grant is more like a Scottish claymore."

Hardee laughed. "A fine analogy, Patrick!"

Cleburne's eyes narrowed in confusion. He hadn't been attempting humor.

Hardee went on. "In any case, as we again have the Chattahoochee River between us and the enemy, we can hopefully prevent the Yankees from coming any closer to Atlanta than they already are."

"Sherman got across the Chattahoochee without too much trouble. Why should Grant not be able to accomplish the same feat?"

"A fair question," Hardee replied.

They had finished passing by Lowrey's Brigade and had begun walking past Granbury's troops from Texas. Cleburne noticed that they were not as well turned out as the men from Arkansas, Mississippi and Alabama. They also were not as good at drill, but they carried themselves with a much greater air of confidence. Indeed, they seemed to swagger with bravado even as they stood completely still. Cleburne wasn't surprised. Texas was the frontier, where violence was more common and where men were expected to defend themselves against any and all comers.

He looked at the stern, sturdy men with a sense of wonder in his eyes. Their uniforms contained scarcely a hint that they had once been clean and gray, and many of the men looked as though they had not shaved in months. Still, he thought they looked more impressive than the finest gentleman in London. These troops had left their blood on countless battlefields over the past year, holding every position they defended and capturing every position they attacked.

He recognized James McFadden, the soldier who had captured George Thomas on the battlefield of Peachtree Creek. Now wearing the uniform of a lieutenant and having exchanged his Enfield for a pistol and sword, he seemed to be doing well.

"Best brigade in your division," Hardee said admirably.

"Best brigade in the army," Cleburne replied.

"The Orphan Brigade might disagree with you. So might Cockrell's Missourians."

Cleburne nodded, acknowledging Hardee's point. In truth, though, rating units in such an arbitrary manner made little sense. They were not racehorses, after all. The important thing was that everyone did their duty.

As they filed past the last ranks of Granbury's Texans, they turned and looked back. The division stretched out perhaps a quarter of a mile. The men had patiently waited until their commanders had completed their inspection of the entire division, remaining steadily at attention. Now they exchanged final salutes with the officers of Granbury's Brigade and moved to mount their horses, which had been held by staff officers for them at the end of the line. As they rode away, they could hear shouted orders from the officers directing their men to fall out and resume whatever chores they had been doing before the inspection had begun.

"Join me for lunch, Patrick?"

"Of course."

The two men began to ride together back toward Hardee's headquarters. As they left the troops behind, Hardee brought up the inevitable subject.

"I'm afraid Johnston will want to discuss the newspaper rumors about your old proposal at this meeting, Patrick."

Cleburne nodded. "I assumed so."

"General Cooper is on his way from Richmond," Hardee said. "Apparently he is going to conduct some sort of investigation. I imagine that he intends to interview us both regarding the circumstances of when and how your proposal was made." Samuel Cooper held the dual positions of Adjutant General and Inspector General of the Confederate Army.

"I feel like a Christian about to be fed to the lions," Cleburne said.

"Cooper is an honest man," Hardee said reassuringly. "I don't think you have anything to worry about. You did nothing against the law or against the regulations of the army. The President just wants to be able to say that he looked into the matter."

"I do not fear prosecution by the courts," Cleburne replied. "It is the newspapers I'm worried about. In their pages, I am already being crucified."

Over the past few days, at Cleburne's request, Major Benham had forwarded to him copies of most of the major newspapers of the Confederacy. To his intense disappointment, not a single one had defended the proposal. In fact, most of the editorial writers had bitterly denounced the proposal and called for Cleburne's head. Only a few had acknowledged Cleburne's patriotism and military record, but even those had still dismissed his idea as horribly misguided and ill-timed.

Cleburne knew that he had broken no law by making his unprecedented proposal. But he also knew that this didn't matter. The very public that had only recently lionized him as the hero of Ringgold Gap and Peachtree Creek was now turning furiously against him. Cleburne knew that President Davis wouldn't hesitate to exile him to some obscure command where he would quickly be forgotten.

"You're worried about being removed from command," Hardee said, reading his mind. It was not a question, but a statement.

Cleburne nodded.

"You shouldn't be," Hardee said. "They cannot remove you at such a delicate time, with Grant soon to renew the Union offensive against Atlanta. And rest assured, if they try to remove you, I myself will resign in protest."

"Thank you, my friend."

"Have you discussed the matter with your officers?"

"Yes. I have spoken with every brigade and regimental commander and all report that the men continue to have complete confidence in my leadership."

"That doesn't surprise me, although I imagine it will dismay Walker. Have you heard from Susan?"

Cleburne shook his head. "Her last letter arrived just before the story got into the newspapers. She knows all about my proposal. I told her about it before I asked her to marry me. She said that she agreed with me entirely. Still, I know she will be greatly upset. Many of her friends are married to large plantation owners. It will cause trouble, to be sure."

"She loves you very much. You need not fear anything on that score."

"I know. But I hate the idea of her being troubled on account of my own politics."

Hardee chuckled. "You'll make a good husband, Patrick."

"I pray so. My anxiety over that question has caused me greater unease these past few months than any concerns I have had regarding the war."

"I understand how you feel. After all, I am a recently married man myself."

Cleburne turned in his saddle and looked hard at Hardee. "Do you ever fear leaving Mary a widow?"

Hardee's eyebrows went up. "A morbid question, my friend. Even in the middle of a war. But the answer is yes. I'd be lying if I denied it. So many of the senior commanders on both sides in this war have been killed. Even the commanders of armies are not immune from the bullets, as poor old Albert Sidney Johnston found out back at Shiloh."

"The thought preys on my mind sometimes," Cleburne admitted.

"You are not afraid of death," Hardee said emphatically. "You are a man without fear, near as I can tell."

"I don't think I fear death, no. But I worry about the sadness my death would bring to Susan."

"Worrying about it does no good. We have been in more fights than I care to remember. How many bullets have passed so near our heads that our ears could feel the air move? How many tore holes in our jackets? Did any of these bullets miss us because we were worried about them? No, not one. They just missed us. Simple as that."

"God's will be done," Cleburne said simply. He was comfortable in his quiet Episcopalian faith.

"Truth, indeed," Hardee agreed. "Even if we don't understand it very well. But I will venture to say that it was obviously God's will that brought you and Susan together. Having done so, it would make no sense for Him to tear you apart from one another."

*   *   *   *   *

August 28, Evening

"Cooper should arrive in Atlanta tomorrow," Bragg said, flipping through a stack of papers in his hands.

"And his instructions are clear?"

"I told him precisely what you told me to tell him. He is to interview all officers who were present at the January meeting, compile a full account of exactly what happened then and after, and inquire into what each officer thought of Cleburne's proposal. He will then write up a comprehensive report for you."

"Good, very good," Davis said, nodding. "An ideal assignment for a man of Cooper's talents." Davis actually considered Cooper's investigation entirely irrelevant, for he had learned of Cleburne's proposal within weeks of when it had been made and felt no particular need for additional information about it. Nevertheless, with dozens of newspapers clamoring for Cleburne's head and half of Congress up in arms, it was imperative that he be seen as doing something. Cooper's investigation would be useless, but at least it provided the appearance of action.

"We should begin considering what actions we shall take based on whatever Cooper's investigation reveals."

"My hope is that the whole matter will soon blow over. I don't want to lose the services of Cleburne. With Grant again commanding the enemy forces in the West, fighting will surely resume very soon. I want Cleburne at the head of his division, with both the army and the people focused on the need to defeat the Yankees."

"That is what concerns me," Bragg said sourly. "Suppose Cooper's investigation finds that Cleburne is an active abolitionist? The men of his division will surely throw down their weapons and refuse to fight under such a commander. Suppose Cooper finds that Hardee and Johnston share Cleburne's abolitionist views? The other officers of the Army of Tennessee will refuse to follow their orders. General Hood tells me that the other corps and division commanders, Hardee aside, were already disillusioned with Johnston because of his support of Cleburne's proposal, or at least his refusal to denounce it."

"Well, we must wait and see what Cooper finds. Perhaps with the resumption of fighting, the newspapers will find other stories to write about. Now, what else?"

Bragg looked down at his papers. "Something rather disturbing, unfortunately. A group of soldiers from Forrest's command who were taken prisoner at Franklin and subsequently escaped are giving an account of Forrest's death that, to say the least, raises a number of questions."

"What kind of questions?" Davis asked impatiently.

"They are saying that General Forrest did not die in combat, but was killed by negro soldiers after he had been taken prisoner."

A look of horror crossed the President's face. "They killed him in cold blood after they captured him?"

"It would seem so, Mr. President. Not only that, but according to one eyewitness, he was hanged like a common criminal rather than shot, with white officers standing by and making no effort to intervene."

"He was a major general in the Confederate Army! If he was captured, he was entitled to be treated as a prisoner-of-war!"

"I know, Mr. President. I certainly contrast the Yankee treatment of Forrest with our own treatment of General Thomas. Though he is a despicable man who betrayed his state, we have treated him with all the respect to which he is entitled under the rules of warfare."

Through the cloud created by his anger, an uncomfortable truth intruded upon Davis's mind. The men of Forrest's command had been accused of carrying out a massacre of black Union soldiers when they had captured Fort Pillow in February. Though the details were unclear to Davis, the Yankee newspapers had repeated the story so often and embellished it so much that it was now being taken for the gospel truth. Forrest's own report had not helped matters, for in it he had all but bragged about how his men had shot down the black soldiers after they had surrendered.

Fort Pillow was not the only place where Confederate soldiers had massacred black troops, Davis knew. It had happened during the Battle of the Crater not even a month before. It had happened in February after the victory in the Battle of Olustee down in Florida. Almost certainly, it would happen again before the war was over.

Davis blamed the Yankees. In his mind, by setting the slaves at liberty and making them into soldiers, the forces of Abraham Lincoln were inflaming the unavoidable tensions that existed between whites and blacks, which the institution of slavery had previously kept in check. Indeed, the Yankees were violating a tenet of natural law which Davis believed had been decreed by God Himself. His mind refused to entertain any other possibility.

"Please send a telegram to General Johnston. Ask him to send a message to General Grant under a flag of truce describing the reports and demanding an explanation."

Bragg nodded. "I will do so immediately, sir."

"I will not allow myself to be distracted by what may be a false report. We must verify the information before we decide upon a course of action."

"And if the reports prove true? What shall be our course of action?"

"I confess that I do not know. But we cannot allow the execution of one of our generals to go unpunished."

*   *   *   *   *

August 29, Noon

Marble looked around in astonishment. The fact that he had expected it made it no less wondrous, for he doubted he had ever seen so many people crammed into a single building all at once. More than ten thousand people had crowded into the Wigwam, an enormous two-story wooden arena that had been built four years earlier to accommodate the 1860 Republican convention that had nominated Lincoln. The fact that it was now being used by the opposition party to nominate Lincoln's opponent struck Marble as a fine example of poetic justice.

Marble looked up and down the endless rows of people, who were chanting and cheering various slogans. A brass band down on the stage was playing patriotic tunes, although Marble noticed with satisfaction that they never played *The Battle Hymn of the Republic* or any other song which might have been construed as supporting abolitionism. Red, white, and blue bunting hung everywhere. Many people waved small American flags, and larger signs held aloft identified each state delegation. The noise and bustle was deafening.

Marble sat with the New York delegation, by far the largest at the convention. He wasn't quite sure in which capacity he was attending the event. On the one hand, he considered himself a journalist there to cover the event for the *New York World*. But he also knew he was a major player at the convention, exerting an influence on events that was matched by only a handful of other men who had come to Chicago. Finally, there remained a part of him that simply considered himself a good American citizen, doing his civic duty by representing his state at the national convention of his chosen political party, just as Thomas Jefferson would have wanted him to do.

Down on the stage, Governor Horatio Seymour began pounding the gavel loudly, trying to hush the enormous mass of humanity that filled the Wigwam to the breaking point. The music of the brass band abruptly ceased. Gradually, after a long pounding and many shushes from hundreds of people, a sufficient level of quiet descended to allow Seymour to begin.

"Having been duly selected as presiding officer by the Democratic National Committee, I, Governor Horatio Seymour of the State of New York, do hereby declare the 1864 Democratic National Convention open!"

These words, rather mundane to Marble's ears, brought the crowd to its feet again in a roaring cheer. Marble frowned. At this rate, it would take the convention hours to accomplish even the most simple task. The notepaper on his lap had yet to receive a single scratch from his pen, as nothing worth noting had yet taken place.

Seymour went on to make what Marble thought was a fairly solid speech. Much of it was essentially a eulogy for Clement Vallandigham, who Seymour held up as a martyr cut down by the wickedness of the Lincoln administration for trying to restore the Union through peace rather than war. Marble certainly had respected Vallandigham in his own way and was sorry that he had been killed. But as he looked over the crowd in the Wigwam and saw many people wiping away tears as they listened to Seymour tout Vallandigham's virtues, Marble considered it all faintly ridiculous.

Having eulogized Vallandigham for rather longer than Marble thought proper, Governor Seymour went on to castigate the Lincoln administration for its unconstitutional abuse of power, its incompetence in managing the war, the enormous casualties that had been suffered in Virginia and Georgia, and every other sin, real or imagined, that the Democrats had been able to craft into rhetorical language.

The crowd cheered at virtually every sentence. Marble could see that they were worked up, that they were determined to win the election, and that they would be willing to do whatever was necessary to achieve victory when the time came. When the convention was over, they would disperse to their home states and spread the

Democratic gospel of a cessation of fighting and the opening of negotiations. Their words would spread across the length and breadth of the Union.

Seymour finally concluded his speech, perhaps three-quarters of an hour after he had started it. To Marble's dismay, however, he had merely been the first speaker of many. For the next few hours, Marble sat and listened to speaker after speaker. Congressman Daniel Voorhees of Indiana, Congressman Fernando Wood of New York, and Governor Joel Parker of New Jersey each had their turn at the podium, as did many lesser lights of the Democratic Party. The message was the same every time: the war was a disaster, too many men had died, too much money had been wasted, and it was time to bring the fighting to a halt and restore the Union through negotiation rather than further bloodshed.

Marble smiled when he saw General Joseph Hooker, who had only just days before submitted his resignation to the War Department, take the podium. The man who had the undesirable record of having suffered a major defeat at the hands of both Lee and Johnston spent twenty minutes castigating the Lincoln administration for its poor management of the war. He denounced Grant as a butcher who cared nothing for the lives of his men and ridiculed Sherman as a lunatic unfit to command a company. When he left the podium to rousing applause, Marble recalled their meeting in Cincinnati several weeks before. It had obviously been a good investment.

The hours passed. A long succession of speakers came and went from the podium, representing the various factions of the party and the geographic regions of the Union, all saying more or less the same thing. Marble's hand began to cramp from all the notes he was taking, and he eventually had to blink hard repeatedly to keep himself from falling asleep. He wished very much that he could have a glass of strong whiskey.

Finally, Seymour returned to the podium.

"We shall now hear the report of the Committee on Resolutions regarding our party political platform."

A hush descended over the Wigwam. At long last, something significant and substantial was about to take place. Congressman Wood, who had been appointed chair of the committee, strolled back up to the podium and began to read the platform plank by plank.

The first few planks were greeted with impatient silence. The first dealt with purely economic issues such as the party's support for free trade, while the second described the need for a transcontinental railroad. The next three were basically a rehashing of the previous speeches, denouncing Lincoln's unconstitutional abuses of power. It was when Congressman Wood got to the sixth plank that the crowd heard what it had been waiting for.

"Resolved, that the continuing bloodshed and needless loss of life, as well as the unnecessary expenditure of vast amounts of public monies, must be brought to a halt at the earliest practicable moment. For this purpose, we demand an immediate cessation of hostilities and the opening of good faith negotiations with our Southern brethren with a view toward a termination of the present military conflict."

As one, the crowd stood and cheered wildly and at great length. Marble was taken aback by the outpouring of support for the peace plank. He had expected support for it would be solid and certainly hadn't been expecting any opposition. But to hear such an immense roaring of approval demonstrated to him that support among the party faithful for a termination of the war through negotiation was even stronger than he had imagined. He only hoped that the rest of the country felt the same way.

As he scribbled the wording of the peace plank onto his note paper, he marveled at their sheer ambiguity. It could mean practically anything anyone wanted it to mean. The term "good faith negotiations" might include any position from insisting on an immediate Southern surrender to an instant acceptance of Confederate independence. Still, the point had been made. In the 1864 election, the Democrats were going to be the party of peace and the Republicans were going to be the party of war.

The platform was shortly thereafter approved by a simple voice vote. As near as Marble could tell, there was no meaningful opposition to any part of it, which was a very good sign. But there was more for the convention to do before the night was over. They had to get on with the business of selecting their candidate for President.

*   *   *   *   *

August 29, Evening

Grant was coming.

Johnston sat quietly in his office, staring down at the maps. The stunning news that Sherman had been sacked and none other than the Union general-in-chief himself was coming to take charge had been forwarded to him from Richmond a week before, but somehow the surprise of it had yet to wear off. Johnston had imagined Grant's progress by ship and train from Petersburg through Washington, Cincinnati, Louisville, Nashville, and Chattanooga as if he were looking at the inevitable approach of a horde of locusts.

In retrospect, Johnston realized that he shouldn't have been all that surprised. Sherman had suffered the worst defeat inflicted upon any Union general since the beginning of the war. Many other generals had been removed from command for much less. With General Thomas languishing as a prisoner in Camp Oglethorpe, there was no other Union officer in the Western Theater with enough experience and prestige to replace Sherman. McPherson was too young, and Schofield and Howard had only recently been promoted to the level of army command.

Conceivably, a general from the Eastern Theater might have been sent out to take command. General Meade, the victor of Gettysburg, certainly would have commanded sufficient prestige, as would have Winfield Scott Hancock. For whatever reason, Grant had decided to take on the job himself. Worse, he was bringing heavy reinforcements with him. With Forrest and Wheeler both dead and their commands defeated, thousands of Union soldiers who had been guarding the railroads were now free to join the Union army on the north bank of the Chattahoochee. It all pointed to a major enemy operation in the near future.

Johnston estimated that the Army of Tennessee had perhaps fifty-five thousand to sixty thousand men ready for action. Although the enemy forces had been whittled down by their losses at Peachtree Creek and the large number of regiments leaving upon the expiration of their enlistments, the arriving reinforcements were beginning to make up for this. He calculated that the combined Union forces on the other side of the river would soon amount to approximately ninety thousand men.

There was a soft knock on the door, which Johnston recognized from long experience as being Mackall's. His chief-of-staff entered and handed over a note.

"Telegram from the War Department, sir."

Johnston took it and read, frowning. He chuckled bitterly when he finished reading.

"Not what you wanted, I suppose?"

"Indeed not, William. Our request for cavalry reinforcements from Virginia has been denied." Johnston had hoped that the dispatch of Union forces from Virginia to Georgia would allow for Confederate troops to be shifted in a similar fashion. Any additional reinforcements would help in the coming struggle against Grant, and the need for additional cavalry was particularly serious.

"Well, that cannot come as a surprise, considering the President's animosity toward you."

"No, but it gets worse. The President is again urging us to cross to the north side of the river and launch an offensive against the enemy before Grant arrives and before all the enemy reinforcements are in place."

Mackall snorted in contempt. "It's easy for a man sitting in Richmond, hundreds of miles away, to think he can look at a couple of colored pins on a map and know the situation better than does the general on the scene."

Johnston nodded. They had already discussed the President's proposal for an offensive at some length. The idea of an offensive was utter madness as far as Johnston was concerned and his opinion had been corroborated by Hardee, Stewart, and Cheatham at a meeting of the high command. Most likely, an effort to cross to the north bank of the Chattahoochee would simply result in the Southerners being pinned against the river by superior numbers and then being destroyed.

Johnston had requested that his corps commanders attach their names to the telegram he had sent the President expressing this opinion. They had willingly done so, but Davis had responded by behaving like a piqued and spoiled child. In the days since they had sent their telegram, Davis had sent no less than four further telegrams urging some sort of aggressive action against the Yankees. Johnston found the whole thing very irritating.

He stared down at the map, trying to put himself in Grant's place. Would the Union commander cross the river and attempt a frontal attack on Atlanta, as he had tried to do outside Richmond when he attacked Lee at Cold Harbor? Would Grant attempt to outmaneuver him by moving his army against the railroad connections of the city, as he had done when he moved against Petersburg? Or would Grant do something completely unexpected, as he had done more than once during the Vicksburg Campaign?

"We are keeping the crossings of the Chattahoochee under constant surveillance, yes?" Johnston asked.

"All of our cavalry are constantly on patrol, sir. Of course, we have only half the number of horsemen we had two months ago, when Sherman first crossed the river. Consequently, our ability to carry out reconnaissance has been severely curtailed."

Johnston frowned and nodded. The disastrous failure of Wheeler's raid against Sherman's supply lines had not only gotten Wheeler himself killed, but brought about the destruction of half of the cavalry of the Army of Tennessee. Four thousand horsemen who should have been patrolling the Chattahoochee River and scouting out the movements of the enemy were instead dead on the fields of northern Georgia or had been shuffled into the confines of Northern prison camps.

"It's like trying to fight a boxing match with our eyes half-closed," Johnston complained.

"That's one way to put it," Mackall said. "Which is why it is so infuriating that President Davis denied our request for any cavalry reinforcements. Surely they could have spared at least a brigade. Even a single regiment of horsemen would have been very useful."

"As always, William, we can expect no help from Richmond. Davis's mind remains fervently poisoned against us." Johnston felt that the animosity the President held toward him had already nearly caused the fall of Atlanta once. He hoped that it would not do so again. He looked back up at Mackall. "Anything else?"

"Yes. I received a message from General Cooper's aide advising us that they have arrived in Augusta. Barring any trouble with the railroad, they should be here tomorrow afternoon."

Johnston grunted. "Why did Cleburne ever have to put forward that damnable proposal?" he said bitterly. "It has caused nothing but trouble." He was no friend of slavery himself and personally saw nothing all that shocking in the idea of freeing slaves and enlisting them in the army. However, the distraction it was creating within the ranks of the Army of Tennessee and the Confederacy as a whole was coming at the worst possible time. With Grant soon to arrive, a major Union offensive was clearly imminent. Just when his army needed to be united, the Cleburne proposal was threatening to tear it apart.

He dearly wished that Cooper was not coming. The investigation, which would obviously involve interviews with most of the high command of the army, would only inflame the situation and set his generals against one another. President Davis, were he a man of any wisdom whatsoever, would have simply ignored the firestorm generated by the publication of Cleburne's proposal and waited for it to blow over. Instead, he had caved in to the extremists in the Confederate Congress and initiated the Cooper investigation for purely political reasons.

"You've made arrangements for General Cooper's lodging?"

"Yes. It's all taken care of. He'll be staying at the Trout House Hotel."

"That's fine," Johnston said, satisfied. Although a bureaucrat, Cooper was technically the highest-ranking officer in the Confederate Army and deserved to be treated with the utmost respect. The Trout House provided the best accommodations to be found in the Atlanta area. "When he arrives, give him my greetings and tell him that I would like to have him for dinner here at my headquarters. It would seem proper for me to talk with him before he begins his interviews."

"He will, in all likelihood, ask to interview you as part of the investigation. Davis and Bragg may intend to entrap you in the same web in which they seem intent to entrap Cleburne."

Johnston nodded, having considered this. As he had many times before, he wondered whether his most dangerous foes were to be found among the Yankees or among his own kind.

*   *   *   *   *

August 30, Morning

Becoming an officer meant that McFadden had been given a sword and a pistol, but the promised horse had yet to materialize. He doubted that it ever would. Relatively few horses had been captured at Peachtree Creek because the Yankees had been able to shoot most

- 459 -

of them before they had fallen into Southern hands. Good horses had long been in short supply in the Army of Tennessee and the few that were available were obviously needed by the cavalry and artillery. Besides, the heavily forested terrain was not well suited to riding. McFadden was perfectly content to walk, as he had been doing since he had first joined the army.

The men of Granbury's Texas Brigade marched with a cocky swagger that exuded arrogance, their rifles held every which way, their feet moving to no beat but their own. It was as if they were challenging any observer to comment on their apparent lack of discipline. McFadden had always liked it that way. The men chattered happily and loudly with one another as they walked, filling the air around them with laughter.

They were moving steadily northwards toward the Chattahoochee River, having left their encampment north of Atlanta about an hour before, immediately after sunrise. Had a battle been imminent, they probably would have been awoken long before dawn, but the recent lull in campaigning did not seem likely to end anytime soon.

The 7th Texas was the second regiment in line, following behind the 18th Texas Dismounted Cavalry, which had fought as infantry for as long as McFadden could remember. He dearly wished that his regiment could have marched as the vanguard of the brigade, for the dust was always considerably less bothersome in that position. As it was, all the dust being kicked up by the men ahead of them was choking the eyes and throats of the 7th Texas and annoying them to no end.

"I don't believe a word of it," Pearson said, just loudly enough for McFadden to hear. "No way old Pat Cleburne wrote anything like it. It's a damn lie, I tell you."

"I don't often agree with you, Pearson," Balch said. "But this time I do. If you ask me, it's all just a story cooked up by William Walker to make Cleburne look bad."

The rest of the 7th Texas took up the conversation as McFadden listened with a deep interest. The rumor that General Cleburne had put forth some sort of proposal to free the slaves had reached the brigade's camp a few days earlier. A corporal working as a brigade courier, who claimed he had been in downtown Atlanta to deliver a message to the army quartermaster, said that everyone in the city was talking about it. The rumors had only been confirmed when a copy of the an Atlanta newspaper containing the story had arrived in camp the previous night.

McFadden was interested in what the men were saying for two reasons. First, as an officer, it was important for him to see how the rumor was affecting the morale of the regiment. Second, the subject was interesting in and of itself. He did not know what to think about it, so listening to the opinions being tossed about by his men might help give him a proper perspective.

Pearson was still talking. "Well, I'll tell you this, boys. If it is true, then Jeff Davis is going to bump Cleburne down to a private, just like us. No way they'll let some abolitionist order us around. We're fighting this war to keep our slaves, after all. Why would Cleburne want us to fight so hard only to give them up?"

"You say what you want, Pearson," Balch replied. "If they do anything to Pat Cleburne, I won't fight any more. No, sir! I'll throw my rifle into the Chattahoochee and go on back to Texas, by God!"

McFadden was momentarily tempted to reprimand Balch for talking in such a way, but decided against it. One of the hallmarks of the Army of Tennessee was that the enlisted men were allowed to speak their minds. Besides, he seriously doubted that Balch, trickster though he might be, was actually contemplating desertion. More importantly, he knew the men would rapidly lose respect for him if he beat them down for such minor infractions. They would have seen it as a needless abuse of power.

McFadden had never given any thought to what Cleburne's opinions about slavery might have been. Why should he have? The private thoughts of the commander of his division were obviously no business of his. Still, if Cleburne had actually proposed freeing the slaves, and this fact was now being splashed across the newspapers, what had been private thoughts had become public proposals. Needless to say, that made it the business of every man in the Army of Tennessee.

Though he knew no one would bother to ask him his opinion, McFadden had to admit that he saw nothing particularly shocking in Cleburne's proposal. The Confederacy was outnumbered by the Yankees, so it made perfect sense to enlist black troops in the army if any were willing to fight. Those Southerners who had an ingrained and instinctive need to defend slavery, such as Teresa Turnbow, had always struck McFadden as vain and absurd.

He personally doubted that any slave would fight for the Confederacy, even if they were offered their freedom. After having been enslaved for the entirety of his life, why would a man want to fight on behalf of the people who had enslaved him? McFadden felt it much more likely that the slaves would simply turn their guns against the Confederacy and call for help from the nearest Yankee army.

As he listened to his men discuss the news, McFadden did not hear anyone express any disloyalty to Cleburne. This didn't surprise McFadden. For one thing, every soldier in Cleburne's division had a deep love for their commander. For another, the men of the regiment were largely drawn from the Texas frontier, where slavery was not well established.

The response of Granbury's Texas Brigade, however, would not be duplicated in other units of the Army of Tennessee. Cleburne would get little sympathy from men from the states east of the Mississippi River, where slavery was as deeply ingrained in the culture as the blood which flows through a human body. Cleburne's long and patriotic record would count for nothing against their furious prejudices. They would demand Cleburne's head. McFadden was worried that they might well get it.

Major Collett, mounted on one of the few horses that had been captured from the Yankees at Peachtree Creek, rode up alongside the column.

"How's it going, Jim?"

"Fine, sir."

"The river's about a quarter of a mile ahead. Your men okay?"

"They're fine, Major. They just keep talking about these rumors regarding General Cleburne."

"Rumors are just that, McFadden. Rumors." He raised his voice so that all the men could hear him. "It is not the place for the men of this army to raise questions about the commander of their division. You'll be sure to make that clear to them, won't you, Lieutenant McFadden?"

"I will, sir!" he said loudly.

Collett spurred his horse and trotted off down the column, intent on checking on the rest of the regiment. Cowed by their commander's words, the men stayed relatively silent for the remainder of the march.

A few minutes later, McFadden could see the column of the 17th/18th Texas Dismounted Cavalry veer sharply to the right. It soon became obvious that the road turned in that direction in order to run parallel with the Chattahoochee River. They had reached their destination. Another few minutes marching brought the 7th Texas to its assigned position along the picket line, which had been held by the 45th Alabama.

The Texans relieved the Alabamians, who happily departed with the usual exchange of good-natured insults. As the men settled into position, McFadden gazed out over the river. Across the water, only a few hundred yards away, Yankee pickets could be clearly seen on the opposite bank, standing around quietly. A few fires were visible, over which the Northern soldiers appeared to be cooking food.

This was the fifth occasion since the Union army had withdrawn across the river that the 7th Texas had arrived on the picket line. On each occasion, an informal ceasefire had prevailed. McFadden hoped that such would be the case again.

He cupped his hands. "Hello over there!" he called.

"What?" a Yankee shouted back.

"May I speak with your commanding officer?"

After a few minutes, a man in an officer's uniform appeared at the bank.

"What do you want, reb?"

"The 45th Alabama has been relieved! We are the 7th Texas!"

"Well, hello there, Texas! Welcome to the picket line! We are the 20th Ohio!"

"20th Ohio?" Private Montgomery said thoughtfully as he removed his knapsack and sat down to rest. "Aren't those the same bastards we tangled with at the Battle of Raymond?"

"I think you're right, Ben," McFadden answered. He cupped his hands and called out again. "Ohio! No need for any unpleasantness! We won't shoot if you don't!"

"It's a deal!" the Yankee officer shouted back. A few moments later, he attempted a joke. "Remember the Alamo!"

McFadden posted his troops. The 7th Texas stretched out in a line several hundred yards long. Their job was to watch this portion of the river and report any unusual enemy activity. In the unlikely event of a major Union effort to cross to the south bank, they were to delay the Yankees and send word higher up the chain of command about what was happening. Their previous stints on the Chattahoochee picket line had been uneventful and McFadden saw no reason to expect this one to be any different.

*   *   *   *   *

August 30, Evening

The long table in Lincoln's White House office was strewn with newspapers and telegrams being sent by friendly reporters covering the Democratic National Convention in Chicago. Off to one end, largely ignored for the time being, was a pile of military maps. Outside the window, a late summer storm was drenching the city and the occasional rumble of thunder could be heard. In the distance, the still uncompleted Washington Monument was visible, as if waiting for the war to be over so work on it could resume.

Lincoln grinned wistfully as he watched Stanton and Seward sift through the mass of paper on the table, trying to obtain any information they could about what was going on in Chicago. Both men were puffing on large cigars. Occasionally, Hay and Nicolay would enter the room with more newspapers and new telegrams. To the President, his closest advisors were following the news of the Democratic National Convention in much the same manner as he had often seen them follow the events of a developing battle.

Stanton grunted. "It looks like their nominee for Vice President is going to be Congressman George Pendleton of Ohio."

"From where do you have that?" Lincoln asked.

Stanton glanced at the by-line of the paper he was reading. "Noah Brooks of the *Sacramento Daily Union*."

Lincoln nodded. "Brooks generally knows what he's talking about."

Seward laughed bitterly. "Pendleton? That spineless little man? The Democrats are scraping the bottom of the bucket, indeed. He's been a defeatist since the very beginning of the war."

"Don't pooh-pooh too soon," Lincoln warned. "McClellan can't rightly be accused of defeatism because he served as the commander of the Army of the Potomac. By choosing Pendleton as his running mate, the Democrats are moving with public opinion."

"How can nominating a defeatist vice presidential candidate help the electoral prospects of the Democrats?" Stanton angrily demanded. "Since the loss at Peachtree Creek, we have won the Battle of Mobile Bay and successfully defeated the rebel attempts to cut our supply lines to Georgia. Joseph Wheeler and Nathan Bedford Forrest are both dead. Surely these successes should be helping to rally public support for the war effort?"

Lincoln shrugged. "It's impossible to say. Of course, the news of Forrest's death ran in giant letterhead across the front page of the *New York Times* and all the other Republican papers the day after the news arrived. But the Democratic papers scarcely mentioned it at all. If you got your information from the *New York World*, you'd probably have no idea that Forrest was even dead."

"Manton Marble is a miserable little bastard," Stanton spat. "I hope he rots in hell."

"Don't matter, anyway," Lincoln said. "Mobile Bay and the killing of Forrest are all fine and well. But the attention of the nation is on Richmond in the east and Atlanta in the west. Unless and until one of those cities falls into our hands, the public will keep thinking that we're losing this war. And if they still feel that way in November, the three of us will soon be looking for new employment."

A particularly disturbing roll of thunder sounded through the room at that moment.

"If Grant can somehow defeat Johnston and capture Atlanta, all may yet be put right," Seward said.

"From his last telegram, he should arrive at Vining's Station, where our forces are encamped on the north bank of the Chattahoochee, tomorrow morning," Stanton said. "Assuming he has some sort of plan, he should be putting it into effect within the next few days."

"If he has a plan, he hasn't told me about it," Lincoln said. "But I trust Grant. I allow him to keep his own counsel. For all his faults as a commander and a man, he is the best we have. We must roll the dice and hope for the best."

"Of course," Stanton said. "But we must also prepare for the worst. If Grant fails, we must continue to do whatever is necessary to ensure the reelection of our administration."

"We are already doing all we can," Lincoln protested. "Every Republican mayor, governor and congressman is barnstorming the country, giving speeches to every crowd that can be gathered, no matter how small. Raymond had his printing press running day and night, churning out pamphlets by the thousands. Meanwhile, I have to debase myself here in Washington, promising every low-level clerkship in every post office or customs house in the Union to unscrupulous scoundrels in exchange for their support."

Stanton shook his head. "No, Mr. President. I am talking about measures that are considerably more stern than that."

Lincoln folded his arms and stared at Stanton, wordlessly asking him to explain himself.

Stanton went on. "Missouri, Kentucky and Maryland are all under military occupation. We can use the troops we have there to control access to polling places. We can do the same in New York City, using the troops we sent there to restore order after the recent riots. Without New York City, the Democrats cannot win New York State. If needs be, we can do the same in other cities where there has been civil unrest. Philadelphia, for instance."

As Stanton spoke, Lincoln's face become more and more gloomy. Seward stared on impassively, shrouded in a cloud of cigar smoke.

Stanton went on. "If we take these measures, it would ensure that the Republican ticket will carry the border states, as well as New York and Pennsylvania. Combined with your own state of Illinois and the abolitionist strongholds of New England, it would give us more than enough electoral votes to secure your reelection."

"Mr. Stanton," Lincoln said sternly. "We cannot have free government without fair elections. What you are suggesting would effectively turn me into a military dictator."

"Perhaps, Mr. President. But what if the alternative is the dissolution of the nation?"

Lincoln said nothing, pursing his lips and staring down at the table.

Seward spoke up. "If God favors us, which I am sure He does, we shall not be forced to make any decision on these matters. Grant will defeat Johnston, capture Atlanta, and swing public opinion back in the direction of Union and abolition. When the election is behind us, we can move forward forcefully with the war effort, defeat the Confederacy, and get on with the business of building the nation."

Lincoln nodded. "I pray you are right, Mr. Seward. If I am ever forced to choose between seeing the nation severed and leaving the blacks in chains or adopting the measures just now suggested by

Mr. Stanton, I'd rather have an assassin put a bullet in my head than make such an appalling decision."

*   *   *   *   *

August 31, Morning

With the piercing sound of a mighty steam whistle, the train slowed to a halt at the station at Marietta. A few minutes later, an immense cigar stuffed into his mouth, looking perfectly calm and rather sloppily dressed, Ulysses S. Grant emerged from the passenger car.

A nearby officer sharply turned and gestured to a brass band, which proceeded to belch out a tune of some kind. Grant had no idea what song was being played, as he had never understood music and considered it an unintelligible annoyance. But the men of the band appeared to be enthusiastic, so he indulged them by nodding in what he hoped looked like an approving fashion before turning away.

There were several companies of troops in and around the train station, for Marietta was the primary supply base for the Union armies encamped on the northern bank of the Chattahoochee River. Upon seeing Grant, the Union troops spontaneously began cheering. Grant did not smile, but lifted his hat in a gesture of appreciation. He instantly knew that the men belonged to the Army of the Tennessee, rather than either the Army of the Cumberland or the Army of the Ohio. He knew it in the manner that a parent might recognize a child that had been lost for many years. The Army of the Tennessee was his old command, which he had led from the earliest days at Fort Donelson through the terrible Battle of Shiloh, the long struggle to capture Vicksburg, and the final triumph at Chattanooga in late 1863.

Grant felt as if he were coming home. The Army of the Potomac in Virginia, however much he respected it, had never been anything but a stepchild to him. Valiant though its men might be, the Army of the Potomac had often disappointed him in the battles against Lee. While leading the Army of the Tennessee, however, Grant had known nothing but victory. He prayed that this would be true once again. The cheering the men were giving him was the first sign of reassurance he had had in some time.

Twenty yards from the track, McPherson, Schofield, and Howard stood together, decked out in their finest uniforms. As if they were still cadets at West Point, they snapped to attention and saluted at the sight of the general-in-chief. Grant merely took a long pull from his cigar, entirely unimpressed by this display of military ostentation. He himself wore a uniform that would not have looked out of place on a private, and only the dust-covered stripes on his shoulders identified his rank of Lieutenant General, which had been held by no one else in American history except George Washington.

"Good morning, gentlemen," Grant said as he strode up to the three generals.

"Good morning, sir," the three answered as one.

"Was that brass band really necessary?"

"I knew you wouldn't like it, General," McPherson answered apologetically. "But it was thought that it would be good for the morale of the men to see their old commander greeted by appropriately martial music."

Grant grunted, taking another long puff on his cigar. A few minutes later, he mounted Cincinnati, a marvelous horse that had been given to him by an admirer from Missouri. He and his three subordinate commanders then rode away from the Marietta station toward the central command post down at Vining's Station.

The four men were trailed by the predicable mass of staff officers and an escort consisting of a company of troopers from the 1st Ohio Cavalry Regiment. As they rode south, they passed by regiment after regiment of Union infantry, some newly arrived from other theaters and some having been in the region for months. The regiments cheered Grant one and all, though he affected no acknowledgement of it.

"My orders regarding the reorganization of the forces have been carried out?" Grant asked.

"Completely, sir," McPherson answered. The other two generals remained silent, content to let McPherson speak for them. Not only was he their senior both in rank and age, but his close personal friendship with Grant gave his words greater weight.

Grant nodded, trusting that McPherson would not give such assurance unless he were certain he was correct. For the campaign Grant envisioned, he had wanted a more nimble organization of the federal armies in the West than Sherman had employed when he had first set forth from Chattanooga four months before. Therefore, through careful allocation of reinforcements and the shifting of some divisions from one army to another, there had been a significant change in the makeup of the three armies on the Chattahoochee.

The Army of the Cumberland and the Army of the Tennessee were now roughly equal in size, with Howard and McPherson each counting about thirty-five thousand men under their command. The Army of the Ohio was somewhat smaller, with Schofield being able to count on about twenty-five thousand men. For reasons which thus far had not been explained by Grant, the Army of the Ohio held most of the cavalry present with the Yankee forces in Georgia. Indeed, nearly half of Schofield's force consisted of horsemen. What this fact suggested for the shape of the coming campaign, or whether it held any significance at all, the three army commanders had not ventured to guess.

"How is the morale of the men?" Grant asked.

"Better now that you're here," McPherson answered.

"Give it to me straight, James."

"I am giving it to you straight, Sam. Morale has improved considerably since news came that you were coming to take personal command."

"News of the failure of the rebel cavalry to cut our supply lines has also had a positive effect on the men," Schofield added. "The deaths of Wheeler and Forrest have been especially well-received. It's like two bogeymen have been done away with by an exorcism."

"He's right," Howard interjected. "Several of the regiments greeted the news of Forrest's death with spontaneous celebrations. Many units got rather too drunk, if you ask me." The three other generals paid little mind to Howard's last comment. They knew well that, as far as Howard was concerned, even a single drop of liquor was one drop too many.

"I don't want any of you to sugarcoat anything," Grant said. "I need to know the exact truth. If the men here on the Chattahoochee are reading the same newspapers as the men in the trenches around Petersburg, they cannot help but have been affected by the news of riots and war-weariness in the North."

"It cannot be denied," Howard said.

"I suppose not," Schofield said. "Although there are some positive signs, I must admit that the morale of our men is still somewhat shaky. They still have not fully recovered from the defeat at Peachtree Creek. The bad news from up North, and from other fighting fronts, has also not helped."

"We've all been in such situations before," Grant said. He gestured toward McPherson. "James here was with me at Shiloh, where we were pounded badly on the first day but came back to win on the next. General Schofield, if I'm not mistaken, you fought at Wilson's Creek, where our side suffered a heavy defeat. But we eventually triumphed and took back the lost ground. And General Howard, your men were roughly handled on the first day at Gettysburg, but went on to play a critical role in winning the battle."

"The men are not beaten," McPherson said. "But they need something onto which they can hold, some promise of victory. With so much talk of peace, of stopping the war and letting the rebels have their own way, they need some sort of reassurance. No man is willing to be the last man to die in a losing war."

Grant did not agree with McPherson's last point. He found himself thinking of the Battle of Chapultepec during the Mexican War, nearly two decades before. He had been part of the American assault force on that memorable day, and he well remembered the courageous Mexican military cadets, none older than twenty. They had gallantly fought to the death rather than surrender, even after they had to have known that any hope of victory was gone. He would never forget the sight of the final surviving cadet, who wrapped himself in the Mexican flag and hurled himself off the ramparts of the

Chapultepec fortress, plummeting to his death rather than be taken prisoner.

All of those men, needless to say, had been perfectly willing to be the last man to die in a losing war. Unable to help himself, Grant found himself thinking that if the men of the North would only show such devotion to their cause as those brave men of Mexico had shown to theirs, the South would have long since been crushed. He would not only have to call upon such reserves of heroism and manliness within himself, but somehow call them forth from his men, if he were to prevail. If he could, the Union would be saved and the abominable institution of slavery would be destroyed forever. He chose not to think on what would happen if he could not.

Schofield now spoke. "The main problem for the men, General Grant, is the inactivity of the past month. True, the Army of the Cumberland needed time to recover from Peachtree Creek and all our forces have needed time to assimilate reinforcements and build up supplies. But now that we are again ready to move, the men are wondering why we yet remain static."

"You needn't worry on that score, General Schofield," Grant replied. "Moving forward is precisely what I intend to do, and soon."

"And what shall be our plan of operation?" Schofield asked.

Grant said nothing, responding only by taking a longer pull on his cigar and kicking Cincinnati into a faster trot.

      *   *   *   *   *

September 2, Noon

"And was the reaction from your fellow officers what you expected?" Cooper asked.

Cleburne looked across the table at the man who held the dual posts of Adjutant General and Inspector General of the Confederate Army. Samuel Cooper had been born when John Adams had been in the White House and his advanced age was the primary reason he had never held a field command. But Cleburne, who had never met the man before sitting down at the table with him a bit over two hours earlier, was convinced that he couldn't have led men into combat even in the prime of his life. Although obviously intelligent, Cooper lacked the inner fire that burned within all true warriors. He was a man seemingly formed by nature to sit at a desk and scrawl his signature onto papers.

Cooper had appropriated one of the rooms of Johnston's headquarters at the Niles House in order to hold his interviews. He had spoken with Johnston himself, as well as Hardee and the other two corps commanders, the day before. Now it was Cleburne's turn. Before he was done, he had let it be known, he intended to speak with every officer who had been present at the now infamous January meeting.

The interview, which Cleburne felt was increasingly taking on the character of an interrogation, was dragging on interminably. His mind kept telling him that this was how men accused of heresy in centuries past must have felt when they had been dragged before the Inquisition.

Cooper leaned his head forward slightly. "General Cleburne?"

"I'm sorry, sir. In truth, no. Their reaction was not what I expected. I rather expected the majority to support my proposal. A few did support it, but most were opposed."

"This disappointed you?"

"Of course. I knew that some men would oppose the proposal, but I did not expect so many to do so, nor did I expect the opposition to be so ferocious."

Cleburne's mind went back to the meeting in January, held when the Army of Tennessee was camped in the tiny hamlet of Dalton, the men thinking of nothing but how to keep themselves warm as the snapping cold of winter enveloped them. He had felt confident as he had begun reading the text of his proposal. However, even before he had finished, he had noted the looks of unbelieving horror on the faces of many of his fellow officers and, most especially, the look of unrestrained hatred on the face of William Walker.

"With respect, General Cleburne, it seems to me that you approached the question with a dangerous level of naiveté. The officers with whom you serve are mostly slave-owners themselves, with a vested economic interest in maintaining our peculiar institution as it presently exists. You seem to have thought that it would be a simple matter to persuade them to accept a complete reformation of the Southern way of life which, more to the point, would be completely against their own interests."

"I freely confess that the matter is more complicated than I initially gave it credit for, sir. I also maintain that I made my proposal with the best of intentions."

"I don't question your intentions, General Cleburne. I simply question your judgment."

Cleburne felt his face flash with heat. He felt Cooper's tone was patronizing. In the small, self-contained world that was his division, his brigade and regimental commanders accorded him deep and unconditional respect, even when they disagreed with him. They would freely tell him when they thought he was wrong, as Major Benham often did, but never in such a discourteous manner.

Still, Cleburne knew how to be deferential to his superiors. After all, before immigrating to America, he had spent years as an enlisted man in the British Army, where disobedience was punished in the same manner used by American slave-drivers to punish their slaves. Cleburne recalled with distaste the memory of seeing men whose backs had been torn open to the bone by repeated floggings, often for very minor offenses. The lesson had been rammed home to him at an early age. One must keep an independent mind, but it did not do to anger one's superiors.

That lesson seemed especially pertinent at this moment. While he knew he had committed no crime, Cleburne was well aware that he was in grave danger of being removed from his command and having his beloved division taken away from him. Many of the newspapers were clamoring for it and there was even a rumor that a petition was circulating among general officers demanding it. Cleburne doubted if the latter were true, for his fellow general officers were mostly honorable men. But if the rumor were true, such a plot could only have been hatched by William Walker.

Cooper went on. "General Cleburne, do you not realize the disorder unleashed among the officer corps of the Army of Tennessee by your actions? If I may speak frankly, this army has been beset by personal distrust and professional rivalries between its general officers from nearly the beginning of the war. The departure of General Bragg and the assumption of command by General Johnston offered a chance at smoothing over these troubled waters, but your proposal to free the slaves disrupted what could have been a sustained period of calm. You might as well have set off a bomb within the heart of the army."

"That was not my intention, sir."

"Of course it wasn't. But your intentions do not matter. What matters is the impact of your actions."

Cleburne was tired of being lectured. "Respectfully, sir, I believe that the impact of my actions would have been of great benefit to the Confederacy had my brother officers embraced my views and had the government been supportive. Freeing at least the most courageous of our slaves and enlisting them in the army would have allowed us to meet the Yankees on terms of numerical parity, would have perhaps prompted Britain and France to extend us diplomatic recognition, and would have undone the deceptive lies of the Lincoln administration that the North is fighting to abolish slavery rather than to subjugate the South. Considering how well the blacks have fought in the Northern army, exemplified by their assault on Fort Wagner and in recent actions around Petersburg, we could expect them to fight equally well for us if we promised them freedom."

Cooper listened to this with raised eyebrows. Cleburne could see instantly that he was not buying it. Whatever his administrative gifts, Cooper did not seem like the kind of man who could easily embrace new and unorthodox ideas. Cooper's view of the world had been formed before Cleburne had been born and he was not about to change it now.

"It should have been made very clear to you by now, General Cleburne, that the government does not share your views on this matter. Nor do the considerable majority of your fellow officers. You were given specific orders to cease promoting your proposal."

"Which I followed," Cleburne said sternly, fearful that irritation was beginning to creep into his voice. "From the moment General Johnston ordered me to stop discussing the subject, I have not discussed it."

"Not at all?"

"Not at all." He paused for a moment and considered his next words, wanting to be truthful. "Except, I suppose, in private conversations with personal friends who are already aware of my views."

"Such as General Hardee?"

Cleburne did not answer right away, for he found this question rather disturbing. Why would Cooper want to single out Hardee? Cleburne considered giving an evasive answer, but the close friendship between Cleburne and Hardee was well known and anything other than the truth would not have been believed. Besides, Cooper had spoken with Hardee the day before. Hardee had been ordered not to discuss the interview and had not done so, though he had seemed somewhat uneasy. Cleburne could only guess what answers he had given Cooper.

"Yes, I have discussed the matter with General Hardee. But, as I say, it took the form of private conversations between personal friends. I do not see how it would be the business of the army or government."

Cooper grunted as he scribbled something down on the paper in front of him. It outraged Cleburne that a mention of private conversations between gentlemen was being taken down as evidence.

Another half hour passed. The questions and answers came and went, becoming increasingly repetitive in Cleburne's mind. He had decided within the first few minutes of the interview that it was an entirely futile exercise, but he was astonished at exactly how meaningless the questioning was. Whatever facts Cooper gleaned from his answers had been known to Jefferson Davis for many months. Thanks to the newspapers, pretty much everyone else in the Confederacy had learned them in the past few weeks as well. Nothing whatsoever was being accomplished by Cooper's questions and every minute Cleburne sat at the table was one minute he was not drilling his men or working with his officers on how to improve combat readiness.

At long last, Cooper set his pen down. "Well, General Cleburne, I believe that you and I have covered all the ground. You are free to go. However, as I shall remain with the Army of Tennessee for the next few days, I may have reason to call you in for another interview if I decide there is more you and I need to discuss. Would that be all right?"

"Of course, sir." In truth, Cleburne had no choice and both he and Cooper knew it.

Both men rose from their seats, Cleburne's legs feeling cramped from having been seated for so long. They exchanged salutes. "I bid you good day, General Cleburne."

"Thank you, sir."

He turned and walked out the door, emerging into the small central hall of the Niles House. Several of Johnston's staff officers were visible in one of the side rooms, engaged in an animated discussion that had to do with bringing in sufficient fodder for the artillery horses in Stewart's corps. Cleburne briefly saw General Mackall walking up the steps toward what Cleburne knew was Johnston's private room, presumably to speak with the army commander about something or other.

Sitting in a chair across from the door to Cooper's room was General William Walker.

"Finished, are you?" he asked, dark humor in his voice.

"Yes," Cleburne said simply, turning toward the front door.

"Good. I've been waiting here for nearly an hour. Did the interview go longer than expected?"

Cleburne stopped walking and faced him. He could not simply ignore Walker and depart, however much he wanted to do so, because he was a brother officer and such disrespect would surely invite unfavorable comment. Besides, Cleburne knew he was on shaky ground and inciting further trouble would not help him maintain command of his division.

"I suppose so," Cleburne said. He noted that Walker did not deign to rise from his chair.

"Well, you and General Cooper certainly had much to discuss, I'm sure. With that abolitionist idea of yours now in the press for all the world to see, it's only to be expected that the government would look into the matter."

"He's interviewing you next?"

Walker nodded. Cleburne knew how that interview would go. Walker would denounce Cleburne as a abolitionist set on tearing apart the Army of Tennessee. He would misconstrue the facts so as to cast Cleburne, and perhaps Hardee as well, in the worst possible light. In truth, he had plenty of material with which to work.

"Yes, he's interviewing me next, all right. Surely you recall that I was at the meeting. I heard you read your proposal. You sent me a copy of it a couple of days later. I know as much about it as any man. Only stands to reason that Cooper would want to hear my side of the story."

Walker had requested a copy of Cleburne's proposal, it had turned out, only so that he could forward it to Jefferson Davis in Richmond with a note bitterly attacking both the proposal and the man who had made it. Cleburne had given Walker the copy in the hopes that it would be an indirect way for his idea to come to the attention of Davis. He had not counted on Walker being so duplicitous.

"Well, I hope your meeting with Cooper is not as boring as mine has been," Cleburne said, again making to walk for the front door.

"Boring? Oh, I doubt it will be boring. He will surely want to know the extent to which abolitionist subversion has penetrated the officer ranks of the Army of Tennessee."

Cleburne again stopped and turned toward Walker. "Explain your words, sir," he said firmly.

Walker still did not rise from his chair. Combined with the sneer on his face, it was clearly calculated to demonstrate his lack of respect for Cleburne. Tellingly, the audible conversations among the staff officers in the side rooms had ceased. Several pairs of eyes and ears were now being training on the two generals.

"Abolitionism," Walker said simply. "You know, people saying that we should set the blacks free. It's here in the army. It goes against everything our Southern Confederacy stands for, but it's here. Your proposal is proof of that, by God."

"I care nothing for the slaves," Cleburne said sternly, though he himself did not know whether or not this was true. "I care only about the success of our cause. A cause you and I share, I might note."

Now Walker did rise, causing Cleburne to tense somewhat. Though he was many years older than Cleburne and partially crippled by wounds he had suffered in the Seminole and Mexican Wars, Walker still somehow presented a threatening appearance. Cleburne reminded himself that he carried his saber and pistol, though the latter was unloaded.

"We do not share the same cause, Cleburne. My cause is the supremacy of the white man. I don't know what your cause is, but if it involves freeing the blacks and placing them on the same level as whites, it's not my cause. It's something that I will fight against with every drop of my blood."

"You and I both fight for the independence of the South," Cleburne said. "If freeing the slaves makes it more likely that we shall be free of the tyrannical rule of the North, I support freeing them."

Walker shook his head and chuckled bitterly. "And tell me, Cleburne, what is the South without slavery?"

"I did not propose abolishing slavery. Only that we free some of the slaves."

"If you free some, eventually you will have to free them all. The Confederacy would be awash in free negroes, wandering about as though they owned the country. You're such a fool, Cleburne. You know nothing of the South. You're just worthless Irish flotsam cast onto these shores because you couldn't make it in the British Army."

Cleburne's eyes flashed fire. "You will retract those words this instant, General Walker!"

"Or else what, you Paddy bastard?"

"General Walker!" a familiar voice boomed from above.

Cleburne glanced upwards and saw Johnston standing halfway up the staircase. He did not know for how long the army commander had been standing there, but obviously long enough to have heard the last few moments of the conversation. Cleburne and Walker both turned and stiffly saluted Johnston, who descended the stairs with a kingly bearing and stood between the two division commanders. He glanced back and forth between the two of them for a few moments before speaking.

"General Walker, you will immediately apologize to General Cleburne for your unwarranted comments."

Walker hesitated but a moment before speaking. "I apologize, General Cleburne."

"General Cleburne, you will immediately accept General Walker's apology."

Everything inside Cleburne revolted at the idea of obeying this order. Walker had spoken to him in so rude and disrespectful a manner that the dueling ground was the only proper place to settle the dispute.

Walker had insulted Cleburne's Irish origins. In a society that prized aristocratic family bloodlines above practically everything else, such an insult was the lowest to which a man could sink. Cleburne had had to work his way up the social ladder the hard way, rising on his own merit with no family wealth or connections to help him. Both despite and because of his great success, Cleburne was resented and despised by many throughout the Confederacy simply because of where he had been born. Combined with the charge of abolitionism, Walker's slur could not be allowed to stand.

However, Johnston had ordered Cleburne to apologize. It was his duty to obey his commanding officer. If he refused, he would surely be removed from command, especially considering the thin ice on which he was already treading. His division needed him, he knew. The Confederacy needed him. As misguided as many in its leadership clearly were, the Confederacy was where his loyalties lay and he would not do anything to detract from the goal of winning its independence.

"I accept your apology, General Walker."

"Good," Johnston said, relieved. "Now, there shall be no more of this nonsense. It is the Yankees we must fight, not one another. The two of you are brother officers fighting in the same army for the same cause. I cannot ask you two to like one another, but I can and do order that you set aside whatever personal differences you may have and fight alongside one another against the common enemy. Do you agree?"

"Yes, sir," Walker said instantly.

"Yes, sir," Cleburne said a moment later, only a trace of hesitation in his voice.

"Good. General Cleburne, you may return to your division. General Walker, I believe General Cooper is waiting for you."

Walker saluted, turned, and walked into Cooper's room. Johnston was already walking back up the stairs. For just a moment, Cleburne stood still in the center of the hall, the eyes of all of Johnston's staff officers on him. Then, he strode out the front door, where Red Pepper was waiting for him.

*   *   *   *   *

September 3, Morning

"Hello, Reb!" a voice called from across the river.

McFadden stirred himself. He had been quietly reading the biography of Thaddeus Kosciuszko, happy that the quiet days on the picket line had finally presented him with an opportunity for uninterrupted reading. He was now approaching the end of the book, drinking in the story of Kosciuszko's desperate struggle to free Poland from Russian tyranny. Still, he had already been reading for a few hours and the diversion from the Yankees across the river was not unwelcome.

The same was true for his men. They had spent the past few days engaged in all manner of activities to keep their minds occupied. Some read newspapers, others wrote letters that had little chance of reaching Texas, while the more devout studied the Bible. A few men were engaged in gambling over dice or decks of cards. McFadden saw gambling as a rather foolish way to spend one's time and lose one's money, but had decided to do nothing to interfere. Had he tried, they would only have done it behind his back.

He stood up and cupped his hands. "What do you want, Yank?"

"Got any tobacco?"

The men raised their heads and looked at McFadden intently. There was only one commodity in short supply in the North which the South happened to have in abundance and that was tobacco. To obtain it, Yankees were known to trade anything and everything. Coffee, in such short supply in the Confederacy, was particularly prized by Southern soldiers. The Army of Tennessee had captured an enormous amount of Yankee coffee during the Battle of Peachtree Creek, but that supply had already become exhausted.

As much as he wanted coffee, both for himself and for his men, McFadden did not like such contact with the Yankees. Hearing his men shout good-natured insults across the river was one thing, but meeting the enemy and shaking their hands was something else. Moreover, General Johnston had issued strict orders against any fraternization with the enemy. The fact that this directive was routinely ignored did not sit well with McFadden's conscience, for he believed in following orders.

At the same time, he understood that his role as an officer of the 7th Texas inescapably required an element of flexibility. If an opportunity were presented for the acquisition of real coffee and he prohibited his men from taking it, they would deeply resent it. It would make it more difficult to run the half of the regiment for which he was responsible. Moreover, he could not deny that he greatly desired a decent cup of coffee.

"Yes!" he shouted. "We have tobacco! Do you have any coffee?"

"We have so much coffee that we don't know what to do with it!"

The men of the 7th Texas raised a happy cheer. McFadden, however, struggled to decide how to conduct the exchange over the river.

"How do you want to do it, Yank?" he shouted when the cheering had died down.

"River's not too deep here, Reb!" the Northerner shouted back. "You could come over here to drop off your tobacco and pick up your coffee! Or the other way around, if you prefer!"

He considered this. If he or any of his men went across to the north bank of the river, they could quickly be overwhelmed and captured. After all, he had to consider the possibility that the Yankees were playing a dirty trick in order to take some prisoners for interrogation. He did not think this very likely, but as an officer he had to take into account all possibilities.

"You started this!" McFadden shouted over the river. "Why don't you come pay us a visit over here?"

"Okay!"

McFadden turned to Montgomery. "Ben, make sure some of our men have their rifles loaded and ready. I don't expect any trouble, but best to take precautions."

Montgomery nodded quickly, ready as always to spring to action at McFadden's word. McFadden also ordered some of his men to collect whatever tobacco they happened to have, wrapping them into small packets made from folded handkerchiefs tied with string. Glancing across the river, he could see the collection of Union soldiers engaged in similar activities, collecting their coffee.

For a moment, McFadden's mind went back to *The Wealth of Nations* by Adam Smith, which his father had made him read when he had decided his mind was mature enough to comprehend it. In a quick flash, notions of supply and demand and the natural and market prices of commodities passed through his mind. The South had tobacco and the North did not because the soil of the South was more conducive to the growing of the weed, whereas the North had coffee and the South did not because, as it was a foreign product not produced in North America, the Union's control of the seas and blockade of the Confederacy allowed the North to import it and deny the South the ability to do the same. Trading Southern tobacco for Northern coffee was, therefore, the most natural thing in the world.

McFadden winced slightly when he realized that the tobacco with which they would be trading was the product of slave labor. Unexpectedly, he found himself feeling somewhat guilty on this point. Thinking again of the ideas of Adam Smith, McFadden found it perfectly obvious that a free man working for wages would be more productive than a slave working merely to avoid the sting of the lash. He found himself wondering how prosperous the South might have been had it never created an economy based on human bondage.

He set those thoughts aside. They were interesting and important, but for the moment he had to focus on the matter at hand.

"You ready, Reb?" the Yankee called from across the river.

"Ready!" he shouted back.

About half a dozen Union soldiers, as naked as the day they were born, strode into the water, holding over their heads their uniforms and the packets McFadden assumed contained the coffee. Oddly, McFadden felt somewhat apprehensive as they crossed the Chattahoochee toward the picket line of the 7th Texas. The men were unarmed and could have been killed within seconds without any difficulty. Still, years of warfare had instilled in McFadden a certain amount of anxiety whenever Yankees were approaching, no matter what the situation.

A few minutes later, the Yankees clambered up onto the south bank of the river. They set down their coffee and quickly put on their trousers, then their shirts.

"Top of the morning to you, boys," the leader of the small group said with a smile.

"And you are?" McFadden asked without much politeness.

"Sergeant Charles Wilkinson. 20th Ohio."

"Lieutenant James McFadden. 7th Texas. You brought the coffee?"

"We sure did," Wilkinson answered, apparently unconcerned with McFadden's attitude.

"How much?"

"Twenty pounds, give or take."

McFadden nodded. "We'll give you twenty packets of our tobacco for it, then."

The Yankee's eyebrows shot up. "Wait a minute, there, Texas. How much tobacco is in each of these packets you're talking about?"

He pointed down to the ground, where the packets had been stacked. "See for yourself."

Like a starving man suddenly offered an immense amount of food, the Yankee soldier eagerly clawed at the packets of tobacco, unfolding them and carefully examining their contents. McFadden grimaced, disgusted by the sight of such unrestrained avarice. He could not say that he felt any differently as he watched his own men carefully examine the contents of the coffee pouches. His own taste buds could already sense the delightfully bitter and sharp sensation of the coffee.

McFadden and Wilkinson haggled over prices for the next fifteen minutes. Wilkinson was of the opinion that the amount of coffee they had brought across the river was worth about the same as the tobacco the Confederates were offering. McFadden actually agreed with this, but tried to wrangle a better deal from the Northerners. At last agreeing, the two men shook hands and their respective comrades raised a cheer, each contemplating the enjoyment of their newly-acquired commodity.

Pearson proposed a dram of whiskey to celebrate the deal. Despite his irritation that the ever-annoying private made the suggestion without consulting him, McFadden agreed. The Yankees might be enemies, but they were men. Besides, if he extended a demonstration of goodwill toward his foes, perhaps they might return the favor later on. For all they knew, their two regiments could be facing one another across the river for several more days.

Pleasant conversation between the erstwhile enemies ensued, the six Yankees trading stories with twenty or so Confederates while all but three teetotalers enjoyed their whiskey. The two sides reminisced about fighting one another in the memorable Battle of Raymond during the Vicksburg Campaign the previous May. McFadden was struck by how they discussed the desperate and bloody engagement as though the 7th Texas and the 20th Ohio had been opposing teams in a sporting match. Some of the men also talked of what they had done at home before the war or exchanged stories about their wives and children.

McFadden, watching all this from a distance, found it so absurd as to be almost laughable. Aside from their accents, the Ohio men seemed little different from the Texans. They were all just men caught up in a war they had no part in starting, trying to do their duty and hoping to live to see their homes again.

He would not have thought this way a few months earlier, he realized. Back then, he could only see the Yankees as the men who had tortured and killed his brother in the New Mexican desert. Now Annie Turnbow and her family had come into his life, allowing him to see beyond his old hatreds. It was not a whole people who had killed his brother, but a single man.

He didn't want to think about Cheeky Joe, but the incident during the Yankee evacuation of the south riverbank could not be shaken from his mind. Without consciously thinking about it, he acted.

"Wilkinson?" he asked.

"Yes?"

He struggled to keep his voice at a tone of friendly conversation, concealing his purpose. "Do you Yankees have regiments of the same state in each brigade, like us?"

Wilkinson's eyes narrowed. "I'm not sure what you mean."

"All the regiments in our brigade are from Texas. Lots of the other brigades in the army are made up entirely of regiments from the same state. Same in Lee's army. Is that the way you do it?"

"Oh, I see. Sometimes, but not always. We used to be in a brigade that only had other Ohio regiments. Now we're in a brigade with regiments from Illinois, Michigan, and Wisconsin. Why do you ask?"

"I have a friend in the 118th Ohio," he said cautiously. "Were you ever brigaded with them?"

Wilkinson shook his head. "Not that I recall."

Another Yankee soldier, overhearing the conversation, gestured toward one of his comrades, who was trying to lit a hurriedly-rolled cigar. "Patrick's brother-in-law is in the 118th, I think. Isn't he, Patrick?"

"He sure is," Patrick responded. "A rotten scoundrel, if you ask me. Only good thing he ever did was to take my good-for-nothing sister off the family's hands. Bastard owes me ten dollars. Better try to get him to pay up again soon."

"Is the regiment nearby?" McFadden asked. "I'd like to get a message to my friend, if I can."

"Who's your friend?"

"An officer named Joe." It was honestly all the information McFadden had.

Patrick looked confused. "Probably lots of officers named Joe."

"He has a big scar across his check, like this." McFadden drew a line with his finger across his face.

"Oh, him," Patrick said emphatically. "That fellow's a crazy one, sure as hell. Only seen him a couple of times. And when I say crazy, I mean crazy. I think lots of the soldiers in the 118th are scared of him."

McFadden felt himself tense. What he had seen on the river had not been his imagination. It had been his enemy, present and in the flesh. The man who had tortured and killed his brother, who had tortured him and left him for dead, was perhaps less than a mile from the very ground on which he was standing. The thought of his proximity put McFadden on edge, as if Cheeky Joe would materialize out of the river at any moment.

He talked more with the soldier named Patrick, finding out which brigade and division the 118th was serving in. The Yankee did not know exactly where they were posted, although he had the impression that they were southwest down the river. McFadden filed this information away in his mind, wondering how he might make use of it later.

James McFadden did not intend to let Cheeky Joe get away.

Chapter Thirteen

September 4, Noon

Emerging from the front door of St. Paul's Episcopal Church, President Davis inhaled deeply, relishing the first rush of cool air which heralded the return of autumn to Richmond. He might have smiled, but there was a large multitude of people crowded around him and he therefore maintained the stony and serious expression for which he was well known. He had to shake the hands of several men before he could begin to descend the steps of the church.

"Mr. President, you should hang Pat Cleburne and Bill Hardee," one man said earnestly as he shook his hand for rather too long. "The last thing we need are a bunch of damn abolitionists commanding our troops!"

"I have understood you quite clearly, my friend," Davis said in reply. The man smiled and departed, clearly thinking that the President's ambiguous words constituted agreement.

"A beautiful day," Varina said, her arm in his as they began walking down the steps.

"Indeed, my love," Davis replied. "I have greatly enjoyed the autumns we have spent together here in Virginia. The crispness of the Virginia air this time of year is to be preferred over the humidity of Mississippi."

"Must you go to work today?" she asked. "It's Sunday, Jeff. Exodus 31:15 comes to mind."

"Others have the luxury of observing the Sabbath day, but the obligations of a chief executive allow me no escape. In fact, I can see the Secretary of State is waiting for me."

At the bottom of the steps, Judah Benjamin stood quietly in a reserved black suit. Davis noted immediately that his perpetual smile did not grace his face and momentarily feared that his closest advisor had some sort of bad news to impart. Davis then relaxed, recalling that he had seen a sour expression on Benjamin's face on many Sundays in the past. As a Jew, Benjamin was isolated from his fellows as they filed into the various churches throughout Richmond. For a naturally vivacious personality who craved the company of others, this was not easy for Benjamin to endure. More to the point, it hammered home his status as a member of a distrusted minority far more than could even the most vile anti-Semitic screed.

Benjamin's eyes lit up when he saw the Davises approach and the smile quickly reformed on his face. "Mr. President!" he said happily. "Did you enjoy church?"

"We did, indeed, my friend."

"And Mrs. Davis. Are you taking good care of your husband and preventing him from causing too much trouble?"

Varina smiled, her natural affection for Benjamin easily shining through. "I am doing my very best, Judah."

"I am afraid that I shall have to borrow your husband for the afternoon, as he and I have much business to discuss. As a matter of fact, we have a special friend to meet. I do hope that you shall not hold this against me."

"No, not at all," Varina said resignedly.

"Very well." Benjamin motioned to a carriage which had been waiting on the side of the street.

"I will see you when I return home, my dear," Davis said to Varina, tenderly kissing her cheek. This caused a flurry of whispers among the crowd of people still gathered around the door of St. Paul's, as such public displays of affection were certainly uncharacteristic of the President. He made a mental note to be careful about such actions in the future.

"Try not to be too late," Varina said, holding his hand briefly before letting go and turning toward her own carriage.

A minute later, Davis and Benjamin were sitting opposite one another as the driver clicked his horses into motion. Benjamin directed him to take them to the Executive Office building.

"Who is this special friend of whom you speak?" Davis asked.

"A prospective friend, I should say. But first, have a look at these." He pulled a bundle of newspapers out and handed them to the President. "Yankee papers," he said. "Four days old. One from Washington, one from New York, one from Baltimore. They have much detail about what transpired at the Democratic National Convention and should make for some interesting reading."

"Can you give me a summary?"

"Well, you already know that they did what we expected them to do and nominated McClellan as their presidential candidate. These papers also confirm the rumors that Congressman George Pendleton will be McClellan's running mate."

"And he's an outspoken proponent of a cease-fire, yes?"

"Yes, Mr. President. McClellan has been evasive on the question of a cease-fire, as he must be in order to attract the votes of moderates. But Pendleton has favored a termination of the war since the earliest days. By nominating him as the vice presidential candidate, the Democratic Party is sending out a clear message."

Davis nodded and motioned for Benjamin to continue.

"The really important information we have obtained from the papers concerns the Democratic party platform. Here, let me read it to you." Benjamin unfolded one of the newspapers. "Most of the platform is a rehashing of the attacks on Lincoln's unconstitutional usurpations of power. Suspension of habeas corpus, closing down newspapers, that sort of thing. One plank specifically condemns the Lincoln administration for the death of Clement Vallandigham, though it stops short of using the word 'murder'."

Davis nodded again, impatient for Benjamin to continue.

"Ah, here we are. The sixth planks reads as follows: 'Resolved, that the continuing bloodshed and needless loss of life, as well as the unnecessary expenditure of vast amounts of public monies, must be brought to a halt at the earliest practicable moment. For this purpose, we demand an immediate cessation of hostilities and the opening of good faith negotiations with our Southern brethren with a view toward a termination of the present military conflict.'"

"Most interesting," Davis said. The carriage rode over a particularly bumpy part of the street, and Davis heard the driver shout a low curse to his horses. He hoped that they would soon arrive at the Executive Office building.

"Indeed," Benjamin agreed. "There is no mention of slavery at any point in the Democratic platform, which confirms for me that they still believe we will be willing to return to the Union if we receive guarantees on the slavery question."

"Let them believe whatever they want, so long as they get elected and bring about their promised cease-fire. The independence of our nation shall date from the moment that official emissaries of the United States sit down with official emissaries of the Confederate States."

"Perhaps so. The prospective friend I wish you to meet may have some interesting things to say on that point."

"And who is this gentleman?" Davis asked, growing impatient.

"A young man named Edward Malet."

The name meant nothing to Davis. "Who is he? More importantly, why should I care about him?"

"He has arrived in Richmond, having run through the blockade into Wilmington, with letters addressed to you from Lord Lyons, Her Majesty's Minister to the United States. In other words, Malet is an emissary from the British government."

Davis found Benjamin's words astonishing. If an official emissary from the British Empire had arrived in Richmond, it was an event of tremendous importance. The Secretary of State, however, was playing one of his usual games, acting coyly and pretending that the matter was of no significance. Davis was about to reprimand him when the driver shouted out for his horses to halt and he felt the carriage quickly slow to a stop. Glancing out the window, he saw the familiar Italianate architecture of the Executive Building of the Confederate government. A moment later, a slave was opening the door and helping the President and Secretary of State out onto the street.

The two men walked into the building and, after a few minutes spent in exchanging greetings with the officers and officials who had also forsaken the Sabbath, began walking up the stairs.

"Where is he?"

"I told him to wait in your office."

"How do we know he is legitimate?"

"I ordered my clerks to comb through the newspapers for any mention of him when he announced his presence to me yesterday. He has been the secretary of the British legations in a few European cities and is currently serving as the personal secretary to Lord Lyons."

"Very well. He has certainly piqued my interest. Let's meet this fellow."

Benjamin opened the door and they both stepped inside. Looking across the room to his desk, Davis saw a well-dressed man in his late twenties rise to his feet, a sharp look in his eyes and an expression of curiosity on his face. He bowed his head respectfully.

"Mr. Davis, I presume?" in a crisp English accent.

"I am President Davis."

"You'll forgive me if I cannot use that title at present. As you know, my government does not currently recognize the Confederate States of America as a sovereign state."

Davis crossed the room and shook Malet's extended hand. "I do hope that this unpleasant state of affairs may be resolved at some point in the near future."

"We shall see, sir."

Davis sat in his chair, while Benjamin took a seat beside Malet. For a moment, he stared across the desk, sizing up the British visitor. "My Secretary of State tells me that you have letters for me from Lord Lyons?"

"I do. My instructions were to confer with you in person, leaving the letters only to ensure that there is no possibility of misunderstanding."

"Very well. Am I to assume that this is an official communication from Her Majesty's Government to the Confederate States of America?"

Malet smiled. "No, sir. Our position is that these letters constitute only a private communication between two gentlemen."

Davis grunted with irritation. "Well, what is it that Lord Lyons wishes to say to me?"

Malet cleared his throat before beginning. "It has become clear to Her Majesty's Government that the political situation in the United States, specifically with regards to the upcoming elections, make it increasingly unlikely that the North shall be able to compel the entity calling itself the Confederate States of America – you will apologize that I must use such terminology – to return to the Union by force of arms. Owing to the fortunes of war, you have halted the Northern advance in both major theaters of the war, inflicted a decisive battlefield defeat on one of the two main Northern armies, and inflicted tremendous losses on the Northern forces."

"I am glad to know that London is paying such close attention," Davis said.

Malet ignored the quip. "The reality of the military situation obviously makes it more than likely that the Lincoln administration will not be reelected in November and that a Democratic administration led by George McClellan will take office in March. The recently announced platform of the Democratic Party and the various political promises McClellan has had to make further indicate that, when the McClellan administration is inaugurated, the North shall offer a cease-fire to the South with a view toward ending the war by negotiation."

"And if such an event comes to pass, what shall be the position of the British government?" Benjamin asked.

"If a cease-fire goes into effect and negotiations between the two opposing sides in the present war are initiated, the British government believes it would be in its interest to recognize the government of the Confederate States of America and offer to mediate the dispute between yourselves and the United States."

Davis's heart quickened. After the twin disasters of Gettysburg and Vicksburg the previous year, he had all but abandoned hope that diplomatic recognition would ever be granted by Britain. The fruits of Peachtree Creek now revealed that pessimism to have been misplaced.

"I am very glad to hear that," Davis said.

"Of course. But before the British extend diplomatic recognition to your Confederacy and offer mediation, we require certain assurances."

"Assurances?" Davis asked, confused. "What sort of assurances?"

"Firstly, we wish to know what terms you shall seek in any peace negotiations with the United States."

Davis furrowed his brow, wanting to collect his thoughts before answering such a broad and critical question. Without speaking, he rose from his chair and opened a cabinet next to his desk. Producing a bottle of Kentucky bourbon, he poured three glasses and set two of them in front of Benjamin and Malet.

"You drink bourbon?"

"I have just recently discovered it," Malet responded, his eyes flashing. "I confess I did not expect it to be as good as the scotch to which I am accustomed, but I have found your bourbon to be its equal and occasionally its superior."

Davis took a lingering sip, delighting in the fiery alcoholic feeling the bourbon lit in his throat. As he waited for the liquor to descend to his stomach, he pondered Malet's question more carefully. Benjamin and the British envoy waited patiently, sipping their own glasses with appreciation.

After a few minutes of silence, Davis again spoke. "Obviously, the single most important item shall be a full acknowledgement by the United States government that the Confederacy is a sovereign and independent nation. It must be made clear that the United States government has no more right to intervene in the affairs of the Confederacy than does the Emperor of Japan."

"Of course," Malet said with a grin. "But that's the easy part, isn't it?"

"You're correct. There are many other issues."

"Her Majesty's Government would appreciate knowing your positions on those issues."   "First, we must get Tennessee back. Its secession cannot legally be in doubt, but most of the state is currently under Union occupation and we do not expect the Yankees to simply pack up and leave. Second, the status of the border states of Missouri and Kentucky must be clarified, as must the status of the Indian Territory and New Mexico. West Virginia, too. Finally, any peace agreement should include a rational settlement on fortifications and deployed military units along the respective border."

Malet nodded. "I agree with what you say. Any peace agreement must include clear statements about your respective borders. I would expect, however, that the United States shall require a provision for free navigation of the Mississippi River, so as to ensure that the agricultural produce of the Great Plains shall not be deprived of its most convenient route to world markets."

"We would have no objection to that."

"Good."

"We do, however, expect significant financial compensation for the damage wrought by Union forces against civilian property in the Confederacy." For a moment, his mind drifted to his plantation at Brierfield, on the Mississippi River just south of Vicksburg. He had spent a lifetime building it, but it had been completely destroyed by Union soldiers in 1863. He wondered for a moment what had become of the two dozen slaves who had lived at Brierfield and silently said a prayer for their well-being.

"I do not believe that the British government would support such a claim, as it strikes me as unlikely to be accepted by the United States government."

"You asked for our position. I gave it."

"Of course, Mr. Davis."

Benjamin chimed in. "Perhaps there are concessions the Confederacy might extend to the British Empire in exchange for support from Her Majesty's Government for our claims?"

Malet took another sip of his bourbon. "Obviously, the British Empire hopes to have friendly relations with the Confederacy in the event that it emerges victorious from the present conflict. Certainly, there are actions your government might take which would promote such a relationship."

"Such as?" Davis asked, mildly irritated. He did not like the idea of Malet dictating anything to him. After all, Malet was a mere boy in his late twenties, whereas Davis was an experienced politician and soldier who served as the chief executive of an entire nation. Davis had to remind himself that Malet was the representative of the British Empire, whose mighty Royal Navy bestrode the world like a colossus.

Davis remembered the story of Gaius Popillius, the diplomat dispatched by the Roman Republic to order the withdrawal of a Greek king, Antiochus IV, who was on the verge of conquering Egypt. Alone and in full view of the Greek army, Popillius had taken his staff and drawn a circle in the sand around Antiochus, ordering him to decide whether or not he would obey the Roman demands before stepping outside the circle. Cowed by the might of Rome, distant though it was, Antiochus had caved in and ordered his men to retreat out of Egypt. One unarmed man had forced the withdrawal of an entire army merely by the threat of what he represented.

Malet was talking. "Before the war, the textile mills of England were supplied with Southern cotton of good quality and in tremendous quantity. When the war is over and the blockade is gone, we hope to restore this mutually beneficial economic partnership."

"That would also be our wish," Davis said.

"We would like to codify this in the form of a treaty guaranteeing free trade."

"The Senate would obviously have to ratify any trade treaty, but I do not foresee a problem there." Davis had been a fierce opponent of tariffs before the war and knew most members of the Confederate Senate shared his views on the subject. Indeed, it was one of the few things Southern politicians actually agreed on, aside from a few who represented sugar producers on the Gulf Coast.

"What else?" Benjamin asked, his voice sounding concerned.

Malet hesitated just a moment, then withdrew several pieces of paper from an envelope he was holding and passed them over to Davis. "Her Majesty's Government hope and expect the Confederacy, should it emerge victorious and independent, to agree to the terms of this treaty."

Davis frowned and quickly put on his reading spectacles. As he read, his heart turned to ice. Finishing five minutes later, he looked up at Malet.

"A treaty for the suppression of the slave trade?"

"Precisely."

Davis frowned and dropped the papers onto the desk. "Such a treaty is unnecessary. The Confederate Constitution already prohibits the importation of slaves from overseas. As far as I'm concerned, that settles the matter."

"The laws of the United States have also prohibited the slave trade for more than half a century, but slave ships have continued to ply the seas between Africa and America. Destroying the slave trade requires more than words on a piece of paper. The provisions of the treaty we propose will allow for the proper enforcement of the ban."

"What you are proposing would allow the Royal Navy to stop and search our merchant vessels on the high seas. That would represent an infringement upon our national sovereignty."

"The language of the treaty states clearly that those ships enforcing the ban would only stop vessels if they were suspected of being slave traders. Ordinary vessels would not be bothered. If you genuinely believe that the constitutional prohibition against the slave trade is sufficient in and of itself, the Royal Navy will never have to stop any Confederate ships and therefore the treaty should present no difficulties for you."

"But who would make the judgment as to which ships are to be stopped and searched?" Benjamin asked. "Are such powers to be delegated to every British naval officer in the Atlantic Ocean?"

"The treaty, as you can see, specifies the nature of the vessels which shall be stopped and searched. In fact, the treaty I am proposing is identical to the one signed between the United Kingdom and the United States two years ago."

Davis shook his head. "I cannot see the Senate going along with this. Setting aside concerns about our sovereignty, many Senators would object to any suggestion that slavery is not completely acceptable by all moral and ethical standards."

"If that is the case, why does the Confederate Constitution ban the slave trade?"

For a moment, Davis found that he was unable to answer.

Malet went on. "The attitudes of your Senate aside, you must be aware that the British people are firmly opposed to slavery. Had it not been for the existence of slavery in your Confederacy, we should have extended you diplomatic recognition long ago. Twist the truth any way you like, you cannot deny the fact that the reason the Southern states seceded from the Union in the first place was to protect the institution of slavery. Had there been no slavery, there would have been no war."

Anger flared in Davis and his lips curled into a grimace. "I tried all in my power to avert this war. I saw it coming. For twelve years I worked night and day to prevent it. But I could not. The North was mad and blind. It would not let us govern ourselves. So the war came. Now it must go on until the North acknowledges our right to self-government. We are not fighting for slavery, sir. We are fighting for independence. And that, or extermination, we shall have, even if it leaves every Southern field in ruins and every Southern city in flames!" He ended with a powerful bang of his fist against his desk, rattling the papers and pens which sat upon it.

"Calm yourself, Mr. Davis," Malet said evenly, not even slightly perturbed by the emotional display. "Unless the Confederacy can give Britain, and the world, some measure of reassurance on the slavery question by agreeing to this treaty, we shall not grant you the recognition you seek, nor shall we offer to mediate your dispute with the North. Your country shall simply be a pariah, assuming it succeeds in obtaining its independence and not immediately falling into economic and political chaos. After all, although we would prefer the convenience of importing Southern cotton, the shortage caused by the Union blockade has turned us toward other sources, including Egypt, Brazil, and our own colonies in India. We can make do without Southern cotton if we so wish."

Davis felt as though Malet was holding a gun to his head. The story of Gaius Popillius again resonated through his mind. Britain was the workshop of the world. It had been economic gospel before the war that the textile factories of Manchester and Birmingham would slow to a halt without the flow of Southern cotton. If the British could obtain cotton from other producers, however, the South would have nothing on which to build their postwar economy.

"I do not have the constitutional authority to agree to such a treaty on my own. The most I can do would be to sign it and then submit it to the Senate for ratification."

"That alone would be met with great approval by Her Majesty's Government."

"And that would suffice as the gesture against slavery you claim Britain requires in order to mediate a peace agreement?"

Malet grinned. "Not quite. We would also require that the Confederacy accept the loss of those slaves freed under the Emancipation Proclamation."

"Those slaves are the property of Confederate citizens."

"That is not the position of Her Majesty's Government."

Doubts flooded Davis's mind. He had long acknowledged to himself that only the most deluded fire-eater could believe that the slaves already freed by the Yankees could ever be returned to servitude. After any man, white or black, had tasted freedom, he could never abide losing it again. In every portion of the Confederacy that had been subjected to Union occupation - Tennessee, the

Mississippi Valley, northern Virginia, much of the Atlantic seaboard - the infrastructure of slavery had been systematically dismantled. Hundreds of thousands of slaves had been set free. Many thousands of former slaves now served in the ranks of the Union Army and Davis knew from long experience how the pride of a man was infinitely magnified by wearing a uniform and shouldering a musket.

Malet was only saying what was obviously true. If the Confederates demanded the return of the slaves who had been freed by the Emancipation Proclamation, they were demanding the impossible.

"At the very least, would Her Majesty's Government support a call on our part for the United States to pay financial compensation to the owners of the freed slaves for their lost property?"

Malet thought for a moment. "I do not know. On that question, I shall have to consult my superiors."

Davis was tired and very much wished the discussion were at an end. "How long are you in Richmond, Mr. Malet? I should like to continue this conversation at a later time."

"I can remain in the city for only three days. But during that time, I am at your service. I am staying at the Spotswood Hotel."

"Very good. I should like to discuss your proposals in more detail with Mr. Benjamin and meet with you again tomorrow. Perhaps we could hold these discussions over lunch?"

"That would be agreeable, Mr. Davis."

The three men rose. Davis and Benjamin shook hands with Malet, who bowed his head with a smile and showed himself to the door. The Confederate President and his Secretary of State then sat back down, to begin several hours of intense discussions about the import of the meeting they had just had.

*   *   *   *   *

September 6, Evening

Johnston was in the midst of yet another meeting of the high command of the Army of Tennessee. It had already gone on for more than three hours. Johnston removed his glasses and gently rubbed his eyelids, a wave of fatigue sweeping over him. He had not slept much in the past few nights. The simple act of remaining awake almost caused him physical pain, but he had to do it for the good of the army.

They had gone over a hundred different points, ranging from a shortage of rations to the letter being sent across the lines to Grant under a flag of truce asking for an explanation of Forrest's death. Yet the meeting was only now getting to the more important questions. Johnston forced himself to concentrate on the point then being

- 491 -

discussed, though it took great effort. General Stewart was the one doing the talking at the moment.

"Our own lack of cavalry makes it possible that an enemy mounted force might descend on the railroad which leads east to Augusta and render it inoperable before any of our cavalry units have a chance to intervene." From his tone, it was clear that Stewart considered this possibility a serious danger.

Johnston nodded. The three railroads which snaked out from Atlanta to the east, south, and southwest were the veins and arteries of his army, the only thing which kept his troops fed and supplied. The railroad to Augusta was particularly important, as it connected Atlanta with the Carolinas and Virginia. Sherman's men had largely wrecked it during their brief occupation of the area in July, but the damage had since been repaired. If Grant launched a powerful cavalry raid against it or either of the other railroads as part of his forthcoming offensive, it would present a very difficult challenge as the Confederate cavalry was now perilously weak.

Hardee spoke up. "According to the accounts of his recent operations in Virginia, Grant dispatched his cavalry under General Sheridan to attack the railroads south of Lee's army as part of his general offensive against Lee back in May. It is conceivable he might try something similar on this front."

Johnston glanced up at General William H. Jackson, recently promoted from the temporary to the permanent command of the cavalry of the Army of Tennessee. The look on his face was quite perturbed, and Johnston suddenly felt sympathy for him.

"General Jackson, do you believe you have the strength to both protect the railroads and properly reconnoiter the enemy in order to ascertain his movements?" Johnston asked.

"Frankly, sir, I do not," Jackson replied without hesitation. "I have but four thousand men both armed and provided with sufficient mounts. To guard the fords over the Chattahoochee, combined with dispatching patrols to the north bank of the river to scout the positions of the enemy, stretches my resources to the breaking point. I cannot spare so much as a single regiment to guard the railroads."

Johnston frowned, but nodded. He appreciated Jackson's frankness, a rare quality in an officer only recently promoted to a senior position. Far too often, eager young men anxious to prove themselves to their commanders made promises that they could not keep. This frequently resulted in failed operations and lots of dead soldiers. Wheeler himself had been a case in point. It was refreshing to see that Jackson did not fit into that mold.

"We have positioned all of the Georgia militiamen that we can spare from the defenses of Atlanta to the critical points on the three railroads," Johnston said. "For the moment, that will have to do."

Stewart shook his head. "If the enemy cavalry cuts the railroads, our supply lines will be severed. Even a temporary loss of access to food and ammunition could us this campaign."

"I understand your concerns, General Stewart. Rest assured, I fully share them. But the primary mission of our cavalry, reduced in strength as it is, must remain the scouting of the positions and movements of the enemy. We would have a hard enough task defeating Grant under the best of circumstances, but we shall surely fail if we attempt to fight him blind."

The four commanders nodded agreement. Johnston went on. "When Sherman came, we lured him onto the south bank of the river in order to ambush him as he crossed Peachtree Creek. Grant will not make a similar mistake, for he has Sherman's example before him. Therefore, I intend to fight him directly on the south bank of the Chattahoochee. The moment our cavalry discover the main crossing point of the enemy, we shall converge on that point with our three corps and destroy whatever forces Grant has managed to place on the south bank of the river. This, I am confident, will cripple Grant's army to such an extent that he shall be unable to resume operations before the end of the present campaigning season."

Cheatham cleared his throat deliberately. "Pardon me, sir?"

"General Cheatham?" Johnston said.

"Sir, should we not consider the possibility that the blue-belly bastards won't even cross over to the south bank of the Chattahoochee?"

Johnston's eyes narrowed. "Surely you don't mean to suggest that Grant shall not attack us?"

"No, the bastard's going to come after us, sure as hell. But Grant has a history of doing the unexpected. We're assuming that he will take a direct approach in an attempt to defeat our army and capture Atlanta. What if he actually intends something entirely different?"

"Such as what?" Johnston asked. He valued Cheatham's intelligence, despite the man's uncouth manners and tendency to drink.

"If you'll permit me?" Cheatham said, gesturing down to the table. Johnston nodded, and Cheatham shuffled through the maps until he found one which covered the whole western theater of the war, from eastern Georgia to the Mississippi River. He traced his finger along the Chattahoochee River.

"We stand between Grant and Atlanta," Cheatham said. "Suppose instead he moves southwest, keeping to the north bank of the Chattahoochee, bypassing us altogether and heading off toward Alabama?"

Johnston looked down at the map. "To what end?"

Cheatham's fingers thumped down on the map in central Alabama. "The capture of Montgomery and Selma," he replied with conviction.

Johnston grunted, thinking the idea over. Montgomery had huge symbolic importance to the Confederacy, as it had been the site of the convention in 1861 at which the seceded states had written their constitution and formed the Confederate government. If any place could be said to be the birthplace of the Confederacy, it was Montgomery. Furthermore, it had emerged over the course of the war as a critical transportation link and production center of war material.

The city of Selma was, if anything, an even greater prize. Aside from Atlanta and Richmond, no city was as important as Selma to keeping the Confederacy's war industry going. Selma's iron foundry was one of the largest in the South, turning out hundreds of cannon, iron plating for warships, and other critically-needed war material. Rifles and pistols were also manufactured there in great numbers and it was one of the Confederacy's centers for gunpowder production.

After quietly thinking for perhaps two minutes, Johnston slowly began to shake his head. "No, it's too great a distance. The distance from the Union camp at Vining's Station to Montgomery is a hundred and fifty miles, give or take. The roads are not that good, and they'd have to carry their supplies with them by wagon train. A logistical impossibility, I'd think."

"Grant did something similar during the Vicksburg Campaign, didn't he? Moving his whole damn army across the river south of the city, abandoning his supply line in order to move faster?"

Johnston drew back a moment, remembering those confusing days in the spring of 1863. He recalled the frantic telegrams he had dispatched to General Pemberton, asking him for Grant's location and direction. Grant's men had marched so far so quickly that he had never really been able to keep track of where the Union forces were. In a matter of weeks, Grant's army had marched nearly a hundred miles, defeated the Southerners in five battles, driven Johnston himself out of the state capital of Jackson, and besieged Vicksburg.

Johnston's role in the Vicksburg Campaign had been more supervisory than active, but he would never forget the psychological shock he had experienced when Grant had caught the Confederates flat-footed. As the memory coursed through his mind, he wondered if perhaps Cheatham was correct and that Grant might indeed do something as unexpected as march toward Alabama.

"Grant commands nearly one hundred thousand men," Hardee said. "There would not be enough wagons in the entire Union to carry sufficient supplies for such a large force."

"We must never underestimate the logistical capacity of our enemies," Johnston found himself saying. The more he thought about Cheatham's theory, the more plausible it seemed. "Besides, Grant would obviously not take his entire force with him. He would have to leave a large force in its present position in order to prevent us from attacking northwards toward Chattanooga."

"I am troubled," Jackson said. "As I mentioned earlier, my troops are already stretched thin merely maintaining watch over the river fords. If a major portion of the enemy force were to detach itself and march southwest along the north bank of the river, it might march for several days without being detected."

In his mind, Johnston cursed Jefferson Davis yet again. By forcing him to send Wheeler off on his idiotic raid into northern Georgia, the President had indirectly destroyed half of the army's cavalry. Had Johnston been allowed to make his own decision in the matter, Wheeler would not have been sent on his fool's errand and the Army of Tennessee would now not be worrying about detecting the movements of the enemy army.

"I am sorry to add to your burdens, General Jackson," Johnston said apologetically. "I'm afraid we have no choice. You shall have to dispatch one of your brigades to the southwest and post it on the north bank of the Chattahoochee River. There it shall remain, sending back word to us at once if it detects any movement of the enemy in that direction."

"You are aware, sir, that this will leave me with fewer men to monitor the fords."

"Yes, I am. But as I said, we have no choice."

Johnston intended for the meeting to end at this point, but Cheatham cleared his throat again.

"Respectfully, sir, there is another matter I wish to discuss."

"Very well," Johnston said, knowing what the subject was likely to be.

"I don't like saying this, since it concerns a brother officer, but some of my subordinates have expressed reservations about continuing to serve alongside General Cleburne."

Johnston glanced at Hardee, seeing the clouds of anger cross his face. Cheatham also looked over at his fellow corps commander, clearly uncomfortable with raising the subject in his presence.

"General Cooper has not yet issued any report on his findings," Johnston said, as though this fact were somehow relevant. "Tell your division commanders that they are expected to do their duty and accord General Cleburne all the respect to which he is entitled by his rank and his status as a brother officer."

"I shall do so, sir. But my brigade and division commanders are, as you know, a rather hot-headed bunch."

"You do not need to remind me of that, General Cheatham," Johnston said sourly. If anyone knew how hot-headed Confederate army officers could be, it was Johnston.

"Which of your commanders has spoken ill of General Cleburne?" Hardee asked, a little too forcefully. Rather to Johnston's surprise, Cheatham answered immediately.

"General Patton Anderson has made his feelings clear more than anybody else. But all of my brigade and division commanders have stated at least some desire to avoid serving alongside Cleburne."

"So the men under your command are informing us that they shall refuse to follow orders?" Hardee asked. He looked over at Johnston. "Are they not therefore guilty of gross insubordination?"

Johnston knew that Hardee was right, but he did not want to say so. Among Hardee's own division commanders, William Walker had long despised Cleburne and William Bate was probably of the same mind. If anger against Cleburne was now rising in Cheatham's corps, the generals among Stewart's corps were likely to follow suit. After all, Johnston recalled that Stewart himself had been greatly angered by Cleburne's proposal when it had been made.

"Every one of you must make it perfectly clear to all officers in your corps that they are expected to follow their orders without question," Johnston said.

"I will do my best, sir," Cheatham said.

"As shall I," Stewart chimed in. Neither man had spoken with as much enthusiasm as Johnston would have preferred.

Johnston knew he was walking on extremely delicate ground. On the one hand, he did not want to lose the services of Cleburne. Not only was he the best division commander in the Army of Tennessee, but the soldiers of his unit were so loyal to him that they might well become mutinous if their beloved leader were dismissed. On the other hand, if the rest of the brigade and division commanders of the army were reluctant to continue serving with Cleburne, and this attitude filtered down the ranks to their men, what could Johnston do other than relieve Cleburne? As outstanding an officer as Cleburne was, it would probably be better to lose the services of a single division commander than have all of the others in a potentially rebellious mood.

Johnston had been inwardly outraged by Walker's insult to Cleburne a few days before, but had not felt able to do anything aside from ordering him to apologize and then ordering Cleburne to accept the apology. He might have placed Walker under arrest for clearly attempting to provoke a confrontation, but this would have made the situation worse. Walker, although not as talented as Cleburne, was a gifted combat leader and Johnston did not feel he could afford to lose him, either. Arresting Walker would also have created resentment among many of the other officers and men as well.

He felt as though he were walking a tightrope. If he could keep his balance, he might be able to save Cleburne and keep the officer corps of the Army of Tennessee more focused on fighting the Yankees than eating themselves alive.

For a moment, Johnston found himself feeling intensely jealous of Robert E. Lee, his old friend and occasional professional rival. Lee's commanders in the Army of Northern Virginian were every bit as hot-headed and arrogant as those of the Army of Tennessee, yet Lee somehow managed to pour oil over the turbulent waters of his own command and keep personal tensions from boiling over. To himself, and in unguarded moments with Lydia, Johnston could admit that he was not nearly as talented as Lee in this regard.

The meeting broke up shortly afterward. Watching his corps commanders mount their horses and ride off to their respective commands, Johnston felt distinctly troubled. He did not know what Grant intended to do. More forbiddingly, whatever Grant was going to do, Johnston did not know if the Army of Tennessee would have sufficient trust in itself to be able to stop him.

*   *   *   *   *

September 6, Night

McFadden stepped carefully out of the water and onto the northern bank of the Chattahoochee River. Dropping his pack onto the ground, he used one of the two shirts he had brought to dry himself off, then began putting his uniform on. The coat he threw on over his shirt was not Confederate gray, but Union blue.

He had been apprehensive while crossing the river. Confederate troops on the southern bank might have fired on him, assuming that he was a deserter going over to the Yankees. The enemy, by contrast, might have done the same out of fear that he was the vanguard of a raid across the river. But he had chosen a spot he thought was devoid of pickets. As far as he could tell, no one on either side had observed his crossing.

McFadden picked his pack up and begin to walk. He had left his weapons behind, for they did not fit into the plan he had spent many long hours putting together. He admitted to himself that it did not have a good chance of success, but it was the best he had been able to come up with. Even the slight possibility of being able to find Cheeky Joe and avenge the death of his brother was worth the risk.

He had elected to play the part of a Union prisoner who had escaped from the infamous prison camp at Andersonville and made his way up to the Chattahoochee in order to reach the Union lines. The idea that a man in a Union uniform could walk over a hundred miles through hostile territory would obviously strike many as unlikely. He had considered pretending to be a man captured in the recent fighting around Atlanta, who would have had a much shorter distance to cover. But that would have required his false identity to be from one of the nearby Union regiments and his ruse might easily have been discovered. The only way it would work, McFadden had decided, would be to portray a soldier from one of the Union regiments fighting in the Eastern Theater, and that would require him to say he had come from Andersonville.

By going through some old newspaper stories on the heavy fighting that had recently taken place in Virginia, McFadden had picked out a Union regiment from which he would say he had come, the 7th Michigan Infantry. Few other Confederate soldiers could have pulled off the deception, as their Southern accents would have given them away in an instant. As McFadden spoke with a Scottish brogue, that would not be an issue for him.

He had considered declaring himself to be a Southern deserter. This would have been a far easier deception to successfully pull off. It would also have limited his options, as he would no doubt be sent to some sort of depot under guard for proper processing. By disguising himself as an escaped Union prisoner, he would have a much better chance of obtaining the freedom of movement he would need to make his way to the camp of the 118th Ohio, wherever it was.

There were no roads nearby, as near as he could tell. The sky was overcast, blocking the light of the moon and stars. He had been in the army long enough to know that he could easily get lost if he attempted to walk under such conditions. Having successfully crossed the river, he decided it would be best to wait until the coming of morning to seek out the nearest Union troops and put his plan into effect. Until then, he would try to sleep.

He decided against making a fire. Instead, he simply wrapped himself in his blanket and sequestered himself under the low branches of a tree. Unfortunately, he found that sleep did not come easily. The nature of his errand preyed on his mind.

He was certain that he had seen Cheeky Joe on the river, and what he had learned from the Yankees during the parlay two days earlier had confirmed that his enemy was nearby. Two months earlier, this information would have filled McFadden with a sinister joy and he would have set off without the slightest hesitation. Killing Cheeky Joe was the only way to avenge his brother and, though he could not understand why, he felt that it would somehow avenge the deaths of his parents and sisters as well.

McFadden now felt only resignation. He was doing it not because he wanted to, but because he had no choice. Annie would not have wanted him to go, for the mission he had embarked upon posed far more danger to him than even the fiercest battle. Were he to be discovered in the Union camp wearing a Union uniform, the odds were that he would be executed as a spy.

He had written Annie a letter and entrusted it to Montgomery, asking him to deliver it to her as soon as the 7th Texas went back into camp after concluded their picket duty. In the letter, McFadden told Annie what he had done and apologized for doing so without saying goodbye. He expressed his fear that his actions would lose him her respect and that of her parents, which he had worked so hard to earn and which had come to mean more to him than he could have previously imagined.

He had ended the letter with words he had never expected to write.

If I do not return, my dear Annie, know that I love you.

The memory of scratching those lines at the bottom of the page caused McFadden to wince, as though it actually inflicted physical pain. Still, as awkward as he had felt when had signed his name at the bottom of the letter, he had also felt a certain relief that Annie would know of his feelings if he failed to return.

For a horrifying moment, he felt disgrace and despair. How stupid had he been to embark upon such a fool's errand as this? A happy and contented life had been beckoning to him. He was a hero, had been promoted to an officer, and had begun courting a woman with whom he had fallen in love. All that he had now thrown away.

McFadden did have the satisfaction of knowing that he had not deserted his comrades in the 7th Texas. After all, he was infiltrating the Union camp in order to kill a Union soldier. He fully intended to return to his men as soon as his personal mission of revenge was completed. How could that be considered desertion?

He had told Major Collett of his plan earlier in the day, reassuring him that he would be back within a few days. Collett had not exactly given him permission to go, but had promised to "close his eyes" when the sun went down. He had also warned McFadden that if he did not return within five days, he would report him as a deserter. Since McFadden had confided in Collett about Cheeky Joe, perhaps he had acquiesced because he knew McFadden would simply disobey him if he tried to prevent him from leaving.

It didn't matter if he had made the right decision or not. Indeed, it was not worth worrying about now. He had sent his letter to Annie and crossed the river. There was no going back. For better or worse, he was committed to his pursuit of Cheeky Joe. Even if the rational part of his mind told him that it had virtually no chance of success, he had no choice now but to do his utmost to succeed. If he did eventually stand over the dead body of his enemy, clutching a bloody knife, he would at least have the satisfaction of knowing he had avenged his family. Whether it was worth destroying his relationship with Annie and losing the respect of her family was a question that he could try to answer later, assuming he survived.

These uncomfortable thoughts rocked back and forth in his mind like the swaying of a ship at sea until he finally drifted off into a fitful sleep.

September 7, Afternoon

The major emerged from the darkness of the tunnel, clutching a long line of twine in his hand. Although he was breathing hard and clearly exhausted from his exertions, he had a beaming smile on his face.

"We did it!" he said exuberantly. "A hundred and ten feet!"

Thomas felt his heart quicken and he could sense the stirring among the half-dozen other officers inside the hut. If the major had measured the distance correctly, the tunnel had now reached beyond the fence line, presenting the tantalizing possibility of freedom to at least some of the Union prisoners in Camp Oglethorpe.

Thomas quickly reminded himself that tunneling past the fence line was only a single step in the escape process. It was an important step, to be sure, but much work remained to be done. They now had to dig at an upwards incline for a certain distance in order to break through to the surface just before the escape attempt itself. This would be a dangerous moment, as it would be easier for the rebel guards to discover the tunnel. But there was no alternative.

The assembled officers began excitedly discussing the plan for creating a diversion to distract the guards when the escape attempt was actually made. Thomas felt that this was not the proper time for such a discussion, but let the men continue talking for the moment. Some of them had been imprisoned for more than a year and the fact that their tunnel had extended past the fence line was possibly the most exhilarating news they had had during that entire time. Excited chatter about the diversion might not have been productive at that moment, but it was good for morale.

Seymour manfully slapped Thomas on the shoulder.

"Good news, eh, George?"

Thomas nodded. "Good news, indeed. But we should not celebrate prematurely."

Thomas's serious demeanor quickly sobered Seymour. "Yes, you're right."

"I do not want the excitement of the men to cause any lack of discipline. A single stray word overheard by an enemy will mean the end of this entire enterprise."

Seymour nodded. "Of course."

There was a sudden, frightening sound: three loud thuds against the door. It was the signal that rebel guards were approaching.

"Concealment!" Thomas said urgently and harshly, trying to keep his voice below the level of a shout. Everyone sprang into action. The major who had been down in the tunnel ducked into it once again, as his dusty and dirty appearance would certainly have given the game away. Seymour and a colonel rapidly pushed the wooden cover into place over the entrance to the tunnel, while Thomas and a captain hurriedly grabbed either end of a bed and pulled it over the cover. The two other men, both majors, snatched up a deck of cards and hurriedly dealt them out onto the bed.

Just over one minute since the warning sound had first been heard, the door slammed open and Captain Gibbs, with half a dozen guards armed with rifles visible behind him, peered into the cabin. He saw six Union prisoners playing cards on the bed.

"Attention!" Gibbs called out.

With a slowness that demonstrated their disrespect for the rebel officer, the six Union officers in the cabin rose from their game and stood straight, facing the door.

Gibbs looked down at the bed. "You were playing cards?"

"Obviously." The tone managed to be polite and mocking at the same time.

"Very well." The Southern officer paused a moment before continuing. "General Thomas, I have been ordered by my commanding officer to inform you that the Confederate government has learned that Major General Nathan Bedford Forrest, during a battle in central Tennessee, was executed by Union soldiers after having been taken prisoner."

"Is that so?" Thomas asked. He found this information to be genuinely fascinating and hearing any news of the war was welcome. While he did not approve of any violations of the sacred rules of warfare, he could not deny that a certain satisfaction crept into his heart upon hearing of Forrest's death. The man had been both an enemy of the United States and a thoroughly vile human being. The world was a better place with Forrest dead.

"It is," Gibbs said. "As you are aware, executing soldiers who have been captured in battle represents one of the most egregious violations of the articles of war."

"Forrest would know that better than most," Seymour chimed in. "How many prisoners did his men slaughter at Fort Pillow?"

"Don't rightly know," Thomas said with a grin. "But I imagine he's explaining it to Old Scratch even as we speak."

"Silence!" Gibbs snapped. "You will not be making jokes much longer, General Thomas. My commander orders me to inform you that the government in Richmond is considering their response to Forrest's unlawful death."

The smiles instantly vanished from the faces of the Union officers. There was an uneasy pause.

"What do you mean?" Seymour asked. "What sort of response?"

"General Thomas is the highest ranking Union officer currently held as a prisoner by the Confederacy. We have sent a message under flag of truce to General Grant, requesting an explanation for the manner of General Forrest's death. If a satisfactory answer is not received, I am informed that the government in Richmond shall order the death of General Thomas by hanging."

"What?!" Seymour exclaimed.

"You heard me perfectly well, General Seymour."

Thomas said nothing, but his stomach clenched tightly. He did not fear death, but the manner of death being described was not how he had envisioned going to his maker. He had expected either to be struck down in battle or to die of old age in the comfort of his own bed. He had certainly never imagined having a noose pulled around his neck and being dropped through the gallows trapdoor.

His fellow Southerners regarded him as the worst of traitors. His name was used throughout the Confederacy in the same manner as Benedict Arnold's name had been used throughout the whole country before the war. He could imagine the sheer glee the newspapers of Richmond, Charleston and Atlanta would display in their headlines when they announced his execution.

"Do you have anything to say, General Thomas?" Gibbs asked.

"No," Thomas said simply.

Gibbs smiled impolitely and nodded. He touched his hat. "In that case, I bid you good day." A moment later, the door closed again, leaving the Union officers alone.

Thomas sank down onto the bunk, his mind racing and his heart pounding. For several minutes, the men looked down at their leader in silence. Seymour finally spoke up.

"We have to get you out of here, George. We need to move up the timing of our escape plan."

Thomas shook his head. "Absolutely not," he said firmly.

"The rebels are going to kill you, George."

"And if I escape, what will they do? If they have announced that they are going to retaliate for the death of Forrest by executing a Union officer of equal rank, they will do so. Therefore, if I escape, they will select some other general to be hanged. How can I have that on my conscience?"

One of the majors spoke up. "Sir, you are the best general the Union has. You need to be at the head of the Army of the Cumberland, not dead at the hands of the rebels in this stinking prison camp!"

"Mind your place," Thomas said to the lower-ranking officer. The realities of life in a prison camp necessarily blurred military formalities, but the chain of command remained intact and Thomas did not like having a mere major speak to him with such familiarity. "In any event, the chances of any of us reaching the Union lines are not good. I shall not force another man to go to the gallows in my place merely on the off chance that I might make it back to my army."

"Well, we should at least discuss the possibility of changing our plans in view of this new development."

"What does this have to do with the escape plan?" Thomas snapped. "Our goal is to get as many men out of this prison as possible. No, we shall carry on with the plan as we have crafted it. The only change is that I shall not be among those who will make the attempt."

"You cannot be serious!" Seymour protested. "If you remain here, you will be executed!"

Thomas shrugged. "If that is what honor demands, that is what I shall do. Now follow my orders."

*   *   *   *   *

September 7, Night

"7th Michigan, you say?"

"That's right, sir," McFadden answered.

The Union colonel's eyes narrowed. "And your name again?"

"Samuel Stephens, sir. A private, sir."

It was the fourth time he had said the name to the Yankee officer. It was clear that the man was testing him, trying to find some hint that his story was a falsification. McFadden was struggling to both maintain his false identity and not to appear too nervous while doing so. After all, if he really was who he said he was, he should not be nervous at all. He should be overjoyed at having gotten to the Northern lines.

He had encountered a Union patrol within half an hour of daylight that morning. He had called to them from a distance, luckily not drawing rifle fire, shouting that he was an escaped prisoner and asking for help. They had given him some food and water and escorted him back to their camp. Once there, he had been kicked steadily up the chain of command and was now being debriefed by this particular colonel, who struck McFadden as a man with a decidedly mediocre mind.

"Where are you from, Stephens? Originally, I mean."

"Aberdeen, sir. In Scotland."

"And you're telling me that you walked all the way from the prison camp at Andersonville to the Chattahoochee River?"

"That's right, sir."

"Hundreds of miles of enemy territory? Land swarming with rebel troops?"

"Hid in slave quarters most of the way, sir," McFadden answered. "Most of the negroes were very anxious to help me escape."

"I'll bet they were," the Union colonel replied. "Wherever we go across the South, they flock to our lines. It's the same everywhere.

Tennessee, Mississippi, Georgia. They want to be free like everybody else, no matter what lies the rebels try to spread about them."

"Not just the blacks, sir. Quite a few whites in these parts are Unionist."

His eyebrows went up. "Are they, now?"

"Yes, sir. Some gave me shelter and food. More food than I ever got in Andersonville, by God."

"I'll wager that's the truth. You look rather stout for a man that's just come out of a prison camp. Tell me, is it really as bad as they say?"

McFadden waited a moment before answering. "It's worse, sir."

McFadden didn't know this from the evidence of his own eyes, for he had never been to Andersonville. But the rumors about the place which circulated in the camps of the Army of Tennessee painted a picture of horror that defied any attempt at description. The prison guards, uneducated militiamen in their teens, were known to shoot down Northern prisoners at the slightest provocation and sometimes merely out of a desire for amusement. Food for the prisoners was virtually nonexistent and the shelters the prisoners were allowed to build did not even suffice to protect them from the elements. Andersonville was, in short, about as close to hell as a man could get without dying as an unbelieving sinner.

He was willing to overlook the lack of food for the Union prisoners. After all, the Confederacy had enough difficulty feeding its own soldiers and refugees, so how could it be expected to feed the men who had been captured while fighting to reduce the South to subservience? He reminded himself that Confederate captives in Northern prison camps fared little better than the Yankees held captive in the South. Before McFadden had joined up with the 7th Texas, the regiment had done its own stint in Yankee prison camps after being captured at Fort Donelson in early 1862. The other regiments in Granbury's Texas Brigade had also endured captivity after being captured at Arkansas Post in early 1863. Before being exchanged, the regiments had lost hundreds of men to disease and hunger, despite being held in the midst of wealth and prosperity.

He forced these thoughts from his mind. If he was to successfully pull off his facade as an escaped Union soldier, it would be far better for him to pretend to despise the Confederacy with every fiber of his being. He described the horrors of Andersonville, hoping that his acting would be sufficient to make the Yankee officer believe that he had been there himself. He also related the story he had made up of how he had escaped by bribing one of the guards to let him through the stockade in the middle of the night.

As he spoke, McFadden became worried. The story had sounded good when he had devised it in his own mind, but as he heard the words coming out of his mouth it seemed increasingly implausible.

Nevertheless, the smile on the face of the Yankee officer did not falter. Despite himself, McFadden realized that the man was believing everything he said.

"Well, I must say. Well done! Well done, indeed!" The colonel extended a hand across the table, which McFadden firmly clasped.

"Thank you, sir." He paused a moment. "What will I do now, sir?"

"Well, we can probably put you on a train and get you back to your regiment in Virginia. Alternatively, you might just start serving with one of our units here in Georgia. Makes no sense to have a good man waste his time travelling for a couple of weeks when there's going to be plenty of action right here."

"Action?"

"Yes. Probably some serious action, too. Orders are coming in. The entire Army of the Ohio and Army of the Tennessee are moving out the day after tomorrow. Nobody's knows where. But I reckon that wherever Grant orders us to go, we'll go."

McFadden wondered what the Union army was up to. When he set out to infiltrate the enemy camp, a month had passed with scarcely a shot being fired across the Chattahoochee. Somehow, McFadden had assumed that this inactivity would continue indefinitely, allowing him plenty of time to find and kill Cheeky Joe. But if serious campaigning was about to start again, it would make it much more difficult for him to make his way to the 118th Ohio.

Moreover, the idea of renewed fighting caused a guilty clenching of McFadden's stomach. If a battle were coming, his proper place was with his men in the 7th Texas, not on the other side of the river pursuing a personal vendetta of his own. But there was no point in second thoughts now. He was in the Union camp and there was no going back.

"Well, I guess I might as well join up with one of your regiments, sir."

"Good. Very good."

McFadden certainly did not want to be put on a train to Virginia. Not only would that have been the end of his quest to find Cheeky Joe, but it would have placed him in an absurd and dangerous situation from which it would have been difficult to extract himself.

The colonel, clearly wanting to end the interview as quickly as possible in order to move on to more important business, wrote out an order directing McFadden to report to the chief-of-staff of one of his regiments, which turned out to be 15th Illinois. How he would proceed from there, McFadden had no idea.

September 8, Noon

"Take a seat, Mr. Marble. General McClellan will be in to see you shortly." The butler, whose back appeared so ramrod straight that Marble wondered if he had a wooden plank hidden in his shirt, turned and left the room.

He glanced around the sitting room, sipping on the glass of wine which had been provided for him. It didn't surprise Marble that George McClellan's house was as impressive as it was. In the years before the war, McClellan had made a respectable fortune as a railroad engineer and executive, and the use to which he had put the money was obvious in the fashionable furnishings and decorative artwork that graced the room. Some of the china and silverware on display appeared so stylish that Marble speculated the general had acquired them in France during his pre-war travels.

Marble had no interest in matters of art and decoration himself, but he did value the light such things threw on the characters of the people who desired to acquire them. Marble had long since determined that McClellan was a vain and silly man, but the additional evidence of the fact provided by the ostentatious display in his house was a welcome confirmation.

He shifted uncomfortably on the couch. Glancing at a grandfather clock, Marble realized that nearly twenty minutes had passed since the butler had left the room. While he considered himself considerably less vain than most of the powerful people with whom he came into contact, Marble did not like being forced to cool his heels any more than anyone else.

Finally, after thirty minutes of waiting, George McClellan strode into the living room with the air of a Roman senator. He was dressed in an impeccably tailored suit far superior to the one Marble himself was wearing. The editor rose from the couch and politely bowed his head to McClellan.

"Mr. Marble, " McClellan said with a restrained amount of warmth. "I am delighted to welcome you to my humble home."

"And I am delighted to be here, General McClellan."

"As you probably know, I have received the official notification from a committee of delegates from the Chicago convention of my nomination as the Democratic Party's candidate in the upcoming presidential election."

"And allow me to offer my personal congratulations."

"Thank you. I am very glad to see you. As I said to you when we last met in New York City, I trust your political instincts better than those of most other men, and I would be very interested in hearing your opinion of the present political situation. I would be especially interested in your view regarding what course of action I myself should follow to maximize my chances of winning the election."

McClellan gestured to a table and both men sat down. The butler reappeared and refilled Marble's wine glass, while pouring one for McClellan. Marble found this annoying. Obviously the butler had been in an adjoining room the entire time, and might have refilled his glass at any point during the thirty minutes he had been kept waiting.

"So," McClellan said simply. "The convention is over and done with. The platform has been decided upon. We shall soon be coming to the heart of the matter, the election itself."

"That's right," Marble said. "Little time remains between now and November 8."

"We are quickly approaching the time of decisive events," McClellan grandly added.

"Let me ask you, General McClellan. Are you in full accord with the platform adopted by the Democratic Party at the Chicago Convention? I speak particularly about the plank calling for an end to military hostilities with the South and the opening of negotiations."

McClellan sighed, the first display of actual emotion Marble had seen since arriving at his house. "I am a soldier. For the first two years of the war, I led armies against the rebels. It pains me greatly to think that the thousands of men who were killed or wounded under my command suffered and died for no good cause."

Marble suddenly felt a rush of alarm, though he maintained a composed expression. If the presidential candidate repudiated the party platform, it would make the Democratic Party appear fractured and confused. The Republicans would pounce, expressing to the people the idea that such a disunited and disorganized party had no business attempting to govern the country.

When McClellan continued, it was greatly to Marble's relief. "However, I have long since determined that the failure to subdue the Southern rebels is entirely the fault of the incompetence of the Lincoln administration and does not reflect on the valor of the men I commanded in any way. The series of disasters suffered by federal forces in the current campaign season has amply demonstrated the futility of continued efforts to suppress the rebellion by force."

"So, you will publicly back the peace plank of the party platform?"

McClellan nodded. "I shall. Only with the greatest reluctance, but I shall."

"Very good," Marble said, feeling the weight lifted off his shoulders.

"Now, can you tell me where you think we stand in the various states? I received a comprehensive report on the subject from the convention's delegation, but I fear they were telling me only the good news. I would like information I can count on, if you please."

Marble proceeded for the next fifteen or twenty minutes to give McClellan as honest and comprehensive an account of the situation in the various states as he could. The news was generally good. New York State, with its precious thirty-three electoral votes, was now considered by many observers to be virtually locked down for the Democrats. Prospects also seemed excellent in the vital states of Ohio, Pennsylvania, and Indiana. Combined with McClellan's own state of New Jersey, these states gave the Democrats an even one hundred electoral votes.

However, the situation was not entirely positive. Aside from Connecticut, the Democrats had failed to make much headway in strongly abolitionist New England, which meant that thirty-three electoral votes there were almost certain to go to Lincoln. Combined with the votes of his home state of Illinois and a few other states that seemed likely to go Republican, Lincoln could count on between sixty and seventy electoral votes.

There were troubling signs from the border states of Kentucky, Maryland, and Missouri. Rumor had it that the federal troops occupying those states were making preparations to intervene on election day by barring Democrats from going to the polls. If the Lincoln administration lowered itself to such dirty tricks and threw those states into the Republican column, then the vote total for Lincoln would jump to ninety-nine.

The outcome in the northwestern states of Minnesota, Wisconsin, Iowa, and Michigan would obviously play a decisive role in the election. Marble had to report to McClellan that information from those states was so sketchy and uncertain that any predictions about them would be would be nothing but guesswork.

McClellan snorted. "I had been told that I had all those states in the bag."

"I feel it my duty as your friend to tell you the unvarnished truth. I would have to say that they could still go either way, as could the election as a whole."

"I appreciate your frankness. Now answer me this. With the Confederate victory at Peachtree Creek and the clear disaffection spreading through the cities of the North, as demonstrated by the riots in New York City and elsewhere, why is this even a competition? Should my victory at the polls in November not already be certain?"

"The victory at Mobile Bay raised hopes of greater military progress before the end of the year, and the defeat of the rebel cavalry raids on our supply lines in Georgia and Tennessee has been portrayed by the Republican press as a tremendous victory. The death of Nathan Bedford Forrest, in particular, has been front page news across the country." McClellan grunted, and Marble went on. "Furthermore, the news that General Grant has taken personal command of the Union armies outside of Atlanta has caused much of the voting public to expect a big victory in the Western Theater very soon."

McClellan laughed with scorn. "Grant is a drunken fool. Whatever successes he has achieved have been due entirely to luck rather than skill, and don't let anyone deceive you otherwise. I have no doubt that our army outside Atlanta will soon meet with disaster. Were I in command, I would expect to enter Atlanta easily and quickly. I could begin siege operations with mathematical and engineering precision that the rebels would be unable to resist. But with Grant, I anticipate nothing but defeat."

Marble said nothing in response. He did not want to appear to be wishing for a Union defeat, as he was a loyal citizen of the United States in his own way. At the same time, he knew that every Confederate victory made the election of McClellan more likely. McClellan's words suggested that he actually wanted Grant to be defeated and it was best not to encourage such talk. If a reporter sympathetic to the Republicans were to get wind of it, the results could prove damaging for the Democratic Party.

Besides, loathe him though he might, Marble was not so disdainful as to belittle Grant's obvious military gifts. The campaign to capture Vicksburg had been a work of genius and his victories around Chattanooga had been nearly as impressive. It was entirely possible that Grant would work his magic once again, defeat the rebel army under Johnston and bring about a major Union victory in the Western Theater. If he did, the complicated political situation which Marble had just explained to McClellan would have to be completely reshuffled.

McClellan was still talking. "Besides, the so-called victory at Mobile Bay and the successes against the rebel cavalry are of small import to the overall course of the war. Were it not for the fact that the Union is desperate for good news, they should not even merit a mention in the newspapers."

Marble smiled. McClellan was the greatest master of self-deception that the editor of the *New York World* had ever encountered. Such men were easily manipulated, which is why McClellan would make the perfect President of the United States as far as Marble was concerned.

"I agree with you that these recent successes of Union arms are only temporary and minor," Marble said. "With such foolish leaders at the head of our affairs, it is clear that the war cannot be brought to a successful conclusion."

"I hope to be the one to provide the leadership this country needs. And if the mistakes made by Lincoln, Stanton, Seward and all those other incompetent puppies in Washington have made it impossible to restore the Union as it was, then I shall endeavor to secure peace with honor and bring the bloodshed to an end."

"I am honored to be a part of the effort to secure the presidency for such a distinguished person as yourself, General McClellan," Marble said, using the most ingratiating tone he could muster. "Rest assured that your candidacy enjoys the full backing of the *New York World* and that the support of the newspaper shall continue after you have arrived in the White House."

"I do hope it shall be within my power to amply reward you for your generous support. Pray tell, assuming that we are victorious at the polls in November, are there any kindnesses within my power that I might extend to you?"

Marble's heartbeat quickened. A crucial step in his own road to power was about to be made. "Your generosity does great credit to your character, General McClellan. But as I said, I am but a humble citizen doing what I think is right for the good of the country."

"Of that I have no doubt," McClellan said, taking another sip of wine. "But I insist. Your support has been crucial to bringing me this far on the road to the White House. If I win, as I think I shall, I will owe you a great deal."

Marble pulled out the letter he had written during his rail journey to Chicago a week and a half before and, without a word, passed it over to McClellan. His face suddenly becoming apprehensive, McClellan took it and read through its contents. It took him a few minutes.

"A steep price, Mr. Marble." McClellan's tone was now much less friendly.

"A fair price, I should say."

"You want final say in who fills half of the federal offices in New York City?"

"Considering the benefit the support of the *New York World* shall give to your candidacy, not only in New York State but throughout the Union, it seems reasonable, I should think."

"Governor Seymour may disagree. He has already approached me about who should be promised certain offices."

"Do you think I would have put this question in writing without Governor Seymour's permission?"

McClellan grunted, then went on. "Which begs the question. Why do you need my answer in writing?"

"There are some influential figures who remain on the fence regarding the choice between you and Lincoln. If I can go back to New York City with your signature on that piece of paper, my credibility with them shall be much improved. Unless I have it, I will be seen as making promises on which I may not be able to deliver."

McClellan grunted again and was silent for several minutes. He stared at Marble as though he were attempting to see through him, but Marble knew that his own impassive expression was a suit of armor through which no man could see. Eventually, after nearly two full minutes of silence, McClellan picked up a pen from the table and calmly signed his name to the bottom of the paper. Without a word, he passed it back over to Marble. The editor took it with a smile, folded it up, and stuffed it in his jacket pocket.

"Oh, one other thing," Marble said.

"What now?" McClellan's voice was rapidly losing its previous serenity.

"I should like to have a say in who shall fill the position of official Printer of the United States."

"And who would you like in that post?"

Marble smiled. "Me," he said simply. "With a considerably increased salary, I should think. And an understanding that I shall continue as the editor of the *New York World* while holding the position, the main duties of which I shall turn over to a subordinate."

"Your steep price keeps getting steeper, Mr. Marble."

"Even the steepest price is worth paying for the biggest of prizes, General McClellan."

McClellan was silent again for a minute. Then, he slowly nodded.

*   *   *   *   *

September 9, Morning

The morning air was fresh and considerably cooler than had been the case of late. This made Grant very happy. He was about to ask his men to commence what would surely be a long and difficult march that would likely culminate in a very bloody and grueling battle. Such a physically demanding task would be much easier to accomplish in the autumn than it would have been during the brutal summer they had all just endured.

As Grant rode Cincinnati down the long column of infantry arrayed in marching order, in a large field set amidst enormous clusters of pine trees, the thousands of faces from regiment after regiment looked up at him with expectation in their eyes. They were all doubtless wondering where his orders would take them, and instinctively scanned his face for any conceivable clues as to their destination.

The men whose ranks he trotted past, trailed only by a single aide and a flag bearer, belonged to Schofield's Army of the Ohio, who would be leading the advance. Grant knew that calling the force an "army" was being generous in the extreme, as it consisted only of a single corps of infantry plus two cavalry divisions. Its total strength, following the reinforcements which Grant had allocated to it, was about twenty-five thousand men. But its small size made it more nimble than many other comparable forces, and that meant it was ideal for the mission he had in mind for it.

Reaching the front of the column, Grant found General Schofield mounted on a black charger, with a small gathering of staff officers around him.

"Good morning, General Schofield."

"Morning, sir."

"Fine day for a march, eh?"

"Indeed, sir."

Grant glanced over at Schofield's staff officers, a suspicious look on his face.

"Gentlemen," Schofield said simply, tossing his head to indicate that they were to withdraw a discreet distance. But Grant grunted a protest and waved a dismissive hand. The men remained where they were.

"You understand your orders?" Grant asked.

"I believe so, sir. I am to march the Army of the Ohio southwest along the north bank of the Chattahoochee River."

"Correct. The Army of the Tennessee will be right behind. You and General McPherson have exchanged liaison officers?"

"Of course, sir."

"Good."

Schofield cleared his throat. "The orders did not specify our destination, but considering the vast amounts of ammunition and supply wagons which have been allocated to my force, I can only assume that this march will be a long one." The words were dangled forth like bait from a fishing line.

"Yes, it will be, General Schofield."

"May I ask where we are going, sir?"

"Your initial destination is the town of Opelika, about ninety miles down the river."

"Opelika?"

"Just over the Alabama border. If we move swiftly, we should be able to reach it in about a week. The roads aren't too good, but there should be no significant rebels forces in the way. I marched through rougher country during the Vicksburg Campaign. From Opelika, it's just a fifty mile march to Montgomery, and then another thirty miles or so to Selma."

Grant said all this with complete composure, but the look of consternation on Schofield's face belied the momentous nature of his words. What Grant was saying meant nothing less than a complete transformation of the war in the Western Theater for the remainder of 1864.

"Montgomery? Selma?" Schofield asked, incredulous.

"That's right, Schofield," Grant said, unable to repress a slight grin. "Atlanta is no longer the goal of this campaign. We are shifting the focus of our efforts to Alabama and our new goal shall be the capture of the two cities of Montgomery and Selma. Both are critical logistical and transportation hubs and Montgomery in particular has immense political importance as the birthplace of the so-called Confederacy. If we can capture these two cities, we can inflict a devastating blow against the rebels."

"You say there are no rebel forces in the way? What about Richard Taylor and his army?" Taylor was the overall Confederate commander in Alabama and Mississippi.

"I wouldn't call it an army. Most of Taylor's men have long since been sent to reinforce Johnston at Atlanta. Besides, the victory achieved by Admiral Farragut at Mobile Bay has forced the enemy to divert most of Taylor's remaining troops to the city of Mobile itself, as they fear an amphibious operation down there. And before leaving Washington I dispatched orders to our commanders in Vicksburg and Memphis to launch new incursions into central and northern Mississippi, which shall hopefully divert some of Taylor's troops in that direction before they become aware of our new movement."

Schofield had a stunned look on his face. "I'm sorry, sir. My mind has been so unalterably fixed on the capture of Atlanta for so long that I find it difficult to contemplate such a change in strategy."

"Contemplate it or not, it is what we are going to do."

"What is to prevent Johnston and the Army of Tennessee from striking northwards toward Chattanooga?"

"Only the Army of the Ohio and the Army of the Tennessee are making this march. The Army of the Cumberland shall remain in its present position as both a blocking force and to pin down Johnston's men in and around Atlanta, preventing them from intervening in Alabama. In other words, sixty thousand men will march to Alabama, while about thirty-five or forty thousand remain at Vining's Station."

Grant grinned again as he saw Schofield's mind whirl. He could easily imagine what Schofield was thinking. The fall of Montgomery and Selma would represent an overwhelming victory for the Union cause and a dreadful defeat for the Confederacy, equivalent to the capture of New Orleans in 1862 or Vicksburg in 1863. Such an achievement would demonstrate to the Northern public that the victory was not only possible, but within their grasp. It would likely be enough to swing public opinion to such an extent that the Lincoln administration would be reelected. If that happened, the triumph for the Union cause was only a matter of time.

Schofield smiled and shook his head. "I am overwhelmed, sir."

"How's that?"

"I was preparing myself and my men for a knock-down, drag-out fight for Atlanta. I never imagined that I would be participating in such a dramatic military maneuver as the one we are now embarking upon. I must say that I am honored to be a part of it. If we succeed, it shall go down in the annals of military history as one of the most daring operations ever conceived."

Grant shrugged. "And if it fails, I shall go down in history as a blundering and perhaps drunken fool. But no sense worrying about that now. I am confident that we shall succeed."

"I pray so, sir."

Grant turned in the saddle and looked back down the row of infantry in marching columns. He again saw the expectation in their eyes and could sense the anticipation they felt. "Do you think your men are ready?"

"I believe so, sir. I know I am, at any rate."

"Let's march, then."

Schofield turned and nodded to a staff officer, who saluted and trotted over to the commander of the nearest brigade. A series of shouted orders followed. Within a few minutes, the cry began to go up, starting with the lead regiment.

"45th Ohio! Forward! March!"

Drums rolled. A fife band began playing as the men stepped off. Grant walked his horse over to the men and proceeded to move at a steady pace beside them. One after the other, the regiments of Schofield's army received the order to march and the long column of men began their trek. Within an hour, the Army of the Tennessee would begin following behind. The red clay soil of Georgia was gradually chewed into a thick paste by the passing feet of sixty thousand Union soldiers marching to the southwest, away from Atlanta.

*　　　　*　　　　*　　　　*　　　　*

September 11, Noon

"Well, gentlemen," Lincoln began. "I have here a telegram I think you would both be interested in seeing." He pushed it over the table to Seward and Stanton.

Mr. President,

I wish to inform you that the Army of the Ohio and the Army of the Tennessee have commenced an offensive operation against the rebel forces in the Western Theater. There is no particular reason for you to know the specific details of this operation, but rest assured I shall keep you updated as necessary regarding our progress.

General Grant

Stanton grunted as he finished reading. "Are you not bothered by his refusal to disclose more information about this offensive?"

Lincoln shook his head. "What good would it do me to know the details of his plan? I make no pretensions to understanding the minutiae of military operations. Three month's service as a captain in

- 514 -

the Illinois militia during the Black Hawk War, during which I never heard a bullet fired in anger, hardly qualifies me to comment intelligently on military affairs."

"McClellan spoke to you many times in a similar manner during his tenure in command of the Army of the Potomac," Stanton reminded Lincoln. "It always was a prelude to an infuriating lack of activity."

"Yes," Lincoln replied. "But there is a big difference between Grant and McClellan. Grant fights. McClellan doesn't."

"That's true, by God," Seward interjected.

"No one is happier to hear criticisms of George McClellan than myself," Stanton said, a hint of ruthlessness seeping into his voice. "I will never forget how that arrogant blow-hard would keep me waiting in his headquarters, as though I worked for him rather than the other way around. But that's beside the point. I would be more comfortable about whatever operation Grant has launched if we had specific details concerning it."

"I trust Grant," Lincoln said. "When I appointed him general-in-chief of the Union armies, I told him that I neither knew nor sought to know the specific details of his operations. His record of victories spoke for itself. I do not see how our exact knowledge of his plans would benefit the Union cause in any way. It should suffice that we know he has begun a forward movement and that he hopes to achieve a significant victory over the rebels."

"I agree," Seward said. "By removing from ourselves the responsibility of managing tactical military movements, we can focus on matters of more importance. In particular, how Grant's offensive relates to political matters."

"Ah, yes," Lincoln said. "It is politics which I wish to discuss with you two gentlemen today."

"Indeed," Seward said, preempting Stanton by a moment. "I wish I could bring you better news from my state, Mr. President, but every letter I receive from home tells me that New York remains all but certain to fall into the Democratic column this year."

"I won't write off New York until Election Day itself," Lincoln said. "But our hopes of victory seem to lie with the states of Ohio, Indiana, and Pennsylvania. I can only trust that my own state of Illinois will remain true to the cause."

"What I hear from those three states gives me cause for some hope," Seward said. "Our people continue to trumpet the victory achieved by Farragut at Mobile Bay and the destruction of rebel cavalry in Georgia and Tennessee. They also stoke the hopes for a more decisive victory now that General Grant has returned to the Western Theater of operations."

Lincoln nodded sharply. "I am increasingly persuaded that the fate of many states has already been set. New England will favor us on November 8, save perhaps for Connecticut, while New York and some other states will fall into McClellan's camp. What the voters of Ohio, Indiana, and Pennsylvania shall decide on Election Day shall be determined by the operations of General Grant over the next few weeks. If he succeeds in inflicting a major defeat on the rebels, we shall win. If he fails, we shall lose. It's as simple as that."

Stanton shook his head. "I would not count even on New England. Too many of the abolitionists seem willing to cast their votes for that fool Fremont and his so-called Radicals. They'd succeed in demonstrating their commitment to abolitionism at the price of helping elect a ticket which is determined to leave the slaves in chains. The idiocy of the whole thing astounds me. If Fremont gains even five to ten percent of the vote in states like Rhode Island or Connecticut, it might be sufficient to push those states into the Democratic column."

There was a momentary silence, broken when Lincoln chuckled slightly.

"Mr. President?" Seward asked.

"Gentlemen, the situation in which we find ourselves reminds me of a friend I had once in Springfield. He was a local horse breeder and he often entered some of his better horses in the local races, where they usually did quite well. One day, he came into my office in a state of demoralization. I asked him what was the matter, and he told me that in the midst of a race one of his horses had collapsed, throwing the jockey to the ground in a nasty tumble. The locals all blamed my friend, calling him an incompetent buffoon, a disgrace, and every other insult their minds could devise. The next month, however, one of my friend's horses won by a margin never before seen in Sangamon County. The same folks who had derided my friend the previous month now called him a genius, the greatest horse breeder of all time, and every other compliment their minds could devise. So you see, gentlemen, the feelings of the people are often quite fickle."

Seward smiled broadly, but Stanton simply looked annoyed. "Mr. President, as much as I enjoy your little stories, there is a matter of some importance which I wish to bring to the attention of yourself and Mr. Seward."

"By all means, Mr. Stanton."

"About four days ago, some of our troops near Gordonsville, Virginia, took into custody a man trying to cross into rebel-held territory. His behavior immediately raised suspicions that he was a spy of some kind, so I ordered an investigation conducted. It was quickly established that the man was Alexander Humphries and that he has been working for some time as an agent of the rebel government."

"I see," Lincoln said, trying to keep the impatience out of his voice. The capture of Southern agents engaged in espionage was not uncommon.

"I ordered Humphries to be hanged as a spy. Unsurprisingly, upon being told of his sentence, he protested his fate. According to the report of the district commander, he claimed that he had important information which would be of interest to the government and offered to provide it if his life were spared. I thought this was intriguing enough to warrant a closer look, so I took the train down to Fredericksburg two days ago."

"And?" Seward asked.

"This Humphries fellow had an interesting tale to tell, to say the least. He claims to have received a substantial sum of money from Judah Benjamin, the Jew who serves as chief advisor to Davis. Humphries was told to journey to the North and use the money in such a way as to contribute to the victory of the Democrats in the fall election. He shipped out of Wilmington on a blockade runner a few months ago, went first to Bermuda and then sailed to New York City. Since then, he has been travelling across the country, seeking ways to use the funds provided to him to impact the election."

"So, you're saying that the Democratic election campaign is receiving direct financial assistance from the rebel government?" Seward asked.

"Apparently so."

Lincoln rubbed his chin. "How much money are we talking about here?"

"A hundred thousand dollars, at least."

"And to whom was this money distributed?"

"To a dozen or so Democratic operatives and editors. But chief among them was Manton Marble, the editor of the *New York World*. Humphries said that he gave him no less than twenty-five thousand dollars."

"Dear God," Seward said. "We should have that bastard arrested at once!"

Lincoln grinned, his mind turning over the possibilities. "Is there any way that Mr. Marble would know that this Humphries fellow has been arrested?"

"I doubt it, Mr. President," Stanton answered. "I am not sure if Marble is even aware that the money came directly from the rebels."

"We should still arrest him," Seward said. "We have cause, and arresting him would certainly remove what has been a large thorn in our side. Marble's editorials are quite damaging to us."

"We should not be rash," Lincoln said, rubbing his chin. "If we are clever, we can make more hay out of this than simply having Marble thrown in jail. This is valuable information, gentlemen. We can surely find a way to use it to our advantage."

"How to do it?" Seward asked.

"Mr. Stanton, please forward a copy of the report your people have no doubt prepared on this incident to Mr. Raymond in New York City. I am sure that the *New York Times* and other newspapers friendly to the Republican cause will very much like to know about Mr. Humphries and his activities, specifically as they relate to Mr. Marble."

"With pleasure, Mr. President."

"Once we find out how the people feel about this, we can decide how to deal with Mr. Marble."

Seward shook his head. "Marble had to know, or at least suspect, where that money came from. He may be a bastard, but he's not stupid. I imagine the same is true for every other Democrat who took money from Humphries' hand."

Lincoln looked back at Stanton. "Bring this Humphries fellow to Washington. See how willing he is to give full details of how much money he distributed and, most importantly, to whom. If you think it worthwhile, you may drop the hint that a full presidential pardon might be in order if he cooperates with us. And remind him that the alternative is the noose."

Stanton nodded sharply, as if impatient to run off and issue the orders.

Lincoln smiled broadly. "Let's put this pot on the fire, gentlemen, and see what kind of stew emerges. With Grant on the move, and this new scandal about to blow up in the faces of our opponents, we may yet emerge triumphant."

*   *   *   *   *

September 12, Morning

Davis stared hard as the officer sent over from the War Department updated the colored pins on the map. His lips pursed tightly and he could feel his heartbeat increasing.

"Tallapoosa?" he said, turning to Seddon. "Union cavalry are reported to be in Tallapoosa?"

"It's unconfirmed, Mr. President," Seddon said unhelpfully. "General Taylor was told of it and he thought it sufficiently important for it to be brought to your attention."

"That town is over a hundred miles from where Grant is reported to be."

"If the report is accurate, it could signify a large-scale cavalry raid, designed to clear the region southwest of their railroad supply lines of our forces."

"Or a major offensive in that direction."

"It's impossible to know for sure, sir."

Davis grunted, looking intently at the map. From the moment that Johnston withdrew across the Chattahoochee River two months before, Davis had feared receiving a report like this. While the river provided a geographical shield that protected Atlanta from the Yankees, it also prevented Johnston's army from interfering with the

Northern forces should they attempt to head west and southwest into Alabama.

"Has General Johnston said anything to you about this?" Davis demanded.

"Nothing at all, sir."

Davis nodded, sitting down in his chair even as he continued to stare at the map. Johnston had always been uncommunicative.

"Please send a telegram to Johnston immediately, asking him if he knows anything about an enemy cavalry movement to the west."

"Certainly, sir."

The door opened and Judah Benjamin entered. "Begging the pardon of you gentlemen. I apologize for being late."

"Not at all, Mr. Secretary," Davis said, waving to the seat across the desk. At the same time, Seddon motioned for the staff officer to depart. As the door closed, Davis was staring across the desk at his two closest advisors. He could not keep himself from glancing over at the map, however, and quickly filled in Benjamin on the reported Yankee cavalry movement.

"Have you any news from the North?" Davis asked.

"Nothing unexpected," Benjamin answered. "Now that the Democrats have finally settled on their ticket, the traditional phase of the election campaign has begun. Rallies, speeches, canvassing for votes in every town and city from Kansas to Maine, and out on the Pacific coast as well. It's shaping up exactly as we expected, with New England remaining mostly solid for the Republicans, New York emerging as a Democratic stronghold, and the major prizes being Pennsylvania, Ohio, Indiana, and Illinois."

"Let me ask you this, Mr. Benjamin," Davis said. "Suppose that Grant wins a major victory at some point in the next month. What impact would this have on the outcome of the election?"

"A major one, obviously. It depends on the precise nature of the victory. If Grant simply wins a tactical success over Johnston, something along the lines of Shiloh, it might not make too great a difference. But if he succeeds in capturing Atlanta, or some other prize of similar importance, it would certainly shift the balance decisively back in favor of Lincoln."

Davis grunted.

Benjamin went on. "Furthermore, even if the Union armies do not achieve sufficient success over the next two months to allow Lincoln to win the election, they might achieve victories large enough to persuade McClellan to repudiate the peace plank of the Democratic Party and, upon his taking office, continue the war until victory is won."

"I had not considered that," Seddon said. This didn't surprise Davis, who had little respect for Seddon's political instincts.

"I have considered it, many times and at length," Davis said. "McClellan is a political weather vane. He will turn in whatever direction public opinion blows him. Any significant setback might be sufficient to persuade McClellan to abandon the peace plan, and he could persuade enough of the Democratic Party to go along with him that it would scarcely matter whether we enter 1865 with Lincoln or McClellan in the White House."

Davis removed his spectacles and rubbed his temples, feeling as though his head were about to explode. He glanced up at the map again, worried over the blue pin at Tallapoosa. There were no red pins between it and the vital Confederate cities of Selma and Montgomery. When he put his spectacles back on, he thrust an angry finger in Seddon's direction.

"When you send that telegram to Johnston, don't just ask him if he knows about a Yankee movement to the west. Order him to find out what Grant is up to and to do it immediately. Make sure the communication is framed as an explicit order. Not a request or suggestion, but an unambiguous and unmistakable order."

"Of course, Mr. President."

"Johnston usually doesn't respond well to such communications," Benjamin pointed out.

"Johnston can go to the devil for all I care," Davis said. "I am the President and he is one of my generals. If he refuses to obey orders, I shall not hesitate to remove him from command. I could order General Hardee to take command. It's also my understanding that General Longstreet has recovered from his wounds, so he might be an acceptable replacement as well."

"Considering the victory he obtained at Peachtree Creek two months ago, public opinion might object to Johnston being removed from command," Benjamin said.

"When a man is right, he should care nothing for public opinion. Unlike Lincoln, I do not have to worry about being reelected."

*　　　　*　　　　*　　　　*　　　　*

September 12, Afternoon

"Telegram from the War Department, sir." Mackall's voice was apologetic.

Johnston scoffed disdainfully as he unfolded the piece of paper.

General Johnston,
General Taylor informs the War Department of the presence of enemy cavalry in the vicinity of Tallapoosa near the Georgia-Alabama border. The enemy force is estimated to be at least of brigade strength. You are ordered to scout in this direction with your own cavalry and determine whether or not this represents a major

movement on the part of the enemy. Please obey these orders immediately and notify the War Department of the results.
    Secretary of War Seddon

"Has General Jackson said anything about this?" Johnston asked.

"Nothing, sir."

Johnston thought for a moment. He recalled General Cheatham's concerns at the last meeting of the high command that Grant might move southwest toward Alabama rather than attempt to cross the Chattahoochee River and move against Atlanta. Was it possible that this movement of enemy cavalry was the beginning of such an offensive? Or was it a minor raid of no particular significance?

"General Jackson dispatched a brigade to the north bank of the Chattahoochee downriver, yes?"

Mackall thought for a moment. "That was decided at the meeting on September 6. I wrote the orders out the following morning, directing that the brigade be positioned near the town of Campbellton. I have no reason to believe they were not carried out. General Jackson is a competent officer, if I may say so."

"More so than General Wheeler ever was," Johnston replied. Mackall looked at him with some surprise and Johnston immediately felt guilty for what he had said. It was best not to speak ill of the dead. Whatever he faults, Wheeler had at least been a brave man.

Johnston stared down at the map. For the thousandth time, his eyes swept out the immense region between the Union encampment and the vital industrial and population centers of central Alabama. The distance was immense, but the fact that the area between them was practically devoid of Confederate troops was disquieting.

If Grant was undertaking an operation to capture Montgomery and Selma, Johnston would be forced to go to their defense. The obvious counter would be to shift his own forces from Atlanta to Montgomery using the railroad which linked the two cities, as his troops could move by train far faster than the Union troops could move by marching. However, this would require him to know the precise nature of Grant's movement, so that he could issue the orders for his forces to move to Alabama in time for them to arrive.

If Grant were somehow able to steal a march on him, as he had done to Pemberton during the Vicksburg Campaign and to Lee in the early stages of the Petersburg Campaign, Union forces could be halfway to Montgomery before Johnston had time to react. If that happened, then even the fastest rail movement in military history might prove insufficient as it would have begun too late.

"Send a message to General Jackson," Johnston said. "Ask him to send a reconnaissance force northward from Campbellton to scout out the area between Smyrna and Tallapoosa if at all possible. A regiment should suffice."

"Very well, sir."

There was something in Mackall's tone that caught Johnston's attention. "You disagree, William?"

"Not at all, sir. It is just that the communication from Richmond expressly orders us to conduct such a reconnaissance. We are merely inquiring of Jackson whether or not it is possible."

"True, but despite what Richmond may want, the operations of the Army of Tennessee shall be dictated by reality. I shall follow the order to the best of my ability, but in the end, we can only do what is possible. If I received an order from President Davis to launch an attack on New York City tomorrow afternoon, would the people criticize me for not attempting to follow it?"

Mackall laughed. "Considering the intelligence of the man we are forced to acknowledge as our president, I should not be all that surprised if we received such an order from Richmond. I do hope that our next President at least has some substance inside his head."

"Odd that you should mention that." Johnston paused a moment before continuing. "When I attended the banquet in Atlanta a few weeks ago, Senator Wigfall and others suggested that I run for president when Davis' term is up in 1867."

"Really?" Mackall asked, his eyebrows shooting up and his voice slightly excited. "What did you tell them?"

"That I had absolutely no interest in politics and that such talk was silly."

Mackall thought for a moment. "Well, if you ever do turn your mind toward political office after the war is over, rest assured that you would have my full support."

Johnston shook his head. "I am but a simple soldier."

"Best not to let such talk get too much attention," Mackall suggested. "If word reaches Davis that people are beginning to speak of you as his potential successor, it will increase his distrust of you even further."

Johnston shrugged. "The Confederate Constitution gives the President only a single six-year term. Davis is out after the 1867 election no matter what happens."

"True, but I highly doubt that he would want you to be his successor."

Johnston threw his head back and laughed. He was about to make a humorous response when a staff officer entered the room and handed Johnston two messages. He immediately began reading the first one.

General Johnston,
I commend to you the bearer of this letter, Mr. John Maxwell,
who brings with him an ingenious torpedo device. Using a clock

mechanism that he has devised, the device can be set to explode after an interval of twenty minutes has elapsed. He has already used the device in a successful operation against the Union supply base at City Point in Virginia, where he destroyed a large vessel bearing a great quantity of artillery and small arms ammunition.

As security has been increased at City Point due to his actions, he inquired whether his services might be useful in the Western Theater. Hence, my letter of introduction.

> *Colonel Josiah Gorgas*
> *Chief of Ordnance*

"Where is this man?" Johnston inquired of the messenger.

"I believe the name of the hotel where he is staying is written on the back of the letter, sir."

He flipped it over and saw the address. Johnston frowned. The idea of using time bombs to attack the enemy covertly seemed dishonorable to him. The danger to innocents would also be extreme. He decided not to bother with the matter and dropped the letter on the table. One of his staff officers would file it away presently, he was sure.

He opened the second message and began reading. As he did so, his face went white.

"What is it?" Mackall asked.

"It's from General Jackson," Johnston said with alarm. "He says that the brigade he has posted in Campbellton is under attack by a strong force of enemy cavalry."

Mackall tensed. "How strong a force?"

Johnston's eyes darted as he read through the entire message. "It doesn't say, but we can only assume one of superior strength. Not only that, but Jackson says that some of his scouts observing the fords over the Chattahoochee report seeing enemy infantry marching southwest along the north bank of the river and that another force of Union horsemen have occupied the town of Riverton."

"My God," Mackall said, somewhat breathlessly. He quickly fluttered through a pile of maps on the table before him, found what he was looking for, and did some quick calculations. "Riverton is several miles farther downriver than Campbellton," he observed.

"The enemy force which has occupied the town must have circled around our troops at Campbellton, then."

"What does this mean? Enemy cavalry at Tallapoosa, a hundred miles to the west? A combined Union force of infantry and cavalry moving down the Chattahoochee River?"

"Grant could conceivably be preparing to cross the Chattahoochee River at Campbellton or Riverton, or perhaps both, in order to approach Atlanta from the west."

"That approach would make it difficult for him to keep his forces supplied. It's much farther from the railroad head at Vining's Station than the crossing points to the north."

"Yes, but crossing to the south and approaching from the west would allow him to avoid the obstacle of Peachtree Creek."

"True."

"But perhaps Cheatham was correct. Perhaps Grant has given up on the idea of capturing Atlanta and is attempting to shift his main effort to Alabama." Johnston stared intently at the maps, wishing that they could simply whisper to him the answer to the riddle.

"Maybe," Mackall said. "We have no solid information on the strength of the enemy infantry to which Jackson refers."

"No," Johnston said indignantly. "And without sufficient cavalry, there is really no way for us to find out." He clenched his teeth in bitterness, silently cursing Davis and Wheeler for their stupidity.

For the next twenty minutes, Johnston and Mackall pored over their maps, reread reports which estimated the size and strength of the Union cavalry force, and dispatched riders to all senior commanders asking for any information which they might be able to provide.

"William, issue orders for Cheatham's corps to march to Campbellton at once. Prepare plans to have Stewart and Hardee move to the region as well, if that becomes necessary. If Grant is intending to cross the river there, I want our troops to be in position to contest the crossing. Cheatham can hold Grant off long enough for the other two corps to arrive, perhaps allowing us to concentrate our entire force and defeat Grant in detail."

"You are willing to leave Atlanta undefended?"

"No. If it does prove necessary for Stewart and Hardee to go to Campbellton, I want one division left behind in the city as a precaution, along with the Georgia militia."

"Very well. Which division?"

Johnston thought for just a moment. "Cleburne," he said simply.

Mackall's eyebrows went up, but he said nothing. Johnston knew it was a decision likely to cause comment, as it would mean going into battle without his finest division commander. But protecting Atlanta would be a serious responsibility and Johnston trusted Cleburne more than he trusted the commanders of any of his other divisions. It also was a sound idea to keep Cleburne and Walker as far apart as possible.

Another messenger arrived and Mackall read the note. The color left his face, and he glanced up at Johnston with an expression that told the commanding general he was about to receive very bad news.

"Tell me," Johnston said.

"I am sorry, sir, but it appears that the brigade Jackson stationed at Campbellton has been destroyed. He reports that most of the men appear to have been taken prisoner, although some managed to regain the south bank of the Chattahoochee."

Johnston's eyes widened in shock. When the day had begun, Johnston had already been so short of cavalry that every horseman had been precious. If the brigade at Campbellton had been destroyed, it made an already difficult situation nothing short of disastrous.

"If the force which Grant has sent southwest along the river is strong enough to defeat a brigade of cavalry so quickly, it can only be the advance guard of a very large force of infantry."

"They could either be trying to cross at Campbellton or they could be headed downriver toward Alabama."

Johnston shook his head sharply. "We have to assume that they're trying to cross the river. Add Stewart's corps to the movement toward Campbellton, tell Hardee to get all of his boys ready to move as well, and inform Hardee that Cleburne will remain behind to ensure that Atlanta remains garrisoned."

"Of course, sir." Mackall immediately took up pen and ink and began writing out the orders.

As his chief-of-staff labored quickly, Johnston stared down at the map. His fingers brushed over the small town of Palmetto, about twenty-five miles southwest of Atlanta. It was a fairly nondescript place, but it sat on the Atlanta & West Point Railroad, which linked Atlanta with Montgomery. Just a few miles south of Campbellton, it would make a useful gathering place for the divisions of Cheatham and Stewart if it became necessary to send them to Alabama by train.

"William, I want sufficient rolling stock dispatched to Palmetto to provide for the quick transportation of Cheatham's and Stewart's troops if it becomes necessary."

Mackall looked at the map, saw immediately what his commander was thinking, and nodded quickly before going back to writing. As the sun began disappearing over the western horizon, the headquarters of the Army of Tennessee became alive with activity. Staff officers bent over maps with rulers, calculating distances and marching times. A steady stream of orders flowed from Mackall's pen, quickly being handed to messengers who dashed off on horseback.

Leaving nothing to chance, Mackall ordered a copy made of each order and had these duplicates separately delivered by a different rider in case some accident befell the first. Johnston approved of this. Having been an obsessive student of military history since his days at West Point, he knew better than most how simple miscommunications could derail even the best plans. He had discovered the truth of this to his cost at the Battle of Seven Pines two years before, when his carefully planned attack on the Army of the

Potomac had gone awry simply because his commanders had not understood their orders.

The memory made Johnston tense. Clearly, Grant's big move had begun. If he kept his wits about him, as he had done leading up to Peachtree Creek, he could achieve a great victory and perhaps win the war for the Confederacy. But if he failed, as he had at Seven Pines, his name might go down in history as the man who brought defeat upon the South.

Chapter Fourteen

September 13, Noon

The sound of thousands of marching men was something that couldn't really be imagined by a person who hadn't heard it. To Grant, sitting astride Cincinnati with a cigar stuffed between his teeth, it sounded as though a giant from some tale of Greek mythology was chewing up a mountain he had eaten for dinner. The sight was astonishing to behold, too. Sixty thousand blue-coated warriors, a gathering of humanity larger than any but a handful of cities in North America, were moving steadily southwest in vast columns running parallel to one another. As Grant looked across the countless regiments that filled his field of vision, he was reminded of the waves of the ocean.

"Three cheers for General Grant!" a man of the 15th Michigan Infantry shouted as they marched past. The men responded with three hearty cheers. Grant didn't smile, but doffed his hat to show his appreciation. He never sought the adulation of his troops, for his naturally shy nature made him feel distinctly uncomfortable when faced with such displays. Whatever else he was, Ulysses Grant was not George McClellan.

Nevertheless, it was good to know that his men had confidence in him. On his orders, they had cast themselves loose from their supply lines and were now moving through enemy territory without so much as a clue as to their final destination. Yet they did so without a murmur of complaint. Of all the men in the army, only Grant himself knew where they were going. In order to pull the wool over the eyes of the enemy, it had been necessary for him to pull the wool over the eyes of his own men.

Things were going well. Since setting our four days before, the Army of the Ohio and the Army of the Tennessee had covered about sixty miles, which was not bad considering the difficulty the wagon trains were having. The Confederate cavalry brigade stationed across from the small town of Campbellton had been dispersed and there still seemed to be no effective opposition in his way.

Grant turned at the sound of a troop of horsemen approaching and recognized General McPherson. A moment later, the commander of the Army of the Tennessee was reining in beside him.

"How's it going, James?"

"Well enough, sir. No good roads around these parts, though. My boys are taking it all in stride, but the wagon trains are having it mighty rough."

Grant merely grunted.

"I have my engineers hard at work constructing corduroy roads, which should speed the advance."

Grant almost told him that there was no need for him to do so, but decided against it. Instead, he merely nodded. It was not yet time for him to bring his three army commanders into his confidence. Until then, Grant wanted every soldier serving with the Union forces, from generals down to privates, to think they were on their way to Alabama. For if they thought they were moving toward Montgomery, they would obviously continue to act as though they were moving toward Montgomery. One way or another, this information would get back to General Johnston. So long as Grant's plan was contained within the confines of his own mind, it would remain unknown to everyone else, most importantly his opponent across the river.

"Have you dispatched scouts to the south side of the river?"

"No, sir," McPherson answered. "From my reading of your orders, I did not believe that you wished me to do so."

"I do now," Grant said. "But not in large formations. Dispatch picked squadrons with instructions to detect any movements of large enemy infantry units and report back immediately. They should endeavor to avoid direct contact with the enemy and do nothing which might attract attention."

"Very well, sir."

Grant nodded. He was attempting to dupe Johnston, but he had to know whether or not the trick was working. The thought suddenly made him tense, and he found that he distrusted himself. Johnston was far from a fool. At the war's opening, the Southern general had won the First Battle of Bull Run by anticipating and then outwitting his Union opponents. He had also constantly thwarted Sherman's flanking maneuvers during the Union advance on Atlanta. Grant found himself wondering if Johnston might successfully get into his head and deduce his plan.

Grant shook the thought from his mind, angry at himself. He recalled a skirmish in Missouri against some rebel guerrilla leader nearly three years before when he had been a low-ranking officer. It had been his first taste of combat since the Mexican War and he remembered how frightened he had been. But upon discovering that the rebel guerrillas had fled in haste at the approach of his own troops, Grant learned a lesson which he had tried to burn into his mind. The enemy was as much afraid of him as he was of them.

It had been this simple confidence that had allowed Grant to go toe-to-toe against Robert E. Lee earlier in the year in the nightmarish fighting of the Wilderness, Spotsylvania, Cold Harbor, and Petersburg. It had not been easy. At the end of the first day's fighting at the Battle of the Wilderness, during which Lee had outwitted and outfought him, Grant had been reduced to sobbing on his cot in his tent. But Grant had quickly recovered, just as he had after the disastrous first day of the Battle of Shiloh, and came out swinging the following day.

Some might call Grant a military genius, but he didn't see himself as one. As far as he was concerned, so long as one was smart enough to get his troops onto the battlefield and give them a bit of faith in themselves, victory would go to whichever commander kept his wits about him.

It was impossible to know exactly what the coming days had in store, but one thing was certain. Sooner or later, the men under his command were going to fight a bloody battle, which might well determine the outcome of the war. As he gazed over the sixty thousand men he was leading to the southwest, and as he thought of the forty thousand men of the Army of the Cumberland still encamped across the river from Atlanta, he knew that a great many of them would not be going home.

It was the brutal truth. But if he had anything to do with it, the deaths of so many of his men would not be for nothing. Grant would bend every sinew of his strength to make sure, no matter how many of his men might fall under Southern bullets and blades, that the Union would be restored and that the sin of slavery would be eradicated from America.

*   *   *   *   *

McFadden blinked rapidly, trying to cleanse his eyes of the dust kicked up by the tramping feet of the forward regiment. He was used to hard marches and never complained, but this made the treks no less unpleasant. Having started just before dawn, he had already been marching for more than four hours and his legs ached painfully. For a moment, he found himself thinking that if he ever made it back to Texas, he would forever refuse to walk more than a quarter mile on any given day.

He marched in the ranks of the 15th Illinois, the regiment to which he had been assigned. Ahead of them were several brigades and following behind were two limbered artillery batteries. Cavalry units and generals with mounted escorts regularly trotted by on either side of the column, filling the air with ever more dust. Angry officers continually shouted orders. It seemed that the whole Army of the

Tennessee was on the move, travelling southwest down the north bank of the Chattahoochee River. He had heard chatter among the men that some scattered fighting had taken place at the point of the advance, but it did not seem that any major battle was yet happening. McFadden didn't think any large Confederate units were nearby.

It had taken him a few days to get over the strangeness of serving with a regiment of Yankees. They were, after all, the very men had had spent the last two-and-a-half years doing his best to kill. Upon arriving in the regiment's camp, he had kept to himself and tried to avoid conversation. After the first few attempts to approach him had been rebuffed, most of the Northern soldiers had decided that he simply wanted to be left alone and paid him no more mind.

Living in the Union camp was certainly different. The coffee was wonderful, but McFadden had expected that. What had taken him by surprise was the sheer abundance and variety of the food. McFadden and other Confederate soldiers had been told that Forrest and Wheeler had torn the Union supply lines to pieces, but his eyes now told him a different story. There was plenty of bacon, fresh bread, a seemingly endless quantity of sugar and molasses, fresh fruit and vegetables, and even luxuries such as cakes and ice cream.

The sight of so much plenty in the Union camp had filled McFadden with dread. If the Union had the logistical ability to feed its soldiers so well and so easily, how could the Confederacy hope to win the war?

He set these thoughts aside and tried to focus on why he was in the Union camp in the first place. From what he had learned before setting out from the Confederate camp, the 118th Ohio was not in the Army of the Tennessee, but rather in the Army of the Ohio. Therefore, McFadden was in the wrong army. He didn't blame himself for this, for he could not have known which Federal unit he would first encounter when he crossed the river. It had just been bad luck.

He had gathered from listening to the chatter of the men around him that the Army of the Ohio was marching ahead of the Army of the Tennessee. He realized that he would have to desert from the ranks of the 15th Illinois very soon, perhaps that very night, if he wanted to make his way forward in order to find his quarry. If he was lucky, the men would assume that he had changed his mind and decided to return to what they thought was his former regiment in Virginia. But in any event, looking for a single deserter would probably not be a priority for a regiment about to go into battle.

There was a sudden rustling among the men. The mounted commander riding at the head of the regiment turned in his saddle to look behind him. His face lit up and he quickly removed and waved his hat.

"Three cheers for General Grant!" he called.

McFadden turned and saw the Union general, riding just ahead of a swarm of mounted staff officers. It was the first time McFadden had laid eyes on the commander of a Union army. The Illinois soldiers gave three hearty cheers, waving their hands energetically. Grant's face did not change, but he politely touched his hat as he rode past. McFadden was struck by his unpretentious appearance, for the supreme Union commander wore the uniform of an ordinary private. In that regard, he reminded McFadden of General Cleburne.

"Impressive, isn't he?" the man marching beside McFadden said.

He turned. "I'm sorry?"

"General Grant. He's an impressive fellow, wouldn't you say?"

McFadden shrugged. "I suppose so."

"Archie O'Connor," the man said, extending his hand.

For a moment, McFadden's mind became careless and he was about to speak his actual name. He caught himself. "Sam Stephens," he finally replied.

"You're the new one, right? They say that you escaped from Andersonville."

"That's right."

"What was it like down there?"

"I'd really rather not talk about it," McFadden said, trying to sound stern without being rude.

"Okay, okay," O'Connor replied. "A man's got a right to privacy. But I do think Grant's an impressive fellow. Don't you agree?"

"I suppose so," McFadden repeated.

"Everywhere he goes, he wins. Fort Donelson, Shiloh, Vicksburg, Chattanooga. All those battles against Lee. Now that that crazy loon Billy Sherman is gone, we can have a right decent fight against the rebels. And once we've beaten them, Old Abe will be reelected and everything will be just as it's supposed to be. Don't you think?"

"We'll see, I guess."

"And when the war's over, I'll go home, marry my sweetheart, and settle down to life on the farm. Had to join the army, you know. When the war started, I mean. Not like a man can sit out the fight. Not when the country is at stake. Got to preserve the Union and free the slaves, you know. Everybody's got to do his part, you know what I mean? Anyone who tries to sit the fight out is a coward. A damn rascal, if you ask me."

"You have a sweetheart back home?" McFadden asked. He immediately wondered why he had bothered asking.

O'Connor smiled. "Alice is her name. Grew up not more than a mile away from her family's farm. God, she's pretty. Can't wait to see her again. The day I enlisted, I asked her to marry me. She said yes. Since then, she's written me a letter every week, without fail. I try to write back just as often, but it's not easy. What with the marches and battles and all that."

McFadden thought about Annie. By now, she had probably received his letter. He wondered how she had reacted. McFadden supposed that she would have nothing further to do with him, even if he somehow made it back to Confederate lines alive. After all, he had deserted his post for a personal vendetta, trying to satisfy the dark and angry forces within his soul, the very forces he had hoped Annie would banish. In short, he had rejected the gift of a new life with Annie in order to seek out and kill a fellow human being. How could she respect him after he had done such a thing?

For the thousandth time, he told himself that it did not matter and that such thoughts were useless. Whether it had been the right thing to do or not, he had committed himself the moment he had left his regiment and crossed the river. He could not abandon his quest for vengeance now. The only way he could even hope to have a future was to find Cheeky Joe, send him to the grave, and then somehow escape back to Confederate lines. Not being able to deceive himself, he knew that the chances of success were fairly small. More than likely, he was going to end up dead.

*   *   *   *   *

September 14, Afternoon

Having left behind the tiny hamlet of Campbellton a few minutes before, Johnston walked his horse slowly toward the south bank of the Chattahoochee River. Behind him, keeping a respectful distance from their chief, were Hardee, Cheatham, Stewart and Jackson. All around them milled thousands of Confederate infantrymen, some getting fires going to cook their food and brew their coffee. Many pointed to the collection of generals and talked excitedly as they passed by.

A few minutes later, the five men reached the banks of the river and pulled their horses to a stop. Along the bank were Confederate pickets, mostly sitting quietly and gazing across the river. Without dismounting, Johnston removed his field telescope from his saddlebag and raised it to his right eye. Scanning the northern bank of the river, he saw blue-coated pickets keeping vigil in much the same way as his own men. Beyond them, he saw the white tents of what looked like a full infantry brigade. Altogether, he estimated that within his field of sight there were perhaps a thousand men.

He spotted a Union officer staring back at him with a telescope of his own. It was too far to make out what rank the man held, but he appeared to carry himself with a self-assured air. He waved when he saw Johnston looking at him. Seeing no reason to be impolite, Johnston waved back.

"A brigade?" Stewart asked, scanning the area with his own telescope.

"At least," Johnston answered. "But there's no telling how many other Yankee troops may be in the area."

"Well, they can't cross the river here," Cheatham said emphatically. "We have two entire infantry corps, plus half of a third, either here in Campbellton or within a few hours' march of it. That's upwards of fifty thousand men. If the Yankees tried to cross, the river would run red with their blood."

Johnston nodded. "A fact Grant no doubt knows perfectly well."

"The main force is already several miles down the river," Jackson said. "This, near as my boys can tell, is just the brigade bringing up the rear. The tail of their army, if you will."

Johnston let out a deep breath. "It's quite clear, gentlemen. Grant does not intend to cross the river. Not here, at any rate. If he intended to cross the Chattahoochee and attack Atlanta from the west, this would be the most distant ford from which to do so."

"What is Grant doing, then?" Hardee asked.

Johnston snapped shut his telescope and put it back in his saddlebag. "It would seem that General Cheatham was correct, gentlemen. Grant is moving directly against central Alabama, seeking to capture Montgomery and Selma before we have a chance to assemble enough troops there to defend them. A simple plan, but potentially a very effective one."

Cheatham couldn't help but smile. "I thought that's what he'd do," he said with a certain smugness.

"General Cheatham, the army is in your debt," Johnston said. "But for your warning, I might not have properly planned a course of action for the situation that we now see unfolding."

"And what is that course of action?" Hardee asked.

Johnston turned his horse about so that he directly faced his corps commanders. "Stewart and Cheatham will march their corps to Palmetto, there to entrain for the trip to Alabama. I have already arranged for sufficient rolling stock to be assembled. Even though the enemy has a head start, by traveling by rail while Grant's men are marching on foot, we shall be able to arrive well before the Yankees. Rather than marching into undefended cities, Grant's men will be faced with forty thousand troops on a selected battlefield some miles to the east of those cities. Having just completed a long march and being far from their sources of supply, we might even be able to attack and defeat them in pitched battle."

"And my corps?" Hardee asked.

"William, you and your men shall remain here in the vicinity of Atlanta, in order to properly garrison the city and keep an eye on the Yankee troops who remain encamped at Vining's Station."

"My scouts report that those troops are the Army of the Cumberland, or at least a considerable portion of it," said Jackson, who was trying to sound helpful.

"My corps numbers only about eighteen thousand men," Hardee protested. "If I am not mistaken, the Army of the Cumberland now numbers around thirty-five thousand men. If they decide to make a play for Atlanta, I don't much care for those odds."

"You have the river," Johnston reminded Hardee. "And even if they get across the river, you have the defenses of Atlanta, with its fortress artillery. The Georgia Militia can also provide some assistance, weak though its men may be. Enough supplies of food and ammunition have been stored in the city to allow it to withstand a long siege, if necessary. I know the odds are long, but our forces have always faced long odds."

Hardee nodded. "True enough, sir."

"I will leave your precise dispositions up to you, of course. But I would suggest that you leave one of your divisions within the defenses of Atlanta itself while the others are deployed at the most likely crossing points."

"And cavalry? I must have cavalry to properly keep an eye on the Army of the Cumberland."

Johnston tilted his head in frustration and frowned. "Our lack of cavalry is our greatest weakness. But you are correct. General Jackson, you shall assign one brigade to General Hardee's corps." The commander of the cavalry nodded his assent.

"They're setting up an artillery battery, sir," Stewart said, eyeing the enemy on the opposite bank through his field telescope.

Johnston turned in his saddle and looked in the direction Stewart was pointing. He saw a distant puff of white gunpowder smoke and, a few moments later, heard a dull booming sound. Seconds after that, a cannonball slammed into the ground less than twenty yards away from the cluster of Confederate generals. It buried itself into the soggy ground and failed to explode, but Hardee and Stewart were splattered with bits of mud.

"We should retire," Hardee said calmly.

"Not yet," Johnston said, straightening himself in the saddle and staring defiantly across the river. "I shall not allow the Yankees to think they frightened us off."

"Remember how General Polk was killed."

"I haven't forgotten."

Another artillery blast was heard from across the river and the cannonball slammed into the ground a few yards closer than the previous one. This time, the shell did explode, but the muddy ground in which it had buried itself muffled the detonation and no one was hurt. Two more shells followed, both as unproductive as the first two. Through it all, the five Confederate generals sat motionless in their saddles, staring impassively at the Northern gunners trying to kill them. They looked for all the world as though they cared less about the artillery fire than they did about the remote possibility of rain.

"Very well, gentlemen. We've made our point. Let us retire."

With infinite patience, Johnston lightly kicked his horse into a walk and, trailed by his four subordinates, slowly moved away from the riverbank. The Yankee gunners fired a few more shots as they departed, but none came close to hitting them. As they left the river behind them, Johnston kicked his horse into a trot, with the others keeping pace.

"General Stewart, General Cheatham, I want your corps on the march to Palmetto within the next two hours. I want the first train loaded with troops to be on its way to Alabama before the sun rises tomorrow morning. General Mackall will have all the details regarding rolling stock ready for you when you arrive at Palmetto."

The two generals grunted their understanding, and Johnston went on. "General Hardee, I shall obviously be accompanying the main force to Alabama, which leaves you in command of the region around Atlanta. I have full faith in you, of course. Make your dispositions with extreme care."

"Of course, sir."

"Very well. To your commands, gentlemen."

*   *   *   *   *

"Retaliation of this sort has been done as long as there has been warfare," Cooper was saying calmly, as if explaining the matter to a child. "One can find examples in the books of the ancient historians, I believe. Herodotus and such."

"Do you think I give a damn about the ancient historians?" Seymour bellowed back. "You know and I know that there is absolutely no justification whatsoever for hanging General Thomas. It's murder, plain and simple!"

Cooper shrugged, as if the matter were no concern of his. Thomas, sitting silently off to one side of the room, was not surprised. He had known Cooper slightly before the war, when both had served in the United States Army. As far as Thomas was concerned, the man was only a single step above senility. Having come to Georgia on some other business, Cooper had decided to make an inspection tour of the prison camps at Andersonville and Camp Oglethorpe. Despite Thomas's own objections, Seymour had loudly and repeatedly demanded an interview with Cooper to discuss the announced plans to execute Thomas. Thus far, the interview was going pretty much as Thomas had expected.

"Forrest was murdered after he had been taken prisoner," Cooper said. "That much is clear. Obviously, as the Union authorities have proven unwilling to hand over the perpetrators of this monstrous act, the Confederacy is left little choice but to retaliate against a prisoner of equal rank. Failing to do so would only encourage more such executions of Confederate prisoners, would it not?"

"Oh, spare me," Seymour said contemptuously. "How do we know these stories about Forrest being murdered weren't just cooked up by your Southern newspapers?"

"I would be happy to provide you with written copies of the eyewitness accounts, if you would like," Cooper replied. "In any case, it is not for me to decide matters of government policy. I am merely communicating the intentions of the Davis administration as a professional courtesy."

Seymour stared daggers at Cooper. "It's perfectly obvious to me that General Thomas is being singled out only because he is the most prominent Southerner to remain loyal to the Union. Were Thomas a Northerner, this execution would never have been proposed."

"A uniformed officer of the United States is the same as any other, as far as the Confederate government is concerned," Cooper answered. "General Thomas has been selected for execution because he is the only Union officer currently in Confederate custody with a rank comparable to that of General Forrest. There are no other considerations, as far as I can see."

Thomas regretted having agreed to come to the interview. Cooper was in no mood to discuss the issue of his impending execution and, even had he been, he did not speak for the administration in Richmond. As it was, Thomas now feared that Cooper would interpret his silence as cowardice. He did not want the rebel general to think he was going to allow Seymour to fight his battles for him.

Seymour was still shouting. "Even if Forrest was killed by Union troops after having been taken prisoner, is that any less than the bastard deserved? How many Union soldiers were killed by his troops when he captured Fort Pillow, after they had surrendered? Do you expect us to weep for the bastard?"

Cooper was unmoved. "General Seymour, it is unbecoming for you to refer to General Forrest as a bastard. I would expect an officer of the United States Army to maintain a certain level of decorum."

"You refer to the army of which you were an officer before you decided to turn traitor, yes? You and all the rest of the Benedict Arnolds in your so-called Confederacy!"

Cooper drew back, his face fixed in a frown, seeming more aggrieved than angered. Thomas guessed that Cooper had not had many occasions to discuss such matters with Union officers since the commencement of the war, so when it was thrown into his face he simply reacted with surprise.

Something snapped in Thomas at that instant. Perhaps it was the pent-up rage he had felt due to his defeat at Peachtree Creek and the destruction of his army. Perhaps it was simply the frustration resulting from his long confinement. Whatever it was, it exploded.

"Enough of this nonsense!" Thomas roared, smacking his leg and standing bolt upright from his chair. The teenage guards who stood nonchalantly behind Cooper were suddenly stirred into something resembling attention, bringing their muskets up in such a way that they could quickly be brought into firing positions. Cooper and Seymour were both stunned into silence, staring intently at Thomas and clearly wondering what he would do next.

"Listen to me, Cooper," Thomas said forcefully. "You think I give a damn that the rebel government is going to kill me? We all have to die sooner or later, don't we? At least I will have the consolation to know that I died while remaining true to the oath I took at West Point, an oath that you and all the other rebels saw fit to ignore. But I will say this. I don't want a hanging. If I'm going to die, I want to die a soldier's death. I demand a firing squad!"

Cooper's eyebrows went up. "Forrest was hanged, according to the eyewitness accounts. I understand the thinking in Richmond to be that since he was hanged, you should be hanged also."

"At worst, Forrest's death was an unauthorized action by overzealous soldiers," Thomas said. "My execution, by contrast, would be an official decision by a group of people claiming to be a legitimate government. If you rebels have even a shred of honor and decency, you'll do me the favor of executing me by firing squad rather than having me hanged. We hang criminals, after all. Soldiers are executed by firing squad."

Cooper considered this. "It does not much matter to me which method is used for your execution. If you like, I shall pass on your concerns to Richmond."

Thomas nodded. "Please do," he said, with all the politeness he was able to muster under the circumstances.

"Has a date been set?" Seymour asked, casting a concerned glance at Thomas.

"Not to my knowledge," Cooper replied.

"The sooner the better," Thomas spat. "As long as it's a firing squad. So long as I'm allowed to die a soldier's death, the earlier I meet my Maker, the happier I will be. And the first thing I'll do is tell God what a bunch of bastards all of you are!"

September 15, Noon

Hardee arrived at Cleburne's tent and slid off his horse with ease. No spoken orders were necessary to ensure that a nearby corporal took the reins and tied the animal to a nearby tree. Cleburne was waiting for him.

"What's the word?" Cleburne asked, his voice mixing excitement with apprehension.

"Stewart and Cheatham are headed for Alabama. Their troops are marching to Palmetto and are probably starting to board the trains even as we speak."

"And us?"

"We're to remain here to protect Atlanta and keep an eye on the Army of the Cumberland."

Cleburne nodded sharply, even as his mind whirled with various calculations. Their corps would be outnumbered two-to-one by the Army of the Cumberland. With the agony of Peachtree Creek now two months in the past, the Yankee force was probably back to the same level of effectiveness it had been when it had crossed the Chattahoochee River in mid-July.

Hardee could see what he was thinking. "We still have the river between them and us, and we have the fortifications of the city. If they try to advance against us, they will have numbers on their side, but we would hold every other advantage. We will be fine."

"Do you think they will advance against us, William?"

"I frankly doubt it. Grant is taking his dog and pony show to Alabama. In fact, it would not surprise me if a fair chunk of the Army of the Cumberland has joined the other two armies in the march southwest, leaving perhaps only two corps or so at Vining's Station. I suspect their purpose is entirely defensive. They don't want us getting back onto the north bank and heading up toward Chattanooga."

"If that's so, then we might be in for a quiet time." Cleburne said these words with some regret. He was a warrior, and his instinct was to be where the battle was raging. If the rest of the Army of Tennessee was soon to be locked in a deadly battle somewhere in Alabama, Cleburne would feel ashamed if he were not present.

But there was more to it than that. If Cleburne and his division were to play a major role in a Confederate victory, perhaps the newspapers would stop talking about his old proposal and instead turn their attention to his military service to the Confederacy. The people who were now calling for his head might remember that he was a patriotic Southern general. It would be just what his reputation needed.

And yet, there was a part of Cleburne which felt a certain measure of relief. Every day, the inevitable onset of winter came closer. When the snows came and the roads froze, the movement of large armies would become impossible and the campaign season would come to an end. If he remained alive when winter finally arrived, he would finally be able to secure a furlough from General Johnston, travel to Mobile, and be married to Susan.

Hardee was still talking. "Nothing wrong with a little peace and quiet. Until it is proven otherwise, we will assume that the enemy across the river will attack Atlanta and we will make our dispositions accordingly."

"Of course."

"We have only four divisions of infantry and a brigade of cavalry. I hesitate even to count the Georgia Militia among our forces, as they are so very useless. But I suppose we shall have to bow to convention and kiss the ass of Governor Brown."

Cleburne chuckled, and Hardee went on.

"I shall keep one division in Atlanta itself, to keep the Georgia Militia company. The three others will be stationed on the river, with their brigades stretched out to cover as much ground as possible without moving so far apart that they would be unable to support one another if attacked. The cavalry, of which we have far too little, will be deployed out on the flanks, with a few picked men to serve in roving patrols."

"A sound plan," Cleburne said. "It allows us to cover as much ground as possible considering our limited resources, while keeping a central reserve in Atlanta. Now, who shall go where?"

"A map?"

Cleburne gestured toward a small table set up in front of his tent, on which a map of the Atlanta region lay. Hardee thumped it in various spots as he spoke.

"Bate's Division will serve as the central reserve in Atlanta. Maney's Division will be positioned here, on the Chattahoochee at Howell's Ferry, directly across from the Yankee encampment where the old railroad bridge is. I'll send Walker's Division upriver, to keep an eye on the same fords the Yankees crossed over the first time around."

"If they do cross the river, I doubt they'll try to come the same way they came before. They're not going to want to have to cross over Peachtree Creek again, by God!"

"Certainly not."

"And my division?"

"You'll be posted downriver, keeping an eye on the fords down by Sandtown."

"Fair enough."

"Good to keep you and Walker as far apart as possible, I think," Hardee said with a grin.

"I can't help but notice that if the Army of the Cumberland does make a try for Atlanta, they are more likely to cross downriver and approach the city from the west. Doing so would allow them to avoid the obstacle of Peachtree Creek."

"Precisely where your division will be located, yes. It only makes sense to have my finest division commander at the point of greatest danger, does it not?"

"As always, sir, it is a honor to me that you display such confidence in my abilities and those of my men."

"How many times in the past has your division been the rock on which the attack of the enemy was broken? Nothing shall ever cause my confidence in you to falter." He then forced the serious expression off his face, reached across the table and cuffed Cleburne on the shoulder. "In any case, it doesn't matter. I doubt that the Yankees across the river will stir out of their encampment."

"Likely not. We are rather like the actors of a four-act play who are never seen again after the second act."

"Speaking of plays, we should inquire what shall be showing at the Athenaeum, now that Mayor Calhoun has allowed it to reopen. Whatever the play is, we should make plans to attend."

*　　　　*　　　　*　　　　*　　　　*

September 15, Evening

It felt good to be back in New York City. Marble's journalistic profession and political interests required him to move across the length and breadth of the United States. He sometimes thought he had traveled more miles by rail than any other person in the country. Still, New York City was where he felt most comfortable and at home. Whenever he left it, Marble felt rather like a dragon having to leave its lair.

As he stepped off the passenger car and onto the platform of the New York Central Railroad, he realized he had been gone too long. Watching the bustle and listening to the chatter of hundreds of fellow New Yorkers, he smiled with genuine warmth. He was back among his own kind of people.

He strolled to the street, clutching both his own carpetbag and the one containing the money given to him by Humphries. He had distributed most of it while he had been in Chicago and at several other places during his return journey. But he still had about five thousand dollars remaining and intended to use it all in New York City itself. A few minutes later, he was rolling through the city streets, happily listening to the clip-clopping of the horse pulling his cab and the curses of the driver constantly berating people who got in his way.

As the cab approached his house, Marble's head swirled with ideas. He would get a good night's sleep, of course, but as early as possible the next morning he would be back at the offices of the New York World to repair whatever damage negligence had inflicted during his extended absence. In the meantime, he would dispatch messages to the most important Democrats in the city, arranging meetings to discuss how best to divvy up the remaining five thousand dollars still in his possession.

He arrived and stepped out of the cab, quickly paying the driver. When he turned and began walking up the steps toward the door, he was stopped dead in his tracks.

Standing on either side of the entrance to his house was a squad of Union infantrymen. They had been lazily leaning against the wall before he had arrived, but upon his appearance they came to attention. They did not look like proper soldiers, leading Marble to suspect that they were probably just militiamen. This didn't surprise him, as any soldier worth his salt would have been at the front in Virginia or Georgia.

But if the soldiers themselves did not have a frightening appearance, the officer standing in their midst certainly did. Marble immediately recognized General Benjamin Butler.

"Good evening, Mr. Marble," Butler said with a charm tinged with something sinister. To Marble's eyes, Butler looked like a haggard clown, whose flabby cheeks seemed to droop down his face like melting makeup, while his arms and legs seemed like the appendages of an overweight octopus. Though Butler might look like a buffoon, Marble knew that he was the last person any rational man wanted to have for an enemy.

Despite the surprise he felt and the anxiety gripping him, Marble refused to be intimidated. He forced himself to smile. "And good evening to you, General Butler. To what do I owe this unexpected pleasure?"

"Do I need an excuse to come see an old friend?"

"We're not friends."

"Sure we are."

"One does not normally require an escort of soldiers to come to pay a call on a friend."

Butler shrugged. "New York City has become rather dangerous of late, as you may have noticed. Perhaps you've heard of the riots that took place recently?" The sarcasm dripped from his mouth like sour syrup.

"I was here when they happened," Marble said wearily.

"Were you?" Butler said with mock concern. "I am surprised. I assumed you had been out of town at the time. When the troops under my command restored order in the city, I couldn't help but notice that the rioters did not lay a finger on the New York World building, though the offices of the New York Times and New York Tribune went up in flames."

"An odd coincidence."

"Odd, indeed."

Marble thought the game had gone on long enough. "What do you want, General Butler?"

"To ask you a few questions."

"I do not give you permission to enter my home. There are still constitutional rights in the United States, you know."

The phony smile on Butler's face had vanished, replaced by a more grim and implacable expression. "In case you didn't notice, Marble, New York City is under martial law. President Lincoln has appointed me to command the city in order to prevent any further insurrections against the authority of the legitimate government. Constitutional rights, you say? In New York City, I am the Constitution."

Marble felt a chill go down his spine as Butler said these words. Coming from another man, they could be dismissed as simple vanity. Marble knew Butler was of a different type altogether. A politician with the qualities of a chameleon, Butler had been a Democrat when the war broke out, but had gone over to the Republicans the moment it had suited his purposes. He was now among the most radical partisans of Lincoln's party. He owed his commission as a general to his political connections and his military career had been little short of disastrous, but Butler had still managed to make huge amounts of money when he had served as military governor of occupied New Orleans. Benjamin Butler was always in business for the cause of Benjamin Butler. Neither vanity nor idealism affected his actions, for he was motivated only by his ambition. Finding oneself an enemy of such a man was to find oneself in very dangerous waters.

"Must be nice to be a dictator," Marble said.

Butler ignored the remark entirely. "You have two choices. We can either talk here at your home or I can have these soldiers take you, by force if necessary, to my headquarters and we can talk there."

"I have already said that I do not give you permission to enter my home."

"Then come with us, if you please."

"Am I under arrest?"

"Call it whatever you want," Butler said. He glanced toward the troops and jerked his thumb in the direction of a carriage across the street. One of the soldiers politely asked Marble to come with him, and Marble decided against resisting, as it would have been both undignified and useless. As he began walking across the street with Butler at his side and half a dozen soldiers behind him, he heard some of the other soldiers bashing in his front door.

"I'll take those bags for you, Mr. Marble," said one of the soldiers. Without a word, Marble passed them over. He doubted he would see the five thousand dollars returned to him. By all odds, the soldier would happily keep the money for himself, for five thousand dollars would be an astounding fortune to most men. If he didn't, Marble had no doubt that Butler would arrange for the cash to mysteriously disappear and somehow find its way into his own coffers.

Marble clambered into the carriage, with Butler taking the seat across from him and two soldiers sitting beside them. With a shout and the snap of a whip, the carriage moved off. As his house faded into the distance, Marble could see the door finally give way to the blows of the soldiers, who dashed inside. No doubt he would return to a home that had been searched from top to bottom and thoroughly ransacked.

"For what cause is my home being broken into?" Marble demanded.

Butler stared across the carriage with eyes that seemed to pierce through his soul. "I think you know why your house is being searched perfectly well, Mr. Marble."

He shook his head. "No, I assure you I do not. Though I oppose the unconstitutional actions of the Lincoln administration, all my opposition to it has been perfectly legal. The Constitution protects my right to publish whatever criticisms I choose against Lincoln and to seek his defeat through regular political means, does it not?"

Benjamin said nothing in response, merely staring out the window of the carriage as the city of New York floated by. A less astute man than Marble might have assumed the silence of the political general to be a good sign, but Marble found it threatening.

After a twenty-minute ride, the carriage pulled to a halt in front of the New York City Hall, which Butler had taken over as his headquarters for the duration of the military occupation of the city. The building, done in the French Renaissance style that had been so popular when it had been built sixty years before, was surrounded by clusters of tents housing Union soldiers. Marble looked out at them with disgust. His beloved New York City was being treated as though it were an enemy metropolis that needed to be held down by military force.

Some soldiers gathered around the carriage and sharply saluted as Butler got out. Two men gathered on each side of Marble as he exited the carriage and remained by his side as he followed Butler inside the building. A few minutes later, Marble found himself escorted into a small room with a table, illuminated by the pale yellow light of a few oil lamps. He was directed into a chair and Butler sat down across from him. He looked deep into Marble's eyes.

"Alexander Humphries," Butler said simply.

"I'm sorry?" Marble responded.

"Do you know the name Alexander Humphries?"

"No," Marble said. He hoped he sounded convincing, but things were suddenly becoming clear to him. He hadn't bothered asking Humphries any details about where he had obtained the money he had given him to support McClellan's campaign, nor had he asked him for whom he worked. As far as Marble was concerned, it was best simply not to know such things.

"No?"

"Never heard of him."

"That's odd," Butler said. "According to our information, you rode with him on a train from New York City to Kingston just three weeks ago."

"If I did, I was not aware of it. I do not know who this Humphries person is or what on Earth caused you to connect him to me."

Butler leaned forward and spoke with a more direct tone. "Listen here, Marble. You are about to learn just how big a mistake it was to even speak to Humphries, much less do what he asked of you. And I know what happened, Marble. Humphries has been arrested."

Marble's heart rate increased sharply and he could feel sweat beginning to form on his forehead. With a horror that he prayed was not apparent on his face, he suddenly realized that the second carpetbag contained not only the remaining five thousand dollars, but the itemized list of how he had spent the other twenty thousand, which he had prepared for Humphries in order to prove that the money was being spent according to his instructions. That bag was certainly being gone through by one of Butler's men at that very moment.

"I don't know what you're talking about," Marble said, his mind racing. If Butler was telling the truth and Humphries had confessed everything, the game might well be up. But Marble had run enough stories about criminal investigations to know how interrogations worked and he sensed that Butler might well be bluffing. Besides which, Marble could at least honestly say that he did not know who Humphries was. "Just who is this Humphries fellow you're talking about?"

Butler scoffed a bit, either as an act or as an intentional display of contempt. "Alexander Humphries is a rebel agent, Mr. Marble. He entered the United States several months ago, having run the blockade at Wilmington on a British ship. He had been entrusted with a large amount of money from the rebel government in order to finance efforts to ensure the defeat of President Lincoln in the upcoming election. You took money from this man, didn't you, Mr. Marble?"

"No!" Marble said, now sounding desperate. Had he known Humphries had been a Confederate agent, he probably would not have touched the money with a ten-foot pole. But then, Marble couldn't deny that the thought had crossed his mind a few times.

Though not a religious man, Marble suddenly found himself earnestly praying that the soldier who had earlier taken his carpetbags had stolen the five thousand dollars for himself, as the money and the list in the bag with it could now become serious evidence against him.

His prayers were not answered. A moment later a soldier came in with the carpetbag. He laid it down on the table between Butler and Marble, taking out the five thousand dollars in greenbacks and the itemized list Marble had prepared and setting them before Butler. Butler picked up the cash and the letter, looking at them intently as the soldier spoke quietly in his ear. After a few moments, Butler looked back over at Marble.

"The evidence lies here before us, Marble. Humphries gave you twenty-five thousand dollars. You have already dispensed with twenty thousand, as specified here in this list you so kindly have provided. Five thousand remains. Do you deny it?"

Marble said nothing as his mind raced to find a way out of his dilemma.

"Do you deny it?" Butler asked again, his voice raising.

Marble remained silent.

Butler frowned and shook his head. "You need say nothing. This evidence, combined with the testimony of Humphries, is more than enough to convict you. You shall be placed under arrest and confined until an investigation is complete. Needless to say, if it is demonstrated that you knowingly took funds from a rebel agent in order to influence the course of the election, a court might easily find you guilty of giving aid and comfort to the enemies of the United States."

Marble felt a terrifying tightening in his stomach, for he knew what punishment the law provided in cases of treason. Butler's lips curled into a sneer as he ordered a soldier to take Marble to his cell.

*　　　　　*　　　　　*　　　　　*　　　　　*

September 16, Afternoon

Davis enjoyed his late afternoon rides. They were his only real opportunity to have any time to himself. During his rides, Davis could reflect on the situation facing the Confederacy without being pressured by his wife, or Judah Benjamin, or another member of the Cabinet, or some random person he happened to pass by on the street.

He did not ride out alone. As always, Colonel William Browne, one of his most trusted aides, followed at a respectful distance, armed with two pistols and a saber. Davis had not given him permission to follow him and had, in fact, been mildly annoyed when he had first seen Browne trailing him several months before. Still, with regular threats to his life arriving by mail and the Executive Mansion itself having narrowly avoided destruction by arson a few months earlier, Davis had to admit that Browne's precaution made sense. After a few excursions, the Confederate President had essentially forgotten Browne was there. He might as well have been a shadow.

Davis would have preferred to ride out into the countryside east of Richmond, as he found the air fresher and the countryside more pleasant there. But circumstances had long since forced him to confine his rides to the area west of the city. The steady rumble of Union artillery off to the east, a sound which had scarcely diminished since it had first been heard back in June, bore grim testimony as to the reason why. But even if he could not be completely alone and could not ride exactly where he pleased, Davis was still determined to relish his afternoon horseback rides.

As he deeply inhaled and exhaled the Virginia air, increasingly crisp and cool as autumn gathered strength, Davis tried to think about anything other than military or political matters. The purpose of these rides, after all, was to allow him to relax and to clear his mind. But he found the task impossible. When he tried to focus on an interesting-looking plant or bird, his mind would immediately wander off into thoughts of how difficult it was to supply food to Lee's men or how frustrating it was to go for days without any communication from Johnston in Atlanta.

Even if he were able to force thoughts of military matters out of his mind, any momentary sense of calm was disrupted by concerns over politics. While he still hoped and expected McClellan to defeat Lincoln in the upcoming election, Davis worried over the state of flux into which the politics of the North had descended. The Battle of Peachtree Creek was now two months in the past and the Union could point to victories at Mobile Bay and elsewhere in the intervening time. The continued unrest in New York City and other Northern urban centers boded ill for the Republican ticket, but Davis worried that they might also give Lincoln an excuse to employ the army to ensure his reelection under the guise of maintaining public order.

Davis tried to shake these thoughts away and enjoy his ride, but just when he had succeeded in getting his body to relax somewhat, he heard a rider approach. The man kicked his horse into a greater speed when he spotted Davis, then quickly reined in alongside him. He wore the uniform of a Confederate major.

"Mr. President, I beg your pardon, but Secretary Seddon wishes for you to come to Mechanic's Hall with all speed. He says it is most urgent."

"Has there been some disaster?"

"Not that I know of, sir."

Davis sighed heavily. "Very well, Major."

Accompanied by Colonel Browne and the messenger, Davis kicked his horse into a canter and headed back toward Richmond. He wondered what it was that Seddon wanted. The Secretary of War was not normally in the habit of interrupting his afternoon rides, so whatever it was had to be important. Davis felt a sharp sense of anxiety, but told himself that the news he was about to receive might just as easily be good news as bad.

The three men entered the outskirts of Richmond and slowed to a trot. As they gradually approached the city center, citizens out on the streets glanced up at the anxious expression on the face of their President. Davis had no doubt that the look on his face would become the fodder for endless rumors in the bar of Spottswood Hotel that evening, but he would not have cared even had he been able to do anything about it.

Eventually, Davis reined in before Mechanic's Hall. A sentry dashed forward to claim the honor of holding the President's horse and Davis walked inside. A few minutes later, he was being ushered into Seddon's office.

"What is it?" Davis asked, not wasting time with pleasantries.

"I've just received a telegram from General Johnston. It seems that the rumors about Grant advancing toward Montgomery and Selma have been proven correct. Johnston informs me that he is entraining the corps of Cheatham and Stewart for Alabama, and leaving Hardee behind in Atlanta to act as a garrison."

Seddon held up the paper, which Davis snatched from his hand as he sat down in the chair across from the Secretary of War. He spent a few minutes reading through it.

"Johnston felt justified in taking this course of action without receiving permission from the War Department?"

"His message was written more as a notification than a request for permission, Mr. President."

Davis shook his head. "I think the esteemed commander of the Army of Tennessee needs to be reminded that I am the President of the Confederacy, not him."

"Of course, sir."

"Has Johnston coordinated his movement with General Taylor? Montgomery and Selma fall within his department, after all."

"If he has, he says nothing about it."

Davis grunted, then read through the telegram once again. As much as he was irritated at Johnston taking such a momentous decision without consulting with him first, Davis had to admit that the man's judgment was correct. With Grant marching toward the industrial centers of Alabama, it was imperative for Confederate troops to get there first. With virtually all his infantry long since sent to the Army of Tennessee and much of his cavalry destroyed in the unsuccessful raid that had led to Forrest's death, it was quite clear that General Taylor lacked the necessary strength to protect Montgomery and Selma from Grant's offensive. Indeed, his forces were stretched thin as it was merely to protect the city of Mobile from a possible Union amphibious attack. If Grant's advance was to be opposed, it would have to be done by the troops of the Army of Tennessee.

"Mr. President?" Seddon said.

The words shook Davis out of his thoughts, and he realized he had not spoken for an awkwardly long time.

"I apologize."

"That's quite all right, Mr. President."

"It seems to me that Johnston has made the correct decision from a purely military point of view. But it is entirely unacceptable that he did so without referring the matter to the War Department first."

"I agree, Mr. President. Entirely unacceptable."

"Please send a telegram to General Johnston immediately. Say that we understand the purpose of his movement toward Alabama and believe it to be the correct decision, but demand an explanation for why he did not request permission from the government before embarking upon such a large-scale movement of troops."

Seddon nodded sharply. "I will do so at once, Mr. President."

"Good," Davis said, his mind already turning elsewhere. He felt a sudden need for the counsel of Judah Benjamin.

A few minutes later, Davis walked out the front door of Mechanic's Hall. He didn't bother to mount his horse, as the executive offices were only a few hundred yards down the road. Less than ten minutes after leaving the office of his Secretary of War, the Confederate President walked into the office of his Secretary of State.

"I'm not disturbing you, I hope?"

"Not at all," Benjamin said, waving to the seat across the desk. "To what do I owe this visit? Is something the matter which cannot wait until tomorrow's meeting of the full Cabinet?"

"I'm not sure," Davis admitted. "We have received a telegram from General Johnston informing us that he is moving the bulk of his army by train from Atlanta to Alabama in order to counter the move by General Grant in that direction."

"I see. I shall not venture to express an opinion on the military merits of such a decision, as I am entirely uneducated in the arts of war."

"It is not the military aspects of the decision which worry me. I am concerned that Johnston saw fit to make such a decision without receiving permission from the government to do so."

"Ah," Benjamin said. "Now that I understand completely. You fear that Johnston is appropriating to himself the strategic direction of the war, which is your responsibility."

"I am the President, and the Constitution states emphatically that the President is the commander-in-chief of the armed forces."

"Indeed. As with most of the rest, that clause was lifted directly from the United States Constitution. I imagine that the

James Madison and his friends knew what he was doing when he elected to give control of the military to the President."

Davis shook his head. "Johnston publicly socializes with Senator Wigfall, Governor Brown, Vice-President Stephens, and just about every other prominent critic of our administration. These are the very people who say that I have no business being the President of our Confederacy."

"Not only that. They are discussing Johnston as possible presidential candidate in 1867."

Davis scoffed. To him, the idea of Joseph Johnston being the chief executive of the Confederacy was ludicrous. "So, what am I to do with a general who constantly consorts with my political enemies and now refuses to communicate with the government before making major strategic decisions?"

"I confess I do not know. History is full of politically ambitious generals who gradually began to raise themselves to a higher level than the government they ostensibly served. Look back to the Roman Republic and the lives of Sulla or Marius or, for that matter, Julius Caesar. Look at Cromwell in England or Bonaparte in France."

"General Johnston was already the darling of our political enemies before Peachtree Creek. In the months since, they have raised him to the level of a mythical hero. God help us, Judah. If we do not do something to deal with this nonsense, we might find ourselves facing a military coup the moment the war against the Yankees is over."

*　　　　*　　　　*　　　　*　　　　*

September 16, Evening

Down on the stage of Ford's Theater, Shylock was raging against the injustices he felt had been committed against him by his fellows.

"He hath disgraced me!" the booming and magnificent voice of Edwin Booth thundered. "And hindered me half a million! Laughed at my losses! Mocked at my gains! Scorned my nation! Thwarted my bargains! Cooled my friends! Heated my enemies! And what's his reason? I am a Jew!"

"Shakespeare didn't like the Jews, clearly," Seward said, leaning over to whisper in Lincoln's ear. No one in the audience could have heard a conversation going on in the President's Box, but the Secretary of State still felt compelled to whisper.

Lincoln looked over at him in some surprise. "How do you figure?"

"Shylock is the only Jewish character Shakespeare ever wrote. He made the man an unspeakable villain, motivated by nothing but avarice and revenge. Just like Christopher Marlowe did in The Jew of Malta."

"Listen further," Lincoln said, tossing his head toward the action on the stage.

"Hath not a Jew eyes?" Shylock was pleading. "Hath not a Jew hands, organs, dimensions, senses, affections, passions? Fed with the same food? Hurt by the same weapons? Subject to the same diseases? Healed by the same means? Warmed and cooled by the same winter and summer, as a Christian is?"

"You see?" Lincoln said.

Seward nodded quickly, but was too intent on the action of the play to respond to the President.

"If you prick us, do we not bleed? If you tickle us, do we not laugh? If you poison us, do we not die? And if you wrong us, shall we not revenge? If we are like you in the rest, we shall resemble you in that!"

Lincoln turned back to Seward with a smile. "You're right that Shylock is a villain. After what he did to Antonio, how could he be otherwise? But can you not see that he was driven to such evil by his endless persecution at the hands of the Christians of Venice? The people in this play who we are supposed to see as the protagonists – Antonio, Bassanio, and all the women – they created Shylock's evil, even though they cannot recognize this."

Seward shrugged. "I suppose so."

"Hmm," Lincoln said thoughtfully. "If you think about it, one can see parallels between how the Christians of Venice treated their Jews and how the whites of the South treat their blacks. The Venetians reviled the Jews of the community for engaging in usury, even though the legal restrictions the Venetians themselves had placed on the Jews left them with no other choice than to engage in money-lending. Similarly, the Southern whites deride their blacks as ignorant brutes fit only to be slaves, even though it is the Southern whites themselves have made the blacks ignorant by ensuring that they never learn to read or write."

"No one who has met with Frederick Douglass can say that a man born a slave is naturally an ignorant brute."

"Indeed not!" Lincoln said, rather too loudly. He heard a rustling in the audience below him and realized he had not kept his voice sufficiently quiet. No one present would dare shush the President of the United States, but they could still make their displeasure known indirectly. "Indeed not," Lincoln said again, this time in a whisper. "The man may skewer me in the columns of his newspaper from time to time, but what a fine man he is! And how hard he has worked at recruiting men for our black regiments!"

"When a man is oppressed, when a man is pushed far enough, he shall push back. Rather like Shylock, I suppose. But Douglass is a

considerably more dignified and honorable man than Shylock is."
Seward chuckled softly.

Lincoln greatly enjoyed coming to the theater. Since he had arrived in Washington three years earlier, he had been to the performances at Ford's Theater and Grover's Theater over a hundred times. Sitting in the darkness of the President's Box, he felt somehow insulated from the pressures of the war and the demands of his office. While at the theater, Abraham Lincoln could be a human being, at least for a few precious hours.

"Edwin Booth is in fine form tonight," Lincoln observed.

Seward nodded. "The finest actor of our age, I'd reckon. I had him over to my house for dinner not too long ago. We had a lovely conversation."

"A good Union man?" Lincoln asked. He recalled that the Booths were from Maryland, which meant that their loyalties might lie on either side.

"Oh, beyond any doubt. He is very loyal to the government. The same cannot be said for his brother John, alas."

"John Booth? Also an actor, yes? I seem to recall him playing Cassius in Julius Caesar at Grover's Theater not long ago."

"Yes, that's the one. I think he played Brutus, though."

The two ceased talking and continued to watch the play. The scene had shifted to a silly conversation between the love-struck Portia and her suitor Bassanio, neither of whom had the slightest conception of the disorder and anguish they were inadvertently causing through their actions. Lincoln reflected for a moment on the Bard's meaning. How much agony was brought about by people who simply had no idea what they were doing?

A man slipped into the back of the box, quietly cleared his throat, and handed Lincoln a message. He quickly unfolded and read it.

"Secretary Stanton is outside," Lincoln said quietly.

"Did you not invite him to the play?" Seward asked.

"He said he didn't want to come. You know that he considers the theater a waste of time." He turned to the messenger. "Could you ask the Secretary to come into the box, please?" The man nodded and left.

Lincoln went back to watching the play. Bassanio was now engaged a game in which he had to answer a riddle in order to win Portia's hand in marriage. It was all the more moving as Bassanio has just realized that he truly loved Portia. For a brief moment, Lincoln felt grief tug on his heartstrings as the image of the face of Ann Rutledge passed through his mind. She had been his first love, with whom he shared more pure and unadulterated affection as a young man that he had ever enjoyed with his wife in later years. She had been taken from him at the tender age of twenty-two during a typhoid epidemic. He wondered how different his life would have been had she lived.

Lincoln was distracted from these melancholy thoughts when the messenger returned.

"Mr. Stanton will not come into the theater, Mr. President. He says that he wishes to speak to you outside."

A look of intense irritation crossed Lincoln's face. He rose from his chair with the deepest reluctance. Though he rather wished Seward would remain seated and continue to watch the play, Lincoln did not protest when the Secretary of State rose to follow him.

They emerged out onto 10th Street, which was crowded with people and carriages despite the late hour. Torches hanging from iron braces on the façade of Ford's Theater illuminated the scene. A troop of infantry was marching by amidst the bustle, unaware of the presence of the President.

Stanton, looking irritable as always, was waiting.

"Well, Edwin? What's so important that we needed to be disturbed while at the theater?"

"I really wish you wouldn't waste your time with such amusements, Mr. President. What does one achieve by watching people frolic around on a stage pretending to be people they are not?"

"Come with us to a performance and you might learn," Seward replied with a grin. He always had found Stanton's seriousness amusing.

Stanton politely ignored the comment. "I've gotten some telegrams from both New York City and Chicago in the last hour. It seems that some of the newspapers will run stories in their morning editions tomorrow that Grant has abandoned the effort to capture Atlanta and is instead advancing into central Alabama."

"Are they?" Lincoln said. "Well, I can honestly say that I really don't know what Grant is doing."

"Some of the reporters are already showing up at the War Department, asking questions." From the tone of his voice, it was clear that Stanton did not think the reporters had any right to ask questions about anything unless he deigned to give them permission to do so.

"Let them speculate," Lincoln said. "All I can say is that I know which hole Grant has gone into, but I do not know which hole he will come out of." Seward smiled at the analogy, but Stanton's face remained cold.

"Grant has not informed me of his destination, nor has he said a word to Chief-of-Staff Halleck. It really is unseemly, Mr. President. I am the Secretary of War, after all."

"Yes, yes, Edwin. I hope you take no offense at Grant's secretiveness. But as he is the one general we have capable of delivering results, I humbly request that you indulge him in this. He clearly knows what he is doing."

"Very well, Mr. President," Stanton said in a voice which sounded more like a grunt. "We must assume that the rebels in Richmond will have access to the newspapers within a few days at most." Try as they might, the commanders in the field had never been able to stop the informal trade that went on between the lines of the opposing armies around Petersburg, in which Yankee coffee was traded for Southern tobacco and each side traded its respective newspapers.

Lincoln shrugged. "Chances are that the rebels are already aware of the movement, if indeed it is taking place. One cannot move a large army a great distance without someone noticing, after all."

Stanton cleared his throat. "There is also the matter of Manton Marble."

Lincoln chuckled, amused at the alliteration. Stanton's eyes narrowed in disapproval.

"Oh, do cheer up, Edwin! Now, tell me about Marble."

"Butler arrested him, and claims he found evidence on his person that he did indeed receive money from Humphries and has been using it to finance the Democratic election campaign. He has now placed him under arrest."

"I assume that Butler, being Butler, has prepared a complete and concise summary of the evidence mentioned?"

"He did, yes."

"Very well. Make sure that this report accidently finds its way to the newspapers. In particular, anything linking Marble directly to McClellan needs to be mentioned."

"Easily done, Mr. President."

Lincoln smiled broadly, then slapped his thigh and laughed. "The people will be up in arms when they discover that the same rebels who are daily killing their sons and husbands are also financing the political campaign against our administration."

"We may have the Democrats over a barrel, Mr. President," Seward said happily.

"Quite so, quite so. And if Grant sends us news of a victory in the West, confidence shall be restored both among the public and in the financial markets. Things are definitely looking up, my friends!"

"I will reserve my judgment for the time being, Mr. President," Stanton said, refusing to smile. "But I agree that our situation seems to have improved."

"Will you join us for the remainder of the play?" Seward asked Stanton.

"No, thank you. Too much work to do. I bid you both a pleasant evening." Stanton touched his hat and walked off down the street.

"Come, Mr. Seward," Lincoln said happily, taking the elbow of the Secretary of State. "If we hurry, we can still catch the courtroom scene."

September 18, Noon

The men of the Army of the Tennessee were continuing to trudge southwest along the bank of the Chattahoochee River. When the march had first begun, they had occasionally spotted Confederate cavalry shadowing them from the opposite bank, but these men had not appeared for a few days. Aside from a few men injured in wagon accidents, the march thus far had been utterly uneventful.

General McPherson was riding at the head of one of his divisions, happily contemplating the fact that the day was going to be both dry and cool and therefore good for marching. He then saw Grant approach at a canter with only a small escort behind him.

He touched his head. "General Grant."

Grant nodded. "How does the day find you, James?"

"Well, sir. Very, very well. My boys seem to be in fine spirits."

"Excellent."

"How is it with the other armies?" McPherson asked.

"Schofield and his boys are fine. I believe that Howard the Army of the Cumberland are feeling rather lonely back at Vining's Station."

McPherson chuckled. It was not like Grant to make such a joke, so the junior officer assumed that his chief must be in exceptionally good spirits. "Is there any sign of rebel opposition up ahead?"

"None," Grant said. "Some local militia in a few towns, who quickly surrender when they see the size of our force. A few cavalry scouts. Not many, though."

"Well, that's good."

Grant shook his head. "No, it's not. I'd much rather have more cavalry on us than has been the case. Perhaps our defeat of Wheeler inflicted more damage on the rebel cavalry than I thought. In any case, though, it doesn't matter. The important thing is that Johnston and the authorities in Richmond see that we're headed to central Alabama and take steps to stop us."

McPherson's eyes narrowed. "I'm not sure I understand."

"Well, James, that's why I have come to you today." He handed an envelope over to McPherson. "Your new orders. The Army of the Tennessee is to halt its march southwest, turn around, and return to Campbellton with all speed. You will be met there by advance elements of the Army of the Cumberland."

McPherson looked through the first few lines of his orders. "March back to the northeast? Why have we come all this way only to turn around and go back the way we have come?"

"It's quite simple, really. You and the Army of the Ohio have been taking part in a ruse, designed to make the enemy believe that we had abandoned our effort to capture Atlanta. In fact, the capture of Atlanta has been my goal all along. We've received word from our spies in the city that General Johnston has been successfully deceived. Two corps have been entrained at Palmetto and are now on their way to Montgomery. Only a single corps now holds Atlanta. If we cross the river and move on the city quickly from the west, we shall have such an overwhelming numerical advantage that we should be able to defeat this force and capture Atlanta before Johnston realizes his mistake and brings the other two corps back."

As he listened to what Grant was saying, a smile gradually spread across McPherson's face. He was silent for nearly a minute, while Grant eyed him closely to gauge his reaction to the news.

"Well, James?" Grant finally asked.

"General Grant, I applaud you. You certainly fooled me. And you seem to have fooled Johnston as effectively as you fooled Pemberton last year during the Vicksburg Campaign."

Grant grunted. "Let's hope so. But there is a lot of work to be done before we congratulate ourselves. You and your men must move to Campbellton at once and secure a bridgehead across the river. The Army of the Cumberland will march to meet you there, excepting one corps which shall remain at Vining's Station to protect the railroad from any rebel attack."

"And Schofield?"

"He shall continue downriver with his men for the time being, as will most of the cavalry, to keep up the appearance of a threat to Alabama."

"And when we're across the river in force?"

"Why, James, it should be obvious. When we're across the river in force, we shall move directly on Atlanta, smash the rebel force remaining there, and present the city as a gift for President Lincoln."

*   *   *   *   *

September 19, Night

The light of the campfires and the sounds of the singing faded into nothingness with every step McFadden took away from the campground of the 15th Illinois. He doubted if anyone had seen him slip away. If they had, they would only have assumed that he was going to relieve himself. Hopefully, they would not notice that he had not returned. McFadden doubted he would be missed in any case, as no one in the regiment had spoken to him all that much, with the single exception of Archie O'Connor.

Somewhere off to his left, he thought he heard the flowing of the Chattahoochee River. The sky was cloudless and through the treetops he could see the waning moon and innumerable stars dancing overhead. Using a simple skill his father had taught him, McFadden quickly used the Big Dipper to pick out Polaris, thereby determining which direction was north. That established, he began walking southwest, toward what he assumed was the encampment of the Army of the Ohio. Every step he took brought him closer to Cheeky Joe.

He walked slowly but steadily. The light of the moon and the stars provided sufficient illumination to allow him to avoid the low-hanging branches of the innumerable trees. Fireflies blinked all around him and, aside from his own steps, the only sound he could hear was the chattering of cicadas and the distant, almost ghostly laughter of encamped Northern troops. Occasionally he could see flickers of campfires through the sea of trees.

McFadden wanted to avoid any unnecessary contact with Union troops, as they might want to know who he was and where he was going, so he kept his distance from the encampments and continued steadily southwest. The task of staying on course became monotonous, requiring only occasional glances at Polaris to know he was still heading in the right direction.

As the minutes turned into hours, McFadden's mind began to wander. He started wondering what he would do after he had killed Cheeky Joe. Would it make any sense to try to get back to Confederate lines? Even if he was able to evade capture and return to his regiment, he would most likely be brought before a court martial on a charge of desertion. His superiors would be justified in hauling him before a firing squad, for he had indeed deserted his post. It had been his responsibility to lead his men and he had abdicated his duty in order to pursue a personal vendetta.

Perhaps he might simply vanish into the wilderness of northern Georgia and wait for the war to end. The pine forests were as vast and endless as the sea, after all. It would probably be a simple matter to find a quiet place, hunt and fish for food, and survive for a few months until the fighting came to an end. And what then? He wouldn't be able to remain in the South, not after having deserted the army. Might he journey north to one of the great industrial cities and find work? What kind of life would that lead to for a man like him? And having fought against them for two-and-a-half years, could he ever be comfortable living amongst the Yankees?

He could, of course, attempt the arduous journey across the Mississippi River to get back to Texas. As far as he understood, he still legally owned the farm that had belonged to his father. But other returning veterans would pick him out as a deserter. No, he could not possibly return to Texas now.

The thought saddened him, but what saddened him even more was what Annie must now think of him. She had probably read his letter in despair, her stomach tightening as she went through each word. As unworthy as McFadden felt himself to be, he knew that Annie had begun to fall in love with him. Perhaps their relationship had begun to awaken in her some of the hope and faith that it had awakened in him. Had she stayed awake at night, dreaming of a happy life together after the war, as he had often done?

It didn't matter now, of course. Whatever his relationship with Annie was or might have been, it now lay in ruins. His quest for revenge had destroyed his last chance at happiness.

McFadden's thoughts suddenly turned to Patrick Cleburne, which he found rather odd. Somewhere, many miles away, Cleburne was sitting in his headquarters tent wondering whether the Confederate government was about to cast him to the winds for having made his emancipation proposal. The men of the division loved Cleburne as though he were their father. McFadden didn't feel quite the same way, but he certainly respected Cleburne for his military brilliance and for how carefully he cared for his soldiers.

Cleburne had seen fit to promote McFadden to lieutenant after the Battle of Peachtree Creek. Although he had been ambivalent at first, McFadden now knew how much he appreciated this gesture of confidence. And how had he returned the favor? By deserting his post. It was shameful. Both Annie Turnbow and Patrick Cleburne had put their faith in McFadden, but he had been weighed in the scales and found wanting.

McFadden continued on, trying to navigate a pass between the yellow orbs on either side of him that suggested Yankee campfires. But the task became increasingly difficult after another half hour, which probably meant that he was approaching the general encampment of an enemy division. He moved very carefully, trying not to make a sound. But it turned out not to be good enough.

"Halt!" a voice demanded.

McFadden turned toward the sentry, who had been standing so still that he had mistaken him for a tall tree stump. In the darkness, it had been impossible to tell the difference.

"Friend!" McFadden said quickly.

"Identify yourself!"

He struggled to remember his façade. "Private Sam Stephens! 15th Illinois!"

"The hell you say! Drop your musket!"

McFadden dropped his rifle and raised his hands. The man moved forward a few steps to get a better look at him.

"Come back to the camp with me, if you please."

The sentry's tone had shifted to one slightly more polite. It was natural to be tense and alert in the dark, but the man probably knew that no Confederate units were thought to be nearby and that his regiment was camped in the midst of an immense Union army. The possibility of an enemy attack was exceedingly remote.

McFadden strolled with him toward the nearest cluster of campfires. It turned out to be the encampment of the 5th Tennessee, made up of Union loyalists from the eastern part of the state. Such men were despised as traitors throughout the Confederate army, much in the same manner as was George Thomas. For just a moment, he wondered what had become of the man he had captured that memorable day at Peachtree Creek, but quickly dismissed the thought as irrelevant.

A few minutes later, he was brought before a Union major, who turned out to be the second-in-command of the regiment.

"15th Illinois?" he asked. There was whiskey on his breath.

"That's right, sir," McFadden answered. "I was supposed to deliver a message to a neighboring regiment, but got lost in the darkness." It seemed as good an explanation as any.

The major smiled in amusement. "Lost, indeed. Hell, boy, you wandered completely out of your army. The 15th Illinois is in the Army of the Tennessee. You've stumbled into the Army of the Ohio!"

He laughed heartily and was joined by many of the men who were cooking around their campfires. McFadden maintained a confused expression on his face, hoping his act of playing dumb would work. He felt a sense of accomplishment, though. Accidentally or not, he was at least getting closer to Cheeky Joe.

"You'd better find a way to get back to your regiment as soon as you can, son," the major was saying. "Word is that the Army of the Tennessee is turning around and marching back northeast first thing tomorrow morning."

"What?" McFadden asked, genuinely confused. "Why would it do that?"

"Do I look like General Grant to you, boy? I don't know why the armies do what they do. Hell, sometimes I don't even know what my own regiment is doing! All I know is that orders came down this afternoon for us to keep marching southwest and telling us that the other army is heading back northeast."

McFadden's mind automatically began to weigh the information, initially just as an exercise in curiosity but then with increasing concern. Why on earth would the Army of the Ohio be continuing to the southwest while the Army of the Tennessee was turning around to go back the way it had come? For that matter, why had most of the Union force left the area of Atlanta and marched southwest in the first place?

He knew he was a simple soldier. By rights, he felt that he probably shouldn't even be an officer. He knew nothing of high strategy, but he could visualize a map as well as anyone. He did not recall there being anything important to the southwest of Atlanta for a hundred miles or more. Could Grant's entire force be moving far out to the west in order to cross the river away from the main Confederate force and then move on Atlanta? Or was something else afoot?

The major had said that the Army of the Ohio was continuing to the southwest. They were already sixty or so miles away from the main Union encampment across from Atlanta. If they continued marching in that direction, their final objective could only be central Alabama. But if they were heading toward Alabama, it made absolutely no sense for the Army of the Tennessee to come halfway and then turn around.

An unpleasant memory intruded upon McFadden's mind. In May of 1863, the 7th Texas had been attached to the Confederate army defending the fortress of Vicksburg on the Mississippi River. Grant, having been stymied in half a dozen earlier attempts to capture the town, had engaged in an elaborate deception to throw the Southern forces into confusion, causing them to think that the main threat was to the north of the city even as Grant marched south and crossed the river below Vicksburg. It was in the midst of this mayhem that the 7th Texas had found itself embroiled in the Battle of Raymond, during which the regiment had nearly been destroyed.

McFadden also recalled something he had read in the newspapers months earlier, about how Grant had successfully deceived Lee in Virginia by swinging his army toward Petersburg and crossing the James River without being detected. If Grant had done something like that twice before, he could certainly be trying to do it again.

In an instant, everything became clear to McFadden. Grant was moving two of his three armies southwest, but only as a feint to draw Johnston away from Atlanta. Having apparently succeeded, he was now ordering the Army of the Tennessee back in the direction of Atlanta to reinforce the attack on the city, while the Army of the Ohio continued on to maintain the deception. McFadden had the sinking feeling that neither Johnston nor any other general in the Confederate army knew what Grant was up to.

But McFadden knew.

He was now within the encampment of the Army of the Ohio. Very likely, Cheeky Joe was within a few miles of the ground on which he was standing. The men of the 5th Tennessee had no idea that he was a Confederate soldier. If his disguise had worked here, it could work elsewhere. All he had to do now was press on just a little further. He could find the man who had tortured and killed his brother and send him to the Hell he deserved.

But something else tugged on McFadden. The call of duty began to struggle with his desire for revenge. A trick of fate had brought him into possession of critically important information which had to be brought to his superiors without delay. If Grant's deception had succeeded in fooling Johnston, the Confederate commander had probably moved the Army of Tennessee into a disadvantageous position, leaving Atlanta weakly defended. If his superiors remained in the dark about what the Union army was doing, the city might be taken before Grant's subterfuge was revealed, along with however many troops had been left behind to defend it. Even a simple soldier like him could tell that a defeat of such magnitude might well prove fatal to the Confederacy.

The Unionist Tennessee soldiers had resumed singing around the campfire, while the major who had earlier questioned him had begun taking more swigs from his bottle of whiskey. No one was paying the least attention to him. Without saying another word to anyone, McFadden quietly slipped back into the darkness of the woods, this time walking directly northeast.

Chapter Fifteen

September 20, Noon

"Welcome to Alabama, General Johnston!" Stewart said, saluting.

The commander of the Army of Tennessee returned the salute as he stepped off the passenger train and glanced around. Stewart was technically incorrect, for the town of West Point was actually just inside Georgia on the Alabama border. It was little more than a tiny hamlet. Aside from the train station itself, there seemed to be nothing of any importance. It certainly bore no resemblance to the beautiful town on the Hudson River in New York, where Johnston and so many of his fellow officers had been educated. The name of the town only indicated that it marked the final western point on the railroad from Atlanta. Farther west, the Montgomery and West Point Railroad ran towards the center of Alabama.

Johnston looked up and down the environs of the train station. Everywhere, infantry companies were disembarking from livestock cars, forming up for a quick inspection before being marched off to their assembly points. Johnston could also see artillery being carefully unloaded from flatbeds. Everywhere there was shouting and swearing by hard-working men. As far as he could see, all was going smoothly.

"Any sign of the enemy?" Johnston asked. Stewart had arrived two days before and would be the best informed person.

"Rumors of Yankee cavalry north of here, but nothing confirmed."

"What sort of rumors?"

"Chatter from the locals, mostly."

Johnston nodded. "Looks like we beat Grant to the Alabama border."

"I think so, sir."

"You hear that, Mackall? We won the race!"

Mackall, stepping off the train himself, smiled and nodded.

Johnston turned back to Stewart. "You've deployed your men?"

"Yes, sir. As each division has arrived, they have assembled outside the station and marched northwest to the town of Lafayette. General Loring informs me that there is good ground in that vicinity. They have begun entrenching there, in a defensive position facing to the northeast."

"Good. Very good. When Grant arrives, he will encounter an unpleasant shock. Rather than marching into Alabama against no resistance, he will bump into two entrenched corps of the Army of Tennessee, ready and eager for battle. And he will have to deal with us before he can move on either Montgomery or Selma. A good strategic situation, I think."

A staff officer handed Mackall a handful of telegrams. The chief-of-staff began reading through them quickly.

"Anything interesting?" Johnston asked.

"The last brigade of Cheatham's corps is departing from Palmetto. The transfer appears to be running with exceptional smoothness."

"I am happy to hear it. Any word from Hardee in Atlanta?"

"Not that I can see. I would imagine that no news is good news, since he would have reported anything unexpected or out of the ordinary."

"True. Atlanta is in good hands with Hardee. We now need to focus on our interception of Grant."

"Hmm," Mackall said, reading through another telegram.

"What is it?"

"It's from the War Department. Secretary Seddon wishes to know why we have decided to move such large forces into Alabama without first receiving permission from Richmond. He also wishes to know if we have coordinated our movement with General Taylor, as we have crossed into the territory of his department."

Johnston grunted.

Mackall's eyebrows went up. "How do you want me to respond, sir?"

"I don't want you to, William. We are in the middle of a highly complicated logistical undertaking here. I have neither the time nor the inclination to flatter the vanity of mindless government officials who are hundreds of miles away and have no knowledge of the situation here."

Mackall tilted his head. "Very well, sir."

"For God's sake, William! Don't the idiots in Richmond know that we're trying to win a war here? I hope that history will faithfully record how much the operations of our army have been hamstrung by meddling officials in Richmond, especially Jefferson Davis himself."

"If historians have the archives of the Confederate Army and the government to look at, the story will tell itself."

Johnston thought about that for a moment. "Would it be too much trouble to begin preparing copies of the more important documents? Telegrams, orders, that sort of thing?"

Mackall considered this. "All our staff officers have their hands full coordinating this movement, but I could see what I can do."

"Do it, then. If, God forbid, this movement fails and we are defeated, I will want the people to know the truth about where the blame lies."

For just a moment, Johnston again found himself haunted by the thought of what the people of the South would think of him if they lost the war. As early as the fall of 1861, there had been grumblings in certain quarters that he should have pushed on to capture Washington after he had won the First Battle of Manassas. Davis and others blamed him for the loss of Vicksburg, a defeat which cut the Confederacy in two. If he failed against Grant now, his great victory at Peachtree Creek would be forgotten and he would go down in history as the man who had brought the South to defeat.

But if future historians had his own records to pour over, they would no doubt conclude that General Joseph Johnston had acted honorably and appropriately at all times.

*   *   *   *   *

September 21, Morning

The five hundred men of the 8th Michigan Cavalry Regiment slowed from a canter to a trot as they approached the north bank of the Chattahoochee River, then from a trot to a walk, and finally came to a halt on the riverbank itself. For several minutes, they gazed southward across the river, keenly observing the tiny hamlet of Campbellton.

A week before, two corps of the Army of Tennessee had been camped around Campbellton. Now, however, there were no Southern troops to be seen anywhere.

The water at this point in the river was fairly shallow and it wasn't long before the Michigan troopers found a spot where their horses were able to walk across without too much difficulty. Slowly and cautiously, the first few squads crossed to the south bank and began to fan out throughout the town. As they did so, more cavalry arrived on the north bank and began to cross over as well. In the distance, as the sun began to peek over the eastern horizon, long snake-like columns of infantry were coming into view. The steady crunching sound these columns produced was the rhythmic footsteps of thousands of marching men.

Two hours after the first troopers of the 8th Michigan established themselves on the south bank, Grant arrived on the north bank, mounted on Cincinnati. There to greet him was McPherson, who had arrived half an hour earlier.

"Well?" Grant said without preamble.

"Three regiments are across. The town of Campbellton has been secured."

"Any resistance?"

"There was a force of about twenty or so Georgia militia sleeping in the Masonic Lodge. They were taken prisoner without a shot fired. They hadn't woken up yet." McPherson grinned with satisfaction.

"None got away? You're sure about that?"

"Completely, sir."

Grant nodded. "Good. I want our friends in Atlanta to be kept in the dark for as long as possible."

"They'll find out sooner or later."

"True, but if we're both lucky and careful, we might have a full day or so to get our troops across and on the road to Atlanta before the enemy knows we're coming."

Grant turned in the saddle and looked behind him. Right on schedule, the men of the 58th Indiana Regiment were scurrying forward, skirting past the edge of the infantry column and dragging with them the enormous number of wooden frames that made up the pontoon bridge. Sherman had told Grant that these were men who could be counted upon without hesitation, as they had rapidly thrown pontoon bridges over every river between Dalton and Atlanta.

They didn't disappoint Grant. Within a matter of hours, the pontoon bridge was secured across the Chattahoochee river.

When the last pontoon was finally in place, bugles blared and drums rumbled in the infantry column that had been patiently waiting. With the fife band at their head playing *The Battle Hymn of the Republic*, the men of the Army of the Tennessee stepped forward and began marching onto the bridge and over the river. Grant sat in the saddle atop Cincinnati, watching the men move past without his placid expression changing a jot, incessantly smoking one cigar after another.

McPherson, who had gone off to attend to the various details of the crossing, returned to Grant in the mid-afternoon. His expression was one of an immensely pleased man.

"All seems to be going well, Sam."

Grant grunted. "We need to be going faster. I want at least twenty-five thousand men on the south bank by the time the sun goes down."

"I think we should be able to achieve that. And the men will continue to cross all night."

"Good. I have just dispatched a courier to General Howard, telling him to bring the bulk of the Army of the Cumberland to Campbellton with all dispatch. He shall first send one of his corps marching northeast, as an additional feint to fool the rebels. This corps will shortly return to Vining's Station, to prevent any sudden rebel lunge at our railroad."

"Very good, sir."

"If the information we have received from our spies is correct, the last rebel troop train departed from Palmetto the day before yesterday. We shall only have Hardee's corps to deal with."

McPherson grinned. "How very kind of General Johnston to send two-thirds of his army away. I should like to send him a note of thanks."

Grant ignored the joke. He had never had much of a sense of humor. "When your army is formed up on the south bank, you shall advance directly eastwards on Atlanta, but detach a force of cavalry to the southeast in order to cut the railroad and prevent Johnston from bringing his men back to the city. If we are lucky, we shall be able to mass sixty or seventy thousand men against Hardee's single corps, which does not number more than twenty thousand, according to our latest information."

"I can accept odds of three-to-one," McPherson said.

"Don't get overconfident. The defenses of Atlanta are very strong. Hardee's corps has some of the best troops the rebels have in the field. We may have the advantage of numbers, but we still have a difficult task ahead of us."

"True enough, sir."

Grant said nothing for a time, watching intently as yet another regiment marched onto the bridge and began crossing the river. A few hundred yards downriver, the pioneers were putting into place a second pontoon bridge, which would allow the flow of men and material onto the south bank to be doubled.

He turned to McPherson. "Have you established a headquarters on the south bank yet?"

"Yes, sir."

"Why don't you go ahead and cross over yourself, then? I shall join you at your headquarters this evening."

"Very well, sir." McPherson stiffly saluted, then kicked his horse into a walk and ventured onto the bridge. His color bearer and a few staff officers followed. Grant watched them go, sticking yet another cigar into his mouth and congratulating himself on so skillfully reestablishing the Union presence on the south bank of the Chattahoochee River.

* * * * *

September 22, Morning

"Did you see the *New York Times?*" Lincoln asked excitedly as Seward entered the room. When the Secretary of State shook his head, the President quickly passed a copy over the table as Seward sat down. He quickly picked it up and perused the front page. Lincoln sat back quietly, a smile on his face, pouring Seward a cup of steaming coffee.

"Well, this story is first rate," Seward said after a few minutes. "Raymond is doing a lovely job, as always. He seems to have laid the entire Marble issue before the people in a concise yet comprehensive manner, connecting him with the money provided by the rebel agent Humphries and highlighting his close involvement with the effort to elect McClellan." Seward glanced at the date. "This is yesterday's paper?"

"Yes. The story will be in papers all across the country tomorrow, I would guess."

"Our papers. The Democratic ones will either ignore the story altogether or claim Raymond is making the whole thing up."

"Oh, they are already doing that," Lincoln replied. "Raymond wired me this morning, telling me that the *New York World* has denounced the story as false and is calling for Marble's immediate release from custody. There have also been some demonstrations on the streets, with Democrats clashing with our people outside the offices of the *New York Times.*"

Seward shook his head. "I deplore the possibility of civil unrest as we come closer and closer to the election. The riots in New York over the past two years are deeply unsettling to me. The fact that immense armies roam across the land slaughtering one another is bad enough, but must we have violent death far from the battlefields as well?"

"Jefferson and Madison did not expect democracy to be quiet and peaceful. We would be naïve if we didn't agree with them."

Seward put the paper back down on the desk. "Yes, well, that is beside the point. I must say, I am very pleased with how things are going. As this story disseminates throughout the country, the people will begin to associate the Democratic Party directly with the rebellion. They start seeing the people who support McClellan as being in league with the same people who are killing their sons, husbands, and brothers in Virginia and Georgia merely to protect their so-called right to own other human beings. It could promote a complete shift in popular opinion back toward our party."

"Appealing to patriotism has always been at the forefront of our electoral strategy. With this story resonating throughout the country, our underlying message that the Democratic Party is uncommitted to defending the Union will seem vindicated. Which, if combined with a military success by Grant, should be more than sufficient to ensure our reelection."

There was a knock on the door and, before Lincoln could call out to ask who it was, the door opened and Stanton walked in.

"Ah, Mr. Secretary. Would you like some coffee?"

"No, thank you," Stanton said as he took his seat. "I have had too much this morning as is."

"Any news from the battlefield?" Seward asked.

"Yes, that's why I have come. Grant has sent a message by coded telegram, finally giving me a summary of his operational plan."

"And?"

"Grant informs me that the movement toward central Alabama was merely a ruse intended to compel General Johnston to shift most of his army to that state by railroad. Grant's actual plan, near as I can tell, is to cross to the south side of the Chattahoochee River west of Atlanta and move on the city from that direction."

"Is it?" Lincoln said. "Well, I must say that Grant can never be counted on to do the expected. The man's more wily than a fox."

"It would have been better if Grant had told us of his plan before he marched."

"I've made it clear repeatedly that Grant enjoys my full confidence," Lincoln said. "He is free to keep his own counsel."

"Well, we'll see," Stanton said.

"I would think the rebels would still have a formidable force holding Atlanta," Seward observed. "And I am sure its defenses are strong."

"No doubt," Stanton said. "But Grant has certainly taken that into account. And if he has succeeded in diverting the bulk of the Army of Tennessee to Alabama and thereby concentrated almost the full force of his own army against only a portion of that of the enemy, then his prospects for success will be very great."

"You hear that, Seward?" Lincoln said playfully. "I had a feeling that Grant had some scheme afoot. Marching his entire army to Alabama seemed rather unsubtle, in my opinion. But then, I am no military man."

"None of us are, Mr. President," Stanton said. "That is why we have generals."

*   *   *   *   *

September 22, Noon

Cleburne, accompanied by Lieutenant Hanley, barely stopped his horse before he expertly slid off the saddle and onto the ground. A waiting orderly grabbed the reins as Cleburne walked quickly up the steps onto the porch of the Dexter Niles house and stepped inside the door. Hanley followed at a respectful distance.

When Johnston had delegated the command of the forces remaining in Atlanta to Hardee, it had been decided that the Dexter Niles house would continue to serve as the general headquarters for all Confederate forces in the area. All the couriers were familiar with its location, the roads in its vicinity were adequate and had been improved by the engineers, and the telegraph wires would not need to be restrung anywhere. It had been a sensible decision.

Hardee glanced up from a map-strewn table as Cleburne walked in. He had a worried expression on his face, but beamed a smile upon the sight of Cleburne.

"How are you, Patrick?"

"Very well. Your message sounded urgent."

"It was." Hardee gestured down to the map. "It looks as though the Army of the Cumberland is on the move. Part of it, anyway."

"Show me."

Hardee's fingers traced his words. "Hard to make out, actually. It seems as though a strong force of infantry, perhaps the size of a full corps, is marching northeast up the river, toward the fords which the Yankees used to cross the river back in July. A considerable body, maybe two corps, is remaining in its previous position at Vining's Station."

"Can we not send scouts to the north bank to determine the strength and exact direction of this movement?" Cleburne asked.

Hardee shook his head. "We have insufficient cavalry. Indeed, we are lucky that we have been able to detect this movement at all."

Cleburne silently cursed Joseph Wheeler before going on. "Is it possible that this is merely a diversion designed to prevent us from sending additional troops to Alabama? It stands to reason that Grant would want Howard to pin as many of our troops as possible here in their present positions."

"It's possible, I suppose. But it's also possible that they are attempting a movement against Atlanta. We have to assume they are, at any rate."

Cleburne thought quickly, his eyes never wavering from the map. "But if they seriously intend to cross the river to threaten the city, why would they move to the north? Crossing there would force them to come up against Peachtree Creek again before they attack the city. Considering their previous experience with that little rivulet, I imagine that they would wish to avoid it."

Hardee grinned. "Nevertheless, I shall instruct General Walker to keep a close watch on the fords to the north."

"Are you going to notify General Johnston?" Cleburne asked.

"Of course, but I shall not present the situation as serious. Johnston has enough on his mind worrying about Grant. If this turns out to be merely a feint designed to keep us from sending additional troops to Alabama, I would hate to have distracted him. Besides, I am optimistic that we can repulse any attack by the enemy with our own resources, without having to call for help from elsewhere."

Another thought crossed Cleburne's mind. "Is it possible that the Army of the Cumberland might also be moving troops southwest, toward the fords of Sandtown or Campbellton? This move to the north might be a diversion intended to deceive us rather than General Johnston. And our lack of cavalry would make any such move hard to detect."

Hardee stared down at the map and thought for a minute. "No, that cannot be. The entire Army of the Cumberland numbers only about thirty-five thousand men, near as we can tell. The troops moving northeast number at least fifteen thousand men. That would leave far too few for them to attempt a simultaneous movement in the other direction."

Cleburne nodded. "Yes, they lack the strength to attempt to catch us in a pincer movement. If they attempted to attack the city from both the north and west, we could concentrate all our force against only a part of the enemy army and crush them before the other could come to its assistance."

"Quite so. Howard's not a great general, but nobody would be that stupid."

"What do you want my division to do?"

"Leave one brigade in place at East Point to watch things to the southwest and move the other two into Atlanta to serve as the reserve. From the city, they can be dispatched immediately to the point of greatest danger."

Cleburne nodded again. Although no Union troops were reported anywhere to the west or south of Atlanta, leaving a single brigade to guard those approaches seemed like a reasonable precaution.

"Sir?" a staff officer tepidly asked.

"What is it?" Hardee replied.

"A man by the name of John Maxwell wishes to speak to you. He says that he provided General Johnston with a letter of introduction from Colonel Gorgas of the Ordnance Bureau about a-" the man fumbled with the pronunciation- "a horological torpedo that he has invented."

"What the hell is a horological torpedo?" Hardee snapped.

"Some sort of infernal device with a clock."

Hardee shook his head abruptly. "I have no time for nonsense, Lieutenant. Tell this man that I shall see him just as soon as I can but that I am presently very busy. In the meantime, he should go back to his lodgings."

Cleburne grinned. "Time is not something we are likely to have much of in the coming days, by the looks of it." He had no idea how right he was.

September 22, Night

McFadden thought that he had chosen a good spot. The tree branch upon which he was now perched was thick and sturdy enough to bear his weight, almost like a smaller, secondary trunk that the tree had thrust out to its side. This allowed him to hover directly over the path beneath him. It could not have reasonably been called a road, but was just some old and godforsaken trail. It had probably been carved out of the woods by the feet of generations of Cherokee Indians, who had ruled the region for centuries before they had been driven out by white settlers thirty years before.

He breathed slowly and deeply, trying to move as little as possible. The branch onto which he clung was thickly covered with smaller, leafy branches, giving him a reasonable amount of cover. But even without it, McFadden felt perfectly safe. The darkness of the night combined with the blue uniform he was wearing made him effectively invisible. Moreover, as he had learned from observing the Yankees who had occasionally passed beneath him, people seldom looked up.

He had not seen all that many Yankees, though. He had gradually moved toward the southern, right flank of the great Northern army that was assembling on the south bank of the Chattahoochee River, miles away from the great concentration that was taking place at Campbellton. Occasional squads of enemy cavalry had passed beneath him from time to time over the past two hours, guided by torch-wielding horsemen, but he had not yet seen what he had been waiting for.

It had taken McFadden nearly two days to catch up to the Army of the Tennessee. True to what the drunken Unionist Tennessee major had said, it had indeed halted its march to the southwest, turned around, and begun a countermarch back to the northeast. McFadden had passed by countless regiments moving up the river road, always keeping up his pretense of being a messenger. It was a thin pretense, he knew, but the sight of an ordinary-looking man in a Union uniform had continued to attract no attention in the midst of a giant Union army.

McFadden had expected that crossing to the south side of the Chattahoochee would be his most difficult task. When armies crossed bridges, a legion of staff officers was usually present overseeing the operation and security was commonly much higher as well. He had considered waiting until nightfall and swimming over the Chattahoochee before deciding that this would lose him too much time. But despite his fears, getting over the bridge had proven surprisingly easy. Unable to come up with a better plan, he had simply walked behind the column of the nearest regiment, a Wisconsin unit, when it had marched across one of the bridges. Nobody had thought his presence worthy of note and, as soon as he was on the south bank, he had continued on his way.

Simply by listening to the conversations going on around him, he picked up a good deal of information. The entire Army of the Tennessee was indeed moving to the south bank of the Chattahoochee and preparing for an advance on Atlanta, just as he had feared. He had even heard some of the men saying that the Army of the Cumberland was crossing the river not far off and would be moving on the city from the west as well.

The more McFadden thought about it, the more fearful he became. It was entirely possible that he, a lowly lieutenant bumped up from the ranks, was the only Southern soldier who knew anything about what was happening. By the time his comrades in the city discovered the truth, it could well be too late.

There was a sound of approaching horsemen. Through the mass of tree branches, he spotted the flicker of a torch coming nearer. He tensed, willing himself to remain as still as possible. He had waited for hours for the proper prey, a solitary Union horseman. Even with the advantage of surprise, he could not hope to successfully ambush a group of enemy soldiers by himself. But like any army, Grant's host needed to communicate with itself over long distances during the night and this could only be done by messengers. Presumably some would be travelling alone.

He heard a man's voice, which meant that the noise was created by a group rather than an individual. His muscles relaxed, for now he only had to remain still and not steel himself for leaping down off the branch. Minutes later, a squad of a dozen Union cavalrymen passed underneath him, never suspecting for a moment the presence of an enemy.

He relaxed and resumed his waiting, even as his concern was growing. Dawn would begin to break in the east within a few hours and light would eventually force him to abandon his ambush position. If he could not find a horse to carry him the rest of the way to Atlanta, there would be no way for him to warn his superiors of the approaching Union threat in time to make any difference. Moreover, he would be trapped outside the city when the Yankees began their attack, meaning that he would likely never see Annie again.

He couldn't tell how much time had passed after he had seen the squad of Union cavalry when he again heard the sound of an approaching horse and saw the flickering of a torch. His ears told him that the noise was much quieter than it had been before. McFadden stared hard until he saw a solitary figure on a brown horse emerge into his sight below him. The torch the man carried seemed to create a small and vulnerable bubble of pale light around him, tenuously keeping the darkness at bay.

McFadden waited until the man walked his horse close enough to the overhanging branch, then pounced. He made no shout or yell as he dove down through the air, but the motion and sight of an unexpected attacker caused the Union trooper to cry out in alarm. It was useless, for it took less than a second for McFadden to land on him. The weight and speed of McFadden's body effortlessly pulled the soldier out of his saddle. The startled horse neighed loudly in confusion. An instant later, McFadden and the Yankee both slammed roughly into the rocky ground, though McFadden's landing was cushioned by the body of the man he was attacking.

Silence had been punctuated by a moment of noise and brutal violence, but it came back almost immediately. It was as though a heavy door had slammed itself shut. McFadden picked himself up and quickly examined the enemy soldier. To his satisfaction, he had been knocked senseless. The torch remained lit on the ground and McFadden quickly picked it up in order to prevent it from going out.

McFadden stood still for a time, allowing his heart to resume a more placid rhythm. He turned toward the horse, which eyed him with some measure of confusion but without hostility. He tightened the saddle and stirrups as best he could, then mounted the horse. Turning to the east, he began leading the horse through the darkness toward Atlanta.

*   *   *   *   *

September 23, Noon

"How large a force of cavalry?" Johnston asked, hunched over a map.

"At least a brigade, sir," Mackall answered. "I'd say it's probably screening the advance of a large force of infantry."

"And they've occupied the town of Roanoke?"

"Yes, sir. About twenty miles north of our present position."

Johnston grunted and looked at the map more closely. Since arriving two days before in the town of Lafayette, he had been striving to memorize the terrain over which he expected the coming battle to be fought. He had carefully deployed his forces to cover the different approaches he thought Grant might take on his approach to Montgomery. Some were lightly fortified and held by relatively small detachments, deployed there only to detect the approach of the enemy before falling back to more defensible strongholds. He had dispatched what little cavalry he had into roving patrols throughout the area. The bulk of Johnston's forty thousand men were busy fortifying a position northeast of Lafayette itself.

"I think we're in a good position," Mackall said. "Assuming that this cavalry is preceding the main infantry force, Grant is doing exactly what we expected him to do."

"I agree. With our main force entrenched here at Lafayette, Grant will either have to attack us head on or attempt to bypass us. If the former, he will have no choice but to throw his men directly against our entrenchments and suffer a bloody repulse. If the latter, he would leave his flank open to a devastating counter attack."

Mackall nodded sharply. "In either case, I believe we should emerge the victor. Grant will be left with a defeated and shrunken army of demoralized troops, at the end of a very precarious supply line. Easy prey, in other words."

"And with a good road connecting us to the railhead at West Point, we need have no fears for our own supplies."

An orderly walked in and extended a paper. "Telegram from General Hardee, sir."

Johnston thanked the man and quickly read through the message.

"What is it?" Mackall asked.

"It appears that the Army of the Cumberland has begun a movement of some kind. One of the three enemy corps has set out from the Yankee base at Vining's Station, moving upriver. As of yesterday, when this telegram was dated, Hardee did not think the enemy had crossed over to the south bank."

"Sounds like a feint to me. Grant may be trying to spook us into sending some of our troops back to Atlanta."

"Or at least prevent us from bringing any more troops from Atlanta down to our position here." Johnston read through the message once again. "Hardee does not seem to feel that the matter is very serious. He states at the end that he believes he can deal with any situation that might develop with his own troops."

"Nothing to concern us, then," Mackall said. "We should keep our attention firmly focused on Grant."

Johnston nodded. "Get my horse saddled up, William. Yours, too. I want to make a personal inspection of the fortifications."

*　　　　*　　　　*　　　　*　　　　*

September 23, Afternoon

Marble paced back and forth, fretting furiously at his lack of freedom. Most men in the Union treated him with a wary respect, fearful of the power he could wield through the pages of his newspaper. Benjamin Butler, however, was not an easy man to intimidate and he had no compunction whatsoever about tossing Marble into a dank and uncomfortable jail cell. Having now spent more than a week behind bars, he was beginning to suspect he was going mad. The journalist in him was hungry for information about what was happening and the political operative in him despaired at his lack of ability to influence events.

Even if he couldn't know what was happening beyond the walls of his cell, he could make some educated guesses. He had no doubt that the information that linked him with money provided by the Confederate government had been immediately handed over to pro-Lincoln newspapers. His close relationship with George McClellan, in turn, would be used as political fodder to promote the reelection of Lincoln.

Marble was angry and disgusted with himself. It had been his own arrogance and ambition which had caused him to accept Humphries' money in the first place. In retrospect, he could see that it had been an incredibly foolish thing to do. He might partially blame the debacle on Humphries, for having been captured during his attempt to escape back into rebel-held territory, but he knew that the principal fault lay with himself.

Just beyond the bars of his cell stood two Union soldiers, each holding a musket with a fixed bayonet. He had tried to engage them in conversation, but the only response they had ever given him was to state that General Butler's orders prohibited them from speaking to him. Out of boredom, he had attempted to spark their anger by mocking them, alternately insinuating that they were buffoons without intelligence or that their wives were unfaithful. Their only reply had been to blankly stare at him and he had given up the game after several fruitless hours.

It had only been after three days that Butler had deigned to allow Marble paper and ink. Since then, Marble had been writing furiously, hour after hour. He feared that he would certainly lose his mind if he stopped writing, for he needed to find some activity besides sleep that would occupy his endless time. More importantly, he had to find a way to strike back at his enemies, even if he had to do it from behind bars.

He heard a clanging sound, and his heart leapt at the smallest break in the monotony. The door to his cell block opened with a grating squeak and two soldiers escorted a well-dressed man into the hall. It was Horatio Seymour.

"You men wait outside," Seymour said to the guards.

"I'm sorry, sir, but we have been given strict-"

"I am the Governor of New York State," Seymour said forcefully. "I can have your families tossed out of the tenements with a single word. You will wait outside."

The men glanced at one another, fear evident on their faces. "We shall have to remain on the other side of the door," one of them said.

"Very well. Now, out with you."

The guards nodded and quickly stepped out, closing the door behind them.

"Governor Seymour," Marble said, bowing his head.

Seymour didn't respond right away, standing on the other side of the bars and shaking his head. "Damn you, Marble," he finally said. "You've made a thorough mess of things, I don't mind saying."

"How bad is it?"

"As bad as it could possibly be!" Seymour's voice rose to a shout. "Every Republican newspaper in the country is running with the story that the Democratic Party is being directly financed by the rebels! The *New York Times*, the *Chicago Tribune*, the *New York Tribune*, and dozens of other papers! They are scarcely talking of anything else! Even some papers which previously supported us are joining in the chorus!"

Marble's countenance fell. Although he had assumed that the situation was very much as Seymour described, to have it confirmed so forcefully felt like being punched in the stomach. He sat down on his cot, holding his head in his hands.

"I thought the money would be useful," he said. "It was like getting manna from heaven."

"Did it never occur to you that the money might be from the rebels? Dear God, Marble, how stupid are you?"

"I have written a letter explaining my side of the story. I was hoping you could have it delivered to my offices at the *New York World* so that it could be printed."

"What good is that going to do?" Seymour asked.

"I simply want it on the record that I did not know that Humphries was a Southern agent."

Seymour shook his head. "Sorry, Manton. It was all I could do to persuade the high and mighty Butler to be allowed to visit you. Among his conditions was a stipulation that I not deliver any writings from you to anyone outside the jail."

Marble instinctively clenched his fists in anger. Butler had given him writings materials only as a sadistic ploy to get his hopes up so that he could dash them down later on. The politician-turned-general was trying to break Marble's will, but the newspaperman could not figure out why.

"What is the news from the war?" Marble asked.

"Rumors are flying that Grant has launched a big offensive against Johnston. Considering the trouble you have gotten the Democratic Party in, if Grant wins a big battle against the rebels, we have as much chance of winning the White House as Satan has of being elected Pope."

"Is there any chance you might bring me some newspapers? The lack of news is one of the worst things about being in here."

"Butler says that you are to have no newspapers."

"Why not?" Marble said loudly. "Is he trying to torture me or something?"

"I don't know. But you know what, Marble? I don't really care. Our party's election chances are in ruins and your actions are a major reason why. I find it odd to agree with Benjamin Butler about anything, but as far as I'm concerned, the more unpleasant things are for you, the happier I am."

Marble's heart sank. His dreams were crumbling into dust before his eyes. He had come within a hairsbreadth of serious political power, a foundation on which he could build a big future for himself. Now his closest political allies had turned against him and he faced the very real prospect of being hauled before a firing squad for treason. Even if he eventually got out of jail and somehow managed to get out of the Andrew Humphries imbroglio, his political ambitions were effectively over. He would be lucky if he could somehow remain in the newspaper business. After all, both the Republicans and the Democrats would do their best to prevent the circulation of the *New York World*.

"If you have nothing but bad news for me, why did you visit?" Marble asked.

"To tell you that we're going to lose the election and that it's your fault. And now, if you'll excuse me, I have to go pick up the pieces from the political party you have broken."

*　　　　*　　　　*　　　　*　　　　*

September 23, Evening

"Sir? A lieutenant is here to see you. He says it is most urgent."

Cleburne looked up at the words of Lieutenant Hanley. "Who is he?"

"Lieutenant McFadden of the 7th Texas, sir."

Cleburne thought for a moment. "Isn't that the man who captured General Thomas at Peachtree Creek?"

"I believe he is, sir."

"Very well. Send him in." Presumably McFadden was delivering a message from Granbury. He wondered what could be so urgent.

McFadden entered a moment later. Cleburne saw that he was exhausted and covered in dust, concluding that he had just ridden on a horse for a very long time. Perhaps the matter was important after all.

He saluted. "General Cleburne."

Cleburne saluted back. "Well, what's the matter, Lieutenant?"

"The Yankees have crossed the river, sir," McFadden said quickly.

Cleburne's eyes narrowed. For a mere lieutenant, this McFadden fellow had a certain assurance about him that Cleburne had rarely seen elsewhere. "Crossed the river?"

"Yes, sir. And in great force. It's the Army of the Cumberland and the Army of the Tennessee, sir."

Cleburne shook his head. "That cannot be. The Army of the Tennessee is over a hundred miles away, on the Alabama border."

"Believe me, sir. It's less than fifteen miles away, approaching the city from the west alongside the Sandtown Road."

"That cannot be," Cleburne repeated dumbly. He thought for a moment. The Army of the Cumberland, as far as he knew, was on the north bank of the Chattahoochee River, with two corps positioned around Vining's Station and one corps marching northeast. The Army of the Tennessee was marching with Grant into Alabama. At least, that's what it was supposed to be doing.

But the look on McFadden's face was certain. He recalled briefly looking over the man's previous record before confirming his promotion to lieutenant. He had found nothing to suggest incompetence. Quite the contrary, in fact.

"You have seen them yourself?" Cleburne asked.

"I have, sir, yes. I was in the Yankee camp myself just a few days ago. They crossed the river at Campbellton three days ago and have been building up their forces since. They are now on the road to Atlanta and are approaching quickly. As I said, they are only fifteen miles from East Point."

"You were in the Yankee camp?"

"Yes, sir."

"Under orders?"

There was a momentary pause. "No, sir."

"Explain yourself."

McFadden's tone became irritated. "I'd be happy to explain, sir. But it is a long story and there is very little time."

Other generals might have been angered to have a mere lieutenant speak to them in such a manner, but Cleburne took no offense. Without thinking, he looked away to the west. There was no telltale cloud of dust that one would expect to be created by a large column of marching soldiers. But then, it had rained a bit in recent days, which might have prevented much dust from being kicked up at all.

He shook his head. What McFadden was saying seemed impossible. Still, the movement of the single corps of the Army of the Cumberland to the northeast had made little sense when Hardee had first told him about it. If what McFadden was correct and the Yankees had crossed the river far to the southwest of Atlanta, then the movement could have been a feint designed to distract Confederate attention away from the point of real danger.

McFadden was adamant that the Army of the Tennessee was part of the Union force already on the south side of the river. Could Grant have hoodwinked Johnston? Might the perceived threat to

Alabama be nothing more than a deception, designed to pull away the bulk of the Confederate army defending Atlanta?

"Lieutenant Hanley?"

"Sir?"

"Send a message to General Hardee, informing him of a possible sighting of a large Union infantry force on the south side of the Chattahoochee to the southwest of the city, on the Sandtown Road."

"Yes, sir."

"Then get Red Pepper saddled up. I'm going to investigate this myself. And get McFadden a horse, too. His is probably too worn out." Cleburne turned back to McFadden. "A long story, you say?"

McFadden nodded.

"Well, you can tell me on the way."

*   *   *   *   *

Davis sat alone in his office, furiously scribbling. There was simply too much to do and too many messages to write. In his mind, he went over the list of items he had to take care of before he went home for the evening. Blockade runners were ignoring the government requirement to reserve half their cargo space for military supplies, so Davis had to write an order to have it looked into. Some idiots in Congress were attempting to pass a ridiculous bill requiring the government to provide newspapers to the soldiers free of charge, so Davis had to dispatch a message to friendly legislators to quash the useless distraction. There had been complaints from Richmond citizens that the men of the local provost marshal were hoarding food, so Davis had to ask that it be investigated.

These and a thousand other worries weighed on his mind. He remembered reading how a man found guilty of witchcraft during the Salem Witch Trials had been executed by having a large wooden board laid over his prostrate body, which had then been slowly covered with stones until the immense weight crushed the life out of him. Davis knew exactly how that man must have felt.

Although the fury which had initially greeted the news of Cleburne's emancipation proposal had died down somewhat, it still dominated the newspaper headlines across the South. From what Davis had been told, it was also the main topic of conversation in the bars and hotel lobbies of Richmond. General Cooper had concluded his investigation, but no proper course of action had been agreed upon before Johnston had begun moving most of the army to the southwest to counter Grant's movement.

The coming battle in the West also weighed heavily on the President's mind. He stopped writing for a moment and glanced up at the military map. From Johnston's latest report, the bulk of the Army of Tennessee had taken up position on good ground several miles northeast of Lafayette. Firmly entrenched there, they would be in a perfect position to block Grant's movement toward Montgomery and Selma. The most recent telegram, which had arrived just that afternoon, reported that lead units of the Army of the Ohio had been identified about ten miles to the north, with the Army of the Tennessee presumably nearby as well. The battle was expected to begin at any time.

Meanwhile, Hardee's corps was hunkered down in Atlanta, keeping a wary eye on the Army of the Cumberland just over the river. Davis was pleased that Hardee and Cleburne were away from what would soon become the center of the action. With so much controversy swirling around them, Davis was happy that their names would likely not appear in the papers anytime soon.

Military news on the other fronts was good. Confused fighting continued in the northern Shenandoah Valley, but Jubal Early remained undefeated. Lee had recently inflicted a heavy defeat on a large Union force which had been attempting to cut his railroads south of Petersburg. In distant Arkansas, the withdrawal of some Union divisions had enabled General Kirby Smith to push back the Yankee forces in several parts of the state, reoccupying valuable agricultural land. Sterling Price was preparing a large-scale cavalry raid into Missouri.

Militarily, then, the situation appeared promising. The Confederacy would be able to hold its own for a few more months. So long as the Democrats emerged triumphant in the upcoming elections in the North, all would be well.

There was a knock on the door and Secretary Benjamin entered the room. His habitual smile was nowhere in evidence as he quietly took a seat.

"What's wrong?" Davis asked.

Benjamin shook his head. "Trouble up north."

"What sort of trouble?"

"I guess I can't even try to sugarcoat it." Benjamin spent the next several minutes describing the scandal surrounding Manton Marble, word of which had reached him via a Baltimore newspaper smuggled through the lines.

Davis frowned as Benjamin finished the story. "So, Lincoln and his cronies have found themselves a political stick with which to beat the Democrats?"

"Yes, Mr. President. And a pretty good one, too. It is my fault, Mr. President. I judged Humphries to be a careful and cautious man. Clearly, he was anything but."

Davis took a deep breath. "How bad could this be, Judah?"

"Bad, Mr. President. Potentially very bad. While I do not think it will be enough to swing New York State back into the Republican column, it could certainly shake things up in Pennsylvania, Ohio and Indiana. If Lincoln wins one or two of those states, and if these stories of using military forces to control the vote in the border states are true, it could change the political equation completely."

"It might be enough to give Lincoln the electoral votes he needs to secure reelection, in other words."

"That's about the size of it, Mr. President."

Davis shook his head. "It all comes down to Grant, then, doesn't it?"

"It's looking increasingly like that. If Johnston can beat Grant, it will surely swing public opinion in the North against Lincoln and against the war once again. But with this scandal having exploded in the face of the Democrats, the people might be tempted to cast their votes for Lincoln if they can at least look to a meaningful victory."

The Confederate President said nothing in reply, placing his fist under his chin and staring up at the military map for a long time. After awhile, he looked back at Benjamin.

"Was there anything else?"

"Yes, though hopefully a minor matter. It concerns George Thomas."

Davis grunted. He preferred not to think about the traitor Thomas. For Davis, the man's betrayal was all the worse for the fact that he had fought side-by-side with Thomas at the Battle of Buena Vista during the Mexican War. Davis had also secured Thomas his appointment as a major in the 2nd Cavalry Regiment in the mid-1850s. Davis regarded Thomas's decision to remain loyal to the Union as not only dishonorable on moral grounds but also as a violation of personal loyalty to him.

"Well, what about Thomas?"

"You have not yet responded to his request to be executed by firing squad rather than hanging."

"I know. I have had rather more important things on my mind."

"Secretary Seddon informs me that he has received letters from General Johnston and General Lee asking you to show clemency to Thomas. Johnston, for one, says that he personally assured Thomas that he would be well treated when they met on the evening of his capture."

"I don't particularly care what Johnston says to anyone," Davis replied. "I am the President of the Confederate States, not Johnston." He decided not to comment on the fact that Lee was weighing in on the issue. He had followed Lee's advice in maintaining Johnston at the head of the Army of Tennessee and he was beginning to wonder if that had been entirely wise.

Davis shook his head. "I'm more concerned about other things right now. Thomas must be executed, but there is nothing that demands he be executed right away. I will read these letters of

Johnston and Lee when I have the time, but I am simply too hard-pressed right now."

"That's hard on Thomas," Benjamin said softly. "Is it not a bit cruel to keep him in suspense?"

"Perhaps so, but I am not overly concerned with how that traitor feels."

*   *   *   *   *

September 23, Night

The pale white light of the waning moon illuminated the open ground southwest of Atlanta. McFadden thought that he, Cleburne and Lieutenant Hanley looked like wraithlike ghosts as they rode silently down the Sandtown Road. For an hour or so, having left the lights of the city and the campfires of the encampments behind, McFadden had the strange feeling that the three of them were the only human beings in existence.

"So, are you going to tell me why you were in the Union camp?" Cleburne asked.

"I was not attempting to desert, if that's what worries you, sir."

"I didn't think so. Had you been a deserter, you obviously would not have returned to the army. So, why were you there?"

McFadden paused a moment before replying. "I had to kill a man."

Cleburne turned in his saddle and stared at McFadden for a moment. Hanley, riding out in front, simply stared ahead. McFadden was not sure whether he was even listening to their conversation, but it made no difference one way or the other.

"You had to kill a man? There's plenty of killing going on these days, in case you haven't noticed."

"A specific man, sir. A man who killed my brother and who tried to kill me."

"Who?"

McFadden told his story. Throughout the retelling, Cleburne was silent as he listened intently to what McFadden was saying.

"It was then that I found out what the Union army was doing," McFadden concluded.

"And you came back to warn us?" Cleburne asked. It was the first time he spoken in nearly twenty minutes.

"I did, sir, yes."

"You abandoned your quest for vengeance in order to do your duty, then?"

McFadden nodded.

"As you know, McFadden, going absent from your regiment without permission is a serious offense. Under the laws of war, I

- 581 -

could have you shot. But, if your information turns out to be correct, we shall say no more about it. Agreed?"

McFadden nodded. "Agreed, sir." He decided not to ask what would happen if his information turned out to be incorrect.

They rode on in silence for another hour. McFadden was exhausted, being kept awake only by an intense nervous energy. He was not sure what time it was, but it had to be a few hours past midnight. The moon had risen, its light being defused through the trees off to the north. In the distance, the Chattahoochee River shone like a thin sliver of mercury.

After a long time, Lieutenant Hanley pulled his horse to a stop. McFadden and Cleburne halted on either side of him.

"There, sir," Hanley said quietly, pointing down the road.

McFadden saw what looked like a long, dark snake in the distance. There seemed to be hundreds of glittering points of white light within it. As Cleburne raised his field telescope and scanned the column, McFadden realized the points of light were bits of metal in the tack and bridles of large numbers of horses.

"Yankee cavalry," Cleburne said calmly.

"A brigade?" Hanley asked.

"Looks like it. The infantry will be close behind, if what McFadden says is true."

"It is, sir," McFadden said.

"I believe you, Lieutenant. I have the evidence of my own eyes."

"We should get back, sir," Hanley said. "We must assemble the division and alert General Hardee."

"I agree," Cleburne said, snapping shut his telescope. "Let's go."

Cleburne turned his horse and kicked it into a trot, followed by McFadden and Hanley. McFadden was happy to begin back toward their own lines, for three men armed with revolvers would have been easy prey for even a squad of Yankee cavalrymen armed with carbines.

"Would it not be wise for us to go faster, sir?" McFadden suggested.

Cleburne shook his head. "Our mounts are tired. They've been walking all night. Besides, it's probably best not to make too much noise."

McFadden nodded, embarrassed at having made such a silly suggestion.

There was a sudden sound of thundering hooves. The three Southerners jerked their heads toward the sound and saw two dozen Union horsemen several hundred yards away, but approaching at a gallop, heading directly for them.

"We've been spotted, sir!" Hanley said with alarm.

"Looks like you're right again, McFadden!" Cleburne said anxiously. "We've got to make a dash for it!"

The three Southerners kicked their horses into a gallop as quickly as possible. McFadden watched as Cleburne and Hanley both pulled their revolvers from their holsters, but he hesitated to do so himself. Adept neither at firing a pistol nor at riding a horse, he feared that he might lose control of his mount while attempting to do both at the same time. He had scarcely ever galloped on a horse before. At such a speed, he might be thrown from the animal at any moment.

"Halt!" distant voices shouted. "Halt, you rebel bastards!"

Shots rang out, but McFadden did not hear the sharp buzz which would have indicated the bullets were passing near them. Cleburne and Hanley both fired their pistols in the general direction of the Yankee horsemen and McFadden was impressed by their ability to shoot and ride simultaneously. He doubted that either the general or the staff officer would hit anything. Most likely they were simply shooting to cause the Union troopers to hesitate in their pursuit.

"Draw your weapon, McFadden!" Cleburne shouted. "What's the matter with you?"

Keeping a tight grip on the reins with his left hand, McFadden struggled to pull his revolver out of his holster with his right. After a minute of struggle, during which several shots rang past his head, he finally succeeded. Pulling the cock back, he fired off a single round toward the cluster of Union horsemen. Nothing happened. He fired the remaining five shots in quick succession. To his amazement, one of the troopers let out a cry of pain and fell off his horse.

"Good shot!" Cleburne shouted with a smile.

The Union horsemen slowed and veered away. For just a moment, McFadden wondered if perhaps it was because he had hit one of them, but he quickly dismissed that idea as absurd. Most likely, the troopers had orders not to venture too far away from the main column. A few of the Yankees raised their carbines and fired off a few parting shots as they turned away from the Confederates.

Lieutenant Hanley gasped and clutched at his throat, dropping his revolver. McFadden heard a sick gurgling sound which he instantly realized was Hanley trying desperately to breath.

"Stephen!" Cleburne shouted. He reined in alongside Hanley's horse, grabbing its bridle. They continued to ride a few hundred yards, as Hanley struggled to maintain his grip on the reins. Cleburne led Hanley's horse into a small copse of trees. McFadden followed, looking back for any sign that the Union cavalry was still following. He could see them off in the distance, still moving in the other direction.

"McFadden! Help me get him down!"

Cleburne slid off his horse and wrapped his arms around Hanley as he collapsed out of the saddle. McFadden, less agile, took a few seconds to get down off his horse. He rushed to help Cleburne lay Hanley down onto the ground.

Hanley looked up at Cleburne, a pleading and terrified look in his eyes. McFadden had seen the look before on many battlefields and he was certain Cleburne had as well. Blood was pouring out of the young man's mouth. The general grasped his hand firmly and placed his other hand behind Hanley's head. Hanley tried to speak, but the only sound that came out was a sort of watery rasping.

"We cannot stay, sir!" McFadden protested, hurriedly reloading his Colt Navy revolver and looking around. "There's nothing we can do for him! The Yankees could be back at any moment!"

Cleburne looked up at McFadden, his face momentarily a mask of rage. But he calmed instantly as the import of McFadden's words sunk in. He looked back down at Hanley. Life was seeping out of him quickly.

"I'm sorry, my friend," Cleburne said. "I'm sorry."

Hanley died within two minutes. McFadden continued to scan the area, expecting to see more Union troopers arrive at any time. However, he knew he had to give Cleburne at least a few moments. Cleburne stood slowly and looked down at Hanley's body, sadly shaking his head.

"We can't take him back," Cleburne said. "It would slow us down too much. We must return to our lines at once in order to take the necessary measures to meet the enemy."

"Yes, sir."

"Are you Episcopalian, by any chance?"

"No, sir. Presbyterian."

Cleburne nodded. "Of course. Scotsman. An Episcopalian and a Presbyterian can say a prayer together, I should think," Cleburne said.

"Yes, sir."

They bowed their heads and spent a minute praying over the still body of Lieutenant Stephen Hanley. Then, they sadly mounted their horses and rode back to the east, toward Atlanta.

Chapter Sixteen

September 24, Morning

Johnston walked Fleetfoot along the portion of the fortified line held by Loring's Division. The men cheered him as they saw him ride past, but his eyes remained fixed on the Union infantry several hundred yards away, drawn up in a battle line opposite their defenses.

His men had used their time well, constructing an immensely strong fortified position. For miles in both directions, the countryside blistered with parapets, trenches, abatis, and palisades. Strong redoubts butted out from the main line, each containing a battery of artillery and a regiment of infantry, posted to deliver a devastating cross fire at any Yankee troops unwise enough to launch a direct attack.

Stewart's corps held the left and Cheatham's corps held the right. The line itself was four divisions in length, with one division in reserve and the sixth division protecting the road back to the railhead at West Point. It was, to Johnston's eyes, one of the strongest fortified positions he had ever held.

"They're making no move to attack, sir," Mackall said, riding close behind.

"They did not expect to find us here," Johnston replied. "Right now, General Grant is trying to recover from the surprise we have just sprung on him."

"It won't take him long. Grant is not shy about attacking strongly fortified positions, you know. You read the newspaper accounts about his attack on Lee at Cold Harbor, I assume?"

"Very carefully. It is possible, though, that the beating he received there has persuaded him not to attempt such an attack again. Suicide holds little appeal for most soldiers, I should think."

"Well, if he does attack us here, we shall give him a proper bloody nose."

"Yes," Johnston said with a smile. "And if he attempts to move around either of our flanks, we have sufficient reserves to catch him with a counter attack."

"We're in a good spot, all things considered."

Johnston nodded. As he and Mackall continued along the line, his men stood up and cheered. All of them felt the same elation as he did, having successfully outwitted the vaunted Union general and blocked the path to his objective. Now, all he had to do was await Grant's next move.

A cavalry major rode up and reined in near them, quickly saluting.

"We got some prisoners, sir. It's the Army of the Ohio opposite us."

"That's surprising," Johnston said. "Any sign of the Army of the Tennessee?"

"No, sir."

Johnston frowned. "I wonder where it is."

"Perhaps it's bringing up the rear, sir," Mackall offered.

Johnston turned back to the cavalryman. "Have any of the scouts penetrated to the rear of the Union column?"

"I don't think so, sir. There's lots of Union cavalry about, especially out to the northwest of the enemy force. It's not easy to get any of our people through their screen."

There was a soft boom of artillery and a few shells began landing in front of the fortified line. Johnston was unconcerned. His men were so well dug in that even the heaviest bombardment was unlikely to inflict many casualties. Some of the Confederate batteries opened fire, though most remained silent. He had given orders to conserve ammunition until the main Yankee attack.

"The shelling could be the prelude to an infantry assault," Mackall said.

Johnston shook his head. "No, I don't think so. Not yet, anyway. They're just feeling us out. Trying to determine our strength. They are probably unaware that it's the Army of Tennessee and imagine that they are just facing some of Richard Taylor's troops."

"Well, if that's what Grant thinks, he's sadly mistaken," Mackall said with a wry grin.

The artillery duel continued for about half an hour. Then both sides slowed their rate of fire and eventually stopped the shelling altogether. It was as if the opposing gunners had silently come to a mutual agreement that there was little point to it.

Johnston frowned, troubled. Mackall saw his chief's discomfort.

"What is it, sir?"

"I'm not sure. Something doesn't seem quite right."

"What do you mean?"

Johnston pointed to the Union forces across the line. "Sherman never used the Army of the Ohio in this fashion. It was always a maneuver force. To my knowledge, it was never assigned the central position in a battle."

"That's correct. But Grant is not Sherman."

"True, true. But judging from everything I have studied about Grant's operations, I would have expected him to assign the most important role to either his beloved Army of the Tennessee or the more experienced Army of the Cumberland."

Mackall shrugged. "It is unusual. But I see no cause for concern. If I had to guess, I would assume that the Army of the Tennessee was simply behind the Army of the Ohio during their march into Alabama. If that is the case, they are probably forming up somewhere behind the Army of the Ohio even as we speak."

Johnston thought hard for a moment, watching as a thin line of Yankee skirmishers filtered out of the main enemy line like a host of tiny beetles. A few Southern troops fired at them, but the distance was so great that none of them hit anything. The Confederate officers shouted orders for the men to hold steady, as the deployment of skirmishers could indicate that an attack was in the offing.

The Union force made no move to attack. Johnston found this irritating. It was as though two boxers were in a ring, but each was simply sitting in the corner and smiling at the other.

Johnston turned to Mackall. "Send word to the cavalry. I want the Army of the Tennessee located. I don't care how they do it, just that they do it. No excuses. I want to know exactly where the Army of the Tennessee is and I want to know by the time the sun goes down tonight."

"Yes, sir," Mackall said. He turned his horse and kicked it into a canter, heading back toward their headquarters. Johnston turned and looked across the lines at the Union forces again, even more troubled than he had been before.

*   *   *   *   *

"Sir, the telegraph line to Lafayette appears to have been cut."

Cleburne cursed, which was a rare thing for him. It really should not have come as much of a surprise. Had he been in Grant's shoes, the first thing he would have done would have been to cut the telegraph line to the main Confederate force in Alabama, thus preventing Johnston from learning about the predicament in Atlanta until it was too late.

"Any word from Hardee?"

"Yes. General Hardee requests that you report to him immediately at the Niles House."

"Tell him there's no time for that!" Cleburne snapped. "The Yankees could be here at any moment! Tell him that he must come to East Point at once!"

The telegraph operator nodded and dashed off to send the message.

Cleburne swore again, then stared down hard at the map. He was exhausted, having not slept so much as a minute during the previous night. He was in the tiny hamlet of East Point, southwest of Atlanta on the Western and West Point Railroad, the line that linked Atlanta with the cities of Alabama. Granbury's Texas Brigade held the post, along with a couple of companies of the Georgia Militia. Even counting the latter as soldiers, a mere two thousand men were in position at East Point. It was now estimated that something like sixty thousand Federal troops were heading their way.

On his own initiative, he had sent riders back to Atlanta with orders for his other two brigades to march to his assistance at once. In addition to bombarding him with telegrams every half hour, Cleburne had also sent two staff officers to the headquarters at Niles House in order to give Hardee the news of the unexpected Union advance on Atlanta from the west.

Warfield's Brigade was now expected to arrive within the hour, and Hardcastle's Brigade was not far behind. When they reached him, they would add roughly four thousand men to the force holding East Point. Even then, they would be outnumbered ten-to-one. If the other divisions of the corps did not march immediately to their assistance, there would be no way they could maintain their position.

The loss of East Point would be a heavy blow to the Confederate corps defending Atlanta. With only about eighteen thousand men against Grant's oncoming host of at least sixty thousand, they would certainly fail without assistance. Their only hope, it seemed to Cleburne, was to hold out long enough for word to get to Johnston and for the commander of the Army of Tennessee to get the corps of Stewart and Cheatham back to the city.

The cold and inescapable logic of this meant that the Confederates would have to keep the railroad line to Alabama open. And that, in turn, meant that they would have to hold East Point.

The next few hours were among the most tense in Cleburne's life. He had no cavalry, so he sent out scouts singly or in pairs using the few horses available. They confirmed Cleburne's worst fears. The cavalry division he had encountered the night was screening the advance of a very large infantry force, at least several divisions strong. If what Lieutenant McFadden had told him was true, it was the entire Army of the Tennessee and a fair chunk of the Army of the Cumberland.

He thought for a moment about McFadden, who had left him when they had arrived at East Point in order to return to the 7th

Texas. He imagined that he was somewhere in the trenches preparing to meet the attack along with his comrades. Had McFadden not abandoned his quest for vengeance, the first warning anyone would have had of the approach of the enemy would have been the moment they had started lobbing artillery shells into downtown Atlanta.

Cleburne wondered if McFadden fully understood how great a contribution he had made to the Confederate cause. Only a few months before, he had been a mere sergeant. He seemed to possess a sharp intelligence, so Cleburne figured he knew perfectly well what he had done. He doubted, however, that McFadden would discuss it with his comrades. He did not seem to be the sort of man to brag, even when it involved telling the truth.

To his great relief, just after ten o'clock, one of their few cavalry regiments arrived near East Point. Cleburne immediately directed its companies to fan out through into the area. It was critically important to get an exact picture of where the Union forces were, in what strength, where they were going, and how fast they were moving.

Even better was the arrival, around eleven o'clock, of General Hardee. He had barely dismounted his horse when he shouted out to Cleburne.

"What the hell's going on, Patrick?" He rushed into the tent.

"Heavy formations of Union infantry, at least a few corps strong, are less than seven miles away. One column is moving directly toward the city. The other is headed this direction. We cannot be absolutely certain, but it appears that the column to the north consists of two corps of the Army of the Cumberland. The column to the south appears to be the Army of the Tennessee."

"My God!" Hardee exclaimed. "I didn't want to believe your telegram. We've been hoodwinked. Completely and utterly hoodwinked."

Cleburne nodded soberly. "While Johnston awaits Grant's arrival in Lafayette, the Union commander-in-chief is in reality moving on Atlanta with an overwhelming force."

"Have you notified him?" Hardee asked.

"I can't. The telegraph line to Lafayette has been cut."

Hardee thought quickly and dictated an order to a staff officer. The telegraph operator at the Car Shed in Atlanta was to dispatch a message to Macon, where it would be routed through Columbus and thence on to Johnston's command post in Lafayette. It would take several hours for the message to reach him, but it was the best that could be done.

Cleburne quickly explained the orders he had given to his brigade commanders, and Hardee nodded quickly in agreement.

"Bate will come to your support here at East Point, as this appears to be the point of greatest danger. Maney's division will take position on the western front of the Atlanta fortifications themselves. I will station Walker to cover the space between Bate and Maney, able to move quickly to one or the other."

"And the cavalry?"

Hardee frowned. "We have but one brigade."

"I know. And I sent one regiment out to scout just before you arrived."

"When they get back in, we'll send them down to check the railroad. If I were in Grant's shoes, I'd send my own horsemen to strike at the railroad at other places than just East Point. We'll hope our own troopers can keep them away."

Cleburne nodded quickly. "We do not have nearly enough troops, but we must do the best we can."

"The enemy will try to take East Point first, to cut us off from any possible reinforcement from Johnston. You must hold this position at all costs. But if the worst happens, you and Bate must be prepared to rapidly withdrew your troops to the inner fortifications of Atlanta. Considering their strength, we might be able to hold out for a time even against such superior numbers."

"Thank God Johnston saw fit to extend the defenses of the city southwest toward East Point," Cleburne said. "Were it not for his foresight, we would be in a much worse situation."

Hardee chuckled bitterly. "Had he had better foresight, he would not have been so completely duped by Grant. As it was, he was tricked into sending two-thirds of the army over a hundred miles away to deal with a threat that didn't exist."

*   *   *   *   *

September 24, Noon

Grant rode with McPherson at the head of one of the infantry divisions of the Army of the Tennessee. His smile curled around the ever-present cigar. Behind them, tens of thousands of blue-coated soldiers were marching with confidence and swagger.

"Cincinnati is a fine animal, sir," McPherson said. "I assume you acquired him after the Battle of Chattanooga, as I do not remember seeing you ride him previously."

"He was given to me about a month after Chattanooga by a fellow in St. Louis, whose name was also Grant. I am still not sure if he was a relative or not."

"How interesting."

Grant leaned forward and patted the animal's neck. "He is a fine animal, as you say. His father was named Lexington, who I understand held the national speed record for the four mile race for a number of years. I've never seen a more beautiful horse, and I have certainly seen my share over the past few years. He carried me through all the battles against Lee in Virginia. I hope he shall soon carry me into Atlanta."

The booming of artillery was suddenly heard up ahead. Grant and McPherson both squinted in the sun to see where it was coming from. They sensed the men in the marching column tense, as they must have felt the probability that they would be in the midst of a bloody battle in the near future.

A cavalry captain rode up. "Less than a mile to East Point, General Grant. The rebels are dug in strong, looks like."

"How many?" McPherson asked.

"Maybe a brigade, sir. But looks like another one is on its way from the north."

"Better hurry up, James," Grant said. "We got awful close before they found us out, but they'll be trying to get all their boys in our way now that they know we're here. Best hit them fast and hit them hard, and knock them out of those trenches before they can get too many rifles into them."

There was a rattling of musketry from somewhere ahead. It sounded heavier than would have been expected from mere skirmishing.

"Any idea what that is, Captain?"

The man shook his head. "No, sir. There was nothing going on in that direction when I left the front to report to you."

"Well, let's have a look." Grant kicked Cincinnati into a trot, followed by McPherson and their staff officers. A company of Illinois cavalry followed to protect them, sending up a cloud of dust.

They rode about fifteen minutes, passing by several brigades of infantry as they did so. The men did not cheer this time. Most of them, hearing the steadily increasing sounds of musket and artillery fire, knew that battle could be joined at any moment. No one's courage faltered, but the tension was obvious.

As they got closer to the front of the Army of the Tennessee, the marching columns slowed and eventually stopped. The sound of musketry was getting louder. Looking on ahead, Grant could see Union formations that had deployed into battle lines. This irritated Grant considerably, for he had not wanted to deploy the men until they were much closer to the Southern line.

A breathless lieutenant rode up.

"What the hell is going on?" Grant demanded.

"The rebels, sir! A brigade came out from the line and charged toward our left flank. We had to go into a battle line to beat them back. They fell back a bit, then came forward again."

"Can you identify them?"

"Kentucky regiments, according to their battle flags."

"The Orphan Brigade," McPherson said. "Bloody hell. One of Johnston's best."

Grant grunted. "They're trying to make us deploy early, to delay us from reaching their main line. Most likely they're rushing reinforcements to the spot. They must have just realized we were approaching some time during the night."

They continued forward until they were just a few hundred yards behind the battle line. Half a mile away, clearly visible in the open terrain, was a line of roughly a thousand men in Confederate butternut. They were keeping up a brisk fire against the Union infantry. A full Union division of three brigades had deployed, outnumbering the Southerners by at least three-to-one.

"Why do these Kentuckians fight for the Confederacy?" McPherson wondered aloud. "Their state didn't even secede."

"They say it did," Grant observed. Kentucky had been bitterly divided between pro-Union and pro-secession factions back in 1861, and each had claimed the authority of a legitimate government. The secessionists had controlled much of southern Kentucky for several months, during which the regiments that eventually became the Orphan Brigade had been recruited. They had fought gallantly on the Southern side ever since.

"I wonder what will happen in that state after the war," McPherson mused. "Thousands who fought for the South and thousands who fought for the Union will return home to Kentucky. How will they respond to each other?"

"The same way the country as a whole will, I suppose. Of course, we have to win the war first."

McPherson chuckled. The two men stopped talking as they watched the unfolding engagement. The Orphans were taking heavy fire and high losses, but they gamely stayed in the fight. Their regiments kept moving forward and back like so many dancers, delivering repeated volleys of musketry into the Union ranks as they did so. Grant shook his head. The whole thing was very annoying.

Eventually, a four-gun battery was brought up and began firing canister. At the same time, another Union division completed deployment on the Union left. It slowly wheeled to the right to overlap the rebel flank. Their mission to delay the Yankee advance having been achieved and unwilling to sustain further losses, the Orphan Brigade began to fall back.

"Shall we pursue them, sir?" McPherson asked.

"No," Grant said with conviction. "See how they're pulling away to the northeast? They're hoping we'll follow them."

McPherson looked hard and nodded. "Yes, I see. They're trying to draw us away from the railroad."

"Quite so. The Army of the Cumberland will handle them. Press on to East Point as planned. We should not let the rebels dictate the events of this fight. It's much more important to cut the railroad than to chase a single brigade."

"Indeed, it is. Do you think Johnston has learned of the situation yet?"

Grant shrugged. "Probably. Even though we cut the direct telegraph line, there are other routes for the message to reach him. In any case, it's too late for him to do anything about it."

"If our cavalry has done their job on the railroad, there's nothing Johnston can do about our attack."

Grant nodded. Two brigades of Union cavalry had been ordered to veer southwards away from the main force to strike at the Western and East Point Railroad in various places. Though they would not have the strength to destroy the tracks completely, they could inflict substantial damage. With any luck, this would make it virtually impossible for the Southern troops now deployed in eastern Alabama to get back to Atlanta anytime soon. This was simply an additional precaution, as Atlanta would be cut off the moment they captured East Point.

He pulled out his pocket watch. "It's getting on to one o'clock. Do you think you can get East Point by five?"

McPherson considered. "Another half hour of marching. An hour to deploy the divisions and arrange the lines. A few hours of fighting. Yes, I think so."

Grant nodded. "Then do so. No holding back, James. You have an overwhelming numerical advantage. Smash through those trenches and get that town. Understood?"

"Completely, sir."

"Very well. I am going to speak with Howard up north. Please keep me informed."

The two men saluted. Grant turned Cincinnati off to the left and headed north.

*   *   *   *   *

September 24, Afternoon

Davis looked up sharply. The pounding on the door sounded much louder than usual, meaning that the news had to be important. Perhaps the battle near Lafayette had finally begun.

"Come in!"

The door opened and Seddon quickly walked in. He shoved a paper toward the President. "Read this immediately, sir."

President Davis,

The Army of the Cumberland and Army of the Tennessee, with a combined force estimated at sixty thousand men at the least, have crossed the Chattahoochee River to the southwest of Atlanta, undetected until now. They are advancing rapidly toward the city. The telegraph line to Lafayette has been cut but we are attempting to notify General Johnston via a different route. We urgently request any reinforcements that can be spared to be sent to Atlanta at once. The situation is critical. This is the great crisis.

> *General Hardee, commanding at Atlanta*

As he read the telegram, Davis felt his heart began pounding. His breath quickened and a layer of sweat formed instantly on his forehead. He lowered the paper down on the desk.

"I do not understand," he said. "The Army of the Tennessee is supposed to be with Grant in Alabama, marching on Montgomery."

"It would seem that Grant has fooled Johnston, Mr. President. The movement into Alabama now appears to have been a feint, designed to draw our forces away from Atlanta, which has remained the main Union objective all along."

Davis looked sternly into Seddon's eyes. "So you're telling me that General Johnston rushed two-thirds of the Army of Tennessee into Alabama, without authorization, to confront an enemy that was not even there? To protect cities that are not actually under threat?"

"That's about the size of it, Mr. President."

Davis slammed a clenched fist down onto the desk. "Damn that Johnston!" he shouted with all his might. He looked up at the door. "Mr. Harrison! Get General Bragg! And Secretary Benjamin! I must meet with them at once!"

"It's a disaster, sir," Seddon noted somberly. "Hardee has less than twenty thousand men in and around Atlanta. The Yankee force outnumbers them by more than three-to-one."

Davis felt he was living in a nightmare. Only twenty-four hours previously, all had appeared well. There had been nothing but good news from the military fronts in Virginia and the Trans-Mississippi for weeks and it had appeared that Johnston was on the verge of catching Grant in a trap in eastern Alabama. Lincoln's reelection prospects had been as dim as ever. The hue and cry caused by the revelation of Cleburne's emancipation proposal was bothersome, but being dealt with.

In a flash, everything had changed. First, Benjamin had told him about the Manton Marble affair, which had been bad enough. Indeed, he had been unable to sleep the night before on account of it. What Seddon was telling him now was infinitely worse.

If Atlanta fell now, at the height of the fury generated by the Marble scandal and with the election only forty-five days away, Lincoln would almost certainly be reelected President. With Lincoln in the White House for another four years, the Confederacy would inevitably be ground into dust.

The door opened and Bragg and Benjamin walked in. While Davis sat silently, Seddon passed around Hardee's telegram and briefed them on what they knew about the situation in Atlanta. As he heard the summary once again, Davis sadly shook his head.

"I should never have appointed Johnston commander of the Army of Tennessee. I should have refused your resignation, Braxton. I should have kept you in command of the army. Barring that, I should have given the post to Beauregard, or Kirby Smith, or Longstreet. Perhaps I should have ordered Lee west to take command. But I certainly should never have appointed Johnston. His incompetence and lack of vision will be the death of the Confederacy."

"We should not think of the past now, Mr. President," Bragg said.

"What of Atlanta's defenses?" Benjamin asked, uncharacteristic concern in his voice.

"They are among the most formidable fortifications in North America," Seddon answered. "Our engineers have had literally thousands of slaves working on them for months. But fortifications require troops. The defenses of Atlanta were designed with the assumption that the entire Army of Tennessee, with fifty thousand men, would be manning the trenches. Hardee has less than twenty thousand at his command."

"Dear God," Davis said. "What help can we send them?"

"None, I'm afraid. We stripped the defenses of Charleston and Savannah of all the regiments we dared spare in order to send a brigade's worth of reinforcements to Johnston last month."

"A brigade that is now sitting uselessly in Alabama!" Davis spat.

Seddon nodded. "Besides which, even if troops from the coast boarded trains this very hour and the transfer to Atlanta went perfectly, they still would not arrive for at least a few days."

"And if troops from Charleston cannot arrive in time, there is no way for troops dispatched from Virginia to arrive in time," Bragg said.

"Quite so," Seddon agreed. "We don't have weeks. The fate of Atlanta will likely be decided within the next few days."

"How long will it take for Johnston to get any of Stewart's or Cheatham's divisions back to Atlanta?" Davis asked.

Bragg leaned forward. "When I commanded the Army of Tennessee, I was able to move most of the army from Corinth in northern Mississippi to Chattanooga in southeast Tennessee in about a week. But that's not the problem. I would imagine that Grant's main objective right now is to secure the Western and East Point Railroad in order to prevent Johnston from sending any aid."

Seddon nodded. "If Grant is marching toward Atlanta from the west, I would expect some of his forces to veer southeast in order to gain possession of the railroad. If we can keep it in our hands, then reinforcements from Johnston could start arriving within a few days. But if Grant manages to seize the railroad, all may be lost."

"Get a message to Johnston immediately and order him to get as many of his troops back to Atlanta with all speed," Davis said. "For once, I doubt it will be necessary to explain to the man just how serious the situation is."

"I would explain it anyway," Benjamin said dryly. "What else can we do?"

Davis laughed bitterly. "I suppose I shall send a circular to all the clergymen in every church in Richmond, asking them to pray for divine intervention. After all, if Joe Johnston is no help, at least we can always appeal to God."

*   *   *   *   *

McFadden glanced nervously up and down the line. The 7th Texas was stretched thin, with six or seven feet between each man. Even with such extreme measures, the weakened regiment could only cover about a hundred and fifty yards of the line. There was no denying how strong the fortifications were, but McFadden thought ruefully that even the best defenses were only formidable if they had an adequate number of troops in them.

Looking out from under the head-log set on top of the parapet, McFadden saw what looked like a solid wall of blue infantrymen advancing toward them, less than half a mile away. He could see more than a dozen battle flags, which meant that the force was at least a division in size. Already, off to the right, Confederate cannon were thumping out explosive shells that burst in the Union ranks, killing and wounding several men each time. The enemy continued moving forward doggedly, seeming to shrug off the artillery fire as though it were not a concern.

McFadden's return to the 7th Texas had come as a great surprise to his men and particularly to Major Collett. As he had threatened, Collett had indeed reported him as a deserter when he had failed to return within five days. All that was quickly forgotten when McFadden had arrived bearing a note from Cleburne that he was to be instantly reinstated without penalty. Moreover, the shock of the news McFadden had brought and the realization that their brigade was almost all that stood between the Union army and Atlanta quickly thrust all thought of McFadden's actions out of mind.

The 7th Texas held the center of Granbury's line. The entire brigade numbered less than a thousand men and was expected to cover nearly a thousand yards of front. From what he understood from Major Collett, Granbury had pulled the 10th Texas back behind the line to serve as an emergency reserve. Off to the left, the consolidated 6th/15th Texas Cavalry, whose men fought as infantry despite their name, held a position at a right angle to the rest of the regiment, forming the line into an "L" shape and hopefully blocking any move by the Yankees to get around their left flank.

Just to their right, between them and another regiment, was a company of Georgia Militia, numbering about forty men. McFadden did not put much stock in their fighting abilities. Most of them were old men and young boys, but a few were also healthy and fit-looking men who had somehow managed to avoid military service up to this point. The men of the 7th Texas had nicknamed the militia "Joe Brown's Pets." Collett had put McFadden in charge of the militia company as well as his own men, though he couldn't help but wonder if they were going to be more trouble than they were worth.

"They've just gone to the double quick, Lieutenant!" Collett said loudly as he walked back and forth just behind the center of the regiment's line.

McFadden looked out toward the enemy. Sure enough, they had moved from a slow walk into a slow jog. They were now only about a quarter of a mile away. Within a matter of minutes, they would charge the line. The artillery had switched from shot to canister fire, with every blast tearing away numbers of men. Still, the Yankees came on, clearly determined to overwhelm the position through sheer force of numbers.

"Prepare to fire!" McFadden shouted. The Texas veterans leaned forward on the parapet so that their weapons emerged from the space between the head-log and the parapet itself. He drew his sword and revolver, holding the former in his right hand and the latter in his left.

He glanced over at the militiamen, irritated to see how long it was taking many of them to load their weapons. None of the men had more than a few hours of training, but the process did not strike McFadden as being particularly hard. Making the problem worse was the fact that the militiamen were not carrying standardized weapons. Every member of the 7th Texas was armed with an Enfield rifle brought through the blockade from England or captured from the Yankees. The militiamen, however, were armed with a variety of Enfields, Springfields captured from the Yankees, shotguns left over from before the war, and even some old flintlocks that could have been used against the British during the Revolution. McFadden thought that they looked less like a fighting unit and more like a traveling circus company.

Observing the militia prepare to receive the enemy, he saw something else that worried him. The look on their faces and the way their hands shook as they tried to ready their weapons told him all that he needed to know. Many of them jerked sharply any time the cannon to their right were fired. Clearly, the militiamen were frightened out of their wits. As he watched, a smelly puddle of yellow liquid formed at the feet of one young militiaman, who could not have been more than sixteen-years-old.

He wanted to turn away in disgust. Then he remembered how frightened he had been at his baptism of fire at the Battle of Valverde.

He especially felt sorry for the young ones. Many of them were certain to die in the upcoming battle, when they had barely begun to live. For a moment, he wondered where their mothers were.

The bugles within the Yankee ranks blew the signal for the charge and the drummers began pounding their instruments much more quickly. The Union infantry went from a jog to a run and from thousands of throats rose the deep, manly battle cry of the Northern soldiers.

"Don't fire until I give the command!" McFadden cried. He wanted to wait until the enemy soldiers were about a hundred yards away, so as to make every shot count. If he ordered his men to fire before the Yankees got within a hundred yards, his men would simply be wasting their fire with inaccurate shots. He waited as long as he dared.

"Fire!"

The Texas infantrymen and Georgia militia all fired their weapons at the same moment. Looking out over the parapet, McFadden saw several federal troops fall dead or wounded. However, the effect was not as devastating as a volley normally was. His men were simply spread too thinly and the attackers numbered too many for the volley to have much of an impact. It was like throwing pebbles at a locomotive. The Yankee horde kept right on coming.

"Fire at will, boys! Let the bastards have it!"

Blue-coated soldiers dropped every second, as the Southerners poured out as heavy a fire as they could manage. But within two minutes, the Yankees reached the trench fronting the parapet. This was edged with abatis and the Union soldiers had considerable difficulty passing between the sharpened wooden stakes. This allowed the Confederates more time to fire at them.

Still, numbers told. Many of the Yankees began dropping down into the five-foot gulley in front of the parapet. As McFadden's men leaned forward to depress their weapons and continue to pour fire down upon them, Union troops to the rear began passing forward short ladders and walking planks to enable men to climb up the parapet. At the same time, a long and deep row of Union infantry paused at the edge of the trench and opened up a heavy fire, giving cover to their comrades. Others began tearing away at the abatis to make more space through which to push forward.

It was a tense few minutes. The Southern troops could not fire at the Yankees at the base of the trench without dangerously exposing themselves to enemy fire. Unwilling to do this, most of his troops continued to blaze away at the bluecoats standing unprotected at the edge of the trench. A great many of these men were struck by musket balls and fell unceremoniously into the trench.

Having anticipated this situation, McFadden had distributed a few live artillery shells to some of his more steady men. They now lit the fuses on these with matches and tossed them quickly over the parapet. Seconds later, they exploded, killing or wounding several Union soldiers. McFadden listened to their screams, but took no pleasure from them.

Despite the improvised defense, more and more Yankees were filling the trench and beginning to scale up the parapet. The first men scrambled up over the head-log and onto the mound of dirt, screaming frenzied battle cries. To McFadden's horror, many of the Georgia militiamen now threw down their weapons and ran for the rear. His disgust was increased when he saw that most of those running away were the fit middle-aged men he had observed earlier. Most of the old men and young boys remained at their posts.

"Cowards!" McFadden shouted at the runaways. "Get back into the line and fight!"

Few paid any attention, continuing their flight. He looked back at the Union troops. He pulled back the cock on his revolver and began firing off his six shots. He realized he was getting better with the weapon, as two Union soldiers fell. Before he knew it, his pistol clicked harmlessly. Unwilling to take the time to reload it, he shoved the weapon back into its holster and charged forward with his saber, screaming the Rebel Yell.

His men were now engaged in hand-to-hand fighting. The advantage of their defenses was now turned against them, as the Yankees towered over the heads of the Southerners the moment they were able to scramble onto the parapet. The sound of musket fire faded quickly, replaced by dull smacking sounds as men used the butts of their muskets as clubs or sickening squelchy sounds as bayonets were thrust deep into human bodies. Horrifying screams began to emanate from the line of defenses held by the 7th Texas. Several Yankees had had the foresight to load their rifles just before going over the top of the parapet and they fired off their single shot before attempting to run the nearest rebel through with a bayonet. The Bowie knives many of the Texans carried were doing bloody work.

McFadden jumped onto the top of the parapet and slashed at the nearest Yankee with his saber, neatly slicing a perfect gash across the man's neck. The bluecoat pathetically clasped his hand to his throat and fell backwards onto his comrades, who were trying to get on top of the parapet themselves. McFadden kicked the nearest one in the face, causing him to fall backwards as well. Bullets buzzed past all around him and he felt a tug at his shirt as one passed through his clothing. Miraculously, however, he remained unhurt. He now felt certain that God was protecting him for some reason and therefore felt no fear.

Off to both the left and right, McFadden could hear the frantic booming of Southern artillery. The defensive line had been built with small redoubts thrust out from the main line, allowing cannon to fire into the flanks of any attacking force. These guns now spewed forth their deadly canister fire into the massed ranks of the attacking force.

At such close range and with such a large target, the gunners couldn't miss. Scores of Union men were literally sliced into pieces with each blast, their tormented screams lasting only a fraction of a second.

McFadden glanced backwards to see a line of Confederate soldiers advancing at a rush. He smiled quickly. Major Collett had seen fit to commit the 10th Texas in a counter attack to drive the Union troops back. The Southern troops halted perhaps twenty yards behind the parapet, raised their rifles, and delivered a heavy volley of musketry into the mass of Union troops standing on top of the parapet. With that, they charged forward with the Rebel Yell to join their comrades in hand-to-hand fighting.

The infusion of two hundred fresh Confederate troops combined with the persistent firing of artillery into both flanks of the attacking force somehow made the difference. The Yankees who had gotten over the parapet were killed or knocked unconscious. Those remaining on the parapet were shot down. The artillery fire continued to butcher those massed in the trench on the other side. Eventually, McFadden began to hear the cries of Union officers for their men to fall back.

He dropped back into the defenses, angry at himself for having remained exposed on top of the parapet for so long. He quickly decided that it was not a time to be chivalrous.

"Get back onto the fire-step!" he shouted to his men. "Keep shooting!"

As heavy as the attack had been, McFadden knew that it was only a prelude to more massive assaults to come. The more troops he and his men killed now, the fewer would be coming at them later.

His men were now a complete mish-mash of troops from the 7th Texas, the 10th Texas and the Georgia Militia company. He was grateful to spot Major Collett, apparently unharmed, directing troops fifty or sixty yards to the left, also ordering them back into position to fire at the retreating enemy troops. The defenses resounded with the continuous popping of musket fire, but it lacked the strength of regular volleys because there were simply too few troops. Still, several Union soldiers were killed as they sought to climb out of the trench, get back through the abatis, and dash back out of range.

The last shot was finally fired, perhaps forty minutes after the Union buglers had first blown out the call for the charge. The combat had been hellacious. In the trench before the parapet and across the ground for a considerable distance beyond were hundreds of dead and wounded Union soldiers. Within the line itself, both Northern and Southern casualties were intermixed. The Yankees had come within a hair's breadth of breaking through.

Collett ran up to him. "You're hit!" he said, pointing to McFadden's waist.

McFadden glanced down and was surprised to see a messy red blotch on the left side of his waist. He had not felt any sensation of pain during the fighting, though the moment he saw it an intense sting flashed through his body. Quickly, but trying to show no concern, he removed his shirt. Collett leaned forward and carefully inspected the wound.

"Just a graze," he said, relieved. "It'll hurt like a devil, but the surgeon should be able to patch you up."

"Thanks, Major," McFadden said. His voice did not betray the relief he felt. Had a bullet actually entered his body, the wound almost certainly would have become infected and possibly cost him his life. He wondered what Annie would have thought about that. He still had not had time to contact her since his return to the army.

"You deserve it, you silly bastard," Collett said. "I saw you standing out in the open right on top of the parapet. Dammit, man, you must have been up there for five minutes!"

McFadden shrugged. He hadn't really been thinking all that much during that time.

Collett looked out over the ground in front of their defenses. "That was close. They almost broke through."

"Would have been easier to repulse them if the damn Georgia Militia hadn't run away."

"True enough. But the important thing is that they were repulsed."

"Yeah, but this is just the start of things. The Yankees will be back."

*   *   *   *   *

Sitting astride Cincinnati in the midst of the marching columns of the Army of the Cumberland, Grant could distinctly hear the fading sounds of the fighting around East Point, five miles to the south. He wondered what the result had been. It had been something of a risk to send McPherson forward in an attack so quickly, when the men were tired from a long march and without any artillery preparation.

"Fighting seems to have stopped," General Howard observed.

Grant grunted his agreement, lighting his twenty-fifth cigar of the day.

"Do you think he captured the town, sir?"

"Don't know," Grant replied. "I'm sure we'll get word one way or another soon enough. Hopefully East Point is now under our control, but if not I will not be concerned."

Howard's eyes narrowed. "No?"

Grant shrugged. "I think we'll be in Atlanta soon, but there are bound to be setbacks along the way. The rebels fight like devils and they need to keep Atlanta as much as we need to take it."

Howard nodded. "I have always wondered why so many men fight so hard and so bravely for a cause so utterly unworthy of their sacrifice. To give one's life so that rich men might keep fellow human beings as their personal property? It is obscene."

"I agree," Grant said. "I have often wondered the same thing myself. There seems to have been no justification for the secession of the Southern states. It was not the act of rational men."

"Indeed. I shall pray to God for the salvation of their souls."

"Let's not worry about that now. We must win the war first, then deal with such questions."

Sometime later, a messenger arrived with a note from McPherson. Grant read it quickly.

"Well?" Howard asked.

Grant frowned and shook his head. "We were repulsed. McPherson put two divisions against a rebel force of only two brigades. They broke the line in a few places but were not able to hold their gains. Losses estimated at fifteen hundred."

'Dear God," Howard said.

"Not so bad, really," Grant replied, folding the paper up and stuffing it into his pocket. "Not nearly so bad as Cold Harbor was. Or Kennesaw Mountain, from what I have heard. There's going to be a lot more blood spilled between now and when our boys march into the city, so you might as well steel yourself for it."

Howard nodded. "Of course, sir."

Grant gazed over the heads of his men toward the distant Confederate fortifications protecting the city, perhaps a mile-and-a-half away.

"How far to the center of the city, do you think? As the crow flies, I mean."

"Two miles or so, I would guess."

"Hmm," Grant muttered, thinking quietly. "Perhaps it would be a good idea to fire some shells into the city. Hardee has certainly called for help and I would not be surprised if rebel troops are even now on the train from Charleston or Savannah. Maybe even from Lee's army in Virginia. If we can inflict damage on the railroad facilities in the center of town, we can make it more difficult for them to receive help from outside."

Howard looked sharply over at Grant. "What of the civilians, sir?"

"Surely most of them have fled."

"Most, I'm sure. But I imagine that there are many who have been unable or unwilling to leave. Hundreds at least."

Grant shrugged. "Too bad."

Howard took a deep breath. "Well, the rebels have sown the wind, so now they will reap the whirlwind."

"Something like that. It's a war, Howard. I'm not trying to be callous. But it's a war. If we can cause disruption in the city and make it harder for the rebels to bring in reinforcements, it means that the war is that much closer to being over."

Howard nodded slowly and looked out over the distance to Atlanta. "I'm sure that twenty-pounder Parrot rifled guns could hit the center of the city from here."

"Good. See to it."

*   *   *   *   *

September 24, Evening

Lincoln had not left the telegraph office of the War Department for hours. Every time a telegraph arrived, he snatched it up the moment its dictation was complete and read through it with furious speed. During the long stretches of time between messages, he paced anxiously back and forth. Stanton, as usual, was visibly annoyed.

"Mr. President, you're achieving nothing here except distracting my clerks. Perhaps you might go back to the White House?"

Lincoln smiled and shook his head. "I cannot, Edwin. Now that the battle has begun outside Atlanta, I must remain here. I shall be on tenterhooks otherwise."

Stanton grunted and went back to his paperwork, which had something to do with a complaint about defective cannon being delivered from an arsenal in Massachusetts. Lincoln went back to pacing.

As he walked back and forth, waiting for the familiar clicking sound from the telegraph machine, the President could feel optimism pushing away his anxiety like a morning sun burns away the mist. The Manton Marble scandal had swung the political situation in Lincoln's favor for the first time since the spring. Although he was not so sanguine as to think it put the great electoral prize of New York State back into play, Lincoln did expect that Ohio and Pennsylvania might now be salvaged, and perhaps Indiana as well. Victory in the upcoming election, which had begun to feel impossible, now seemed within his grasp.

The latest telegrams from Grant indicated that the long-awaited assault on Atlanta had finally begun. Word of this would spread throughout the North within the next day or so. He imagined that the tension he felt would be mirrored by the nation as a whole. If Grant succeeded, Lincoln expected his reelection would be assured.

Grant appeared supremely confident of victory, judging by the tone of his telegrams. However, giving Grant his overwhelming numerical superiority had required the Union to strip other fighting fronts of many of their troops. Near Petersburg, Lee had defeated every effort by Grant to cut off his railroad links south of the city. In the Shenandoah Valley, Jubal Early's army continued to stoutly resist Union efforts to gain control of that critical region.

In more distant theaters, the withdrawal of several Union divisions from the Trans-Mississippi had unfortunately allowed the rebels to regain the initiative there. A large enemy cavalry force was now rampaging through Missouri, while a rebel army was moving to recapture Little Rock. Grant had assured Lincoln that, given Union control of the Mississippi River, this theater of war was not strategically important. Still, Lincoln was wary of the political price he would pay if Northern voters read about further Union defeats in their newspapers.

The sound of the telegraph clicking abruptly terminated Lincoln's thoughts and he jerked his head toward the sound. Major Eckert, as calmly as though he were making a sandwich, jotted down the message on a piece of paper. Although he was technically supposed to wait for Stanton's instructions, he immediately handed the telegram to the President.

Stanton, who had emerged from his office next door the moment the clicking had begun, walked in hurriedly.

"From Grant?" he asked.

Lincoln nodded, continuing to read.

"Well, what does he say?"

Lincoln frowned and shook his head. "It appears that the first attack on East Point, which we need in order to control the railroad, has been beaten back by the rebels."

"A disappointment. Casualties?"

"He doesn't say."

Stanton shrugged. "This is going to take a few days, Mr. President. Our first attack on Vicksburg was repulsed, if you recall."

"It took Grant a month-and-a-half to capture Vicksburg after he had reached its defenses," Lincoln said sourly. "We don't have that much time."

"I wouldn't worry, Mr. President. Grant will bring up more men and do it right. Probably tomorrow."

"Let's hope so."

The door opened and Seward entered, a pensive look on his face.

"Ah, Mr. President, Secretary Stanton. Good to see you both here."

"Is something wrong?" Lincoln asked.

"Chief Justice Taney has died." He let those words fall about the room.

Stanton beamed. "Well, that's good."

Seward's eyes narrowed. "Show some respect, Edwin. We're talking about a man's life. A man who was the Chief Justice of the Supreme Court, I might remind you."

"Respect be damned, William," Stanton replied. "Had it not been for Taney and his stupid and unforgivable decision in the Dred Scott case seven years ago, this infernal war might never have happened. And how often have his rulings undermined our prosecution of the war against the rebels? He's cost us more trouble than Jefferson Davis. Good riddance, I say."

As Seward and Stanton continued to argue, Lincoln said nothing. Within a minute of hearing Seward's news, he was already silently mulling over in his mind whom he would appoint to be the new Chief Justice of the Supreme Court, happy to have a distraction from the events taking place around Atlanta. But he knew the distraction wouldn't last long.

*   *   *   *   *

September 24, Night

"They have withdrawn?" Johnston's voice betrayed his incredulity.

"So it would seem, sir," Mackall answered. "Stewart and Cheatham are both reporting the same thing. It seemed strangely quiet after the sun went down, so both sent forward skirmishers, who soon returned with word that the enemy positions before them were completely empty. They then sent forward some cavalry to locate the enemy, who found them a mile down the road, marching northeast, back the way they came."

Johnston shook his head, thoroughly confused. The strange behavior of the enemy was all the more baffling because, despite their best efforts, Johnston's scouts had been unable to locate the Army of the Tennessee. This was making him increasingly uneasy.

"Is it possible that Grant has decided our position is too strong to assault?" Mackall asked.

Johnston shook his head. "That cannot be. Of course, our position is a very strong one, but Grant has never been one to turn away from a fight. McClellan, yes. McClellan would never have considered attacking us here. But Grant? Considering how he hurled his troops against Lee's defenses at Spotsylvania and Cold Harbor, I see no reason why he would refuse to attack us. He also had no hesitation to assault the works at Vicksburg, which were much stronger than our defenses here."

"I agree it is a mystery, sir. Shall I give orders for our men to pursue?"

Johnston considered this. It was almost midnight, so he assumed that the Yankees were using the cover of darkness to conceal their withdrawal. His instinct was to pursue them, but it was exceedingly difficult to control an army in total darkness. The prudent thing to do would be to wait until daylight, then locate the enemy and take actions accordingly.

A horseman galloped up, reining in outside the tent. "Where is General Johnston?" he shouted. "I have an urgent message that General Johnston must get at once!"

Moments later, Johnston unfolded the message.

General Johnston,

The Army of the Tennessee and the Army of the Cumberland, minus one corps which remains at Vining's Station, have crossed to the south bank of the Chattahoochee River southwest of Atlanta and are now moving in force against the city from the west. I repeat that the Army of the Tennessee is not in Alabama but is near Atlanta. It is estimated that the enemy force numbers sixty thousand men. Prisoners report that General Grant in person commands the force on my front.

I urgently suggest that the corps of Stewart and Cheatham be brought back to Atlanta with all possible speed.

The direct telegraph wire between Atlanta and Lafayette has been cut. To communicate, I recommend sending the message via Columbus and Macon.

General Hardee

Johnston's eyes widened in shock. He leaned forward against a chair to steady himself. "No, that cannot be," he said firmly, even as he passed the message over to Mackall.

"My God," Mackall said simply.

"I think General Hardee is seeing double."

"Hardee is usually a very thorough officer, sir."

"The last time we had certain intelligence on the whereabouts of the Army of the Tennessee, they were marching southwest toward Alabama directly behind the Army of the Ohio, yes?"

Mackall nodded. "Yes, sir. That was about a week ago."

A chill went down Johnston's spine. Hardee was not one to make mistakes about such matters. If they had not conclusively seen the Army of the Tennessee for an entire week, could that have given Grant sufficient time to countermarch it back to Atlanta? Was it possible that he had been the victim of a massive act of deception?

He thought about the events of the day. The Union infantry, all of whom belonged to regiments identified as belonging to the Army of the Ohio, had engaged in sporadic artillery bombardments and occasionally pushed forward skirmish lines as though they were preparing to attack. Beyond that, though, they had done nothing. He had assumed that the Army of the Ohio was waiting for the Army of the Tennessee to come up before commencing its attack. Was the truth that they were simply presenting themselves as a decoy?

Another messenger arrived with a telegram from the War Department.

General Johnston,

We are informed by General Hardee in Atlanta that the great bulk of Grant's forces are not moving into Alabama but are in fact attacking Atlanta on this very day. You are directed to move your army back to Atlanta by rail with all possible speed to defend the city against Grant's attack.

Secretary of War Seddon

He felt as though an enormously powerful hand was clenching his stomach and his heart. He and Mackall began going over every report they had received from the cavalry over the past few days and a picture gradually began to emerge. Every prisoner they had taken and every regimental flag that had been spotted belonged to the Army of the Ohio. Accurate reconnaissance had been difficult because of the swarms of Yankee cavalry that had constantly hovered on the edges of the Union force.

For a moment, Johnston's mind went back to his West Point history lessons. He recalled how John Churchill, the Duke of Marlborough, had successfully deceived his French enemies into thinking that he was threatening their strategic fortresses in Flanders when in fact the main effort of the British general was being directed against the French army in the Danube Valley. The result had been Marlborough's great victory at Blenheim. Was it possible that he had been the victim of a similar trick?

"William, you say the Union force on our front is withdrawing?" Johnston's voice sounded much more tired than it usually did.

"Yes, sir," Mackall responded sympathetically.

"We've been duped."

"I fear you are correct, sir."

"Pull Cheatham's corps out of the line. Get them on the road and march them back to the railroad depot at West Point. We need to get them back into the trains and get them back to Atlanta at once. Have Stewart extend his line to cover the length evacuated. Once the first of Cheatham's divisions is dispatched, have Stewart withdraw one division at a time and march them to the depot as well."

"You believe General Hardee is correct, sir?"

"I do, yes."

"Yankee cavalry have been raiding the rail line, sir."

Johnston nodded. "Well, we will have to identify the points where they have broken the line and do the best we can to repair them. Whatever must be done to get our troops back to Atlanta as quickly as possible."

"Grant may have already seized the railroad at East Point, sir. If he has, our two corps here will be cut off from Atlanta."

"I know. I've been made to look a fool, William. Right now, even as you and I sit here speaking, Jefferson Davis, Braxton Bragg and Judah Benjamin are damning me to high heaven in Richmond. Hood, wherever the hell he is out in Arkansas, will be telling everyone who will listen how stupid I am and how much better everything would be if he had been given command of my army in July. It's a disaster, William. A complete and unmitigated disaster."

Mackall looked almost offended and pulled himself back to stand bolt upright. "Well, sir, if the Yankees have seen fit to trouble us with their tricks, I don't see why we shouldn't repay the favor. And with interest, sir."

*   *   *   *   *

McFadden and Collett had counted their losses. During the Union attack, the 7th Texas had lost twenty men killed or wounded. This had reduced it to a mere fifty soldiers, half the strength of what a single company would have been at the outset of the war. In return, they had killed a vast number of Yankee soldiers in front of their defenses and many of the bluecoats who had gotten over the parapet had been marched to the rear as prisoners.

Every time McFadden moved, a sharp pain tore through his left side. The wound might have been a slight one, but it still felt like a red-hot flame was being shoved up against him. He checked once again to make sure the bandage was secure and tried to ignore the pain.

"It doesn't make any sense to keep the old company structure," Collett was saying. "It has to stay intact on paper, of course. The idiots in the War Department insist on such matters. But as far as we're concerned, the 7th Texas will be divided into two companies. You'll take one and Lieutenant Russell with take the other."

McFadden nodded. "Makes sense, I reckon."

"A major and two lieutenants should be able to handle fifty men, I would think." He said this with a sarcastic grin. McFadden realized he was attempting to lighten the mood. The only reason they were discussing the reorganization at all was because so many of their friends had been killed.

"How are the men?" Collett asked.

"Good," McFadden answered. "I put them to work repairing the abatis on the far side of the trench. The Yankees pulled a bunch of them down during their attack."

"Okay. When they're done, see if we can get them anything to eat and then make sure they get some sleep. This battle is not over by a long shot. The Yankees are going to try again tomorrow, and probably with greater numbers than they did today."

"Any chance of reinforcements?" McFadden asked.

"Granbury says that Bate's division has finished deploying on our right. One of his brigades will be in reserve, which we might be able to call on if we get into serious trouble."

"I imagine Bate's men will have problems of their own."

Collett chuckled. "Most likely."

"I don't know if we'll be able to hold them tomorrow, sir. We were barely able to hold them today."

"General Cleburne had told us that we must hold this position and hold it we shall. If we lose it, our rail link to General Johnston will be cut and Atlanta will be lost. Make sure your men understand just how serious the situation is."

"I will."

The dull thudding sound of artillery broke the silence of night. Instinctively, McFadden and Collett glanced at the direction from which the booming came. It was far off to the north, several miles away. A few seconds later, explosions could be heard coming from Atlanta, off to the northeast.

"What the hell is that?" McFadden asked.

Collett's eyes furrowed in confusion. "I think the Yankees are shelling the city."

"What for?"

"Going after the Car Shed station, perhaps?"

"But there are over a thousand women and children in the city!" McFadden exclaimed in anger. He clenched his fists in a fury. While most civilians had fled the city in early July during Sherman's initial approach, a few never left and a great many had returned after the Battle of Peachtree Creek.

"Tell that to General Grant," Collett said contemptuously.

"Barbarians," McFadden spat. "What sort of people would open fire on defenseless women and children?" He thought about the Turnbow family. The thought of Annie being under fire from Yankee artillery sickened and infuriated him. He wanted nothing more than to rush up to Atlanta and find her and her parents, but knew he could not leave his men.

"The Turnbows will be all right," Collett said.

"I hope so."

"A city is a big place. The chances of a shell landing anywhere near their house are pretty slim."

"The Yankees have plenty of ammunition. By the sound of the firing, lots of guns are involved."

"I read in the papers that Petersburg has been shelled every day for the last few months. Relatively few civilians have been killed or injured." He watched McFadden closely for a moment. "Tell you what. If any of the brigade staff officers go into Atlanta to get ammunition or rations, I'll ask them to see if they can find out anything about the Turnbows."

McFadden nodded. "Thanks, Major."

September 25, Morning

The steam whistle piercing the early morning air around West Point added to the tumultuous sounds of scarcely controlled chaos around the railroad yard. Thousands of men stood about in great crowds, impatiently waiting for their turn to scramble into the large boxcars which, they had been told, would take them back to Atlanta. More were marching down the road from Lafayette. Angry officers struggled to maintain order, repeatedly shouting the same commands over and over again until they had been understood. The enlisted men, clutching their rifles, spoke with concern to one another, at a loss to explain what was going on or what was soon to happen.

Johnston had decided to set up his headquarters within the main building of the railway station itself. Properly organizing the transport of his troops back to Atlanta was such an important undertaking that he had felt it necessary to be as close to the scene as possible. Although crisp autumn winds blew outside, the atmosphere inside the office seemed stuffy and stifling. He felt nervous. Indeed, he could not recall ever have been so agitated. If the trains did not maintain a precise schedule, or if there was so much as a single accident or delay, everything might be lost.

Mackall came into the room at a jog.

"The first train is off, sir. Manigault's Brigade is on their way."

Johnston walked from the table to the window, gazing out over the rail yard. In the distance, an engine was chugging away, smoke bellowing from its funnel and its wheels slowly accelerating. It dragged a dozen boxcars behind it, carrying a thousand tough soldiers from Alabama and South Carolina. Johnston nodded, relieved.

He turned to Mackall. "Who's next?"

"Benton's Mississippi brigade, sir. I hope to have them on the way in the next hour-and-a-half."

"Good. Very good." Johnston thought hard and swiftly. It would take the trains at least a day to reach Atlanta, but it would inevitably take time to disembark them when they arrived, properly organize them, and march them to their positions. Under ideal circumstances, the men then packing into the boxcars could be in the city's defenses within forty-eight hours or so.

Johnston shook his head, for circumstances were far from ideal. Yankee cavalry had struck at the Atlanta and West Point Railroad at various locations between the city and the border with Alabama, tearing up short sections of track. Engineers had already been dispatched on small trains before dawn to locate these breaks and make repairs, but there was no telling how bad the damage was or how long it would take for them to patch it up. Even worse, any flawed repair to the track might result in a derailment, which would not only kill or injure large numbers of soldiers but would cause another unacceptable delay.

All of this, of course, assumed that Hardee would be able to maintain control of the crucial town of East Point, southwest of Atlanta. If Grant were able to seize control of it, the railroad link to Atlanta would be severed. Judging by the scattered information that had trickled in on the telegraph, the Yankees had already made a heavy attack on the town which had been beaten off by Cleburne's division. Johnston had no doubt that they would try again. Indeed, he found himself tormented by the idea that the enemy was at that very moment pouring over the Confederate defenses just outside the town. If they did, all his efforts would be for naught.

A courier came in and handed Mackall a telegram.

"It's from the War Department. They demand an update on the situation."

Johnston thought for a moment and started to reply, then waved a dismissive hand. "Make whatever response you feel is suitable. I have no time right now to spare for Davis, Bragg or any of those other fools."

Mackall glanced around awkwardly Some staff officers and railroad officials had looked up at these words, but the expression on the face of the chief-of-staff persuaded them all to remain tactfully silent.

"Anything on the Army of the Ohio?" Johnston asked Mackall.

"No, sir. According to the latest report from the cavalry, which came in about four this morning, they are continuing to march back to the northeast. They're already about fifteen miles from their earlier position and show no sign of stopping. My guess is that they are on their way back to their starting point at Vining's Station or going to join Grant's attack."

Johnston pursed his lips. Had he been in Grant's place, he would have left Schofield in position to pin down Confederate forces in Alabama. However, having moved away from their own railroad supply line, the Yankees could only have as much food as they carried in their supply wagons. Foraging might have subsisted them for a few days, but the surrounding countryside would have quickly become exhausted.

Of course, it would take days for two entire corps to be entrained and on their way back to Atlanta. If Schofield's army suddenly turned up once again, whatever forces had not yet begun the movement would be on hand to fight. Johnston decided to stop worrying about it. He had to avoid the temptation of becoming afraid of his own shadow.

"Send a telegram to Hardee, via Columbus and Macon. Inform him of the dispatch of Manigault's brigade and give him a general update on the situation."

"Of course, sir," Mackall answered.

"How long before we expect Benton's Mississippi brigade to be off?"

"Perhaps an hour."

Johnston nodded, making a decision. "General Stewart and select staff officers will remain here to coordinate the transfer operation. You, General Cheatham, and I will be on the train with the Mississippians. It's time for us to get back to Atlanta."

*   *   *   *   *

Grant, McPherson, and Howard stood around a map-strewn table in the headquarters tent Grant's staff had erected on the Sandtown Road just south of Utoy Creek, west of Atlanta. Outside, in numerous other tents, a small army of staff officers went about their business, while a regiment of the United States Colored Troops, made up of freed slaves, stood guard. Autumn had clearly arrived, for the air was crisp and fresh. There was not a cloud in the sky.

A few hundred yards away, two four-gun batteries of 20-pounder Parrot rifled cannon occasionally thundered, firing their explosive shells across two miles toward the center of Atlanta. Of course, no one knew what sort of effect they were having inside the city, but the simple fact that they were striking at the rebels was a pleasing thought to the Union troops.

"The plan for today is simple, gentlemen," Grant said gruffly. "James, you'll deploy your army with two corps up front and one in back, like so." He indicated what he was saying on the map. "It doesn't look like the rebels have more than two divisions in the defenses of East Point, and each of your three corps has more than that. It will cost us some casualties, but our force will be overpowering. You are to swamp the rebels with both forward corps, drawing on the divisions of the third corps for reinforcements as needed. I want East Point under our control by the time the sun goes down. I don't care how many men it costs us. The more that die now the fewer will have to die later."

McPherson nodded. "It will be done, sir."

Grant turned to Howard. "The Army of the Cumberland will demonstrate against the defenses on the western side of Atlanta, and against the division holding the line between the city and East Point, here. If you break through, all well and good, but the important thing is to tie down rebel forces in these parts so as to prevent them from going to the aid of the divisions holding East Point."

Howard nodded. "With God's help, we shall succeed."

"Have you secured the south bank of the Chattahoochee below the railroad bridge?"

"Yes. The rebel division that had been deployed there has withdrawn into the defenses of Atlanta and Twentieth Corps is now crossing over. There are no longer any rebel troops on the Chattahoochee at any point, so far as I know."

"Very good," Grant said. "How is the Twentieth Corps?" The formation had been virtually destroyed at the Battle of Peachtree Creek and much effort had gone into rebuilding it.

"I am pleased, sir," Howard replied. "It has spent the last two months resting and reorganizing. We have received substantial reinforcements. I do not think the men will flinch from combat. If anything, I think they are determined to exact revenge from the rebels for what happened two months ago."

"Do we have any information on whether the rebels are receiving any reinforcements?" McPherson asked.

Grant shook his head. "We can't be sure. Our cavalry have torn up sections of track along the Atlanta and West Point Railroad and we know for a fact that no trains have passed from Alabama to Atlanta in the last few days. There do seem to be some trains coming into the city from the direction of Augusta, conceivably bringing in some new troops. Not many, but some."

"It's possible they are bringing in reinforcements from the Atlantic coast," Howard said. "I believe they still have large numbers of troops around Charleston."

"And they cannot bring in too many of them without risking the loss of that city," Grant replied. "At most, only a few regiments are arriving from the east. Not enough to affect the overall situation."

"The fact that they are receiving reinforcements at all disturbs me," McPherson said. "And Johnston cannot be sitting idly by in Alabama, either."

"Of course," Grant replied. "That is why we must not tarry. We must press on as fast as possible. Tomorrow will be the big day, gentlemen. Having captured East Point, McPherson will move against Atlanta from the south, while Howard will attack from the west. It will be bloody. Very bloody, in fact. But we shall succeed. I expect us to have captured the city within the next three or four days."

*   *   *   *   *

"You look awful, William!"

Cleburne intended the comment mostly as a joke, but it was not a lie. Hardee and his staff, who had just arrived at Cleburne's divisional headquarters, looked exhausted and disheveled. Some of the men were covered in soot.

"Sorry I could not wear my best dress uniform," Hardee said apologetically as he dismounted and stepped inside Cleburne's tent. His tone then turned serious. "Fires are burning throughout the city. The damn Yankees have not stopped shelling since yesterday. I had to task a whole regiment of Georgia militiamen to serve as firefighters."

"And the good citizens of Atlanta?" Cleburne asked.

"Mostly hunkered down in their homes, thank God. Some of them fled to the area south of Five Points, expecting that the Yankees would avoid shelling that part of town due to the large number of churches there. No such luck. If you ask me, the Yankees are using the church steeples as targets for their guns."

"My God," Cleburne exclaimed. "Have the Yankees no shame?"

Hardee shrugged. "They're doing it to hinder the arrival of our reinforcements. Were we in their place, would we not do the same?"

Cleburne drew his head back in surprise, for he would never have considered firing artillery into the midst of a civilian population. But he knew that the same could not be said for many of his comrades.

"Now, to business," Hardee continued. He looked down at the map on the table. "Your division still holds the line protecting East Point. A telegram arrived from Johnston just before I departed headquarters. He says that the first brigade of reinforcements has departed West Point. Yankee cavalry have torn up track at various points on the railroad, though, and it may take some time to repair these breaks."

"So we should not count on the arrival of any reinforcements until the day after tomorrow?"

"If that," Hardee said sourly. "It depends on how badly the tracks have been damaged and how well the railroad transfer goes. Even then, it will be several days before the bulk of our troops get back to us."

"And until then, we're outnumbered three or four to one."

"Probably more than that. I won't sugarcoat it, Patrick. We're hanging on by our fingernails here."

The dull thudding of artillery from nearby caused both men to look up. A few seconds later, explosions begin pounding the earth a few hundred yards away. The Federals were shelling Cleburne's front line. Reflexively, Confederate batteries began returning fire, seeking to silence the guns of their foes.

"It begins," Hardee said. "What are your dispositions?"

"Granbury's Texans are on the left, Warfield's Arkansans in the center and Hardcastle is on the right, linking with Bate's division."

Hardee nodded. "Good, except for the left flank. It's completely in the air."

"I know. I had Granbury refuse his flank with the 15th Texas Dismounted Cavalry, but that only protects the flank for a distance of a few hundred yards."

"I'll have Bate station his reserve brigade on your left flank. It's the best we can do."

"The Orphans?" Cleburne asked hopefully.

Hardee shook his head. "No, they were too badly beat up in their spoiling attack yesterday. It will be Finley's Floridians."

"Very well," Cleburne said. The Florida brigade was a tough enough unit.

"Walker is in the line just south of Atlanta and Maney's division is holding the west side of the Atlanta defenses themselves. The Army of the Cumberland is beginning to feel for the end of Maney's line, so he's having to deploy one brigade to the north side of the city as well. I'm trying to place the Georgia Militia in the gaps that are starting to form between divisions. Not sure how that will go."

"The Georgia Militia did not impress me yesterday. Many of them dropped their weapons and ran as soon as the Yankees got close to the line."

"Bad troops are better than no troops."

Cleburne snorted. He was not sure he agreed with this sentiment.

"Answer me truthfully," Hardee said with grim seriousness. "Do you think you can hold the line?"

Cleburne thought carefully. In his heart, he could not honestly answer the question in the affirmative, but neither was he a man who could succumb to defeatism.

"William, if any troops can hold the line, my men will hold the line."

*　　　　　*　　　　　*　　　　　*　　　　　*

September 25, Noon

Johnston felt an enormous sense of relief when he sensed the train jerked slightly as it finally began moving forward. Every mile it traveled brought him closer to Atlanta, where the true battle was being fought, and farther away from Lafayette, which he would forever associate with the humiliation of having fallen for a classic *ruse de guerre.*

Johnston and his staff, along with General Cheatham and his officers, had been allocated a regular passenger car. Needless to say, most of the thousands of soldiers now filling the trains chugging between West Point and Atlanta were crammed into uncomfortable boxcars, with barely enough room to sit down on the hard wooden floors.

Mackall sat across from him, intent on some paperwork. The rest of the officers in the car were doing much the same. For the first time in as long as he could remember, Johnston had nothing to do. He relished the moment, staring out the window as the west Georgia countryside rushed past him.

The few telegrams which had reached him from Richmond had been furious and disjointed demands for an explanation as to what had happened and what he intended to do about it. He could easily imagine the insulting and disrespectful clamor going on between President Davis, Secretary Seddon and General Bragg. Johnston had no doubt that some of them, particularly Bragg, were getting a certain satisfaction at seeing him in such difficulties. They would see it as confirmation that Davis had made a mistake when he had appointed him to command the Army of Tennessee in December and when he had decided against replacing him with Hood in July.

Johnston burned with resentment. As he gazed out the window, he silently shook his head. If the Confederacy were going to be destroyed, the architects of its destruction would be Jefferson Davis and Braxton Bragg far more than Abraham Lincoln and Ulysses Grant.

Hardee's frantic requests for assistance had been almost as difficult for him to read. He loved the Army of Tennessee as though it were his own child and the idea that he had left thousands of his men in a position of terrible danger gnawed at him remorselessly. His men had put their trust in him. They had faithfully followed his orders from the earliest days of the campaign at Dalton, which now seemed a lifetime ago. They had sacrificed their lives to win the great victory at Peachtree Creek and now he had put at risk all that had been gained by their valor and blood.

Johnston's head suddenly jerked up. The train was slowing down. He glanced about with irritation, but the looks of confusion on the faces of the other officers in the car told him that they had no more idea what was happening than he did. Eventually, the train lurched to a halt.

Mackall was sent to find out what was going on. When he returned five minutes later, he reported that they had come upon the first break in the track caused by enemy cavalry. The earlier train that had departed West Point with Manigault's brigade had been stopped for a few hours. Although it was only a few hundred yards long, it would take some time for it to be repaired.

Johnston sat back heavily in his seat, frustration eating away at him. It was going to be a long ride to Atlanta.

*   *   *   *   *

September 25, Afternoon

The sun had peaked in the sky and begun its long descent to the west. McFadden walked back and forth behind the line of the 7th Texas, staring out over the parapet. He had thought the Union force which had assaulted them the previous day had been enormous, but the number of bluecoats he saw assembling for an attack this time was much larger.

Up on the fire-step of the position, Private Pearson shook his head.

"We're dead men, sure as hell."

"You said that just before Peachtree Creek," Montgomery replied.

"Odds were even then," Pearson replied. "Today, they're about as lopsided as they can be."

McFadden had to admit that Pearson was correct. Granbury's brigade had been so weakened that it was now considerably smaller than a regiment would have been at the outset of the war. The day before, they had been assaulted by a full-strength division and had barely survived. By the look of things, the Yankees were about to throw an entire corps at them.

He shook his head. Even Granbury's Texans couldn't beat those odds. Without thinking, he glanced up at the regimental battle flag, posted firmly in the dirt of the parapet and fluttering defiantly. Next to it was the distinctive blue and white flag of Cleburne's division.

He glanced anxiously back to the northeast. Pillars of smoke continued to rise from the city, which made his stomach clench more than even the upcoming Union attack. Any one of those fires might signify the death of Annie Turnbow. He tried not to think about it. Major Collett had asked a brigade commissary officer to ask after the Turnbows when he went into the city to collect ammunition and rations, but the man had come back with absolutely no information. McFadden had to concentrate on leading his half of the regiment and thoughts about what had become of Annie would only distract him.

Another half-dozen artillery shells landed on or just in front of the parapet, exploding and sending up showers of dirt. The Yankees had been bombarding them all day. Altogether they had lost two men killed and four wounded, but the defenses had been constructed so stoutly as to be essentially unharmed by the artillery fire. McFadden speculated that the main purpose behind the barrage was to keep the Confederates from getting any rest.

"Lieutenant!" Pearson's voice called out. "They've started forward!"

McFadden ran up to the fire-step and peered out from beneath the head-log. The enormous formation of Union infantry, at least three divisions strong, had indeed begun marching slowly forward. McFadden was struck by the disturbing image of an elephant about to stomp on a mouse.

"So many Yankees," Montgomery said soberly.

"Yeah," Pearson answered. "Where the hell are we going to bury them all?"

Laughter resounded through the position of the 7th Texas. Despite himself, McFadden chuckled as well. For once, he was happy with Pearson, as his joke helped steady the nerves of the men. If one could laugh, he mused to himself, then all was not lost.

Confederate batteries intensified their fire as the Union infantry advanced. Each exploding shell took several Yankees with it, just like the previous day. But the Northerners simply closed up whatever gaps were created and kept on coming. The buglers and drummers in their ranks sounded the double quick and they moved from a walk to a jog.

"Get ready, men," McFadden said with as much firmness as he could muster. He glanced over at Major Collett, a dozen yards away, and received a reassuring nod. His men loaded their weapons and held them steady. He had ordered them not to fix their bayonets, for they would interfere with the reloading process. Only when the Yankees got into the trench and started scrambling up the parapet would he order the blades affixed to their rifles.

As he watched the Yankees advance at the double quick, the only thing which gave McFadden any reassurance was the large surplus of ammunition. Being so close to the depots of Atlanta, all of the troops holding the defenses of the city had been issued more cartridges than they could possibly fire before the barrels of their rifles melted. Whatever the outcome, McFadden was certain that a good number of Northern men would be slain before the defenses of the 7th Texas.

As the Union attackers approached the abatis fronting the trench, the buglers blew the signal for the charge, the Northern battle cry went up, and the drumbeating accelerated to a swift pounding. During the night, McFadden and his men had worked to link the sharpened wooden stakes together with chains brought in from the city. It was hoped that this would make it more difficult for the Yankees to tear them down. But McFadden now saw that the leading men in the attacking columns were wielding axes rather than muskets. They must have been pioneers, whose role would be to cut gaps in the abatis.

The moment the first Union soldier hacked at one of the stakes, McFadden gave the order to fire. Collett and Lieutenant Russell did the same, and the whole line of the 7th Texas exploded in a rattle of musketry. On either side of them, the other regiments of

Granbury's brigade fired their first volleys at almost the same instant. A sheet of lead flew forth from the Southern defenses into the exposed Union troops struggling through the abatis on the other side of the trench.

Union troops began falling in droves, but McFadden saw that the fire was not intense enough. At various points, pioneers succeeding in hacking down the wooden stakes. Like water bursting through a cracked dam, blue-coated soldiers poured through these small gaps, dropped down into the trench, and charged forward toward the parapet.

McFadden drew his sword and pistol. The wound he had suffered the day before, minor though it had been, still seethed with pain and he worried it would affect his ability to fight. He would simply have to ignore the agony if he was to do his duty.

His men continued firing. Scores of Union men were falling beneath a hail of Southern lead, but more and more of the abatis stakes were being hacked away and the trench before the parapet was rapidly filling up with Yankees. Some were beginning to scramble upwards. McFadden fired six shots from his Navy Colt down into the trench. He didn't bother to see whether he hit anything, although there were so many enemies in front of him that it seemed impossible to miss. He quickly reloaded his weapon, wondering if he would ever get a chance to do so again.

The first Union soldier appeared on top of the parapet, firing his musket down into the space on the other side. One of the Texans was hit in the stomach, but the Yankee was immediately struck by five bullets and tumbled backwards into the trench. Almost instantly, though, three more Yankees rose to take his place. They fell immediately, two tumbling back into the trench and one falling forward over the parapet.

McFadden pulled three of his men out of the line, ordering them to fire only at enemy troops who appeared on top of the parapet. The others remained on the fire-step, pouring fire as quickly as they could down onto the Yankees in the trench. As they had done the day before, some of his men tossed lit artillery shells over the head-log, so that they tumbled down the parapet and exploded in the midst of the attackers.

A bullet snapped the flagpole holding up the 7th Texas battle flag. One of the men dropped his rifle and scrambled up onto the parapet toward the fallen banner. McFadden screamed for the man to get back to the fire-step, but he either didn't hear the order or decided to ignore it. Bravely, he raised the flag and shook it in the direction of the attacking Yankees, screaming defiantly. Almost instantly, he was struck by three or four bullets, dropping the flag abruptly onto the parapet and tumbling down into the trench.

Rage filled McFadden at the loss of the regimental flag. Almost as disturbing, a Union flag bearer topped the mount and planted his colors into the parapet. Glancing at it quickly, McFadden saw that it was the flag of the 48th Illinois. The man turned and waved his flag, calling for his comrades to join him.

"Come on, men! Come on!"

McFadden expected the man to fall, pierced by Southern bullets, at any moment. But he yet remained unharmed, continuing to wave his flag and call to his comrades. Frustrated, McFadden raised his pistol and fired six shots in rapid succession. All missed.

More and more Yankees were now appearing on the top of the parapet, firing down into the space behind it. Several of the Texans were hit. Even worse, many of the blue-coats were now jumping down into the defenses, swinging their rifles like clubs and jabbing with their bayonets.

"Fix bayonets, men!" McFadden shouted, feeling stupid for having waited so long to issue the order. "Fix bayonets!"

It took only a few seconds for his well-trained men to unsheathe their bayonets and fix them onto their rifles, but their fire slackened during that brief space of time. Seeing their chance, Union officers screamed for their men to go over the top. Their battle cry increased in intensity as hundreds of Union soldiers scrambled upwards at the same moment, flooding over the parapet like a tidal wave over a tiny breakwater.

As the bluecoats plunged down into the defenses, a vicious hand-to-hand struggle ensued. McFadden had managed to reload his revolver, but within seconds he had expended all six shots once again. He looked around for Major Collett, but could not find him. The men of the 7th Texas were now intermingled with the other regiments of Granbury's brigade, but all told they numbered only a few hundred men, drowning in a sea of federal troops. More and more Union battle flags were now waving from the top of the parapet.

He plunged into the melee, swinging his sword. He realized that the Yankees using their muskets as clubs would have an advantage over him, for their muskets were so much heavier than his sword. Still, he gashed the arm of the nearest Yankee, just before slamming his head into the man's nose and then embedding his saber deeply into the man's chest.

The roar of a cannon fired from very close by nearly deafened McFadden. It took him a few seconds to realize that the gun crews of one of the nearest artillery batteries had pulled their pieces back from the parapet, turned them toward the Yankees massing inside the defenses, and were now firing at point blank range. Although they killed huge numbers of enemy soldiers with a single blast, they also cut down some of their own men in the process.

As he watched, dozens of Yankee soldiers descended vengefully on the offending battery. In a matter of seconds, the artillery crews had been clubbed or bayoneted. There was nothing now to stop the Yankees from turning the artillery pieces against the Confederates.

"Major Collett!" McFadden called, looking about frantically for his commander.

One of the Texans pointed and McFadden saw Collett leaning heavily against the parapet, sword in one hand and clasping a bloody leg with the other. He dashed over.

"Get them out, James!" Collett screamed in his ear. "Get as many of the men together and get out!"

There was no time parting words. McFadden backed away from the parapet, waving his sword in a circle over his head.

"Rally to me, Texans! Rally to me!"

He realized that his shouting and waving made him a prime target for Yankee bullets and several did zip past his head. But by ones and twos, soldiers in gray and butternut extracted themselves from the fighting and backed away from the parapet, slowly coalescing around him in a rough semicircle. They began reloading their rifles and firing at the Yankees. Within three or four minutes, perhaps a dozen survivors had assembled around McFadden. Keeping up a weak rate of fire, they slowly backed away from the position they had held with such tenacity.

The enemy fired back but made no effort to follow them. Dozens of Yankee battle flags were now firmly posted on the parapet, while cheering bluecoats were waving captured Confederate standards about them as trophies. One of them, McFadden could see, was the flag of the 7th Texas.

"Let's go," he said loudly to the group.

They turned and marched away, determined to put as much distance between them and their victorious enemies as possible. As they departed, the cheers of the victorious Union troops grew louder.

*   *   *   *   *

Through his field glasses, Grant could see his men waving captured rebels flags about, while the standard of the United States was firmly planted on the enemy defenses in many places. The sound of shooting had nearly stopped, indicating that whatever rebel defenders had not been killed or captured had run away.

He scanned the enemy defenses all across the line, noticing with satisfaction that several of the artillery batteries had been captured. While he had an immense amount of artillery already, the captured cannon would prove useful after they had been incorporated into his own forces. More important, however, was the denial of their use to the Southerners.

He turned to one of his aides. "Send a telegram to the War Department. Inform them that we have smashed the enemy defenses around East Point and that we expect to control the railroad within the hour."

"Happily, sir." The man saluted and rode away.

A long column of rough, disheveled men slowly snaked out of the rebel fortifications and wound its way across the intervening ground. On each side were bluecoats holding rifles with fixed bayonets. Realizing that the group was one of Southern prisoners, Grant tapped Cincinnati with his spurs and walked out toward them.

"What brigade are you?" he asked the first man to come within speaking distance.

"Why don't you go to the devil?" the man replied with irritation in his voice.

"We are Granbury's Brigade," another answered.

"Shut your mouth, John!" the first prisoner snapped. "Why would you answer any of their questions? Any information just helps them!"

The second man shrugged. "Never hurts to be polite."

Grant ignored the conversation between the two prisoners, satisfied as to the identity of the unit that had just been overrun. If he recalled correctly, Granbury's brigade was a unit of Cleburne's division, which meant that his beloved Army of the Tennessee had just taken on and beaten the best troops the Confederacy had in the field outside of Virginia. That was all the more reason for celebration.

He turned to see McPherson and some staff officers riding up to report.

"Congratulations, James!" Grant said warmly.

"Thank you, sir."

"Those trenches look every bit as strong as the ones which repulsed the Army of the Potomac at Cold Harbor. Your men did a stellar job getting through them."

"We have suffered heavily, sir," McPherson replied, not sounding nearly as happy as his commander. "Four thousand casualties in both corps. At the least, sir."

Grant nodded. "And in exchange we captured a strong line of entrenchments, smashed two enemy divisions, and cut the critical railroad to the southwest. A fair trade, if you ask me."

"What now?" McPherson asked.

"Prepare for a counter attack. I don't see how the rebels would have the strength to strike back, but best to be on the safe side. Then, see to the wounded and the prisoners. Send forward ammunition and get your divisions in proper order. In half an hour, I want you to advance eastward until we are on the tracks of the railroad."

McPherson nodded. "Easily done, sir."

The two generals exchanged salutes and McPherson rode off. Grant pulled out another cigar and quietly lit it, watching as the long column of rebel prisoners continued to march to the rear. Seeing so many prisoners highlighted the victory more than any dispatch from a courier could. It was one thing for people in Washington to push colored pins into a map so as to indicate that a particular piece of ground had been captured, but to hear concrete numbers of enemy soldiers taken prisoner, battle flags captured, and pieces of artillery seized was infinitely better.

It would also make for good press, which Grant realized was almost as important as any strategic advance gained. He made a mental note to send the War Department exact figures on the number of prisoners, battle flags, and artillery captured, so that Stanton could ensure they would find their way into the headlines over the next few days. Lincoln had not discussed the upcoming election with him, but he had not needed to. Better than most generals, Grant understood perfectly well that political considerations were every bit as important in war as military ones.

*   *   *   *   *

September 25, Evening

The scene north of East Point was one of utter pandemonium. Thousands of Confederate soldiers milled about in confusion, having become separated from their units and trying to find any officers who might be able to give them any sort of orders. Fires were burning in East Point itself, as many Union shells had landed in the town during the fighting. Everywhere there were men shouting and arguing with each other. Pervading the entire panorama was an overriding sense of fear, for a renewed Union attack was expected at any moment.

Hardee and Cleburne rode through the confusion and looked on dispassionately as their officers tried to bring order out of chaos. Of the six brigades that had been holding the defenses around East Point, only the Florida Brigade of Bate's division and the Arkansas Brigade of Cleburne's division had succeeded in maintaining a semblance of organization as they had retreated to the northeast. The other four brigades had simply disintegrated under the weight of the Union attack.

Beneath Cleburne, Red Pepper was far from happy. The horse instinctively sensed the disarray around him, which seemed to trouble him more than even the noise and bedlam of a battle. He shook his bridle repeatedly to make his displeasure known. Cleburne responded by gently patting the faithful animal on the neck to calm it down.

"It's a damn fiasco, Pat!" Hardee said angrily. "We've lost the railroad!" Scattered reports had the first regiments of Union infantry on the Atlanta and West Point Railroad a mile south of East Point.

Cleburne nodded. His men had fought as bravely as any men possibly could, but all their valor and courage had counted as nothing against the overwhelming numerical superiority of the enemy. The

Yankees had not so much beaten then as simply rolled over them like a deluge.

"We made them pay for it," Cleburne said. "The ground in front of my division's position is covered in dead and wounded Yankees."

"Doesn't matter," Hardee said. "They've got more than enough men. They can wheel around to the north and crush us anytime they want to."

Cleburne nodded again. He wanted to be stoic in order to cheer up an obviously dispirited Hardee, but he could not argue with his assessment of the situation.

Looking around at the confused soldiers nearby, he saw a group of about a dozen men being led by a lieutenant he recognized.

"McFadden!" Cleburne called out, waving.

The Texan heard him and his eyes lit up with relief when he recognized Cleburne. He walked over to the two generals, his soldiers trailing behind him.

"Good to see you, Lieutenant!" Cleburne said. "I am very glad to see you alive."

"Thank you, sir. Likewise."

"General Hardee, this is Lieutenant McFadden of the 7th Texas. He is the man who captured George Thomas. I might also add that he was the man who warned me of Grant's movement."

Hardee nodded. "Pleased to meet you, Lieutenant. I thank you for your service, although after today I must frankly state that it may have come too late to do any good."

McFadden shrugged. Cleburne speculated than many other men might have taken offense to Hardee's words, but McFadden seemed entirely disinterested. Looking at him, Cleburne only saw an exhausted and defeated man.

"Where is the 7th Texas?" Cleburne asked.

McFadden waved to the west. "It's lying out there in those trenches, General. The regiment has been wiped out."

Cleburne's face contorted into horror. "Major Collett? Lieutenant Russell?"

"Either dead or prisoners, I suppose."

Recovering, Cleburne nodded. "That means you command the 7th Texas, McFadden."

"Don't think that means much. I think these men around me are all that's left of the regiment and a lot of them started the day with other units."

"Form them in a line here, if you please. We're trying to rally as many men as possible."

McFadden nodded and started barking orders. His men spaced out in a long line before the two generals. As soldiers came by individually or in small groups, McFadden's men halted them and pulled them into their line, which gradually grew longer and more compact.

A courier rode up. "General Hardee, sir! I regret to inform you that General Bate has been killed!"

"No!" Hardee said, casting a quick glance at Cleburne. In such a situation as this, with chaos and confusion having already swept through the disorganized troops, the death of a division commander was a disaster too terrible to contemplate.

"Yes, sir. He insisted on personally leading a counter attack after the Yankees got over the lines. I saw him fall myself, sir."

"Find any of the brigade commanders you can," Hardee said to the courier. "Tell them that they are to report to General Cleburne."

"Yes, sir!" The man dashed off.

Hardee turned to Cleburne. "Consider Bate's brigades as now attached to your division. Bate's brigade commanders will be far too busy getting their own men back into some semblance of order, so I can't burden one of them with the additional duties of taking command of the whole division."

Cleburne nodded quickly. "Understood, sir. What are my orders?"

Hardee angrily shook his head and stared southwest, toward the massed Union formations that were just over the horizon. "No way to knock them out of there, is there?"

"No, William. We have only two reliable brigades at the moment and both of them are shaken to the core."

"But we cannot allow the Yankees to secure the area. If they dig in here, we will never be able to pry them out."

"If we try to counter attack now, we will fail and we will lose those two brigades as well."

Hardee was starting to say something about bringing in reinforcements from the divisions of Walker and Maney, when a series of explosions ripped through the area a few hundred yards south. Instantly, cries of fear rose from hundreds of Confederate soldiers, many of whom began running wildly to the northeast in a panic.

"The Yankees are shelling us again!" Hardee said.

Cleburne nodded. "They're trying to keep us from reorganizing."

"We've got to get these men out of here. We've got to-"

The commander's words were cut short when a Union shell exploded on the ground directly between their horses. Cleburne was thrown off of Red Pepper by the force of the detonation, flew several yards to the left, and landed roughly and painfully on the ground. His vision faded for a moment and he couldn't hear a thing. He realized he was losing consciousness.

Time passed, though how much he did not know. Everything seemed slow and murky. His mind struggled to reassert itself. He felt as though he had been run over by a horse and wagon. Gradually, he realized that someone was shaking his shoulder.

"General Cleburne? Are you hurt?"

It was McFadden. His words struck Cleburne as ridiculously inane, seeing as he had just been thrown off of a horse. Cleburne tried to push himself up off the ground, but his arms were so sore that they refused to make the effort and he fell back onto the ground.

"Sir, General Hardee is wounded!"

This woke Cleburne up as though water had been splashed in his face. He glanced over to where McFadden was pointing and saw his worst fears realized. Hardee had been thrown in the opposite direction and lay on the ground several yards away. Large red splotches were visible on his left leg, which could only have been due to shell fragments having embedding themselves in his body.

Painfully, Cleburne stood up with the help of McFadden. He had been momentarily knocked unconscious by the force of the blast and the fall from his horse, but he did not appear to be seriously hurt. Having verified that, he walked over to Hardee as quickly as he could.

Hardee was still conscious, wincing in pain. Two of McFadden's men were trying to apply a tourniquet to his leg to staunch the bleeding. As they tightened it, Hardee let out a scream that deeply unsettled Cleburne. He had seen countless severe wounds during his years in the army, but the man he now saw in agony was his closest friend.

Nearly delirious with pain, Hardee's eyes focused on Cleburne. "Are you all right?" he asked through gritted teeth.

"Yes, William. I'm fine."

Cleburne looked at the wound. It was clear that Hardee's leg would have to be amputated. If it wasn't, infection would inevitably set in and the result would be a slow and painful death. But it was entirely possible that the surgery to remove Hardee's leg would be so shocking and painful that he would not survive. The rational part of Cleburne's mind told him that the odds of his friend's survival were, at best, fifty-fifty.

"Take command," Hardee said, his words coming in painful fits. "Get all the troops into the Atlanta defenses. Hold out to the last bullet."

"I will, William. I will hold the city." Cleburne tried to sound confident as he spoke these words. The railroad was now in Union hands. The Confederates had taken massive casualties and suffered a demoralizing defeat. Much of their artillery had been captured. The defenses of Atlanta might be strong, but the odds against the Southerners were even longer now than they had been when the day had begun.

"Johnston is coming," Hardee said weakly. His head fell as he lapsed into unconsciousness.

McFadden had located a stretcher and detailed four men to carry Hardee away. He was speaking to Cleburne, telling him that his men would take Hardee into the city as soon as they could find a horse and wagon. Cleburne barely heard him. He was consumed by something resembling panic.

In an instant, all the collected burdens of the entire Southern Confederacy had descended onto the shoulders of Patrick Cleburne. Grant's army was on the verge of taking Atlanta, the fall of which would not only cripple the South's ability to continue the war but would almost certainly ensure that Abraham Lincoln would be reelected President of the United States. The divisions of the Army of Tennessee in and around Atlanta would be destroyed, leaving Johnston's remaining two corps easy prey for Grant's victorious forces. The Confederacy would be left with no effective army outside of Virginia. If this came to pass, Cleburne doubted that the Confederacy would survive more than a few months at most.

And who was he? An Irish orphan who had come to America penniless and obscure, who still spoke with a strong Irish accent. If men like William Walker and Braxton Bragg were to be believed, he was no Southerner at all, but an abolitionist agitator who was unfit to command a company of infantry. How was it that everything had suddenly fallen to him?

"Sir, what shall we do?" McFadden asked.

The question snapped Cleburne out of his thoughts. "Keep your men with me, McFadden."

"Of course, sir. Where are we going?"

"We're pulling back into the city. Where is my horse?"

"Sorry, sir, but I'm afraid your horse has had it."

He looked where McFadden was pointing and saw a grievously wounded Red Pepper whimpering in pain. Two of the horse's legs had been torn off by the same shell explosion that had wounded Hardee and some of the animal's entrails were spilling out onto the ground from a massive slash made by shrapnel in its belly. Nevertheless, Red Pepper was struggling to stand up, frightened, confused, and obviously in agony.

"Oh, Red Pepper," Cleburne said sadly. A man at least could understand what the war was about and why he was being asked to risk his life. A horse had no such solace. It merely went to where its master directed it to go. The poor animal had no idea why it had to die an agonizing death.

"I'll do it, sir," McFadden said, drawing the pistol from his holster.

"No," Cleburne said sharply. "Thank you, Lieutenant, but I'll do it."

He sighed as he walked over to his beloved horse. It neighed softly in recognition, perhaps asking if Cleburne could do something to help it. He pulled his pistol and pulled back the cock. Seemingly understanding what was about to happen, the animal moved its head slightly before laying it calmly back down on the ground. A second later, a single pistol shot ended Red Pepper's pain.

Cleburne shook his head. There was no time for grief of any kind. Right now, his job was to get all the men back into the Atlanta defenses and hold out for as long as possible. He did not consider it likely that they would be able to hold out long enough for Johnston to arrive, but it was his duty to try.

*   *   *   *   *

September 25, Night

Marble has almost drifted off to sleep when the rusty creaking of the prison door startled him into wakefulness. He stood up from his uncomfortable cot. The cell and the hallway beyond the bars were illuminated by the flickering light of three torches, casting a pale yellow light. Two guards still stood impassively outside the cell, as startled as he was to receive a late night visitor.

Benjamin Butler entered the cellblock, looking as sinister and oafish as usual. Marble thought he saw something else under the rubbery exterior of the man's face, though he couldn't say what. Marble considered himself a good reader of minds, but he had always found it frustratingly impossible to know what Butler was thinking.

"Wait outside," Butler said to the guards. They immediately saluted and departed, shutting the door behind them.

"General Butler," Marble said with mock warmth. "To what do I owe the pleasure?"

Butler didn't respond right away. He stepped forward until his face was almost between the bars of Marble's cell, eyeing him closely and warily. Marble found this deeply unsettling. It was though he were being examined by a predator to determine whether or not he would make a decent meal. No one who knew Butler well could help but be afraid of him.

Butler took a step back. The next words were among the most surprising of Marble's life.

"Do you want to get out of here?" Butler asked. His tone was simple, as though he were asking Marble what he wanted for dinner.

"I'm sorry?"

"You heard me."

Marble snorted. "But General Butler, I am so enjoying your hospitality that I-"

"Drop the pretense, Marble. You shall never succeed in impressing me. I asked you a question. Do you want to get out of here or not?"

There was stone cold silence. The flickering of the torches and the dripping of a trickle of water onto stone were the only sounds. For a long minute, Marble tried to make sense of what Butler was saying.

"Perhaps if you explained yourself?" he finally asked.

"I am willing to offer you a deal. If you do what I want, I am willing to let you out."

"And why on Earth would you do that? You are Lincoln's errand boy, aren't you?"

"I am my own errand boy."

"And what is it that you want me to do?"

"It's quite simply, really. I want to be the Secretary of War. If McClellan wins the election, as I believe he shall, I want to be included in his cabinet as the Secretary of War."

Marble's eyes widened in shock. The unadulterated audacity of the man was enough to win his admiration, if not his respect. Butler had been a ferociously partisan Democrat before the war, pushing for Jefferson Davis to be nominated as the party's presidential candidate and stridently working against Lincoln's election throughout 1860. When the Southern states had seceded and the war had begun, Butler had effortlessly switched over to the Republicans and become one of Lincoln's staunchest supporters. Now, by the looks of things, he was ready to switch sides yet again.

"You amaze me, General Butler," Marble said. "At least Benedict Arnold had the decency to betray only one side."

"Spare me. I made you an offer. What say you?"

Marble raised his hands in a gesture of helplessness. "George McClellan has said he wants nothing more to do with me. Governor Seymour probably doesn't trust me any longer, either. I want to get out of this jail as much as any prisoner in history, but what makes you think I can persuade anyone in the party to make you Secretary of War?"

"If I release you from this jail, I am also willing to make a statement to the press that your arrest was unwarranted and that the evidence against you was contrived. In a flash, your credibility with McClellan, Seymour, and the other power players in the Democratic Party will be restored. Indeed, it will be enhanced, as you will become a symbol for what you have been calling the unconstitutional abuse of power by the Lincoln administration."

"But what has become of the evidence? The list you confiscated from me?"

He withdrew a piece of paper from his uniform coat pocket. "Is this the list to which you refer? If we have an agreement, I shall place it over one of these torches."

"And the remaining five thousand dollars?"

Benjamin said nothing, staring impassively through the bars at him. Marble took that to mean that the money had already found its way into Butler's own coffers.

"Why do you think McClellan is going to win the election? From what Governor Seymour told me, Grant is knocking on the gates of Atlanta and the people are enraged at the idea of the rebels funding the Democratic Party. It seems to me that Lincoln's chances for reelection are now excellent."

Butler slowly shook his head. "The scandal you speak of, once I let you out and release my statement to the press, will be like the tide reversing itself. As for Grant, I do not expect him to succeed at Atlanta. Indeed, I expect that he shall eventually be repelled by the enemy and will suffer enormous casualties. At least, that is the outcome I choose to bet on."

"Quite a risk," Marble said.

Butler looked up at the ceiling, staring at nothing in particular. "If I were to remain a Lincoln man and the Republicans emerge triumphant in the upcoming election, I would expect to be rewarded. I shall be guaranteed a seat in the House of Representatives. Perhaps I should even be the Governor of Massachusetts. But a Cabinet post? No, Lincoln would never have that. It will be his policy to reconcile with the South once they are defeated, and that task would be made much more difficult were I in the Cabinet."

Marble nodded in understanding. As far as the Confederates were concerned, no Union man was more despised than Benjamin Butler. During his stint as the military governor of New Orleans, he had executed a man for tearing down the United States flag, issued an order allowing his men to treat as prostitutes any woman found to be disrespecting a Union soldier or sailor, and lined his own pockets and that of his brother through corrupt deals in confiscated cotton. He had bent himself to the task of recruiting both former slaves and Confederate prisoners into the Union army. Jefferson Davis himself had issued a proclamation stating that Butler would be immediately shot if he were ever to be captured by Confederate forces.

"Why is it so important for you to be in the Cabinet?" Marble asked. "I would have thought a lifetime seat in Congress or the governorship of Massachusetts would be enough, even for you."

"If you don't know the answer to that question, Marble, than you have no business being a newspaper man."

Marble considered this for a moment, and then all became clear. A seat in Congress or the governorship of a state would, for all their prestige, confine Butler to a relatively small geographic region of the country. At most, he might exercise a dominating political influence over New England, but in practice his power would be limited to his home state of Massachusetts. For most men, that would be the culmination of all their dreams, but it would not be enough for Butler.

A cabinet post, on the other hand, would instantly transform Butler into a figure on the national stage. His influence would be seen across the country. Moreover, his ability to offer an inexhaustible number of military contracts to businessman from one end of the United States to the other would put almost unchecked political influence in his hands. With clout like that, there was literally no limit to the heights of power Butler might obtain. And his ultimate goal was suddenly crystal clear to Marble.

His machinations might well tear the country apart, but the politician-turned-general staring at him through the jail bars clearly intended that whatever was left of the United States when all the dust had settled would be fertile ground for an eventual accession of Benjamin Butler to the presidency. All his heart and soul craved it, no less than the Medici family had craved the power of the papacy. He would have it and he could not have cared less how much death and destruction he left in his wake.

"So, Marble?" Butler asked. "Do we have a deal?"

Slowly, ever so slowly, Marble nodded his head.

An unpleasant smile crossed Butler's face. Without another word, he held the list of the names of people to whom Marble had distributed the money from Humphries over the nearest torch. Within seconds, the paper ignited and the soft crackling sound of its fiery incineration echoed through the cellblock. A few moments later, Butler dropped the gray ashes onto the stone floor.

"Guards!" Butler called.

The two soldiers opened the door. Butler tossed his head toward Marble's cell.

"Let him out."

Without hesitation, one of the guards produced a large set of keys and, fumbling only momentarily, unlocked the door to Marble's cell. As the door swung open, Marble felt the refreshing sensation of freedom, which overpowered his spirit with a much greater force than he had expected. He stepped out into the hall, smiling from ear to ear.

"You'll have my press statement tomorrow."

Marble nodded. "Very well, sir."

"Perhaps you and I could meet for dinner at Delmonico's the day after tomorrow? Seven o'clock, perhaps? We are good friends now, after all. Aren't we, Marble?"

Marble smiled more broadly and bowed his head. "That we are, General Butler. And dinner at Delmonico's would suit me just fine."

Chapter Seventeen

September 26, Morning

The train carrying Johnston, his staff, and some regiments of Benton's Mississippi brigade had arrived in the town of Newnan, roughly midway between the Alabama border and Atlanta, shortly after midnight. Because of a delay needed to repair yet another break in the line made by Yankee cavalry, Johnston had decided to try to sleep. Mackall had appropriated a local house whose owner had been more than happy to vacate temporarily in order to accommodate the commander of the Army of Tennessee.

Though he had scarcely slept more than two or three hours out of the previous forty-eight, Johnston had found it difficult to fall asleep. The sun was just beginning to illuminate the eastern horizon with a long, thin, reddish glow when Mackall stepped quietly into the room. He gently shook his commander awake.

"Sir?"

Johnston opened his eyes and, after a moment, sat up in the bed. He saw trouble on Mackall's face.

"What is it?"

"We've just received word, sir. East Point fell yesterday evening. The railroad into Atlanta is blocked."

He kicked off the sheets and turned, placing his feet on the floor. He waited for his mind to fully clear away the cobwebs of sleep, trying to make sense of what Mackall had just said. If East Point had fallen to the enemy, then it would be impossible to simply run the trains directly into the city with their precious cargo of reinforcements. The plan he had devised was in tatters.

"What happened?"

"From the telegrams we have gotten, sir, it seems that the Yankees overwhelmed the two divisions that were holding the defenses of East Point by sheer force of numbers. Two entire Yankee corps attacked them, essentially destroying both divisions and

- 632 -

capturing the railroad. General Bate has been killed and General Hardee has been badly wounded."

"What's that? Bate killed? Hardee wounded?"

"Yes, sir. Hardee was hit by shrapnel from a Yankee artillery shell."

"Who is in command in Atlanta?"

"General Cleburne, sir."

Johnston's eyes widened. "Good Lord," he said without thinking. Cleburne was an outstanding division commander, but how would he respond to the responsibilities of commanding an entire corps, without any supervision from a superior officer? Johnston had seen the burden of being an independent commander break more than one general. Moreover, with all the swirling controversy about Cleburne's proposal, how would the rank and file respond to his leadership?

With a sudden shock that hit him with the power of a fist, Johnston realized that events had made Cleburne into Walker's immediate superior. Would Walker even take orders from Cleburne? Considering the man's fiery temperament, it seemed rather doubtful.

"General, what shall we do? We cannot continue on to Atlanta now."

"How far south along the railroad do the Yankees control?"

"We're not sure right now. The situation up north is changing rapidly."

"Is Palmetto still free of Yankees?"

"We have not heard that the city has been occupied by the enemy, but we cannot be certain."

"We have no cavalry here?"

"No, sir."

Johnston nodded. "Pick a good regiment. Send a locomotive and enough boxcars for the troops north along the railroad. If they can get to Palmetto without encountering resistance, we shall continue moving troops up to that point and assemble the army there."

"That's still twenty-five miles short of Atlanta," Mackall pointed out.

"A good day's march, I know. But it puts us in a position to strike the rear of Grant's army. It will force him to divert some troops away from Atlanta. It's the best we can do, William. If you have any better idea, please let me know."

Mackall thought for a moment before shaking his head.

"Do we still have the ability to send telegrams to Atlanta?"

"Indirectly, yes. It takes quite a long time, though."

"Good. Send a message to Cleburne telling him to hold on as long as he can. Tell him that we are coming. I would rather have the city reduced to rubble than for there to be any thoughts of withdrawal or surrender."

"Very good, sir."

"Oh, and one more thing. Please address a message directly to General Walker. Tell him that he is to obey the orders of General Cleburne as though they were coming directly from me."

Mackall snorted. "I'll send the message, for whatever good it may do."

"If nothing else, I just want that to be on the record."

"Okay, I'll send that scouting train north and I'll get the two telegrams off."

"Are the other units still on their way from Lafayette to here?"

"Yes. We have two brigades here already. Two more should arrive by this afternoon, I think."

"Very well. Off with you, then."

*   *   *   *   *

"General Cleburne?" the voice said.

"Yes?" He didn't immediately recognize to whom the voice belonged. Lieutenant Hanley, of course, was dead. Most of the rest of his staff had been dispersed throughout the area the night before, trying to bring order out of the chaos caused by the defeat at East Point.

"General Finley is requesting your presence on the southwestern portion of the defenses, sir. He says it is most urgent."

He opened his eyes and recognized Lieutenant McFadden. His memories of the previous night instantly reasserted themselves. McFadden and his small band of Texans had remained with him, essentially serving as military police for a time and helping to reorganize the scattered bands of Southern troops as they had come into the inner defenses of Atlanta. Cleburne assumed that McFadden and his men had bedded down for the night nearby, not having any better idea where to go.

"What's that?" Cleburne asked.

"General Finley, sir. A courier has arrived from him. He needs you on the southwestern defenses."

Cleburne nodded. He expected the Union attack to begin at any time. Presumably Finley, who had taken over command of Bate's division following the latter's death, had observed something that led him to believe the attack was imminent. He rose from the ground, where he had slept wrapped in a simple blanket, grabbed his hat and sword, and followed McFadden.

The sun was still just peeking over the horizon. He recalled that the red glow of dawn had already been visible when he had lain down on the ground for a brief bit of sleep. It had been one of the most exhausting and confusing nights of his life. For hours, he had striven to reorganize the shattered brigades of the two divisions that had been defeated around East Point. It had not been an easy task, especially as so many of the officers had fallen during the ferocious fighting that had taken place over the previous two days. After the sun had gone down, the hours had seemed endless as an immense stream of thousands of confused Confederate troops filtered north into the inner defenses of Atlanta.

Things had only gradually started to come back together. Granbury, to his relief, had made it out alive and unharmed, but so few of his men were left that his entire brigade now numbered less than five hundred rifles. He had considered amalgamating them into the Arkansas Brigade, with Granbury in command, then decided that the middle of a battle was no time for such reorganization efforts.

The survivors of the two divisions had been rallied along the southern defenses and the remnants of the six brigades had been put back together. Cleburne had forwarded ammunition from the city's depots and sent forward rations, but the men were so shaken from the strain of two day's combat and the shock of their heavy defeat that their reliability was questionable.

Cleburne mounted the horse McFadden was holding for him, feeling a great sadness washing over him at the memory of firing a bullet into the head of his beloved Red Pepper the night before. A horse was not a man, of course, but that mattered more to his mind than it did to his heart. Cleburne knew he would never forget the expression of infinite sadness and forgiveness with which Red Pepper had looked up at him just before he pulled the trigger.

He was worried that he felt the loss of his horse more deeply than he did the loss of one of his men. What did this say about his moral character?

"Come along with me, McFadden," Cleburne said. It seemed sensible to bring him along. Though not officially attached to his staff, McFadden and his men had served him very well the previous night. It wouldn't do for the men to see their commander riding around by himself, and he might need a good man to send on an errand at some point. McFadden nodded, mounted another horse, and followed.

After a few minutes riding, they arrived at the redoubt where General Finley had set himself up. As he dismounted, Cleburne saw Finley pointing over the rampart.

"Riders from the enemy lines with a flag of truce, sir!"

Cleburne's eyes narrowed in confusion. What on earth did the Yankees want to talk to him about? He looked out over the parapet and saw three blue-coated men, though from the distance it was impossible to make out any details of their appearance or rank. One of the men was carrying a white truce flag. They had reined in halfway between the lines and were waiting.

He suddenly felt nervous, being wholly unfamiliar with the procedures and protocols involved with communicating with the enemy. Over the course of the war, he had occasionally arranged temporary truces with Union units opposite him so as to allow both sides to assist the wounded and bury the dead. But Hardee's incapacitation had elevated him to the supreme command of all Confederate forces in and around Atlanta. Whatever it was that the Yankees wanted to discuss with him, Cleburne was uncertain what sort of authority he had. There was no time to send a telegram to Richmond to clarify the situation, either.

"What do you think they want?" Cleburne asked Finley.

"No idea at all, sir."

"Well, I suppose I have to go."

"Alone, sir?"

Cleburne started to reply, but realized he had no idea what to say. Would it be proper for him, now the commander of all Southern troops in Atlanta, to venture forth alone to meet with the enemy between the lines? But he reasoned that he would be perfectly safe. Not even the Yankees would be so uncivilized as to attempt to kill or capture a Southern officer under such circumstances, in plain sight of thousands of soldiers on each side.

He nodded at McFadden. "Come with me."

"Of course, sir."

Cleburne remounted his horse and, taking a deep breath, tapped it with his spurs, trailed by McFadden. They rode through the gate of the redoubt and, not wanting to waste time, kicked the horses into a canter. He headed directly for the Union officers. Only half a mile away, thousands of Union soldiers were watching his approach. Behind him, his own troops were viewing the proceedings with concern as well. Cleburne wondered what they all were thinking.

He reined in less than ten yards from the three enemy officers and stiffly saluted.

"I am General Cleburne," he said. "I command the Confederate forces in Atlanta."

The officer returned the salute. "I am General McPherson, commander of the Army of the Tennessee. It is an honor to meet you, General Cleburne."

Cleburne nodded. "And you, General McPherson."

"It was my understanding that General Hardee commanded in Atlanta."

"General Hardee has been wounded."

"Oh? I pray not seriously. He was one of my instructors at West Point."

"I believe he will survive. I shall extend your best wishes to him."

McPherson nodded. "Thank you." He cleared his throat before continuing. "Let us come to the matter at hand. I have been authorized by General Grant to speak with full authority."

"Very well. I am listening, though I confess I have no idea what you want to discuss."

"General Grant wishes me to give you the following message. The result of yesterday's fighting must surely convince you of the hopelessness of further resistance. To remove from the United States any responsibility for the further needless effusion of blood, he calls for the surrender of the city of Atlanta and all Confederate forces within it."

Cleburne laughed softly. "We will never surrender. Of that you can be certain."

McPherson leaned forward. "General Cleburne, when you return to your command post, you will be told that our cavalry has managed to reach the railroad linking Atlanta to Augusta. All rail traffic in that direction has been halted. We already hold the railroads to both the south and southwest. You will also be told that all telegraph lines have been cut. You are surrounded and cut off from any hope of resupply or reinforcement."

Cleburne tensed at these words. He had to assume that McPherson was speaking the truth. A bluff under such circumstances would have made no sense, since he could easily check it for himself within an hour. The Southerners themselves had no cavalry to counter such a move, for all their mounted units had been destroyed. He tried to look as calm as possible.

McFadden, of course, had said nothing. Cleburne wondered what he was thinking. From what Cleburne had learned in their conversations, he had served in New Mexico under Sibley in 1862, fought in Arkansas the following winter, and served in the 7th Texas since the spring of 1863. The man did not waver in his courage, and Cleburne's command was filled with soldiers like McFadden. The thought gave him confidence.

"Surrounded or not, Atlanta will not be surrendered. Our defenses are strong and we have an enormous reserve of ammunition for both rifles and artillery. Our food supplies are also more than adequate."

"Even if that is so, you are outnumbered by an impossible margin. You found that out yesterday, did you not? Your strong defenses meant nothing against our numbers."

Cleburne shook his head. "It doesn't matter. So long as a single one of us remains alive, we shall resist. If you want Atlanta, you shall have to kill every single one of us in protracted fighting amidst the rubble of the city."

"Are you really going to condemn your men to suffer and die in the ruins of Atlanta, General Cleburne?" McPherson said, the polished tone of persuasion slipping into his voice. "What will be gained by their deaths? You and I both know that the Confederacy is doomed."

"You're wrong, General McPherson. You cannot crush the spirit of the South, for there is a fire in our hearts which you cannot hope to extinguish. We shall continue fighting for our rights, no matter how long it takes, until the North acknowledges our right to decide our own destiny in our own way."

"Why do you fight for them, General Cleburne? You are not a Southerner. You're an Irishman. You should be fighting to free Ireland from British rule, not fighting to maintain the power of a corrupt slaveholding aristocracy which cares nothing for the welfare of ordinary people. The leaders of your so-called Confederacy only want to keep their slaves and their plantations. They don't care about you or your men."

Cleburne tilted his head, looking back at McPherson in some confusion. Did McPherson seriously think he might be able to persuade him to surrender? If so, he was deluding himself.

"I am a Southerner," Cleburne said firmly. "I may have been born in Ireland, but I am a Southerner. These people have been my friends. They welcomed me into their midst with open arms when I arrived, penniless and obscure, from another land. The South is where I have made my home. And I will fight for it."

"No matter how many men must die?"

Cleburne's eyes flashed with anger. "You spoke of Ireland. England has lorded it over Ireland for centuries. What is the North doing today but trying to establish a similar rule over the South? You invade our land under the pretense of freeing the slaves, but your true objective is to establish an absolute tyranny over the South and deprive us of our rights."

"Your rights?" McPherson asked mockingly. "You mean the right to own other human beings?"

"I do not own slaves, sir. You Yankees say you are fighting to free the slaves, yet you burn our towns, loot our farms, and kill our people. Of course I will fight you to the death, slavery be damned. In my place, you would do the same."

"You are willing to fight for the South, yet the South seems distinctly unwilling to fight for you," McPherson said. "How many newspapers and politicians, not to mention your fellow officers, have called for your removal from command since your proposal to free the slaves was revealed to the public?"

Cleburne shifted uncomfortably in the saddle. He decided to respond to McPherson by saying nothing.

McPherson went on. "If you favor freeing the slaves, why do you fight for the Confederacy?"

"Slavery is not what I fight for, General McPherson, nor is it what my men fight for. We are fighting only in defense of our right to decide our own destiny as we see fit." He spoke these words as firmly as he could, though part of his mind wondered whether he was trying to persuade himself as much as McPherson.

"I've read the newspaper accounts. I know all about your proposal. If what you're saying is true, if the South really is fighting only for its own freedom and not to maintain slavery, why was your proposal rejected? Why was your proposal not embraced with open arms by your comrades? Why have you been humiliated and disgraced for writing it, rather than being honored as a visionary?"

Cleburne looked at McPherson with what he hoped was an expressionless face. In fact, McPherson's words stung badly. McPherson's question was one for which Cleburne had never found a satisfactory answer. He thought of how his proposal had engendered the visceral hatred of William Walker and many of his other fellow officers. He thought about how quickly President Davis had ordered all discussion of the subject terminated and how he had been passed over so many times for corps command. He thought of how the public revelation of his proposal had nearly ended his career and destroyed his reputation.

"This conversation is serving no useful purpose, General McPherson."

"I shall ask one final time. Will you surrender Atlanta?"

"I will not, sir."

"In that case, we have nothing further to discuss. Farewell, General Cleburne."

"Farewell, General McPherson."

The two men saluted and simultaneously turned their horses away from one another. Cleburne tapped his horse into a walk and headed back to his own lines. He did not want to move very fast, as he wished to give the Yankees the impression that he was entirely unconcerned.

"An odd conversation," McFadden said simply.

Cleburne turned and looked at him in some surprise. Although he was on easy and familiar terms with his staff officers, several of whom had served with him since the beginning of the war, he had only just recently met McFadden. To have a mere lieutenant show such familiarity was unusual, but it also showed a level of confidence.

"Indeed," Cleburne replied. "One of the oddest of my life, I must say."

"Do you think it's true? About the enemy already being on the railroad to Augusta?"

"Probably. He wouldn't have said it otherwise. We can easily check."

"Well, if I can speak for the men, sir, we have every confidence in your leadership. We will fight for this city with every sinew of our strength."

"Thank you." He paused a moment before continuing. "Do you own slaves, McFadden?"

"No, sir. My mother held emancipationist views. She told my father that no one would ever be held in servitude under the roof of her house."

"Do you favor emancipation, as she did?"

McFadden thought for a moment. "I suppose I never really considered it, sir. Holding slaves has certainly caused the South a great deal of trouble, to say the least."

Cleburne nodded sharply. "It has prevented the nations of Europe from recognizing the Confederacy. And whenever Northern armies have invaded our territory, slaves flock to them in the hopes of being set free. Tens of thousands of them have enlisted in the Union Army. Their claim to be fighting to destroy slavery has also given the North a feeling of moral superiority that Lincoln has used well, false though it is."

"That's all true, sir. But I was speaking more in the sense that slavery is what brought the war on in the first place. Had there been no slavery, there would never have been a war. And then we would all have been much better off, I think."

Cleburne laughed softly. McFadden's observation was so simple and obvious that it was little wonder it had escaped the notice of the vast majority of people.

"Sir, may I ask you a favor?"

"Of course, McFadden. What is it?"

"My men have been with you since last night. If you no longer need us, we would like to find whatever is left of Granbury's brigade."

Cleburne nodded. "Yes. Your services have been very useful, McFadden. I appreciate your efforts."

"Thank you, sir. Also, if I might be excused for an hour or two, there is someone in the city I need to check on."

Cleburne grinned. "A lady friend?"

"Yes, sir."

"How can I deny a request like that? Take your men back to Granbury, then go check on your lady friend. But stay no longer than necessary before rejoining your men. The Yankees will attack soon, and I will need every man at his post. Especially my best men, a group in which I include you."

"Thank you, sir."

They crossed back into the Confederate lines and, without another word, McFadden kicked his horse into a canter. Cleburne watched him go, finding him an even more interesting fellow than he had the night before.

*　　　　*　　　　*　　　　*　　　　*

September 26, Noon

"Well, Seward, things seem to be going well outside Atlanta," Lincoln said with a smile.

"Oh? Pray tell."

"Stanton received a telegram from Grant late last night. I read it this morning. McPherson's men smashed the Confederate defenses around the town of East Point and captured the place. This is important, so Stanton tells me, because it cuts Atlanta off from railroad communication with Johnston's army in Alabama."

"Well, that's good news."

"Indeed, it is. Grant says that McPherson will now attack the west and south side of the Atlanta defenses, while Howard pins the enemy down with feints on the north side and tries to get around to the east to surround the city."

"Not like him to be so specific," Seward noted. "He must be unusually confident."

"I believe so."

"Where is General Johnston's army?"

Lincoln eyebrows went up. "Grant did not mention Johnston. Presumably he is still in Alabama."

"Who, then, is commanding the rebel forces in Atlanta?"

"Stanton told me last night that it was General Hardee."

Seward smiled and nodded. "I thought so. How fascinating."

"How's that?" Lincoln asked.

"When my wife was in Europe about twenty years ago, she was riding in a carriage through the Alps on a sightseeing expedition when the horses became spooked and bolted, carrying the carriage with it. She would surely have been carried over a cliff had not an American army officer, who just happened along in the nick of time, grabbed the bridles of the horses and stopped them. Turns out it was Hardee."

"Fascinating, indeed. What on Earth was he doing there?"

"If I remember correctly he had been granted a sabbatical to study at a school for French cavalry officers."

Lincoln chuckled. "The United States spent many years and huge amounts of money training these Southern officers. Now they take what they have learned to lead armies against us. Strange, don't you think?"

"It is strange."

"But thank God Hardee happened to be there."

"Oh, yes. I have no doubt that he saved my wife's life. When I learned what had happened, I wrote to Hardee to tell him that he would always be able to count on me if it were ever in my power to provide any service for him."

"What a odd world we live in," Lincoln observed with a smile.

Seward reached for his coffee. "Quite true, quite true. In any case, Mr. President, I think the news from Atlanta is very good. With the Democrats in disarray on account of the Marble scandal and the military situation considerably improved, I think we can go forward toward the election with confidence."

They discussed issues only indirectly related to the war for the next half hour. The French armies of Napoleon III were continuing to gain ground in Mexico, which was obviously a matter of great concern but about which little could be done until the Confederacy was defeated. Seward wanted to lodge a complaint with the British regarding the economic damage caused by Confederate commerce raiders that had been constructed in British dockyards, but Lincoln also felt that such an issue should wait until the war was over.

Seward briefed Lincoln about events in Europe, including the unfortunate war Prussia was waging against Denmark and the failure of a Polish rebellion against Russia. None of this had much to do with the war, but Lincoln felt it was good for him to be kept aware of what was happening in the wider world.

A messenger arrived with what he said was a telegram from Henry Raymond in New York City. With a smile, Lincoln unfolded the message and read it. As he did so, his smile quickly disappeared.

He stood up from the table. "Oh dear God," he said, his face whitening.

"What is it?" Seward asked, instantly troubled.

"Raymond telegraphs that Butler has released Marble from jail!"

"What?"

"Not only that, but the *New York World* is running what it purports to be an official statement from Butler that the charges against Marble were false and politically-motivated!"

"Surely that's concocted!" Seward exclaimed.

Lincoln continued reading to the bottom of the telegram, his eyes frantically searching for any good news. "If there were any evidence that it was concocted, I would assume Raymond would say so. Besides, how could it come so quickly after Marble's release from jail unless Butler and he had planned it together?"

Seward leapt to his feet in anger. "Damn Ben Butler! That lying, scheming bastard has betrayed us!"

Lincoln threw the telegram down on the table, anger sharpening his features. He leaned forward with his hands on the table to support himself, letting his chin fall to his chest. All the happiness and exuberance of a few minutes earlier had been instantly sucked out of the President.

"We should never have trusted Butler," Lincoln said tiredly. "Such an unscrupulous man, with only his own interests in mind. How could we not have anticipated such perfidy?"

Seward shook his head. "He must have cut a deal with the Democrats. God knows what sort of bait they dangled before his greedy, fat face before he bit into it."

Lincoln sat back down, letting out a heavy sigh. "The worst possible news at the worst possible time."

"It will certainly cost us New York," Seward said. "Up until this moment, I had some hope that our recent successes had a chance of bringing the Empire State back into the Republican column on election day."

Lincoln waved his hand dismissively. "New York was going to be for McClellan, anyway. I am more concerned about the other big prizes. Pennsylvania, Ohio, and Indiana."

Seward nodded quickly. "Yes, the news will reverberate in those states, I'm afraid. The Democrats had been discredited by the Marble scandal, but this will shatter all the gains we have made in those states over the past few weeks."

"And unless the laws of mathematics no longer apply, those states going to McClellan will give him more than enough electoral votes to secure the presidency."

"I'm afraid so, Mr. President."

Lincoln paused for a moment. "So, it all hinges on Grant outside Atlanta then, doesn't it? Only the capture of Atlanta will be enough to bring the Northern public back into our orbit after this disaster in New York."

Seward nodded soberly. "I believe so, Mr. President. If Grant fails at Atlanta now, I think it entirely possible that the United States will be two nations instead of one."

*　　　　　*　　　　　*　　　　　*　　　　　*

McFadden rode northeast along the cut of the Atlanta and East Point Railroad toward the center of Atlanta. He wished he could trot or canter, but both he and the horse were simply too tired. By rights, he should have simply found his men and tried to get some rest before the upcoming battle. However, he needed to find out if the Turnbows were safe.

All around him he could see the results of the Union bombardment. Several homes and buildings he passed were punctured with large holes created by solid shot or shrapnel, while many others were blackened and burned by the fires caused by exploding shells. There was still smoke rising from the city in many places and, in the distance, he could occasionally hear the thumping sounds indicating shell detonations. The Yankee bombardment of Atlanta, clearly, was far from over.

As he rode to the Turnbow house, for the first time in quite awhile, he had the time to think about all the events that had transpired over the last few days. He still could not quite believe that he had come so close to finding Cheeky Joe only to abandon his quest when he became aware of the deceptive Union movement. Why had he thought that his efforts to warn the high command would matter in the end? Surely, he should have expected Hardee, Cleburne and the rest to discover what Grant had been doing on their own. From what Cleburne had said, they had been entirely unaware that anything was afoot until McFadden had told them. Cleburne had even told him that he deserved credit for saving the city. McFadden was far too modest to acknowledge anything like that.

From what McFadden understood, the two Union armies now attacking the city were the Army of the Tennessee and the Army of the Cumberland. The Army of the Ohio, near as he could tell, was nowhere nearby. That meant that Cheeky Joe was nowhere nearby. He tried to put the thought out of his mind. He had had a chance to avenge his brother, but now that chance was gone, perhaps forever. He had paid the price for doing what he felt was his duty.

Since coming back, he had seen his beloved 7th Texas destroyed in battle. Of the remnant of Granbury's men that had attached itself to him, Pearson and Montgomery were the only survivors of the old Lone Star Rifles and only six other men were from the old regiment. The other half dozen or so had been picked up from other Texas regiments. The disorganization and loss of so many men appalled him. As soon as he confirmed that the Turnbows were all right, he intended to get back to his men and then try to link up with whatever other Texas troops still remained in the ranks of the Confederate forces holding Atlanta.

He thought about Cleburne for a moment and wondered why his division commander had taken such an obvious interest in him. Being the man who had captured George Thomas at Peachtree Creek had obviously put his name in Cleburne's mind and bringing the news of Grant's movement toward Atlanta had kept it there. But that didn't explain why he had asked McFadden to ride out with him as his color bearer to meet with General McPherson. Perhaps he simply happened to be the most convenient nearby officer.

He turned right down Hunter Street, now heading southeast. In the distance, he could see the shattered ruins of the Car Shed. The last time he had seen it, the rail depot had been bustling with people and activity as innumerable crates of ammunition and supplies had been offloaded from the trains and countless refugees had been trying to gain space on the next train out of the city. A series of direct hits had reduced the building to a heap of rubble.

The streets were largely deserted. In front of a few houses, white women and an occasional black man sat with stern expressions on the porches, nestling shotguns on their laps, a clear warning for looters to stay away. A small number of people went to and fro with baskets of food, having obviously gone forth to find something to eat. McFadden nodded politely to each passerby, but no one seemed interested in talking. The fear hung so heavily over the city that he could almost smell it.

The sound of breaking glass caught his attention. He glanced at a nearby house and saw three men, two of them in Confederate uniforms, breaking the window panes on a window and forcing their way inside. Clearly, they were looting. He glanced around, seeing no provost marshals or, for that matter, anyone else of any authority. Presumably the men were deserters trying to help themselves to plunder in the midst of the surrounding chaos. He considered trying to stop them, seeing as he was an officer, but thought better of it. If men were willing to desert the colors in order to pillage, they would just as likely be willing to kill an irritating officer. McFadden rode on.

He thought back to the extraordinary conversation between Cleburne and McPherson. He had never heard anything like it. Until quite recently, McFadden had given relatively little consideration to the cause for which he fought. As far as he had been concerned, he had fought simply to fight. He had sought to burn away the rage and hate that consumed him. Meeting Annie had quenched that rage, though.

This had left him with the disquieting question. What exactly was he fighting for now?

It was obvious to McFadden that Cleburne knew what he was fighting for. The general was fighting to free the South, his adopted nation, from what he perceived as Northern tyranny. His commander obviously had no interest in the slavery question. Neither did McFadden or, for that matter, most of the men in the Confederate army. For all the talk about Northern tyranny, however, what had the North done before the war that might be considered tyrannical? At most, the Republican Party had been making noise about preventing slavery from expanding into the territories. This did not strike McFadden as especially tyrannical. It certainly would have had no impact on him. How, then, could the secession of the Southern states have been justified in the first place?

McFadden was not an admirer of Abraham Lincoln, but the man was obviously no despot. After all, he knew all about despots. His parents had taught him about the kings of England who had ravaged Scotland until defeated at the Battle of Bannockburn. In reading the Kosciuszko biography, he had learned about the czars of Russia who had done the same to Poland. President Lincoln could not be compared with such tyrants, no matter what the politicians of the South said.

As with Cleburne, McFadden's decision to fight for the Confederacy had nothing to do with slavery. But what did motives matter? He was fighting for slavery, whether he wanted to or not. McFadden had told Cleburne as much: had there been no slavery, there would have been no war. If the Confederacy triumphed, slavery would triumph. If the Confederacy were defeated, slavery would be defeated. McFadden and Cleburne both might try to deny it, and so might tens of thousands of other Confederate soldiers, but it was the truth.

In a certain sense, McFadden and Cleburne were the same. They were both outsiders. McFadden was isolated from his fellows by the wall his heart had erected around him in the wake of the tragedies of 1862. Cleburne, for his part, was isolated by his foreign birth and his lack of understanding of Southern society.

Even the Yankee general, James McPherson, had sensed this when he had called out Cleburne as an Irishman rather than a Southerner. McFadden remembered the conviction he had seen in the face of General McPherson. He realized that he actually admired the Yankee, which was a surprising thought. McPherson had clearly believed the preservation of the Union and the destruction of slavery were sacred causes for which he would have happily sacrificed his life. For a long time, McFadden had seen the Yankees as little better than barbarians come to loot and burn. He had at times grudgingly admitted a respect for their courage in battle, but that had been the limit of any positive feelings he had held toward them.

In McPherson, though, McFadden had seen Cleburne's doppelganger. Cleburne's idealistic motives revolved around his conviction that the South must be free to determine its own destiny. McPherson's motives, no less idealistic, revolved around his belief that the Union must be preserved and slavery must be extinguished. Neither man was entirely right or entirely wrong. Whatever idealism the South possessed was tarnished by its connection to slavery, while that of the North was tarnished, at least in McFadden's mind, by burned towns, destroyed farms, and shattered lives all across the South.

The biography of Thaddeus Kosciuszko was still in his knapsack. He envied the Polish patriot. Fighting the British in America and the Russians in Poland, Kosciuszko had not been burdened by doubts and questions such as those now tormenting McFadden. He had simply fought as a pure son of liberty, both for his own native Poland and for the whole of mankind. McFadden found himself wondering which side Kosciuszko would have chosen in the conflict between North and South. From his reading, McFadden knew that the man had been a ferocious opponent of slavery.

What looked like a regiment emerged from a side street and moved at the double quick past him, heading to the west. Presumably they had been ordered to move from one position on the defenses to another, more threatened sector. He exchanged a quick salute with the captain leading the small column, but said nothing. The looks on the faces of the men, officers and enlisted men alike, were all pensive. Trapped and besieged, with a massive enemy attack likely to come at any moment, the Southern troops holding Atlanta were all under a severe psychological strain.

McFadden shook his head, trying to clear his thoughts. Perhaps it was not wise to question what he fought for. If he did, it might drive him insane. He had a duty to his commander, Patrick Cleburne, as well as the men under his command. He had a duty to protect Annie Turnbow and her family. Moreover, he needed to survive the war so that he might have some future with Annie when the guns finally fell silent.

The thought brought a smile to his face, as did the fact that he was getting closer to the Turnbow house. Despite the animal's fatigue, he kicked his horse into a trot, now more anxious than ever to see Annie. As he turned from Hunter Street onto Mitchell Street, which would bring the house into view, his heart turned to ice.

The Turnbow house was nothing but a charred and burned-out shell.

*   *   *   *   *

September 26, Afternoon

"It's confirmed, sir," the staff officer was saying. "There is at least a brigade of Union cavalry on the railroad just west of Decatur. They've been tearing up the track for the last few hours. The telegraph line has been cut, too."

Cleburne nodded, having expected the news. With East Point lost to the Yankees and enemy cavalry on the Augusta railroad, Atlanta was now completely cut off from the rest of the Confederacy. Not only could the railroads no longer bring any men or material in or out of the city, but the severance of the telegraph lines meant that he could no longer send or receive messages. Cleburne was entirely on his own, as cut off from the outside world as a ship in the middle of the Atlantic Ocean.

Cleburne had set up his headquarters in City Hall. It made pretty good sense. The building was centrally located, allowing him to remain abreast of developments on the southern, western, and northern defenses of the city with equal ease. It also was spacious enough to accommodate the entire staff.

He leaned over a large map that showed the city and its defenses. Throughout the morning and early afternoon, the staff officers had done a fairly good job of reorganizing the troops. His old division, now under the command of General Granbury, held most of the southern portion of the defenses. What was left of Bate's division, now under the command of Finley, held the southwestern portion and much of the western section. Walker's division held the remainder of the western defenses, the northwestern portion, and some of the northern sector. Maney's division, composed entirely of Tennessee troops, held the remainder of the northern sector, although one brigade had been detached to serve as the emergency reserve.

The eastern sector was held by the five thousand men of the Georgia Militia. Aside from the enemy cavalry reported near Decatur, there did not seem to be much Union activity on the eastern side of the city, leading Cleburne to believe that the area would not be subject to any serious attack. Still, he needed to maintain some sort of defense there and the militia seemed ideal for the task.

According to reports sent back by the two divisions that had fought at East Point, the two days of fighting had cost them about four thousand casualties. Though they had inflicted more than twice that number of casualties on the enemy, these losses meant that he had only around fourteen thousand men left to defend the city of Atlanta. It was estimated that Grant had between fifty and sixty thousand under his command.

Despite the loss of so much artillery at East Point, Cleburne still had plenty of cannon in the Atlanta defenses, as each redoubt along the lines held at least two guns. Another comforting fact was that he had plenty of ammunition for both the infantry and the artillery. The Atlanta depots bulged with crates of munitions and Johnston had not had enough rolling stock to take it all with him when he had departed for Alabama. Whatever problems his men were soon to face, running out of bullets and shells would not be among them.

He lifted his head as the sound of artillery fire suddenly increased in intensity. The Yankees had continued throwing shells into the center of town, which was making it more difficult to move troops from one location to another. The fire now sounded like it was being concentrated on the southern defenses, near where his own division was posted. He felt a tingling of fear. If the Union forces launched a determined attack on that sector, his men might be too worn down to beat it back.

The men of his own division and that of the late General Bate were exhausted and many of them had suffered minor wounds. The men under the command of Walker and Maney had not experienced serious fighting as yet, having been called on only to repel probing attacks from the Army of the Cumberland. He quickly wrote out a dispatch to General Walker.

General Walker,
You are directed to pull a brigade out of the line and send it at once to General Granbury. His section is weak. Extend the lines of your remaining units to cover any gap thus created. The choice of which brigade to send is left to you.
General Cleburne

Cleburne had two copies of the order made, then sent off two couriers to take them to Walker, instructing them to take different routes. With so much confusion in the streets of the city, and with Union artillery shells continuing to fall randomly throughout Atlanta, he did not want to risk one courier becoming lost or incapacitated.

His thoughts turned to Hardee, lying unconscious in a hospital that had been set up in the Second Baptist Church, just across the street. His leg had been amputated sometime during the morning and he had survived the operation. Now the waiting game began. Cleburne had asked the hospital staff to periodically update him about Hardee's condition, but he could not recall hearing anything for the past two hours or so. In any event, he had far too much on his mind to be distracted, even if it was regarding the life of his closest friend.

Over an hour passed. Cleburne and the corps staff officers frantically tried to do the work that would have taxed three times as many men. He was busy sending a message to Mayor Calhoun, responding in the affirmative to a request that he issue some of the army rations to hungry civilians, when one of the couriers he had sent to Walker returned, a dismayed look on his face. Without a word, the man handed him Walker's reply. It chilled Cleburne's heart to read it.

General Cleburne,
I have received your message and respectfully decline to dispatch the brigade. Please be advised that I shall not respond to any further such messages, as I do not consider myself under your command.
General Walker

*   *   *   *   *

September 26, Evening

McFadden galloped up to the sound of the firing and rapidly dismounted, a shell exploding scarcely fifteen yards to the left of him as he did so. Not wanting to bother with the horse any longer, he smacked its flank, causing it to canter away on its own.

Granbury ran up when he saw him.

"About time," the general said with a grin. "Enjoy the time with your lady friend?" He instantly became more serious, however, when he saw the vengeful expression on McFadden's face. Almost timidly, Granbury pointed to a part of the line. "There are the survivors of the 7th Texas. Twenty five men, all told. We haven't seen either Major Collett or Lieutenant Russell since yesterday, so they're all yours."

McFadden gave a single, sharp nod and jogged over to his men. A quick glance revealed that Pearson and Montgomery were there, but he didn't see any other men from the Lone Star Rifles. Some of them waved or nodded when they saw him, but he did not acknowledge their greetings.

The men were firing from under the head-log at a group of attacking Union troops. The Yankees were a bit more than a hundred yards away and in great numbers, but their attack was not being pressed. The bluecoats had halted their approach and were now simply blazing away at the Confederate defenses with musketry. It happened many times in combat; men could not gird themselves to push forward yet could not bring themselves to retreat. The Southerners were delighted, pouring fire into the ranks of their enemies with only a minimal chance of being hit in return.

McFadden spent less than a minute looking around at the remnants of the once proud 7th Texas. He didn't give any orders or say anything. Then, he pulled his pistol out of its holster and without any preamble simply clambered up over the head-log and stood tall on top of the parapet. He quickly fired the gun six times in the general direction of the enemy formation, but they were so far away as to be out of effective range. Bullets zipped past his head and smacked into the parapet near his feet. Once he fired off his sixth round, he started to reload.

"Get down, Lieutenant!" Montgomery yelled. "What the hell do you think you're doing?"

McFadden ignored him. The rest of his men, confused looks on their faces, called for him to find cover, but he paid no attention to them, either. Completing his reload, he again fired off his shots. Even at the great distance, he saw a Union soldier fall from what he was reasonably sure was his shot. Dark elation filled him. As he fired his weapon, he let forth a scream of primal rage. All that was animal in him had been unleashed.

He could see Union officers gesturing at him, yelling for their men to shoot him down. A demonic smile crossed his face, for that was exactly what he wanted them to do. The incinerated corpses he had found inside the Turnbow house had seen to that.

He was out of bullets, so he threw his pistol back behind the parapet and drew his sword. He was just about to charge off the parapet toward the Yankees when he felt an arm wrap itself around his upper chest. It yanked him roughly backwards before he could react. He was pulled down onto the parapet, landing with a crash that sent up a cloud of dirty dust. He then felt himself being dragged over the head-log and back down into the space behind the parapet.

"Let me go!" McFadden yelled. "Let me go!"

He pulled himself up and turned to look at whoever had pulled him down. He came face-to-face with Private Pearson, who looked back at him with an almost childlike expression.

"How dare you!"

"You would have been killed, sir!"

"Mind your business, damn you! Get back to the firing line!"

Pearson said nothing and did not move for an endless second. Then, he picked his rifle up off the ground and took his position on the fire-step, quickly entering into the repetitive process of loading and shooting.

McFadden stood still for a moment, breathing deeply. His men remained focused on firing , but McFadden caught quick side glances from Private Montgomery and a few others, who eyed him warily. He picked his pistol up from the ground and put it back in his holster. Then, he began slowly walking up and down the lines.

"Keep up your fire, men!" he called. "Pour it into them!" He attempted to make his voice sound as authoritative and enthusiastic as possible.

It took a conscious effort to control his breathing. He tried to understand what he had just done. He had to keep his mind clear, to concentrate on his duties as an officer. Cleburne and Granbury had told him that he was in charge of the 7th Texas, because he was the only officer who was not either dead or a prisoner. He had to remain focused, otherwise his leaderless men would lose their discipline and probably their lives.

But he couldn't keep his mind clear. He felt like he was on fire, like something was trying to eat him alive from the inside. The Yankees had killed his beloved, the woman he would have made into his wife. He had seen the charred and blackened remains of what had been her body inside the house, which itself had been shredded and burned by exploding shells. His mind could not stop imagining the terror and confusion that her last moments on Earth must have been like.

The agony that coursed through him was too terrible to be contained within a human soul.

"Sir!" Montgomery called. "They're pulling back!"

He shook his head vigorously, then turned toward the fire-step. Peering under the head-log, he saw that Montgomery was correct. The Union officers, having given up on getting their men to mount a charge and unwilling to endure further casualties, had ordered a withdrawal. The Yankee bugles were blaring the notes for a retreat.

He glanced up and down the line. One of his men was holding a bloody cloth up to the side of his head, a look of anger and irritation on his face. Aside from him, though, there did not seem to be any casualties. He ordered the man to the rear and hoped for the best. McFadden knew from experience that head wounds often looked much worse than they actually were, so he was optimistic that the man would be back in the ranks in a few hours.

Some of his men were still shooting at the Yankees as they pulled back. He considered ordering them to cease fire, as it was unlikely they would hit anything at such a range and it was a shame to waste ammunition. However, Cleburne had said that there was plenty of ammunition in the Atlanta depots. The simple act of having his men continue to fire on the bluecoats was pleasing to him. Eventually, as the Yankees continued to pull back and the range became impossible, his men stopped firing on their own account.

Silence descended on the portion of the line held by the Texans. Off to the north, they could hear the steady booming of artillery and the rattle of musketry, indicating that the Yankees were attacking other portions of the Atlanta defenses as well. McFadden speculated for a moment that perhaps the assault the Texans had just repulsed had merely been a diversion. It certainly would explain why it had not been pressed home with much enthusiasm.

The quietude did not last long. As the Union infantry pulled back out of range, two enemy artillery batteries opened fire and shells began to burst in front of the trenches. McFadden ordered his men to the ground to shield them from the storm of shrapnel. Private Montgomery crawled over to him.

"Lieutenant, are you all right?"

"Yes, private. I'm fine."

"Sir, the way you jumped out onto the parapet like that. I just-"

"I'm fine, Montgomery. Don't worry about it. I appreciate your concern, but I'm fine."

Montgomery nodded, then crawled into a better position.

McFadden looked over his shoulder at Private Pearson. The man had been an irritant to him for a long time, but had just risked his own life to save McFadden's. He nodded stiffly and Pearson nodded back.

*　　　　*　　　　*　　　　*　　　　*

September 26, Night

The train lurched to a halt as it neared the overhang of the rail depot in Palmetto. The second it came to a complete stop, Johnston stepped out from the car and onto the platform. Almost as quickly, officers and depot workers were sliding open the boxcars, out of which began pouring hundreds of Confederate soldiers. Others had made the trip from Newnan to Palmetto on the train's roof; these men patiently waited for the ground below them to clear before they began climbing down. Slaves stood about with torches to illuminate the area.

"General Johnston!" a waiting staff officer cried, waving. "This way, please!"

Johnston nodded and followed, with Mackall close behind. The man guided the two of them to a large tent that had been set up a few hundred yards away from the train depot. Inside, a dozen staff officers were hard at work. The headquarters post of the Army of Tennessee had been set up shortly after the previous train had arrived, with an efficiency that impressed and pleased Johnston.

"Where are Grant's forces?"

"Here, sir," an officer said, indicating the map. "All his forces are concentrated around Atlanta. The southern, western, and northern portions of the line are invested and we believe that enemy cavalry have seized the railroad to Augusta as well."

"Has there been any effort to communicate with General Cleburne?"

"No, sir. The telegraph lines have all been cut. There does not seem to be any way to get in or out. The city is completely surrounded."

Johnston shook his head. "God help them."

"The sounds of battle are never-ending, sir. The city is under constant attack and bombardment."

Johnston walked quickly outside the tent, staring intently to the north and listening carefully. Although Atlanta was more than twenty miles away, he could distinctly hear what sounded like a low roar rolling over the Georgia countryside. The booming of artillery was clearly audible, carried by the wind. The sound was almost pleasant, like a distant thunderstorm on a summer day, but he knew that the sound signified death.

Mackall had walked out beside him. "We've got to help them," he said simply.

"Indeed, we do, William. And not just for their sakes, but for the sake of our cause. If the Yankees take Atlanta, the game may well be up."

They went back inside and bent over a paper-strewn table. Johnston looked over at the chief-of-staff.

"Well?"

"Manigault's brigade arrived before we did, as you know. Its regiments are deployed around Palmetto to ensure security. Benton's brigade is unloading now. The telegraph boys have managed to reconnect the line between here and Newnan."

"They did? That's impressive."

Mackall shrugged. "It's a miracle that any of our telegraphs are working these days. I've long since started to chalk it up to divine favor."

Johnston smiled and waved for Mackall to continue.

"The rest of General Brown's division is going to arrive during the night, assuming everything goes well. After him will be Stevenson's division, and Clayton's division is third."

"How long?"

"I think we can have Cheatham's entire corps here by nightfall tomorrow. Then we can start bringing Stewart's men up."

"The trains will be busy," Johnston noted.

"They will be, sir. They'll be steaming up and down the railroad between here and West Point for the next two days. It will be difficult, but we've done it before."

Johnston nodded. Despite the ramshackle nature of Confederate railroads, the South had become adept at moving large numbers of troops by train since the beginning of the war.

"So, in a best-case scenario, Cheatham's corps will be fully up in Palmetto by tomorrow night, and Stewart's corps perhaps two days after that?"

Mackall nodded. "That sounds about right."

"We have only two brigades here at present. If Grant catches wind of what we're up to, he could descend on Palmetto with an entire corps and have us for breakfast."

"Well, there is no indication that he knows we have arrived here as yet. And we will have all night to bring in the rest of Brown's division. Palmetto will probably be defensible when the sun rises."

Johnston nodded. "In any event, every division we can get Grant to deploy against us is one less division attacking Atlanta."

Mackall nodded. "And suppose Grant either does not notice us here at Palmetto or elects to ignore us and continue the assault on Atlanta? What then?"

"Why, we shall march to the rescue of our comrades, of course."

*   *   *   *   *

Cleburne dismounted his horse and handed the reins to one of Walker's staff officers without a word. Lieutenant Learned Magnum, his personal aide-be-camp now that Lieutenant Hanley was dead, reined in behind him and remained on his horse, watching as he stormed toward Walker's command tent. Cleburne was not normally a man given to anger, but the furious look on his face was clear for all to see.

"General Walker!" Cleburne yelled as he ducked under the flap of the tent.

Walker, with three of his own staff officers around him, looked up from his table. "Ah, General Cleburne! How kind of you to visit my headquarters. May I offer you some whiskey?"

Cleburne fumed. Walker knew perfectly well that he was a teetotaler. He held up a piece of paper.

"Would you be so kind as to explain this?"

"I would, if you would tell me what it is."

Cleburne wanted to shout, but managed to keep his tongue. "On three occasions, I have ordered you to send a brigade to reinforce our troops on the south side of the city. The only reply I have received from you is this single note, refusing the order and asserting that you are not under my command."

"I'm sorry, Cleburne, but that Irish accent of yours makes it difficult for me to understand you. Perhaps you could speak more slowly?"

"You heard me very well," Cleburne responded firmly.

"Oh," Walker said, indifference evident in his voice. "Well, my own troops have been rather hard-pressed today and I felt I needed all my men here. Simple enough explanation, I should think."

"General Walker, you will obey my orders or I shall have you arrested for insubordination. I would have thought that had been made clear by my last message."

"Well, let me make something clear to you, Cleburne. If you think I'm going to follow the orders of abolitionist scum like you, you are even more stupid than I thought. I would no sooner follow your orders than I would kiss the ass of Abe Lincoln."

Cleburne tensed. Things were rapidly getting out of hand. He realized his mistake in coming to Walker's headquarters. First, it gave Walker the psychological upper hand, as he had forced Cleburne to come to him rather than have Walker come to Cleburne. But if Cleburne had summoned Walker to his headquarters, he obviously would have refused to come. Cleburne's second mistake was in coming with only a single staff officer. His threats to have Walker arrested were meaningless unless he had the means to carry them out.

He glanced around the headquarters tent. Most of the men there looked at him with the same sort of contemptible sneer as Walker. If it came to any kind of showdown, he realized instantly than these men would side with Walker over him. He wondered if the same might be true of Walker's brigade and regimental officers.

His pulse quickened. The Union assault was over for the night, but on many points of the defenses they had come close to breaking through.

"I command all Confederate forces in Atlanta," Cleburne said sternly. "You will obey my orders."

"I'd sooner rot in hell."

"What is the date of your commission as major general, Walker?" Cleburne asked sternly.

"I'm sure you'll remind me."

"I will. Your commission dates from May 23, 1863. My commission dates from December 13, 1862. I am senior. I am in command."

Cleburne knew Walker would not care a whit about commission dates. He was saying this in the hopes that they would have a beneficial effect on the men watching in the tent and, no doubt, listening from the outside. If the men of Walker's command realized that they were participating in what amounted to a mutiny, they might reconsider their support. Everyone knew the penalty for mutiny. What worried Cleburne was that, at the moment, he lacked the ability to enforce the implied threat.

Walker, to Cleburne's fury, simply shrugged as though their respective ranks were a matter of no concern to him. "Considering what the newspapers have been saying about you of late, I doubt that the good men in Richmond will pay much attention to the date on your commission paper. More likely that you'll be cashiered out of the army altogether. We are fighting a war to ensure the supremacy of the white man over the black man. The South does not take kindly to those who believe the respective positions of the races should be reversed."

"The laws of the Confederacy are clear, General Walker. If you do not follow my orders, you shall be guilty of mutiny. And if any of your men choose to follow your orders that are in conflict with mine, they shall be guilty of mutiny as well."

For the first time, Cleburne thought he sensed hesitation, a dark uneasiness, in the faces of the staff officers. There was an uncertain rustling.

Cleburne continued. "We are in the midst of the most important battle of the war. Your insubordination is threatening our ability to fight effectively. Is your pride and arrogance such that you would willingly endanger not only our army, but the survival of the Confederacy itself, simply for the sake of spitting in my face?"

Walker smiled and shrugged. "Might I simply suggest that you look after your sector of the line and allow me to look after mine?"

Cleburne felt he had done all he could. He had made his position clear to Walker and had hopefully introduced some element of fear into the minds of his men. As for Walker himself, no words would ever be able to persuade a man with such a poisoned mind.

He turned and ducked out of Walker's tent. Lieutenant Magnum was still waiting on his horse. Cleburne mounted and rode away without another word. He would let Walker think he had won for the time being. Foolishly, he had hoped the man would see reason, but that clearly had been wishful thinking. Cleburne's mind was already turning over a new idea.

Chapter Eighteen

September 27, Morning

The fierce red glow along the eastern horizon clearly announced that sunrise was imminent. Grant, McPherson, and Howard, along with a smattering of corps commanders and staff officers, huddled together under the immense command tent that had been set up not far from the banks of the Chattahoochee River just to the northwest of Atlanta.

The Union army had moved into the area just hours after the rebel troops had withdrawn into the Atlanta defenses. Since then, they had been very busy. Three pontoon bridges had been erected and more were already being constructed. An endless stream of supply wagons were now crossing over, bringing vast quantities of food, ammunition and other supplies from the railroad depots at Smyrna and Marietta. As the Union generals debated the course of the coming day's battle, they were drinking coffee that had been sitting in a Chicago warehouse only five days earlier.

The engineers were already in the process of laying track over the stone pillars which were all that remained of the old Western and Atlantic Railroad bridge. They had told Grant that the first trains should be able to use the bridge within the next few days.

Securing both river banks across from Vining's Station and throwing the bridges across the Chattahoochee meant that the fords and crossing points downriver near Campbellton were no longer necessary. These accordingly had been abandoned and the men who had been assigned to guard them had been brought northeast to join the main force.

Sitting amidst the generals and staff officers, Grant calmly smoked a cigar and whittled away on a large stick with a knife. One who did not know him well might have assumed that he was paying no attention to the ongoing discussion, though in fact he was listening intently.

"The rebels are proving unexpectedly resilient," Howard was saying. "None of my attacks have been able to penetrate their defenses and we have suffered heavy casualties."

"My troops have broken the rebel lines in a few places, but in each case we were driven back by enemy counter attacks," McPherson replied.

"They are fighting like devils, these blasted Southerners," Howard said.

Grant chucked, as the adjective Howard had used to describe the rebels was the nearest he had ever heard the man come to swearing. Still, what the commander of the Army of the Cumberland was saying reflected a pattern Grant had noticed. The rebel troops on the north side of Atlanta seemed to be fighting more effectively than those on the western and southern sectors. A plan had been forming in Grant's mind since late the previous evening and he now took the opportunity to explain it.

Tossing away his half-shredded stick, Grant rose from his chair and stood over the map. Using his fingers, he described what he wanted.

"Howard, you'll leave one corps on the north side of Atlanta to keep the rebel troops there pinned down and to protect our depots from any sudden enemy sortie. You'll move your two other corps to the west side of the city and launch an attack there. McPherson, I want you to move all the troops you currently have on the western sector to the south. When that is done, we shall have two corps of the Army of the Cumberland attacking the west side and all three corps of the Army of the Tennessee attacking the south side."

McPherson nodded. "A sound plan. If you ask me, I think the rebels are weaker on the south and west than they are on the north."

Grant grunted his agreement. He liked McPherson very much, but the man did have a habit of stating the obvious.

"If we can concentrate our attacks on just the west and south side of the city, we will be throwing five entire corps at just two or three divisions," Grant said. "Even with stout entrenchments, we will surely overwhelm them. I expect the attack to be launched promptly at noon. Any questions?"

The men shook their heads. There was a brief silence, then Grant asked a question that was always on everyone's mind. "How many men have we lost so far?"

Howard answered quickly. "In three days of fighting, I have lost about eight thousand men."

"And the Army of the Tennessee?" Grant asked.

"A bit more," McPherson answered. "Ten thousand, give or take."

These answers were given so casually, Grant thought, as though they did not represent the totality of existence for thousands of human beings and signified infinite grief for so many Northern families.

"Nearly twenty thousand men," he said simply. It was a steep bill for the butcher, but not quite on par with the carnage of Chickamauga or Gettysburg. Grant reminded himself, however, that the battle was far from over.

A courier arrived and handed Grant a quick message. It was from one of the cavalry divisions that was screening the right flank of his forces, engaging in constant patrolling to the south.

"Well, this is interesting," Grant said. "Confederate infantry has been reported in the vicinity of Palmetto."

"Could be Johnston coming up," McPherson said, a slight trace of foreboding in his voice.

"The cavalry cut the Atlantic and West Point Railroad in many places," Grant replied. "Surely the rebels could not have affected repairs so quickly."

Howard chimed in. "Though they possess but a fraction of our resources, they are capable of great efforts of improvisation."

Grant dropped the note on the table. "It doesn't matter. Even with a fully functioning railroad, it would take Johnston several days at least to bring his two corps up to Palmetto. We will be in Atlanta by then."

"Perhaps," McPherson said. "But it wouldn't do to be incautious."

"No, it wouldn't. I shall dispatch a stronger cavalry force to verify the information. If any of Johnston's troops have arrived, we can always detach a sufficient number of divisions to hold them in check. I want you to concentrate on the attack scheduled for noon. If we succeed, we can be in Atlanta as early as tomorrow."

*   *   *   *   *

September 27, Noon

Buglers blared their instruments and drummers pounded their drums as the men of Brown's division stood to attention. After herculean efforts by the staff officers and railroad workers, a complete Confederate division was now deployed in Palmetto.

Johnston, standing stiffly with his hands behind his back, walked along the line with a critical air about his face, staring at the men intently. To his left walked the division's commander, the inaptly-named John Brown, while the faithful Mackall walked beside him on his right. The men being reviewed were clearly tired, as many of them had clambered out of the railroad boxcars only an hour or so earlier. Their officers had done a good job getting them organized and cleaned up.

"Your division looks excellent, General Brown."

"Thank you, sir."

The looks on the faces of the men were eager and anticipatory. Almost all the men in Brown's division were from Alabama and Mississippi, although there was a scattering of South Carolina regiments among them as well. Rumors were doubtless swirling through the ranks that Atlanta had come under a massive attack and Johnston hoped that the urge to go to the rescue of their comrades would inspire the men.

The scream of a train whistle reminded Johnston that more troops were arriving all the time. The men of Stevenson's division and Clayton's division were disembarking from the boxcars and, according to the telegraph, Stewart's corps was busy entraining in West Point for their trip north.

Johnston had elected to leave one division of Stewart's corps behind in Lafayette to make sure the route into Alabama was secure from any major enemy force. Having been fooled once by Grant's maneuvering, Johnston had no wish to be fooled again. This decision would reduce the strength of the force he would be able to assemble at Palmetto, but it gave him the comfort of knowing his rear was somewhat secure. It also freed up rolling stock and made the transfer of the other divisions an easier task.

"We should hurry, sir," Mackall said in a quiet voice. "There is much work to be done."

"I know, William. Believe me, I know."

Mackall's words reminded Johnston of just how tired he was. It had been three days since he had received the shocking telegrams from Atlanta and Richmond which had torn the wool from his eyes and revealed Grant's deception. His mind had been in a fever of activity and calculation since then.

There were already about eleven thousand Confederate troops in Palmetto. He hoped that twenty thousand would be on hand by the end of the day and perhaps thirty thousand by the afternoon of the next day. When he had the force completely assembled, he could move north to confront Grant. At the very least, this would force the Union general to stop his attacks on Atlanta, presuming that it had not fallen by then.

Union cavalry had been spotted hovering a respectful distance away to the north, telling Johnston that Grant was now aware of their presence in Palmetto. He wondered what Grant's reaction would be. Conceivably he might break off the attack on Atlanta, leave a few divisions to cover the city, and march on Palmetto with an overwhelming force. However, Johnston assumed that Grant would take the opposite tack and try to capture Atlanta before the army assembling at Palmetto was strong enough to intervene.

Late the previous night, Johnston had called for volunteers to attempt the dangerous task of taking dispatches to General Cleburne in Atlanta. Three men had volunteered and set off just after two in the morning, taking different routes. Unsurprisingly, nothing had been heard from them since. Johnston frankly had not given the men much of a chance of success, thinking it much more likely that they would be either killed or taken prisoner rather than reach the Confederate lines. The Union forces had the city completely encircled and were heavily patrolling the surrounding countryside.

Still, it had been a risk worth taking. It was important for Cleburne to be notified that a relief force was being assembled. This news would not only raise the morale of the men but would certainly squelch any thought of capitulation from the minds of the officers. Johnston was confident that Cleburne, his fighting Irishman, would never allow any thought of surrender to enter his mind, but the same was not necessarily true for the other officers.

He wondered how Cleburne was doing. Indeed, the question deeply worried him. Cleburne was an outstanding division commander and would probably have made an effective corps commander as well. Yet he had never been in the position of an independent commander, where ultimate responsibility rested on his shoulders. He had always had Hardee nearby to provide a guiding hand to his operations.

There was a greater concern. The public revelation of Cleburne's proposal had stirred up no end of trouble. How would General Walker, with his militant views on slavery and white supremacy and his hatred of Cleburne, respond to taking orders from Cleburne?

Johnston shook his head. He was consumed with worry regarding things about which he could do nothing. He had to focus on getting the army assembled in Palmetto and going to Atlanta's relief. Whatever was happening within the defenses of the city were sadly beyond his control.

*   *   *   *   *

Cheeky Joe was pouring kerosene onto Annie, who was tied to a stake on top of a pile of dry wood and kindling like those used to burn witches back in the old days. He was laughing maniacally, while Annie herself was screaming for help. Robert and Teresa Turnbow were there, too, berating McFadden for not protecting Annie. McFadden would have helped, but found that he could not move his feet, which had somehow become solidified into the stone floor on which he stood. In fact, he realized with a shock that he himself had turned into stone, except for his head. As he continued laughing, Cheeky Joe struck a match.

McFadden awoke with a start, his heart pounding. He instinctively glanced around, searching for danger, but all he saw were other Confederate soldiers in the artillery redoubt. The sun was bearing down, glinting off the polished metal of the guns.

Realizing it had been another nightmare, he took a deep breath and tried to calm down. He had had nightmares on most nights after he had come back from New Mexico, but they had faded and eventually gone away altogether after he had met Annie. He wondered if, now that she was gone, they would return with renewed energy.

He looked around quickly to see if anything had changed while he had been asleep. Granbury had given him command of one hundred soldiers drawn from the various regiments of the old brigade and ordered him to provide infantry support to Battery Bate, a redoubt on the southern sector of the Atlanta defenses which had just been renamed after the fallen division commander.

It was called a battery, but in truth it was more like a small fort. Battery Bate held eight 12-pounder iron Napoleon cannon and four double-banded 7-inch Brooke rifled cannon. The latter guns had been sent up to Atlanta from Mobile during Sherman's initial advance on the city. The Napoleons were meant to protect the redoubt from an infantry attack, while the Brooke guns were intended to dominate the ground for a considerable distance all over the southern sector of the Atlanta defenses.

"A nice nap, Lieutenant?"

McFadden looked over at the man asking the question. It was Major James Horwood, commander of the battery, whom he had just met that morning.

"Good enough, I suppose." Nightmare or not, he had badly needed the sleep.

"Glad you're awake," Horwood said. "I wanted to suggest that I give some of your men rudimentary instruction on how to load and fire the cannon. That way, they can help man the guns if any of my gun crews become disabled."

"A good idea," he said with a nod. He ordered his men, one company at a time, to stack arms and take Horwood's instruction.

While the artillery officer was giving his lesson, McFadden walked up to the port for one of the Napoleons and looked out over the field. Perhaps a mile away, large formations of Union infantry waited patiently, their battle flags fluttering in the light breeze.

"They've been getting in position all day, sir," Private Pearson said. He was sitting on the redoubt's enormous parapet, cradling his Enfield on his lap, watching the Yankees in the distance. "We saw another division arrive while you were sleeping."

"They'll attack soon," McFadden said firmly.

"Think so?"

"They haven't come all this way just to give up and go home because a few of their attacks were repulsed, have they?"

"We've killed lots of them over the past couple of days," Pearson said, with no more emotion than one would have used to describe duck hunting.

"There are always more."

"Yeah, but now we're behind the walls of this fort. Nice, I think. Better than anything we ever built in the field. Walls are good and thick enough to stop Yankee shells."

"I know."

"Looks like a big bucket, don't you think?"

McFadden was distracted. "What's that?"

"This fort. It looks like a big bucket. That's what the men are calling it. Not Battery Bate, but just the Bucket."

"Oh," McFadden said. He hadn't thought about it, but in truth the long convex curve of the fort's rampart combined with its height did give one the impression of a giant bucket.

"Pearson?" McFadden said.

"Yes, Lieutenant?"

"I have not yet thanked you for saving my life yesterday."

Pearson chuckled. "No, I suppose you haven't."

"Well, thank you."

"You're welcome. But I would rather you apologize for punching me that day on the riverbank. My head hurt for the rest of the day."

"That I shall not do." He chuckled, but the memory pained him, for it had been that day when he had first met Annie.

There was a sudden boom of a cannon from the Union lines. Without a word, McFadden, Pearson and all the other Confederates on the parapet rapidly scrambled back inside. Seconds after the sound, a shell impacted on the ground a few dozen yards in front of Battery Bate and exploded, showering them all with dirt.

Over the next few minutes, it seemed that the enemy shells were landing at a rate of one every two or three seconds. Clearly, the enemy was concentrating their fire on Battery Bate in an effort to knock out its guns. McFadden and his Texans took cover as Horwood and his artillery crews bounded into action. He was impressed by the coolness the gunners displayed as they danced about their cannon, as they had spent most of the war sitting idly in the coastal fortifications around Mobile.

Within three minutes of the first shell, the four giant Brooke rifled guns thundered their response. McFadden had neglected to cover his ears, imagining that the sound would be more or less the same as that of a regular cannon. He could not have been more mistaken, for the booming sound pounded his eardrums. He clapped his hands over his ears as tightly as he could and hugged the ground.

The artillery duel between the Brooke guns and the Yankee cannon went on for some time. The eight Napoleons remained silent, their ports covered with thick bundles of dirt and straw to absorb the impact of enemy shells. The men were well-protected from the bombardment by the stout ramparts of the redoubt and McFadden felt little fear.

"Lieutenant!"

McFadden wasn't sure if he had heard his name shouted or not. The ringing in his ears caused by the four Brookes was extremely distracting. He glanced over in the direction from which he thought the call had come and saw Major Horwood gesturing excitedly at him.

He pulled himself from the ground and jogged over. Horwood pointed over the ground.

"The Yankees are advancing!" he shouted.

It was true. Several hundred yards away a thin line of skirmishers was advancing at a jog. Behind them, moving in tight column formations, were at least two Union divisions.

"How long until we can fire the Napoleons?" McFadden asked.

Horwood shook his head. "I wouldn't want to waste them on the skirmishers. Better to fire into the packed formations. We'll kill more Yankees that way. And I don't want them to know how much firepower we have until it's too late for them to do anything about it. If we fire off our guns too early, they'll just wait and pound us with their artillery longer before they launch an infantry attack."

McFadden nodded. "Makes sense." Horwood seemed to have a decent grasp of tactics.

"Just make sure you and your boys keep those skirmishers at bay long enough for the main formation to come within range. Then we'll send these Yankees straight to hell."

McFadden nodded sharply. Looking again at the approaching Yankee skirmishers, he thought that they were advancing far too quickly. At the rate they were coming, they would come into musket range several minutes before the main assault column. Being relatively few in number, they were liable to be cut to pieces by the Texans long before their comrades could mount a charge. He shook his head. Perhaps the commander of the attacking force was inexperienced or there had been some sort of miscommunication. He wasn't going to waste time wondering, though.

He walked calmly back to where most of the infantry were huddled against the back of the parapet. "On your feet, men! Yankee skirmishers approaching!"

The Texans stood up and coolly loaded their Enfields. They mounted the fire-step and slotted their rifles through the space between the parapet and head-log. McFadden drew his sword and pistol, more for the sake of appearances than anything else. He stepped up between Pearson and Montgomery, the only other survivors from the Lone Star Rifles, and watched as the Yankee skirmishers came closer.

He noticed something strange. The weapons the skirmishers were carrying appeared to be shorter and lighter than the Enfield or Springfield rifles with which Union forces were normally armed. Conceivably the skirmishers were dismounted cavalry armed with carbines. He dismissed the thought as irrelevant and continued waiting for the enemy to come within range.

A shell impacted directly on the mount of one of the Brooke rifled guns, killing or wounding most of the gun crew and knocking the enormous weapon onto its side. The screaming of wounded men was added to the cacophony of sounds amid Battery Bate. McFadden frowned, more displeased by the loss of a valuable cannon than by the casualties they had just sustained.

"Open fire, boys!" McFadden shouted. "Fire at will!" The enemy were now within range. Against skirmishers, massed volley fire was ineffective. The rifles along the fire-step began cracking as each individual soldier picked his target with deliberation. He hoped that they would deal with skirmishers quickly, so that they could focus on the task of repelling the oncoming assault column.

Bullets began splattering into the head-log and parapet as the Union skirmishers fired back. This was only to be expected, but very quickly McFadden realized that something was wrong. The rate of fire coming from the skirmishers was so rapid as to defy belief. His men noticed it as well, having to duck down below the parapet to avoid the well aimed shots coming at them with such intensity.

McFadden felt a tug of anxiety as he realized the Union skirmishers were armed with repeating rifles. He had heard stories about these weapons but had yet to encounter a federal unit equipped with them. If the rumors were correct, each Yankee soldier had the ability to fire ten shots in the same space of time it would take for one of his men to fire twice.

He kept having to duck below the parapet to avoid the attention of the repeating rifles, but he stole enough quick glances to see axe-wielding Yankee pioneers hacking away at the abatis to clear a path through for the oncoming assault column.

McFadden waved to get Horwood's attention. "Fire the Napoleons!" he cried. "Canister fire!"

Horwood energetically shook his head. "Not yet!"

A sudden human roar filled McFadden's ears and he realized that the main assault column had broken into a charge. The enemy skirmishers were still filling the air with bullets like so many swarms of angry bees and the Texans were having difficulty returning the fire. As he watched, one of the Texans raised his head over the parapet and attempted to aim his Enfield but was unable to fire before his head exploded like a watermelon dropped from a great height. The blood and brains of the man were scattered over the soldiers on either side of him, who cried out with disgust and irritation.

McFadden couldn't understand why Horwood refused to fire the Napoleons. A quick burst of canister fire from the eight guns would sweep away the skirmishers and end the troubling fire of their repeating rifles. The infantry could then focus its fire on the oncoming assault column.

Shells began landing on the parapet once again, which surprised McFadden. With the assault column so close, the Union gunners should have ceased fire in order to avoid hitting their own men. That they were so intent on keeping the defenders pinned down as to risk the lives of their own soldiers showed how determined they were that the attack succeed. Two or three of the Yankee shells fell amidst their own men and exploded, scattering clumps of dead and wounded men in every direction. Horwood must have noticed the Union gun crews in the distance preparing to fire, which was why he had yet to unleash his Napoleons.

More of his men were falling dead or wounded as they attempted to fire back at the skirmishers. During the quick glances he was able to steal beneath the head-log, McFadden was gratified to see several of the enemy soldiers lying dead or wounded. At least some of his men were finding their targets.

As the main assault column reached the chopped up remnants of the abatis, Horwood finally ordered the crews of his Napoleons into action. The men braved the fire of the skirmishers to tear away the bundles of dirt and straw, then ran the guns out of their ports. Aiming directly into the mass of the Union troops, Horwood gave the command.

"Fire!"

The eight guns fired almost at the same instant, sending forth a wave of canister that swept through the Union column like a manifestation of death on earth. Scores of Northern men were killed instantly, literally cut to pieces as McFadden watched, while many others fell to the ground with bloody wounds, shrieking in agony. The acrid smell of gunpowder smoke filled the air.

The first rank of the assault column faltered at the loss of so many men. McFadden spotted one man on his knees, instinctively picking his left arm up from the ground as though he would be able to reattach it to the bloody stump where it had once been. But the halt was brief and the endless ranks behind the front of the column continued to push forward. Weaving their way through the paths cut in the abatis by the pioneers, the blue-coated troops came on.

Ignoring the fire of the repeating rifles of the skirmishers, the Texans poured forth as heavy a fire as they could manage, while Horwood's men loaded and fired the eight Napoleons as quickly as they could. The Brooke rifled cannon were put to use as anti-personnel weapons as well, although their mounting made it difficult to aim them at the infantry. Some of the gun crews were struck down by the bullets and flying shrapnel and McFadden was gratified to see some of his own men drop their rifles and run over to help serve the artillery.

The skirmishers kept up a steady fire with their repeating rifles as the men of the assault column plunged into the trench and dashed up to the parapet. Hearing a sharp cry of pain, McFadden turned to see that one of his men had been struck in the face by a bullet, his eye now dangling out of its socket like some sort of grotesque child's toy.

McFadden unloaded his revolver into the mass of Yankees at the edge of the trench. It occurred to McFadden that Horwood was likely to concentrate his fire on the men of the main assault column now getting into the trench. It would be better, McFadden thought, to sweep the ground just behind the trench clear of the skirmishers and their annoying repeating rifles. He turned to call this to the attention of Major Horwood, just in time to see the artillery commander be struck in quick succession by two bullets, first in the shoulder and then instantly afterwards directly in the chest. He was thrown backwards and was dead before his body reached the ground.

McFadden sensed that what had happened during the second day of fighting around East Point was about to happen once again. For all the valor of his men and the strength of their fortifications, they were to be overwhelmed by the sheer force of irresistible Yankee numbers.

There was a sudden swarm of Union soldiers through the gun ports of the disabled Brooke gun and one of the Napoleons. The crew of the Napoleon was killed very quickly by rifle shots at point blank range, but one man stayed on his feet long enough to yank the lanyard a final time, sending a last blast of canister directly into the mass of Yankee attackers. At such close range, ten Northern men were simply erased from the earth in a shower of shrapnel, blood, and torn flesh. But others came right after them, pouring through the gun port like water through a break in a dam.

"The guns!" McFadden cried. "Right wing! Fire at the guns!"

Half his men redirected their fire toward the guns. Within seconds, half a dozen Yankees were killed or wounded, but more continued to pour through. Forbiddingly, he could see some of the Yankees attempting to turn the Napoleon around, clearly intending to use it against its former owners. To be subjected to canister fire at such close range would certainly mean a very quick and bloody death for him and his men.

He was about to shout an order for withdrawal when he heard a loud battle cry from the rear area of the battery. McFadden turned to see a row of Confederate soldiers advancing into the redoubt at the double quick. A glance at the flags revealed that they belonged to Finley's Florida Brigade, come to reinforce the redoubt. They charged forward into the fight, screaming the Rebel Yell.

September 27, Afternoon

"Calm down, Lieutenant!" Cleburne said loudly. He tried to keep his voice from rising to the level of a shout. "What is happening at Battery Bate?"

The question was very important, as the sounds of battle had been roaring from the general direction of Battery Bate for the past three hours. Clearly, the Army of the Tennessee was making a heavy attack all along the southern sector. Unable to get any solid information from the officers on the scene, Cleburne had dispatched Lieutenant Magnum to see for himself.

"I've never seen anything like it, sir!" Lieutenant Magnum replied, his tone a mixture of excitement and fear. "I've never seen so many men fighting in such a small space! It's a slaughterhouse, sir!"

"I don't understand," Cleburne said, feeling frustrated. "Have the Yankees been repulsed or not?"

Magnum shook his head. "No, sir. At least, I don't think so, sir. The fighting is still going on. The Texas and Florida troops are all in, but the Yankees just keep pouring more men in, too. The Yankees can't push out us, but we can't push the Yankees out, either!"

Battery Bate was one of the most important positions on the southern sector of the city's defenses. If it fell into Union hands, the entire Confederate position in Atlanta would be compromised. It had to be speedily reinforced. If the worst had already happened and the position had already been taken, a counter attack would have to be mounted to recapture it.

He looked up at his chief-of-staff. "Major Benham? Has there been any response from General Walker?"

Benham shook his head. "No response at all, sir."

Cleburne let out a deep, heavy sigh. Walker's division had not been strongly attacked, nor did there appear to be a serious threat on the northern sector. Cleburne's own division had been all but shattered, Finley's division had been badly cut up, and Maney's division was now heavily engaged on the western sector. Yet Walker retained all of his three strong brigades in their relatively comfortable positions despite repeated orders to dispatch one of them to reinforce the south. With Battery Bate clearly on the edge of capture, the situation was critical. It was no longer a matter of honor and obeying the proper chain of command, but of saving the city of Atlanta.

"Very well," Cleburne said. "Let's put our plan into effect."

He rose from the table, pausing to grab his sword and pistol belt and carefully putting them on. Major Benham, Lieutenant Magnum, and two other staff officers did the same. Around them, the other corps officers looked on with knowing expressions, even as they continued to do their work.

Cleburne and his men walked outside and quickly mounted their horses. Nearby, twenty or so other mounted men, Kentucky troops of the Orphan Brigade, had been patiently waiting. He would have preferred using men from his own division, but all of them were now fighting on the southern defenses. Could he count on the Kentuckians to support him over Walker? As Cleburne spurred his horse into a canter, Major Benham waved for the Orphans to follow. Commander, staff, and soldiers all rode off to the north, leaving a cloud of dust in front of the Atlanta City Hall.

As they rode northwards, Cleburne could hear the constant roaring of battle to the south around Battery Bate. He thought of his men fighting for their lives inside the imperiled position and his anger toward General Walker increased.

Thankfully, the city streets were mostly empty. Artillery continued to pound the city and many buildings they passed had been reduced to rubble. With fighting raging all around them, most of the good citizens of Atlanta were holed up in their own homes.

Only a few people were spotted. A few slaves could be seen dashing about, perhaps having been sent by their masters to find food or run some other errand. Conceivably they were trying to take advantage of all the confusion to escape.

It took about twenty minutes to arrive at Walker's headquarters. Compared to the headquarters of the other three divisions, Walker's command post looked remarkably clean and tidy. The uniforms of the men remained clean, the horses appeared to have been recently brushed and washed, and there was even a pig roasting over a fire in preparation for dinner. This sector had seen less artillery fire than the others and the attacks made against the line by the Army of the Cumberland paled in comparison to the intensity of the attacks made by the Army of the Tennessee on the south and west.

"General Walker!" Cleburne cried.

A minute passed. Cleburne tensed up. Was it possible that Walker was not even going to acknowledge his presence? It was something he had not anticipated and for which he had no planned response.

The tent flap was pulled back and Walker emerged, an irritated look on his face.

"What do you want, Cleburne? We're rather busy here."

"You are ordered to dispatch the brigade of General Gist to Battery Bate at once. It is under heavy attack and needs reinforcements immediately."

"Yes, well, as I told you before, why don't you look after your sector of the line and allow me to look after mine?"

"Are you refusing to follow my orders, General Walker?"

Walker laughed. "I don't acknowledge your right to give me orders, Cleburne. I take no orders from abolitionists."

Cleburne calmly nodded to Benham, who walked his horse a few steps forward.

"General Walker, on the authority of General Patrick Cleburne, commander of all Confederate forces in Atlanta, you are under arrest. If you will please come with me."

These words created a commotion. There was an uneasy rustling and low shouting throughout the headquarters. Cleburne's heart began pounding as he watched some of Walker's men grab their rifles. Many stepped forward to defend their chief. Cleburne and his staff officers, as had been decided earlier, remained still and impassive, but behind them the mounted troops from the Orphan Brigade quietly and calmly readied their weapons.

After a minute of tumult, silence descended. Both sides stood uneasily, watching one another. Cleburne was more nervous than he had ever been in the midst of a battle, for it would not take much for the situation to blow up into full scale violence.

Walker stared up at him, rage and hatred filling his fiery eyes. "You're arresting me, Cleburne?"

"I am. Your insubordination and refusal to follow my orders has left me no other choice."

"You know what the newspapers will say about this? You will be damned from one end of the Confederacy to the other."

"Are you going to go with Major Benham or do you intend to resist?"

"My men will protect me if I ask them."

"And then you, rather than me, will be the one damned from one end of the Confederacy to the other. You would be known as the man who ordered his troops to open fire on their fellow Confederates while the Yankees were beating down the door to Atlanta."

Walker looked around at his men, who were staring expectantly at him, their hands gripping their rifles. Clearly, Walker was telling the truth when he said that his men would resist if he asked them to do so. Neither Walker's men nor the Orphans pointed their weapons at one another, which reassured Cleburne. He was willing to employ the threat of force, but he had already made the decision that he would not actually use force if it came to that.

Cleburne was bluffing. He just hoped Walker wouldn't call his bluff. If he did, then Cleburne would be humiliated and his ability to exercise effective command in Atlanta would be at an end. So would his career and, very possibly, whatever chances the Confederacy had of obtaining its independence.

An endless minute of silence passed, broken only be the distant sounds of battle to the south. Then, Walker frowned and took a deep breath. He looked over at Benham.

"Major, that damned abolitionist commander of yours has ordered my arrest. I am to go with you, yes?"

"That's correct, General Walker," Benham replied.

Walker turned to one of his own staff officers. "Get my horse, Captain."

Cleburne still didn't move, even as the captain slowly strode over to the headquarters stable. Walker continued to glare up at him.

"What else do you want, Cleburne? I'm going with your man, just like you asked."

"General Gist's brigade," Cleburne said simply.

"Ah, yes." Walker turned to another staff officer. "Lieutenant, take a message to General Gist. He is in command of the division and he is to report immediately to General Cleburne for further orders." He turned back to Cleburne. "Satisfied now?"

Cleburne said nothing, but merely nodded.

Walker mounted his horse and, without a word, walked it over to Major Benham. "Lead on, Major."

Benham and Cleburne nodded at one another. Benham rode off, followed by Walker and the men of the Orphan Brigade. Cleburne looked around at the men of Walker's division, who were staring up at him with a grudging respect. His bluff had succeeded.

General Gist appeared a few minutes later. Cleburne informed him that he was now in command of the division and that he was to send his brigade down to Battery Bate without delay. That task done, Cleburne rode back toward his headquarters at the Atlanta City Hall, a much relieved man.

*   *   *   *   *

September 27, Evening

"Please tell me you know something new about the situation in Atlanta," Davis said, his voice sounding like a plea. "Any news would be very deeply appreciated."

Seddon sadly shook his head. "I wish I had something to tell you, Mr. President. But we have had nothing new since this morning's telegram from Johnston. Atlanta remains under attack and the Army of Tennessee is being assembled at Palmetto."

Davis sank back into his chair and fumed. He looked up at the military map yet again, having done so hundreds of times already. He paid no attention to Petersburg, or the Shenandoah Valley, or the Trans-Mississippi. His eyes fixated on the colored pins around Atlanta and on them alone.

He shook his head in frustration. "I must say, Mr. Seddon, that this endless waiting is the worst aspect of being in my position. Though I am safe here in Richmond, I find myself envying Cleburne in Atlanta and Johnston at Palmetto. They, at least, are active and busy. By contrast, I can do nothing but wait for the next telegram. It is intolerable, I must say."

"I understand, sir," Seddon replied.

"No, I do not think you do, Mr. Seddon. Unlike you, I do not have the soul of an administrator. The day they told me that the Montgomery Convention had selected me to be the president of our Confederacy was a dark day in my life. I had hoped and expected to be chosen as commander-in-chief of the army. In that position, at least, I could have taken an active part in the war. I could have commanded troops in the field, rather than push endless amounts of paperwork back and forth across this damn desk!" Davis slammed his fist down onto the desk so hard that it sounded as though a gun had been fired.

Seddon waited a moment before replying. "The Confederate Constitution says that the President is commander-in-chief of the army. Washington led troops during the Whiskey Rebellion while he was serving as President of the United States, as I recall. There is nothing preventing you from taking the field yourself. And you would undoubtedly make an outstanding field commander, sir."

Davis didn't respond. Although he was sadly susceptible to flattery, he had heard such sycophancy from Seddon often enough to have learned to recognize it for what it was. What Seddon said reminded him of words John Bell Hood had said to him nearly a year before, when the man had been in Richmond convalescing from his wounds. It had been largely because of such statements of support that Davis had come so close to giving Hood command of the Army of Tennessee.

Davis thought for a moment about Hood, now commanding troops in Arkansas and participating in an offensive to retake the state capital of Little Rock. The diversion of Federal troops from west of the Mississippi to the fighting in Georgia had been of great benefit to the Confederacy in that theater. But Davis had no time for it. Atlanta was all that mattered. Everything else was secondary.

There was a knock on the door and Secretary Benjamin entered. He was beaming a broad smile.

"Good news?" Davis asked.

"Very good news, Mr. President."

Seddon's eyes narrowed. "You know something about Atlanta that we don't?"

"Of course not, Mr. Seddon. I know nothing of military matters, nor would I ever presume to step on your toes. No, my news is about something far more important than any battle."

"Well, out with it, then!" Davis spat.

Benjamin took a seat. "I just read the most recent dispatch of Yankee newspapers sent in by General Lee. It seems that Manton Marble has been released from jail by General Butler. Not only that, but Butler has released a statement saying that Marble's arrest was unconstitutional and that the evidence against him was contrived."

"I don't understand. Marble is released?" Davis asked.

"You heard correctly, Mr. President."

"But I thought Butler was Lincoln's creature," Seddon said.

Benjamin shook his head. "Butler is a political chameleon. He has judged that the wind is blowing away from Lincoln and toward McClellan. I own that I would not have agreed with him before today. If anything, the momentum in the race was with the Republicans. But Butler has decided to become a turncoat and once again embrace the Democratic Party."

Davis rubbed his chin. Despite how much he detested Butler, the Confederate President had to admit that his actions were now serving Southern interests quite well.

"How do you imagine this news will affect the election, Mr. Benjamin?" Davis asked.

"The Democrats had been hammering the Republicans on the issue of unconstitutional war acts. You know, newspapers being shut down, dissenters intimidated or jailed, the suspension of habeas corpus, and of course conscription. The Democrats have made a lot of hay with this line of political attack, but the recent revelations about Marble and the money coming from us to fund their campaign caused it all to go off the rails. With this single act, Butler has basically erased all the advantages the Republicans gained from the Marble scandal and reinforced the Democratic message about Lincoln's unconstitutional rule."

"But why?" Seddon asked. "What Butler has done doesn't change the fact that Confederate money did fund a lot of Democratic campaign activities."

"It's politics, my friend," Benjamin said with a twinkle. "Reality is irrelevant. In any case, the Northern public will buy Butler's claims of the evidence against Marble being fabricated."

"Why?" Seddon asked.

"Because it makes for a better story. Everyone loves a good story, you know. Especially if scandal is involved. In such cases, the people will believe whatever they were last told."

Davis nodded. "This will certainly contribute to Lincoln's defeat at the polls."

"Indeed, it will. It could be enough to push Indiana, Ohio, and Pennsylvania into the Democratic column. And that would be enough to give McClellan the presidency."

"Unless we lose Atlanta," Davis said. His lips pursed tightly and he again damned Joseph Johnston.

"Yes, Mr. President. If we do lose Atlanta, it could yet again swing the election in Lincoln's favor. And I must admit, if the latest reports are true, the fall of the city is not a possibility, but a probability."

September 27, Night

"This is it, Truman," Thomas said soberly. "Are you ready?"

Seymour nodded nervously. "I think so, yes. As soon as you and the others draw the attention of the guards, we'll move back to the cabin and get through the tunnel." Throughout the camp, the hundred men who had drawn the shorter straws the night before were anxiously waiting. Seymour has been among the lucky ones and his rank as a general entitled him to go through the tunnel first.

The diggers had broken through to the surface the night before. They were close enough to the tree line that those who emerged from the tunnel could dash into the woods immediately upon coming out of the ground. Assuming that the guards lining the stockade were distracted, there was at least a possibility of getting away from the camp without getting shot.

"I'll pray for you, my friend. God willing, you'll be back in the army commanding a division or a corps within the next week or so." In truth, Thomas gave Truman and the others a less-than-even chance of even getting away from Camp Oglethorpe, much less back to the safety of the Union lines. Even those odds were preferable to remaining imprisoned, however.

"Is it too late to persuade you to make the attempt with us?" Seymour asked. "You know what happens if you remain here, George."

"The firing squad if I'm lucky and the noose if I am not. Yes, I know. But if I escape now, after having had a death sentence pronounced against me, the rebels would simply choose another man to die in my place. That is not something I am willing to have on my conscience."

Seymour pursed his lips tightly and shook his head. "If I do manage to get back to friendly territory, I'll make sure that the whole country is told that you could have escaped but chose to remain behind. Your courage will not be forgotten."

Thomas gave a slight, bitter chuckle. "Yes, it will. But I don't care."

"Can I do anything for you, George?"

"Yes. If you do get home, tell my wife that I love her." He paused just a moment. "Now, let's get on with this, shall we?"

Seymour nodded sadly and slowly walked away. Thomas watched him go, wondering if he would ever see him again. Amid the crowd of Union prisoners milling about in the center of the camp, there was a noticeable stirring. Perhaps a quarter of the men were privy to the plot in some way. Now that the attempt was actually going to be made, a few others had surely been told as well. If discipline failed to hold, some of those just now learning of the existence of the tunnel might try to find it and demand to be let through, thus spoiling all the careful planning. It was also possible that some desperate prisoner might succumb to the temptation to inform the guards of the plot, thereby winning his own freedom at the expense of the freedom of others.

There were many unknowns. It was entirely possible that not a single man would succeed in escaping. If Thomas could do anything at all to help his comrades reclaim their freedom, he was willing to try.

Trailed by several dozen other prisoners, Thomas walked slowly to the "line of death" on the opposite end of the camp from where the tunnel was located. Although there was no physical marker, it was understood that any prisoner who came too close to the stockade could be shot without warning. The young, undertrained militiamen serving as guards on the stockade did not have a reputation for restraint in such matters.

He glanced back and forth at the men watching him, just as he might have done while inspecting a line of infantry in the midst of a terrible battle. Then, he began to shout.

"More food!" he called up to the nearest pair of guards. "We want more food!"

"Yes!" another prisoner shouted. "More food! We want more food!"

The two guards, who could not have been more than fifteen-years-old, looked down at the crowd of prisoners with confusion in their eyes. "Shut up, you Yankee bastards!"

"We demand more food!" Thomas bellowed.

"I said shut up!"

More prisoners took up the call, shouting loudly for more food. Within less than a minute, the scattered calls had become a deafening chorus. As the noise intensified, Thomas could see guards moving along the stockade toward the disturbance. Every guard that came to his side of the stockade meant fewer on the other side, thus giving the escapees the chance they had been waiting for.

The shouting continued. "More food! More food! More food!"

Two guards fired their muskets into the air, hoping to frighten the mass of prisoners into silence. It didn't work and the shouting grew even louder. The pent-up frustrations of the captives seemed to feed off the discomfort they were causing the guards, who had tormented them for so long.

Someone threw a rock. Within seconds, other rocks filled the air. Thomas glanced worriedly back up at the guards. The shouting by itself was having the desired effect of drawing the guards from the other side of the stockade. Engaging in actions that would prompt violent retaliation would only endanger lives unnecessarily.

Thomas saw one rock glance off the shoulder of one of the guards, who had looked especially nervous. Now, his face coiled into an expression of anger and he fired his musket directly into the crowd of prisoners. Colonel Benjamin Harrison, a brigade commander who had been captured at Peachtree Creek, was struck squarely in the chest. He was flung backwards into the crowd and was dead before he hit the ground.

A stunned silence fell on the prisoners, like a curtain falling abruptly on a stage. For an infinite moment, no one moved. Then, Thomas stepped forward from the crowd, boldly walking beyond the line of death until he was directly beneath the guards overhead.

He was happy to see more than two dozen guards lined the stockade above him. That meant that most, possibly all, of the guards who normally covered the perimeter on the other side of the camp had come over in the face of the developing riot. The diversion had already cost the life of Colonel Harrison, but it was also accomplishing its mission of distracting the rebels long enough for Seymour and the others to make their escape.

"I am General George Thomas!" he yelled defiantly. "I am a Southerner who fights for the Union! If any of you rebel bastards wants to shoot me, shoot me now!" He stretched his arms out and raised them level with his head, inviting the gunfire of the guards. He wasn't sure whether or not they would fire, but he found part of himself hoping that they would. Jefferson Davis had not yet responded to his request that he be executed by a firing squad rather than by hanging. Perhaps he could take the decision out of his hands.

The guards and the prisoners were both absolutely silent. Amidst the rebels above him, all of them aiming their rifles down at him, Thomas saw the figure of Captain Gibbs.

"What do you think you're doing, Thomas?" he called down.

"Calling on your men to show the courage of their convictions."

"Have you lost your mind, man? What is the purpose of this demonstration?"

"We are demanding more food, obviously! And better food!"

Gibbs drew his head back in surprise. "A man just got killed, Thomas. You think that complaining about the food we provide you here is worth a man's life? You think it's worth your own life?"

Thomas knew that every moment he could keep the conversation going was one more minute in which the attention of the guards would not be focused on the point of the camp perimeter where the exit of the tunnel was located.

"The food you give us is garbage that isn't fit for pigs!" Thomas shouted. There was a stir and murmur in the crowd of prisoners at these words, causing some of the guards to shift the aim of their rifles away from Thomas and back toward the other prisoners.

"The food we give you is the best we can provide," Gibbs replied.

"Hogwash!"

Anger clouded the Confederate captain's face. "If you don't like the food, you have only yourselves to blame! Your raiders have torn up our railroads! Your armies have destroyed our farmland! Your navy blockades our ports! We can scarcely feed our own women and children! How can we be expected to feed you prisoners more food that we already are?"

"The South brought the war upon itself the day it seceded from the Union!" Thomas yelled back. These words were greeted with cries of agreement from the crowd of prisoners.

"Be silent, Thomas! Your own day with the hangman is soon to come. Causing trouble like this will only blacken your name further!"

"Like I told your General Cooper, I'd rather be shot than hanged. So have one of your little boys shoot me now and be done with it!"

Several of the guards again raised their weapons to a firing position, perhaps hoping that Gibbs would give exactly such an order. But the camp commandant held up his hand as a signal not to fire. He looked down at Thomas for some time in silence.

"Tomorrow morning, General Thomas, I shall meet with you in my office and we will discuss what can be done to improve the quantity and quality of the food in the camp. In exchange, you will tell these men to go back to their cabins. Do we have a deal?"

Thomas thought quickly. If he continued making a ruckus, the distraction of the guards would be prolonged. However, if he failed to agree to Gibbs' sensible proposal, the enemy captain might realize that what Thomas was doing was a diversion and therefore discover the escape attempt. He figured that the attention of the guards had been sidetracked for perhaps half an hour, which should have provided enough time for Seymour and the others to get away.

"I will see you tomorrow morning, then, Captain."

Gibbs nodded and the guards begin filtering back to their assigned positions on the stockade. The crowd of Union prisoners begin drifting back to their habitations, still grumbling. After detailing some men to take Colonel Harrison's body away from a proper burial, Thomas walked back to his own cabin, his heart pounding. He tried not to be so quick as to attract unwanted attention from the guards who were still eyeing him carefully.

He stepped inside the cabin. There was no sign of Seymour or any of the other escapees.

*　　　　　*　　　　　*　　　　　*　　　　　*

Night had brought no respite from the fighting. Fires had been started in the woodwork by exploding shells or inflamed cartridge wadding and now were burning out of control in certain parts of the redoubt. Many men had fallen wounded into the flames and the screams they had let forth as they had burned to death had shaken the nerves of many men. The fires cast a disturbingly macabre light over the whole scene. With the clouds of gunpowder smoke obscuring the light of the moon and stars, it was the only illumination by which the men could fight. Unfortunately, it was enough.

Inside the confined space of Battery Bate, thousands of men were doing everything in their power to slaughter one another. Union forces were trying to cram into the redoubt from the gun ports they had captured and at other points along the rampart, while Confederate troops dashing in from the rear of the battery were just as intently trying to push them out. Hundreds lay dead all over the fort, cut down by gunfire, bayonets, or swords. Others lay wounded and found themselves being trampled to death by the feet of both their friends and foes as the fighting continued to swirl unmercifully around them, their desperate cries for help going unanswered. Everywhere were the sounds of gunfire, metal clanging against metal, wood smacking against wood, and bare fists pounding bony faces.

McFadden stood toward the rear of Battery Bate, directing the fire of a line of two dozen troops he had assembled. He was struck by the terrifying idea, which his mind refused to entirely discount, that Battery Bate had become some sort of opening into Hell itself. There no longer appeared to be any unit cohesiveness whatsoever. The men to whom he was shouting orders were a combination of survivors from the Texas and Florida brigades plus a smattering of troops from South Carolina, Mississippi, and Georgia.

The men of Gist's brigade from Walker's division had arrived about an hour-and-a-half earlier. McFadden had thought them not a moment too soon. The remnants of Granbury's Texas Brigade and Finley's Florida Brigade, after several hours of fighting, had been on the brink of collapse and had been about to abandon the redoubt when the reinforcements had arrived. However, the newly-arrived troops had simply been swallowed up by the fighting within Battery Bate.

The enlisted troops had confused and often terrified looks on their faces. Their overriding concern, besides simply staying alive, seemed to be finding an officer to give them any kind of order. But most officers had already fallen, dead or wounded, as anyone waving a sword and shouting orders immediately made himself a primary target for the rifles of the opposing side.

McFadden was at a loss to know who was actually in command inside Battery Bate. When Gist's brigade had arrived, he had assumed that the commander was the highest ranking Confederate officer in the redoubt. Gist had not lasted for than ten minutes before his chest had been ripped open by a blast of canister fire from one of the Napoleon 12-pounders, which the Yankees had captured and turned on the Southerners. While McFadden had seen captains and majors running about, none of them seemed to be exercising any command responsibilities. It was as if the entire Confederate force inside Battery Bate, now numbering in the thousands, had degenerated into nothing more than an armed mob.

McFadden had his rough line of riflemen pouring as much fire as they could into the mass of Northern troops still forcing their way inside the redoubt through the captured gun ports. There was no end to the constant stream of Union reinforcements pouring into Battery Bate. Artillery shells passed by overhead, the eerily sparkling light of their lit fuses casting a strange white light over the proceedings before they exploded in the area behind the redoubt.

"Lieutenant!" an unfamiliar voice called out. It was a man in a major's uniform, running up to him. "Who are you?"

"Lieutenant McFadden! 7th Texas!"

"I'm Major Dunlop, 46th Georgia!" He pointed to one of the gun ports on the top level, which had contained one of the Brooke rifled cannon until it had been struck by a Yankee shell near the beginning of the battle. "See that?"

McFadden looked. Directly facing a steep ramp to the upper level, Yankee troops were pouring in through the gun port. They had to have erected ladders in a considerable number to be coming through so quickly. He nodded sharply.

"I've got a dozen men with me," Dunlop said, shouting to make himself heard over the din of the fighting. "Why don't we rush those Yankees together? We can push them out and then fire down onto them from the top of the rampart!"

McFadden nodded again. Dunlop waved for his men to come up. Together with McFadden's band, around thirty-five Confederate soldiers now huddled together near the center of the battery, loading their rifles quickly. McFadden had long since run out of ammunition for his revolver, so he tightly gripped the hilt of his saber, the only weapon he now had. Dunlop glanced up and down the cluster of men. There was no time to lose, for if they didn't move soon they would become an obvious target of Union riflemen.

"All right, men!" Dunlop shouted. He pointed his sword toward the gun port. "Charge!"

With a shout, the Southern troops dashed forward, running up the ramp as quickly as they could. The shout attracted attention and almost immediately men began to fall as Union troops redirected their fire into the charging mass of men. McFadden ran with them, waving his sword in the hopes of getting more Confederate soldiers to join the charge. Dashing up the ramp was tiring for leg muscles that were already exhausted from endless hours of combat, but the sheer nervous energy he felt coursing through his body, magnified by his constant fear of death, was enough to keep him going.

Within a minute, despite losing a third of their number, they were in among the Union troops at the gun port. There was a sudden explosion of gunfire as the attackers discharged their weapons, but there was then no time to reload. Major Dunlop was killed instantly by a Federal officer who shot him at point blank range with his pistol, though the Yankee was immediately skewered by a bayonet.

McFadden swung his sword, slashing through the uniform coat of one Yankee near the right shoulder and seeing a thin splatter of blood fly through the air. The man cried out in pain and covered the wound with his left hand. Considering him disabled, McFadden paid him no further attention, instead ramming his saber up to the hilt into the belly of a big, hulking bearded Yankee. Even as he heard the man scream in pain and terror, McFadden realized his mistake, for the man instinctively grabbed the blade with all his might to prevent it from being twisted inside his body and McFadden was unable to pull it out.

As he struggled to extricate his saber, McFadden caught a momentary glimpse through the gun port of the ground outside Battery Bate. Through the dim light cast by the fire of the burning woodwork, he could see a veritable ocean of blue-coated uniforms, like an immense army of insects, crowding its way forward toward the battery. All along the rampart, ladders had been raised and Northern troops were scrambling up to get inside. There were probably more Union soldiers trying to get inside Battery Bate than there were Confederate soldiers in all of Atlanta.

His heart sank. Against such numbers, there was no hope of holding the city.

McFadden finally was able to withdraw his sword after placing his foot on the man's chest and pushing as hard as he could. But while he was doing this, the Yankee whose shoulder he had earlier slashed had recovered and picked his musket back up. His face a mask of rage, he swung the heavy wooden butt of his weapon as a club down on McFadden's head. Everything went black.

*   *   *   *   *

"Shall I have Major Eckert bring some coffee, Mr. President?" Stanton asked.

"Yes, thank you," Lincoln replied. "It is going to be a long night and as I doubt I will be able to sleep some coffee would be appreciated."

Stanton nodded at Major Eckert, who quietly rose from his desk and walked out the door to get the requested coffee. Lincoln, who had been pacing back and forth across the length of the telegraph office, finally stopped and sat down on the couch, still intently reading the paper in his hand.

"What does Grant say?" Seward asked. He had come over from the State Department to get the latest war news.

"Nothing new, I'm afraid," Lincoln replied. "They are still attacking Atlanta."

"Any word on the casualties?" Stanton asked.

"Grant says that their losses since the fighting began have reached twenty thousand."

"Twenty thousand?" Seward exclaimed in astonishment. "Dear God!"

Stanton grunted. "It's been four days of constant fighting around Atlanta. Heavy casualties are to be expected. Remember, Grant lost seventeen thousand men in the Battle of the Wilderness, which only lasted two days."

"Most of the troops in the army outside Atlanta come from the western states," Seward said gravely. "Ohio, Indiana, Illinois, Michigan."

"Yes," Stanton replied. "What of it?"

"Well, I doubt that our electoral prospects there will be much enhanced by thousands of families receiving a telegram informing them that their sons were killed."

Stanton's face curled into anger. "Those men are out there fighting and dying for the Union and all you can think of is the political angle? You should be ashamed of yourself, William!"

Seward returned a fierce expression. "And if we lose the election, then all the suffering and dying that has gone on for the last four years will have been for nothing!"

"Calm down, gentlemen," Lincoln said. "We will not be helping anyone, much less helping our nation, by losing our tempers."

"I beg your pardon, sir," Seward said, sounding genuinely apologetic. Stanton, for his part, went back to reading the telegram in his hand without a word.

"It is no matter, William," Lincoln said reassuringly. "All our tempers are frayed, what with the uncertainty over Atlanta and all this trouble with Butler."

Stanton grunted at the sound of the man's name. "This business about Manton Marble and his allegedly illegal arrest is sweeping over the country like the tide coming in. So is the news that Butler has switched sides and gone back over to the Democrats. It makes our administration look weak and incompetent. Worse, it makes us look like fools."

"Perhaps we are fools," Lincoln said, laughing softly. "Perhaps I was foolish when I set out from Springfield after winning the election four years ago, thinking that I could somehow persuade our Southern friends to come to their senses. Perhaps I was foolish to think we could bring them back into the fold through strength of arms." Lincoln paused for a moment and chuckled bitterly. "Perhaps I was a fool for thinking I should ever try to be anything more than a small-town lawyer in a rustic Illinois town."

Major Eckert returned with a tray of coffee, prompting Lincoln to stop talking. It was one thing to speak so personally in front of his two Cabinet secretaries, whom he counted among his personal friends. It was quite another to do so in front of a staff officer.

Seward's eyes lit up for a moment. "Have you considered the possibility of using the Democrats' own trick against them?"

"What do you mean?" Lincoln asked.

"Whatever the means, they pulled Butler out of our orbit and into their own. This robbed us of the powerful political instrument of the Marble scandal as well as Butler's own extensive political network. Could we, perhaps, choose a similar target amongst the Democratic Party and offer them a sufficient inducement to abandon McClellan and come over to our side?"

"I've already parceled out every position in every post office and customs house in the nation. We even approached Governor Joel Parker of New Jersey about becoming Minister to Russia if he would switch parties, though that was no use. There are simply too many chickens and not enough chicken feed."

"You have one gold nugget now, Mr. President," Seward said. "You must choose a new Chief Justice of the Supreme Court."

Lincoln considered this. He had been wondering what to do about the vacancy ever since he had heard about the demise of Chief Justice Taney. The man who held the office of Chief Justice was only a few steps below the level of the President in terms of prestige. To make it even more enticing, the office of Chief Justice was a lifetime appointment.

Moreover, it was an office that Lincoln could now offer to anyone he wished on a silver platter. The Senate was still controlled by the Republican Party and, barring any difficulties with Charles Sumner and a few others, could be trusted to go along with whatever choice he saw fit to make.

"I don't much like the way this conversation is going," Stanton said warily. "Are you suggesting we offer some prominent Democrat the position of Chief Justice in order to get him to switch sides?"

"If it can help us win the election, it might be worth the cost," Seward said.

"And just who do you have in mind as the fish who would snap at this bait?"

"Governor Seymour, perhaps?" Seward said. "His defection to our cause would likely give us New York and its thirty-three electoral votes. Or perhaps Congressman Voorhees? He could potentially bring Indiana into our column."

"Have you lost your mind, Seward?" Stanton demanded, his voice rising. "You would hand over the supreme judicial power in our nation to such villains as Seymour or Voorhees? Damn Copperheads! Queen Victoria might as well ask the Devil to become the next Archbishop of Canterbury!"

Lincoln listened only slightly as Seward and Stanton embarked upon one of their habitual arguments. He actually agreed with Stanton. It would be an unforgivable crime to turn over such power to a person like Horatio Seymour or Daniel Voorhees, more so because the Chief Justice was effectively impervious to recall or impeachment. Moreover, Lincoln knew that he would be excoriated as the most corrupt politician in American history the moment the deal became public.

There was another consideration. If the worst happened and McClellan won the upcoming election, Lincoln would technically remain in office until the official handover of power took place on March 4. Between the election and the inauguration, Lincoln would therefore still have the power to appoint the new Chief Justice. If McClellan won the Presidency, it was likely that the Democrats would also gain control of the House of Representatives, leaving the Republicans with only the Senate.

Lincoln began to imagine what a McClellan presidency would be like. The former general would owe his election to the Copperheads within the Democratic Party. Allowing the South to go its own way would be only the beginning of the disasters visited upon the nation by a McClellan administration. Efforts to pass the 13th Amendment abolishing slavery would be abandoned and forgotten. Corruption of the Tammany Hall variety would infect the federal government at every level. Lincoln's stomach turned as he imagined Copperhead Democrats or Tammany Hall thugs representing the United States before Queen Victoria in London or Czar Alexander II in St. Petersburg. The United States would become the laughingstock of Europe.

To combat such a measureless disaster, Lincoln had to maintain the option, after the election results were known, of appointing a Radical Republican who could be counted upon to oppose McClellan on every measure with such energy as to keep alive the fire of abolitionism and Union that would otherwise perish from the face of the Earth. It would be the most effective manner of thwarting the ambitions of the Democratic Party. Since the appointment would be for life, Lincoln could count on the man fighting the good fight for many years to come.

"This discussion is at an end," Lincoln said, calmly but firmly. "I have decided to make no decision on who shall replace Chief Justice Taney until after the election."

Seward and Stanton stopped yelling at one another long enough to hear what Lincoln said.

"Are you sure?" Seward asked. "If we were to offer the position to Seymour we might-"

"I have made my decision, William," Lincoln said, in such a tone as to entertain no argument. "There shall be no more discussion of the issue of the Chief Justice position. Not in my presence, anyway.

And let me be very clear when I say that this is a decision that I shall make in my own good time. When I require your advice on the matter, I shall ask you. Not before."

By their silence, the two cabinet secretaries acknowledged their understanding.

The telegraph machine began clicking again, and Lincoln waited impatiently for one of the clerks to transcribe the message.

*   *   *   *   *

September 28, Morning

The eastern horizon had only just begun to glow, but already the Confederate soldiers around Palmetto were awake. Johnston had ordered them up at four o'clock and had instructed all commanders to make sure they had breakfast. They were likely to be doing a good deal of marching and fighting this day and the army commander wanted to make sure that at least they did so on a full stomach.

Johnston looked out over the enormous bivouac from his headquarters tent. Thousands of campfires twinkled in the pre-dawn twilight as the men cooked the last of their rations. There was an uneasy rustling, for the men could sense that they were on the verge of another battle. From the moment of their arrival in Palmetto, the sound of fighting twenty miles to the north had been clearly audible. Now, at long last, the Army of Tennessee was ready to go to the rescue of their embattled comrades.

By now, the rumors had flowed through the camps like countless messages over a vast number of telegraph wires. The men doubtless knew that Grant had initially outwitted Johnston and sent them all on a wild goose chase into Alabama. From what Johnston could tell, however, they still had confidence in him. The regiments still cheered him as he rode by. The trust he had earned during the long retreat from Dalton that had culminated in the great victory at Peachtree Creek had been sufficient to survive the fiasco. Still, Johnston had spent a lifetime as a soldier and he knew that the men might not be so charitable if he failed them a second time.

As the sun began to rise, the camps gradually filled with the sounds of beating drums and blaring bugles. The men stuffed the remnants of their food into their mouths and began to prepare themselves for the coming battle. Regiments lined up to be inspected by the captains and majors. Commissary officers struggled to complete the distribution of ammunition. The cavalry double checked the condition of their horses, while the artillerymen ensured that their batteries were ready for battle.

Mackall strode up beside him.

"Reports from the cavalry, sir," he said.

"Well?"

"Fighting raged along the southern portion of the Atlanta defenses all through the night. It apparently only tapered off a few hours ago."

Johnston nodded. It confirmed what his own ears had been telling him. He wondered whether the silence now prevailing to the north meant that the great attack had been repulsed or that Atlanta had fallen to the Yankees. He said a silent prayer that it was the former.

"Is Walthall's division all up yet?"

"Not all of it, sir," Mackall said, not bothering to hide the fact behind an apologetic tone. "There was a minor derailment at Newnan that has delayed the last two brigades. Only Cantey's brigade is here."

"How long?"

"With a little luck, the other two brigades will arrive here sometime around noon."

Johnston chuckled. "A little luck, eh? I think we're going to need a lot of luck if we are to relieve Atlanta."

He did some mental calculations. All three divisions of Cheatham's corps were on hand, but only a single division and one additional brigade of Stewart's corps had managed to arrive. All told, it amounted to perhaps twenty-five thousand men. Assuming the two other brigades of Walthall's division arrived on schedule, their total strength would rise to about thirty thousand by midday.

"We could wait," Mackall said, reading his chief's mind. "We could delay our march north until those final two brigades arrive."

Johnston considered this. Was the addition of five thousand additional men worth the price of a few hours' delay? He quickly decided that it was not. They had to begin moving north toward Atlanta sooner rather than later. Conceivably, Grant had broken off the attack on Atlanta in order to move south to confront the Confederate force assembled at Palmetto. Any delay in moving north would allow the Yankees to select the ground on which the battle would be fought. Johnston, with the eye of an engineer, knew the critical importance of being able to choose the battlefield.

Going forward without those extra five thousand men would be significant, as he was sure to be outnumbered in the coming battle. From what information they had gathered, Grant had arrived outside Atlanta with between sixty and seventy thousand men. No doubt, they had suffered heavy casualties in the Battle of East Point and their attack on Atlanta, but exactly how heavy was impossible to determine. They would also have to leave a covering force outside Atlanta or, if the city had already fallen, a garrison to secure the place and watch the prisoners.

Johnston assumed that the force Grant would bring to bear would number around forty-five thousand men. He was going to be outnumbered significantly even if he waited for the two delayed brigades. The best policy was to move north to select the battlefield and hope that the two brigades would be able to reinforce the main body in time to play a role in the upcoming battle.

There was something else that Johnston had to consider. Having already fought against the defenders of Atlanta for several days, the Union forces were likely to be quite shaken. He would never discount the courage and steadiness of the veterans of the Army of the Cumberland or the Army of the Tennessee, whom he knew were formidable warriors. Still, attacking fortified positions was the most mentally straining action a soldier could be asked to perform and the men under Grant's command had been doing it for several days. His own men, by contrast, were fired up with the urgency to go to the aid of their comrades trapped in Atlanta.

Johnston had been a soldier long enough to know that matters of morale often meant the difference between victory or defeat. He recalled one of his West Point instructors repeating to him one of Napoleon's most important military maxims: an army's effectiveness depends on its size, training, experience and morale, but morale is worth more than the other three put together.

As he listened to the distant shouting of regimental officers, their voices filled with determination and confidence, Johnston was satisfied that his army would be marching forward into battle with its morale at a high pitch.

He turned to Mackall. "No, we cannot wait. Issue the orders for the march north to commence. And have Fleetfoot saddled up. I intend to ride at the head of the army."

Chapter Nineteen

September 28, Morning

McFadden awoke. At first everything was hazy and uncertain, as if he had one foot in the real world and one foot in the realm of his unconscious dreams. For a moment, he wondered if he was dead. Perhaps the light that was now flooding his eyes was the great light of the Lord which everyone said you were supposed to see when you passed from one world to the next. He figured he couldn't be dead, though, for his head was throbbing with a pain that he thought quite out of place in the afterlife.

As his senses gradually came back, he realized he was lying on the ground. He focused his eyes and could finally see that he was a few hundred yards behind Battery Bate, or rather what was left of it. Much of the woodwork had collapsed after being burned to a cinder and the ramparts of some sections had been pounded into dust by the relentless Union artillery barrage. McFadden saw, with infinite relief, that the Confederate flag still waved above the remnants of the redoubt.

The absence of the sounds of musket fire or artillery made it eerily quiet. The sun was well up in the sky, shining down on him. He assumed it had to be mid-morning. He tried to sit up, but the act of moving caused more pain to scream through his head. Instinctively, his hands moved to grasp his temples in the hopes that light pressure might ease the agony.

"Oh, you're alive," an unfamiliar voice said.

His eyes focused on a black man looking down on him, an amused grin on his face.

"Good thing you woke up when you did. Otherwise, we might of carted you off with all the dead bodies. You could have been tossed in a mass grave and covered over with dirt."

McFadden wasn't able to do anything other than grunt. Very slowly, he sat up, feeling as though every muscle in his body had been subjected to brutal punishment. He suddenly realized that he had been lying amidst several dozen corpses, laid out in neat rows. Had he been fully conscious, he would have found this unsettling, but all his mind could focus on was the throbbing pain in his head.

"Water?" the slave asked.

McFadden nodded. The man had been carrying a bucket of water, presumably on his way to the wounded, and held out a ladle. McFadden took the ladle in his hand and drank the water gratefully. He could almost feel the hydration flow to his aching muscles. Having spent most of the previous day fighting in the midst of a hellhole without so much as a sip of water, it was as though the slave with his bucket was an angel sent from heaven. The black man smiled, nodded, and moved on.

He stood up, looking about. Black laborers were walking back and forth, some carrying wounded soldiers on stretchers toward the rear while others were laying corpses out for later disposal. A good many of the dead and wounded, McFadden noted, wore blue uniforms rather than gray or butternut ones. He supposed this was something to cheer about, yet he didn't.

Along what was left of the redoubt's parapet, a line of tired and dusty-looking Confederate soldiers stood quietly, gazing out across the ground in front of Battery Bate. McFadden wondered what they were looking at, and forced himself to start walking over to find out. Each step was painful, but as he moved he felt the achiness gradually seep away.

He clambered up the ramp that had been the scene of the charge the night before and soon reached the parapet. As hardened a veteran as he was, what he saw caused him to gasp in shock. For hundreds of yards in front of Battery Bate, in every direction, there lay a sea of Yankee corpses. He had seen the aftermath of many a ferocious battle over the past few years, but he had never seen so many dead bodies in a single place.

Moving out there among them like little ants were teams of stretcher-bearers. A truce had obviously been agreed upon so that the Yankees might collect their wounded. Burying the dead would likely take much longer, such was the sheer number of bodies. Disturbingly, flocks of buzzards were descending for the traditional post-battle feast.

"Oh, McFadden," a voice said. "I thought you were dead. Saw you lying out there with the corpses."

He turned to see General Granbury among the Confederates viewing the enemy bodies. He said the words without warmth, as though the fact that he still lived was of only a passing interest to the commander. McFadden took no offense.

"Quite alive, sir."

"Well, that's good. Wish I could say the same for the rest of the brigade."

"Oh?"

Now a hint of sadness crept into Granbury's eyes and he shook his head. "I doubt there's even a hundred men left alive from any of our eight Texas regiments."

McFadden nodded. He was greatly saddened, even though it was what he had expected. Having been in the thick of the fight at both the Battle of East Point and the ferocious combat in Battery Bate, how could it have been otherwise? The men of Texas had shed more than their fair share of blood in the struggle for Atlanta.

McFadden did the math in his head. If the law of averages held, what Granbury said would mean that there were perhaps ten or so survivors of the entire 7th Texas. He wondered whether Pearson or Montgomery were among them. If not, then he himself would be the only survivor of the Lone Star Rifles.

"The brigade took a lot of Yankees down with it, by the look of things," McFadden said.

Granbury nodded. "Yes. Eighteen hours of continuous combat. They just kept coming at us, throwing regiment after regiment after regiment at this battery. The damn redoubt changed hands five times over the course of the night!"

"Five times?" McFadden asked, incredulous. He tried to imagine the fighting that had to have raged for hours around his unconscious body. It was a miracle that he hadn't been killed.

"The men are calling it the Blood Bucket."

"What's that?"

"The Blood Bucket," Granbury repeated. "It's what the men have nicknamed Battery Bate, since it sort of looks like a bucket. Appropriate, don't you think?"

"A waste," McFadden said. "A godawful waste. All those men dead. And for what?"

The other Southerners on the rampart eyed McFadden somewhat warily. He decided to stop talking further.

Granbury went on. "The Yankees requested a truce to gather their wounded when the sun came up. No attacks anywhere along the line, though we have seen lots of their troops marching south in the far distance."

"Maybe the Yankees have had it," suggested someone that McFadden didn't recognize. "Maybe they realize they can't capture the city and they're retreating."

"Not likely," said another. "If they were retreating, they'd be heading north, not south."

For the first time since waking, a positive thought entered McFadden's mind. "It's Johnston," he said firmly.

"What do you mean?" Granbury asked.

"Johnston. Brought up the rest of the Army of Tennessee on the railroad as far as he could. Now he's marching north to help us and Grant's going south to meet him."

Granbury shrugged. "Maybe. Hard to tell, really."

McFadden shook his head. "No, it's Johnston, sure as hell. Old Uncle Joe has come back to Atlanta."

*　　　　*　　　　*　　　　*　　　　*

September 28, Morning

Grant rode at the head of a division of the Army of the Cumberland as it marched south, throwing up a tremendous cloud of dust. On either side of the marching column floated a cloud of cavalrymen whose job it was to protect their commander. General Howard and General McPherson rode beside him, along with the ubiquitous collection of staff officers. Grant had an irritated and disappointed look on his face.

"I am afraid I have to admit that the rebels are not playing the role which I had assigned them when I initially drew up my plan" Grant said glumly.

"Sadly, no," Howard replied.

"I had hoped to be in Atlanta days ago. Certainly long before Johnston would be able to return to the vicinity of the city with his army. The stubborn resistance of the defenders of Atlanta is proving most difficult to overcome."

McPherson nodded tiredly, his head almost jerky. Grant looked over at him sympathetically. Not only was McPherson exhausted, having scarcely slept for several days and now subsisting only on nervous energy, but he was in shock at the high casualties his army had sustained during the assault on Battery Bate. The Army of the Tennessee had launched a series of ferocious attacks on the key position. Despite enormous casualties on both sides, the rebels had managed to hold on until mutual exhaustion had finally brought an end to the fighting shortly before sunrise.

Grant had seen a similar look on the faces of many of his commanders before. When he had led the Army of the Potomac into battle against Lee's Army of Northern Virginia in the spring, he had fought three ferocious battles in less than a month. The Battle of the Wilderness had cost seventeen thousand men, the Battle of Spotsylvania nearly twenty thousand men, and the Battle of Cold Harbor had seen seven thousand men lost in less than an hour. The heavy casualties had strained the nerves and spirits of the generals to the breaking point.

What he had seen in the looks of his corps commanders then he saw on McPherson's face now. Grant knew his subordinate was haunted by the enormous loss of life, so many men sent into battle to be slain on his orders. Although he had done his best, Confederate flags still waving defiantly from the rampart of Battery Bate testified to his failure. Heavy casualties were bad enough when the outcome was a victory, but were hardly bearable when it was a defeat. Grant did not blame McPherson for the repulse and had tried to console him by pointing out that heavy casualties had also been inflicted upon the enemy. McPherson was a sensitive man. Grant knew that he would hear the screams of his dying men in the dark corners of his mind for the rest of his days.

Grant fumed, curling his lips around his cigar in an annoyed frown. He had to momentarily turn his attention away from Atlanta. The buildup of Southern forces at Palmetto could no longer be safely ignored. He had hoped that the cavalry raids on the Atlanta and West Point Railroad would have been sufficient to delay the return of Johnston, but they had apparently been ineffectual. Grant recalled Sherman's warning that the mounted arm of the Western armies was worse than useless and certainly no match for the Confederate troopers.

If he had continued to assault the defenses of Atlanta, Grant knew that he would have eventually overrun them, even if it took a day or two longer. However, with a rebel force estimated to be about thirty thousand strong coming up from the south, he could not risk doing so without suffering a devastating attack from that quarter. If Johnston were bold enough to attack him from the rear, Grant's forces might be caught between him and the defenders of Atlanta. Johnston's threat had to be eliminated before Atlanta could be taken.

He had therefore ordered Howard to withdraw two corps of the Army of the Cumberland from the north and northwest sides of Atlanta and march them around the city to the south, leaving a single corps in place to protect the bridges over the Chattahoochee that were now serving as the critical supply line for all Union forces in the area. McPherson had similarly been ordered to leave his most battered corps in a defensive position south and southwest of the city, keeping Cleburne's men hemmed inside, and move his two other corps to link up with Howard's men.

It had taken some doing, and the tired men had grumbled about marching such a great distance in the dark. Things were now finally coming together. Grant was moving south against Johnston with a total force of four corps, two from each army, numbering perhaps forty-five thousand men. That would give him a significant numerical advantage.

Would a numerical advantage be sufficient? Grant knew that the morale of his men was shaky after the many days of combat around Atlanta. Nothing strained the nerves of infantrymen more than assaulting heavily fortified defensive positions and the men of his two armies had been doing exactly that for the past few days. They had suffered heavy casualties and not gotten much rest. As with his generals, Grant had seen the way the strain of constant combat in Virginia had reduced the fighting strength of his infantry. Might the same be true here and now?

Grant knew the battle toward which he was marching would be perhaps one of the most important he would ever fight, for it would determine whether or not Atlanta fell and, therefore, determine who would win the upcoming election in the North. The fate of the country hung in the balance of what was about to happen. Yet he found that he was strangely unconcerned. He knew that he would do his best, he knew that Howard and McPherson would do their best, he knew that the foot soldiers stomping through the dust of the Georgia countryside would do their best. Beyond that, what else could they do?

The outcome, after all, was in the hands of fate.

*   *   *   *   *

September 28, Morning

"Five thousand?" Cleburne said, incredulous. "That's all?"

The staff officer, one of the men Cleburne had inherited from Hardee, sadly nodded. Of the eighteen thousand men who had manned the defenses of East Point and Atlanta when Grant had begun his offensive less than a week before, not even a third of that number had answered the roll call that morning. The rest had been killed, taken prisoner, or were now crowding the nightmarish hospitals in the center of the city. The once proud corps had been reduced to a shadow of its former self.

Even worse, those who still held their muskets were exhausted and nearly broken. Cleburne had seen it when he had ridden out along the lines that morning. Many of the survivors of the fighting in the Blood Bucket appeared to be mentally and emotionally shattered. He had seen uninjured veterans of regiments that had charged into battle on over a dozen battlefields lying on the ground in fetal positions, rocking themselves gently back and forth. Not every war wound was physical, as Cleburne well knew.

He looked around at the staff officers trying to maintain some semblance of order in the Atlanta City Hall. It was almost useless. For one thing, casualties among the corps and division staffs had been horrible. More than half of the corps staff officers were gone, either killed, wounded, or missing. Moreover, there was very little organization left to manage. The constituent units of the four divisions were hopelessly intermingled with one another. Some regiments had literally vanished off the face of the earth, every man a casualty. Simply getting an accurate count of the number of men still under the colors that morning had been a difficult task.

Cleburne stopped what he was doing for a moment and listened. For the first time in several days, there was no sound of artillery fire. When the assault on Battery Bate had finally ceased, the Yankees had also silenced their artillery batteries all along the lines, which had until then been pouring fire into both the

Confederate defenses and the city beyond. The officers on the ramparts had reported that most of the Union batteries were now being withdrawn. The silence that had descended over the city was comforting and ominous at the same time.

Major Benham arrived, looking dusty and exhausted. Behind him was a captain Cleburne didn't recognize, whose head was wrapped in a bandage stained with blood.

Benham wasted no time with pleasantries. "General, this is Captain David Hay. He says he rode in from General Johnston's headquarters with dispatches."

"Does he?" Cleburne said, his tiredness fading for a brief moment. "Are you all right, Captain?"

The man saluted. "Got nicked by a Yankee ball on the way in, sir. Otherwise, I'm tolerable." He handed over an envelope, which Cleburne quickly opened.

General Cleburne,
I have been notified of the wounding of General Hardee and your assumption of command. Be advised that the main body of the Army of Tennessee is now in Palmetto and moving north to your assistance. There must be no thought of surrendering or abandoning Atlanta to the enemy. For God's sake hold on. Help is coming.
General Johnston

Cleburne read the message through twice more. The news was not entirely unexpected, but it still rejuvenated him like a welcome splatter of water on his face. Since the moment the enemy shell had incapacitated Hardee, Cleburne had felt more alone than he had ever felt in his life. It had seemed as though the entirety of his universe had been encompassed by the defenses of the city and that nothing outside of them actually existed except in his own imagination. To receive a message from General Johnston gave him confidence and reminded him of the existence of the outside world.

"Major Benham, please draw up a circular for distribution among all commanders. Tell them the contents of this message." He handed over the paper and Benham headed directly for the nearest table.

"Captain Hay, if you'll go to the surgeon's tent outside, they can take a look at that head wound of yours.

Hay nodded. "Thank you, General."

"It is I who thank you, Captain, for bringing a message that shall restore hope to the defenders of Atlanta."

It was important, Cleburne thought, that the men be informed of General Johnston's efforts to relieve the besieged city. It would give them hope that their struggle would soon have a victorious outcome. Without such hope, the men would still have sold their lives dearly before the Yankees overwhelmed them, but Cleburne had been a soldier long enough to know that hope was a better motivator of men than was despair.

As Benham wrote out the circular, Cleburne thought things over. Johnston's arrival at Palmetto explained the halt in Union attacks and the withdrawal of their artillery batteries. Although no scouts had been able to get out of the city through the Union siege lines, many officers had observed large formations of Federal infantry in the distance, circling around Atlanta to the west before heading south. Obviously, Grant was moving the bulk of his forces into a position to strike at Johnston.

He assumed that Johnston had not been able to bring up all of the two corps which had been sent to Alabama. Despite their proven brilliance at improvisation, the railroad engineers of the Confederacy were not supermen and the rails themselves were worn down and ramshackle. They could only move so many men within such a short space of time. Although Cleburne's men had inflicted terrible casualties on Grant's army, the Union commander would undoubtedly still be able to bring a much larger force to bear against Johnston than the Confederate commander would be able to field.

The battle that was about to be fought south of Atlanta would surely decide the fate of the city. If Johnston somehow managed to inflict a defeat on Grant, or even fight him to a standstill and remain as a force-in-being somewhere to the south, the Union commander would not be able to return to the assault on Atlanta. On the other hand, if Grant succeeded in smashing Johnston's army and forcing it to retreat, the Yankees would be able to resume their attack. Cleburne knew his men might be able to hang on for a day or two longer, but with all hope of reinforcement or relief ended the outcome would no longer be in doubt.

He tried to a way in which he could help Johnston. With a mere five thousand men, all of them exhausted and of questionable fighting readiness, and with twice that number of Union troops still ringing the Atlanta defenses, was there anything he could do?

There had been no Union attacks all day, which meant that his men had had a few hours to recover from the strains of the recent fighting. Assuming that the night also passed quietly, perhaps the next day could begin with an artillery bombardment of the Union positions and a few sorties by his troops to keep the Yankees off balance? There was still plenty of ammunition left and the heavy guns in the Atlanta defenses would be ideal for such work.

He nodded. It would be worth doing, but would probably have only limited effect. Grant was not an easily rattled man and would not be fooled into bringing any of his troops back to the north.

Grant might have moved to the south, but the main Union supply depots were still near to Atlanta, deployed along the southern bank of the Chattahoochee around the Western and Atlantic Railroad bridge, which the Yankees had rebuilt as they had occupied the area.

Perhaps some sort of strike could be organized against the supply depots?

Thinking on it, Cleburne shook his head. With only five thousand men, he could scarcely spare even a single squad of troops from the defenses of the city. Even if he somehow managed to organize half his men into an attacking column, twenty-five hundred troops would stand no chance against ten thousand Yankees.

He recalled the impromptu "university" that he had established in his division's encampment during the previous winter, just before the onset of the Atlanta campaign. He and his brigade and regimental commanders had spent several hours a day discussing military strategy and the art of war. One of the ideas he always tried to ram into the minds of his subordinates was never to do what the enemy expected, to always try to keep him guessing, and to constantly seek a way to strike at the enemy's most vulnerable point.

The enemy's most vulnerable point within his immediate reach, as should have been obvious, was the reconstructed Western and Atlantic Railroad bridge.

"Major Benham!"

The chief-of-staff looked over at his commander. "Sir?"

"Are you finished writing the circular yet?"

"Just about, sir."

"Good. When you're done, I will need you to draw up a new set of orders. We need to get the men ready for tomorrow."

"Tomorrow, sir? What's happening tomorrow?"

"I'll tell you shortly. But first, there was a man who arrived in Atlanta some time ago. I don't remember his name, but he delivered a letter of introduction to General Johnston and later tried to see General Hardee. Something about a time bomb."

Benham looked confused. "A time bomb?"

"An infernal device he had invented. I forget exactly what he called it. In any case, find that letter, or comb through the city until you find the man. I want him here as quickly as possible."

"Yes, sir," Benham said faithfully, though the sound of his voice revealed his doubts.

"Oh, and Major?"

"Yes, sir?"

"Get me Lieutenant McFadden."

*   *   *   *   *

September 28, Noon

Johnston had set up his headquarters in a small farmhouse just north of the tiny hamlet of Fairburn, about fifteen miles southwest of Atlanta. The staff officers were setting up shop, placing maps on the tables and generally getting comfortably situated.

"The cavalry says it's good ground, sir," Mackall was saying. "A low ridge running northwest to southeast, behind a stream called the Pontic Fork." The cartographer was busy sketching the terrain onto a makeshift map of the area.

"The flanks?" Johnston asked.

"The right flank is covered by thickets, streams, and broken ground. Would be hard to move large numbers of troops around the edges of the ridge very quickly. The left flank is much the same, but rather more passable, they say."

Johnston thought for just a moment, then nodded sharply. "All right. Deploy the army. Cheatham on the left and Stewart on the right. Tell Cheatham to form his line in such a way as to have his leftmost division facing north rather than northeast, if the ground allows for it."

Mackall turned and began issuing orders. Clerks frantically copied down what he was saying, before handing the orders over to the couriers, who rapidly mounted their horses and galloped away. At the same time, the small army of staff officers rode off to ensure the proper posting of infantry brigades and artillery batteries. All became controlled chaos in Johnston's headquarters for the next few hours.

He dictated a telegram to an aide for transmission to Richmond.

President Davis,
The Army of Tennessee is taking up a position near the town of Fairburn, southwest of Atlanta. Grant's army is marching to meet us. The decisive battle for Atlanta is likely to be fought in this vicinity today or tomorrow. I trust that Almighty God shall grant us victory.
General Johnston

The message was brief and to the point. The President was always complaining about a reticence in his communications, but Johnston considered such pestering to be irrelevant and annoying. He told the President what the President needed to know. What else was there for him to say?

A courier arrived and handed a message to Mackall.

"Cavalry reports Union infantry a mile north of Pontic Fork," he said simply.

"In what force?"

"At least a division."

"There will be much more behind them. Can they identify them?"

"They say nothing about unit identification."

"I do wish our cavalry would be more thorough in their reports," Johnston said with irritation. His mounted troopers had been too heavily influenced by Wheeler, who had focused much more on obtaining good newspaper headlines through useless skirmishes than doing the hard but necessary work of reconnaissance.

More reports came in over the next hour. The approaching Union force was very large, with at least two infantry corps and assorted cavalry. It quickly became clear to Johnston that it was the main body of Grant's army. It was headed directly for Fairburn, which suited his needs just fine. The more troops Grant was bringing south, the fewer there were around Atlanta. The city was safe, at least for the time being.

"Is Fleetfoot saddled up?"

"Yes, sir," Mackall replied. "I took the liberty of getting him ready half an hour ago."

"Good man. I would like to inspect the front line."

Minutes later, Johnston and Mackall rode out from the farmhouse northwards, trailed by a squad of cavalrymen from the 8th Texas Cavalry. The road was now mostly cleared of infantrymen, but artillery batteries and ordnance wagons continued to clog up the route. Johnston and his coterie stayed mostly to the side of the road to prevent any unnecessary encumbrance.

He paid close attention to the faces of the artillerymen he passed. They seemed anxious but determined, clearly anticipating a major battle in the near future and knowing exactly what he expected of them. There might have been some fear in their faces as well, for the last time these men had faced an army under Grant had been at Missionary Ridge, when the Army of Tennessee had been shattered.

As they approached the front line, they encountered the final infantry brigades coming off the road and deploying to their positions. Finally, they reached the ridge. In a long, continuous line, Confederate infantry was arraying itself in a formidable position facing northeast toward the enemy. The men were busying themselves digging trenches, but as they passed by each regiment in turn, the soldiers stopped what they were doing long enough to give Johnston a hearty cheer.

Looking out to the northeast, there was not much to see, for the ground was heavily wooded. Men were out there with axes, hacking away at the trees in order to provide clear fields of fire, but Johnston was not sure if they had enough time to make much progress. The stream of Pontic Fork was clearly visible at certain intervals a few hundred yards in front of the ridge. This would be a benefit, as having to wade through the water would slow down any attacking Union force. Moving northwest to southeast, Johnston noted that the ground in front of the rightmost portion of his line was more heavily wooded than the rest.

Johnston pointed. "The woods here are thicker, William."

Mackall squinted in the sunlight. "Yes, sir."

"How large a force could be concealed there?"

Mackall thought a moment. "Perhaps a division? Maybe more?"

"I want pickets posted there. Grant might use it to conceal an advancing force."

"I shall notify General Stewart right away, sir."

Johnston looked at the woods for some time, lost in thought. Something about them seemed troubling, yet also promising. He filed the thought away in his mind for future reference.

Somewhere out there in the distance was the Union army. It would take several hours for it to march the remaining distance and to properly deploy for an attack. By then, the Southerners would have finished constructed rudimentary earthworks and be in a solid defensive position. Grant might attack during the evening, in the hopes of driving his men off the ridge before their defenses became too strong. But there would not be much daylight left by then and the Yankees would be tired from having marched such a great distance.

If Johnston had been facing Sherman, he would have expected no attack at all. Sherman would have simply closed up to the Confederate position and launched a few probing attacks to pin him down while seeking to maneuver around his vulnerable flanks. Grant was more likely to confront him directly, seeking to crush him in an overwhelming attack.

That was exactly what Johnston was counting on.

*   *   *   *   *

September 28, Afternoon

"It's a strong position, sir. But the rebels have only arrived within the last few hours. They have not had much time to entrench."

Grant nodded to the reporting scout and glanced over at McPherson, wordlessly asking his opinion. The commander of the Army of the Tennessee looked at his pocket watch.

"It's almost three. We could attack within the hour with plenty of daylight remaining. I would think we should try to knock them off that ridge before they have time to properly entrench. If they are still there when the sun goes down, then next morning they will be so strongly fortified that an attack would be inadvisable."

Grant nodded. McPherson didn't need to say what was obviously true. Having spent the last several days hurling themselves against enemy fortifications around Atlanta, the men might shrink from doing so again. Grant had seen the veterans of the Army of the Potomac hold back from energetic attacks at Petersburg after the nightmarish slaughter at Cold Harbor. It could easily happen here in much the same way. If an attack was to be mounted, it would have to be before Johnston had had time to entrench.

Grant turned to Howard, nodding for him to speak.

The commander of the Army of the Cumberland shook his head. "I don't like it, General Grant. Even unfortified, the position on the ridge will be strong, and the rivulet running along the base of it will be an impediment. Why not pin the rebels in place with my force and send McPherson around the enemy left, which appears vulnerable?"

Grant considered this. It certainly was what Sherman would have done in Grant's place. Howard, ever the Christian gentlemen, did not want to expend the lives of his soldiers if he could see any possible alternative. What he was suggesting could at least force Johnston to abandon his position and fall back to the southwest.

Simply forcing Johnston to retreat would be meaningless, though. So long as the Army of Tennessee remained a force-in-being outside of the city, Grant would not be able to focus on the assault on Atlanta. Even forcing Johnston to retreat a hundred miles would not matter, for so long as the rebel force remained formidable it could simply return to its previous position the moment the Union armies returned north to resume the attack on Atlanta. Grant made up his mind and pointed southwest toward the enemy position.

"It's not about forcing them to retreat, gentlemen. We have to smash Johnston's force. Nothing else will do. Therefore, we must attack at once. Deploy your men. Howard on the right, McPherson on the left. I want the attack to commence within the next two hours, gentlemen. By nightfall, we must have possession of that ridge. Understood?"

Both men nodded.

"Get to it, then," Grant said simply.

The two commanders saluted and departed, kicking their horses into quick trots and being followed by their respective staffs and escorts.

It seemed a lifetime ago that Grant had led his two armies across the Chattahoochee River, though in truth it had been only a week. During that time, he had won a clear victory over the rebels at the Battle of East Point and had launched a succession of heavy attacks on Atlanta itself. For all this, he had paid the price of roughly twenty thousand casualties.

He didn't flinch from the price in blood, which was sadly the nature of modern warfare. It was not the loss of life in itself that troubled Grant, but rather its political implications. Grant was not a politician, but he was aware that suffering such heavy casualties was a serious political blow to the Lincoln administration. Unless he could obtain a decisive victory, every Union casualty was another argument for the Northern public to vote the Lincoln administration out in the upcoming election.

Quite calmly, Grant told himself that the situation was more critical than any in which he had previously found himself. He had to defeat Johnston here at Fairburn. After Johnston was beaten and

Atlanta captured, news of the twin victories would spread over the telegraph wires across the North in a matter of hours, completely transforming the political situation and hopefully ensuring the reelection of President Lincoln. The defeat of the Confederacy would then be a mere matter of time.

On the other hand, if Johnston somehow avoided defeat, it was possible that Atlanta would not fall before the election. If November came with Atlanta in rebel hands and the Army of Tennessee undefeated, Lincoln would suffer a heavy defeat at the polls. Grant didn't need to remind himself what that would mean.

Colonel Wright, the engineering office in charge of bridge construction, rode up and saluted.

"The Western and Atlantic Railroad bridge has been rebuilt, sir."

"Already?"

"Yes, sir."

"You amaze me, Colonel Wright. You and your men are truly miracle workers."

Wright shrugged, neither wanting nor needing the compliment. "It wasn't that hard. The stone pillars of the old bridge were still in place, obviously. It was a simple matter to lay the track across."

"Still, you are to be commended."

"Thank you, sir. The first train should be moving across within the next hour or so. I believe Colonel Anderson is already arranging for the main supply depot to be transferred from Marietta to the south bank of the river."

Grant nodded, greatly relieved. During the fighting around East Point and Atlanta, his two armies had expended a massive quantity of ammunition. Although the wagon trains using the pontoon bridges were able to keep the troops supplied, Grant did not feel entirely secure with the Chattahoochee River between him and his main ammunition reserve. As it was, he had only enough ammunition for a few days of severe fighting. Now that he was about to fight a major battle against Johnston, bringing the ammunition reserve onto the south side of the river was a matter of urgency. The rebuilding of the railroad bridge had therefore come not a moment too soon.

Grant turned Cincinnati and, without a word to the dozens of staff officers and cavalry escorts who had been silently watching him think, headed back to his headquarters. The battle was about to begin.

September 28, Afternoon

Johnston had mounted Fleetfoot the moment he had heard the sound of musketry. The Union artillery had begun shelling their positions twenty minutes earlier, but the sound of infantry fighting meant that the enemy attack had begun. The shelling had been briefer and lighter than normal, which told Johnston that the Yankees had not yet been able to bring up all of their artillery. Leaving Mackall to manage things at the army headquarters, Johnston rode north toward the front lines, determined to show himself to the troops at the scene of danger.

He was not surprised that Grant was proving so aggressive. It only made sense for Grant to try to smash the Army of Tennessee before it had time to firmly entrench. As it was, his men had had time only to construct rudimentary earthworks, consisting mainly of shallow trenches and low parapets. The ground in front of the line had not yet been cleared of trees, so the enemy would have a reasonable amount of cover as they approached. Although the ridge on which the army was deployed would give the Southerners an advantage, Grant's superior numbers were likely to make the battle a near-run thing.

The sound of the firing was coming from the right of the line, where Stewart's corps was deployed. He considered this as he rode in that direction. It made sense for Grant to concentrate on his right flank. In the event that his right collapsed, the army would likely be forced to retreat toward the west, pushing it farther away from Atlanta. The left, with its flank refused, was more difficult for the Yankees to approach. Still, Johnston knew that his left would soon come under attack as well, if only to prevent him from shifting troops to the right.

As he came closer, it became clear that the attack was falling most heavily on Loring's division. This gave Johnston some comfort, as Loring had fought well during the Battle of Peachtree Creek and the men of his division, a mix of Alabamians and Mississippians, were tough fighters. Johnston was certain that the attacking Yankees were about to receive a nasty surprise.

The roar of battle grew louder the closer to the front lines he approached. He sensed the hesitation in the trailing staff officers and cavalrymen, but he himself felt no fear. He had been wounded so many times in battles against the Seminoles, the Mexicans, and the Yankees that battle no longer held any terror for him. If he was going to die, he was going to die.

The line came into view. Loring's men appeared to be holding their position without too much trouble, for Johnston could see the men still arrayed in well-ordered lines in their shallow trenches, loading and firing calmly and quickly. Several of his men had fallen, killed or wounded, but the line seemed to be holding firm. In front of the line amidst the trees, Johnston could just make out through the smoke a line of Union troops pouring fire toward his men.

After a few minutes of searching, he located General Loring and rode up beside him.

"How's it going, General?"

Loring saluted quickly. "Fine, sir. The attack started about half an hour ago, but the Yankees aren't pushing very hard."

Johnston glanced back out over the field, ignoring a few bullets that zipped by close enough to hear. He saw immediately that Loring was correct. The Yankees had halted about a hundred yards away, almost at the edge of his vision. There were no fallen bodies of enemy soldiers closer than that. He could see Union officers walking back and forth just behind the line, shouting and exhorting to their men. However, the bluecoats were making no effort to close the distance. They huddled behind trees or large rocks, reloading and blazing away at the Confederate line.

In a flash, Johnston knew what was happening, for he had seen it before. There was only so much that a soldier, even a hardened veteran, could stand. The officers might urge the men to charge, but the minds of the soldiers simply could not bring themselves to order their legs to move them forward into the hail of enemy fire. Because they had some cover behind the numerous trees, the Yankee soldiers could remain where they were and fire at the Confederates with some measure of safety. That being the case, they would not charge.

Johnston thought quickly. Grant's men had spent the last few days launching attacks against the immensely strong fortifications around Atlanta. As these were held by some of the toughest soldiers in the Confederate Army, the Union troops were certain to have suffered heavy casualties and to have been extremely shaken by the experience. Their nerves were likely to be unsteady. With a sudden feeling of elation, Johnston realized that the damaged morale of the Union troops might offset their numerical superiority. If so, the Army of Tennessee had a good chance of victory.

Johnston remained mounted on Fleetfoot fifty yards or so behind the line, walking the horse slowly between the trees and ignoring the bullets that occasionally zipped by his head. Loring's men loaded and fired methodically, not rushing and trying to save their strength. The atmosphere was one of calmness amidst the noise and chaos, for these men knew they were holding their position without much difficulty.

After half an hour, the Union officers on the other side of the line recognized that the attack was not going to ever get moving and withdrew their men out of range. In the distance through the trees, they could be seen reforming their lines and sending wounded men to the rear. Over the heads of the bluecoats, artillery shells began screaming through the air and impacting the Southern lines, causing Loring's men to lie prone on the ground for better protection. It was clear to Johnston that the Yankees would soon try again.

"I assume you can handle things here, General Loring?"

"Yes, sir. If the Yankees attack again, we'll give them the same treatment."

"I will support you with whatever I can if you find yourself in difficulties."

"Thank you, sir."

Johnston and Loring exchanged salutes and the army commander was off. For the next hour, he rode along the length of the line, meeting with other division commanders, as well as with General Stewart and General Cheatham. Everywhere, the story was the same. The Yankees were attacking all along the line, but few of the attacks seemed especially threatening. General Cheatham reported that the enemy had broken General Clayton's line at one point, but a counter attack by his reserve brigade had easily sealed the breach. In most places, the Yankees had not come within a hundred yards of the line. The battle had essentially been a repeat of Kennesaw Mountain.

Satisfied, Johnston rode back to his headquarters. The fact that he had received no message from Mackall during his excursion to the front line told him that there were no pressing emergencies that required his attention. A glance at the sun told him that a perhaps two hours of daylight yet remained, which meant that Grant might well try again before nightfall. Having repulsed the first attack, Johnston felt confident of repulsing the second.

It was at that moment that Johnston realized what he had to do.

*   *   *   *   *

September 28, Afternoon

McFadden tried to bite through another piece of hardtack but found that, like the one he had had for lunch, it was as hard as granite. He wondered where the commissary got the things, for they were almost impossible to eat. As he had done before, he dropped the large cracker into his tin of water and waited for it to soften.

Around him, perhaps a hundred and fifty men of what had been Granbury's Texas Brigade bivouacked under some trees not far from Atlanta City Hall. Cleburne had pulled the men out of the line after their ordeal in the Blood Bucket. As it had turned out, McFadden was one of three surviving officers of the entire brigade, one being a captain from the 10th Texas Infantry and the other a lieutenant from the 24th Texas Dismounted Cavalry. Every single regimental commander had been killed or wounded, as had the considerable majority of the enlisted men. General Granbury himself had survived and was now commanding the remnants of both Cleburne's division and Bate's division.

As they had come in, most of the Texas survivors of the Blood Bucket had promptly laid down beneath the shade of the trees and fallen dead asleep. Rations had been distributed and, for the first time in many days, the Texans would have something to eat when they woke up.

Without the nervous anxiety caused by stress and combat, McFadden was feeling the physical agony that the last several days had inflicted upon his body. Although it had slowly faded over the course of the day, his head still ached from the blow of the Union infantryman's rifle butt. The torso wound he had received in the Battle of East Point, minor though it was, still caused him a good deal of discomfort. More than anything else, though, he was simply tired. As soon as he finished eating, he wanted nothing more than to go to sleep.

He knew sleep would not come easily. He tried to distract himself by focusing his thoughts on the needs of his men, but he could not push the image of Annie Turnbow's incinerated body from his mind.

There was a different tinge to the way he fought now. He had assumed that, with Annie now dead, his feelings would quickly return to their former state and he would again enjoy killing. If anything he should enjoy it more, as the death of Annie and her parents had been caused directly by the enemy.

Yet he didn't enjoy it. He now saw it only as his duty. He killed Yankees, but it was now more out of loyalty to his men and to General Cleburne than anything else. When he realized that war had turned him into a killing machine, a being of which neither Annie nor his family would not have been proud, he hated the war itself far more than he hated the Yankees.

"Ah, there you are, McFadden."

The man looking down at him was only a darkened silhouette, for he stood directly between McFadden and the setting sun. His murky form set against the yellow glare of sunlight seemed to present a sinister picture, but the voice was friendly. McFadden struggled to recognize it.

"Major Benham?" he finally guessed. He had met Cleburne's chief-of-staff a few times previously.

"Indeed. If you would please come with me, Lieutenant, I would be most obliged. General Cleburne wishes to speak with you."

"With me? What for?"

"Come and find out."

Benham turned and began walking toward City Hall. McFadden reluctantly rose to follow. While his loyalty to Cleburne had always been without question, and he had been honored by the recent interest the commander had taken in him, McFadden at the moment wanted to do nothing except go to sleep. He found Benham's sudden summons annoying.

Minutes later, McFadden followed Benham through the front door of the building. The interior was strangely subdued. Some staff officers were quietly laboring at the map-strewn tables, writing orders or reports, although McFadden could see several lying asleep on blankets near the walls. He envied the sleepers very much.

"Ah, McFadden," Cleburne said, gesturing him over to one of the tables. A man Cleburne didn't recognize stood by his side, while a strange-looking device lay on the table itself. "How are you?"

"Tired, sir."

"I can imagine. How is the Texas Brigade?"

"Virtually gone, sir," McFadden replied, not wanting to sugarcoat it. "Less than two hundred men left."

Cleburne nodded sadly, clearly having expected the answer. "Same is true in many other brigades. Finley's Floridians. Lewis's Kentuckians. The entire corps has been bled white."

McFadden, not really knowing what to say in response, merely nodded. He was very tired and hoped that this interview would not last long.

"McFadden, this man is John Maddox. He has come to us from the East, where he has been serving as a clandestine operative."

He nodded toward the man and extended his hand. "Pleased to meet you."

"Thank you," the man responded in a thick Scottish drawl. "Nice to encounter a fellow Scotsman."

"Likewise," McFadden said, though he didn't really care.

"Mr. Maddox has brought to Atlanta an infernal device of his own invention," Cleburne said.

"I call it my horological torpedo," Maddox said proudly. He gestured to the object on the table, which consisted of a large glass jar filled with powder and was topped by a clock with two cylinders on each side. "It is a bomb packed with fifteen pounds of concentrated gunpowder. It is designed to explode thirty minutes after this timing device is started." He patted the clock.

"Interesting," McFadden said, wondering what all of this had to do with him.

"Mr. Maddox here succeeded in planting one of his devices on a Union supply ship at City Point in Virginia," Cleburne said. "As the ship was packed with ammunition, it was blown to pieces, destroying much of the dock and causing great damage to the surrounding area as well."

McFadden nodded. "I believe I read about the incident in the newspapers."

"So, you know a bit about my handiwork, eh? I only wish more people knew that it was my doing. Apparently, the Yankees suspect it may have been some sort of accidental explosion." He smiled and shook his head. "You should have seen it. It was a thing of beauty."

McFadden found the smile on Maddox's face distasteful. He wondered how many of those killed by the agent's bomb had been innocent dock hands rather than armed soldiers. Many of the fatalities were likely to have been freed slaves. The idea of killing people from a distance with explosives seemed somehow dishonorable.

"If I may ask, sir, what does all of this have to do with me?"

Cleburne nodded. "I want you and a small group of men from the Texas Brigade to lead Mr. Maddox toward the Union supply depot on the south bank of the Chattahoochee by the Western and Atlantic Railroad bridge, find a suitable place to plant this bomb, and inflict whatever damage you can."

McFadden took a deep breath. Aside from his own incursion into the Union camps to find Cheeky Joe, he had never been involved in a clandestine operation of this sort.

"Why me, sir? I could do with some rest, I don't mind saying."

"You penetrated the Union lines before. Your Scottish accent will help disguise the fact that you are a Confederate. Besides which, you are a reliable, quick-thinking fellow. Just the sort of person for this kind of work."

"I would have thought you had other men for such a mission. Partisan rangers and such."

"Oh, we did. But most of them are dead."

McFadden pursed his lips in frustration. He had no desire to undertake what could well be a suicide mission, but he knew he couldn't say no to Cleburne.

"I won't order you to go, McFadden," Cleburne said with a sincerity that was clearly genuine. "But I very much want you to."

"I will go," McFadden said simply. He wondered if he had just signed his own death sentence.

*　　　　　*　　　　　*　　　　　*　　　　　*

September 28, Evening

"It's no use," McPherson said firmly. "The men are just not up to it."

Grant could see the truth of what his subordinate was saying. The regiments within their field of view looked utterly exhausted. Many men, with no wounds evident, sat silently with their backs resting upon trees, having fallen into a deep sleep. The bluecoats of his two armies were approaching the limits of human endurance.

A rare expression of irritation crossed Grant's face. The attacks had been launched on schedule all along the line, but nowhere had they been pressed with much vigor or energy. A momentary break on the enemy's left had briefly raised his hopes, but somehow the orders for the reinforcing brigade to exploit the breach had gone awry and the men of the advance division had been unable to hold their gains.

Grant sighed in exasperation. "How many men have you lost?"

"Not sure," McPherson replied. "Reports from my division commanders are still coming in. But I would guess about fifteen hundred."

Grant assumed that the same would be true for the Army of the Cumberland, though he'd have to wait for a solid confirmation from Howard to be certain. If so, the three hours of fighting had brought losses of three thousand men and gained no advantage. The Southerners had suffered comparatively light casualties. While it had not been a defeat on the scale of the slaughter at Cold Harbor, it had certainly been a frustrating setback.

"Do you wish me to prepare another attack, sir?" McPherson asked. By his tone, it was clear that he hoped the answer would be in the negative.

Grant glanced upwards through the trees to see the sun. "Only about an hour of daylight left. Probably not enough time for another attack."

"Perhaps, sir," McPherson said with relief. Even if they could get another attack together and seize a portion of the rebel-held ridge, the approaching darkness would make it almost impossible for reinforcements to find their way to the breakthrough, allowing the enemy sufficient time to organize and mount a counter attack.

"No more attacks today," Grant finally said. "Let the men be. They've been marching and fighting all day. See to the distribution of rations and pull the men back from the rebel line. I want them to have some rest. Tomorrow, after all, will see more bloody work."

"What do you intend?"

"I'm not sure," Grant admitted. "The rebel position will become much stronger during the night, so another frontal attack is inadvisable. Better to try to smash one of the enemy flanks."

"Their right seems difficult to approach," McPherson offered. "The ground is very bad and broken there. Our brigades would have difficulty remaining in formation if they moved in that direction."

"The enemy left flank is more vulnerable, or so Howard says at any rate." Grant thought for a few moments. "Perhaps the best course of action would be to mount a attack with one corps on Johnston's right while using the other three to smash his left. Considering our greater numbers, such an attack would have a good chance of success, providing that our boys have a decent rest during the night and some food in their bellies."

McPherson nodded. "Probably the best course of action available to us. But perhaps we might wait for additional reinforcements?"

Grant shook his head. "No, we must smash this army of Johnston's without delay, then hurry back north to take Atlanta. We have no time to lose. The election is barely a month away. If we don't win a victory here, within the next day or so, our cause may be lost."

McPherson looked at Grant in some confusion. While the upcoming election was on the minds of every general officer in the army, who supported Lincoln almost to a man, it was unusual for Grant to speak about it so openly. Somehow, correlating military operations with politics seemed inappropriate, perhaps even sordid. Grant knew better. To speak of them at the same time was simply a concession to reality.

"I will pull my boys back, then," McPherson said. "I'll have them dig shallow earthworks in the event that Johnston decides to attack, but I'll not keep them at it for an unreasonable amount of time. As you say, they need their rest."

Grant nodded. "Be at my headquarters at ten o'clock. We'll go over tomorrow's plans then."

*   *   *   *   *

September 28, Night

"General Mackall!" Johnston called as he dropped off of Fleetfoot and onto the ground.

The chief-of-staff appeared at the door of the farmhouse housing the headquarters seconds later. "Yes, sir?"

"My maps!" Johnston snapped. The commander hurriedly stepped inside and strode toward the table as Mackall frantically motioned for the staff officers to lay the maps out. Johnston leaned against the table, his hands clenched into fists, staring down hard at the representation of the battlefield. For several minutes, he neither moved nor spoke.

The staff officers watched silently, knowing their general's moods and not wishing to interrupt his thoughts. They quietly went about their business, the headquarters now illuminated by the pale yellow light of several hanging lanterns.

At long last, Johnston slowly nodded. "William, you remember that the woods here appeared to be thicker and heavier than the rest of the surrounding terrain?" He thumped the map just to the north of the right flank of the Confederate line, where Stewart's corps was located.

"Yes, I think so."

"You said they were thick enough to conceal a division?"

"Yes. As you requested, sir, I had General Stewart post additional pickets there to prevent the Yankees from approaching our right flank undetected."

Johnston nodded hurriedly, his mind racing. When he had first considered the heavy woods on his right, he had been concerned about the possibility of Grant hiding a division within them. For the same reason that the woods were a potential threat, they might also provide an advantage.

"What is it, General?" Mackall said. He had grown adept at reading his commander's mind over their time in service together. He could tell that Johnston already had some scheme afoot.

"William, if a Union division might be concealed undetected in the woods, so might one of our own divisions, yes?"

Mackall thought for a moment. "I suppose so."

"General Cheatham has pulled one of his divisions into a reserve position, yes?"

"That's right," Mackall answered. "Stevenson's division is in reserve."

Johnston frowned. Stevenson was a competent officer, but his troops had often showed a lack of offensive punch. At the Battle of Knob's Farm, fought a few days before the engagement at Kennesaw Mountain, they had demonstrated a marked reluctance to come to grips with their Yankee foes. While he would not have hesitated to assign them the task of holding any position against an attack, for what he now had in mind he would need a more hard-hitting outfit.

"Clayton's division is in the line?"

"Yes, sir. They fought off the most serious Yankee attack today."

"Casualties?"

Mackall shrugged. "Not bad, from what I understand."

Johnston nodded. "I want General Cheatham to pull Clayton's division out of the line and replace it with Stevenson's division. General Clayton shall march his men to the right flank and report directly to army headquarters until further notice. Understood?"

Mackall's eyes narrowed in confusion, yet he nodded. "I shall have the orders drawn up at once, General."

"Let me know when Clayton is in position. I shall want to speak to him myself."

*   *   *   *   *

September 28, Night

Through breaks in the clouds, McFadden could see the stars dancing overheard. For the first time in many months, he actually felt cold, occasionally rubbing his arms roughly to warm them through friction. He and the ten picked men of his clandestine force were kneeling silently on the ground just outside the northwestern Atlanta defenses. No one spoke, but the tension mounted appreciably. The men tightened their grips on their rifles, impatiently waiting for the signal to advance.

Maddox, armed with a pistol and cradling the carpetbag containing his time bomb, showed no sign of anxiety. Despite only having known him for a few hours, McFadden had taken an instant dislike to him. He knew his type, the sort of man who regarded life as nothing but a game and seemed to delight in causing mayhem. While he would hopefully prove useful to the army in the operation they were about to launch, McFadden was eager to be out of his presence as quickly as possible.

The plan they had agreed upon was simple enough. A quick surprise attack organized by General Granbury would open a gap in the Union line through which McFadden, Maddox and a few chosen men would slip through. All of the infiltrators were wearing Union uniforms, taken off the corpses of enemy soldiers who had died in the Blood Bucket. This would obviously aid their penetration of the Union lines but, as had been carefully explained to the men who had volunteered for the mission, it would also mean that they would be shot as spies if they were captured.

To better disguise themselves, the Texans had exchanged their Enfield rifles for Springfield rifles. Although both models were in use in both armies, the proportion of Enfields to Springfields was slightly higher in the Confederate army. The men were grumbling, as the Springfield was longer and heavier than the Enfield. McFadden wondered if the bother would be worth the comparatively small impact the exchange would have on their disguise.

"Mind if I join you, Lieutenant?" a familiar voice asked.

Private Pearson scurried up to the group of soldiers, a sly smile on his face.

"Pearson!" McFadden said, trying to keep his voice down. "You damn son of a bitch! I thought you were dead."

"Nah, just got separated from the brigade. Been on the rampart with some of the Arkansas boys today, till somebody told me where you were."

McFadden noticed that Pearson was wearing a Union uniform. "Someone filled you in?"

"Yeah. I told them I wasn't about to let you go into the Union lines all by yourself again."

McFadden nodded. Despite his long distaste for Pearson, it was nice to be reunited with a member of the Lone Star Rifles once again. His little band had grown from ten men to eleven, not counting himself and Maddox.

Granbury came by, walking with a deep stoop and as quietly as possible.

"Are your men ready, McFadden?" he asked in a whisper.

"Ready when you are, sir."

"Good. Almost time." He smacked McFadden's shoulder and scurried on to the next team.

McFadden glanced around at his men, wishing that he had had more time to acquaint himself with them. Six of them were soldiers from other regiments in the Texas Brigade, while the other five were Kentuckians from the Orphan Brigade. They had been selected by their commanding officers for their coolness and steadiness under fire. Those were qualities they would certainly need over the next few hours.

He sadly thought to himself that most of the men around him would probably lose their lives in the mission, either by being killed outright or shot as spies after being taken prisoner. Though he would obviously do his best to obey Cleburne's orders and inflict as much damage on the Yankee supplies as possible, he still thought that the undertaking was a fool's errand and probably a suicide mission.

"What's going to happen down south tomorrow, do you think?" someone asked. Rumors as to the result of the day's fighting between the two armies around Fairburn were sweeping through the army, though no one had any way to verify any of them.

"Either Johnston's going to attack Grant or Grant's going to attack Johnston," another answered. McFadden found this response annoying, since it was merely stating the obvious.

"Never you mind, men," he snapped. "Nothing we can do about it, anyway. Stay quiet, stay ready. The signal to advance can come any second."

McFadden's words were prophetic, for less than a minute had passed before the sound of a solitary musket going off momentarily broke the silence of the near-darkness. About twenty yards ahead of them, the men saw the advance team, totaling about two hundred and fifty men, move forward without making a sound. Their officers had ordered the men to tie white stripes of cloth around their left arms, so as to help distinguish them from the enemy in the hand-to-hand fighting that would soon be taking place.

The Yankee lines were a few hundred yards away. Enemy sentries had been spotted making the rounds, but there had not seemed to be any undue alarm among the federal troops. It couldn't be more than a few seconds before the pickets spotted the attacking Confederates, for all their efforts to avoid making noise. Every additional second they remained undetected would mean fewer of them being killed.

A sudden chorus of confused cries emanated from the Yankee lines, followed by scattered gunshots.

"The rebels!" a voice cried. "The rebels are coming!"

McFadden and his men waited tensely, straining their eyes to peer through the darkness at what was happening. The Confederate troops vanished into the Union lines and they could soon hear the sounds of hand-to-hand fighting. Gunfire was also heard, but only in the form of sporadic single shots rather than full volleys. McFadden distinctively heard the short screams that he easily recognized as men being bayoneted to death.

The wait was excruciating, for the instinct of everyone in McFadden's company was to charge forward to help their comrades. Yet that was not the plan. Finally, after what seemed like an infinity but was probably no more than two or three minutes, the sounds of fighting seemed to diminish. Almost at once, McFadden heard the call from Granbury.

"Go, McFadden!"

They got up and began walking quickly forward. The men held their loaded rifles ready to be fired, scanning ahead of them searching for enemies. Within their midst, McFadden gripped his Navy Colt pistol and, beside him, Maddox clutched his deadly carpetbag.

Fighting could now be heard to both the left and right of the small gap the storming party had torn in the Yankee line. McFadden and his men hurried to the northwest, soon lost to the sight of their comrades as they vanished into the darkness.

Chapter Twenty

September 29, Morning

Grant sat impatiently on a tree stump amidst the half dozen tents containing the headquarters of the Army of the Cumberland, already smoking his second cigar of the day even though the sun had not yet risen. Behind him, he could hear Howard and his staff officers talking with one another, coordinating the complicated movements involved with approaching the enemy flank. Grant made no effort to intervene in their discussions. He assumed Howard knew what he was doing and the orders he had given him were fairly straightforward. During the night, one of the two corps of the Army of the Cumberland present on the battlefield had quietly marched westward a few miles before turning south, placing it in a position from which it could strike the exposed left flank of the rebel army.

Grant was calm, although he knew that the day's battle would probably be the most important of his life. Johnston was out there, dug into a strong position but with considerably fewer men than Grant had on the battlefield. Moreover, when the previous day's attack had failed, Grant had ordered the troops fed and rested rather than attempting further assaults. Figuring that Johnston himself would not consider taking the offensive, Grant had decided against having his men entrench. Although they had been awoken well before dawn, he hoped that his men would therefore be in better spirits and more fit than they had been the day before.

Grant momentarily thought about how it had come down to this, the outcome of the war likely to be decided in a battle between two comparatively small armies in an obscure town southwest of Atlanta. Military historians in the future would wonder whether Sherman would have won the campaign and the war had he not made the single mistake, stemming from momentary overconfidence, of allowing the Army of the Cumberland to be separated from the other Union forces and caught in an awkward position south of Peachtree Creek. The same attention would doubtless be drawn to his own campaign against Lee in Virginia. It didn't matter in the end, though. The only thing that mattered was where they were, not how they got there. There was no sense in dwelling on the irretrievable past.

There was a sudden, low boom, which instantly silenced the staff of the Army of the Cumberland. This was followed, at regular intervals of two seconds, by a further three booms. It was the agreed-upon signal for the launch of the Army of the Cumberland's attack on the rebel left. The men of the headquarters began chattering excitedly, checking their watches and congratulating one another on the successful timing of the assault. Grant did not move from his tree stump and quietly continued whittling his stick.

If the plan was being carried out as Grant had laid out the previous night, McPherson was even then moving forward as well, mounting a diversionary attack on the rebel right and center in order to prevent Johnston from detaching troops from that section of the line to reinforce the left. Grant would assume this was being done until he heard otherwise.

Twenty minutes later, his confidence was rewarded when the unmistakable sound of artillery fire was distinctly heard coming from the east, signifying that McPherson's attack had begun as well. The stick upon which Grant had been working had become too small to continue whittling, so he tossed it aside and picked up another, bigger stick and started anew.

One of Howard's officers brought him a cup of strong coffee and some biscuits, which he consumed gratefully. He strained his ears to pick up the sound of musketry, but he could not hear anything other than the artillery fire. The woods were too heavy and the distance was too great. An hour passed, then another.

A courier arrived at the cluster of tents and asked to speak with Howard. After a discussion of a few minutes, the commander of the Army of the Cumberland did approach Grant's tree stump.

"Well?" Grant asked.

"We're driving them," Howard responded. "We smashed into the left flank of the leftmost rebel division and drove them back in confusion."

Grant nodded. "Well, that's first-rate news."

"Indeed," Howard said. "The courier said he saw the attack go in and that we caught the rebels napping."

"Not like Johnston to get so careless," Grant said. Yet such things happened in war. It had not been like Thomas to be so careless at Peachtree Creek, after all.

"My other corps has mounted a frontal attack as well. The rebels facing them are holding for the time being, but I expect them to break as the rebel left collapses."

"Good."

"I'm delighted, sir," Howard said with a smile. "I feel like I'm getting a little payback for the way my corps was treated by the rebels at Chancellorsville."

Grant grinned but didn't pursue the point. "Any word from McPherson?"

"No."

He nodded. "That's fine. No news from him is probably good news. He'd tell us if anything were going wrong on his front, and all he has to do is keep the rebels there occupied."

For a brief moment, Grant wondered if anything worth his attention might be happening around Atlanta. He considered sending a message on the field telegraph inquiring as to the situation around the city, then decided against it. Cleburne's garrison was shattered and incapable of any action aside from manning the city's defenses. The ten thousand men Grant had left to hem them in were more than sufficient to keep the Irishman from causing any trouble. It was best to remain focused on the task of defeating Johnston.

*   *   *   *   *

September 29, Morning

McFadden and his men paused briefly as the sound of artillery fire rolled over the ground from south to north. Instinctively, they gazed toward the sound, despite the fact that they could not see a thing. Obviously, the day's battle between Grant and Johnston had begun.

"Move along, men," McFadden said sternly. "Nothing we can do about it."

It had been three hours since they had departed the lines. Thus far, they had not had any trouble. McFadden had given strict orders to the men that they were not to speak, for he did not want Southern accents to be heard by any Yankee ears. Any talking that needed to be done would be done by himself or Maddox, whose Scottish accents would provide a reasonable disguise.

As soon as they had started to the northwest, they had begun encountering Union troops in large numbers. Initially, there were regiments of infantry hurrying forward to shore up the line, probably in response to word of the surprise attack that had opened the gap for them. When they moved into the area beyond artillery range of the Atlanta defenses, however, they entered into the logistical centers of the Union rear areas.

Still miles away from the Western and Atlantic Railroad bridge, where they assumed the main supply depot was located, McFadden and his men looked around at the profusion of plenty all around them. They passed a well-ordered hospital with hundreds of beds cradling wounded men, who were being waited on by a number of doctors and male nurses. The sheets actually appeared to be clean, which was something a wounded Southerner in an Atlanta hospital couldn't have imagined in his wildest dreams.

As they continued northwest, they passed by several sutler wagons, some of which were surrounded by eager Union soldiers haggling with the peddler for flour, coffee, tobacco, and bags of sugar. The passed by an enormous bakery and the scent of baking bread filled the air. McFadden, who had not eaten anything other than hardtack in many days, felt his stomach ache with desire. He was sure the same was true of his men.

What McFadden found hard to believe was that the Union forces had only been in occupation of the area for about a week. In that time, they had built what amounted to a small city. The logistical power of the Union never ceased to amaze him. He hoped he might now use Maddox's infernal device to inflict some damage on that power, though he still felt the use of hidden explosives to be somehow ignoble.

No one paid them the least bit of attention. With so many blue-coated soldiers milling about, they did not look at all out of place in their Union uniforms. However, McFadden was growing increasingly frustrated at his men for the way in which they stared at the material abundance all around them, their eyes wide in wonder. None of them had seen such plenty in years. He worried that if they didn't shake the looks of astonishment off their faces, some keen-eyed Union soldier would realize they didn't belong there. He wanted to say something, but kept silent out of fear of creating exactly such a situation.

Walking alongside the tracks of the Western and Atlantic Railroad, they eventually passed into a more heavily wooded area and momentarily out of sight of any of the milling bluecoats.

"Stop," McFadden said. "Let's rest a moment."

"Why?" Maddox asked. "We should push right on."

McFadden shook his head. "I'm giving the men just a few minutes. Don't want them to be winded when the time comes."

Maddox gave a skeptical look, then simply shrugged and lit a pipe.

In truth, McFadden wanted to stop as much to give himself some time to think as to allow the men to rest for a few minutes. Though they had passed through what had obviously been a logistical area, the activities there had all involved provisions and medical care. He had not spotted anything resembling an ammunition dump, which would be the obvious target for Maddox's infernal device. With fifteen pounds of gunpowder, the bomb would pack an explosive punch equivalent to a few rounds of artillery detonated simultaneously. Unless it were placed in such a manner as to set off large amounts of Yankee ammunition, the destruction the bomb might cause would never justify the trouble to which they were going to smuggle it into the Union lines.

As these thoughts were moving through his mind, a mounted Union officer appeared coming down the sidetrack road toward them, trailed by two other riders. They were moving at a rather slow walk, in no great hurry. As the man came closer, McFadden was disheartened to see a cautious and inquisitive look on his face.

"Why is a squad of infantry standing idle next to the railroad?" the officer demanded. "Where are you men supposed to be?"

"Our colonel sent us up to pick up more ammunition for our regiment," McFadden said, thinking quickly. He lamented the lack of time which had prevented proper planning for this operation. He should have had a cover story prepared and memorized for exactly this kind of situation, which had been bound to happen sooner or later.

"What regiment are you?"

"13th Iowa," McFadden replied, randomly pulling the name from his mind. He cursed himself. The least he could have done would have been to learn the name of a nearby regiment, and perhaps even the name of its commander. Surely it wouldn't have been too difficult to do that.

The Union officer, a major, looked at McFadden with skepticism. Perhaps it had been the tone of his voice, or perhaps the major knew the whereabouts of the 13th Iowa. Whatever the cause, the man clearly sensed that something was not right.

'What's your name, son?"

As calmly as if he were pouring himself a drink, Maddox produced his revolver and fired a single shot at the Union major. In the quiet part of the woods, the sudden sound of a gunshot echoed like a loud clap. The bullet struck the man squarely in the throat. As a look of shocked horror crossed the major's face, his hands instinctively grasped around his throat in an effort to staunch the loss of blood. It was no use. With every heartbeat, a stream of blood pumped out from between his fingers.

The two staff officers just behind the major were at first too surprised to do anything. Before they could respond, Pearson and one of the other soldiers raised their Springfields to their shoulders. At such close range, they couldn't miss. Two shots brought both men down off their horses within a second of one another.

The mortally wounded major did not give in to terror. While holding his throat with his left hand, he pulled his own revolver from its holster with his right. Pointing it in the general direction of the group of disguised Confederates, he had time to fire off a single bullet before being felled by two more shots.

Pearson let out a sharp cry of pain. The bullet smacked into his belly just below the left side of his ribcage. He fell to the ground even as the Union major tumbled from his horse.

"No!" McFadden cried as he rushed to Pearson's side. Having seen the wound when it had happened, he instantly sensed that it would be mortal. Wounds to the belly usually were, although it sometimes took a long time for the victim to die. As it was, Pearson was still alive and conscious, frantically tearing at his shirt to try and determine where he had been hit.

"Is it bad, Lieutenant?" he asked fearfully. "Is it bad?"

"You'll be all right," McFadden said, trying to sound reassuring.

Pearson's teeth clenched in pain. "You're no good at lying, McFadden."

"Okay, it's bad."

"Leave me here, then. Keep going with that bomb."

McFadden almost chuckled, for he had never heard Pearson say an unselfish thing in his life. He helped Pearson get his shirt off and saw the entry wound. As he had feared, it had all the signs of a mortal wound. Most likely it had struck his left kidney, possibly severing an artery, or more than one, while it did so. He wadded up Pearson's shirt and gently pressed it against the wound in an attempt to staunch the flow of blood.

It took a few moments before McFadden realized that Maddox was speaking to the other men.

"You!" Maddox said sharply, pointing to a specific soldier. "Run back to the hospital quick as you can and come back with a stretcher! If they ask, just tell them that the major has been hit! Act like you know what you're doing and speak normally! They'll not suspect you unless you give them reason!"

The man nodded, set his rifle down, and took off down the path back the way they had come.

"Take off those Yankee uniforms!" Maddox said to the rest of the men. "They'll be here any moment, drawn by the gunfire. Head off in that direction." He pointed to the woods to the east. "We'll stay here with Private Pearson."

McFadden only half heard this, intent on trying to do something for Pearson. Conceivably, they could carry him back to the Yankee hospital. But would they treat him, assuming his identity as a rebel infiltrator were discovered? Even if they did, was there anything any doctor could do for Pearson?

The rest of the men had thrown off their Yankee uniforms, revealing their gray Confederate garb beneath. As ordered by Maddox, they quickly set off at a jog into the woods to the east, being lost to sight after two or three minutes. In the meantime, Maddox was hurriedly removing the uniform coat of the Union major, which was splattered with blood.

Pearson faded into unconsciousness, but the continuing rise and fall of his chest told McFadden that he was still alive. Although it was uncommon, sometimes men survived such grievous wounds. The hope glimmered in McFadden's heart that Pearson had a chance. Pearson had saved McFadden's life at the Battle of East Point, so McFadden felt honor-bound to do what he could to save Pearson's.

A few minutes later, the soldier dispatched by Maddox returned with a stretcher. Maddox gave him the same instructions he had given to the others: remove his Union uniform and flee into the woods to the east.

"What are you doing?" McFadden finally asked, distracting himself from Pearson for just a moment.

"The other men will create a diversion for us. We'll load your man Pearson on this stretcher wearing the major's uniform and continue north. No one will stop two Union soldiers carrying a wounded officer."

"What?!" McFadden shouted. "You sent them away as bait?"

"It was the most logical course of action."

"You bastard!" McFadden spat. "They'll be killed!"

"They might be okay," Maddox said calmly. "They will likely be taken prisoner. Some might even make it back to Atlanta."

Anger filled McFadden. He drew his sword, intent on running Maddox through. He had taken him for a bloody-minded murderer from the moment he had met him. He had obviously not cared a damn that innocent people had been killed when he had destroyed the ship at City Point. He had even seemed to delight in the fact. Now, he had tricked nearly a dozen brave Confederate soldiers, half of them members of McFadden's beloved Texas Brigade, to almost certain capture or death. Moreover, he was proposing to use Pearson as a human decoy rather than taking him to the nearest hospital.

As he stepped forward, Maddox surprised him by showing no sign of fear. Indeed, he smiled, as though McFadden had just invited him for a drink.

"Oh, put the sword away, Lieutenant. We have more important things to worry about. We need to find a good target for this bomb."

"You're a damn, lying bastard who doesn't deserve to live."

"Why do you say that? I'm just the same as you, Lieutenant McFadden. Cleburne's staff officers told me all about you. They say you're a berserker in battle. That you may have killed more Yankees than any other man in the Army of Tennessee. That you refused promotion for more than a year because you thought being an officer would keep you from killing the enemy. You and I are very much alike."

"Shut the hell up," McFadden said.

Having finally removed the Union major's uniform, Maddox stood up. Looking into his dark and empty eyes, McFadden suddenly saw deeper into the man, as if he were opening a door and briefly allowing McFadden to see inside. The man standing before him was a killer, not a warrior. The killing of other human beings was the entirety of his purpose in life. McFadden had killed more men than he cared to remember, but for him killing was either a duty or a desperate attempt to smother his own rage. Maddox was very different. He was a man who killed for the sheer pleasure of killing. In short, a demon.

Although he was brandishing his sword and Maddox had made no move toward either of his own weapons, McFadden felt fear. Although he was a seasoned combat veteran, he sensed instinctively that Maddox could kill him in a hundred different ways so quickly that McFadden would not even realize he was being attacked before he was dead. If that happened, Maddox would just light his pipe once again and continue the mission on his own, feeling no more remorse about killing McFadden than he would have felt after ringing a chicken's neck.

"You and I have been given an assignment by General Cleburne," Maddox said. "Are you going to help me or not?"

McFadden hesitated. He did not want to have anything more to do with Maddox, but abandoning the mission would mean breaking his word to Cleburne.

Maddox sensed his mental disarray. "McFadden, what do you have to live for? They tell me that you have no family. They tell me that your woman was killed by the Yankee bombardment. The Confederacy is what you live for now. That and revenge."

McFadden wanted to tell Maddox that he hated the Confederacy, that he hated slavery, that he hated secession, that he hated the war. He wanted to say that he didn't want revenge, that he simply wanted to forget everything that had happened over the past few years and somehow find a way to go home. However, what Maddox was saying was undeniable. McFadden realized that he was irretrievably trapped. He remembered the conversation he had observed between Cleburne and McPherson out between the front lines and realized that Cleburne was trapped, too.

His mind spun again. Maddox was right. McFadden was with the Confederacy, right or wrong. He had laid his cards down on the table the moment he had joined the Southern army. He had killed dozens of Northern soldiers, he had taken George Thomas prisoner, he had saved Atlanta by warning Cleburne of Grant's approach. It was far too late for him to go back now. Whatever future his life held, and however long he lived, he had to live for the Confederacy.

Maddox's eyes arched up inquisitively. "Are you going to help me or not?" he asked again.

McFadden didn't respond with words, but slowly sheathed his sword.

Maddox smiled. "Good. I didn't want to have to kill you."

Without any further exchange of words, McFadden and Maddox propped Pearson's unconscious body up, took off the private's uniform coat he had been wearing and replaced it with the coat of the major. They were just placing his body on the stretcher when a squad of Union infantry trotted up at the double quick.

"Dear God!" a sergeant said, looking at the bodies strewn about. "What happened here?"

"Rebels!" Maddox responded quickly, the tension in his voice so convincing that McFadden almost believed him. "Must be some sort of raiding party. They took off that way!" He pointed into the eastern woods.

"How many?"

"Six or seven, maybe? If you can flush them out, we'll get the major to the hospital."

The sergeant nodded sharply, then barked orders to his men, who quickly spread out into a skirmish line and vanished into the trees.

"Listen," Maddox said in a vaguely menacing tone as soon as the Yankees were out of earshot. "We'll take your man on this stretcher northwest toward the bridge. That will be where the bigger supply depots are located. Nobody is going to stop two men carrying a wounded officer on a stretcher."

"Makes sense," McFadden responded. No matter how he felt about what was going on, he was committed to it.

"Very well. Let's go."

*   *   *   *   *

September 29, Morning

Johnston couldn't gallop. In fact, he couldn't even canter, so thick were the trees. At times he was able to kick Fleetfoot into a trot, but for most of his ride westward he was limited to walking his horse. His inability to go faster was extremely frustrating. He was desperate to return to his headquarters as quickly as possible.

He hadn't needed the arrival of couriers from Cheatham to tell him that something had gone wrong on the left flank. There had been the sudden crash of artillery and heavy musketry, indicating a sudden outburst of fighting. As he had not given Cheatham any orders but to hold his ground, Johnston assumed that Grant must have launched a powerful attack on the left. This had caught the Confederate commander, who was expecting his opponent to follow the same strategy as the previous day, by surprise.

Johnston had been waiting with General Stewart on the right, ready to spring the ambush he had planned for the moment when McPherson and the Army of the Tennessee resumed their attack on his right. During the night, General Clayton's division had quietly and carefully taken up a position in the thick woods just to the north and east of the main line of Stewart's corps. From there, they would be perfectly placed to crash into the left flank of McPherson's divisions the moment they moved forward to attack the Confederate line. Stopped in their tracks by Stewart's corps and then struck in their flank by Clayton's division, the Army of the Tennessee might be shattered.

What Johnston had not expected was such aggressiveness on the part of the Army of the Cumberland. Having beaten off some half-hearted attacks the previous day, Cheatham had told Johnston that he envisioned no difficulty maintaining his position this day as well. In fact, he had shown no hesitation in dispatching Clayton's division to the right flank to serve as the ambush force. It now appeared that this might have been a mistake, potentially a fatal mistake.

Johnston reined in a few yards from the farmhouse door and dropped quickly from his saddle. He jogged inside and saw Mackall and half a dozen other staff officers huddled over a map. Two couriers who Johnston recognized as being from Cheatham's staff stood nearby, having just arrived with news.

"What is happening on the left?" Johnston asked loudly, storming inside.

Mackall scarcely looked up from the table. "They caught us flat-footed, I'm afraid. Just before dawn, a whole Yankee corps crashed into the left flank of Stevenson's division. They folded like a house of cards, it seems."

"Surely Stevenson left a brigade in reserve!" Johnston protested.

Mackall nodded quickly. "Palmer's Tennessee Brigade. They had just launched a counter attack when these couriers left Cheatham to report to us. No word on the results."

Johnston shook his head. One brigade could not hope to stop an entire enemy corps. At best, they might slow it down long enough for the rest of Stevenson's division to reform. How much time the counter attack might buy was anyone's guess. Johnston didn't think it would be more than an hour at most.

Mackall leaned forward. "Sir, begging the general's pardon, but perhaps we should recall Clayton's division to the left flank? If the Yankees continue to drive forward, they will eventually roll up the entire line."

He considered this. The attacking enemy corps were driving from west to east. Unless the Confederate dispositions were changed radically and quickly, the Union forces would be able to concentrate all their combat power against only a small portion of the Confederate forces at a time. If they continued to push forward, the entire Southern army would be routed.

The scenario that Johnston had most feared was now on the verge of becoming reality. Grant seemed poised to win a decisive tactical victory over the Army of Tennessee. If he succeeded, he could wreck the Confederate army as an effective fighting force, at least for a few weeks. If that happened, the fall of Atlanta was mere days away.

"Dispatch an immediate message to General Cheatham," Johnston said determinedly. "He is to refuse his line at a right angle to its current position, facing to the west, with the point of connection with Stewart's corps serving as the hinge. General Palmer's brigade will fight a delaying action to give the rest of the corps time to fall back."

Mackall and the other staff officers were hurriedly taking all this down. Johnston's orders would pull back Cheatham's corps like a door swinging on its hinges, transforming the position of the Army of Tennessee from a straight line facing north to a right angle, with one half of the army facing west and the other half facing north. The line facing west would be completely unfortified and expected to withstand an assault by many times their number.

"And Clayton's division?" Mackall asked.

An icy grip seized Johnston's heart. Pulling Clayton's division back from its ambush position and sending it to reinforce the left would be the reasonable thing to do. Johnston had always been a reasonable general, cautious and never rash. Even his great attack at Peachtree Creek had only been undertaken after very careful consideration and preparation, with all possible contingencies having been taken into account beforehand.

If Clayton were recalled to reinforce the left, the situation could probably be stabilized and the Union advance brought to a halt. But Johnston would certainly have to abandon his position during the night, for his left flank was obviously shattered and the favorable terrain on the ridge compromised. He would probably have to retreat to the southeast. Having driven Johnston away, Grant might easily march back north and resume the assault on Atlanta.

Caution made perfect sense on a certain level. Still, Johnston could also see that the final outcome would be unfavorable, if not disastrous, to the cause he served. Therefore, perhaps the situation called for something other than caution. He thought for a moment of Robert E. Lee, his old friend, classmate and comrade in the Mexican War, for whom he nursed a silent but intense envy even while holding him in the highest respect. Had Lee been cautious at Second Manassas or Chancellorsville?

"Leave Clayton's division in place," Johnston suddenly said firmly. "McPherson will advance shortly, in support of Howard's attack. Our plan for striking his left flank as he advances is as valid now as it was yesterday evening."

Mackall's eyes widened in surprise. Nevertheless, he nodded. "Very well, sir."

"Has there been any word from Stewart's lines?"

"The Yankees on his front are pushing forward skirmishers, but no serious attack has been mounted."

Johnston nodded quickly. "Tell him to select a brigade and send it to Cheatham's assistance at once."

"Yes, sir."

Johnston knew he was taking a great gamble. One brigade of reinforcements would not be enough to stop the juggernaut of the Army of the Cumberland. It would help slow them down and give Cheatham's corps time to reform its lines. If McPherson did not attack in the next few hours, however, his gamble might prove disastrous.

*　　　*　　　*　　　*　　　*

September 29, Noon

Grant listened to the reports coming in from the division commanders of the Army of the Cumberland. The situation at the front was very confused, with units becoming intermingled and losing their sense of direction in the thick woods. Communication was proving very difficult.

Amidst the muddled reports, it was becoming increasingly clear that the Union forces were pushing forward, driving the rebels back in disarray. Large numbers of prisoners had been taken and it appeared that the rebels were having difficulty reordering their lines to meet the attack.

Grant nodded as Howard finished summarizing the latest report from the front.

"This is good news, Howard," he said slowly. "I don't want the boys to get too disorganized, though. If Johnston has a division in reserve and is able to launch a counter attack with our forces in such disarray, we could quickly lose all the ground we have gained. I saw it happen in the Wilderness."

"Agreed," Howard said simply.

"Send word to your division commanders to halt where they are and reform their lines. You also must ensure that their ammunition is replenished and that batteries are brought forward to those points where clearings in the woods make the use of artillery possible."

"Very good, sir."

Grant checked his pocket watch. "It is twelve thirty. I want the reorientation done within two hours. At three o'clock, the attack shall resume."

"The rebels will use the time to bring forward reinforcements and reform their own lines," Howard pointed out.

"I know. When your attack goes in again, McPherson shall strike the rebel right. Having struck them a heavy blow already today, we have no doubt shaken the rebel army. A swift attack on both flanks may now crush them altogether."

Sending McPherson forward was obviously the best course of action. Grant assumed that Johnston was even then stripping units from his right to reinforce the left. A powerful attack by the Army of the Tennessee could break through the lines where they had been repulsed the day before, even if the fortifications were stronger. If McPherson could break the rebels on his front while Howard continued pushing forward on the other side of the battlefield, the rebels would be caught between two overwhelming Union forces. If things went well, the Army of Tennessee might be destroyed. At the very least, it would be driven away from Atlanta in a bloody rout, ruined as a fighting force.

Grant turned to one of his aides. "Is anything happening around Atlanta?"

"No, sir. The rebels opened fire with their artillery this morning and launched some trench raids, but nothing serious."

Grant frowned. The two corps he had left behind to hold the siege lines around Atlanta had been those which had suffered the heaviest casualties in the recent fighting. Still, he assumed that they were sufficient to keep Cleburne's men pinned down inside the city and prevent them from providing any aid to Johnston.

Cleburne was a wily Irishman who needed to be treated with extreme caution. However, having suffered such heavy losses in the recent fighting and with his survivors no doubt exhausted, what could Cleburne do to affect the outcome of the battle? Grant assumed that the artillery barrage and raids had been an attempt to distract Grant's attention from Johnston. Well, he was not about to fall for such a trick. Cautious fools like McClellan might be taken in by such ploys, but not Grant. Like a bulldog, he had his teeth fixed upon Joe Johnston and he would now tear him to pieces, come hell or high water.

*   *   *   *   *

September 29, Noon

Pearson was still unconscious but alive as McFadden and Maddox carried his stretcher northwest toward the Western and Atlantic Railroad bridge. As Maddox had anticipated, no one hindered their progress. As far as any of the Yankees could tell, the wounded man lying in the stretcher was a Union officer and the two men with him were carrying him to a hospital. No one recognized the terrible danger that had just entered their midst.

McFadden could see that Maddox had been correct in his prediction that the Union supply depots would get larger the closer they got to the river. On both sides of the railroad track, they passed by dozens of wagons parked side by side, all of them packed with crates containing war material. Some were clearly marked as ammunition wagons, while others carried foodstuffs or footgear.

Scores of artillery pieces sat together in assembly areas to either side of the railroad. McFadden found this surprising, as he would have expected all available artillery to have either gone with Grant southwards to take part in the battle against Johnston or to have been deployed against the defenses of Atlanta. In the Confederate Army, every available gun had long since been pressed into frontline service. Seeing such vast Union firepower waiting quietly in reserve demonstrated to McFadden yet again the immense material superiority of the enemy.

Union soldiers milled about, talking amiably and sharing cigars. Many were unarmed, leaning against trees a considerable distance away from their stacked arms. It was apparent that the last thing any of them expected was the appearance of the enemy.

"Plenty of good spots for our bomb," Maddox said quietly, glancing about like a hungry man in a meat market. "If I can get it into one of those ammunition depots, hide it behind a crate or something, the whole place will go up like Mount Vesuvius."

"But we're carrying a wounded man," McFadden protested. "If we set him down and start puttering around in an ammunition depot, it will look suspicious."

"True. We might as well find a place to set him down, then go about our business."

"A hospital, you mean."

Maddox shrugged, indicating his utter lack of concern for Pearson's life.

"He's one of my men. We will leave him at a hospital. There is bound to be one nearby."

"It would appear strange if we left him anywhere else."

"What are you talking about?" Pearson asked weakly.

McFadden was jolted by the sound of his voice. Quickly motioning for Maddox to put the stretcher on the ground, he quickly cradled his hands behind Pearson's head.

"We're taking you to a Yankee hospital. You'll be all right."

"Better you keep me with you."

He shook his head. "No. If you don't get to a doctor soon, you'll die."

"You need me for your disguise. If you're not carrying my stretcher, someone will stop you sooner or later. And when they find the bomb, you'll be shot as a spy."

"Your man is right," Maddox said. "The longer we continue to carry him, the longer we shall not attract the notice of the enemy."

"I'm dead, anyway," Pearson said. "Won't last another hour. You know that." As if to emphasize his words, Pearson coughed roughly, blood trickling out the corners of his mouth. "Better my death be useful."

The sharp sound of a train's steam whistle pierced the air. McFadden was distracted from his tormented thoughts by the noise. Had the Yankees managed to rebuild the railroad bridge since securing control of the ground northwest of Atlanta? If his memory served, the rebels had burned the bridge when they had withdrawn from the north bank of the Chattahoochee back in July, but the massive stone support pillars were still standing. The Yankee railroad engineers had progressively rebuilt the Atlantic and Western Railroad as they had slowly advanced south from Chattanooga. The capabilities of their engineers were legendary, so McFadden supposed they might have been able to build a bridge over the surviving structure and lay railroad track across it.

He felt uneasy. He looked around at the vast amounts of war material all around him, the artillery, the ammunition, the immense piles of food and fodder. All of it had been brought across the Chattahoochee by boat or pontoon bridge. If the Yankees had succeeded in rebuilding a railroad bridge over the river, they would be able to bring forward vastly greater quantities of men and material.

"Let's carry Pearson north toward the bridge," Maddox said. "If the Yankees have trains coming across the river, better we target it for destruction rather than an ammunition depot."

"Sure," McFadden said skeptically. "But fifteen pounds of gunpowder will scarcely put a dent in a bridge. Any damage that is done will probably be repaired by the Yankees in less than an hour." McFadden stomping an ant pile to pieces when he was a child; returning twenty minutes later, he had found the ants hard at work putting it all back together.

"We'll find a way," Maddox said with determination.

*   *   *   *   *

September 29, Afternoon

Leaving Mackall to direct things at the headquarters as best he could, Johnston had swiftly departed as soon as he had finished issuing the orders for the new dispositions Cheatham's corps was to take on the left flank. Now, he was flying back to Stewart's corps on the right flank as swiftly as Fleetfoot could carry him. He took with him only a single color bearer and a handful of couriers.

The Army of the Cumberland had stopped its advance, at least momentarily. This shouldn't have been unexpected, but it nevertheless had taken Johnston by surprise. His worst fear was that Howard's divisions would simply keep driving on, rolling up the entire line of the Army of Tennessee from west to east. When battle took place in such heavily wooded terrain, it was inevitable that any attacking force would find its organization in disarray after a few hours of fighting. Grant had obviously ordered a temporary halt to the attack so as to allow Howard some time to reorder his formations and resupply his men with ammunition.

The realities of fighting a battle in the midst of a pine wilderness had provided Johnston with a priceless hour of time. Cheatham was reforming his two divisions into a new line facing west rather than north, while a brigade of reinforcements from Stewart's corps was arriving to shore up the line. Johnston had also ordered his reserve artillery batteries into the nearby clearings, from which they could lob shells into the general area through which the Yankees would now have to advance. When the Union attack resumed, he hoped his forces would be able to present a stronger resistance than they had earlier.

Johnston could see things from Grant's perspective as well as his own. It would be obvious to Grant that Johnston would use the momentary halt to restore order to his own lines. Consequently, when the attack resumed, it would need additional support. Grant would also want to ensure that the Southerners would be unable to dispatch troops from their right to shore up their left. Because of this, Johnston was certain that the Army of the Tennessee would be sent forward in a supporting assault at the same time the Army of the Cumberland resumed its attack.

Clayton's division, four thousand tough warriors, remained concealed in the heavy woods just northeast of Stewart's corps. As far as Johnston could tell, the Yankees were unaware of their presence. They had made no effort to push skirmishers into the area, for they knew that the broken ground and small rivulets made it poor terrain to push through if they wanted to get around the Confederate flank. Grant's mind was so fixed on attacking the Army of Tennessee that he had not considered the possibility that the Army of Tennessee might attack him.

Johnston reached Stewart's headquarters. As he dismounted, several men sprang forward for the honor of holding Fleetfoot's reins. He strode immediately into the command tent.

"Well?" Johnston asked as Stewart saluted.

"You were right, General," the corps commander answered with a smile. "The picket line has sent back word that McPherson's men are forming for a major attack."

"Excellent!" Johnston exclaimed, unable to keep the delight out of his voice. He restrained himself, embarrassed at exhibiting such an emotional display in front of the men. "Clayton's division is ready?"

Stewart nodded. "Yes, sir. His last report came in an hour ago. A few Yankee skirmishers were feeling their way into the woods, but were held back by his picket line. Nothing in the dispositions of the Army of the Tennessee leads me to believe that the Yankees are aware of his presence."

Johnston thought quickly. He remembered the fiasco at Cassville, where a similar plan of ambush had come to nothing because Hood had pulled back the attacking force at the critical moment. Of course, Johnston had since become convinced that Hood had deliberately botched the attack, but that wasn't important now. Hood could no longer trouble him, being far away on the other side of the Mississippi River. Clayton was an efficient and patriotic officer, the antithesis of John Bell Hood. He could be counted upon.

Still, the memory of Cassville haunted Johnston. He might rightly blame Hood, but he also could admit to himself that the ambush might have still succeeded had he provided closer supervision to the operation.

"I shall go to Clayton myself," Johnston said.

Stewart's eyes betrayed only a hint of surprise. "Of course, sir. I shall provide a guide to lead you directly to him."

Five minutes later, having hurriedly discussed the position of Stewart's corps to face the coming assault, Johnston was back in the saddle. He trotted eastward as quickly as he could, until he reached the right flank of Stewart's line. Then, led by Stewart's guide, he turned north into the deep forest. It took twenty frustrating minutes, but he soon arrived at Clayton's makeshift divisional headquarters, which consisted of a mere two tents with a medium-size table set up between them.

"General Johnston!" Clayton said, snapping to attention and giving a salute. "I did not expect to see you here."

"I hope I am not intruding?" Johnston said as he dropped out of the saddle.

"Not at all. Has there been a change in my orders?"

"No. You are to attack the enemy flank the moment his advance movement crosses your front. It is all just as we discussed last night."

Clayton nodded sharply. With such simple orders, it would not have been unusual for a Confederate division commander to resent the presence of the army commander, especially in as touchy an outfit as the Army of Tennessee. As a grown man might resent the presence of his father at his workplace, the subordinate might assume the visit indicated a lack of confidence. Johnston hoped that this was not the case with Clayton, but could not think of any tactful or appropriate way to ask.

There was a sudden increase in the tempo of artillery fire in the distance. Johnston's experienced ears listened to the high-pitched ringing sound and realized the cannon being fired were Confederate. The guns he had sent to reinforce Cheatham had presumably opened up against the Army of the Cumberland. This meant either that the

Union attack had been resumed or that the Southern artillerymen assumed that it was about to.

"Your men are ready?"

A mischievous grin crossed Clayton's face. "They are ready and eager for the fight, General." He gestured toward the woods just ahead of the command post.

Johnston looked, and saw through the trees a thick line of men, some standing and some kneeling on the ground. All gripped their muskets tightly, looking forward toward the ground over which they expected to soon advance. The hundreds of men in his field of vision were but a small part of Clayton's division, stretched in a line half a mile long. He considered going before them to speak words of encouragement, but he knew that the appearance of the commanding general might induce the men to cheer. The sounds thus created might serve as a warning to the Yankees that they were about to be attacked.

There was another crash of artillery fire, this time much closer. Several cannon fired all at once. He heard the distinct ringing sound of Southern gunpowder as well as the lower booming sound of Yankee guns, meaning that a gigantic artillery duel was taking place. From the closeness of the fire, it could only be between Stewart's corps and McPherson's army. Clearly, the Yankee attack was about to happen.

Half an hour passed. A captain rode breathlessly up to Clayton's command post.

"The Yankees are coming, sir!" he said hurriedly, trying to catch his breath. "I think every damn Yankee south of the Ohio River is on the move, heading straight for Stewart's line." He stiffened and saluted when he noticed General Johnston.

"Are any of them coming into these woods?" Clayton asked.

"Some skirmishers deployed as flankers, but the picket line is holding them back."

"How many flankers?"

"Not many. Maybe a regiment."

Johnston thought quickly. McPherson was a good soldier and would have tried to get some idea of whether there was any enemy presence in the woods to his left. However, if he was only sending in a regiment, at most a few hundred men, he obviously didn't consider the matter very urgent. Clearly, he wanted to concentrate all of his strength in the assault on Stewart's line.

"How long before the Yankee advance is bestride our battle line?"

"Less than fifteen minutes, sir."

Johnston tried to imagine the situation from the point of view of a bird which could see through the foliage. McPherson's army was arrayed in a battle line running from east to west, advancing southwards toward Stewart's similarly set line. The Southerners

- 730 -

were fortified on the ridge, but the Yankees were counting on their superior numbers to break through. This advantage had been increased by the need to send reinforcements from Stewart to Cheatham in order to shore up the shattered Confederate left flank. In any case, McPherson's main objective was merely to pin Stewart down and prevent him from sending any further help to Cheatham. Grant was clearly intending to win the battle with a further attack by Howard against Cheatham. The Yankees did not know the position or intention of Clayton's division, which was Johnston's ace in the hole.

He waited. Soon, the sounds of Yankee artillery faded, which meant that their gunners assumed the infantry was getting so close to the Confederate lines that continuing to fire might risk hitting their own men. It was impossible to tell through the woods. The sound of Southern artillery fire went right on, however. The Yankees were obviously getting closer to the front line.

"Shall I move forward?" Clayton asked.

Johnston shook his head. It was not yet time. He wanted the Yankees to impact on Stewart's line before unleashing Clayton. That would provide the added psychological shock that could throw the entire Army of the Tennessee into rout. Yet every minute that passed was another minute in which the enemy could discover the presence of Clayton's division.

"I'll speak to your men, if you please?" Johnston said.

"Of course, General."

Johnston clambered back into his saddle and, taking the reins, clicked Fleetfoot into a slow walk. He passed between two companies of men and turned to face the entire line. In his field of vision, he could see a few hundred men. He was comforted to know that there were thousands more beyond the obscuration of the trees. The troops he could see were all Georgians and they gave him a single hearty cheer when they saw him. Considering the fighting going on, Johnston was not concerned any longer about the noise. The attack would go in shortly in any event.

He stood up in his stirrups and held his hat high. "Men of Georgia! The eyes of the Confederacy are upon you! The eyes of the world are upon you! Will you be wanting in courage at this moment?"

"No!" came the roaring response from hundreds of throats.

"When you go forward, I want you to give those Yankees cold steel!" Johnston yelled. "We can break the enemy army! We can break them! Here and now, we can break them! We have caught the enemy in a position where we can shatter them! With God's help, we can drive the enemy from our soil and send these Yankees fleeing back across the Ohio River where they belong!"

The men cheered. It wasn't merely a polite cheer such as soldiers might give a routine speech, but a cheer from the deepest recesses of their hearts. It was as if an electrical storm were breaking out in the woods around Clayton's division. Johnston felt his face flush and breath quicken. Fleetfoot sensed the emotional commotion, neighing loudly and momentarily rearing up on his two back feet before Johnston got him back under control.

"This will be the decisive battle of the war!" Johnston roared. "On it shall depend all our hopes for independence! If we win, all of our cherished dreams may come to pass! Go forward, you men of the South! Go forward and free our nation!"

The men cheered again, louder this time. They believed him. More importantly, they trusted him. Johnston felt as though the fervor of his soldiers was infusing him with energy. Part of him wanted to recoil from it, the way a child instinctively yanks his hand away from a fire. Another part of him could not help but lustily embrace it. Johnston felt the earth falling away beneath his feet, as though something were carrying him into the sky.

He stood up in the stirrups again and waved his hat, causing the cheering to rise to a tumultuous crescendo. He kicked Fleetfoot into a quick trot and dashed back behind the lines. Nodding quickly to General Clayton, Johnston heard a series of shouted orders. Within seconds, the men of Clayton's division stepped forward, led by their officers, the faces of the men filled with determination. Johnston rode slowly behind them, not wanting to interfere with Clayton's command but wanting to watch the attack go in. He also issued quick orders to a courier to race to General Stewart's headquarters and inform him that the attack had begun. He wanted to minimize the risk of Stewart's men accidentally firing into Clayton's division.

The troops went forward slowly at first, advancing at a walk until they had cleared the thickest part of the woods. Then the officers begin shouting orders for them to advance at the quick step. The movement forward accelerated, but Johnston still saw no Union infantry in his field of vision. The sound of musket fire crackled loudly throughout the woods, but he couldn't be sure if this was coming from the fighting between the Yankees and Stewart's line or if some of Clayton's troops had made contact with the enemy immediately upon attacking. A few minutes into the attack, the woods cleared sufficiently for the officers to order their men to advance at the double quick.

Suddenly, emerging into his field of vision through the trees as though from a fog, Johnston spotted Union infantry. He couldn't tell how large a formation it was, but they were desperately trying to turn about to face the unexpected attack of Clayton's men. It was no use. The Confederate officers ordered their men to open fire, and a few well-delivered volleys cut the bluecoats down. The return fire was confused and light, but still accounted for some Southern soldiers falling, dead or wounded.

There was firing off to the north as well, and Johnston knew that it could only be coming from Clayton's other brigades. Contact with the Yankees was being made all up and down the line and the Confederates were driving forward. Johnston was elated. His flank attack had caught the enemy exactly in the manner he had planned.

He had walked Fleetfoot forward, trailing two dozen yards behind the advancing infantry. There were more Yankees ahead, trying to form themselves into battle lines, and the Georgia troops were shrieking the Rebel Yell as they pitched into them. The forward momentum was clear, like an avalanche tumbling down a mountainside.

Johnston turned back and rode over to General Clayton, who was advancing on foot behind his own troops.

"You seem to have everything under control, General Clayton," Johnston said with a smile.

"Indeed, I do, sir!"

"Good. I shall leave you now and ride to Stewart. Push the enemy as hard as you can. Do not let up for an instant."

"We will drive them all the way to the Great Lakes if you tell us to, sir!"

Johnston saluted and kicked Fleetfoot into a trot, heading south. The guide previously provided by Stewart led him back to the corps commander's headquarters, for he wanted to consult with Stewart as quickly as possible.

During the twenty minutes it took to ride to Stewart's headquarters, the sound of battle to the north massively increased. Obviously, Clayton's division was now heavily engaged and pushing the Yankees back. Johnston noted that the sound of Yankee artillery fire had sharply diminished, which meant that the batteries were either being overrun or that the Yankee gunners were repositioning to open fire on Clayton. He prayed that it was the former rather than the latter.

Johnston reined in at Stewart's headquarters. He didn't bother to dismount, since he wanted to be off to see General Cheatham as soon as he spoke with Stewart. The corps commander dashed out of his tent as soon as an aide told him of the commanding general's arrival.

"Clayton has gone in!" Johnston shouted.

"Very good, sir!"

"The attack was making good progress when I departed half an hour ago. As Clayton's division advances, it will push the Yankees away from the line of your corps. Like a broom sweeping away debris, you see? As the front of each successive brigade is cleared, you shall advance the said brigade north, wheel to the left, and advance to reinforce Clayton. You understand what I mean, General?"

Stewart's eyes reflected fast and intense thought. He nodded sharply. "Yes, sir!"

"Good. I shall ride to Cheatham now! And make sure your artillery fire does not fall on Clayton's men!"

The two generals exchanged salutes.   Johnston jabbed
Fleetfoot in the belly with his spurs, and the commander of the Army
of Tennessee was off again, still trailed by his color bearer and staff
officers.

*   *   *   *   *

As they had continued northwest, the number of Union men
had remained relatively constant but the number of armed soldiers
had actually decreased. Well over half of the people McFadden could
see were unarmed railroad engineers or other people involved in
logistics in one way or another. There were still hundreds of armed
Union guards scattered about, but none of them seemed particularly
alert.

Still, McFadden was worried. They had not seen anything
resembling a hospital for the last hour and it had occurred to him that
the subterfuge of carrying a wounded man in a stretcher was
becoming increasingly tenuous. If any notice were to be taken of them
by an officer, or even an astute common soldier, they would be
directed to the nearest place where the wounded man could receive
medical treatment. If they did not go there immediately, suspicions
would inevitably be aroused, their mission would fail, and he and
Maddox would probably both be shot as spies.

They set the stretcher down at a spot somewhat more heavily
wooded. Although there were several blue-coated soldiers within
view, none of them were looking at the trio of Southerners.

"We should leave your man here and continue on without
him," Maddox said simply.

McFadden looked down at Pearson, who had again lapsed into
unconsciousness but was still breathing. He still believed that the
wound he had sustained was almost certainly mortal, but could not be
entirely sure.

"We should go back to one of the hospitals, then."

"No time. It's already after four o'clock. If we're going to
accomplish our mission, we need to do it in the next few hours."

It had not occurred to McFadden until that very moment that
they would still be within the Union lines when night fell. Even if
they started back for Atlanta right away, which they could not do as
they had not yet placed the bomb, they would not have enough time to
reach it. The sun would set in perhaps three hours and it would be
impossible to navigate back to the city through the woods.

Even assuming that they successfully deployed the horological
torpedo and escaped the detonation, they would have to find a place to
hide during the night. Presumably the Yankees would be searching
for them, but even in the rear areas of the Union army there were
vast woods in which a man might conceal himself. How could they do
that with Pearson on the stretcher?

- 734 -

"Wake up, McFadden," Maddox said harshly. "Pearson has served his purpose in getting us this far. It's time to leave him behind."

McFadden glared up at Maddox but said nothing.

"There's no help that you can give him, anyway," Maddox said. "If anything, carting him around on the stretcher is making his death more likely. Better that he be allowed to lie somewhere still."

McFadden did not want to abandon Pearson. He had saved McFadden's life and, with Montgomery unaccounted for, was the last fellow survivor of the Lone Star Rifles. Although he had disliked Pearson intensely for most of the war, the idea of giving him up now seemed to McFadden like abandoning the company in which he had fought so many battles and faced death so many times. It would not just be abandoning Pearson, but turning his back on every other member of the company, the closest thing he had had to friends over the past few years. Had it not been for the men of the Lone Star Rifles, and the 7th Texas Infantry as a whole, McFadden was certain that his grief and rage would long since have pushed him over the edge into insanity.

McFadden saw Maddox watching him carefully. He noticed that the clandestine operative always kept his right hand free, which could allow him to pull his revolver out of its holster without any warning. This could simply have been a precaution against the sudden appearance of enemy soldiers, but McFadden also sensed that Maddox was just as likely to use his weapon on him.

"We have our mission, McFadden. Let's not let Cleburne down."

He glanced back up at Maddox, who was still looking intently down at him. For the first time, McFadden thought he detected a hint of hesitation and uncertainty in the murderer's eyes. That reassured him.

"We'll leave Pearson here," McFadden said carefully. "But only on the condition that we come back and get him after we have placed your bomb. Then, we all go back to Atlanta together. Agreed?"

Maddox arched his head slightly upwards for just a moment, then nodded.

"How long does that clock on your device run before the bomb explodes?"

"About half an hour, give or take."

"Fine. Let's go."

They walked without a word toward the river, which was a half mile to the north. A few hundred yards off to their left were the tracks of the Western and Atlantic Railroad, which they used as their guide to lead them toward the bridge. As there were still innumerable Yankees moving about, McFadden felt more vulnerable. Guards who would not have stopped two men carrying a wounded officer were more likely to stop two soldiers moving about at random.

Maddox appeared unconcerned, grinning like a schoolboy as they continued their trek. He obviously relished the thought of the mass slaughter he was about to unleash. McFadden wished he had kept a stern expression, as his foolish smile was more likely to catch the eye of a Yankee soldier than a completely blank face.

The sound of a steam whistle broke over the land once again, much closer this time. McFadden realized that whatever train was emitting the noise had to be on the south bank of the Chattahoochee.

"Interesting," Maddox said. "Not only have the Yankees completed laying tracks over the bridge, but they've already started running trains over them."

"Perhaps we should have a look," McFadden said, thinking aloud. "If we can plant the bomb in the locomotive, it would put a crimp in Grant's logistics."

Maddox snorted. "A minor one," he said dismissively. "How many locomotives do you think the Yankees have? Scores of them. Maybe over a hundred. Wrecking just one of them won't cause Grant more than a minute's concern."

"You have a better idea?"

"I think we should stick to the original plan of placing the infernal device in an ammunition depot. That would be the way to cause the most damage, I would think."

"Perhaps the train is carrying ammunition?" McFadden said. "Didn't you think of that?"

Maddox's eyes narrowed. "That is a possibility."

"If it is, and if we place the infernal device inside of it, we could wreck a Yankee train and destroy a large amount of ammunition at the same time."

Maddox nodded. "Yes, you're right. It's worth looking into, at any rate."

"Come on, then."

They started to the west. They spent several minutes passing through an area of heavy vegetation before they emerged into an opening completely devoid of trees. Trains habitually set off a large amount of sparks as they traveled, which often caused fires in dry brush. As a result, the state government of Georgia had mandated that the area for several hundred yards on either side of the railroad be cleared of any vegetation that might provide kindling for wildfires. It was as though they had emerged from a cave into the bright light of day.

Sitting on the tracks, with steam still rising from its engine, was a locomotive to which were attached a dozen boxcars. Some of them had their side doors open and large numbers of workmen were busy unloading crates from the cars and placing them on wagons.

Maddox pulled out a small telescope and scanned the train. "We're in luck, McFadden. It is an ammunition train. A damn big one, too. I'd wager every one of those boxcars is full to the brim with artillery shells and crates of rifle cartridges."

An image suddenly filled McFadden's mind. If they placed the bomb in one of the boxcars, it would certainly cause all of the ammunition in the car to explode the moment it detonated. This massive explosion, in turn, would cause the ammunition in the adjacent cars to go off as well. A chain reaction would spread like lightning down the length of the train, setting off every single shell stored inside and utterly obliterating the train as well as the ammunition.

"Let's go," Maddox said, stepping forward.

McFadden followed, but his mind was still racing. "Half an hour, you said?"

"About that, yes. Why?"

McFadden stopped. He suddenly realized a way in which they could use the fifteen pounds of gunpowder inside Maddox's infernal device not only to destroy a train and a large store of ammunition, but to inflict an incalculably more severe blow to General Grant and the Yankee army.

Maddox stopped and turned to look at him. "What is it, McFadden?"

"Don't you see, you fool! If we place the torpedo in one of those ammunition cars, start the clock, and put the train into reverse at the right time, the infernal device will go off when the train is halfway over the bridge."

Maddox's eyes widened. The image of the bridge that the Yankees had worked so hard to repair being blown to pieces along with the ammunition train obviously flashed through his mind just as it had McFadden's.

"My God," Maddox said. "The bridge would be reduced to splinters. The explosion might even wreck the stone support pillars." His voice quickened when another thought entered his mind. "The shock wave generated by the explosion along with the falling debris might even damage or destroy the Yankee pontoon bridges on either side of the railroad bridge!"

Maddox turned and walked back to the woods. McFadden followed. When they were again shielded from the sight of the Yankees surrounding the ammunition train, Maddox pulled out his telescope again and surveyed the area long and carefully.

"They're unloading them from back to front, you see?" Maddox said. "It will take them some time to unload each car. Probably a couple of hours to unload the entire train."

"The more time passes, the closer they will get to the engine."

"That is so. We must move quickly, then. It doesn't much matter in which car we put the torpedo, so long as we place it next to some ammunition. When we get over there, I shall place the torpedo in one of the box cars, preferably one close to the engine. While I'm doing that, you take care of whatever Yankees are in the engine itself and get it moving backwards."

"How far is it from here to the river?"

Maddox scanned the area north of the train with his telescope. "I can see the bridge from here. Quarter mile away, maybe? Wouldn't take long at all for the train to reach it."

"We'll have to time it just right," McFadden said.

"No, I don't think you get it, McFadden. It won't take more than five minutes for us to reach the train, maybe ten minutes for me to place the torpedo and for you to take over the engine, and then just a few minutes for the train to be run back over the bridge. If we want the torpedo to detonate when the train is on the bridge itself, we'll have to start the clock before we even begin moving toward the train."

Maddox opened his carpetbag and pulled the torpedo out. A large glass jar filled with dirty gray powder with a strange clock-like device at the top, it looked deceptively harmless to McFadden's eyes. The dirty gray powder, however, was high quality gunpowder that would explode with the force of several artillery shells. The clock at the top had a cylinder on each side of it.

"How does the clock work?" McFadden asked.

"One cylinder contains a spring, the other a percussion cap. When the clock has ticked for half an hour, it flips a small lever that sets off the spring, which in turn sets off the percussion cap and causes the gunpowder to detonate."

"Can it be stopped after it's started?"

"No. If the clock is tampered with, the lever flips and the gunpowder is set off. I designed it that way on purpose. Once the clock is started, the gunpowder is going to go off. There's nothing anyone can do about it."

Maddox began fiddling about with the device, preparing to arm it. McFadden took the time to check his own weapons. His Navy Colt pistol was loaded and ready and he had several rounds of ammunition with which to reload it. He was glad that he had decided to take it with him rather than assume the guise of a regular Union infantryman, as the pistol would be of much more use in the close confines of a train engine than would a Springfield musket. He also felt fortunate to still have his saber, which was likely to come in handy. As a final backup, he had brought a Bowie knife with him as well. He was as ready as he would ever be.

"Do you have a pocket watch?" Maddox asked.

McFadden shook his head. Only rich men carried pocket watches.

Maddox shrugged. "No matter. Nothing to be done about it now, at any rate. Just try to judge the time in your head. When I start the clock, we have exactly thirty minutes until the bomb goes off. No more, no less. You understand?"

McFadden nodded.

"Okay, just to go over it one more time. I shall start the clock here. We shall walk across this open area toward the train together. When we reach the train, I shall find a good place inside one of the ammunition boxcars and conceal the device. While I am doing that, you will take control of the engine and prepare the train to be reversed back onto the bridge. I shall come to you to inform you that I have placed the torpedo. Then, we shall set the train in motion and head toward a place safely removed from the explosion. Yes?"

"Yes, and then we shall recover Pearson and head back to Atlanta?"

Maddox could not stop himself from snorting in contempt. "Yes, of course," he said, though it was obvious to McFadden that Maddox cared nothing for what would happen after they had set their deadly project in motion.

"Very well, then," McFadden said.

"You know anything about trains?" Maddox asked, suddenly concerned.

McFadden shrugged. "I'll manage." In truth he had never stepped on board a locomotive in his life. All he had ever experienced in terms of trains was being crammed into a boxcar with scores of other Confederate soldiers being transferred from one theater of war to another.

"You'll manage?" Maddox asked skeptically.

"I'm not stupid."

Maddox didn't reply, instead finishing his work with the arming device on the top of the torpedo. He wound up the clock, turning it several times. This took about a minute. Finally, he held the winder in his hand carefully, prepared at any moment to let it loose. He turned to McFadden. "Ready?"

McFadden nodded. Maddox let go of the winder and the clock began its unstoppable ticking. Very carefully, he placed the infernal device back in the carpetbag.

"Let's go," Maddox said simply.

He picked up the carpetbag and stepped out into the clearing like it was the most natural thing in the world, as though he were simply going to board the train for a routine trip to see a friend. McFadden followed behind him, hoping his anxiety were not obvious.

"Stay by my side until we reach the train," Maddox said. "It will look less suspicious that way." He glanced over at McFadden. "Try to look calm, you idiot. Imagine you're an actor playing a part on the stage. You might even smile a bit. People trust you more when you smile."

McFadden forced a smile onto his face, but it felt unnatural. He abandoned the effort after fifteen seconds, convinced that it would require too much mental concentration to maintain. He needed to focus his mind on more important matters.

As they got closer, McFadden could see two men inside the locomotive, with two guards armed with muskets outside the engine. They leaned lazily against the wheels, cradling their weapons but not expecting any trouble. He assumed that he would be able to take the guards by surprise and deal with them quickly, but the noise he would make while doing so would surely alert the men inside the locomotive, who would respond by calling for help.

"I'll help with the guards," Maddox said.

McFadden grunted acknowledgement. Much as he hated to admit it, he could not fathom a way to take control of the engine without Maddox's help. He was an infantryman, not a clandestine operative or a partisan ranger. As they came closer to the train, the two guards stood up and looked them over. The sight of two men wearing Union uniforms was not a cause for concern.

"Afternoon," Maddox said pleasantly, a warm smile on his face.

"And to you," one of the guards said.

"Listen, friends. I stole some good Southern tobacco off the body of a rebel the other day. Been selling it a bit at a time since then to pay for my whiskey. Don't suppose either of you fellows wants some?"

One of the guards shrugged, uninterested. The eyebrows of the other went up and he took a few steps forward. "How much?" he asked.

The next few seconds happened in a flash. Maddox opened up his carpetbag, as though the tobacco were inside. As the Union soldier leaned forward to peer down into it, Maddox unsheathed a knife from inside his trousers just above his right leg, a weapon that McFadden had not known Maddox carried. With shocking ease, Maddox raised the knife quickly upwards in a slashing motion so fast it was difficult to see. The blade cut through the man's throat, causing the bluecoat to instinctively grab his neck. The man's eyes went wide in shock.

At the same time, McFadden lunged forward toward the other guard. He considered pulling out his bowie knife, but his brain told him that he needed to waste no time in order to ensure that the element of surprise was not lost. In any event, the knife was unnecessary. McFadden leaped forward, piling all his weight and velocity onto the man's upper body. The guard was violently thrust backward, his head slamming forcefully into one of the large steam pipes on the side of the engine.

The guard attacked by Maddox fell to the ground, unable to scream and rapidly bleeding to death. McFadden glanced up at the forward window of the engine car, but no one appeared to be looking out at them. The sound of the steam engine, even as it idled, was loud enough that McFadden was reasonably sure the two men in the engine car could not have heard anything untoward.

McFadden turned to look at the man he disabled, satisfied that he was out cold and no further threat. Maddox held the mortally wounded Union soldier to the ground until he stopped moving, then placed his knife between his teeth, picked up the body by its boots and dragged it beside the engine. After taking a moment to shove the corpse underneath the car, Maddox dashed forward to rapidly slit the throat of the unconscious man.

"What are you doing?" McFadden whispered harshly.

"Killing the son a bitch!" Maddox spat back. "What the hell do you think I'm doing?"

"I knocked him out cold!" McFadden protested. "You didn't need to kill him!"

Maddox shrugged, unconcerned. He cleaned the blood off his knife by wiping it rapidly back and forth across the dead man's uniform coat. He sheathed the weapon and quickly looked into the carpetbag.

"Twenty minutes remaining. You ready?"

McFadden nodded.

"Then I'll meet you here in ten minutes." Maddox scurried around the other side of the locomotive, staying low to the ground, and was soon lost to McFadden's sight.

McFadden wondered what to do next. He had to enter the engine car, kill or incapacitate the men inside, and then prepare the train to be reversed back onto the bridge. He had to do it all in ten minutes. If he did it too quickly, more Union troops would likely arrive on the scene and realize something was amiss. On the other hand, if he waited too long, someone was bound to wonder what had happened to the two guards.

He picked up the Springfield musket that had belonged to the man he had knocked out before Maddox had killed him. If he was holding the weapon as he entered the engine car, the men inside might think he was one of the guards for a fraction of a second, perhaps giving him enough time to take them by surprise. It seemed a trivial advantage, but McFadden was willing to take any advantage he could get.

It was foolish to stand around any longer, he decided. Two or three minutes had already passed since Maddox had vanished, which meant that little more than fifteen minutes remained until the torpedo exploded. Better to run the risk of acting too quickly than the risk of not acting quickly enough.

He withdrew the bayonet from the sheath on the dead man's belt and fixed it firmly to the top of the rifle. Then he shuffled through the man's pouch, procured a cartridge and percussion cap, and loaded the weapon. Holding the Springfield in his left hand, he clambered up the short ladder and opened the small door to the engine cab.

As he stepped inside, McFadden was surprised by how hot it was. Two men were standing a few feet away, arguing about something. One man was gesturing toward one of the innumerable metal valves on the vast engine that took up the bulk of space within the cab. Below the engine, the firebox glowed a threatening shade of yellow from the burning coal within. The hissing of the steam made it impossible for McFadden to hear what the men were saying.

Seeing McFadden's entrance, the two men turned to look at him. For a single instant, there was no concern at all in their eyes, obviously thinking he was one of the outside guards coming in to deliver a message. As McFadden stepped inside and shut the door, however, confusion entered their expressions as they failed to recognize him.

"Who are you?" one of the men asked.

McFadden brought the Springfield to his shoulder. "I apologize for the inconvenience, gentlemen. But I am afraid that I must confiscate this locomotive in the name of the Confederacy."

One of the men laughed, thinking McFadden was joking. The other man was more astute. After a single moment's hesitation, his hand suddenly darted toward the top of a small metal crate on which sat a LeMat revolver, a small and light weapon ideal for such close quarters as the inside of a locomotive cab. McFadden dashed forward, skewering the man's leg with the bayonet and causing him to scream in pain. Momentarily dropping the Springfield, McFadden punched the face of the other man with all his strength. He then fumblingly pulled out his own Navy Colt pistol from its holster, waving it menacingly at both men.

"Don't move!" he yelled.

The man he had punched was holding his hands up to a bloody nose, but the Yankee who had attempted to grab the LeMat was much more agile and alert. Ignoring McFadden's order and the pain in his leg, he jumped forward, trying to reach the door on the other side of the cab.

"No!" McFadden shouted, having not expected either man to try to escape. He squeezed off a round from the Colt, which missed the man's head by an inch and smacked harmlessly into the metal wall. The sound the gunshot made inside the confined area of the cab was deafening and took McFadden by surprise. A second later, before he had time for another shot, the man had frantically thrown open the door and fallen down onto the ground outside.

"Help!" the man shouted. "Send help!"

McFadden cursed. He considered leaning out of the doorway and trying once again to shoot the man, but just as quickly dismissed the idea as useless. The damage had been done. There were probably dozens of Union soldiers within earshot of the man, and they would bring still more. It wouldn't surprise him if a hundred bluecoats descended on the locomotive within the next few minutes. None of them would have a clue that in approaching the train they were placing themselves in mortal danger.

"You!" McFadden said, pointing his Colt at the Yankee who still remained in the cab. "How do you back the train up?"

"What? Who the hell are you? What are you doing here?" The man was confused and terrified.

"I asked you a question, you Yankee bastard! Can you back the train up or not? Now, answer me or I'll shoot you!"

"Reverse the engine? Shift the slider valve to the other side." He pointed to a contraption on the engine. "That reverses the flow of steam to the pistons and cause the wheels to rotate backwards."

"And how do you get the engine to go?" He felt foolish asking what had to be rudimentary questions, but now was not the time for embarrassment.

"To go? What do you mean?"

"To start moving, dammit!"

The man pointed to another large lever. "Just throw that bar," he said. "It controls the intake of steam into the engine. And release the brake."

He nodded sharply, fear and anxiety coursing through him. He could hear the sound of voices shouting outside the engine, which could only mean that Union soldiers brought by the calls for help were swarming around the train. He wondered if Maddox had yet been able to place the torpedo inside one of the box cars. With a sudden sense of terror, he realized that he had completely lost track of time since he had come into the engine cab. Had it been two minutes or ten minutes?

He wondered if Maddox would even bother to come to the engine after placing the torpedo. Perhaps he had decided that destroying the train and its ammunition was a sufficient success and that the effort to destroy the bridge was too great a risk. In such a case, he certainly would not have thought twice about abandoning McFadden to his fate.

Yet McFadden felt sure Maddox would arrive soon. The man felt a hunger to cause the maximum amount of devastation and would surely be more than willing to risk his own death if it meant he would have a chance to destroy the bridge along with the train and its ammunition. McFadden would therefore wait.

"Get out," he said to the Yankee. "Tell everyone that the train is going to explode and that they'd better get as far away as they can."

The man sharply nodded and without hesitation opened the door and leapt to the ground. He then ran as fast as his feet could take him. "It's going to blow!" he shouted. "The train's going to blow! Get the hell out of here!"

McFadden stood at the edge of the open door, leveled his Springfield as the nearest Yankee, and fired. The bullet missed, kicking up a small plume of dust near the man's feet. McFadden raised his Colt into the sky and quickly fired off his five remaining rounds. The unexpected gunfire combined with the frantic shouts of the engineer's assistant fleeing from the locomotive was enough to cause confusion and hesitation among the hundred or so Union troops assembling in the distance. All knew what cargo the train was carrying and none wanted to get anywhere near the train if it was, in fact, about to explode. Most of the bluecoats turned and ran.

Dropping the rifle to the floor, McFadden stared at the various valves and levers on the engine. All were labeled, but none of the words made any sense to him. He pulled the lever which the Yankee had called the slider valve, until it was in precisely the opposite position it had been when he had come on board. If he had understood correctly, all he had to do now was to throw the other indicated lever and the steam would be introduced into the engine, throwing the train into motion.

A dreadful thought suddenly occurred to him. On several occasions, he had heard stories of train engines exploding because the steam pressure had been too high. If he threw the lever as far as it would go, would the engine simply blow itself to pieces? He had no idea, but he also had no time to worry about it now.

Suddenly, Maddox pulled himself into the car, standing by the doorway. He had discarded his carpetbag and was holding his revolver in one hand. He looked winded but excited, as if he were enjoying himself.

"Ready?" he asked.

"Yes," McFadden responded carefully. "Did you place the torpedo?"

"I shoved it between two stacks of powder bags," Maddox said gleefully. "And I glanced into lots of the other cars. All of them are packed with gunpowder and artillery shells. When the torpedo goes off, the whole train is going to be blown to kingdom come."

"Good."

"Well, then, start the train and let's get the hell out of here."

McFadden threw the lever and released the brake, just as the Northern engineer had told him to do. With a jolt, the train began to move. Very slowly at first, and then with ever-increasing speed, the engine chugged and pushed the cars toward the bridge over the Chattahoochee.

The sound of gunfire suddenly filled the air. McFadden saw two tiny explosions of red near both of Maddox's shoulders. With a cry of pain, he tumbled forward onto the floor of the locomotive. McFadden, with every fiber of his being telling him to escape the train, dashed across for the door on the other side.

"McFadden!" Maddox cried. "Help me!"

He thought of the Texas and Kentucky soldiers that Maddox had dispatched as bait, Maddox's callousness with Private Pearson, and Maddox's sheer glee in causing death and mayhem. For just a moment, McFadden thought he saw the visage of Cheeky Joe on the man lying on the floor.

"Help yourself, you murdering bastard."

The train was now moving at a fair clip and continuing to accelerate. Moving to the edge of the doorway, McFadden hesitated only a split second before hurling himself off of the locomotive. He landed roughly, rolling away from the tracks under no willful control of his own. His heart pounded and every survival instinct inside his brain was screaming for him to flee. Despite the punishing landing, despite the pain of his abdomen wound, he stood up quickly and began running down the track away from the train with every ounce of speed his brutalized body could muster, for he suddenly so wanted to live.

*   *   *   *   *

Cleburne stood quietly, leaning against the ramparts on the southwestern corner of the Atlanta defenses. He was frustrated at the lack of information and activity. The sounds of battle off to the southwest were clearly audible and he was tormented by the thought that most of the Army of Tennessee was even then fighting for its life against Grant while he and his men were powerless to intervene.

He had done all that he could, of course. He had used Atlanta's heavy siege guns in sporadic artillery bombardments of enemy positions, while deploying sharpshooters with Whitworth rifles to pick off any Union officers they could spot. A few trench raids had also been mounted, but with so few troops remaining fit for duty these operations were little more than pinpricks.

Cleburne was doubtful if a single regiment of Union troops had been diverted from the south back toward Atlanta on account of his attempts at creating a diversion. He was only slightly comforted by the knowledge that he was attempting to do his duty to the best of his ability and with every available resource he had.

He had sent out scouts at first light, but only two had returned. They both reported a large battle taking place just north of the town of Fairburn. Neither of them had made contact with friendly forces and both had had to scurry back to Atlanta in order to avoid being caught by Yankee patrols.

Cleburne fumed at the lack of cavalry. Had he had even a company of reliable mounted troops, a serious effort at reconnaissance to the south might have been made. Yankee prisoners might have been captured and interrogated, giving a clearer picture of the overall situation. As it was, all Cleburne had was the short note Johnston had dispatched nearly two days before, urging him to hold the city at all costs. Cleburne scoffed. It was almost an insult to suggest he would have done anything less.

These musings were slowly drifting through Cleburne's mind when they were abruptly interrupted by a bright flash on the horizon off toward the northwest. Instinctively, his eyes turned in that direction. In the far distance, he could see the red glare of what looked like rockets rising into the sky and dark and fiery clouds spiraling away like bizarre tendrils. Moments later, the sound of a titanic explosion punched his eardrums and the ground beneath his feet shook.

Several nearby Confederate infantrymen cried out in alarm. Others quietly snatched up their weapons in case this unexpected noise presaged some sort of Yankee attack. Cleburne quickly pulled his field telescope out of its case and focused on the area where the explosion had taken place. It was impossible to make out any detail on account of the dense woods, but a massive cloud of dark smoke was rising, slowly morphing into the shape of an enormous mushroom. His dead reckoning of the distance placed the plumes of smoke roughly by the railroad bridge over the Chattahoochee River.

The echo of the mighty explosion rolled over the city of Atlanta like a wave over a beach. As it faded and his hearing recovered, Cleburne could hear a sound of continuous rattling, like that of prolonged musketry. It sounded as though a battle were raging near the river, but of course that was impossible.

Major Benham came running up.

"General Cleburne! What the hell was that?"

"If you could tell me, Major, I should be much obliged to you." He passed the field telescope over to his chief-of-staff.

Benham scanned the area. "Looks like it came from the river. Perhaps a train exploded in some sort of dreadful accident."

"But that was the most deafening explosion I have ever heard," Cleburne said in wonder. "It was something much bigger than a train. I would assume that an ammunition depot went up."

Benham shrugged. "Well, if an accident like that is going to happen, better it happen to the Yankees than to us. Think of how much damage would have been done to Atlanta if our ammunition depot went up."

"McFadden?" Cleburne said under his breath, talking more to himself than Benham. Could the Texas lieutenant and his small force have somehow been responsible for the blast? Had the infernal device made by that unpleasant Scottish fellow have done its job better than anyone had expected?

"Might have been McFadden, sir. Maybe he used that infernal device to blow up some Yankee ammunition. That was the idea, right?"

"Stand the men to," Cleburne said. "Tell the division commanders to be prepared for an attack. And they are to report anything unusual in front of their lines, no matter how insignificant it may seem."

"Yes, sir," Benham said. He paused a moment before continuing. "I wouldn't have thought an explosion within the Union lines would be a cause for concern."

"It probably isn't," Cleburne admitted. "But I do not believe in leaving anything to chance."

Benham nodded, passed the telescope back to his commander, and departed to carry out his orders. Cleburne again scanned the area of the explosion. Black smoke continued to bellow up from the ground in a thick and sinister-looking pillar. The steady sound of popping continued to flow over the city, which Cleburne assumed were secondary explosions of artillery shells and cases of rifle ammunition. It was becoming increasingly clear that an enormous amount of ammunition had been blown up.

Cleburne had honestly not given McFadden's clandestine raid much of a chance of success. In truth, he had probably not given the matter more than five minutes thought since he had sent McFadden on his way, for there were so many other things vying for his attention. Cleburne felt guilty about this, for McFadden was obviously a special officer and someone he should keep an eye on.

He wondered what chance McFadden actually had of returning, to say nothing of the dozen or so men he had taken with him. Infiltrating the enemy lines while wearing Yankee uniforms made a certain amount of sense, but it would mean that the men would be executed as spies were they to be captured. Assuming that everything had gone perfectly and the torpedo had been used to destroy some valuable target, every Union commander throughout the area was even now issuing orders to hunt down and capture whatever rebel operative had been responsible. Cleburne told himself that McFadden's chances of survival were slim.

Cleburne wondered if there was anything he could do to help McFadden. He decided that, upon Benham's return, he would issue additional orders to the men commanding the various sectors of the Atlanta defenses. The artillery batteries were to commence another round of bombardments, while a force of a few hundred troops would be massed on the western side of the defenses and make a demonstration toward the Union lines. Perhaps this would frighten the Yankees into thinking that the destruction of their ammunition was the signal for a major sortie out of the city and cause them to reinforce the front lines. Every Union infantryman diverted to guard against such a phantom threat would be one less soldier looking for McFadden and his men.

Benham returned and Cleburne dictated to him the necessary orders. He rushed off again. After that, the only thing Cleburne could do was wait.

*   *   *   *   *

September 29, Night

Illuminated by the light of torches held by members of the cavalry escort, Grant's normally expressionless face wore a heavy mask of disappointment as he rode Cincinnati slowly northward. The fighting had sputtered out less than an hour earlier due to the encroaching darkness and the mutual exhaustion of both armies. It had become increasingly clear that the Union forces had suffered a heavy defeat.

Johnston's flank attack had caught the Army of the Tennessee completely by surprise. The division which had borne the brunt of the assault had simply disintegrated, its men fleeing to every point of the compass between due west and due north, having more than a thousand men taken prisoner by the rebels. Although McPherson had done his best and been in the thick of the fight, he had not been able to restore order until his men had been driven several miles to the northwest. Heavy casualties had been incurred, a considerable amount of artillery had been captured, and the Army of the Tennessee had been decisively knocked out of the battle.

As the extent of the disaster had become known, Grant had temporarily hoped that the Army of the Cumberland, on the other side of the battlefield, might turn the tide with a renewed push against the rebels. However, that attack had been sharply repulsed by the rebel corps, which prisoners had identified as belonging to Cheatham. During the morning, a flank attack against a surprised enemy had yielded a temporary advantage, but the afternoon frontal assault against a ready and waiting foe had earned nothing but dead and wounded men.

The Battle of Fairburn was over. Grant and the Union army had lost.

From a tactical perspective, the defeat was not as serious as the disaster at Peachtree Creek. The Union army, now deployed mostly in a line running northeast to southwest with its back to the Chattahoochee River, had mostly retained its organization and was still capable of fighting, despite losing eleven thousand men over two days. But there was no denying that they had been bested by a considerably weaker opponent. Johnston's rebel troops had fought like lions. All the skill and determination of Grant's own men had been for nothing.

"General Grant!" Howard's voice called.

The commander of the Army of the Cumberland materialized out of the darkness and into the illumination of the torches. Though tired, he still seemed energetic and his eyes were hungry for information.

"McPherson is routed," Grant said laconically. He briefly explained what had befallen the Army of the Tennessee, then described his intentions. "We must pull back to the ferries at Campbellton and Sandtown and then withdraw to the north side of the river. Your men will dig in south of the ferries. McPherson will begin crossing tomorrow and you will go after he has finished."

A look of surprise crossed Howard's face. "My men may have been repulsed, sir. But they are still capable of fighting."

Grant shook his head. Every fiber of his being rebelled against the idea of retreating, but he saw no other choice. "Did you hear the explosion a few hours ago?" he asked Howard.

"I did. The whole army did, I expect. What was it?"

"It was most of our ammunition reserve going up in smoke."

Like tens of thousands of other soldiers in and around Fairburn, Grant had distinctly heard the cataclysmic explosion hours earlier and wondered what it was. His first thought was that the forces he had left outside of Atlanta had somehow become engaged in battle with Cleburne's men. The field telegraph soon brought news of a much more ominous development.

As he explained to Howard, dozens of railroad boxcars had been destroyed in the explosion, which had reportedly been caused by rebel sabotage. Survivors who had been near the train before it had gone up reported gunfire and shouting as unidentified men had sought to seize control of the locomotive. Each boxcar had been loaded with artillery powder charges and shells, crates of rifle ammunition, and various other explosive supplies. A large portion of his ammunition had been destroyed in the blink of an eye, including most of what he had intended to bring down to Fairburn the very next day.

Making the disaster even worse was the fact that the railroad bridge over the Chattahoochee, which had been rebuilt only with great difficulty and effort, had been utterly destroyed. Even the stone pillars had been knocked to pieces, making immediate reconstruction impossible. Two of the nearby pontoon bridges had also been smashed to splinters by the blast's shock wave and the cascade of debris which had rained down upon them.

"Can we not replace the ammunition from our depots at Allatoona and Chattanooga?" Howard asked, incredulous. "Surely more can be sent from our logistical hubs at Nashville and Louisville."

"We could, but not for several days. The loss of the bridges will involve more delay. As it is, here at Fairburn we have only enough ammunition for one more day of heavy combat, if we're lucky."

Howard slowly nodded, understanding the point Grant was making. If they did remain and fight and the result was anything less than a crushing victory, both the Army of the Cumberland and the Army of the Tennessee would be at Johnston's mercy. Without ammunition, an army could not fight. If they remained south of the river, they risked having every soldier in both of their armies becoming rebel prisoners.

"We will withdraw," Grant said. "You will secure your wounded and your artillery and begin pulling back to the northwest, toward the river. Those too badly wounded to be moved will have to be left behind. Dig in a mile southwest of the river. You will remain in position tomorrow to allow the Army of the Tennessee to cross to the north bank first, then commence your own crossing during the night."

"And after we cross back to the north bank of the river?" Howard asked. "What then?"

Grant thought that this was an excellent question, but one for which he did not have an immediate answer. Obviously, there was nothing now to prevent Johnston from linking up with the rebel forces inside Atlanta, which would place the two weak corps he had left outside the city in grave danger. He intended to send orders to General John Palmer, who commanded the troops nearest the city, to pull back from his present lines and fortify himself in a strong position just northwest of the city, rebuilding the destroyed pontoon bridges as quickly as possible.

"General Grant?" Howard asked.

"I'm sorry," Grant said, suddenly reminded that he had not answered Howard's earlier question. "Once we're on the north bank of the river, we shall march back to our former camps around Smyrna and Marietta, there to rest and resupply the men."

That was the logical course of action, but his mind offered him no suggestions for what he might do after that. The men of all three armies were exhausted, casualties had been enormous, much of the ammunition had either been expended in battle or destroyed, and everyone from the highest-ranking general to the lowliest private was utterly demoralized.

His forces under his command were in a pitiful state and it would take some time to restore them to anything resembling fighting readiness. Weeks, at least. Perhaps over a month. The Union cause did not have that much time.

For a moment, he wondered what would happen if he simply crossed the river with his most reliable troops and launched a final frontal assault on its defenses. But such an effort had failed when only Cleburne's men held the defenses. Now the entire Army of Tennessee, reunited under their beloved commander, would be manning the ramparts. Any such attack would be suicidal. Indeed, Grant would not have been surprised if many of the regiments would erupt in mutiny and refuse to fight if given such orders.

What else could he do? The weak and muddled state of his forces precluded any effort to launch a campaign of maneuver against the Atlanta railroads. Even if it didn't, the coming of winter would soon bring active campaigning to an end. His forces were far too weak to commence a regular siege against Atlanta and there was no time for such an operation to be successful anyway.

The more Grant thought about it, the more obvious the truth became. Johnston and Cleburne had won. He had lost. Because of that, the Union was going to lose the war.

It was over.

Chapter Twenty One

September 30, Morning

Lincoln was beginning his morning by sipping on a cup of coffee and reading a letter from Minister Charles Adams, his chief diplomat in London. It had arrived the previous evening, having been dispatched from England eleven days earlier. The letter from Adams contained the latest accounts of what was happening in Parliament, as well as rumors of a new rebel commerce raider which was thought to be near completion in a British dockyard.

The threat of another Southern commerce raider roaming the high seas was not to Lincoln's liking. The destruction which had been wrought by other rebel cruisers, especially the *CSS Alabama* before it had been sunk back in June, had cost the Northern economy millions of dollars and diverted naval resources which would otherwise have been devoted to the blockade. He scribbled a note in the margin of Adams's letter indicating that it should be sent to the Navy Department at once.

Lincoln was about to pick up his next letter, from a delegation of Ohio industrial leaders, when the door was opened by Hay.

"Mr. President? Secretary Stanton requests your presence at the War Department telegraph office immediately, sir."

"Did he say why?"

"No, sir."

Lincoln assumed it had to have something to do with the fighting then going on around Atlanta. If so, he would want to know the details at once. He stood up from the desk, grabbing his coat and top hat as he walked through the door, and was soon strolling across the White House lawn toward the War Department. Scarcely five minutes passed before he walked through the door of the telegraph office.

Major Eckert and his clerks were busy as they rapidly tried to transcribe the messages arriving on the telegraph machines. Stanton, looking even more grim than usual, was slowly pacing back and forth across the office, intently studying the telegram in his hands.

"Well, Mr. Stanton?" Lincoln said upon entering. "You asked for me. Here I am."

Without a word, Stanton handed him the telegram that he had been reading.

Mr. Secretary,

Two events yesterday have compelled me to commence a withdrawal to the north bank of the Chattahoochee River. Our forces engaged in battle near the town of Fairburn received a severe check, with the Army of the Cumberland repulsed in its attack after an initial success and the Army of the Tennessee defeated by an enemy flank attack. Furthermore, rebel saboteurs destroyed an ammunition train using an infernal device, destroying most of our ammunition reserve as well the railroad bridge over the Chattahoochee and some of the pontoon bridges.

Our withdrawal over the river commences today and I expect it to be completed soon. I shall keep you informed.

General Grant

As he read through the telegram, Lincoln knew it was over. He had pinned all his hopes on Grant being able to defeat the rebels outside Atlanta and then capture the city. It would be the victory, he had urgently prayed, that would restore faith to the Northern people, ensure a Republican victory in the upcoming elections, and lay the groundwork for a restoration of the Union. Those hopes now lay in tatters.

So often since the beginning of the war, Grant had been Lincoln's salvation. In the dark opening days of the conflict, following the disasters of Bull Run and Wilson's Creek, Grant had won his first great victory at Fort Donelson. His capture of the key rebel citadel of Vicksburg in the summer of 1863 had torn out the nail which had held the South's two halves together. And after the terrible defeat at Chickamauga, it had been Grant's success at Missionary Ridge which had saved Chattanooga and set the stage for the campaign to seize Atlanta. Each victory had helped Lincoln calm the fears of shaky political allies and discredit the rhetoric of his political enemies, allowing him to continue pushing the war effort forward.

Grant would not save Lincoln this time.

The President looked at Stanton. "Well?"

"It's a disaster, Mr. President."

"But the armies remain intact. They are not routed. It does not seem to be a defeat on the scale of Bull Run, Chickamauga, or Peachtree Creek."

"No, but that doesn't matter. The force near Fairburn is almost out of ammunition, thanks to this rebel sabotage. If Grant continues the battle there, his men may soon be fighting only with bayonets for lack of cartridges and the artillery will become useless for lack of shells. The rebels would cut them to pieces. I don't want Grant to retreat any more than you do, but I agree with him that there is no alternative."

"What is this about rebel sabotage? What happened, exactly?"

"The details are sketchy," Stanton said with irritation. He was a man used to having all the information about every situation. "From what we have been able to gather, a team of rebel partisans or scouts, wearing Union uniforms, killed the guards of the ammunition train in question, planted an infernal device among the powder charges, and reversed the train back onto the Western and Atlantic railroad bridge, where it exploded with tremendous force."

"My God," Lincoln exclaimed.

"Several boxcars of ammunition were lost and the bridge was destroyed. Because the stone pillars collapsed, it will take some time for it to be rebuilt. Needless to say, I am sending orders out to all commanders in the region that the men responsible for this atrocity are to be hunted down like the dogs they are and hanged from the most convenient tree the moment they are in our hands."

Lincoln let out a dry, bitter chuckle. Stanton might salve his own disappointment with such bloodlust, but it held no attraction for Lincoln. He hated the fact that his job often involved approving executions of rebel spies, who were brave men serving a cause in which they believed. Lincoln always feared having hypocrisy seep into his mind. After all, had Union soldiers wearing rebel uniforms succeeded in such a clandestine operation against a Southern army, Stanton would have held the men up as heroes and given them medals.

He wanted to make a joke about this. Throughout his life, Lincoln had used humor to keep despair at bay. This time, no joke came. He walked to the couch and sat down, taking a deep breath. He looked up at Stanton, a pleading look in his eye.

"Can anything be done?"

"I don't think so, Mr. President."

"What of Schofield and his small army? Surely they may be of assistance?"

"They have marched hundreds of miles without a break for nearly a month. From what I understand, they are broken down and desperately in need of rest. Both the Army of the Tennessee and the Army of the Cumberland are used up. They have suffered severe casualties and their morale is at breaking point. The rebel forces, by contrast, will soon be reunited. I cannot see any way for the campaign to be brought to a successful conclusion before the close of the campaign season."

A wave of nausea swept through Lincoln's stomach. He suddenly very much wanted to see Seward, whose optimism would hopefully lift him up from the shadow being cast by the news from Georgia. He decided he would send Hay to fetch the Secretary of State the moment he returned to the White House.

"Do you believe Grant's withdrawal will succeed?" Lincoln asked.

"Yes, Mr. President. I doubt Johnston will do anything to interfere. He usually refrains from attacking unless he has had a long time to plan and prepare and his own forces cannot have escaped suffering serious losses themselves in the past two days."

The President slowly nodded. "Very well. Please send me updates as you see fit."

"Of course, sir."

Lincoln slowly rose and, with a slowness brought on by despair, began walking back to the White House, now certain he would not be residing there much longer.

    *   *   *   *   *

President Davis was scribbling furiously, a characteristic look of irritation on his face. He was responding to a letter from General Kirby Smith, who commanded all Confederate forces west of the Mississippi River. He was irritated with Smith. The general had attempted to initiate local prisoner exchanges with the Yankees, an act which Davis thought well beyond the limits of Smith's political authority. Moreover, among the list of officers Smith had nominated for promotion was that of a captain whose father, a minor Georgia politician, had criticized Davis in an editorial published in a Macon newspaper two years earlier. Davis would be damned if the man in question got his promotion. Officers, after all, had to earn their ranks.

Harrison quietly entered the room and placed a telegram on the President's desk, leaving without a word. Davis scarcely noticed, so intent was he on his letter to Smith. He spent another ten minutes outlining precisely why the captain was unworthy of promotion before finally setting the letter down and noticing the telegram.

> *President Davis,*
> *The Army of Tennessee has won a decisive victory over the enemy's combined forces outside the town of Fairburn. On our left, the enemy launched a heavy attack that was repulsed with heavy casualties. On the right, a flank attack by the division of General Clayton succeeded in routing the enemy and hurling him back. The enemy now appears to be withdrawing toward the Chattahoochee. We are following with caution, while endeavoring to reestablish communication with General Cleburne in Atlanta.*
> *General Johnston*

His pulse quickened, but he did not move. He read the telegram again, then silently set it down on the desk. He glanced up at the military map on the wall, seeing the red and blue pins indicating the battling armies just southwest of Atlanta. For a moment, he tried to imagine the blood-stained ground, the battle cries of brave and determined men, the sounds of artillery and musket fire. He had seen the worst of war during the conflict with Mexico. He remembered the thrill of victory that had filled his soul after the Battle of Buena Vista in 1847. He wondered how many of the young men and older officers of the Army of Tennessee were feeling the same sensation.

The implications of the telegram were immense. If Grant had indeed been defeated and was withdrawing to the river, the threat to Atlanta was at an end. Cleburne and Johnston would be able to join forces and the situation would revert to roughly what it had been a month earlier. The Confederates could cry defiance from the defenses of Atlanta, with the Yankees powerless to do anything to trouble them.

Moreover, news of the defeat had to be even then dancing across the telegraph wires across the North, bringing despair to Republicans and delight to Democrats. This news would be the final nail in the coffin of the Lincoln administration's chances for victory in the upcoming election. Indeed, it had to be. Even as wily a political operator as Abraham Lincoln would not be able to whitewash the failure of the Union army outside of Atlanta.

"Mr. Harrison!" Davis bellowed.

His aide appeared in the doorway a moment later. "Yes, Mr. President?"

He held up the telegram. "Are you aware of the contents of this?"

"I am, Mr. President," Harrison said, unable to suppress a slight grin.

"Would you be so kind as to summon Secretary Benjamin to the office?"

Harrison nodded. "Of course, sir."

For days, Davis had imagined what his response would be in the event Johnston were defeated. It took him rather by surprise that he had not given the same amount of thought to what he would do in the event of a victory. As the President was musing on this, Benjamin walked through the door.

"Atlanta?" he asked, taking his seat.

Davis nodded. "We won." He pushed the telegram over the desk and the Secretary of State hurriedly read it. As he did, a beaming smile crossed his face.

"Well, this is first rate."

"What shall be our response?"

Benjamin shrugged. "Publicly, I really see no particular reason for us to do anything. We should simply allow the situation to unfold. The newspapers will report word of this victory with their usual enthusiasm. The people will be delighted. The currency may recover some of its value, but you'd have to talk to Secretary Trenholm about that."

Davis nodded, mentally noting the need to summon the Secretary of the Treasury later that day. He waved for Benjamin to continue.

"Johnston will be hailed as a hero, of course, but there's nothing to be done about that. The newspapers will ignore Cleburne's contribution, which is too bad but also unavoidable. Right now, it is important that public sentiment is so positive. We shall be ending the campaign season on a high note and this very fact will dishearten the Northern electorate all the more. Lincoln's reelection is now an impossibility."

"And our European friends?"

"This victory will certainly raise our credibility in the eyes of the Europeans, but as the Northern election is scarcely a month away, they shall sit on their hands until then."

"No matter," Davis said. "This seals Lincoln's fate. He will lose in November, and then the Europeans shall surely send their emissaries."

"Perhaps. But even if they do not, they shall have no choice once it becomes clear that McClellan will implement a cease-fire." Benjamin held up the telegram. "The news contained in this piece of paper, Mr. President, ensures the independence of the Confederate States."

Davis held up a finger. "If McClellan is willing to negotiate once he's in office. I'm fairly certain that he will be, but we should take nothing for granted."

"Perhaps some sort of display of goodwill on our part would be of some benefit?" Benjamin suggested. "It might help grease the wheels and make it easier for McClellan to initiate negotiations when he comes into office."

Davis furrowed his eyebrows. "I'm not sure I know what you mean. We have won the victory, have we not? It will now be up to the new administration in Washington to initiate peace talks."

"I'm talking of making a symbolic gesture. A sign to the North that we are not the barbarians they seem to think we are."

"Like what?"

Benjamin paused a moment before replying. "You could grant clemency to George Thomas, for instance."

Davis drew his head back in surprise. "Spare that traitor? Surely you can't be serious."

"Think about it for a moment, my friend. The newspapers are still clamoring for his head in retaliation for the murder of Nathan

Bedford Forrest. Many of our own politicians and generals, Johnston and Lee aside, are forcefully expressing similar judgments. How statesmanlike of you to go against public opinion and be merciful to Thomas, thereby showing the people of the North that you can be diplomatic as well as strong, that you possess compassion as well as vigor. In other words, that you can be the kind of President with whom the new administration can do business."

"Now you're talking like a Yankee," Davis observed, disappointed.

"If we are to secure a peace agreement with the United States, we shall have to out-Yankee the Yankees. Better to learn to think like a Yankee now than be forced to do so later, don't you agree?"

Davis looked down at the table. "Are we to simply accept Forrest's murder, then?"

"Yes," Benjamin said simply, his smile never wavering. "Truth be told, now that the prospect of peace is before us, we must look to the future. Nathan Bedford Forrest was a useful tool, but he had no place in the country we must now strive to create." Seeing that Davis was still uncertain, Benjamin went on. "Besides, Mr. President, if we do execute Thomas, we will simply be creating a martyr, a symbol that the Yankees will use against us for all time to portray us as a savage and faithless nation. And Thomas is a Virginian, don't forget. You and I both know that there yet remain many Southerners who are not fully loyal to the Confederacy. Killing Thomas would push them toward maintaining a loyalty to the United States, whereas sparing him might help conciliate many toward the new order we are creating. It might also have a beneficial effect on the British and French governments, making it politically easier for them to extend diplomatic recognition to us."

Davis nodded slowly, brought his fingers up to the sides of his head and slowly massaged his temples. "I will think on it, Judah. I am not saying that I shall do it, but I will think on it."

*   *   *   *   *

October 1, Afternoon

Johnston spurred Fleetfoot to even greater speed. Two dozen Texas cavalrymen surrounded him, the collective sound of so many hooves making a thundering noise. The church spires of central Atlanta were visible in the distance, just a few miles away, as if beckoning him to hurry. He was anxious to enter the city as rapidly as possible, for only then could he honestly tell himself that he had achieved a complete victory and saved the metropolis from capture. Besides, Johnston felt it necessary to confer with Cleburne as quickly as possible. He wanted to know what precisely had happened in Atlanta over the previous week and whether Cleburne's men were in any shape for continued fighting. He was also anxious to learn the condition of General Hardee and to learn if Cleburne knew anything about the tremendous explosion that had been heard the previous evening.

He had left Cheatham in command of the forces around Fairburn, as he was the senior corps commander. The situation there did not seem to require the presence of the commanding general, as the Yankees were clearly intent on withdrawing over the river. Johnston had given Cheatham orders to observe Grant's actions and keep him fully informed, but not to attack or otherwise hinder the enemy in his front.

Mackall rode alongside Johnston, trying to keep up. His horse was not as easy a ride as was Fleetfoot.

"Are you sure it is wise to return to Atlanta so soon, General?" Mackall asked. "Grant's forces remain intact."

"If anything happens around Fairburn, Cheatham will handle matters. Grant's forces are clearly pulling back in any event."

"They may yet decide to offer battle once again."

"And if they do, it will not take long to return to the main force. But I do not think they will. The Yankees are clearly spent."

"You think so?"

Johnston nodded. "I do. They certainly did not fight at Fairburn with their usual tenacity. Most of their attacks seemed to lack energy and force, with the assault on Cheatham's flank only succeeding, and that temporarily, because they possessed the advantage of surprise. And when our attack struck them, they folded like a house of cards."

"The Yankees are tired and dispirited," Mackall agreed. "From what our prisoners tell us, they had battered away at the defenses of Atlanta for days before being marched south to confront us."

"Well, I hope to soon have a firsthand report from Cleburne on that subject."

They continued northeast. Johnston noticed that smoke was still rising off in the direction of the Western and Atlantic bridge over the Chattahoochee River, which was where his scouts had said the explosion had taken place the day before. If there were still fires burning in that area, the blast must have been enormous, indeed.

He wondered what the people in Richmond were thinking. He had sent a telegram announcing the victory to President Davis, but had not yet received a response. Johnston expected that Davis would consider the Confederate victory at Fairburn a great disappointment, seeing as it was he who had won it. But the rest of the country would see it for the triumph that it was.

Through the trees, a small group of horsemen appeared several hundred yards ahead of them. The captain commanding the cavalry escort shouted a warning and the Texans readied their carbines. Johnston instinctively slowed down, allowing his escort to move ahead and create what amounted to a human shield between him and the unidentified riders.

"Friends!" a man shouted from the group. "Don't fire!"

"Identify yourselves!" the captain of the escort cried.

"7th Alabama Cavalry!"

"We are the 8th Texas!"

Johnston looked warily down the road, wondering if it was some Yankee trick. The morning reports from his scouts had told him that the area between Fairburn and Atlanta was now empty of Union troops, as Grant was retreating to the northwest and the Northern forces around Atlanta were also pulling back. Still, it was possible that cavalry units were still present, either covering the retreat or scouting for the Confederate forces.

Bravely, the commander of the escort walked his horse forward. At any moment, Johnston expected a shot to ring out, at which point he was supposed to turn Fleetfoot around and kick her into a gallop. A few seconds later, though, having gotten close enough to make a proper observation, he turned his head back to the group with a smile on his face.

"It's all right, General! It's the 7th Alabama, sure enough!"

Johnston, Mackall and the escort walked their horses up. When they recognized their commander, the Alabama cavalrymen gave three cheers. The unit was, in fact, only a single company of the 7th Alabama that had been serving as an escort for General Hardee, since the rest of the regiment had gone off on Wheeler's raid back in July and been cut to pieces. They had been ordered to scout to the southwest and make contact with the rest of the Army of Tennessee. Coming across the commanding general struck everyone as a happy coincidence and a hopeful omen.

The combined party headed northeast toward the city. As they traveled, Johnston questioned the lieutenant commanding the detachment of Alabama cavalry. He learned of the terrible fighting that had raged on the ramparts of the Atlanta defenses for several days, as well as the troubling circumstances that had led Cleburne to place Walker under arrest. The lieutenant could provide no details as to what had caused the massive explosion the day before, although camp rumor was that it had destroyed the railroad bridge over the Chattahoochee. The only thing the man knew about Hardee was that the general's life still hung in the balance. The more Johnston heard, the more he wanted to speak with Cleburne.

An hour after making contact with the scouting party, Johnston and the rest of them emerged into the cleared area just south of Atlanta's defenses. There, he was confronted by a horrific sight and had to momentarily restrain himself from retching. Across an impossibly large space, the ground was literally covered with the bloody remnants of what had once been Union soldiers. Confederate soldiers and many slaves with white cloths over their faces were moving about them, gathering them for burial. Johnston had never seen so many dead men in one place in his entire life.

"My God," he said simply. He turned to look at Mackall, who also had a shocked expression on his face.

"It's like something out of Dante's *Inferno*," the chief-of-staff added.

"They're calling it the Blood Bucket," the lieutenant of the 7th Alabama said.

"The redoubt, you mean?" What had once been a stout and well-built battery had been largely leveled, though the Stainless Banner of the Confederate States still waved defiantly over it.

"Yes, sir."

"What on Earth happened here?"

"The Yankees made this battery the central focus of their attack. They launched diversionary attacks on the north and west sides of the city, but stormed this battery with everything they had. I only saw it from a distance, but it was terrible. They just kept pouring troops in like a waterfall. The fighting went on for nearly twenty-four hours. A nightmare, I tell you. But we held."

Johnston put Fleetfoot into a walk and the escort formed up just ahead of him. They passed through one of the gaps in the defenses and emerged just south of where the streets of Atlanta began. Soon, they were moving up McDonough Street toward the Atlanta City Hall, which the helpful lieutenant had told him was the location of Cleburne's headquarters.

As they headed north through the streets of the city, Johnston looked around in astonishment. Everywhere, houses and buildings lay punctured and shattered by Union artillery fire. He had been told by his scouts that the Yankees were shelling the city, but part of him had refused to believe it until he saw for himself. For a moment, he felt a wave of revulsion against all Northerners, for only a beastly people would wage war against defenseless women and children. He wondered how many civilians had been killed or wounded.

The streets were not empty. Men and women scurried about, baskets in their hands, trying to find food. The Union forces had departed from their siege lines and the shelling had stopped days earlier, but the need to find something for themselves and their children to eat was obviously still a matter of grave concern. The Yankees had torn up the railroads leading to the city and the trains could not run in provisions until they had been repaired.

At long last, they arrived in front of the Atlanta City Hall. Johnston and Mackall dismounted, their horses quickly taken into the care of the Texas cavalrymen. The Alabama troopers stood around uncertainly, wondering what their duties now were and waited for someone to give them orders. Johnston left them where they were and strode into the building.

Inside, he saw Cleburne talking urgently to his chief-of-staff, while various other staff officers were busy at tables spread throughout the hall, some writing orders, some placing pins into maps, and others reading reports. Off to the side, along the wall, three men were sound asleep, their snoring providing a rather comic background noise to the headquarters.

Cleburne looked up and saw Johnston enter. A warm smile filled his face and he walked forward with a spring in his step. He stopped just in front of Johnston and saluted. The staff officers rose as one and also saluted, with the exception of those sleeping against the walls, who snored on.

"General Johnston, sir! I am very glad to see you."

Johnston returned the salute, smiling broadly. "And I, you, General Cleburne. Congratulations on a most magnificent defense of Atlanta."

"Defending the city would have been for nothing, had you not come back north in time to save it." Cleburne gestured for Johnston and Mackall to sit down at the table and sent a staff officer to fetch coffee.

"How are your men?" Johnston asked. "What is the overall condition of the corps?"

"We have suffered heavy casualties, sir. We were not able to get an accurate count until this morning, so disordered have our units become. But we believe that there are six thousand, five hundred men present and accounted for who are in condition to fight."

Johnston's eyes widened. If Cleburne's numbers were accurate, the proud corps he had left in Atlanta when he had raced south to Alabama had been reduced to a third of its previous strength.

Cleburne went on to describe the thousands of wounded men suffering in the hospitals, the civilians desperately in need of food and shelter, and other pressing matters. Johnston had Mackall write an urgent message to Richmond, urging them not only to speed repairs on the railroad to Augusta but to rush whatever food and medical supplies were available to the city by whatever means necessary. Mackall took the message to one of the Alabama troopers still waiting outside, ordering him to ride to Fairburn with all speed, as the telegraph line from that town to Lafayette was still intact, and the message could be forwarded on from there to the capital.

"I was told that two corps of Union troops remained near Atlanta," Johnston said. "What happened to them?"

"Yes, two corps commanded by General Palmer, or so say the prisoners we've taken. Yesterday, they withdrew from their positions close to the city and marched northwest a few miles. According to my scouts, they have dug in on the south bank of the river in a semi-circle, with both flanks anchored on the river itself. They number about ten thousand men."

"Ten thousand men in two corps?" Johnston asked.

"They were badly beaten up in their assaults on the city's defenses," Cleburne said.

"I'll say," Johnston replied. A Union corps was typically fifteen thousand strong. Clearly, Grant's two armies had dashed themselves to pieces against the ramparts of Atlanta. This explained why the fighting qualities of the Army of the Cumberland and the Army of the Tennessee had been so greatly reduced when they had gone into battle at Fairburn.

"How is General Hardee?" Johnston asked.

A look of intense concern crossed Cleburne's face. Johnston told himself that perhaps he should have broached the subject more carefully, for he was well aware that Cleburne and Hardee were friends.

"His left leg was shattered by shrapnel during a Yankee artillery bombardment. It had to be amputated. I have visited him in the hospital when I have had the chance, but he has been slipping in and out of consciousness and has not yet fully awakened. The doctors say that he remains in danger. When I asked them point blank as to his chances of survival, they said it was fifty-fifty."

Johnston frowned and nodded. While he did not share Cleburne's warm friendship with Hardee, he had grown very fond of the man. Unlike Hood, Hardee had been a faithful subordinate to him since the day he had taken command of the Army of Tennessee.

"I shall pray for his recovery," Johnston said gravely. "Moreover, I shall issue a circular order to the army suggesting that the men do the same."

"Thank you, sir."

"How many other generals have fallen?"

"Many, I'm afraid," Cleburne answered. "General Bate was killed in the fighting around East Point. General Gist was killed defending the southern defenses. There are several others. I shall have a report sent to you.

"Thank you. Now, if you'll forgive another question, General Cleburne, can you tell me anything about the large explosion we all heard two days ago?"

Cleburne nodded enthusiastically and quickly told the story of James McFadden's mission with John Maddox's infernal device.

"McFadden?" Johnston asked. The name sounded vaguely familiar, then he suddenly remembered. "Was that not the man who captured George Thomas during the Battle of Peachtree Creek?"

Cleburne nodded. "The very man. Really an extraordinary fellow, if you ask me. And he succeeded beyond all expectations. As far as we can tell, the weapon detonated on a Yankee ammunition train as it was crossing the Chattahoochee River bridge. So not only did he destroy an immense amount of Union ammunition, but he destroyed the railroad bridge as well."

"Most impressive," Johnston said. "We shall certainly have to arrange for this lieutenant to be promoted."

Cleburne frowned. "Unfortunately, he has not been seen since the left the city, and that was nearly three days ago. If I had to guess, I would say that he most likely died in the explosion."

Johnston grunted. "Well, that's too bad. But it is an honor to die for one's country. And now, if I may ask, what happened with General Walker?"

"I regret that I had to place Walker under arrest for gross insubordination." Cleburne spent the next few minutes filling Johnston in on the details.

"Where is Walker now?"

"I believe he was installed in the Atlanta jail, which seemed the most convenient place."

"Well, I am sure he will submit a request for a proper court martial. I would recommend that you and your staff record in writing your recollections of the events surrounding the incident."

"I will, sir."

Johnston shook his head. "I do not like this rancor between my generals," he said simply.

"Nor I," Cleburne replied.

Johnston almost responded by saying that Cleburne might have avoided the entire situation had he never written his proposal, but thought better of it. Such words would only exacerbate the situation. He thought the feud between Cleburne and Walker was a great shame, for it had created nothing but trouble for the Army of Tennessee.

He wondered what would happen with the issue now that Cleburne had performed so brilliantly and gallantly in defense of Atlanta. Would Davis and his cronies in Richmond still crow for Cleburne's head or would they now allow the issue to quietly drop? What would the newspapers say when word spread that the man who wanted to free the slaves and hand them muskets had been the very man who beat back Grant's grand assault on the Confederacy's second most important city? Only time would tell.

Johnston knew his own mind, at least.

"General Cleburne, when matters have settled down, I shall send a message to the War Department urging them to promote you to the rank of Lieutenant General."

"Thank you, sir."

*   *   *   *   *

October 1, Afternoon

Marble looked happily at the copy for the next day's paper. The headline said it all.

GRANT DEFEATED IN GEORGIA!
RETREATING NORTH OF THE CHATTAHOOCHEE!

The story itself would contain all the juicy details, summarizing the military events that had taken place in and around Atlanta since Grant had crossed the Chattahoochee River two weeks before. In the fighting around East Point, the assaults on Atlanta itself, and the final Battle of Fairburn, the two armies under Grant's command had suffered roughly thirty thousand casualties. It had all been for nothing. Atlanta remained in rebel hands and Grant was pulling back to his original positions on the north side of the river.

Marble could not have been happier.

"Can you have the text focus more on the heavier casualties sustained by the regiments from Ohio, Indiana, and Illinois?" Marble asked the copy writer who was working on the story.

The man shrugged. "I suppose so, sir."

"Do it, then."

The man went to follow his instructions. Marble wanted the story to dwell on the heavy losses among troops from those states, for it would help turn what few remaining undecided voters there were to cast their ballots against Lincoln in the upcoming election. Not that there was much of a need for such measures now. With the Union defeat at the Battle of Fairburn and the withdrawal of Grant back across the river, there was no longer any chance of a Republican victory in November. The Democrats were surely in and the Republicans were surely out.

Still, every little bit helped. Lincoln's credibility in New York and Pennsylvania, already weak when the year had opened, had been crippled by the huge numbers of casualties among regiments from those two states during the fighting between Lee and Grant in Virginia back in the spring. Now, the casualties suffered by units from the western states in the fighting around Atlanta would serve the same purpose.

Word of the debacle in Georgia had reached New York City that morning. Marble and the rest of the staff at the *New York World* had been scrambling to make the most of it in the hours since. Of course, everyone had known that desperate fighting was raging around Atlanta, with the Southern defenders inside the city holding out against the Union host led by General Grant. The arrival of Johnston and the remainder of the Army of Tennessee had added a certain dramatic flair to the story, which Marble, being a journalist, certainly appreciated.

During the past two days, Marble had slept in a cot at the office, waiting for the telegraph machine to start clicking. Like everyone else, he had been on pins and needles. If Grant had emerged victorious and Atlanta had fallen, the resultant relief and exhilaration that would sweep the nation could well sway a sufficient number of voters to make the difference in key states like Pennsylvania and Illinois. McClellan might then still win the popular vote, but Lincoln would have had a chance at victory in the Electoral College, which was all that really mattered.

The first news to arrive had been confused and disjointed. Atlanta was still in rebel hands, but a fierce battle was being fought south of the city at the small town of Fairburn, which the *New York World* staff had struggled to locate in their atlas. It was obvious even to Marble, a man who knew next to nothing about warfare and military science, that whoever won the battle would emerge the victor of the campaign.

When the dust had settled and the telegraph had begun clicking again, the news was that the victory had gone to Johnston. All had been hectic chaos in the offices of the *New York World* since then.

Even as Marble and his underlings struggled to perfect their copy for the next day's stories about the fiasco at Fairburn and the political situation around the North, there were other stories which were continually catching his attention. He assigned one of his other writers to put together a story on the big rebel offensive taking place in Missouri and Arkansas, which seemed likely to capture Little Rock and was even placing St. Louis itself in danger. Another writer was assigned to write up a summary of the political changes taking place in the United Kingdom, which might soon have an impact on affairs in North America.

As he reveled in his newspaper work, Marble could occasionally spare a moment to contemplate how marvelous life was. Grant had lost, which meant that Lincoln would also lose. McClellan would win, which meant that he himself now would also win. The brief fright concerning the Confederate agent and the unfortunate list of names was over, thanks to the unexpected assistance of none other than Benjamin Butler.

"Mr. Marble?" one of the errand boys meekly asked. "This came for you, sir."

Dear Mr. Marble,

If events in New York and Pennsylvania unfold as we wish them to unfold, your proposal regarding the office of official Printer of the United States will be seen as satisfactory, as will your proposals regarding the various offices in New York City that we discussed. Kind regards.

     George McClellan

     Marble smiled and shook his head, still amazed at the political ineptitude of the former commander of the Army of the Potomac. When Butler had thrown Marble in jail, McClellan had elected never to speak to him again. But when Butler let him out, dangling the possibility of throwing the power of the Butler political machine behind the McClellan candidacy, suddenly Marble was thrust back into favor. Such was the power of the pen Marble wielded through the *New York World*.

     He was determined that this power should increase. Already, he was quietly negotiating agreements with the owners of the *Chicago Times* and the *Cincinnati Enquirer* that would allow him to purchase shares in their respective newspapers. These prospective deals would not give him control of the newspapers, but they would give him sufficient sway over them to exercise a significant amount of influence. He was also laying plans to start a new newspaper in distant San Francisco, giving him a foothold on the Pacific Coast of the United States.

     The future was bright, as far as Marble was concerned. Perhaps, on a certain philosophical level, it was not for the best that the Union was about to be torn apart. Still, whatever form the United States took in the uncertain future, it was clear that Manton Marble would be a major player in it and that was all that really mattered.

*   *   *   *   *

October 2, Morning

     As Grant rode Cincinnati along the column of troops from the Army of the Tennessee awaiting their turn to cross the pontoon bridge over the Chattahoochee River at Sandtown, he could see defeat in their eyes. Many of these troops were men he had led to victory at Vicksburg, who had once looked upon him as a father figure. But now they refused to cheer him, or even to acknowledge his presence as he rode past. They marched with an uncaring step, exhibiting a disrespectful nonchalance that the officers had attempted to correct without success. In many places, discarded equipment littered the ground as the men sought to lighten their burdens by disposing of items they no longer wanted to carry. According to many regimental commanders, desertions had increased sharply, the number of men claiming to be sick had gone up, and many men were refusing to carry out their basic duties.

     The men had behaved poorly during the Battle of Fairburn. The attacks against fortified rebel positions had not been pressed home, with the men going to ground early and either retreating or staying put until nightfall. When Johnston's surprise attack had struck Grant's left flank, the men had run away in unseemly haste. The collapse in morale was evident even during Howard's momentarily successful attack on the rebel left wing, during which many men had broken ranks to loot the enemy camps.

It was little consolation to Grant that the withdrawal, at least, was going according to plan. As he had outlined to Howard and McPherson, the Army of the Tennessee would pull back toward the ford at Sandtown while the Army of the Cumberland retired toward the ford at Campbellton. Two pontoon bridges had been constructed at each location, which would hopefully allow the two forces to pull back to the north side of the river in a reasonable amount of time.

The rebels were shadowing their movements, as if gently nudging the Northerners back toward the river. Although there had been some sharp skirmishes between the forward pickets of the rebel divisions and the rear guard units of Grant's forces, the rebels did not seem to be preparing a major attack. This was a great relief for Grant, as the condition of his men combined with an acute shortage of ammunition made any serious engagement a potential disaster. Grant only prayed that Joe Johnston remained unaware of just how vulnerable the Union forces truly were. If the rebel commander knew that the Northerners had only enough ammunition for a single day's heavy fighting, he might throw off his characteristic caution and mount a major offensive. The result could be a disaster comparable to Peachtree Creek.

If Grant had any second thoughts about deciding to withdraw over the river, they had been terminated when his scouts had reported more trains arriving in Fairburn from the south, bringing the final elements of the Army of Tennessee that had been deployed to Alabama to protect against his phantom thrust toward that state. All told, the rebel army probably numbered between thirty-five and forty thousand men, equal if not superior to the number of Union troops in the field. Their spirits were high and their ammunition plentiful.

Grant knew when he was outmatched. If he stayed south of the river, he risked the destruction of both the Army of the Cumberland and the Army of the Tennessee.

He expected both of his armies to complete the crossing of the river during the night. When it was finished, the pontoon bridges would be destroyed to prevent the rebel forces from crossing over themselves, though Grant highly doubted that they would attempt to do so. Johnston, having beaten Grant and secured Atlanta, would not make any effort at seizing the initiative. Why should he? Having achieved his own objectives, Johnston would need only to wait until the Northern election and the arrival of winter ended the war altogether. One dependability of Joe Johnston was that he would always carefully conserve the lives of his soldiers. Risking them all in an offensive move north of the river would make no sense.

Once his forces had completed their withdrawal over the river, Grant would have the cavalry patrol the river around Campbellton and Sandtown, while the main body returned to the camps at Smyrna, Marietta and Acworth to rest and refit. He expected that Johnston would shift the two corps of the Army of Tennessee back to Atlanta, while leaving sufficient forces to keep an eye on the river crossing as well. Then, both armies would rest and recover from the trauma of the last few weeks.

Grant had not read the newspapers that had been sent down from the North. He had not wanted to. In any event, he knew what the headlines would say. All the blame for the failure to capture Atlanta or defeat the Army of Tennessee, and the thirty thousand casualties they had sustained, would be laid squarely on his own shoulders. Grant was used to harsh treatment from the press, having been denounced for the high casualties at Shiloh and the failures of his early efforts to capture Vicksburg. Those setbacks had later been made right. This time, however, there would be no chance for redemption.

Lincoln would share the blame, too. If his defeat in the upcoming election had appeared very likely a week earlier, it was now all but certain.

As he watched his defeated troops march past, none of them meeting his gaze, Grant's face remained expressionless, but his heart was filled with a great sadness. Four years earlier, just before the winter of secession had torn the country apart, Grant had been resigned to living an obscure life as a penniless failure. The coming of the war had somehow lifted him. Rejoining the army, he had risen steadily through his victories at Fort Donelson, Vicksburg, and Missionary Ridge. At the height of his glory, there was even talk about his becoming President of the United States when the war was over.

Just as it had raised him up, the war had now driven him down. He would, indeed, live out his days as a failure. At least before the war he had been obscure and unknown, his disappointments evident only to his family and friends. Now, his failure was so vast that it would be remembered in the history books for all time to come. Grant would be known to the world as the man whose failings had resulted in the destruction of the American Union.

He did not know what he would do when the war ended. Perhaps he would write a book about his experiences in the great conflict. It might be of interest to future historians and, more importantly, provide some measure of financial stability for his family. Other than that, he supposed he would simply stay out of the limelight as much possible, ignore the disparagement of his name that would float about everywhere, and just fade away.

He put the thought out of his mind, reaching instead for another cigar. For the time being, he had to see that the river crossing was completed successfully.

*   *   *   *   *

October 4, Afternoon

McFadden stumbled more than walked through the door of the building. Every step caused a painful and uncomfortable numbness in his limbs. He had lost track of exactly how much punishment his body had endured over the past few weeks. He had been grazed by a Yankee bullet at the Battle of East Point, been knocked senseless by a clubbed musket during the fighting in the Blood Bucket, and reduced to total exhaustion by an almost complete lack of sleep.

That had all been endured before the train had exploded. His last clear memory had been running away from the train as fast as he could. He remembered hearing the immense sound of the detonation and momentarily feeling the shockwave of the blast, but the memory had a vague and ethereal quality to it, rather like one struggling to recall the contents of a dream.

His next conscious memory had been waking up in the woods near the tree line by the tracks of the Western and Atlantic Railroad. It had been sometime during the night. He had no idea how he had gotten there, nor did he know how long he had been unconscious. The grass along the track was scorched by fire, so he theorized that someone had pulled his body out of the path of the flames, but he could not be certain. There had been debris all over the place, fires burning in the woods, as well as the scattered bodies of many Union soldiers.

McFadden's memory of the rest of the night and the next day was blurry and uncertain. The verse from Corinthians about looking through a glass darkly came to his mind as he struggled to remember exactly what he had done. He recalled trying to find Private Pearson but being unsuccessful after several hours of searching. Perhaps he had collapsed and fallen unconscious again, maybe even more than once. It was hard to say. He eventually gave up the search for Pearson as futile and lay down to sleep in the woods, without a blanket or shelter of any kind.

He had been awoken the next morning by the sound of marching men. Only somewhat revived, he had realized that the Union troops around Atlanta were marching back toward the Chattahoochee River, though he did not know why. He had no longer cared. Having accomplished the mission given to him by Cleburne, McFadden considered his duty done. He did not know what he wanted to do next, only that he wanted nothing to do with the war any longer.

Getting back to Atlanta seemed like the logical thing, though he hadn't considered what he would do when he got there. He remained in the woods, still in his Union uniform, staying under cover and enduring the hunger as best he could. Eventually, the Yankee forces completed their withdrawal from the area, leaving the path back to Atlanta open. Then, it had been a relatively easy matter of discarding his Union uniform and simply walking back to the city. He had to move slowly, however, as his entire body ached.

McFadden had passed back into the Confederate lines without difficulty. He had encountered a Confederate patrol a mile outside of the defenses and told its commander that he was an escaped prisoner, which seemed to satisfy the man. As he passed through the fortifications, he noticed that they were rapidly filling up with additional soldiers, which could only mean that one or both of the other two corps of the Army of Tennessee which had gone to Alabama with Johnston had returned to the city. From what he could tell, the Confederates had defeated Grant and won the campaign.

McFadden scarcely cared. He did not bother to report his return to Cleburne. Perhaps he would do so later, but perhaps not. All he cared about right now was finding a place to rest, both physically and spiritually.

This was why he had come to the Central Presbyterian Church of Atlanta.

The church, like almost everything else in Atlanta, was simultaneously new and heavily damaged. The building had only been constructed four years earlier, not long after the existing Presbyterian congregation in Atlanta had split in two. The separation had been caused by some arcane dispute which had made no sense to McFadden when Robert Turnbow had tried to explain it to him. The church had been nothing fancy to begin with. It had been struck repeatedly by Union shellfire, but if any fires had broken out they had been quickly extinguished. All the windows had been shattered and, as he stumbled inside, McFadden could see that the floor was covered in broken glass and pieces of the shattered wooden beams.

Half a dozen people were inside, one man, one boy, and four women. They were busily cleaning up the floor of the church, and looked up at McFadden when he entered.

"Can I help you, soldier?" the man asked.

McFadden looked at the man in confusion. The authority with which he had spoken suggested to McFadden that he was the minister. But having entered the church, McFadden had no idea what he wanted to do or even why he had come. There had not seemed any better place to go. As far as he could tell, the 7th Texas had been destroyed, so he had no regimental camp to which to return.

Indeed, he did not even know who his immediate superior was at this point.

The minister looked at McFadden sympathetically. "What's your name, son?"

"James McFadden," he answered simply, feeling like a schoolboy.

"I'm John Rogers. I'm the minister of this church."

McFadden nodded. "Yes, sir. I've seen you preach."

"You look like you have had a rough time of things, James."

Despite himself, McFadden almost laughed. "If you only knew, Reverend."

Rodgers nodded. "Is there anything I can do for you?"

McFadden considered this. "Could I possibly have some time to myself here?" He paused before continuing, uncertain if he were using the right words. "I'd like to have some time alone with God."

Rodgers nodded and, without another word, motioned for the other people to leave the church. As McFadden walked slowly up to the altar, he heard the door close behind him, leaving him alone.

He didn't kneel down. It wasn't in his character to get down on his knees, even when he wanted to talk to God. Nor, staring at the crucifix, did it occur to him to actually speak. As his father had told him countless times when he was growing up, God knows what goes on inside a man's head. Simply by thinking, he had said, we are effectively talking to God.

He wanted to ask God why he had suffered so much. Why had his brother had to die such a miserable death? Why did his family have to be butchered? Why had McFadden been allowed to continue living when so many of his comrades, men he had counted as friends, had been slaughtered on a dozen different battlefields? And why had Annie and her parents, who had briefly brought light back into his life, been killed by the guns of the Yankees? Why had the war come in the first place?

McFadden waited for an answer. God said nothing in response.

He frowned, feeling foolish. What had he expected, after all? His father might have raised him as the devout son of a Presbyterian minister, but the bloody years of war had cured him of whatever sentimental attachment to the church had remained. Had he seriously thought that a burning bush was going to appear? Or that an angel would descend through the ceiling to answer his questions?

He was about to turn away in disgust, but a wave of exhaustion swept over him. He sat down in one of the pews. His wounds, the battering his head had taken, and simple lack of sleep were finally catching up with him. The anxiety caused by combat and the mission to destroy the bridge had provided him with sufficient nervous energy to keep him going until this moment. Now that he was safe, the fighting over, and his mission accomplished, his body cried out for rest.

McFadden fell asleep seconds after sitting down on the pew, his chin resting on his chest. He had not slept long before he was awoken when a hand tightly touched his shoulder.

"James?" a voice said hesitantly.

He came awake in an instant, pushing himself up from the pew and spinning around to look at the source of the voice. Standing before him, alive and apparently unharmed, was Annie Turnbow. He had not heard her come in. It was as though she had simply materialized out of nothing.

"Annie?" he asked, his voice barely above a whisper. "It cannot be."

Her eyes narrowed in confusion. "What? What do you mean?"

"You're dead!"

"Dead?"

"I saw you," he said, almost angrily. "I saw your body. Burned. Burned up in your house!"

"The house?" she asked. "It was struck by a Union shell. It caught fire and burned down."

"But there were bodies!" he protested. "Three burned bodies in the house!"

"My parents," she said sadly. "They were trapped inside. A friend of my father, too. Those were been the bodies you saw." She spoke with a deep sadness. McFadden knew the depths of such sadness better than anyone.

"I'm so sorry," he said simply, even as his mind raced to make sense of it all. Annie had been alive this entire time?

"What happened to Jupiter and Mattie?" he asked.

"They abandoned me and ran away to the Yankees."

"Where have you been?" he asked. He wanted to take her into his arms, yet he hesitated. Part of him wondered if she were some sort of phantom who would vanish from his sight the moment he took a step toward her.

"The house was gone. I've stayed here at the church since then. Lots of people sleep here during the night." She arched her head slightly. "I thought that's why you came."

"No," he stammered. "I thought you were dead. I thought you died in the fire."

"Why did you come here, then?"

"I-" he stammered. He glanced at the altar, where the crucifix still stood quietly, as though watching them. "I don't really know."

She smiled hesitantly. "I do."

He smiled back.

"Well, I am very happy to see you alive," she said, cautiously taking a step forward. "I heard that your brigade was in the worst of the fighting around East Point and on the southern defenses. They said nearly all the Texans were killed."

McFadden was jolted by the thought that not only had Annie been alive all this time, but that she had been worried about him. During their all-too-brief time together, it had been difficult to fully grasp that Annie might actually feel love for him. Indeed, he couldn't fathom why she would even look on him as anything other than a barbarian. He had let her into his life and shared with her many of his secrets. She had seen the depth of his rage, but she alone had also seen something in him that could be redeemed, something of which he himself had been unaware until he had met her.

"Were you there?" she asked. "Were you there in those battles?"

"Yes," he said simply.

She looked him over with concern, clearly seeing the physical torment his body had endured over the past several days. She took another step forward. Finally, he reached out to her and pulled her into his embrace. Her face pressed against his chest and her felt her taking long, reassured breaths. He forgot the burning wound to his torso. The pain in his head subsided and then disappeared entirely. As they stood together, the deeper spiritual wounds inside of him, which she had begun nurse months ago, now healed completely.

He would go with her, McFadden decided. He would report to Cleburne, of course, for he was no deserter. As soon as he could, though, he would get out of the army and devote the rest of his life to Annie. For the first time since leaving for New Mexico, he felt he had a place in the world to call home, and that place was wherever Annie Turnbow was.

"The man you said you had to go after," she said softly. "Did you get him?"

"No."

She pulled back slightly and looked up into his eyes.

"He's still out there?"

He shrugged. "I suppose so."

"Are you going to go after him again?"

"No," he said firmly. He meant it, too. Cheeky Joe had been a demon, but McFadden was through dealing with demons. "I no longer care about him, Annie. All I care about is being with you."

Her eyes widened, and he decided to say the words he had been thinking for months.

"I love you, Annie. I want to be with you for the rest of my life."

"Oh, James. I love you, too."

Chapter Twenty Two

November 8, Night

The impersonal clicking of the telegraph machines was the only sound that broke the silence in Major Eckert's office in the War Department. No one had spoken much since the first election returns had begun filtering in three hours before. Outside, an appropriately gloomy rainstorm was coming down, distant lightning and thunder seeming to manifest the angry response of nature itself to what was happening.

The quiet belied the fact that the room was filled with people. Stanton and Seward were both there, as were some other members of the Cabinet, reading the telegrams as they came in. All wore the most somber expressions on their faces. Major Eckert occupied himself with paperwork at his desk, while the telegraph clerks hurriedly transcribed the messages coming in. Two staffers kept the room continually supplied with hot coffee. They all maintained a business-as-usual attitude, as though the news streaming into Washington didn't sound the death knell of the Union.

Lincoln sat silently on the couch, quiet and still with his hands on his knees. An infinite sadness was manifest in his deep eyes. He was lonely. He was so lonely.

Stanton finished reading the telegram in his hand. "More returns from Indiana. McClellan remains ahead of us there by twenty thousand votes."

The President nodded. "Yes. It is as I expected it would be in that state. What do you have, Mr. Seward?"

"Some returns from upstate New York. They favor us, but the tide in the state as a whole remains against us. The Democratic vote in New York City is simply too large. McClellan is ahead in the state overall by over forty thousand votes at present."

"It's Tammany Hall's doing, if you ask me," Stanton said. "They control the votes of all the Irish immigrants in New York City. And that bastard Butler has done nothing to stop them. Probably helping them, in fact. Lord knows what the Democrats offered him to make him turn traitor."

Lincoln shook his head. "It doesn't matter why it is happening. Not now. It only matters that it is happening."

The utter resignation with which Lincoln spoke startled the men in the room. They looked over at him in near despair, wanting to comfort their friend and their chief and yet knowing they could not. Lincoln seemed like the floating debris of a sunken ship, quietly bobbing up and down in the sea that had just torn him to pieces.

"Most of New England remains true," Seward said. Normally the most optimistic of men, Seward's voice now seemed desperate to cling to anything that resembled good news. The voting in Massachusetts and most of the neighboring states had favored the Republican ticket, due largely to the strong abolitionist vote. "Only Connecticut and New Hampshire remain undecided. The other New England states have declared for us. That will account for twenty-eight electoral votes in our column."

"Yes," Stanton replied sourly. "And those are the only states which we can definitively place in our column. On the other hand, we can firmly put New York, New Jersey, Delaware, Maryland, and Kentucky in McClellan's column. That gives him sixty-one electoral votes."

"One hundred and seventeen are needed to win the election," Lincoln said jadedly. "McClellan is more than halfway there and the night is yet young."

"It is not over yet," Seward said firmly. "We cannot yet concede Ohio, Indiana, Illinois, or Pennsylvania. Until those states are called, the outcome of the election is still open."

"We are behind in all those states, according to the most recent returns," Stanton growled. "I have to admit that I think Ohio is a lost cause." The Secretary of War said this through gritted teeth, as Ohio was his home state.

Lincoln nodded. "Vallandigham continues to torment me from beyond the grave," he said. A grim smile crossed the President's face. Had the accidental bullet fired from one of those soldiers in New York City not sent the devilish Copperhead to an early grave, everything might have been different.

"If we tally Ohio with the Democrats, that gives McClellan eighty-two electoral votes," Stanton grumbled.

Seward was handed a telegram that had just been transcribed. "Ah, some good news for a change. We have decisively won the state of Kansas."

"No surprise there," Lincoln replied. The state had been largely settled by anti-slavery radicals during the political turmoil that had preceded the war. "I appreciate the support of the good people of Kansas. Unfortunately, the three additional electoral votes this gives us are unlikely to make much difference. It gives us a mere thirty-one votes to McClellan's eight-two."

"There remains a path to victory," Seward said hopefully. "If Illinois and Pennsylvania go our way, and if Michigan, Iowa and Minnesota favor us as well, we will come close to the electoral margin we need."

"Too many ifs," Stanton replied. "Why should we expect those states to go our way when everywhere else the news has been even worse than we expected?"

"I am simply pointing out mathematical reality," Seward said in response, his voice tinged with uncharacteristic irritation.

The night wore on interminably. As it did so, even Seward's optimism began to fray. At ten thirty, conclusive word reached them that Ohio had indeed gone to McClellan. Less than half an hour later, it was confirmed that Pennsylvania had fallen into the Democratic column as well. Every man in the room made the same quick calculation in his head, finding that this gave McClellan one hundred and eight electoral votes. An hour before midnight, McClellan was within a hairsbreadth of crossing the electoral threshold.

Between eleven fifteen and eleven thirty, there was a brief surge of hope for the Republicans. The telegraph wires hummed with the news that Minnesota, West Virginia, and Missouri had all gone for the Republicans, raising their vote total from thirty-one to fifty-one. Lincoln knew that his victory in Missouri, a slave state that had sent several thousand troops to fight for the Confederacy, was due primarily to pro-Confederate Missourians having boycotted the election. But at this point, he was willing to take any vote he could get.

The momentary rise in Republican fortunes proved short lived, however. Just after midnight, the telegraph begin clicking once again. One of the clerks quickly jotted the message down.

"It's from Illinois," he said simply. Everyone in the room tensed, for all knew that if the Democrats won Illinois and its sixteen electoral votes, George McClellan would be the next President of the United States.

Stanton snatched up the paper the moment the young man had finished writing. He scanned through the message without a word, while every other man stared at him intently, not moving or making a sound. The Secretary of War slowly turned toward the sofa on which Lincoln was sitting, gazing at him sadly.

"Illinois has gone for McClellan."

"It is over, gentlemen," Lincoln said in near despair. He raised his hands to cover his face. "Our effort to reunite our nation has failed. Our armies have been repelled and the people have voted us out of office." He looked up, an expression of infinite sadness on his face. "I have failed."

"You are still the President until March, my friend," Seward said. "Perhaps if we mount a renewed offensive in Virginia, we could"

"To what end, William?" Lincoln snapped. "Do the rebels show any signs of breaking? No. Quite the contrary, in fact. Their armies seem stronger and more motivated than ever. Our own armies are demoralized, desertion is rife, and the men have no stomach for further fighting. Besides, the approaching winter means that any offensive will become impossible in a matter of weeks. How could I live with myself if I ordered thousands of men to die for a cause that has clearly already been lost?"

Lincoln stood and walked over to Major Eckert's desk. He took up pen and paper and quickly scribbled a note, eventually handing it to Eckert.

"Major, would you be so kind as to transmit this message to George McClellan, in Trenton, New Jersey?"

"Of course, Mr. President."

"What are you telling him?" Seward asked.

"I am congratulating him on his victory in the election and offering my support for his efforts to preserve the Union."

"What do you hope to accomplish by such a message?" Seward asked. "He'll simply ignore you."

"Perhaps so," Lincoln said sadly. "Probably he will, in truth. But if I cannot save the Union, I at least want history to know I tried my best."

*   *   *   *   *

January 1, Morning

It was the fourth time President Jefferson Davis had hosted a New Year's Day reception at the White House of the Confederacy. For the first time, he was actually enjoying himself.

Having endured two hours of handshakes in the receiving line, he now happily looked around the room, holding his third glass of champagne. The atmosphere was effervescent, with every guest appearing as cheerful and content as could possibly be imagined. There was General John Hunt Morgan in a fine dress uniform, regaling a small gathering of elegantly attired ladies about his famous escape from a Yankee prison. Rear Admiral Raphael Semmes, recently returned from England, was telling a similar group of females about his exploits when captain of the *CSS Alabama*. On the other side of the room, noble and austere, General Robert E. Lee stood next to his wife, talking politely with Secretary of the Navy Stephen Mallory. Everywhere there was laughter and animated conversation, helped by the copious amounts of champagne and fine food that had been thoughtfully provided by Secretary of the Treasury Trenholm.

He thought for a moment about the previous two months. It had not been until the morning of November 10 that clear word of Lincoln's electoral defeat had arrived in Richmond. In the end, Lincoln had won Kansas, Missouri, Minnesota, West Virginia, Rhode Island, Vermont, Massachusetts and Maine. McClellan had been victorious in every other state, beating Lincoln by one hundred and eighty-three electoral votes to fifty-one. In the popular vote, McClellan had taken fifty-five percent to Lincoln's thirty-eight percent, with seven percent having gone to the Radical candidate John Fremont. It seemed that the Radical vote had been sufficient to guarantee a Democratic victory in certain states where McClellan had not achieved a majority, thereby contributing to Lincoln's defeat. Even better for the Democrats was the fact that they had gained control of the House of Representatives and cut down the Republican majority in the Senate.

With Lincoln's defeat at the polls, everything had changed overnight. It had been just as Davis had predicted several months earlier. The Lincoln administration had declined to communicate officially with any Confederate authorities, still stubbornly refusing to acknowledge the independence of the South. Union military commanders in the field, though, had sent word under flags of truce that they would refrain from offensive military operations if the Southern forces agreed to do the same. Throughout mid-November, the guns had fallen silent on the various battlefronts across the Confederacy. Despite occasional skirmishes, the truce appeared to be holding rather well.

In late November, Thomas Seymour, the former Democratic governor of Connecticut, had appeared in Richmond, having run through the blockade at Wilmington. He had brought with him a personal letter from George McClellan addressed to Davis, which had referred to the Confederate President as "the chosen representative of the South" and had offered to call a "convention of the states to resolve the problems besetting all our people." Seymour had offered to act as a go-between and carry back to McClellan whatever response Davis saw fit to make. The Confederate President had thereupon closeted himself with Judah Benjamin to draft an appropriate response.

Since McClellan had not yet been inaugurated as President of the United States, Davis and Benjamin had decided to treat the letter as simply a courtesy from one gentleman to another. Therefore, they could safely ignore the fact that McClellan did not address Davis by his proper title and that he declined to technically acknowledge the legal existence of the Confederacy. The constitutional and diplomatic niceties, they had decided, could be dealt with later.

Three days after receiving the letter from McClellan, Davis had handed Seymour the response he and Benjamin had carefully crafted. They accepted the idea of a conference but insisting that it take place "between the authorities of the United States and the authorities of the Confederate States". Seymour had dutifully departed with the letter and had not yet returned.

Davis was not much concerned as to how McClellan would respond. If he insisted on holding a convention of the states rather than agreeing on negotiations between two individual governments, it would serve Confederate aims perfectly well. The important thing was to commence negotiations as quickly as possible, so as to make what was an informal and shaky ceasefire into a permanent and official armistice. Once that was done, political realities were such that it would be impossible for the incoming McClellan administration to resume hostilities. If McClellan agreed to official negotiations between the two governments from the beginning, so much the better. Either way, Confederate independence was all but assured.

Davis was in the midst of a pleasant conversation with General John Breckinridge and General Wade Hampton when he noticed Secretary Benjamin enter the room. From long experience, he realized that the look on his friend's face indicated that he had important news to share.

Surprisingly, Benjamin only nodded in the President's direction and did not approach. Instead, he picked up a glass of champagne and strode toward the center of the room, sipping as he went. He then picked up a fork and began tapping loudly on the glass, continuing with the ringing sound until everyone in the drawing room was silent and looking in his direction.

"Forgive me, ladies and gentlemen," Benjamin said with a grin. "I hope I may be excused for interrupting the festivities, but I think that the news I have to impart to all of you will be most welcome."

A hush fell over the crowd. All eyes were intently focused on Benjamin.

"This morning, I received a dispatch from Mr. Mason in London. The House of Commons voted two weeks ago on a resolution to recognize the independence of the Confederate States. I am happy to tell you all that a decided majority of the Members of Parliament voted in favor of the resolution. The United Kingdom has officially recognized the Confederacy as a sovereign state!"

The room erupted in cheers. The surprise was such that several people had to ask the person standing next to them whether they had heard correctly. It took Davis a few moments to fully process what Benjamin had just said. Great Britain, the world's most powerful state, had recognized Confederate independence. France could therefore not be far behind, as Napoleon III had long said he would be guided by the British on the question of Confederate sovereignty. If Britain and France both recognized the Confederacy, Russia, Austria, and the other great nations of Europe would quickly follow.

"Oh, how I wish I could see Abe Lincoln's face at this moment!" Varina Davis exclaimed.

"It is truly wonderful, my dear," Davis replied. "Wonderful!"

Breckinridge proposed three cheers, and the hurrahs filled the room with joy. Davis barely heard them, as his own mind was spinning. Surely, this momentous news had already reached Washington and New York. There could no longer be any doubt that the upcoming peace negotiations with the McClellan administration would be conducted on the basis of two nations speaking to one another as diplomatic equals. All the talk about a convention of the states would be revealed for the nonsense it was.

Benjamin came over and extended his hand. "Congratulations, Mr. President."

"And to you, Mr. Secretary. This is the day we have been waiting for since the beginning of the war."

"The British and French are merely acknowledging reality. With McClellan coming into office and already committed to negotiations with us, they wanted to inject themselves into the situation so as to derive the maximum advantage. With Lincoln now a lame duck, they no longer fear an invasion of Canada. I would expect the arrival of representatives of the European powers, all clamoring for our cotton and tobacco, within the near future."

Davis nodded vigorously. "They will be more than welcome. Every pound of cotton and tobacco that is sold on the wharves of European ports will mean more hard cash coming into the Confederacy."

"The Yankees have not made much of an effort to enforce the blockade since the election. With diplomatic recognition now in the bag, it would not surprise me if the European governments insist that the blockade be completely lifted. The ships will soon be sailing to and from Wilmington and Charleston without much trouble, I should think."

"If Mr. Seymour is on his way back with McClellan's response to our letter, I suspect that he may turn around and get an revised version," Davis said happily. "Everything is changed by this most glorious news."

Davis suddenly experienced an elation rarely felt during one's life, the kind of spinning he had felt in his head and stomach when Varina had accepted his marriage proposal or when he had been chosen to represent Mississippi in the United States Senate. He couldn't quite persuade himself that his dream was coming to pass. The Confederacy was going to be a nation, it was going to govern itself, it was going to decide its future for itself without any outsiders attempting to dictate its fate. All for which he had striven and suffered was going to come to pass.

His mind told him that the war really was over and that he needed to begin thinking about the problems that would beset the

Confederacy when the last Union soldier marched off Southern soil. After all, his term as President would not end until early 1868. Having led the Confederacy through the fires of war, he would now face the even more difficult task of leading it through the early years of peace. The economy was in tatters, the transportation infrastructure had been mostly destroyed, the various factions within the Confederacy would no longer have the Union threat to serve as a unifying force, and good relations between the Union and the Confederacy had somehow to be established.

More than any other problem, however, the Confederacy would have to come to grips with slavery. Perhaps a million slaves had been set free by Lincoln's Emancipation Proclamation and over a hundred thousand of them had joined the Union Army to fight for the freedom of their people. Despite the Confederacy's victory, the European nations as well as the United States remained unalterably opposed to the institution of slavery and this would doubtless be a millstone around the neck of the Confederacy's international relations. Deep in the recesses of his heart, he knew that the South would eventually have to rid itself of an institution that would one day be rightfully damned by history.

What the future held, Davis could not even venture to guess.

"Are you all right, my dear?" Varina asked him. "You look as though you're disappointed in the news." Her voice betrayed understandable confusion.

Davis smiled and laughed softly. The difficult questions could, at the very least, wait until tomorrow. "Yes, dear. I am fine. " He turned and looked into the eyes of his beautiful wife. "Let us have another glass of champagne. I have a feeling 1865 is going to be a very good year."

*　　　　*　　　　*　　　　*　　　　*

January 25, Night

"Sign here, General Thomas. If you please."

The Confederate major passed the pen across the table. Thomas noted in passing that the man's uniform was so immaculate that it could only have been brand new. He had noticed that other Southern soldiers were also wearing much better uniforms than had been the case a few months before. Newspapers were much easier to acquire in Camp Oglethorpe these days and many of them were reporting that the Union Navy was no longer enforcing the blockade with any enthusiasm. With peace so obviously around the corner, what was the point?

He looked over the paper. "And this says?"

"That you acknowledge being properly exchanged as a prisoner-of-war."

His eyebrows went up. "I am exchanged?"

"That's right, General. The Yankees gave us a hundred privates for you. Better to have them in our ranks again rather than dying of starvation and disease at Point Lookout, don't you think?"

He carefully scanned the document. "But this is an exchange, not a parole, yes?"

"Correct. When you return to Union lines, you are an officer of the United States free to again engage in combat against the Confederacy. But we really don't think you'll cause us any trouble. Grant and Meade haven't troubled us since the election and the only fighting going on is some minor skirmishing out in Arkansas. Once McClellan gets in, the war will be over. That's what all the papers say, at any rate."

Thomas grunted and began scrawling his name across the bottom of the document. He felt that a hundred privates was far too low a rate of exchange for a general of his abilities and importance, but it would do no good to complain. It would only damage his reputation, after all.

He finished signing his name and looked up at the major. "Now what?"

"You'll stay with us one more night here at Camp Oglethorpe. Tomorrow you'll be taken to Macon and put on a train north to Atlanta. We have set up an exchange site with your forces at the site of the old Western and Atlantic Railroad Bridge over the Chattahoochee, right at the spot where Grant's big ammunition train was blown up. You've heard about that, yes?"

"Yes," Thomas said sourly.

"The one hundred privates will cross over to the south bank and you'll be escorted over to the north bank. Pretty routine, General."

Thomas nodded. Prisoner exchanges were a fairly simple matter, after all.

The thoughts running through his head, however, were anything but simple. As he was escorted from the office back to his tiny cabin, his head was swirling with conflicting emotions. It was now more than six months since he had suffered the catastrophic defeat at Peachtree Creek. Since coming to Camp Oglethorpe, he had faced both the enticing possibility of escape and the dreaded prospect of the hangman's noose.

Returning to his cabin, he fell onto his pathetically inadequate cot, which nearly buckled under his weight. Tonight would be the last night he would ever sleep on it. He told himself that, no matter what life had in store for him from this day forward, he would never sleep on anything so uncomfortable again.

He could comfort himself with the knowledge that he had aided the escape of Truman Seymour and perhaps two dozen other Union officers back in September. Over a hundred men had successfully scampered through the tunnel to freedom. Though most had been recaptured in the following days by roving bands of Georgia Militia and returned to the camp, nearly thirty remained unaccounted for. The first thing Thomas intended to do when he reached the Union lines was to inquire as to the whereabouts of the men who had broken out. Thomas hoped that at least some of them had made it back to the Union lines. As Grant's offensive against Atlanta was in full swing when the escape attempt had been made, it stood to reason that the rebels had other things on their minds than trying to find a few unarmed escaped prisoners.

Thomas wondered what sort of reception he would receive from General Grant and the others. He didn't expect it to be pleasant. Outwardly, all would no doubt be politeness and relief at his release from prison. Behind his back, Thomas knew, his detractors would do their best to discredit him and lay the blame for the failure of the Union cause squarely on his shoulders. Grant, Sherman, and all their friends from the Army of the Tennessee, to say nothing of Meade and the generals of the Army of the Potomac, would say that everything would have turned out well if only George Thomas had not lost the Battle of Peachtree Creek. The newspapers, always eager for a scapegoat and remembering Thomas's Southern origins, would quickly leap onto the bandwagon.

His name was already reviled in the South. Now, Thomas supposed, it would be the North's turn.

The war over rapidly coming to a close. Whatever name it would eventually be given, the conflict would be written about in the history books long after everyone involved in it passed from the scene. What would they say about George Thomas? Would they remember his victory at Mill Springs? Would they remember how he secured the victory at Stone's River or prevented complete catastrophe at Chickamauga? Probably not. They would remember only his disastrous failure at Peachtree Creek.

But, Thomas thought hopefully, perhaps the story was not yet over. Even if his reputation was blackened, he would still be a major general in the United States Army. The independence of the Confederacy would require that a large army be maintained and he would likely have some role to play in organizing it. There were too many issues remaining between the North and the South to allow peace to settle easily over the land. If war ever did break out again, George Thomas fully intended to play his part in it.

With that pleasant thought, he drifted off to sleep.

February 10, Morning

Cleburne looked at himself in the mirror, pursing his lips and shaking his head in disappointment. He had gone to considerable trouble to turn himself out as best he could, for obviously he should look his best on his own wedding day. The best tailor in Mobile had been paid a pretty penny to provide him with the finest Confederate dress uniform, using gray cloth of the highest quality that had just come in from England. The gold lace was perfectly embroidered and the laborious ironing had insured that not a single wrinkle was visible. At his side hung a ceremonial sword that had been presented to him by the men of the 15th Arkansas Infantry, the regiment he had commanded at the very beginning of the war.

Yet Cleburne was unsatisfied. The uniform and sword might be perfect, but the face looking back at him from the mirror was far from it. He had never thought of himself as handsome, though he had been told that most ladies considered him rather attractive. He had always been a shy man around people he did not already know well.

Susan's father had offered to assign one of his slaves to serve as Cleburne's valet the previous day, but he had decided that he needed to dress himself for his own wedding. Mr. Tarleton had taken his decline with a raised eyebrow. In retrospect, Cleburne realized that it had been a minor test to search out the truth of his alleged emancipationist sentiments. The man was probably happy that his daughter would be marrying the savior of Atlanta, but the publication of his proposal to enlist freed slaves in the army was certainly not being taken kindly in the upper echelons of Confederate society. Cleburne was not expecting many dinner invitations.

There was a quick knock on the door and, before he said a word, it opened. Hardee entered, a broad smile on his face. Every other step thumped on the floor, as his amputated left leg had been replaced by a cork peg. Like most high quality products, it had been imported from England. Hardee was already dressed in his own fine uniform and seemed as happy as a West Point cadet about to go to a rollicking party.

"Well, Pat?" Hardee was saying with boyish enthusiasm. "Doesn't a peg leg make my dress uniform all the grander?"

Cleburne laughed. "Your ability to flirt with the ladies has increased now that you're a warrior gallantly wounded in battle. Your wife has reason for concern."

"I trust you will restrain me from engaging in any untoward adventures," Hardee replied.

He smiled, attempting to fix his collar so that it appeared perfect. In truth, despite his teasing nature where females were concerned, Hardee could no more be unfaithful to his wife than he could be unfaithful to the Confederacy.

Glancing at the peg leg, Cleburne again gave a silent thanks to God that his friend's life had been spared. For nearly a week after the amputation, fever had seemed likely to carry away William Hardee. His strength and endurance had passed the ultimate test, however, and he now seemed healthier than ever. Whereas many men grew depressed and despondent at the loss of a limb, Hardee actually delighted in showing off his new appendage. The man's good humor was simply irrepressible.

"You look passably handsome, my friend," Hardee said. "At least, I do not think you shall make a fool of yourself today."

"I thank you for your vote of confidence."

"All eyes will be on your beautiful bride in any event. The guests will scarcely notice you are there."

"How I wish that were true. But their eyes will be on me, you know. People will be whispering how foolish Mr. Tarleton's daughter is to marry the idiot who wanted to free the slaves."

"Nonsense," Hardee said forcefully. "Let the Senate prattle on for as long as they wish. The people know you as the hero who saved Atlanta. No one can ever take that away from you."

Cleburne shook his head. Although his promotion to lieutenant general had been endorsed by both Joe Johnston and Robert E. Lee, the two great heroes of the hour, his confirmation had been filibustered to death in the Senate. A separate measure to give Cleburne the official Thanks of Congress for his defense of Atlanta had also failed. While a few of the newspapers were lionizing Cleburne for what he had achieved in September, most of them were downplaying his role, giving the bulk of the credit to General Johnston instead.

Hardee was still talking. "Besides which, what do you care about what the people are saying? Today is about nothing except you and your bride. And Susan's love for you knows no bounds. Don't think for a moment that she was not besieged by an army of angry friends when your proposal became public, all of them telling her she should break off her engagement. She has stood by you through the storm. Her parents, too. Focus on that. Today is the happiest day of your life, after all."

Cleburne smiled and nodded. It was, indeed, the happiest day of his life. Within the next hour, Susan Tarleton would be his wife. Against the fact that she loved him, all the words and denunciations of the Confederate Senate did not matter in the slightest. Moreover, the fact that William Hardee would be standing beside him as best man and Calhoun Benham would also be among the groomsmen meant more to him than any number of newspaper editorials.

There was a soft knock on the door and a well-dressed slave entered.

"Begging your pardon, General Cleburne," the man said, using the refined accent that house slaves of wealthy families often possessed. "Mr. Tarleton wishes to know whether you are ready."

Hardee answered for him. "Tell Mr. Tarleton that General Cleburne will be along just as soon as he finishes fiddling with his collar."

"No, don't tell him that!" Cleburne said quickly, forestalling the slave's departure. "Just tell him we'll be along presently."

"Very good, sir." The black man bowed his head and was gone.

"Think he would have made a good soldier?" Hardee asked with a sarcastic grin.

"Give a man a uniform, rifle, a bit of discipline, and a sense of unit pride, and he will be as good a soldier as any who marched with Napoleon."

Hardee shook his head. "You're the bravest man I have ever met, Patrick Cleburne. But not having been born in this country, you still have much to learn about how to be a Southerner."

"Oh?" Cleburne asked, mildly annoyed. "Such as?"

"Learning not to say what you honestly think."

Cleburne, having gotten his collar in as good a shape as possible, turned toward the door, electing not to respond to Hardee's last comment. "Do I look all right?" he asked.

Hardee smiled warmly. "You look like a happy man about to be married to a beautiful woman."

"Let's get on with it, then."

*   *   *   *   *

March 3, Morning

"Is that everything?" Lincoln asked.

"Just about, sir," Hay replied. He and Nicolay picked up a heavy box at both ends, carefully stepping out of the office in order to load it onto one of the wagons waiting outside. He had asked his secretaries to personally load the boxes rather than rely on servants, as he worried that copies of sensitive papers might go missing and find themselves in the possession of unscrupulous newspaper editors.

The President, momentarily alone, looked about the office resignedly. The floor was covered with boxes and crates stuffed with papers of every kind. Since the election results nearly four months earlier had turned him into a lame duck, he had put his three secretaries to work diligently making copies of all the official correspondence that had been generated by his administration so that he could take it back with him to Springfield. This had been intended to simply give them something to do as much as anything else, but the thought had taken root in Lincoln's mind that he might write a book about his time in the White House. If he did so, having easy access to the material would prove invaluable.

The last few months had passed by in a daze. After the election, the winter had closed in and prevented any significant military operations. Rather than waste the lives of men for no purpose, Lincoln had given Grant, Meade, and the other army commanders the authority to enter into ceasefire agreements with the enemy commanders opposing them. Lincoln recalled how his hand had trembled when he had given the message to Major Eckert to transmit to the generals in the field. He would always remember the moment as one of the darkest of his life.

Mary Todd Lincoln had already left Washington, having taken a train to Springfield a week earlier. She had somehow convinced herself that Lincoln had, in fact, been reelected by a wide margin and would continue to serve as President of the United States. It had only been with great difficulty that Lincoln had prevented her from sending out invitations to a victory dinner celebrating his imagined reelection. After that, she had shut herself in one of the White House rooms for nearly two days, crying hysterically. With her mental state clearly unbalanced, Lincoln had persuaded two of her friends to escort her back to Springfield, along with their son Tad. As she was boarding the train, she had reportedly been frantically shouting something about how clothing stores in New York City had robbed her of all her money.

In a certain sense, Lincoln was glad of being freed from the burdens of power. He would now be able to focus his attention on giving his wife the help she obviously needed. He would have to steel himself to endure his wife's insanity the same way he had steeled himself against news of Union defeats like Chancellorsville or Peachtree Creek, but at least the burden would not involve the deaths of thousands of men.

Seward and Stanton entered the room, looking around curiously.

"Good morning, Mr. President," Stanton offered.

"Is it?" Lincoln replied. "It is the morning of my last full day in office. I'm not sure if that makes it a good day, but I suppose it will be better than tomorrow morning is likely to be."

"That's the truth," Seward said sourly. "It is revolting to think that, a mere twenty-four hours from now, that pompous blowhard will be sworn in as President."

Stanton glanced out the window at the gathering gray clouds. "Perhaps there will be a torrential downpour," he said hopefully. "At the very least, the Almighty might express His displeasure by forcing the Copperhead bastards to move the inaugural ceremony indoors."

Lincoln chuckled. "We shall see."

Seward's face curled into anger and he shook his head. "The office of the Presidency has been held by George Washington, Thomas

Jefferson and Andrew Jackson. Now George McClellan is expected to take their place? He would not be fit to shine the shoes of any of those men!"

Lincoln shrugged. "The office has also been held by such men as James Buchanan and Millard Fillmore. Noble men as well as rascals have governed and will govern from within the walls of this house. Democracy, after all, is the manifestation of the will of the people. We cannot always count on the people to make wise decisions, but we must always respect their will whether we agree with it or not."

Stanton only grunted in response. He had never been as infatuated with democracy as Lincoln and Seward, which Lincoln had always found somewhat amusing.

"What will you do now?" Seward asked.

"Go back to Springfield and resume my law practice, I suppose. I asked my old partner, William Herndon, to keep my name on the sign hanging outside our office while I was away in Washington. I'm still a small-town country lawyer at heart. I may travel to Europe at some point, to see all those places I have only read about in books."

"I may attempt to return to the Senate or the Governorship of New York at some point," Seward said. "But first I shall return to Auburn and rest. It should not be difficult for us to find our way home, as the route will be lighted for us every step of the way by our own burning effigies."

Lincoln was pleased to discover that he could laugh at such a morbid joke. Since the election results had come in, he and the members of his cabinet had been violently excoriated by just about every newspaper in the country. He had long been used to such treatment from Democratic newspapers, but now every Republican paper had joined in denouncing him as well. In particular, the abolitionist periodicals in New England had been filled with near-hysterical rage toward him, accusing him of everything from exercising gross incompetence to willfully sabotaging efforts to abolish slavery.

It would be this way for some time, Lincoln knew. Having failed to win the war and having seen hundreds of thousands of their sons, husbands, and brothers lose their lives in the process, the people of the North would need a scapegoat. The President was the logical choice.

Who was to say that the people were wrong in assigning blame to him? Lincoln had wracked his mind time and again wondering what he might have done differently. Had he been wrong to make Grant commander-in-chief? Had it been wrong to issue the Emancipation Proclamation, or had it been too early or too late? There were a thousand things he might have done differently and

Lincoln knew he would spend the rest of his life, however long it would be, asking whether he had truly done his best.

He wondered whether it would be worse to conclude that he had done his best and it had not been enough or to conclude that he had failed because of his own shortcomings. In the former case, he had suffered through the nightmare of the last four years for no purpose, whereas in the latter he would forever blame himself for the fact that the country had been torn apart and millions of human beings remained enslaved. It would be another question he would spend the rest of his life trying to answer.

"And you, Mr. Stanton?" Seward was asking. "What are your plans?"

"I plan on running for Congress at the first opportunity so that I can oppose McClellan in every way I can. And I don't care whether it's the House or Senate."

A broad smile swept across Lincoln's face. "You will be here in Washington to oppose McClellan, Mr. Stanton. But you will not do so as a congressman."

Stanton's eyes narrowed in confusion. "What are you talking about?"

"As you know, I remain the President until the moment George McClellan is sworn in tomorrow. The Senate will not change until tomorrow, either."

"I know that," Stanton said irritably.

"Having consulted our friends in the upper chamber for the past few weeks, yesterday I sent your name to the Senate as my nominee to be the next Chief Justice of the Supreme Court. I suppose it is the last official act of my administration and, if I am not mistaken, the Senate is confirming the nomination even as we speak."

Stanton's eyes widened in shock. Seward, who had been fully informed from the beginning, smiled and extended his hand.

"Congratulations, Mr. Chief Justice."

Stanton was dumbstruck but instinctively shook Seward's proffered hand. "Chief Justice of the Supreme Court?"

"That's correct, my friend. You are the best man possible for the job. McClellan and his Copperhead allies are likely to spend much of the next four years cozying up to the slaveocrats in the Confederacy and undoing whatever good we managed to do in the North over the past four years. He's a silly and foolish man desperate to gratify his own vanity and those who will be his chief advisors in office are self-interested villains. Having a man in charge of the Supreme Court certain to oppose them with every sinew of his strength will allow me to leave the White House slightly reassured."

Stanton nodded, recovering his senses. "I shall do absolutely everything I can in service of the United States," he said with determination.

"I know you will. You shall be the rock on the beach of our national ocean against which the breakers shall dash and roar."

The new Chief Justice nodded sharply once again. Lincoln knew Stanton well and could sense the weight of responsibility he felt coming upon him. Most men would have flinched from it, but it only seemed to give Stanton more strength.

"It is our final night in office," Seward said. "Would you two gentlemen do me the honor of dining at my house this evening?"

"I should be very glad to do so," Lincoln replied.

Stanton shook his head. "Thank you, Mr. Seward, but I must decline. If I am to begin my tenure at the Supreme Court properly, I must get to work at once. I bid you gentlemen a good afternoon."

Stanton scurried out the door just as Hay and Nicolay walked in to get another box.

Lincoln turned to Seward. "I shall see you tonight, my friend."

"I look forward to it." The Secretary of State nodded and left the room.

The two secretaries lifted the box and walked out the door, leaving Lincoln alone once again. He sat down at the desk, thumping its surface with his fingers and wondering what the future held.

* * * * *

May 16, Afternoon

The city of Atlanta was recovering quickly, Johnston was pleased to see. The debris had been cleared from the streets by working gangs of slaves, some of whom had unfortunately been killed after accidentally disturbing unexploded shells. The buildings most heavily damaged by the Union bombardment had been torn down, while those which were only moderately damaged were already mostly repaired. Many of the brick buildings in the downtown area had solid shot or bits of shrapnel lodged in their structures, with some owners having decided to simply leave them there as a reminder of what had happened.

There had been a good deal of suffering on the part of Atlanta's civilian population in the weeks and months after the departure of Union forces. Many civilian homes had been destroyed or rendered unlivable and for a time many people lived in tents provided by the Army of Tennessee. A relief effort by the city's churches, organized primarily by Father Thomas O'Reilly of the Catholic Church of the Immaculate Conception, had distributed needed supplies. Eventually, the railroad to Augusta had been repaired and a supply of food and other necessities became available.

According to what Cleburne and others had told him, the streets of the city had been all but deserted during the bombardment as the people huddled fearfully in their homes. However, on this bright spring day, it seemed that all of Atlanta was out and about, trying to find a good place on the parade route to see the men march past. For today was the day that the Army of Tennessee was holding its long-awaited grand review in the city where it had won its greatest victory.

Johnston sat in the center of a large review stand that had been erected on Mitchell Street by the Atlanta City Hall. His wife Lydia was with him. Various dignitaries were present, including Mayor Calhoun, Vice President Stephens, Governor Brown, and others. Various wealthy citizens of Atlanta had also managed to secure seats on the review stand. The corps and division commanders of the Army of Tennessee would be riding at the heads of their units.

He pulled out his pocket watch and checked the time. The review was supposed to have already begun, but he saw no sign of his troops.

"Something troubling you, General?" asked Vice President Stephens, who was sitting to his left.

"The men should have begun the march by now," Johnston said.

Stephens laughed softly. "Delays in such things are ordinary, my friend. Don't worry."

Johnston nodded, but was surprised to realize that he was almost as nervous as he had been on the eve of the attack at Peachtree Creek. It was very important to him that the review come off without a hitch, as it was quite possibly going to be the final act of his beloved Army of Tennessee.

Stephens leaned closer. "May I tell you something in confidence, General?"

"Of course."

"I received a telegram from President Davis yesterday. He has asked me to serve as a member of the delegation that will discuss a peace treaty with representatives of the United States. I leave for Richmond tomorrow."

"Really?" Johnston said. "McClellan has agreed to direct negotiations?"

"Apparently so. General Breckinridge and I are to lead the Confederate delegation. From the wire Davis sent me, Governor Seymour of New York is to lead the Union delegation. The negotiations are intended to conclude in an official treaty of peace between our two nations."

"I can think of no man better than you to lead our delegation, Mr. Vice President," Johnston said. In truth Johnston did not know the Vice President particularly well. He wondered why Stephens was confiding in him in the first place.

"Thank you. It will be a mammoth task, of course. The Yankees will demand concessions in exchange for their withdrawals from Tennessee and other areas they still control. They will also probably insist that the Confederacy assume a portion of the pre-war national debt of the United States. It will be very difficult to get a treaty to which both sides can agree, but we must do it. We must start our new relationship with the North on good ground."

"What about the slaves?" Johnston asked.

Stephens responded immediately, without having to think. "Asking for the return of the slaves the Union armies have set at liberty will be futile. I still must do it, of course. Too many of our own politicians will demand it. But the Yankees will never agree to it. I doubt we shall even obtain financial compensation for our lost slave property."

"If the United States is now a foreign country, it seems to me that more of our slaves will attempt to escape into the North than was the case before the war." Since the cease-fire, large numbers of slaves had been frantically trying to escape into the Union lines before the Yankees withdrew. Under orders from Richmond, Johnston had organized patrols of the back roads of Georgia and parts of Alabama to try to stem this tide, a duty he found profoundly distasteful and which the men themselves found boring.

Stephens nodded. "Indeed. There will be no Fugitive Slave Law now. The implications of this are obvious."

Johnston was about to ask Stephens what he meant when there was a sudden increase in noise from the crowd, many of whom were gesturing to the east. Johnston looked down the road and saw the first regiment of the Army of Tennessee approaching. The people on the review stand rose to their feet.

Only two corps of the Army of Tennessee, those of Hardee and Cheatham, were actually participating in the grand review. Stewart's corps was encamped in and around the town of Dalton in north Georgia, keeping a wary eye on the Union forces at Chattanooga, to which they had withdrawn following the official announcement of the ceasefire. This decision was hard on Stewart's men, who deserved the honor as much as the rest of the army, but there had been no way to avoid it.

General Hardee, sporting a fine cork peg where his left leg had once been, rode a beautiful black charger at the head of his troops. His beard was neatly trimmed, his gray dress uniform was immaculate and he wore an elegant cream colored sash across his chest. As he passed by, men doffed their hats and several of the ladies threw flowers in his path. Johnston was amused to see a grin form on his corps commander's face. Much as he might try to maintain a stoic expression, his vanity would always be touched when bombarded with female attention.

The troops followed their general. The first unit was Maney's division of Tennessee troops, who had fought so splendidly in so many battles. Then came Bate's division of Kentucky, Tennessee, and Florida boys, now led by General Finley since Bate's untimely death during the Battle of East Point. After him came Walker's division of Georgia, South Carolina, and Mississippi troops.

General Walker rode somewhat sullenly, still smarting from his arrest by Cleburne during the fighting around Atlanta. His court martial had been delayed by the War Department in Richmond, and Johnston suspected that the charges would be quietly dropped in the near future. President Davis and Secretary Seddon had decided it would be best if the matter simply went away. For once, Johnston agreed with them.

All along the route, the people cheered wildly. The younger men and women, along with the children, continually jumped up and down as if they were bobbing in the ocean surf. Older men waved their hats above their heads as they cheered. From the rooftops of the nearby buildings came colorful streamers. The roar and applause of the crowd mixed with the tramping of thousands of marching feet and the shouted orders of the officers. The men paraded with a perfect order that Johnston had seldom seen during the Atlanta Campaign itself. But then, the Army of Tennessee was out to impress on this particular day.

As he watched the men march past, Johnston was saddened. A standard division in the Confederate Army was supposed to number between four thousand and five thousand men. But the divisions he saw marching past were scarcely the size of brigades, perhaps only a quarter of the size they were supposed to have been. So many good men now lay in shallow graves across northern Georgia.

The South might have won its independence, but it had only done so at a terrible cost.

Now came Cleburne's division, with its commander riding at its head. As the troops from Texas, Arkansas, Alabama and Mississippi approached, Johnston noticed a strange phenomenon. The women and children continued to cheer as loudly as before, if not louder. However, a large number of the men placed their hats back on their heads and stood silently as Cleburne rode past. In the review stand itself, most of the dignitaries remained impassive, looking down at the fighting Irishman with obvious disapproval. The single exception was Mayor Calhoun, who saw what was happening and boldly stood from his chair to applaud Cleburne as he walked past. Johnston himself had the luxury of giving his fellow officer a salute, thereby showing neither public approval or disapproval.

"Poor fool," Stephens said, shaking his head. "Were it not for his emancipation proposal, that fellow would today be the greatest hero in the Confederacy. Next to you, of course, General Johnston."

"Patrick Cleburne is a patriot," Johnston said sharply. "I was honored to endorse his promotion to lieutenant general and I believe the Senate was very wrong to reject it."

Stephens glanced up at Johnston. He voiced no opinion, but his eyes seemed to Johnston to be saying that it was not for a mere general to question the actions of the Confederate States Senate.

Cleburne's division completed its march past the viewing stand and the men of Cheatham's corps were now approaching. Johnston told himself that he should stop thinking about politics and slavery and all the rest of it and focus on enjoying the rest of the parade. After all, this was supposed to be his army's special day, its moment of glory.

Joseph Johnston figured that the future would take care of itself. It would be many years before he realized how terribly wrong he had been.

*   *   *   *   *

June 18, Morning

As James and Annie McFadden travelled westward, they had passed through a land that seemed not unlike the tree-clad hills of Georgia they had left a month before, just after the Grand Review of the Army of Tennessee had been completed. The swampy areas of central Louisiana through which they had passed after crossing the Mississippi River had been the only noticeable variation. As they approached the Balcones fault line that roughly divided Texas into two halves, James had begun preparing Annie for the abrupt transformation in terrain that they were about to see.

McFadden had traveled the length and breadth of the South from Atlanta in the east to the deserts of New Mexico in the west. He knew that a squirrel could be born in a tree near the Atlantic coast and, the Mississippi River aside, jump from tree to tree and get all the way to Texas without ever touching the ground. As the wagon carrying their few possessions rolled ever westward, however, they were reaching the point where the squirrel would have to stop.

It happened suddenly, over the course of a single day of travel. McFadden kept glancing with curiosity over at Annie, whose eyes boggled as the trees disappeared and the vast plains of central Texas opened before them like the pages of a book. Endless and vast, like the great waves of the sea his parents had crossed to come to America, the plains seemed infinite.

Somehow, even when he had been a boy, the great plains of Texas had promised possibilities. That had been why his parents had come to Texas after being driven off their land in the Highlands. Their dreams had ended in tragedy and death, but they at least had created him. Now their dreams were his dreams, too.

McFadden focused his attention on Annie's reaction, partly out of sincere interest but also to distract him from the emotional turmoil he knew he would experience the closer they drew to his old home. He honestly had no idea what it would look like. A few days after the wedding, when they had decided to go to Texas, McFadden had written to a Waco lawyer whose name he had recalled but whom he did not remember ever actually meeting. A letter had arrived back several weeks later, confirming that no one was at the farm and, as far as he knew, McFadden still legally owned the place as the sole survivor of the family.

Throughout the journey west from Atlanta, they had encountered many other Texans traveling home, some of them being fellow survivors of Granbury's Brigade from the Army of Tennessee, others having served in the ranks of Hood's Texas Brigade in Lee's Army of Northern Virginia, as well as many other men who had served in various cavalry outfits. Most traveled in small groups, while a few traveled alone. None of the men he talked to had been back to Texas since 1862 and most, like him, had extremely limited contact with anyone in the state. On many nights, James and Annie had pitched camp with such men, not only for the sake of camaraderie but also because much of the countryside was infested with brigands.

The lack of information fed innumerable rumors about how Texas had changed during the war. There were stories that the German immigrant communities in the Hill Country had risen up in some sort of Unionist revolt and that General Kirby Smith, commander of all Confederate forces in Texas, had made himself dictator and was refusing to communicate with the Richmond government. McFadden did not give any of these rumors much credibility, having heard more than his fair share of dubious stories during his time in the service. He kept telling a worried Annie that they should not believe anything until they had the evidence before their eyes.

In addition to wild rumors about Texas, their encounters with other travelers provided hard news of events back east. Newspapers were reporting that some sort of conference had been held in Canada and that a treaty of peace between the Union and the Confederacy had been hammered out after long and intense negotiation. The details of the treaty were sketchy and there appeared to be some question as to whether it would be ratified by the respective legislatures. Every day brought word of some new development, the general consensus being that peace was right around the corner.

The coming peace had made McFadden face the question of what he would do with the rest of his life, especially now that he had a wife. The decision to go west to Texas had not been made lightly. Annie had inherited her father's wealth and the two of them could have lived comfortably in any of the cities of the Confederacy. But McFadden's heart had been drawn back irresistibly to Texas.

Annie, having grown up as the daughter of a prominent businessman, accepted the role of a farmer's wife with such ease that McFadden wondered how much of her reaction was feigned. As they pushed farther and farther west, he realized that she was in fact delighted. Her spirit seemed to rise with each passing mile and with it her appreciation for adventure. She had been uneasy during the first few evenings in which they had camped out under the stars, but now she positively reveled in it. This gave him hope that she would find the life of a farmer's wife agreeable. If she didn't, they could always go back to Atlanta.

They had begun their day's trek early, even before the sun had risen. The scorching Texas summer was still in its early stages, but McFadden knew from long experience how hot it would be before the day was over. Best to get the horses moving while it was still relatively comfortable.

As the hours and miles passed by, they did what they had done every day for the past month. They talked. Throughout the journey, McFadden had regaled her with stories of Scottish history, tales of William Wallace and Robert the Bruce, Rob Roy and John Knox. Even as their wagon bumped along the shoddy roads, he recited to her the poems of Robert Burns while she read to him out of a copy of Shakespeare's collected works that they had purchased before setting out. They had discussed religion, literature, even the bits of philosophy and science they had picked up from their respective reading.

They grew closer the farther they traveled, intellectually as well as emotionally. Most of the women McFadden had known before the war had been rough wives of farmers, so he was unused to the education and articulation Annie presented to him on a daily basis. He regretted his own lack of a university education and had resolved that his children, however many there would be, would not endure such a limitation.

Events soon made that thought more than hypothetical. During their brief stay in Vicksburg, Annie had told her husband that she suspected a baby might be on the way. By the time they were passing through northern Louisiana, she was certain of it. McFadden had resolved to make contact with a doctor in Waco as one of their first priorities when they finally reached their destination.

Having spent so many long days on the road, both of them were increasingly anxious to reach the farm. McFadden grew more and more concerned by what he would find when they arrived. Would there even be a structure resembling anything like a farmhouse? What would be the condition of the soil? It was too late in the season to plant anything, so how would they get by until the spring? There were endless questions, and none of them yet had any answers.

The sun had long since peaked and was approaching the horizon when, at long last, the desolate remains of the McFadden farm came into view. He pulled the horses to a stop and, for an endless moment, sat in stillness and silence. The farmhouse still stood, but the windows were broken and much of the wooden frame around one of the doors had fallen down. Some of the planks in the roof had been blown off by the powerful winds that so often swept through the countryside, leaving numerous gaps that would have to be filled in.

Annie glanced over at him, studying his face as a wave of powerful memories flooded his mind. There was the tub in which his infant sisters had happily splashed while being bathed by his mother. It had fallen over but could easily be set right. There were stones from the chimney that had fallen down. Repairing that would take much more work, but he wanted to do so in order to recreate the evenings by the fire during the brief winters, which he and his family had enjoyed so very much.

He spotted a small stone standing somewhat upright, which he suddenly recalled marked the final resting place of Gus, a white terrier his father had brought back from a trip to San Antonio, despite the protests of his mother than it had cost far too much. Gus had proven his worth, however, largely freeing the house from rats and other rodents before falling prey to the poisonous bite of a rattlesnake at the age of nine. During those nine years, Gus had been McFadden's favorite playmate and the memory of his happy bark now brought a sorrowful smile to his face.

He stepped down from the wagon, beginning a slow walk around the farmhouse. Annie came down and walked beside him, holding his hand but saying nothing. As they passed around to the far side of the house, they saw the graves of his family, the stones marking the resting places of his father, his mother, and his two sisters still standing quietly, as though they had been waiting for him to return. Grass was growing around the graves and he resolved at once that he would clear it away the next morning as his first order of business. He knelt down and gently put his hands on the stones, first on those of his parents and then on those of his sisters, saying nothing and saying so much.

They entered the house. The furniture was long gone, probably taken by passers-by who saw no reason not to help themselves to it. The rooms were entirely empty, the floors covered with a layer of dust. It seemed eerie to think that no one had lived in the rooms for more than two years. No conversation had taken place, no laughter, no crying of children. The rooms had simply been empty, like the endless spaces between the stars, with only the sound of the wind blowing through the windows.

"This house will soon be filled with life," Annie said, smiling cautiously.

He looked at her and returned the smile. "Are you sure you want to live here?"

"I want to be wherever you are, my darling. At the very least, I want us to give it a try. This is where you come from, so it is where part of our child comes from. It is only right that he be brought up here."

"Being a farmer's wife is not easy."

She smiled and playfully slapped him. "So you've been telling me every moment of every day since we left Atlanta. If I didn't know better, James McFadden, I would suspect that you were trying to frighten me away."

He laughed. "Foolish indeed is the man who would ever try to frighten you. And even more foolish is the man who would ever try to persuade you to do anything you didn't want to do."

It was too late in the day to unload much of the wagon, so they simply hauled their blankets into the house to make an improvised bed on the floor. McFadden kept his Navy Colt and sword close at hand, as well as an Enfield rifle he had acquired. With the armistice, Texas cavalry had been deployed on the frontier to chase the Comanches back to their own lands, so he did not anticipate any trouble. Still, it was well to be prepared for anything.

And so James and Annie McFadden went to sleep for their first night in their own home. As they drifted off, neither could possibly have imagined that the child even then growing in Annie's belly, who would be given the name of Thaddeus Kościuszko McFadden, would one day shatter the Confederate States of America.

*   *   *   *   *

September 1, Evening

Sergeant Bayard gripped his Springfield rifle tightly, gazing down the hill at the column of Confederate troops marching down the road. Although his men would have followed whatever orders he had seen fit to give, he had already made the decision not to open fire. His band numbered scarcely more than fifty, most of them fellow veterans of the 13th United States Colored Troops, but some having come from other regiments. The Confederates, by contrast, appeared to be at least five hundred strong, probably being the remnants of two or three regiments headed home together. The Southerners looked to be a jolly group, laughing and talking happily among themselves, carrying their rifles in all sorts of ways.

Had Bayard and his men sprung an ambush, they would have had both the advantage of surprise and the tactical benefit of the high ground on their side. They would certainly have been able to kill a great number of the hated graycoats. However much Bayard detested the Southerners for seeking to keep him and his kin in a state of slavery, he acknowledged their skill as soldiers. After recovering from the shock, the Confederates would have stormed the hill and almost certainly destroyed his unit. Better, for the time being, to wait.

His men sensed his caution and held their fire, the training and discipline they had acquired during the war still holding strong. Not long after they had made the decision to take to the woods, they had elected Bayard as their leader. This was partly because of his previous status as a noncommissioned officer, but mostly because he was the man who had defeated Nathan Bedford Forrest in hand-to-hand combat.

The orders for the 13th U.S.C.T. to withdraw from Nashville back into United States territory had come a month before, not long after the United States Senate had finally ratified the treaty of peace with the Confederacy. His commander, Major Easton, had offered to help Bayard find a decent job in the North, but had made the offer already knowing that Bayard would refuse. Instead, when the train whistle sounded and the regiment was supposed to board, Bayard and roughly half of the regiment had quietly slipped away, taking their rifles with them. Easton and the rest of the white officers had made no effort to stop them. Indeed, they had made a point to leave hundreds of ammunition pouches stuffed to the brim with cartridges lying conveniently next to the railroad depot, which Bayard and his men had gratefully taken with them.

They had made a camp in an isolated part of the woods, many miles away from the nearest town or railroad. They were supporting themselves thus far mostly by hunting, but that would not provide for their needs forever. Soon they would have to begin raiding the smaller communities in order to obtain sufficient food. There was already some discussion among the group about how to make contact with plantation slaves, who might be able to smuggle some food and other supplies out to them.

There would be other groups, Bayard knew. Well over a hundred thousand freed slaves had joined the Union army, been taught military discipline, felt the confidence that comes with shouldering a rifle and wearing a uniform. U.S.C.T. regiments had served in Tennessee, in the lower Mississippi Valley, and along the coasts of Florida, Georgia and the Carolinas. The woods and swamps of these areas would make ideal places from which to conduct a guerrilla war. Many of these soldiers were not about to quit the fight to free their people from slavery. The Confederacy might think they had won the war, but they were about to discover that the war was far from over.

Bayard silently waved his hand. He and his men slowly faded back into the woods.

THE END

Author's Note

Shattered Nation is a novel of alternate history. In actual fact, Jefferson Davis did remove Joseph Johnston from command of the Army of Tennessee on July 17, 1864, and replaced him with John Bell Hood. Hood proceeded to fight and lose three battles against Sherman over the next eight days, including the historical Battle of Peachtree Creek. Hood's army suffered enormous casualties in these engagements while achieving little if any advantage. In late August, the Army of Tennessee was defeated again at the Battle of Jonesboro, which resulted in the Union capture of Atlanta on September 2. The capture of Atlanta, in turn, provided the morale boost that catapulted Abraham Lincoln to reelection that November. The fate of the Confederacy had been sealed.

Davis's decision to replace Johnston with Hood is perhaps the most historically controversial decision the Confederate President made during the whole war. Rivers of ink have been spilled over the question, beginning even before the fighting had ended. In a series of bitter postwar memoirs, Davis and Hood both blamed Johnston for the fall of Atlanta, essentially accusing him of being too cowardly to fight during the months leading up to his removal. Johnston, by contrast, held Hood responsible for the failure to defeat Sherman at Cassville and suggested that Davis's removal order took place just before he was about to launch a long-planned attack on the Union army.

Who was right and who was wrong? The truth will never be known and I certainly don't pretend to know the answer. My novel is an exercise in imagination. In developing the plot for *Shattered Nation*, I made a conscious decision to accept Johnston's claim that he planned a massive attack on the Union army at Peachtree Creek. For all I know, Davis was correct in fearing that Johnston would have abandoned Atlanta without a fight had he been left in command of the Army of Tennessee.

Still, I believe that Johnston's reputation as overly cautious is not entirely deserved. History records that Johnston launched offensive battles on multiple occasions during the Civil War. He attacked McClellan at the Battle of Seven Pines in May in 1862. During the Atlanta Campaign itself, he attacked Sherman at Resaca and Dallas and tried to attack him at Cassville and New Hope Church. In the last days of the war, Johnston launched the last major offensive of the Confederacy at the Battle of Bentonville in March of 1865. I find it entirely plausible to suppose that Johnston would have attacked Sherman at Peachtree Creek had he remained in command.

A few quick notes…

James McFadden and the members of the Turnbow family are completely fictitious.

The 7th Texas was a real regiment and the recounted history of its service before the events of the novel is actual fact. Some of the names of the soldiers depicted are the names of actual men who served in the unit, though the portrayal of their personalities is derived entirely from the author's imagination. The continued existence of Company F of the 7th Texas Infantry – the "Lone Star Rifles" - is fictional. In actual fact, the unit was broken up after the Battle of Raymond and its men transferred to Company A.

The 7th Texas was under the command of different captains during the course of 1864, including Captain James Collett. To avoid confusion, I decided to have Collett in command throughout the novel. I confess that my love for the city of Austin may have had something to do with this, as Captain Collett's grave can be found in Oakwood Cemetery not far from the Texas State Capitol.

Careful observers might note that Hiram Granbury took sick leave in early June and did not resume command of his brigade until July 23, which would be three days after the Battle of Peachtree Creek. But since this is an alternate history novel and because I couldn't bear the thought of Granbury missing the battle, I decided I could overlook this particular factoid.

Some who read my novel before publication suggested that the acoustic shadow which prevents Sherman from hearing the fighting at Peachtree Creek is something of a *deus ex machina*. However, this was what happened in actual fact on July 20, 1864, so I felt comfortable including it in the storyline.

Jeff Brooks
September 12, 2013

Acknowledgements

Writing this novel has been a long, drawn-out process and I would never have completed it had I not had the help and encouragement of many people. I'd like to thank my friend Rob Brown for freely giving his time and talent to create my author website. Thanks also go out to Lana Castle for teaching me the ins-and-outs of modern self-publishing; Steven Stanley for making a beautiful map; and Craig Symonds, biographer of Cleburne and Johnston, for helpfully answering questions asked by a complete stranger.

The editing and publication of *Shattered Nation* was very much a family enterprise. I'd like to thank my sister Meredith, an amazing artist, for creating the truly stunning cover art, and my uncle Brian, a fellow writer, for proving to be an invaluable editor.

My parents, Lonnie and Barbara, helped the project in so many ways that I can't even begin to list them all; it can be truly said that the book never would have seen the light of day without their support. Most importantly, if they had not taken a certain little boy on a visit to Fredericksburg, Virginia, many years ago, the author might never have developed his love for history and this book would never have been written.

My greatest thanks is reserved for my wonderful wife Jill. She not only was the bluntest and most honest editor imaginable, but provided critical and perceptive ideas regarding the plot and characters. More than anything, I thank her for her constant encouragement and support, as well as her willingness to see her husband disappear into his study for hours at a time. I love my wife more than I can express in words.

A quick final word of thanks to my baby daughter Evelyn. It was during a research trip to Georgia, while staying at a friend's house in Acworth, that Jill and I found out Evelyn was on her way. Her arrival eight months later inspired me to the final effort necessary to complete this book.

The Civil War Trust

There were four major battles fought around Atlanta in the summer of 1864: the Battle of Peachtree Creek on July 20, the Battle of Atlanta on July 22, the Battle of Ezra Church on July 28 and the Battle of Jonesborough on August 31. These were some of the most important battles in American history, as they decided the fate of Atlanta and thereby determined the outcome of the American Civil War. Sadly, urban development has completely obliterated the battlefields. The people living, working, shopping and playing golf on the battlefields generally have no idea of the momentous and bloody events which took place on the ground underneath their feet. Unlike the case with Gettysburg, Vicksburg, and many other Civil War battlefields, there has been no major effort to preserve or protect this historically priceless land.

Tragically, this same story is today being acted out on Civil War battlefields across the country. Every year, we lose vast amounts of priceless historic land on which Northerners and Southerners fought for what they believed in. In recent years, an effort to build a Walmart on the Wilderness battlefield was only narrowly defeated. Limestone mining has inflicted terrible damage to the land on the Cedar Creek battlefield in the Shenandoah Valley, just as lignite mining has destroyed much of the battlefield at Mansfield in Louisiana. These are just a few examples. All over the country, urban development is steadily eating away at countless Civil War battlefields, destroying them like the steady dripping of acid.

This is a national disgrace and should not be tolerated.

Those readers who wish to help preserve Civil War battlefields should consider becoming supporters of the Civil War Trust, the nation's largest nonprofit organization dedicated to preserving Civil War battlefields. To date, the Civil War Trust has preserved more than thirty-four thousand acres at over a hundred battlefields in twenty different states. Becoming a supporter of the Trust is by far the best way to help preserve Civil War battlefields.

The website of the Civil War Trust is www.civilwar.org.

About the Author

Jeff Brooks was born in Richmond, Virginia, and grew up in Dallas, Texas. He currently lives in Manor, Texas, just outside the state capital of Austin. He graduated from Texas State University with a double bachelor's degree in history and political science and a master's degree in history. Aside from his writing, he teaches life skills to students with special needs at Anderson High School. He is a certified wine sommelier and a devoted fan of Chelsea Football Club.

Jeff met his lovely wife Jill at a wine tasting in 2009. They married in the Bahamas in 2011. In 2013, their daughter Evelyn was born.

Shattered Nation is Jeff's first novel.

jeff@jeffreyevanbrooks.com
www.jeffreyevanbrooks.com